THE VIC VALENTINE CLASSIC CASE FILES:

FATE IS MY PIMP
ROMANCE TAKES A RAIN CHECK
I LOST MY HEART IN HOLLYWOOD
DIARY OF A DICK

Will Viharo

THRILLVILLE PRESS

Seattle, WA

THE VIC VALENTINE
CLASSIC CASE FILES

Cover art by Matt Brown www.mbrowni.com
Formatting by Wild Seas Formatting
(http://www.WildSeasFormatting.com)

Published by Thrillville Press
www.thrillville.net

INTRODUCTION

by Will Viharo

I will keep this relatively brief, at least by my standards, since much of this backstory was covered in my introductions to *The Thrillville Pulp Fiction Collection* Volumes One-Three, also available from Thrillville Press. Plus this four-in-one omnibus pretty much speaks for itself, and at length.

Quick recap, then:

In 1992 I was being actively courted by major New York editor Judith Regan of Simon & Schuster, who was made aware of my work via one of her authors, Wally Lamb (*She's Come Undone*), whom I interviewed. She kept me on the hook for two years, during which time I wrote the first Vic Valentine novel *Love Stories Are Too Violent For Me*, subsequently published by Wild Card Press of San Francisco in 1995 (long defunct), the founders of which later started Speakeasy Theaters, eventually hiring me as their film programmer, publicist, and host/producer of my own "live cult movie cabaret" (B movies, bands and burlesque), which I called "Thrillville."

Yes, that means Regan didn't publish it, or any of my books written by that time, including *Lavender Blonde* and *Down a Dark Alley*, now paired in The Thrillville Pulp Fiction Collection Volume Two.

However, buoyed by my promising prospects during this period, I wrote four sequels to *Love Stories Are Too Violent For Me* virtually back to back, and this quirky quartet has been assembled into this single anthology. They're all very distinct in terms of content and tone, yet bonded by a creative burst of enthusiasm I've never been able to quite duplicate. I hope this collection finally earns them a proper audience. I think they deserve it. They've waited long enough.

Wild Card Press basically went belly up not long after publishing *Love Stories*, mainly because the owners were focused on their much more lucrative movie theater/restaurant enterprise. I became locally famous (or infamous) around the San Francisco

Bay Area as "Will the Thrill," along with my lovely assistant on and off stage, Monica Cortes, AKA "The Tiki Goddess," whom I married with a Rat Pack/mariachi-themed ceremony/celebration at the Cal-Neva Resort in North Lake Tahoe on May 31, 2001—exactly four years after we'd first met at my midnight screening of *Jailhouse Rock* at The Parkway Speakeasy Theater in Oakland.

Earlier that same year I received a letter at the Speakeasy office informing me that actor Christian Slater had discovered my novel *Love Stories Are Too Violent For Me* and wanted to option it for a film, as both star and director. The renewal checks started coming once a year. My ship had finally come (back) in, or so I thought.

Flash forward to 2012: I finally meet Christian when he graciously flies me out to Miami to do location scouting, so we can set his script of my novel in South Florida instead of Northern California. It was a fantastic experience, one of the highlights of my entire life, but as of this writing, despite aching proximity, this long-gestating passion project is still awaiting that fateful green light, perpetually idling at the corner of Hope and Desperation.

Anyway, the previous year, 2011, I self-published the four Vic sequels as two "double features" via Lulu/Amazon—*Fate Is My Pimp* with *Romance Takes a Rain Check* (cover art by frequent Thrillville event poster artist Rich Black), and *I Lost My Heart in Hollywood* with *Diary of a Dick* (cover art by Rick Lucey). Then in 2013, rising author Joe Clifford (*Wake the Undertaker, Junkie Love, Lamentation*), chief acquisitions editor for Gutter Books of Oregon, contacted me via Facebook when I had mentioned in a status update I was mulling over reprinting *Love Stories* myself, since the Wild Card Press edition was long out of print, and with the movie finally in development, it seemed like an opportune time to put it back on the market. That summer, Gutter issued the freshly edited and slightly revised "definitive edition" of the novel with a new cover by Matt Brown, who was the storyboard artist for Christian's screenplay. Matt also designed the cover of this anthology, as well as *The Thrillville Pulp Fiction Collection* Volume Two. I am very grateful for his talents, which ideally suit the subject.

The text has been technically cleaned up, but the vintage voice remains as down 'n' dirty as ever. These four novels are much wilder than either *Love Stories* or the most recent Vic book, *Hard-boiled Heart*, published by Gutter Books in December, 2015. Frankly, I doubt any other publisher would even consider these "in-betweeners." They're just so *weird*, far from conventional genre fare. But for fans of the character, they collectively constitute the essential appeal of Vic Valentine, Private Eye: lover, loner, loser. Basically, Vic is a more nakedly vulnerable, brutally honest version of most of us, or at least those of us shameless enough to admit it.

Also included here as a "bonus" is a new Vic story I wrote in 2014 but set in 2005, called "Brain Mistrust," originally published in the private eye ebook anthology *The Shamus Sampler 2*, edited by Jochem van der Steen, in 2014. It serves as a bridge, more or less, between the books of the '90s and the brand new, contemporary Vic novel, *Hard-boiled Heart*, foreshadowing some of the changes coming in the increasingly outmoded detective's life. He hasn't changed much, but the world around him certainly has.

By the way, if you're ever in the San Francisco Bay Area, drop by Forbidden Island Tiki Lounge on the exotic island of Alameda, and have an original, exclusive "Vic Valentine" cocktail, my "liquid legacy" as created by Susan Eggett. Hopefully this big book will prove equally intoxicating.

Cheers.

Will "the Thrill" Viharo
Seattle, WA

Dedicated to the memory of my dear,
departed cat "Puss" (1983-1995)
who was my faithful companion
through the writing of all these novels,
and then suddenly he was gone.
His spirit lives in these pages.

RIP, baby.

TABLE OF CONTENTS

FATE IS MY PIMP

A Vic Valentine Adventure

Chapter One
HEART BOARD

San Francisco, 1995

Fate is my pimp. He's really been slacking off lately, though, and there's no percentage in that for either of us.

I was blindsided by this gut wrenching, nerve racking, nut-cracking insight while tossing darts at my brand new, custom-made, heart-shaped dartboard. It was Technicolor red in hue and occupied a rather large space on the otherwise barren wall left of my desk—from my perspective, the barrier to the bedroom. As it were. The dart board was a gift from my good pal Doc Schlock, a.k.a. Curtis Jackson, owner and chief bartender of The Drive-Inn, the combo bar and video store right beneath my office/apartment. I'm Vic Valentine, Private Eye, in case you haven't figured that out yet. Who the hell else would spend his time chucking darts at a big wooden heart, ruminating on cheap, corny metaphors for his non-existent love life? No one *I* knew, that's for sure.

It was springtime in San Francisco, and romance was in the air. I had developed an allergy to the stuff so my eyes were watery and itchy, and I felt achy and lazy. I had just wrapped up a case involving a missing saxophone player and his fiancée, who hired me to find him. I had been infatuated with this babe, Flora Paige, now Mrs. Joey Link after a hastily arranged ceremony in Las Vegas, for a long time and had been hoping she'd dump the sax player for me. She almost did. I'll tell you about it in a little bit, if I feel like it. Like I said, I don't feel much like doing anything lately. It's been one of those years, and it's not over yet. Not by a long shot.

I guess I should explain what I mean when I say that Destiny procures for me. For one thing, I'm basically assuming it does out of sheer desperation, and also so I won't have to take the rap for my wretched existence. Well, *wretched* is too strong a word. I have my health, as far as I know, and I make a living honestly, or with a clear conscience at any rate, and I bear no apparent resemblance to Quasimodo, so going strictly by the book, my life is okay. I shouldn't bitch. I have no right to, really. And I'm not, exactly. Merely objectively observing my solitary situation, which is not of my own choosing. That's why I blame it on God or Fate or whoever or whatever is out there calling the shots. I could be wrong. Maybe no one is calling any shots, and it's all a random masquerade ball, and we choose whatever masks we feel will adequately hide our despair. In that case, it *is* my fault, sitting here on a beautiful day alone in my room, relentlessly piercing my own heart. But I'd rather blame it on Destiny, my old pal. If I'm meant to be a lonely son-of-a-bitch, it's out of my hands. Oh, I could join a dating service, advertise in the paper, go barhopping, but for some reason I don't. I just don't have it in me to actively pursue the one thing in my life that is missing. So I sit and wait for it to come to me. I guess that's why I'm in this racket going on seven years now. To meet women. If Fate really is my pimp, then maybe I am not a john on the make, but a whore, lying in bed, waiting for my next customer. Either way, the analogy works.

Anyway, at least I got laid this year. That's a crude way of putting it, and I'm only assuming this macho detachment in retrospect. I had a fling with the aforementioned Flora Paige, on the hopes that she would permanently break it off with her fiancé. I found the loser holed up in a hotel in Ukiah, playing with his saxophone and weeping. I had once gone all out to win this girl over, even going so far as to take pictures of "The Date That Never Was," photos of potential locations for our magical day together, organized in a folder with funny little captions. I met her at the local blood bank, where I gave blood and she took it. Took it and ran. Then I got mixed up with another case, wherein a ballplayer named Tommy Dodge hired me to find his missing wife. Turns out she was also *my* missing angel, who flew the coop six years before when we were living in New York, in the throes of romantic bliss. Or so I wrongly assumed. I found her, only now she had changed her name from Valerie to Rose, or maybe she found *me*, and I tried to rekindle the old flame but got burned instead. Tommy Dodge found us together and put me in the hospital, and Rose took off for parts unknown. She was the love of my life but I'm resigned to never seeing her again. So then Flora walked into my office, wanting me to find her errant sax player. I did so within two weeks, but in the meantime Flora and I cried on each other's shoulders and then gradually more intimate body parts one night in my office. She told me she never really loved the sax player and would dump him for me after I found him. That's where I went wrong. I should never have found the *schmuck*. But I did. She wanted to iron things out with her past so she could begin her new future with me on a clean slate. So she told me. But once I brought Joey back from Ukiah, Flora took one look at his sorry ass and she fell back in love, and they got hitched by an Elvis impersonator in Vegas. I like that part. It's the lead-in that kills me.

We're still friends, though. That's what I tell her when she calls. But the truth is I get all the friendship I want from Doc downstairs. I'm looking for love, baby. The *dirty* kind.

Rose made me believe in Fate, if only because the alternative—that she deliberately set me up as some neurotic power play—is just too hard to swallow. I'd like to believe Rose still loves me deep down, and that Flora does too. But they're not the ones, or *The One*. I'm still interviewing. Fate is sending them through my door like job applicants. Either Fate or Chance, but the latter is too risky. I'm too lazy even to gamble. I'd like to believe Fate is on my side. If so, I can't lose. If not, I'm terminally screwed. But then so are all of us. Face it: if life is merely a crapshoot, odds are we lose. But if Fate really is on my side, he needs a new watch. We're on a schedule here, dude. No more extended lunch breaks. Let's get this over with so we can call go home happy.

I was lost in this philosophical contemplation illuminating exactly nothing when the phone rang. I let the answering machine pick it up, since it was late in the day and I was tired from sitting around since breakfast waiting for something to happen. The outgoing message on my machine this time was Frank Sinatra singing "Same Old Saturday Night," the part where he goes to the movies and a coffee shop by himself. Even the Chairman is not beyond eloquently moping. Before this I had on the Coasters doing "Searchin'," but that was when I was hoping Rose would break down and call me from Tibet or wherever the hell she was. It would be collect, no doubt, and I was broke, so it was best she didn't call. I was just screening out wackos and clients whose cases I was blowing off while spending their retainers. I was totally unprepared for the voice that emanated from my machine after the beep like a mysterious beacon from beyond.

Julie London was singing the opening lines of "Cry Me a River."

I bolted up from my chair with my last dart in my hand and went to pick up the phone. But I didn't. I couldn't. Something about the music made me freeze. It was eerie, full of pops and hisses like an old 45. Record, that is. Coming over my machine it had the effect of tuning in an obsolete station from the 50s on a radio you picked up at a flea market, like in *The Twilight Zone.* I stood there transfixed as the music continued, then suddenly stopped. *Click.*

I had been waiting for someone to come on the line, either laughing or crying, *something*, but no, that was it. I picked up the phone. Dial tone. I rewound the tape and played it back. Over and over. The objective here was unmistakable, the music carefully chosen to convey a message of forgotten love. But who left it? And had I burned them, or had they burned me? My brain was racing with the possibilities as I played the tape back again and again. I briefly thought of Monica Ivy, the twenty-something young thing who worked for Doc and with whom I nearly had an affair. But she was too young for Julie London, and not imaginative enough to do something like this as a way of communicating her feelings without laying her heart on the line. Monica's idea of a romantic ballad was "Suck My Kiss" by the Red Hot Chili Peppers, anyway. "Cry Me A River" was beyond her. I thought of Flora, my most recent involvement, but she was on her honeymoon somewhere. No, she'd be back by now, actually. She liked this kind of music, jazz standards and all, but then so did Rose. In fact, "Cry Me A River" had been one of our mutual favorites. So it had to be someone who not only knew I liked this particular tune, but had access to it. Did Rose collect old 45's? Did she have a Victrola with her on the road to nowhere? Maybe. But Flora could have done it, too. It was one or the other, I immediately presumed, standing there like an idiot with a dart in my hand, playing the message over and over and over, wondering who had called me with such a mournfully melancholy message. Someone was thinking of me. Someone as lonely as I was. Maybe even lonelier. Someone was also as crazy as I was, since this was definitely a case of someone turning the tables on me with my own M.O. Calling someone and leaving "Cry Me A River" on their answering machine was something I would do, for sure. I was almost jealous I hadn't thought of it first.

I was excited again. I wanted to live. The saga continued. The chase was on. All I had to figure out was who was chasing whom, and why. Same old story, actually, but then this was my life: repeating it till I got it right. As I ran downstairs to tell Doc about it, a third possibility came into my mind that gave me pause—what if this was an entirely *new* player, who just wanted to fuck with my head or, worse, was stalking my sorry solitary soul? Then again, it might have only been a random crank call, or a prank by someone who did know me and wanted to have a good laugh at my expense. By the time I walked into The Drive-Inn I had just one thing to say to Doc.

"Was that you who just called and left that message, god damn it? Just tell me, yes or no. I'm in no mood to play games."

"Easy does it, Vic, just sit down and catch your breath," Doc said, pouring me a beer from the tap. Doc's real name was Curtis Jackson, like I said, and he was black through and through, raised in Oakland, but he forgave me my whiteness as he did many of his patrons. I was black anyway, I told him. On the inside. Charbroiled to a crisp.

The bar was lined with the typical assortment of lonesome losers, exchanging gossip about who wasn't sleeping with whom. The sour grapevine, I called it. The big screen TV behind the bar was showing the usual fare, this time a cult oddity from 1980 called *Fade to Black*, about a loner type who loses it and starts knocking off his enemies in the style and makeup of his cinematic heroes, like Jimmy Cagney, Dracula, and the Mummy. There was a girl in it that was an Australian version of Marilyn Monroe. The sicko in the flick becomes obsessed with her, and I could hardly blame him. Sometimes when I watch these psychotronic movies Doc specializes in, I get more scared by me and my identification with them than by the movies themselves.

"What's up, my man?" Doc asked me. "What now? What are you babbling about?"

I sipped my beer, then gulped it, and said, "Doc, just be straight with me. Did you put someone up to it? Because you couldn't call from here, actually. You're too busy, and anyway I've never known you to appreciate schmaltzy love songs from the Fifties."

"Vic, is this *it*? Have you finally gone bonkers on me? I have no idea what you're talking about. Really. Fill me in, though. You got me hooked. As usual."

I studied his face. I'm pretty good at reading people, part of my profession. I saw no trace of mendacity in his countenance whatsoever. He wasn't lying. He was innocent. I knew he was all the time, anyway. True, he was the only male who knew me well enough to know my taste in music, but he wasn't malicious enough to torment me like that, either. No, it wasn't Doc. I crossed him off the list.

As I explained the message and what it meant to me, he just stood there nodding and grinning, really lapping it up, having a jolly old time with my boyish anxiety. But this was the nature of our relationship, so I let it slide. Anyone else would have made me feel totally humiliated. Even with Doc I was beginning to feel somewhat foolish by the end of my spiel.

"You know what your problem is, Vic?" Doc said, laughing gently.

"No. Light my way, O Wisest of the Wise."

"You're *bored*. Ever since that Flora thing fizzled—as I predicted, once again—you don't know what to do with yourself. So you fabricate these wild ass scenarios to amuse yourself. And me too, don't get me wrong. It was just a crank call, my man. Don't go off on a tangent. Ain't no phantom caller from beyond, Vic. Just somebody messin' with you."

"And it wasn't you."

"Why would I do that?"

"I don't know who else would that actually knows me."

"I like you, Vic, but not in that way."

"I know, I just thought you'd be doing it to tease me, causea Rose and all. You know I still think about her."

"Yea. Like I give a damn."

I looked at him with hushpuppy eyes, and he weakened. Never fails.

He said, "Look, Vic. You know where I stand on this Rose shit. You guys had your thing, long time ago, then coincidence brought you together again."

"Fate, Doc. It was Fate."

"Or my pet theory, as you know, that she set your ass up for a fall."

"Why, Doc? For what purpose? It doesn't make sense."

"*Nothing* that broad did made sense. All that talk about karma is just crap. She's just randomly pulling strings and straws, to see what happens. She's bored, too. That's all y'all's problem. Boredom."

"You're the one who should know it when you see it."

"Amen, brother."

"I'm not saying it was Rose, Doc. Probably wasn't. It just seems strange, is all. That's all I'm saying."

I finished my beer and he poured me another. I looked up at the TV screen and saw the blonde starlet who looked like Marilyn and wondered whatever happened to her. I didn't recall ever seeing her in anything else. It depressed me, for some reason. Hell, maybe *she* called me. Why not? The way Doc made it look, it was just a stranger randomly dialing numbers and leaving weird messages to toss a wrench in peoples' mundane routines. Maybe it was some other lonesome sap, bored as I was, with nothing better to do than torment people he or she would never meet. For some reason this explanation didn't wash with me. The song seemed too carefully chosen, the moment too carefully planned, the effect too carefully predicted. The more I thought about it, the more I went out of my mind wondering who it had been.

"I know who it was, Doc," I said after brooding for a while as he tended to other customers.

"Oh yea? Marilyn Monroe, maybe?"

"Funny guy, Doc, I keep tellin' ya, you're wastin' your world class wit here. You should tell jokes on the side, wear a funny bow tie and all. Turn this joint into a burlesque hall."

"Actually, I've been thinkin' about spicing things up around here in that direction," Doc said, leaning toward me so only I could hear him.

"What? Burlesque? You gonna hire strippers, for Chrissake?"

"Maybe."

"Doc, get real. You're scaring me. Where're they gonna dance, on the bar here?"

"No, no. I was thinkin' of installing one of those cages, y'know? Like go-go dancers used to dance in?"

"Before my time, Doc. You're getting senile on me. Or you haven't been laid in so long the jizz is backing up to your brain."

"It wouldn't be for *me*, Vic," Doc insisted. "It would be for the customers." He nodded toward two overweight women having a heated discussion about something insignificant and a skinny, greasy guy nursing a whiskey sour.

"Yeah, this is certainly the crowd for it," I deadpanned.

"Certainly," he agreed wholeheartedly, to my further surprise and chagrin. He actually seemed serious.

"Doc, if these people wanted to see that kind of sleaze, they'd go where the sleaze is."

"Vic, the sleaze is *here*, and has been here forever, or as long as I have. This place runs on sleaze, and you know it."

"Yeah, but only on tape, Doc. That's different. Safe. People can get down in the dirt in the privacy of their own homes, without rubbing shoulders with bikers and dope fiends. You don't want to attract that sort of clientele, Doc. You'd start losing customers.

Me, for one."

Doc waved me off. "Bullshit, man. You'd practically *live* down here if I go through with this. You upstairs with your Bettie Page videos. This would be the same thing only in 3-D! No, *4-D*! Don't you get it? These are lonely people, Vic. They're here looking for cheap thrills. And I'm here to give it to them, in, right, in a safe environment. I wouldn't allow no scumbags in. If business picked up I'd even hire a bouncer. People need *flesh*, Vic. Man cannot live by video alone."

"And woman?"

"I'd hire a male dancer, too. And shit, *lesbos* dig women too, right? And gay guys dig *men*. Something for everybody. Play some techno shit and rap, or maybe some old school Vegas shit, turn the volume of the TV down but still have it goin', y'know. It would be a feast for the senses!"

"Doc, look at me, and be honest. Is business really that bad?"

He looked back at me for a beat. "Yes," he said grimly.

I sighed. "So who would you hire, Doc? This isn't North Beach. You have to think of the neighborhood, too. You wouldn't want the police cracking down on you for hiring undesirables, would you?"

"I know, I know. But Monica volunteered!"

I was stunned. "Monica? You're kiddin'. You mean to tell me you'd actually exploit your own employees for a fast buck?"

"Exploit, nothin'! I said she volunteered! Fact is, most of this was her idea."

"I dunno, Doc. This just sounds too desperate."

"You should know it when you see it."

I nodded. "Yup."

"So anyway, enough pipe dreamin'. Who was it that called you now? You said you'd figured it out."

"Fate."

"Ah, shit."

"Fate is my pimp, Doc. You know that. He just sent me another one, or an old one."

"Vic, the day you make Fate your *bitch* is the day you start livin'. You got it all backasswards, my man. Fate is your bitch, not your pimp."

"Since when did you start in with the gangsta rap, Doc? I thought you had class."

"What class did you take? I got class, just not your class. You take your own damn classes and I'll take mine."

"Neither of us seems to be learning a damn thing but the blues."

"You and Frank Sinatra. Soul brothers. Only he took misery and made a heap of money out of it."

This was true. That was why I listened to Frank a lot more than his homeboy Dean Martin, the *menefreghista*, the One Who Did Not Give a Fuck. Dino would just as soon be playing golf as go out with a bombshell to a nightclub. Frank and I gave a fuck. We wanted the romance. Frank got it, with Ava Gardner, no less. Sure, she dumped him later, but then his career really took off. If only I could turn cold, hard experience into cold, hard cash. I should have a PhD in rejection by now. I asked for one, but was turned down. "Maybe it was Flora who called," I murmured

"Vic, *why*? Why wouldn't she just call you straight if she had something to say? Anyhow, she's married and all that shit. Forget her. You only dig broads if they're unattainable. *That's* your problem."

"Oh yea? I thought it was boredom."

"Both. Add 'em up, and you got me. That's why I had that dartboard made for you. You ever notice what you do to it? You throw darts at it."

"Thanks for clearing up that mystery, Doc. Now I can sleep at night without wondering."

"But don't you get the symbolism?"

"Yeah, yeah, yeah. It ain't too god damn deep, I hate to burst your bubble, Doc."

"You're hurting your own big heart, Vic. I hate to say it, and more I hate to see it, but you just keep doin' it." He pantomimed throwing darts, like I was a retard who needed visual aides to get the picture. "*Plunk, plunk, plunk,*" he said, adding some sound effects just in case his masterful metaphor was still escaping me.

"Thanks for the boost, Doc. I gotta go take a whiz, and I think I'll do it upstairs."

"Think about those dancers," Doc said as I got up to leave.

"You mean while I'm taking a whiz?"

"Can you think of a better time? No, man I mean whenever. I think it'll work. This is the Richmond District, I know, and I'll keep it clean, not funky. I just need to jazz things up around here."

"You're just bored, Doc," I said, walking toward the door.

"Here we go again," I heard him say just as I walked out.

When I got back to my office, the red light on my answering machine was glowing ominously. My heart stopped as I pressed the playback button and heard the Casinos performing another of my old favorites, "Then You Can Tell Me Goodbye."

That did it. Whoever was doing this knew me, and how to get to me. They just wanted me to guess who they were, so I could— what? Call them back? I had no idea where Rose was, since I hadn't heard from her since her ex-beau had me hospitalized, and I hadn't talked to Flora since she returned from her Vegas wedding, just before she moved in permanently with Joey, whose number I did not have or want. This was getting creepy, but exciting. Doc was right. I was bored. I got easily excited by small things. But this was weird by *any* standards.

Then I thought to call up my old pal Denise, who worked at the blood bank and had acted as my liaison with Flora during my so-called courtship, when the entire blood bank knew me and thought I was a love-struck lunatic from hell. Her husband picked up and when I asked for her he sort of grumbled and then called her name. I don't think he liked me much, from what he'd heard.

"Vic, how's it goin'?" Denise said. "Long time no hear."

"Yea, as far as I know," I said.

"What does that mean?"

"Denise, just tell me straight: did you call and leave those messages on my machine as like a joke or somethin'? Because if you *did.*"

"Hey, hey, slow down. *What* messages?"

I explained them to her and she laughed, predictably.

"Just a crank, Vic. Or some psycho trying to send you over the edge. Just ignore it."

"So you don't think it was Flora."

Again, laughter. "Vic, Flora told me what happened between you. It was just a one-nighter, Vic. She was sad and confused and maybe even horny!"

"Thanks for setting my mind at ease. I thought it was because she actually *liked* me."

"She *does*, Vic. But she loves someone else, and it isn't you. She *married* the sucker, didn't she? Take that as a clue, detective."

I sighed deeply, as I often do. "Maybe she had a change of heart."

"Vic, it wasn't her. She's in the Midwest somewhere with her husband. I think she's moving to Chicago. That's where he's originally from, so they're checking it out for housing. It wasn't her, Vic. Maybe it was that other one, what was her name? Your old flame."

"Rose."

"Yeah, right. She was psycho, right?"

"Yeah, but she knows me well enough, and she likes this kind of music, too, but *I* don't know. Why wouldn't she just call me and leave a regular message? This is just too weird. I mean, someone is obviously trying to tell me something in a very creative way, but what? *Who*?"

"Vic, you're just driving yourself crazy. Anyway, I gotta go, I'm fixin' dinner and my boy is hungry. Call me when you find out who it is, cause now you got *me* wondering."

I said I would and we said so long and hung up. My excitement was starting to ebb. I didn't turn any lights on, I just lay on my bed in the dark, dreaming. Then after a while I got up and turned on a light and put on my Julie London album and listened to "Cry Me A River" over and over in the dark again. I wasn't dreaming of Rose or Flora. I was imagining the phantom caller in my head, a cross between Bettie Page and Donna Reed, all sweetness and sex.

Waiting for Fate is like waiting for a bus. The longer you wait, the more desperate you become, but if you wait too long you get picky. So if you're waiting for ages and a broken down school bus downs up, with broken windows and nasty graffiti, you pass and say you'll look for a luxury charter bus, with air conditioning and plush seats and a portable bar. You've waited this long, so you may as well hope for the best and ride in comfort. The school bus will get you where you want to go sooner, but after waiting for so long it's no longer the destination that counts, it's the journey.

I was hoping the right bus had finally arrived, behind schedule but worth the wait.

Chapter Two
DIM SUM NEON

I awoke late the next day from a dream wherein I was James Bond, conducting myself with stylish aplomb, but hoping no one would catch on that I was too short to be Agent 007. This is a recurring dream, along with the ones where I'm adrift on a ship lost in the fogbound sea. I don't know what it means, nor do I particularly care, since as James Bond I not only have a license to kill, I have a license to *love*. Faceless but beautiful women occupy these dreams, usually posing as my next-door neighbor in an exotic hotel, but then I find them going through my belongings while I'm in the shower. I'm on a ship in a lot of these dreams, Walter PPK in tow, searching for something before being discovered and diving overboard in a hail of misfired bullets. Then I return to my exotic hotel room, find the babe in my closet, kiss her, and hope she doesn't catch on I'm too short to be James Bond. I can't tell if the bad guys on the ship do or not. Maybe they try to shoot me because I'm an imposter. Sometimes in the dream I wonder if I'm *starring* as James Bond in a movie, or if I'm really supposed to *be* him. Either way, I go along with it. If only I could stay asleep past that first kiss.

When I woke up from that dream, I felt the same way I always do when I wake up: I'm still undercover, in the life of a loveless loser, in too deep and begging to get out before it's too late and I lose my mind, merging identities with this hopeless sap forever, lost in this pathetic existence. I beg and plead with my nameless, formless superior to let me out; the mission is a bust, and I'm in perpetual danger. But my contact, whoever sent me into this, is either eluding me or ignoring me. Maybe I've been written off. I'll never get out alive, I fear. I'm caught in a trap, and I can't walk out.

I walked down to Rendezvous, my favorite cafe, for some wakeup espresso and a quick scan of the *Chronicle*. Maybe Doc was right, I thought. The phone calls were meaningless. I had to wake up, or grow up, do something vertical at any rate. This was the hazard of being in too deep in a phony guise—you start believing it's real. I had to keep reminding myself it was only a dream.

For lunch, since it was noon (I wake up late on a regular basis unless a case dictates otherwise), I went into Chinatown and dined at my favorite chop-suey joint on Grant. It was cheap and the Chinese waiters were just off the boat and I felt like James Bond in the Orient on a secret mission. All I really did was order the Number 5 lunch special and stare into space. I especially liked the fortune cookies in this joint. Usually. I remember that day I got one that made me feel vaguely uneasy: *"Life: Lights go on, a brief flurry of confusion, lights go out."* Made me feel like a goddamn cockroach.

I called over the waiter, whose name was Louie, at least in English, and asked him what the hell this fortune was supposed to mean.

"You Wic Walentine, you know," he said, smiling ear to ear, more like a wise guy than a wise man.

"*Vic. Vic* Valentine," I corrected him, as always. "A wick is in a candle. I keep telling you that, Louie."

"Okay, Mister Walentine. You want 'nother cookie?"

"Naw, not this time. Next time, though, make sure I get a cheerier message."

Louie nodded, smiling, inwardly laughing at me, I could tell. I flashed on Chow Yun Fat in *The Killer*, doing some double fisted point blank bullets-in-the-belly action. But I was a little short to be the Killer, too. Something me, my love affairs, and life all had in common: just too damn short.

The only thing in the world that gave me any hopeful notion of longevity was my trusty '63 sky blue Corvair. I took a roundabout route back to my office, just killing time. Or maybe it was killing *me*. Hard to tell. At least the scenery was pleasant on the way to inevitable oblivion. That's why I stay in San Francisco, I reminded myself as I cruised through Pacific Heights, stealing right hand glances at the majestic Bay, the sweeping panorama of Alcatraz, the low fog-bank, the bridges. It was the middle of April somewhere, warming up but still cool and crisp, just like I love it. The architecture was equally awesome up here, Victorian mansions painted in an array of pastels, nestled in well-kept flower gardens. By the time I got back to my dumpy office in the Richmond I was hating life again, envious of those who could afford to live daily surrounded by luxurious beauty. A small-time P.I. like me could never score such comforts. At least we were all equally vulnerable to earthquakes. And I had my Corvair. And my freedom. I sat down at my desk listening to messages, hoping for another mysterious musical message from the phantom phoner. Nada. It was just a fluke after all. I still had my Corvair. And my freedom.

Whoopdee-do.

There was a knock on the door, and my heart jumped. No one on the answering machine had piqued my interest, since they were all people either asking for their money back or demanding money for petty things like rent and electricity. I was way behind on my bills. I owed Doc two months back rent, and if it went any longer it could strain my friendship. I needed a client. I got one. He waltzed in the door like a genie to grant me three wishes. As soon as I saw him I knew he could never give me my first two no matter what, so I had to settle for the third: a wealthy client. And that he was, in spades.

The guy standing in the doorway looked like a cartoon version of a classic wiseguy: dark double-breasted suit, white silk shirt, a tie as deeply red as my heart board, shiny Florsheim shoes, slick black hair, dark wire-framed shades, and pasty East Coast skin, pockmarked with questionable experience. He took off his shades with well-rehearsed flourish, revealing eyes as dark and spicy as Italian meatballs. I noticed a scar from his left cheek down to his upper lip, giving him the appearance of a cleft lip, but when he spoke I could tell this was not the case. His voice was low and even. But I couldn't help noticing that his hand still holding the shades was shaking. A *lot*. Did I make him nervous?

"I'm Shiv," he said. "Just plain *Shiv*. Don't ask for a first or last name. And if you ever—and I mean *ever*—call me Shivers, I'll bury a bullet so far into your skull they'll need to excavate your head with dynamite to get it out."

"Understood," I said simply, acting nonplussed like I did way back when as a paperboy being tracked by a neighborhood dog nipping at my heels. Animals sense fear, and this guy was definitely Mutual of Omaha material.

"New York," I then said, pegging his Wild Kingdom of origin correctly.

"That's right," he said, closing the door behind him and taking the seat opposite me, with casual grace. He was around fifty so his shaking wasn't due to some geriatric condition. I didn't think it prudent to inquire any further into the subject, since it was obviously so touchy he had to lay it to rest as part of his introductory remarks. As long as he wasn't aiming a piece in my general direction I had nothing to worry about, anyway. For now. He reached into the left breast of his suit and I held my breath, but he only produced a handsome gold cigarette case and asked me, "Mind if I smoke?"

"Go ahead," I said, breaking my own office policy. If a cigarette would calm him down, I thought, I'll risk the second hand cancer factor. At least that was a long shot. From where he was sitting, a bullet in my brain wouldn't be. My mind was racing even faster than usual. I wondered if someone had ordered a hit on me, and this guy was just being polite about it. So who would want me iced? The stalker on my answering machine? But no, Mister Shiv had other plans for me that may have entailed my demise indirectly, but this wasn't his intention.

"I want you to find my daughter," he said finally after taking a puff from his trembling cigarette. His fingers were a blur. "I flew in from New York to San Francisco just this morning, looked in the phone book, and picked you simply out of a hunch. I'm good with hunches, so don't let me down."

"I'll try," I said. "What makes you think your daughter is out here, Mister Shiv?"

He closed his eyes and reopened them slowly, massaging his right temple with his right index finger as he did so. "Shiv," he hissed. "Just *Shiv*. That is the final time I'll tell you that." His *voice* didn't quiver at all.

"Like a knife," I said, but it bounced right off of him. He'd heard it all before. For all I knew he got the moniker from carving up guys like me, so I moved the conversation ahead quickly. "What's her name?" I asked.

"Lucy," he said.

"Lucy what?"

"I can't *tell* you that." He sure was a touchy guy.

"Well, Mister, I mean, um, Shiv, I'll need to know as much about her as possible if I'm going to locate..."

He held up a finger as a signal of silence, and I obliged him instantly. Then he reached into the right breast of his suit and handed me a photograph of Lucy. It was all I could do not to bark or whistle out loud. I stifled my instincts in favor of good health, though. She was beautiful in a suburban Sicilian kind of way, a Long Island bad Catholic girl: long wavy dark hair, smooth olive complexion, huge brown long-lashed eyes, full luscious lips. I knew the type from growing up in Bensonhurst, where these girls were on every block like little black widows. I'm half-Italian, but the fathers of these girls wanted nothing but purebreds for their precious little daughters. Despite their advances, the word around the 'hood was hands off the goodies. Hands caught in *that* cookie jar would never see their wrists again. The girls knew this and flirted shamelessly, hoping to trap Micks and half-Micks like me and other WASPs and Jewboys into big trouble with their older brothers. Lucy was very innocent looking but that didn't fool me. And this picture screamed jailbait, dangling from a meat hook. I didn't bite.

I chose my next words carefully. "Anything more recent?"

"That's from her high school last year," he said, watching my reaction carefully. With a daughter as beautiful as this, I understood now why he shook so much. She probably drove him crazy. "Good enough, unless she's shaved her head or something. I'll *kill* her if she did. Kids these days got no god damn style." I looked up briefly at his disco wardrobe but repressed an urge to smile. He went on. "You notice that? All kids dress like nigger ghetto punks these days. Girls, too. Backward baseball caps and shit. Flannel shirts, baggy pants. It makes me sick. I used to pick her up at school in a fucking limo, and she'd walk out of the schoolyard looking like an ex-con in the prison yard instead. I felt like I wasn't her Daddy anymore. She embarrassed me, looking like that."

"She looks very pretty here," I blurted, but then I stammered, "but not *too* pretty. I mean attractive in a nice, natural sense. Not attractive, she's too young to be attractive, at least to me, I mean look at me, but she looks very nice, is what I mean. Nice. Well *mannered.* A nice girl. A nice Catholic girl. Not that she's Catholic, I mean she could be anything, but I don't mean to assume anything, that she's Catholic or *you're* Catholic, but what I'm getting at is that she doesn't look like the MTV type. You know MTV? That's what you meant, right? I mean, I used to watch MTV, when it first started, I was young once, I'm still young, but too old for her, I mean for her generation, I mean, not that I'd ever be in the running for—well, anyway, I used to write about music, mostly new wave type music, you know, of the rock genre, but I really like Frank Sinatra, not that I assume you do, that's just me, but I understand what you mean, I mean my point is I really hate grunge and hip-hop and all that stuff kids like these days, so I'm with you. You're right, they got no style. Not that your daughter hasn't got style, I'm sure she does, but there's such a thing as peer pressure, especially at that age, and..."

"Shut up," he said.

"Okay," I said.

"She wrote me from San Francisco, so I know she's here," he went on as if I'd never said a word. "No return address. I have some relatives in North Beach, but they tell me she never got in touch with them."

"Did she run away?" I asked.

"As opposed to what?" he shot back.

I swallowed. I was already working up a sweat and we hadn't even talked money yet. I hoped the dough would be worth it. "I mean, she ran away without telling you where she was going, or she planned to leave and start a new life, possibly with your relatives out here."

He laughed derisively, and I merely smiled politely. "She's seventeen, what do you mean start a new life? She's only a *baby*, for Christ's sake."

"So if she didn't get in touch with your family here, why San Francisco?"

"That's what I want you to find out, Mister Valentine. You are Italian, aren't you?"

"Sure," I said. "New York, too."

"Yes, I know."

"Oh, I mentioned that? I don't remember."

"I had you checked out."

"Already? By who?"

"I have friends in this town, Mister Valentine. You think I'd hire just any jerk to find my daughter? I need someone low-key like yourself. I avoid high profile business of this nature. My line of work is, shall we say, of a sensitive nature, and I don't like to advertise my whereabouts and business dealings to the general public. Do I make myself clear?"

His words were bubbles in a murky lagoon to me, but I lied to save face. Literally. "Crystal," I said. "What else can you tell me about Lucy?"

"What do you want to know, exactly?"

"Well, how is your relationship with her?" I gulped. I was tired of feeling on the defensive with this quivering hit man. Who cares if he had an itchy trigger finger? This was *my* office he was shivering in. "What I mean is, is she *avoiding* you?"

Again he closed his eyes and reopened them. "Obviously she is *avoiding* me, Mister Valentine. If all I had to do was call her up and go pick her up at the airport, I wouldn't need *you*, would I?"

"So you had a falling out, I take it."

"Of a sort. I don't want to go into detail about my personal life, Mister Valentine."

"Vic. You can call me Vic."

"When and if I know you better. The more I talk to you the less I like you, to be frank. But I trust my sources, so I'll give you a chance."

Speaking of chances, I took a big one just then. I'd had it with this character already, and if he wasted me I only hoped I'd live long enough to write him a thank you note. "Look, Shiv, I feel under no obligation whatsoever to find your daughter. This is business, not personal, as the saying goes. You're not doing me any big favor to hire me for this job, just like I wouldn't be doing you a big favor to take it. We can both ply our respective trades elsewhere. Only after money has changed hands will I feel in a position of obligation to you, and since that hasn't happened yet, you're free to walk out of here and get on with your life without me, and I'll do the same. I mean, without you, not me. I'm stuck with me. You're not. Now, do I make *myself* clear?" If my love life had been better I would never have been so bold. As it was, I felt I had nothing to lose.

He looked at me for a while, studying my face, then he broke into a broad grin, stood up, and reached his shivering hand for a shake. I accepted and found his grip to be firm, uncomfortably so, despite the illusion of weakness. "You're my man, Vic," he said. "I was waiting for you to show some *chutzpah*. The way you were acting, like a freakin' pussy, well, you had me worried. I need a man with two balls knockin' when he walks."

"*Clang, clang, clang*," I said, and he laughed. Then he sat back down and I continued, feeling manly and full of masculine camaraderie, Mafia style. I'd already made up my mind this guy was Mob. Everything about him screamed "import-export." I knew the type from back East, from my 'hood. I could've been wrong, but I decided to coast under that assumption just to play it safe. We weren't exactly old-time goombahs yet, and if I took this case and screwed up there was a chance I'd wind up a sea monkey in San Francisco Bay. I'd never dealt directly with a goodfella before, but I was desperate and I knew he had plenty of cash. If I played my cards right, I'd be able to take a long overdue vacation. And if I didn't, what the hell, I'd be on permanent vacation. Either way, I'd be better off than I was, I figured. So Shiv sat back and relaxed and explained how Lucy was a little wild and rebellious and thought she could live without her Daddy just fine. He chalked it up to normal teenage angst but I could tell with my gift for reading human nature that Lucy was not your average runaway with an attitude problem. After all, her old man wasn't your average authority figure. She was probably real mixed-up, found out her father was a shady character, and took off to escape her evil environs. This was how I read it at the time, anyway. The little he told me about her intrigued me, but I knew what it was that *really* inspired me: Little Elvis, coughing up a storm between my legs, stifled by my pants and my telepathic pleas for restraint. Lucy was a babe, and Little Elvis wanted to meet her. He was a selfish bastard, and ignorant, too, because if Daddy caught me boinking his daughter Little Elvis would be surfing down a sewer pipe, and if the cops caught me he'd wind up doing the jailhouse rock with some unpleasant partners. I wouldn't let him be anyone's punk. I was keeping him under wraps, no matter how much he tried to plea bargain with me. Lucy was not a romantic prospect, I kept telling myself as I looked at the picture and listened seriously to Shiv talk about her privileged childhood, at least in his eyes. *She's trouble*, I said to myself, over and over and over, trying in vain to drown out Little Elvis' cries for release. Nonetheless, after Shiv was finished telling me what a princess his daughter was, and how he'd give his life to save her from any potential jeopardy, I couldn't wait for him to leave so I could get started on the case.

On his way out he paid me my retainer fee plus a generous bonus. We both agreed that New York was the center of the Universe and San Francisco merely a petty satellite. Actually I only pretended to agree, because in truth I could never live in New York again. Too many people like him there. I hoped to one day wind up in Seattle, anyway. I need more rain, man.

When he left all I had were his hotel number and the picture of Lucy to show around town, discreetly, as he'd instructed. He was a very self-conscious guy. That wasn't a good sign. Paranoid clients usually have something to hide that I'd rather not find. But money and Little Elvis talked to me that evening, and like an idiot I listened, forgetting all about the mysterious romantic phone calls, at least temporarily. I thought instead about my fortune cookie for the day, the ominous *"Life: Lights go on, brief flurry of confusion, lights go out."* If only the light wasn't so bright it wouldn't be so bad, I thought. It glared in my vision and made me see spots so I could only stumble blindly down my path, reaching out for landmarks and anchors and other sympathetic hands. I was thinking about this when I went into the bathroom and the light bulb blew out with a pop and I stood there pissing aimlessly in the dark, hoping I was right on target but never being completely sure that I was. When that light goes out, it goes quickly, and without warning. I was having second thoughts about the Lucy case as I contemplated this fact. I didn't want Shiv to put my lights out before my flurry of confusion had run its course. I made a mental note to replace the bulb in the bathroom first thing in the morning, and finally fell asleep.

Chapter Three
LUST FUND

So what happens when a lone wolf meets a loan shark in the woods? Simple: the shark is out of his territory, so he can't breathe and he croaks. But what happens when the lone wolf meets the loan shark in the *ocean*? The wolf drowns, of course. All I had to establish was whose turf I was on, and the answer was: mine. Shiv probably didn't know San Francisco at all, or else why would he hire a small timer like me? I was already approaching this situation as adversarial, which may have been jumping the proverbial gun, but Shiv had put me on the defensive with his threatening demeanor, plus I was secretly entertaining immoral notions about his beautiful teenage daughter, so I figured the gauntlet had already been thrown.

What was happening to me? I used to be such a romantic. Now I actually fantasized about underage Mob brats, based purely on a photograph and my imagination. I hoped Doc would hire some go-go dancers soon. I was obviously desperate and didn't fully realize it.

Actually, I had no real intentions of banging this girl once I found her. For one thing, why the hell would she want me? I was twice her age, and I didn't wear a backward baseball cap. I had slight love handles. She was probably shacked up right now with some longhaired rapping surfer stud with a washboard stomach and an earring. A Philosophy major who worked part time in a hot dance club as a bouncer. I wasn't in her league. But the fantasy gave me impetus. It always does.

I was uncomfortable, too, with the idea of being "checked out" by Shiv's mysterious sources. Maybe he meant Rose. Or Doc. The Mob can get to anybody. I'd seen it in the movies, so I knew it was true. I tried not to let paranoia get the best of me as I set out that day to find Lucy.

Like I said, Shiv hadn't given me much to go on. I knew she had relatives in North Beach—naturally, since it was San Francisco's equivalent of Little Italy—so I decided to start there. I still heard Julie London singing "Cry Me A River" in the back of my head somewhere, but Lucy was front and center for now.

I was already cruising North Beach in my Corvair, trying to find a place to park, when I realized I'd forgotten to change the bulb in my bathroom. The symbolism bothered me, and I almost drove all the way back to take care of it, but decided against it. Doc had brainwashed me with this symbolism crap. I had to think rationally for a change. I parked not far from Washington Square and took a walk around, the photo of Lucy deep in the pocket of my trench coat, my Ray-Ban wayfarers stylishly deflecting the still soft rays of the springtime sun.

I like North Beach. It isn't what it used to be, not even as recently as when I first arrived in this town from New York seven or so years ago. Back then the sex merchants were still thriving, there were fewer boutiques and high falutin' fast food joints, it was less gentrified and not so much an annex of nearby Chinatown. I like Chinatown, too, but it was spilling over its borders and robbing North Beach of its own ethnic charms. Nothing I could do about it, so I let it slide. I can't do much about anything going on around me. As long as I don't allow gentrification of my own soul I'll be content.

I can't offer too much descriptive detail of my surroundings in the course of my chronicles simply because I don't notice them. I'm not as meticulous with details as a professional detective should be. I read a lot of hard-boiled novels about my fictional counterparts, and they're always going on and on for paragraphs or even pages about how someone is dressed or how a room is decorated or how ambient the outdoor scenery is. Personally I don't give a damn about such stuff. I'm too inside my head to notice or care. Truthfully? I'm usually thinking about pussy, and how to get it. I know that sounds very crude, and I don't mean to offend anyone, but in my book dishonesty is truly rude, and I'm only being honest. I'm a standup guy, no kidding. I just find that my head is at its clearest when thrust between two fleshy female thighs. That's the only time my mind is in focus.

Yet despite my self-proclaimed boyish horniness and preoccupations with the feminine mystique as personified by pussy, I am a die-hard romantic. I'm very discriminating. Too much so. I think about it constantly, and avidly fantasize about voluptuous strangers in public whom I don't know and will probably never see again, but when it comes to actually getting some, I'm very shy and picky.

Yes, I need romance. I can't simply pursue sex for the sake of it. I need the whole mess. This is why I am a fuckup in life. My priorities are not conducive to my own well being, or anyone else's. I have little concern for what goes on outside my head. I'm a selfish prick in many ways. I admit it. I have no interest in what goes on in the Middle East or the Midwest for that matter. People are killing each other every day in increasingly random and gruesome fashion. Government and corporations are robbing the public blind, lying to them every step of the way. Racial hatred is rampant. Disease strikes mercilessly, leaving tragedy and heartbreak in its wake. I acknowledge all of these things in the orbit of my puny, ultimately meaningless existence. Yet I really don't dwell on them much. I'd rather think about breasts, thighs, and pussy. And lips. And soft music and candlelight. The rest doesn't matter much in the long run, because nothing matters much in the long run. So I concentrate on what matters in the short run:

Breasts, thighs, pussy, lips, soft music, and candlelight.

But you know, in my experience, which is fairly varied and colorful, given my occupation and background, most people think about sex and physical affection more than most other things, with the exceptions of money and death. Of the three, sex is the most fun, though the hardest to obtain in some cases. Money can buy you sex and often even love or a facsimile thereof. Money can also cause death, a rising commodity in our modern world. People make money off of sex, people are willing to die for sex, people unwittingly die from it. They're all connected. Sex, money and death. The big three. Put them all together and what have you got?

Religion!

This is why religion is such big business these days. The guys who run the show from the pulpit and TV screen are savvy enough to exploit people's simultaneous need for and fear of intimacy, their fear of death, and their ignorance about finance. It's a brilliant if sickening racket. My mother, who eventually went insane and had to be committed, raised my brother (who committed suicide at age eighteen) and me as Catholic. My father never went to church with us because he was generally terribly hung-over on Sunday mornings, either in his own bed or someone else's, usually a whore's. But that's another story. My point is that even though my mother had religion, she had no close contact with true love in her life. I tried to give it to her but that wasn't the kind she needed to sustain her. She needed my father to make love to her more, to buy her flowers and tell her nice things to make her feel good about herself. Without these things, she eventually lost her hold on reality, as well as her need for it. Physical love counts. Spiritual love is nice when it comes in tangible form. Faith in unseen, unfelt deities can only carry someone so far. It's like the difference between an oasis and a mirage. If you can't find your own personal oasis, you cling to that mirage for all its worth. That's where the religious racket comes in and makes a killing.

Myself? I'll settle for pussy.

Anyway, I was wandering around North Beach, basically pissing in the dark in my quest for a lead in the Lucy case. I had the address of her uncle, but if he was anything like Shiv I didn't want to deal with him. I was a nervous wreck as it was. Shiv told me not to bother his brother with a lot of questions about his personal life should I look him up. His name was Antonio and he owned a bakery. Yeah, right, I thought. Nice front for a racket. It's like Marlon Brando said in *On the Waterfront—everybody's* got a racket. I trusted no one judging by face value. I trusted few people on the planet that I actually knew. Doc was one. Little Elvis wasn't. I sat in Café Trieste gazing at Lucy's photo, sipping espresso, listening to opera on the jukebox and wondering whether to knock on Antonio's door for about an hour before I walked up Grant Street and did just that.

Antonio lived with his family on Green Street, actually, right above the bakery, tucked out of the way up Telegraph Hill. It was small and looked to be frequented by the same regulars from the past fifty years. It was called Guisseppe's. I assumed this was Antonio's name and possibly Shiv's by natural extension, unless either changed their original name, but I didn't have the *cajones* to ask outright. But if Lucy had assumed Antonio's surname, and I knew that for a fact, it might be a handy tidbit of info somewhere along the trail, so I made a mental note of it as I entered the little bakery on Green Street and confronted the portly Italian woman behind the counter. She was wearing an apron and an obligatory smile. She looked like she was around fifty, Shiv's age, and I knew right off she must've been the lady of the house, or bakery, so I smiled politely and said, "Hello. My name is Vic, Vic Valentine, and I'm looking for Mister, ahm, Antonio, that is. I'm a, uh, acquaintance of his brother. Sh-Shiv." I felt stupid saying such a name, but that was the only one I knew.

Her face didn't exactly light up when I said it, either. She had a stern, rather worried look on her otherwise pleasant kisser. She was probably real friendly to people who just wanted to buy bread and maybe shoot the proverbial breeze about the old country. She kind of nodded at me with the same expression of suspicion on her face and then walked into the back room, leaving me standing there with a little old man in a musty sweater and a gray Fedora hunched over the display case. Apparently he hadn't noticed me or didn't care I was there. Probably the latter. I knew the type from New York. Italians in their own 'hood were skeptical of outsiders, but never rude. Even if they had a gun pointed at your head, they were generally polite about it, unless you had offended one of their relatives, that is. Then it was No More Mister Nice Guy Time.

Speaking of which, Antonio showed up a few moments later, portly like his wife, with a silver-specked mustache and not much left of his graying hair. He looked a little older than his wife and also Shiv, and not nearly so svelte. He wasn't shivering, though, so obviously this disorder didn't run in the family. His eyes were warm but his face remained stolid as I again introduced myself.

"How you know my brother?" he asked, still not looking happy with my presence. Shiv's name obviously didn't carry much weight around here—either that, or too *much* weight.

"I'm a private detective," I explained to their constipated countenances, "and your brother hired me to find Lucy, your niece. Apparently she's here in San Francisco and hasn't gotten in touch with you, is that correct?"

"You work for my brother?" Antonio asked, his brow still wrinkled.

"Sort of. I'm independent. He just hired me to find Lucy and that's it."

"You're not a button man?" Antonio asked.

I let out a little laugh but then caught myself. "*Me*? C'mon, look at me." Then I realized I still had my shades on. Not being able to see your eyes can intimidate people. Just ask the CIA or CHP. I took them off and smiled. "I'm just a regular fella. I just want to ask you a few questions about Lucy and then I'll be on my way. Okay?" I flashed my P.I. license

Antonio looked at his wife, then back at me. He seemed lost in thought and I was beginning to wonder what the big deal was when he nodded at his wife and she tended to the little old man next to me and Antonio motioned for me to step behind the counter. He then led me into the back room for a private chat. Either that, or he was going to whack me. I had my .38 tucked behind me in my waistband, and while pretending to adjust my pants I fingered it for security. This was all cinematic razzmatazz, though. I liked to be melodramatic on a case for my own amusement, and often I amuse others as well. Antonio was as harmless as a newborn fawn, but it made it more interesting for me to think of him as a charging bear. I didn't think he was Mob, even. I didn't think he even liked his brother. He certainly didn't go for the idea of my association with Shiv, and I couldn't blame him. The back room was small and neat and furnished with a couple of chairs, a table, and a cot. A small black and white TV was on with the sound low, tuned in to some soap opera, and a Victrola was playing Tony Bennett. My mind flashed briefly on the scratchy musical messages on my machine, but then I let it go as Antonio, after offering me some coffee, which I wisely accepted, began to shed some light on the subject.

"I'm sorry if I offended you," he said, sitting in one of the wooden chairs, watching me sip fresh brewed coffee from a cute little cup. "It's just that me and my brother, we don't get along so good since I left New York, you know?"

"That's really none of my business," I said, recalling Shiv's admonition to stay out of family matters without regard to Lucy. "You don't have to explain."

"No, no, it's all right, it's all right," he said. His East Coast accent was beginning to kick in full throttle now. He could probably tell I was a homeboy myself, and this set him a little at ease. But just a little. "I don't want to overstep any boundaries, ya understand. What I mean is, I don't want my feelings about my brother and my family back home to get in the way of whatever business brings you here today."

I was pissing in the dark again. "Um, I *don't* understand."

"It's all right, Mister—what was your name again?"

"Valentine. Vic Valentine." For a second I felt like Sean Connery. But only a second.

"Mister Vic Valentine. Italian, yea?"

"New York, too. Brooklyn."

"You met my brother in Brooklyn?"

"No, no. Right here. I'm local now, transplanted like yourself."

"Oh. You like it here?"

I shrugged with feigned nonchalance. "It's okay. You know. Next to the Big Apple San Francisco looks like Toyland, am I right? But nice weather, nice people, good coffee."

"Yes, we like it, my wife Tina and me, we like it." He seemed to drift off in a reverie, but then he came back as I waited patiently.

"My brother, well, we haven't talked for a long time, until, what, day before yesterday? And then he shows up here, looking for Lucy, but we told him we hadn't seen her. Now you come around—he must suspect something, then. This is why I seem a bit *nervous*."

"Wait—you think your own brother would someone to knock you *off*?" I grinned slightly, feeling a bit tough without earning it. As usual.

"What? Oh, when I asked are you a button man, heh. No. He wouldn't have to hire out. Some people would do it for nothing."

"Who? What for? Or am I prying?"

"You are not, you are not—you are just a private detective, like in the movies, yea?"

"More or less. I know nothing about your brother, except he's Lucy's old man and he wants her found. Says she ran away, he looked you up to see if she'd contacted you, you told him no, she hadn't."

He started to fret again. "So why did he send you, then?"

"He didn't, officially. He told me about you, said I could ask some questions about Lucy that may help me find her. He didn't tell me much about her himself. He seemed anxious to close the deal and get on with his life. Not to suggest he isn't worried. Obviously he is, or he wouldn't have flown all the way out here."

Antonio waved his hand in disgust. "Let me tell you something, Mister Vic Valentine. My brother doesn't give a *damn* about his daughter. He was forced to marry Lucy's mother when she got knocked up, and they're Catholic, you know how it is, so they stayed married, but my brother has no love for her or for Lucy. Lucy's mother was a good woman, and very beautiful. But my brother—I don't know. He wanted her for the bed only, and not just her. He wanted..." He stopped, and seemed to drift off again, and then came back. "The only reason I tell you these things is because if it gets back to him I won't have to kill you. *He* will."

"So you're taking my confidence for granted," I said, and nodded. "Understood." Then I backpedaled a little. "You referred to Lucy's mother in the past tense just now. Is she—?"

He nodded grimly. "About a year ago. Cancer. Found it too late, a lump in her breast. I say he killed her, the louse. She was overweight and smoking and drinking on the sly while he was out playing the field, and Lucy, Lucy wanted no part of him. She only stayed long enough around the house for her mother's sake. The day after the funeral, she came out here."

"I get the impression you have seen Lucy since she's been out here."

He nodded. "Briefly. She stayed with us for a little while, and then she got in with a bad crowd of teenagers and started acting cheap, and she wouldn't go to school, and she said if we told her father where she was she'd kill herself. But she was getting so wild, out of hand, and finally, finally, she ran away from us too. We get a postcard from her now and then telling us she's okay, but I don't know where she is."

"In the Bay Area at least? Shiv says he got a letter postmarked here from her not long ago."

"Shiv?"

"Your brother."

Antonio half-smiled, almost sadly. "*Shiv*," he repeated snidely. "I haven't heard that in years."

"Not the name he was born with, I take it."

"No, that came from his young days. He used to mix it up a lot, carried a switchblade. You noticed his scar. A war wound from the old days. He was some punk. Always in trouble. The Family almost disowned him several times until he finally learned to control his temper."

I fidgeted. "Bad temper, huh?"

"The worst. He's a *killer*. Watch yourself."

Nervously I laughed. "He's got no reason to go off on me. If I don't find Lucy, well, it's only business. If I do, I'll turn her over and that will be that."

"No, it won't," Antonio said, looking me dead in the eyes.

"What's *that* mean?"

"Means Lucy will run away again, or kill herself. If anything happens, my brother will hold you personally responsible."

I gulped in an obvious way. "Me?" I squeaked. "Why *me*? Got nothin' to do with me!"

"You don't get it. Why do you think I'm telling you all this stuff? Because I'm warning you. I don't want any innocent blood on my conscience. Not ever again."

I let the "not ever again" part slide for now, but the "innocent blood" bit was hard to ignore, since he apparently meant *mine*. "Antonio, or Mister Guisseppe, I'm sorry."

"It's all right. Call me Antonio."

"Antonio, I'm getting a little nervous here. I know that's not your intention, not exclusively, anyway."

Antonio held up his hand and made it tremble, doing a dead-on impromptu impersonation of Shiv. "Notice this? Know why my brother shakes?"

I shook my head nervously in the negative.

"Because he's like a *volcano*, trying not to explode. Oh, that's not the clinical explanation, but that's what it boils down to. My brother is crazy, Mister Vic Valentine. And you don't want to get mixed up with him. Why do you think he sent you here, huh? You said he didn't, I know, but he did, just by telling you my address. He knew I'd say the things to you that I have, and try to scare you away from him. He's testing you. Already, he is controlling you. That's my brother, and the rest of the Family, too. This is why I got away from them. Only my brother knows I am here. No one else, not even the Family. And you, a total stranger, he gives my address. There are people who would kill for that information. If they find out that you know..." He threw up his hands and sighed. "Too late now. Would you like more coffee?"

I was trembling a bit myself by now, and it had nothing to do with caffeine. "No thanks, Antonio. But what people would kill for this address? I got a right to know, don't I? Now that I've been let into this little secret society of yours."

"Not mine. Not anymore. That's why the Family wants me dead. But Shiv is my brother. If they knew he knew and wasn't telling, they'd kill him too. You, him, me, everybody. So probably you're safe for now. Listen, I must help Tina up front now with the business."

He started to walk out but I gripped his arm, saw the stern look on his face, and let go, except for my eyes. "What are you telling me? That just by taking this case I've signed my own death warrant?"

He threw up his hands again. "Who knows? Maybe I am wrong. But my brother knew I'd tell you this, or else he wouldn't have sent you here and let you think you decided to come here on you own."

"Antonio, are you in a, you know, like, are you in a Witness Protection Program?"

He put his fingers to his lips and smiled. "*Sssssshhh...*"

Little Elvis was about to dribble down my leg. "Antonio, wait a second here. What about Lucy?"

"What about her, my friend? We are like friends now, yea?"

"Yeah, yeah, bosom fuckin' buddies. Pardon my lingo, but you got me a little bent out of shape here. I don't want any part of this!"

He took my face in both of his warm, hairy hands, and looked at me with avuncular sincerity. "Vic, I cannot help you now. I do not know where Lucy is, and you are better off not finding her."

"But, but you make sound like if I don't, your brother will *kill* me."

"He will."

"And if I do find her, and tell him, she'll kill herself."

"He'll still kill you."

"I don't believe this."

"I am sorry, Vic. Truly."

"That's it? No advice?"

"Leave me your card. If I hear from Lucy, I will call you. What you do then is up to you."

"Either way I'm dead."

"All roads in this world lead to the bone yard, my friend."

"Yea, but Shiv wants me to take the short cut. I'm into long, scenic journeys, nice and slow and easy."

Again he shrugged helplessly. "I am sorry. Lucy will understand. Talk to her. She would be dead too if the Family knew she knew where I was. And Shiv, my brother—I cannot tell you his actual name, not now—and Lucy has taken my new last name, which is her mother's maiden name, to use so the Family won't find her either, but my brother would be dead if the Family knew he knew where Lucy was and she knew where I was."

"So let me get this straight. If the Family knew that Shiv knew that Lucy knew that I knew, then..."

Antonio pantomimed a pistol to my forehead, right between the eyes. "*Pow*," he said, pulling the imaginary trigger. "This is the one reason Lucy does not want to be found. But she loves this city, this area, so she stays. Where? I do not know. If she happens to call again soon, I will tell her you are looking for her."

"*No!*" I said forcefully. "I mean, just tell me. Okay? If you clue her in about me, she may not call you again."

"You're right. In fact, if you find her, don't even mention me. It may make her mad, and she might drop the dime on me herself to the Family. The more I think about this, the more I see how Shiv has woven a web around all of us. I am truly sorry. If it helps, I will offer you a discount on doughnuts. In fact, I'll have Tina wrap up a dozen for free."

"That's okay, really."

"I must go back to my business now, Vic. If you happen to notice some men in dark sunglasses following you sometimes, don't be alarmed. Chances are they are not hit men, but Feds. They won't hurt you if you cooperate. Really, they can be very nice."

Before I could even respond to this I was shooed out the door with my complimentary bag of assorted doughnuts. They were warm and smelled good, like a last meal should. Walking back to my Corvair I realized that my little visit had garnered me no hard information about Lucy but a serious case of paranoia instead. Just what I needed. I no longer wanted pussy more than anything else in the world. Religion was looking pretty appealing all of a sudden. There probably wasn't any pussy in Heaven, and especially not in Hell since how could they call it that then, and Shiv had already booked me on the next flight out of here. I needed religion more than I ever had in my life. At least I'd see my father and brother again, and maybe my mother if she was dead yet. No word from the asylum in a long time. Maybe she'd be sane again up there. It wasn't so bad, after all.

I went home after a stop-off at the market and tried to change the bulb in the bathroom. It lit up and went out again with a pop. It wasn't the bulbs, it was the connection. A bad connection can make all the difference.

Chapter Four
ALLAH SHOOK UP

"I'm fucked," I was explaining to Doc that night in The Drive-Inn. I was really putting 'em away, and Doc, as usual, was sympathetic and amused simultaneously. "Any way you look at this, I'm a dead man." Up on the TV screen was Doc's latest bootleg acquisition: *Bare Knuckles*, a classically bad '70s bounty hunter vs. kung fu serial killer flick. The bounty hunter's name was Zachary Kane, and he had a big black leather-vested partner (played by John Daniels) named, guess what?, *Black*. The soundtrack music sounded like porno Muzak. Yet despite all this, or maybe because of it, I was riveted to the action. Dead men have no taste, I guess.

"Sic Zachary Kane on 'em," Doc joked. Doc really liked *Bare Knuckles*. He could be a strange guy.

"Doc, I don't think you appreciate my predicament," I slurred.

"Vic, if nothing else, I *always* appreciate you."

"You fix that bathroom light yet?"

"Tomorrow, Vic, I told you. And if I can't do it, electrician will. Don't sweat it, my man."

"Easy for you to say. Tomorrow's a safe bet for you, but me?"

"Vic, this baker dude is pulling your leg. That's all movie talk. Witness Erection program my ass."

"Protection."

"Whatever. Why would the Mafia have you hit just for knowin' his address? *Lots* of people do."

"Yeah, but only I know his true identity."

"You've seen too many movies, Vic."

"Look who's talkin'."

"Vic, why should you be privy to this info, man? Why would Shiv set you up?"

"To control me?"

"Then why would the baker dude tell you he's in hiding? How did he know you weren't working for the Mafia, a kind of emissary like?"

"If I were Mob, he'd be dead. No time for conversation. No point. That's how he'd know. C'mon, Doc. *Think*."

"About what?"

"How about your own safety? You could be implicated by association."

"Shit. Then *I'd* kill you. Vic, just go back and talk to the baker, man. Ask him to be straight up with you. But don't even tell this Shiv guy about it. He don't need to know everything."

"He probably already does. Anyway. I plan on going back to visit the baker often, and soon."

"Yeah?"

"Sure. Great fuckin' doughnuts."

"Hey—any more of them phone calls from beyond?"

"Nope, not since coupla days ago. Why?"

Doc shrugged. "Just wonderin', that's all. Somethin' to take your mind off this Mafia shit."

I eyed him suspiciously. "Still no idea who might be callin' me, huh? I told you I got a second one that day."

Shaking his head, Doc said, "Fate, my man. All of your weird-ass experiences with women are being bounced back to you by the Cosmos, sending you messages from the age of romance."

"What the hell does that mean?"

"I don't know, I'm just playin' with you. I don't know, Vic, okay? I don't know. I know *nothing*. Like that Nazi prick on 'Hogan's Heroes.' Just relax. All that beer in you and you're a nervous wreck. Amazing."

"I drank a lot of coffee today too."

"That's not it. Your brain is goin' on hyper drive. Next thing you'll have steam comin' outcha ears. Bullshit overload."

"Yeah, maybe. How's the stripper thing comin'?"

"Nothin', yet! I'm still thinkin' about it."

"Yeah, me too."

"I knew you would be."

"Doc."

"Yeah?"

"Ah, nothin'. Skip it."

"No, what, *what*. I hate half a question, you know that. What."

"I think I've asked you this before, but you believe in a hereafter?"

"Yea. You go upstairs here and beat off right after this, same as always."

"No, no. I mean, y'know. God and all."

"Do I believe in God? Yea, sort of. I don't know which one, it's like a lottery out there, but *I* don't know, Vic. Ask me when

I'm in the mood. Right here, surrounded by all this weirdness and loneliness, I'm inclined *not* to. But then I go home, think about stuff, life and all, people, animals, stars, gotta be *somethin'* puttin' all this together, right? But nobody's talkin' worth listenin' to. Anyway, shit, 'nuff of this. I got work to do. I'll get back to you on that."

I nodded and finished my last beer and headed upstairs to beat off. Only I didn't. I played back my messages and heard Patsy Cline singing "Sweet Dreams." *Click.*

Another old favorite. Patsy Cline was one of my all time favorite female vocalists. Somebody knew that. After that came the cold voice of doom, personified by Shiv: "Hey there, detective. This is you client, your only client that counts. My brother tells me you paid him a visit. He tells me he tells you a few things. We need to talk." *Click.*

I wasn't in the mood for love, not even with myself. I wasn't even in the mood for Sinatra. I went to take a whiz in my black bathroom, feeling aimless in general.

I was thinking about what Doc had said flippantly, but it had resonance for some reason. Maybe the Cosmos were bouncing back messages to me from the age of romance, which was waning around the time I was born. The Age of Romance. At least as long as I was alive there was hope for at least a minor revival. No matter what age I was, I was a romantic.

I decided to call Shiv back right away rather than sit and torture myself. I needed to clear this up before I went any further. If I was already marked for death then being blunt with Shiv couldn't hurt, since I had nothing to lose anyway. Like he said, he admired big balls. Mine were bonging as the phone was ringing, or maybe they were the bells in my head. Whatever.

"Yo, Shiv," I said in my best New York badass tone. "What's up?"

"Vic. Talk to me."

I flubbed. "Ahm, about what, exactly? Lucy?"

"No, advice on San Francisco tourist attractions."

I could tell he was kidding but in a bad mood. "Well, today for instance, I was in North Beach, which has Coit Tower and is near Lombard Street, the crookedest street in the world."

"I heard."

"About Lombard Street?"

Long sigh. "My brother is not in no freakin' Witness Protection Program. Otherwise, how would *I* know where to find his ass?"

I paused. "Oh," I said finally. "So, what else did he tell you?"

"Suppose you tell me. That's why I hired you, isn't it?"

"You hired me to find your daughter," I said, trying to keep my voice from quivering.

"Right. And?"

"Nothin' yet. Gimme a break."

He lost it. "*I'll give you a freakin' broken leg! Now talk to me! What did my brother tell you?*"

"First you tell *me* something. Why was your brother giving me that crap about being put under by the Feds?"

Another sigh. "Look, I told you to stay out of my personal affairs, especially with regards to the Family. My brother had a falling out with the rest of the Family some time ago, but we're okay, him and me. But he doesn't want to deal with my problems where Lucy is concerned. He wants to stay out of it. So he probably gave you that line to keep you away from him."

"Tell the truth, Shiv, he told me to stay away from you." That just fell out, but I didn't regret it. Not yet.

"Vic, I sense building tension here, and it's uncalled for. What can I say that will put your mind at ease so you can concentrate on your work?"

"You can promise not to whack me out if I don't find Lucy."

He laughed. It was a sinister laugh, but a laugh all the same. "Vic, what has my brother been telling you? That I'm a *gangster*?"

"Well..."

"Vic, what did he tell you?"

"Nothin', really. I just assumed it when I met you. Not that I have a problem with it, not unless it affects my life, particularly its length, and when your brother started making with the Family history and how if they found out where he was they'd kill me for the info."

Shiv was laughing again. "Vic, anyone ever tell you you've seen too many movies?"

"I hope that's the case and yes, I've been told that."

"For one thing, say I *was* Mafia. Why would I need *you*? We, I mean, they got their own resources that far outstrip your own. No offense, but they're a major organization and you're small potatoes."

"Granted." I was feeling relieved. Prematurely.

"And two, they wouldn't take you out just for knowing where my brother was. If they asked you and you didn't tell them, they might do some harm, but just enough to get you to talk. And if this were true, why would my brother cop to it right away? You coulda been anybody, just some joker or a hit man. Anybody. He wouldn't tell a stranger he couldn't trust, because the Mob could get to a guy like that. Easy. It would be suicide."

"So what you're basically saying is, you're *not* Mafia?"

Chuckle, chuckle. "Sorry to disappoint you, Vic. I'm just a businessman. With a few connections, maybe, so don't screw me over. But I have no plans knock you off. Why would I?"

"What if I don't find your daughter?"

"But you will. Think positive."

"Hypothetical. I don't."

"Then we part company and I hire someone who is competent enough to complete their given task."

"I'm no bum, Shiv. I just want to know what I'm getting into before I go any further."

"What have I done to make you think I was a mobster, Vic? I'm offended, slightly."

"Well, you didn't say you weren't right away."

"You didn't say you weren't the King of Siam, but I had no reason to suspect otherwise."

"I don't *act* like the King of Siam, either."

"Vic, have I ever threatened you? No, I take that back. What I mean is, have I ever given you an ultimatum?"

"Not in so many words."

"Then cut the crap and talk to me about Lucy. I'm getting tired of this. Already I'm on the defensive. Do you treat all of your clients with the same disrespect?"

"Shiv, look. Your brother kind of shook me up today, so I'm a little on edge. I'm sorry if I jumped the gun, as it were. But in any case, your brother, well, he's seen Lucy, but he has no idea where she is, except she is probably still in the Bay Area."

Long pause. "He *talked* to her?"

"Yep."

"Recently?"

"No, not for a while, he said. She writes and calls sometimes, but he doesn't know where she's living or what she's doing."

"Then why did he lie to me, tell me he hadn't heard from her at all?"

"That's between you and him."

"Don't condescend me, or I'll *kill* you!"

I paused.

"Just kidding," he said flatly. "I mean about the killing you. But don't patronize me—or I'll *hire* someone to kill you."

"Shiv, I'm not in a position to patronize anyone. I can't tell you why your brother lied to you. How could I? What am I, a psychic?"

"I know he told you shit about me, and let me tell you something right now: they're all lies."

"Okay."

"Okay what?"

"Okay—*sir*?"

"*Don't smart mouth me, kid, I mean it!*" He was losing it again. "I don't know for sure what he told you, but he's got some strange ideas about me from talking to my wife, God rest her. He—he was sleeping with her, you know. For years. That's why he came out here, to escape the shame." God damn if he didn't start weeping. I listened patiently. "He slept with my *wife*, Vic. And he came on to my daughter when she was only *twelve*!"

"Shiv, I'm really not equipped to deal with all this. Maybe you should see someone else, a professional."

"Are you calling me *crazy*, cocksucker! *Huh*?"

"Shiv, calm down, please. It's just that you're getting into some areas that are not my field."

"Did he tell you about how he used to fondle Lucy right after fucking my wife while I was *out*? He tell you that? *Answer me*!"

"No, I don't think he mentioned that, actually."

"Of *course* he wouldn't! He'd like you to think he's just a gentle freakin' baker, Pinocchio's old man! He'd even molest a wooden puppet, that sick fuck! Tell me something else then: has he touched Lucy since she's been out here?"

"I doubt it. Shiv, are you sure about this? I mean, he doesn't seem like the type. Maybe he didn't tell you he talked to Lucy because you'd think this weird shit."

"Weird shit, hah? *Weird shit*. You think I'm makin' this up, don't you? Why do you think Lucy ran away in the first place?"

"I really don't know, Shiv."

"To get away from Antonio! Why else?"

"But, Shiv, she came out here, to where *he* is."

"Vic, you call me a liar once more, and I swear, and I'm not kidding now, I'll have you killed."

"Got it." I sighed. I had a headache. In fact, I had the spins, and it wasn't just from the beer in The Drive-Inn. "Anyway, I'll talk to him again and make sure."

"Stay away from my brother! And, Vic, if you have any ideas about my daughter, forget 'em. I don't want to hear that you and my brother were talkin' dirty about my daughter, you hear me?"

"*Shiv.*"

"You know why I shake, cocksucker? People like you, Vic. People like you. Now find my daughter, or I'll do some shakin' that'll make these pussy earthquakes of yours look like a Coney Island roller-coaster." *Click.*

I hung up thinking: Roller-coaster. Exactly what I was on now.

I tossed some darts at my heart board for a while. The phone rang again but I let my machine pick it up, thinking it was Shiv. After the beep, instead of another senseless tirade I heard Patsy Cline singing the opening bars of "Crazy." I knew how she felt. The recording was scratchy like the others, an old LP or 45. At least it wasn't a .45 *automatic.* Same M.O. as the other calls. Same person torturing me. I put my head in my arms and nearly cried from the pressure. I just couldn't take this anymore. My life was just too crazy, man. Patsy's sweet voice only confirmed it.

As it stood, I was more inclined to believe Antonio than Shiv, who was obviously a serious sociopath. Also, it seemed to me that Antonio was trying to say that *Shiv* had been the one who had abused Lucy. That was my distinct impression, even though he pretty much danced around it, but why else would she be so adamant about avoiding Shiv? Maybe they were both lying, to a point. I almost didn't care anymore. I looked at Lucy's picture. She sure was a dish. She deserved better than either Shiv or Antonio, and probably the whole damn Family, Mafia or not. I wanted to rescue her, to take her away from all this. That was my mission, I decided. To rescue Lucy from the Family, and if we wound up trysting, cops and gangsters be damned. Like Antonio said, all roads lead to the bone yard. If I were Big Bad Wolf to Lucy's Little Red Riding Hood, it'd be Primrose Lane, no matter where it led.

But after hearing both Antonio and Shiv hint at alleged molestation by an immediate family member, maybe *two*, I couldn't really think of Lucy in sexual terms anymore, age notwithstanding. I mean, I do have *some* half-assed code of ethics, or at least some general guidelines that I adhere to, however loosely. I didn't even beat off that night, breaking timeworn tradition. Make that *palm*-worn. I had my palm read back in New York by some gypsy fortune-teller in the Village, who told me I had a long lifeline, a long love line, and a deep career line.

Considering how my life has turned out since then, and with these recent threats of impending death, I could only surmise that all that masturbation had covered my promised good fortune with calluses, or buffed my good luck lines down to faded remnants of their former glory. My mother taught me never to jerk off, that it was evil. Maybe she was right after all, in a way. By jerking off so much, maybe I'd really screwed myself out of the life I was originally destined for. It's one possible theory, anyway.

Despite my noble attempts at purity where Lucy was concerned, I fell asleep and had a dream that I was making out with her on a sofa in a large, luxurious living room with a huge bay window in front of us. Suddenly I was distracted from my passion by a presence in my peripheral vision. I turned to face the window and saw to my horror that a thirty foot black dude dressed in basketball attire was bent over and peering at us with a look of bemused malice. I instantly pegged the giant Peeping Tom as her boyfriend and fled, but my movements were in slow motion, and I could feel the jealous giant right behind me, closing in. I awoke in a sweat, wondering what the hell had induced such a strange nightmare. Where did the thirty foot black guy come from, and what did he represent? O.J. Simpson? No, this dude wasn't a football player. Typical white boy fear of having his lady brought to unknown heights of sexual ecstasy by a big bad homeboy? But Lucy wasn't my lady, not by a long shot. Probably never would be. I was planning on being her rescuer, not her seducer. A big brother figure, with no incest on the agenda. In the dream I had a big brother chasing me. It's true I had watched *Attack of the Fifty Foot Woman* down at The Drive-Inn recently, but I didn't follow the Golden State Warriors even out of passing curiosity. Maybe this was left over from when I nearly had a romantic run-in with Doc's employee Monica and then discovered belatedly that he was screwing her himself. I wasn't in love with Monica, though. Nor Lucy. But they were both young and sexy and trouble. Perhaps my subconscious had mentally connected all these disparate thoughts together and threw them into a pot for some nightmare soup. In any case, I didn't sleep well for the rest of the night.

The next day I decided to avoid the bakery and North Beach altogether. I went into Chinatown to my favorite chop-suey joint again. I don't usually visit this place twice in the same week, but I was curious what fortune I would get. Louis the wise guy waiter was on hand to taunt me as usual, but I was good-natured about it. I liked Louie, he was a friendly guy and all, so he never really bothered me even though he apparently tried to.

"Wic Walentine," he greeted me. I still couldn't figure out if he kept saying that to perpetuate a stereotype as a gag or he really couldn't pronounce a 'v'.

I went along with it anyway, to be nice. I really needed a good fortune that day, something about a long life and true love and an upward career change. I'd have settled for any one of them, but with customary avarice demanded all three as compensation for all the shit I'd been through lately. "That's me, Wic," I said. "Burning a candle at both ends."

Louie gave me a mock-quizzical look. "I no understand, Mister Walentine."

"All you gotta understand is that I want the Number Five lunch special," I said with a wink. I wanted to rush through my meal and get it over with so I could get my goddamn fortune cookie. The meal showed up with typical urgency and I wolfed it down and asked for my check. I broke into my cookie like a kid opening a big present on Christmas morning. I stared at it for at least a minute, trying to digest the words and their possible portent. What really freaked me out was how personal they were: "*Do not get so swept away by the melody that you forget to listen to the lyrics.*"

I called Louie over. "You a music fan, Louie?" I asked.

"Music? Yes, I like music. All kind."

"Who do you prefer, Julie London or Patsy Cline?"

His brow wrinkled. "Who?"

"Never mind. And stop calling me Wic. It's Vic, with a 'V'."

"Okay, Mister Walentine."

He *had* to be putting me on.

After leaving the chop-suey joint, looking over my shoulder for the phantom phoner as I walked through Chinatown to where my Corvair was parked, I went into a payphone to check my messages. I listened anxiously but there were no more musical messages yet, only a call from Antonio, telling me he had a lead for me, and if I was interested to stop by the bakery. Since I had nothing to go on I did just that after hanging up.

Antonio greeted me warmly, as did his wife Tina, making me instantly suspicious. I didn't bring up my conversation with Shiv, more out of terror than prudence. For all I knew they were plotting against me. I couldn't even guess a motive for such a conspiracy, but that didn't prevent me from suspecting it just the same. I was pretty sure both were lying to me at least a little, and I had no idea why. But what Antonio had to show me temporarily eclipsed all thoughts of music and conspiracies.

It was a flyer that Lucy had left behind when she'd moved out of the upstairs apartment where Antonio lived with his wife. Apparently Lucy had been sleeping in the guest room, a small alcove with a view of the Golden Gate, and Antonio had found this on the floor beneath the bed. At the time he didn't think much of it, but after I'd left the day before he got to thinking about its possible significance. He said I could have it, so I stuck it in my trench coat pocket and bid him good day, promising to keep in touch. He never brought up Shiv or the fact that they'd spoken about me. All he said as I was leaving after my brief visit was "Watch your back." It reminded me of the final line of Howard Hawks' *The Thing*: "*Watch the skies*." Equally ominous, at least to me.

The flyer was printed on pink paper with black script. At the top in boldface type, capital letters, were the words "ARE YOU LONESOME TONIGHT?" Beneath that was an inartfully inserted photocopied picture of Elvis Presley, a publicity shot from the early '60s, I guessed, when he was still young and handsome but entering his safe, sanitary Hollywood phase, sans sideburns and sneer. Under the picture was a paragraph that read: "Are you following that dream but need a change of habit? Is your tender love returned to sender? Then call 1-800-THE-KING and Deacon Rivers will treat you nice and won't ever be cruel. Get in touch with your Inner Elvis and discover the wonder of you! Deacon Rivers' flaming star will guide you to a big hunk of burning love! Never be lost or lonesome again. Call now—or never."

I couldn't *believe* this crap. Sure, Elvis Presley was an established cult icon, and I'd even named my pecker after him as a kind of tribute to his everlasting greatness in our culture, but this sounded like a David Koresh type attempt at organized brain-washing in the name of The King. Had Lucy really fallen for this obvious scam? Only one way to find out. I went home to call this number, and as I dialed, all I could think of was why hadn't somebody thought to create an actual Elvis religion before, like me?

Chapter Five
POST MODERN FLAKES

Elvis belting out the opening lines to "Heartbreak Hotel" greeted me when I called 1-800-THE-KING. Then the recording cut off and the song segued neatly into a polite, steady male voice saying: "Hello, seeker. This is Deacon Rivers, Minister of the New Church of Elvis." In the background Elvis was now singing "Crying in the Chapel." It was nauseating but mesmerizing, like watching a UHF evangelist soak his audience of suckers for all they're worth with ersatz words of carefully calculated wisdom. It went on: "We are here for you now and always. I am here to help you discover truth through the message of Elvis, for that was his message: *truth*. His voice wasn't just entertaining, it was enlightening. I am ordained to interpret the secret meanings of his songs that will change your life forever! If you wish to pursue this route to salvation, drop by our Berkeley office at…" He gave an address off the beaten path somewhere, and I could tell "office" was a euphemism for "commune." This guy was seriously bonkers, and so was anyone who would fall for such a pitch. I vowed not only to find Lucy but also to bust this racket wide open. I couldn't tell if it was illegal yet—probably Graceland would disapprove at the very least—but it was certainly immoral. And you know me, Captain Morality. My mission was coming sharper into focus all the time. Fate was standing on the corner, directing traffic. He was giving me the high sign to continue.

I drove over the Bay Bridge to I-80 North and got off at the University Ave. exit. The New Church of Elvis was located in the flatlands near Emeryville. I was surprised to discover it actually *was* a church, or a converted one, one of those cozy Frank Capra-on-Sunday-Morning specials, way too quaint for the neighborhood, which was desolate and depressing. Maybe this was Deacon Rivers' intention, to give the illusion of an urban oasis. More likely the real estate was cheap and the property condemned. Rivers probably picked up this building for a song, as it were, and refurbished it to suit his bizarre purposes. I have to admit I was looking forward to meeting this con artist. He was an original if nothing else.

When I got out of the Corvair and walked toward the Church I noticed the details more. On the lawn was a cut-rate statue of The King in his glory days, the '50s rockabilly rebel, posing with a guitar pointed toward the heavens. It was made of stone and painted gaudily, matching the tackiness of the Church itself, which was purple with pink window and doorframes. A sign on the porch read NEW CHURCH OF ELVIS on a cheap gold plaque. Then beneath it was a cheaper hand-made sign that told me the OFFICES ARE IN THE REAR. The whole sight made for a surreal tourist attraction if nothing else. This obviously wasn't the location of the actual commune, though. There had to be one somewhere, I was certain. This Deacon Rivers cat was providing a unique haven for misfits and runaways, but I gathered he wasn't in it for the sake of philanthropy or even profit. He was in it for pussy.

Can't fool a fool for love.

I walked around to the back rehearsing my spiel in my head. My general plan was to go in under the guise of a "seeker," sort of like an undercover operation. If I determined that Lucy wasn't involved with this setup I'd bail right away. Till then I'd have to act sincere and lost and rather stupid, at least gullible, if I were to lend the act any authenticity. I had an interesting job sometimes, I must admit. It sure beat the daily grind most poor stiffs were stuck in. That's for *damn* sure.

I walked around to the back and, sure enough, there was a rear entrance marked OFFICE. I walked up the short flight of stairs and rang the bell and was promptly greeted with what I know as the Main Theme from *2001: A Space Odyssey,* a.k.a. "Thus Spake Kajagoogoo" or something Latin, a classical piece. At any rate, it threw me a bit, since it wasn't the usual "ding-dong" sound a doorbell makes—but then this was no ordinary abode. Just before the door opened I remembered that Elvis' 70s concerts always began with the band playing this melodramatic piece as an introduction to The King's entrance on stage. I was beginning to realize what I was in for here, hoping I was prepared.

The guy who answered the door was instantly recognizable as Deacon Rivers, and I'd never even seen him before. He certainly didn't fit the Podunk image most people have of the typical Elvis fan. If anything, he looked like a goddamn hippie. His hair was reddish and long and tied into a braid down his back that would've made Rapunzel look like Kojak. He had a thin beard and sharp blue eyes that made me think of New England for some reason.

He was tall, at least standing next to me, and he was dressed in a pair of baggy knee-length shorts, sandals with brightly colored socks, I forget what color, and he had on a T-shirt that simply read JESUS IS ELVIS'S PUNK. In my old neighborhood this probably would've been considered sacrilegious. Berkeley was truly the haven for heathens.

"Hey, baby," he said with a crooked smile in a mock Elvis tone. "Wassgoneon?"

"Come again?" I said.

"What's, going, *on*?" he repeated, now enunciating every syllable carefully, subtly insulting me, but since I'm a pro at subtle insults he didn't fool me.

"Well, I got your flyer."

"*What* flyer?" he said quickly, losing his smile.

I was cautious. "You know, your *flyer*. The one with the 800 number on it."

His blue eyes darted around busily. "Where'd you get it?"

"Around. You know."

"I haven't distributed those things for months now."

"Must be an old one, then. Can I come in and talk?"

He barred my entrance. "What for?"

"To talk. You know."

"No, I don't know. Enlighten me."

"But that's why I'm here. So you can enlighten me. Get it?"

He studied my face, searching for a giveaway nuance, but I didn't used to be Poker Champ of Bensonhurst for nothing. "You a seeker?"

"*Ces't moi,*" I said suavely.

"Say *what*?" His voice had a trace of an East Coast accent. He was no hillbilly, that was for sure.

"Yes. I'm a seeker. You were a lot kinder on the phone message. I'm feeling a bit intimidated."

"No, no, come in," he said, stepping aside graciously. "Sorry. It's been a rough morning. I'll fry you up a peanut butter and banana sandwich and tell you about it. Come in, seeker. Come in."

"Thanks, but I'll pass on the sandwich," I said, entering and patting my stomach simultaneously. "I'll take some coffee, though."

"Fudge or raspberry flavor?"

"Uh, how about regular?"

"Sorry, that's the only flavors I got." He shut the door and I was in there.

"Okay, um, f-fudge, then." I felt sick just saying it, but what the hell, when in Rome. Or Graceland, as the case may be. The little office was either Col. Tom Parker's headquarters or the shrine of a psychotic devotee. I knew this joker wasn't the Colonel, so it had to be the latter. I felt claustrophobic all of a sudden. I kept a close eye on him as he whipped up the instant fudge coffee in the little kitchenette adjacent to the office. What a kook, I thought. He wasn't living in the lap of luxury, apparently, so I wondered just how much pussy he was getting to make this operation worthwhile. What the hell, maybe he actually believed Elvis *was* the Messiah. That wouldn't be any more arbitrary than most other beliefs, I decided. Whatever works. I scanned the myriad of memorabilia on the walls as he handed me my coffee in a little plastic Elvis cup and then sat down at his messy desk, beckoning me to join him in the chair opposite him. I did so reluctantly. I didn't feel in danger, exactly, just paranoid that someone would see me here and think I was as insane as this guy, who finally formally introduced himself as the one and only Deacon Richard Rivers.

"Elvis' name in 'Loving You' was Deke Rivers, you know that?" Deacon Rivers said to me seriously. "It all means something, you know. It's all there—in his movies, his music, his *life*. All we have to do is look and listen. That's his legacy to us. *Truth*."

"Uh-huh," I said with a nod, still looking around in irreverent awe. There were movie stills, concert posters, dolls, dishes, towels, toilet paper, pinups, postcards, bottles, beer mugs, paper, pencils, pens, household appliances, videos, books, games, and just plain garbage featuring The King's likeness and visage, wall to wall, ceiling to floor. It was like his career had exploded inside of a microwave, and Deacon Rivers lived inside this combustible cubicle.

He seemed totally oblivious to my antipathy, continuing in earnest, "A lot of people who come to me are, well, shall we say, disturbed. Emotionally. I don't turn away anyone, except for snoopy reporters from Hard Copy and Entertainment Tonight and their ilk. 'Sixty Minutes' wanted an interview once. But publicity would only hurt this enterprise, you know what I mean? Exploit it. The media are to me what the Romans were to Jesus—or Albert Goldman was to Elvis. Who needs 'em? What I do is pure, and even if you are a lunatic, but you're sincere in your devotion to

The King, I'll here for you. We'll be here, I should say. This is an organization now, after all, not a one-man show, like when I first started out."

"Well, I tell ya, Deacon, your highness, sir, I ain't no kook," I said, trying to block out the sarcasm from my tone, probably unsuccessfully. "I'm just a poor lost soul looking for Truth in a world gone mad. If you and Elvis can help, fine. My mind is open."

He was watching me carefully. I could tell he was no idiot, but I hadn't ruled out maniac just yet, so I kept my wits about me. "How about your heart?" he asked. "Is your heart open to The King?"

The way he said it was the way I would've said it—mock-dramatically, lampooning New Age banter even while pitching it. He was good, no question about it. So I just said, "Yeah, my heart's open, but behind a wall, know what I'm sayin'? And that wall ain't comin' down till I know for sure who wants in and why."

He nodded and smiled sagaciously, or maybe it was sardonically. I just wasn't sure yet.

After a minute of this insipid beaming I grew uncomfortable. "What the hell are you smiling at?" I asked him.

"Elvis has a song for everyone," he grinned. "I'm just trying to figure yours out. It'll help me guide you to the Inner Elvis. Of course, I still have to peel away any layers of denial that still may exist. Are you in total or even partial denial of The King?"

"Um, can you be more specific? I mean, denial about *what,* exactly?"

"Then you are. Elvis was much more than a rock 'n' roll singer. He was a savior, at least for those who can see past the glitz and hype."

I rolled my internal eyeballs. Oh, brother. "Well, what can I say. I'm here to learn."

"And I'm here to teach you."

"Good. So, how do we start? I mean, do I go to confession that I listen to Dean Martin and then do twelve Hail Mama's or what?"

He grinned but didn't laugh. "Catholic, huh? I used to be Catholic."

"You and everyone I meet, it seems." I was thinking of the Mafia at the moment.

"I have my work cut out for me, don't I?" he said, looking for affirmation of his quest from an objective observer.

"Yes, you do," I agreed whole-heartedly, "but, what is it

exactly that you offer?"

"Truth. Through Elvis."

"Well, what I'm getting at is, when did you first realize that Elvis was your savior?"

"Why does this feel like an interview—or an interrogation? You a cop?"

I always get asked that sooner or later. It makes me feel kind of tough but it breaks my stride and annoys me all the same. "No. Just a seeker. Looking for answers. I don't just dive into any lake before I test the water, know what I'm sayin'?"

He nodded. "I first received Elvis when I was thirteen, back in Boston. Well, a suburb of Boston. I was watching 'Fun in Acapulco,' and there's a scene at the film's finale where he dives off of a cliff to conquer his fear of heights. That's when I first realized it. I threw away all of my Beatles and Stones and Zeppelin albums and made a full conversion. Then he began talking to me, first through his music, then whispering in my ear. It was *magical*. I realize this must sound completely crazy to an unbeliever or outsider like yourself, but Truth is Truth."

"I see," I said with a nod, casually glancing at the door and measuring the distance in my mind in case a quick exit was warranted. "But didn't it ever occur to you that Elvis probably used a double in that movie? For the cliff diving sequence, I mean. I saw that flick too."

He was giving me a cold stare. "You just don't get it, do you? I was looking at the meaning beyond the obvious. This was Elvis' method of teaching. He wanted to reach as wide an audience as possible. That's why he knocked himself out the way he did. Three movies a year, album after album, concert after concert—and in each one? A hidden pearl of wisdom."

I let out a little laugh despite myself. "Sorry. I was, uh, overcome with joy for a second there."

He stood up and pointed a finger at me, Elvis-style, natch. "I don't believe you're here to receive The King and his message. You're here to scoff. You're a seeker, all right. A curiosity seeker. Get the hell out of my Church, Mister Whatever-your-name-is."

"Valentine. Vic Valentine." I hadn't budged yet.

"Yeah, sure it is. And I'm Harry Halloween."

"Now who's being the skeptic? This how you treat all your followers?"

"We're *all* following Elvis. I'm just a guide, a gatekeeper. Now are you leaving or not? I don't have time for this nonsense. As I said, I'm having a rough enough day, and now you show up. Now what's it gonna be?"

I shrugged. "I came here with an open mind. I'm not making fun of you. I don't have time to waste, either. But you have to understand, as a recovering Cathaholic, I do have some leftover trepidation about putting my faith in anyone. And yet, here I am." I stood up slowly, shaking my head. "And now. you tell me to leave before I've even had a chance to understand. I guess I'll *never* find the answer," I sighed, heading for the door.

"No, wait," I heard him say, predictably. "Please. Sit back down. It's just that I get a lot of kooks and jerks hassling me, and I have to weed them out, you understand? There's a lot of denial out there, and so little time to deal with it. Please. I'll give you another chance if you give me one. Deal?" He reached his hand out for a shake.

I shook it and sat back down. "I can't make any promises I'll be won over," I said. "I'm just feeling this thing out. I've been to ashrams and cult ceremonies and orgies, you name it."

"*Really*?" He sure lit up all of a sudden. "What *kind* of orgies?"

I *knew* it. "The good kind. Or the bad kind, depending on your POV. Personally, I like sex. But it leaves me with an empty feeling, you know what I'm sayin'? It just doesn't have the answer I need."

"Well, all I can say is, you're on the right track. 'Long Lonely Highway.' That's your song."

"Huh?"

"Your personal Elvis song. Everyone has one, whether they know it or not. Yours is called 'Long, Lonely Highway.'"

"Never heard it. You sure?"

"Trust me. I'll dub you a copy of it, if you wish."

"Ahm, sure." I always thought my personal theme song was "Just A Gigolo" by Barbie and the Kens. Or by Louis Prima. *Anyone* but David Lee Roth. Guess I was wrong.

"Well, I suppose the first thing to do is invite you to an Orientation Meeting. That should help us both decide if you're ready to commit."

Or be committed, I thought. "When's the next one?"

"Friday night, seven PM, right here, or rather, in the Church."

"I'll check my date book, but I can probably make it."

"No hot dates, I take it."

"If I had a successful love life I probably wouldn't be here."

That was the truth, too.

He nodded. "I understand," he said simply. "It really *is* a long, lonely highway, Rick."

"*Vic*, I said."

"Sorry."

"Can I ask you something?"

"Sure."

"Are you really a deacon? I mean, are you officially ordained?"

"I'm doing The King's work," he responded rather curtly. "You either trust that or you don't."

"Well, we'll see." I stood up. I was anxious to get the hell out of there by now. I'd already accomplished what I wanted—an open invitation to a gathering, where I could scout for Lucy, talk to her, and decide what to do next. "I'll see you Friday, then."

"I'm sure it will be very enlightening," he said, standing up and shaking my hand again.

"I'm sure it will," I said, opening the door, nodding so long, and shutting the door behind me. As I was just walking off the porch I heard the deacon announce in a booming voice: "*LADIES AND GENTLEMEN, VIC VALENTINE HAS LEFT THE BUILDING*!" I wasn't sure if he intended me to hear that as a gag or what. I decided it didn't matter. Either way, it was eccentric behavior, and I'd have to tread lightly around this character. I just couldn't see how seventeen-year-old Lucy would get snowed by this guy. It was kind of a long shot, but I had a hunch I was indeed on the right track, riding this mystery train to wherever it took me.

When I got back to my apartment in San Francisco, the electrician was there, fixing the bathroom light at last. I said hello to him and told him I'd be downstairs at The Drive-Inn if he needed anything. Doc was there, and I told him all about Deacon Rivers.

"Why is it every time you meet someone it turns into a confrontation?" he asked me. "It seems people are always trying to fuck with you—clients, women, whoever. Why is that?"

"Sexual tension," I deadpanned.

"Yea, right," he said. "Speaking of which, you're just in for the first show."

"Of what?"

"Monica's gonna do a tryout number for us."

I looked around the place. It was empty except for some guy in a raincoat perusing titles in the Women in Prison section and another weirdo drooling all over the Babes and Bullets section. "*Us*, Doc? You mean me, you, and a coupla perverts?"

"Why not? She's shy, so it's just as well." He then reached over to the sound system and pushed PLAY on the CD deck, shutting out the volume to *The Incredibly Strange Creatures Who Stopped Living and Became Mixed-Up Zombies*, one of my favorites, which was playing on the big TV screen behind the bar. The title summed up most of Doc's patrons as well. Then I heard Nancy Sinatra singing "These Boots Were Made For Walkin'," and Monica Ivy stepped out of the back wearing nothing but neon pink hot pants, a black lacy bra with sequins glued on, glittery cowboy boots and a white Stetson hat, which she flung aimlessly as she danced around, flirting stupidly with the two perverts, who grinned lasciviously. She also had on a holster with two toy six-shooters, or "sex-shooters," as Doc called them, loaded with caps, which she fired randomly as she lip-synced the tune, the lyrics of which she obviously hadn't bothered to learn. It was like watching a poorly dubbed Spaghetti Western cheesecake musical, a whole new genre. Leave it to Doc. I noticed Monica's hair was no longer dyed green, but Mamie Van Doren platinum. She had on a ton of makeup and looked very uncomfortable. She had a very nice figure so I can't say I wasn't slightly titillated, especially since I had made out with her once anyway, and when she took off her bra and flung it at me I nearly grabbed her and kissed her, but I assumed that was against the house rules.

"Whaddya think?" Doc leaned over and asked me just as the number was winding down. Monica smiled at me bashfully as her beautiful breasts bounced in the air. The two perverts were scooping their jaws off the floor and peeling their eyeballs from the wall. "*Well*?" Doc prodded me as Monica ran into the back giggling shamelessly and Doc switched the sound system back to video.

"This can't be *legal*, Doc," I said, still stunned and stimulated. "Don't you need a license for this?"

"That's where *you* come in," he said.

"Where *I* come in?" I said. "You can't mix booze and nudity, for one thing, no way, no where. And I got no clout with that sort of thing, anyway."

"You got friends on the force, right? And for show time I'll serve fuckin' Olvatine and V8 juice, who cares?" He was referring to my now deceased connection, former Police Captain Al Marcus, an old buddy of my old man's from the old neighborhood, who took me under his wing when I came out here, helped me set up shop and got me out of a few scrapes in deference to the memory of my father, who was gunned down in an alley one night while off-duty near a Brooklyn pool hall. I suspected that my father was killed by bookies, since he was a notorious gambler and horseplayer, plus he slept with a lot of the wrong women, so it could have been an irate husband or even pimp. Captain Marcus claimed he didn't know, and when he croaked from a heart attack any knowledge he may have been withholding went with him. "Talk to them," Doc said, meaning the cops. "Give me a good word. You can do that, can't you? Promise them some sneak peeks, booze on the house, but not during show time. You can do that, can't you?"

"My connection is dead, remember?"

"You mean your bathroom? Oh. But his friends still cut you slack, right?"

This was true. "I'll see what I can do, but I don't want to draw too deeply from that well anymore. Never know what'll come up bucket full of mud or worse."

He slapped me on the shoulder. "Vic, I have faith in you."

"Put your faith in The King," I reminded him. I was tempted to go in the back and see Monica, tell her I liked the show, but thought better of it. I had my hands full as it was.

Doc laughed at my Elvis crack. He thought Deacon Rivers was a psycho. Coming from Doc, that was kind of funny, I thought, looking around The Drive-Inn. Everyone had their own version of the Truth, and they all seemed odd to me. Maybe that's funny, too.

I told Doc I had some cool albums of Vegas stripper music from the '50s and '60s he could use, and he said great, we're in business. I told him we'd see, then I went upstairs and the electrician was just putting the finishing touches on the light connection. It flickered on finally and I tipped him, like he was a bellboy. He was an older guy and I felt kind of sorry for him, plus I was relieved I wouldn't have to piss in the dark anymore. The old guy politely ignored the urine stains all over the place. I cleaned them up after he left, and then remembered to check my messages.

Billie Holiday was looking for her "Lover Man," Shiv was looking for me, and I was still looking for Lucy, hopefully in the right place. I'd find out Friday night. I played the Billie Holiday song, what there was of it, a few times, straining to hear any telltale background noises, but coming up with zilch. No clues there. Then I called back Shiv, but he wasn't in his hotel, so I left a message that I had a lead and would get back to him Saturday morning with some solid info. I remembered as a kid I used to look forward to Saturday mornings, watching cartoons and cheap monster movies and eating corn flakes. My Saturdays were still full of cartoons, corn, and flakes, but it just wasn't the same.

Chapter Six
TEA AND CHEESECAKE

Crossing the Bay Bridge always makes me think I'm leaving the Island of Misfit Toys for the Island of Lost Souls (interchangeable between San Francisco and Alameda.) But when I cross the Golden Gate bearing north, it's like I'm going from the Island of Lost Souls (or Misfit Toys) to Fantasy Island, rustic retreat for the wealthy weenies. Marin County is slightly more digestible than, say, Contra Costa County, but that's like saying dog dooky is somewhat tastier than a steaming pile of horse manure. I guess that sounds obnoxious and unpleasant. I'm really a nice, charming guy. It says so on many of my ex-girlfriends' restraining orders.

Anyway, I found myself making the journey north the next morning. Fog was billowing in off the Pacific like an avalanche of dry ice on a Hollywood sound stage, giving my mission a much-needed shot of *noir*-ish ambiance. I had the radio tuned to KABL AM, the old fogeys' station, which played a lot of schmaltzy stuff my mother used to listen to. Besides Sinatra, they played Mathis, "Mr. Sandman," "Stranger on the Shore," Dino, Doris Day, Connie Francis, Bobby Darin, Julie London, Ella Fitzgerald, "Theme From Exodus," some big band swing, and occasionally '70s crap like The Carpenters. Whatever. Had to take the bad with the good, I guess. Funny how *I* loved this stuff, *me*, the former punk rock hipster of SoHo. Maybe I was carrying on the tradition of romance in my own way, on my own.

They were playing "King of the Road" by Roger Miller, one of my mother's favorites as well as one of mine, as I contemplated Deacon Rivers and his rock 'n' roll religious ring of retro retards. I had a friend in Mill Valley who was up on local lore and current cults, an Asian babe I would give my eyeteeth to sleep with, and I'm not even sure what the hell eyeteeth are. Molars with vision? If I have 'em, they aren't doing me any good. I'll take the nookie.

The Asian babe's name was Vicki Lee, and I was way too embarrassed to ask her to remind me exactly *which* Asian descent she was of, Korean or Vietnamese or Chinese or Japanese, because then she would correctly peg me as a white ignoramus who can't differentiate between the races. I'm no racist, but unless a Latino tells me, I really can't say if they're Mexican or Salvadoran or Spanish or even Italian or Iranian. Just like people out here can't tell whether I'm from Brooklyn or Jersey or Philly or Delaware or Chicago—it's all the same to these West Coast airheads. I don't mind, it's not their fault. So Vicki Lee would have no right to call me a racist, but she'd have the excuse, and I didn't want to give her that, not in the mood I was in. Besides, it made no difference at the time whether she ate sushi or caviar or pizza, since all I needed from her was some info, if she had any, on this Deacon Rivers cat. Plus I could gaze longingly at her long tan legs and fashion model figure and cherubic face framed by long shiny black hair I would happily suffocate in. And anyway, I did recall that she was raised in San Jose, which made her as American as hamburgers and apple pie. And Elvis Presley.

I idled the Corvair for a bit until Tennessee Ernie Ford's classic "Sixteen Tons" was over, then I shut off the engine and walked up to Vicki Lee's rustic little pad tucked away in some dense foliage and rose bushes. There were maybe a dozen flower types in the garden out front of her place, but unlike many literary observers of nature, I couldn't place any of them. Sorry. You'll just have to imagine a colorful burst of obscure (at least to me) vegetation. I was soured on flowers, anyway. I used to send them to prospective dates, even women I was actually seeing, but in my experience they didn't really work on sustaining a woman's affections. Most women I've known would rather have the cash. Then beat it.

I knocked loudly on the screen door, which was locked. I knew Vicki Lee had a roommate or two, youngish grad student types like herself. An Amazonian girl I didn't recognize answered the third knock. She was dressed in cut-offs and a T-shirt. She was stacked like Raquel Welch, not beautiful like Raquel, but definitely do-able. And *tall*. A romp with her would be on par with the Fifty Foot Woman attacking the Incredible Shrinking Man. That was okay with me. I'd crawl up inside of her and disappear. But I could tell from the scowl on her face that would probably never happen. She looked down at me, snapping her gum and grimacing. "Yeah?"

"Vicki here?"

"Maybe. Who're you?"

Why is it every time I visit someone they're in a bad mood with loads of attitude to spare? "You screening out her psychotic stalker fans?"

She threw her auburn mane of thick hair around with a toss of her oh-so-bored head, rolling her eyes. "That would leave *you* out, I'm sure," she sighed. "She's in the shower. She expecting you or somethin'?"

"Yeah, I called this morning. Name's Vic."

"Okay, hold on." She shut the door on me and I heard her yell for Vicki. I just stood there on the front stoop sucking in the floral scents pervading the atmosphere, aromas which strangely enough struck some chord deep inside of me, jolting childhood memories from their subconscious crypt. I closed my eyes and took a quick nostalgic time-trip back to my days in Brooklyn, watching monster movies on Saturday afternoon TV, then acting out the parts with little chums from the neighborhood. There weren't many flower gardens in Brooklyn, though, so I wondered why those flowers here and now reminded me of those forgotten idyllic times. Maybe I was mentally transported to a past life, a remote time and place recorded in the recesses of my soul. These thoughts made me feel poetic. I thought of one of my favorite poems, which I'd read on the wall of a L.A. restaurant once: "*Roses are red, violets are blue, I'm going to kick your fucking teeth down your fucking throat if you fuck with me cocksucker, you bet your ass.*" I even said it out loud, oblivious to the fact that Vicki Lee was standing behind me, listening.

"Touching," she quipped. "Walt Whitman?"

I swerved around at her, grinning sheepishly. "Mickey Rourke," I enlightened her. "He doesn't just box, you know. He has a heart."

She unlatched the screen door and let me in. She was wearing a skimpy bathrobe and a sardonic smile. The Amazon was stretched out on the sofa watching a soap, and another babe, wearing sweats and glasses, had her nose in a book. A feminist slacker's den, except Vicki was like something out of *Faster Pussycat, Kill! Kill!* I licked my lips as she led me into the bedroom and shut the door.

"You mind if I get dressed?" she said, letting the robe fall down around her ankles immodestly. I didn't pretend to look away as I sat on the bed. Vicki Lee never thought nudity and sex were automatically linked. She often swam at nude beaches, un-self-conscious and justly proud of her smooth, sweet figure. I ducked into a hot tub with her once at a party, but when I tried to put the moves on her she threw champagne in my face. That was all right. It was a sexy gesture considering the context, and after she left the hot tub I climaxed in the warm foam engulfing me. I thought of that distant night as I watched her slip into her undies and a skimpy dress, leaving about as much to the imagination as the robe had.

"It's good to see you," she smiled. "Long time. How've you been?"

"Peachy," I lied. "You?"

"Hm, okay," she pouted. She looked cute when she pouted. Also when she didn't. She couldn't look bad without the aid of fifty years or a sledgehammer. "Just broke up with someone. Again. One of those off and on things, you know. Then I slept with someone I used to go out with last year, a professor, in a weak moment. I think it was a rebound thing, you know?"

I nodded sagaciously. I sure felt odd looking at her just then. I sucked in my gut when she sat next to me on the bed, partly because I didn't want her to notice my bulge and partly because the proximity made me hyperventilate with sexual tension. "You're a crazy kid," I said, playfully slugging her on the chin.

"I'm mixed-up these days," she said sadly "When I get my Masters I think I'll leave the country."

"Oh? Where to?"

"Back home."

"Ah. Where was that again?"

"Hawaii, silly. Oahu. Not really leaving the country, I guess."

So she was *Hawaiian* after all. Maybe. "I thought you told me you're from San Jose?"

"I grew up there, well since I was twelve, anyway."

"Oh."

"And you're from where again? Pittsburgh? Cleveland?"

"New York already."

"That's right." She giggled, putting her legs up and locking them with her arms. God, she was cute. "Whichever," she laughed. "I've never been east of Reno myself."

"You should. Do you some good."

"Maybe I'll move to New York."

"With me?"

She looked at me coyly. "You want to?"

"With you? I'd go anywhere. Besides, I'm sick of the Bay Area already. I miss New York sometimes." Must have been those damn flowers talking.

She lay back on the bed and stretched, driving me crazy and probably realizing it. "How did we meet again?"

"You hired me to find your dog."

She laughed. "Oh, yea! I called you up as a joke sort of, but you were so broke you took me up on it. Anyway, it was a *cat*, not a dog."

"It was neither when I found it," I reminded her.

She frowned, still looking good. "That's right. Don't remind me."

"It's still an unsolved case, as far as I'm concerned. I mean, if there is a Santeria cult in San Francisco, which there probably *is*, that's the only explanation I can come up with. Who else would ritually sodomize and strangle a cat?"

"*Shut up!*" she said, sitting upright, then standing and pacing. "Anyway, that brings us to why you called me. As if I'm the expert on cults. My degree is in Philosophy, not exotic religions."

"Close enough. Ever hear of a dude called Deacon Rivers? Runs a racket based on the legend of Elvis Presley."

She wrinkled her brow. Still a doll. "Elvis Presley? Are you *serious*?"

"*I* am. I just need to know if *he* is."

"Wait a minute. Is he kind of a hippie?"

"Sort of, in appearance only. Why?"

"Well, there's this woman who lives around here, I see her at the Book Depot sometimes downtown, and she's always with this guy with a long red braided ponytail, and he's always wearing some weird Elvis shirt and talking about Elvis in a really loud voice. He's *so* obnoxious. The woman is beautiful, too. Older than him, it looks like. Kind of classy, too. Looks like she has some money. I can't figure them out."

"Must be my boy. Small world."

"This is the Bay Area, dear. Close-knit family of nutcases, all crammed around this foggy body of water. A great big loony bin by the sea."

"Took the words right out of my mouth. C'mon, let's blow this pop stand and go somewhere and talk."

"Like where?"

"This Book Depot joint. Maybe we'll get lucky and run into this woman. You ever talk to her?"

"Nope. Why would I?"

I shrugged and stood up. "Coffee's on me," I said.

"I drink tea."

"Figures."

She led me out though the living room. The Amazon and the

bookworm didn't seem to notice or care.

"Nice room mates," I said, opening the passenger door for Vicki. "Very gregarious, I mean."

"They pay their share of the rent and they don't butt into my business. That's all I need from them. Besides, I'm moving out at the end of the term, when I graduate. I should be working on my thesis instead of hanging out with private dicks."

"Careful or I'll be a *public* dick and embarrass you. What's your thesis on?"

She smiled prettily as I revved up the engine. "Twentieth Century Icons As Latter Day Saints and Mythological Figures."

I raised my eyebrows and whistled in appreciation. "Like I said, small world."

I cruised down to what would have once been quaintly referred to as the Village Square and parked where Vicki told me to, then we got out and walked to the Book Depot, a combo café and bookstore frequented by typical overeducated shitheads with time and income to burn. I felt somewhat uncomfortable in these cushy surroundings. It seemed everyone around me wore flannel and jeans and loafers and carried some type of reading material, whether paperbacks or newspapers or notebooks. Laid-back intellectuals are an inoffensive bunch, on the whole; I just found their company particularly sleep-inducing. A cure for insomnia I *didn't* need. I felt drowsy as I ordered a double latte to perk me up long enough to sustain a conversation with Vicki, then drive back to the galvanizing grit of The City.

Don't let my misanthropic diatribes fool you. I love human beings. They can be very entertaining. In a pathetic kind of way. And my profession affords me a front row view.

Vicki looked around but didn't notice Deacon Rivers' female friend anywhere in the vicinity, so we just sat and chatted for a bit, hoping against hope the object of our conversation would traipse in any minute. Such a coincidence would have been nice and welcome, but nothing to count on. Fate likes to sucker punch you. Expecting something then just having it show up takes all the fun out of it, as far as Fate is concerned. But it was hormonally harmonious just basking in the company of Vicki Lee. I kept up the pretense of shoptalk just long enough to segue smoothly into more erogenous topics.

"Can you really make a living being a detective these days?" she asked me.

"What do you mean, 'these days'?" I asked, mock offended.

"Well, in the old movies all you guys had to do was sit in your hovel and wait for some gorgeous widow to walk in and make a proposition. If you know what I mean."

"I getcha. Well, I hate to tell you, sweetheart, but crime and deceit are just as rampant today as they were in the black-and-white days. Not that I have any recollection of those halcyon times. I watched the same movies you did, probably."

"Except I saw them on TV," she quipped, amusing herself immensely. "No. Really. Being a detective seems so, I don't know. Quaint. Archaic. But cute."

Jesus. Youngsters. "*Cute*? Well, it's not the most lucrative profession in the world, and maybe it is a bit outmoded in this cyberpunk, or make that cyber*bum* culture of ours—of *yours*—but I wouldn't say it was *cute*."

"Don't get mad."

"I'm always mad. As in scientist. Anyway, I'm not charging you for my time. Or for yours, so what difference does it make?"

"Touchy today, aren't we?" She was toying with me and loving it.

"No, just touched as usual."

"My witty remarks are just boomer-ranged right back at me. You're *so* snappy, Vic. The Comeback Kid."

"Flatulence will get you nowhere. Flattery, on the other hand…" I sipped my latte and winked at her. Her foot touched mine beneath the table. She sure was flirty all of a sudden. To hell with the case, I thought. I was on a mission of mercy—for *myself*.

"Why do you need to know about this bogus deacon?" she asked me, shifting paddles midstream, as is a woman's wont.

"Case I'm on. Missing teenage girl. I was hired by her old man to find her, and I have reason to believe she's mixed up with this wacko."

"So you plan to infiltrate the cult and rescue her? How romantic. In a pulpy sort of way."

"Thanks, sister."

She laughed at my anachronism. "Well, from what I've seen of him—providing that *was* him—he seems relatively harmless. This woman seems to have him on a short leash. He's probably just a harmless flake. Forget about him."

"I didn't say she was in danger, this girl. The father just wants her found and returned."

She grimaced. "Like a dog, you mean?"

I shrugged. "Or a cat."

"She should make up her own mind."

"You haven't met her Pop."

"Asshole?"

"Major league. And I suspect he's, well, connected."

"What do you mean?"

"Mob," I whispered, lowering my voice and my face simultaneously, as if what I said carried great portent or an imminent threat.

She giggled at my melodramatic hush-hush tone. "Yeah, right. This is the West Coast. None of that out here."

"He's from back east." That shut her up. I sighed as if fielding wiseguys was old hat for a tough hombre like me. Milk your assets, even if they're phony ones. I was practicing to be a cad, one of the few options open to a failed romantic—*menefreghismo*, the quality of not giving a fuck. More Dino, less Frank. The other options were basically suicidal, and dead I'd have even less chance of getting laid as alive. Or so I chose to believe.

Then something dawned on me, a remote possibility that might shed light on a particular subject nagging me of late. "You haven't called for a while, have you?" I said in a leading way.

"If I'd have, you'd know."

"I'm out a lot. Detective work."

"I'd have left a message. I'm sorry, Vic, but then you haven't called *me*, either."

"You sure you haven't left me *some* sort of message?" I said again. "I mean, maybe you did and forgot."

"What are you driving at, Vic?"

"What kind of music do you like?"

"*Huh*?"

Suddenly it seemed my suspicions were not only unfounded but also ridiculous, the signs of desperation. "Never mind. Somebody's been leaving weird messages on my machine, and I just thought maybe, y'know."

"It was *me*?" She laughed hysterically, way out of proportion, I thought. "Vic, believe me, maybe in grade school, but I don't even think of you that way, and if I did, I wouldn't be so mysterious and subtle. You'd *know*."

My heart sank like it had an anchor tied to it. "Don't think of me in *what* way?"

"Well, you know, as a lover."

I removed my foot from the vicinity of hers. Suddenly I had lost interest in this interview, as it were. Once again I had mistaken friendliness for flirtatiousness. My impulse was to just walk away from the table, get in my Corvair, and head for Mustang Ranch at full gallop. I didn't, though. I still had some half-assed notion of chivalry. My metamorphosis into full-fledged cad was not going too well. So what if she didn't want to sleep with me? She was still a sweet, intelligent person with something to offer other than her stunning, lithe, warm, sensuous, young, firm, tan, curvaceous body. I stifled an ululation as I contemplated what I'd never experience.

"Vic?" I heard her say a few moments later. "Vic, are you okay? I lost you."

"Hm? Oh. No. I mean, yeah. I'm fine."

"Is it what I said? I'm sorry."

"What? Oh, no. No, no, of course not. I don't think of you that way, either." I glanced at my watch and stood up abruptly, spilling my latte and her tea in one graceless motion. "Shit, I gotta get goin'. You need a lift back to your place or what?"

Her facial expression went from remorseful to bewildered. She just stared at me while she wiped coffee off the table with a napkin. "Vic, what is it? What's wrong?"

"Nothing. I told you already. Got some detective work to do, that's all. Confidential. Sorry. I'll call you." I bent to kiss her, thought better of it halfway to her face, then swerved awkwardly away from her, making it look like I was stooping to pick up something next to her. "Thought I'd dropped something."

"What?"

"My gun. I carry a piece. You never know." I patted the inside of my jacket as if reassuringly checking my non-existent holster. I do carry my father's .38 on occasion, but today I didn't think I'd need it. Walking back to my Corvair with a hard-on and no dignity, I realized I was wrong. I could've used a gun on myself. Unless I learned how to be a cad soon, I'd have to start exploring those other options thoroughly.

My so-called "lead" had led me nowhere but the doghouse. I felt stupid and humiliated and horny, so course the only place for me to go was The Drive-Inn, haven for heartbroken heels. At least Vicki had seen Deacon Rivers in the company of an older woman. I didn't know what that meant, but then I don't know what *anything* means. Of course I never thought that Vicki could actually help me on this case. Her college major was just an excuse, not a reason, a feeble link at best. And yet, my initially pointless visit—sex drive notwithstanding—had turned up a tidbit of info. Vicki didn't know anything I needed to know about weird local cults, but she had seen my quarry in her own 'hood, with someone who could throw a kink in my path further down the road. Coincidence? That's not what Fate would say.

Fuck Fate.

Doc seemed a bit glum when I sat down at the bar and ordered a cup of coffee with a rum chaser. Or maybe it was rum with a coffee chaser. In either case I sipped on both as I watched Doc mope.

"What's down, Doc?" I asked him.

"Monica bailed on me," he said after a beat, wiping the same glass over and over until it squeaked.

"Whaddya mean—she *quit*?"

"Yea, man. Gave me some feminist shit 'bout how I'm exploitin' her sexuality or some shit. Where did she pick up that lesbo jive?"

I shrugged off Doc's sexism, which wasn't really sexism, but honesty, and said, "Don't look at *me*, Doc. Maybe she's growin' up."

"Aw, man, what the hell's *that* mean? Whose side are you on, Vic? Don't give me no hypocritical bull now, you bein' all goo goo ga ga over Bettie Page, the *queen* of striptease bitches!"

"Whoa, Doc, settle down there. Relax. I ain't takin' sides at all. But maybe Monica wants more out of life than to be a, y'know, exotic dancer."

"What do you think she's doin' on Broadway five nights a week?"

"Beats me. Tour guide?"

"Shit. She's dancin' in a club, man. Takin' it all off for bunch of drunks. At least here it's a bit private and dignified."

"Dignified? Doc."

"All right, maybe not *dig*nified, but at least she's workin' for a guy that respects her."

"So how can she claim you're exploiting her if she's shakin' her booty in North Beach?"

"That's what I'm *sayin*'. It don't make no sense. There's somethin' else eatin' her."

"Not me," I grinned slyly.

"Yeah, but I think you bein' here yesterday had somethin' to do with it. Embarrassed her."

"What? But I *know* her!"

"That's just it, Vic. She respects you, and wants your respect in return."

"Could be the same deal with you, Doc, ever think of that?"

The veil was lifted. "Vic, you may have a point there. Anyway, she moved out this mornin' of that room she was rentin' from me, y'know, since her falling out with her room mates in the Mission, and I don't know where she went, and, so I was wonderin' if, y'know."

"Doc, give me a break. I'm on a case, remember? The Mob brat. I got no time for Monica. Besides, she'll be okay. Give her some time to cool off. Me, I got my own worries."

"You're tellin' me. Guy was here lookin' for you earlier, guy with a face like nightmare pizza. Scary dude, man."

"Shiv?"

"Uh, yeah, man. Shiv, said his name was. He looked pissed, Vic. I mean, the man was *shakin'*."

I started trembling myself at the thought of it. Sex and death, death and sex. I was surrounded. "Shit," I murmured. I put my head on the bar. "Why am I in this spot?"

"You mean The Drive-Inn?"

"This is the *only* place in the known galaxy where I *don't* wonder why I'm here, Doc. I meant in the detective racket. Why can't I just get a job?"

"Same reason you can't get laid. Don't want to bad enough."

"Oh, I don't *want* to get laid? *That's* why I'm a celibate horn dog? I ain't neutered, Doc—mentally *or* physically."

Doc shook his head and sighed. "I don't have the energy for this riff right now. What's up with this Shiv dude, anyway? He the Mob guy gonna dump your ass in the Bay if you don't find his daughter?"

"Yep. Did he say what he wanted?"

"Not in specifics, no. Vic, I gotta tell yaI don't like the looks of this guy. He's bad news. I don't want him tossin' a bomb in your pad one night, 'cause you live just too close for comfort, my man. No offense."

"Doc, earlier you said *I* was hallucinatin'. Now *you're* talkin' this Godfather shit. Nobody's gonna blow up my god damn office, Doc. Anyway, I think I have a line on the little babe."

"She with the Elvis dude, y'think?"

"Yeah. This friend of mine in Marin saw him hangin' around this café with some older broad. At least, the guy she saw fits the description. I can find him when I want him—but who is this older babe, I wonder?"

"What's the difference?"

"Maybe none. Maybe I'm just jealous he's got a sex life. But what's he doin' in Mill Valley? His church is in Berkeley."

"Vic, this may come as a shock to you, but some people actually travel outside their neighborhood on occasion. I know you yourself are content alone in your room jackin' off, but c'mon."

"Can it, Doc. Shiv says he wants me to call him?"

"ASAP."

"A sap," I said, polishing off my rum shot and coffee. "*C'est moi*."

I went upstairs to check messages.

Shiv: "I talked to my brother, Vic, and he tells me you've been harassing him again. If this keeps up I'll have to take appropriate action. Find Lucy, Vic. That's *all*. Leave my brother alone." *Click*.

Whatever.

Vicki Lee: "Vic? It's me. I just hope you weren't upset today. You seemed like it when you left so suddenly. Was it something I said? Give me a call. Also, I just wanted to talk to your machine personally and tell it I'm not the one leaving music on it. Okay? Call me. 'Bye." *Click*.

Whatever. Then:

Elvis on 45 crooning "Surrender."

I went to my desk, sat down, and tossed a dart at my heart board thinking: Whatever. I was tired, confused, and frankly fed up. I wanted to escape all this madness, but then it occurred to me: Madness is my heritage. My old lady was a nutcase, locked up in an asylum. I had it on my agenda to go visit her some day, but kept putting it off. She had been an Elvis fan, I recalled. Maybe some how she found out where I was and *she* was the one leaving weird messages on my machine. The fact that this last number was an Elvis tune seemed beyond coincidence. Someone was either keeping tabs on me or was psychic as all get-out. Or psych*o*. I was like a magnet for maniacs. Maybe the phone company had a conspiracy against me. I paid my bill sometimes, but not always *on* time. Hardly ever. Still, I called them up and asked for that special service where you could automatically dial back the last person who called you by dialing Star 69. I just had to clear this business up if I was to continue on the Lucy case unfettered by petty distractions. I'd pretty much ruled out Rose as a suspect, as well as Flora. Vicki, too. Monica? No, not her style, and anyway she had other things to deal with these days. Whoever was phone stalking me was either bored or obsessed with me for some reason. I liked the idea of that, in a way, but once the phone company hooked up the callback service I could decide whether it was worth pursuing.

Then suddenly this rock came flying through the open window behind me, sailing though the blinds, which I always kept closed since I hate sunlight. The rock was small but could have done some damage had it connected with my cranium. As it happened, it landed on the floor in front of my desk, zipping past my shoulder at uncomfortable proximity. Of course there was a note attached with a rubber band. Before picking it up, however, I ran to the window and flung open the blinds to scan the street below. I saw no apparent suspects. The thrower would have anticipated my looking out the window and if they'd wished their identity to remain a secret they'd have planned it so they were out of sight within seconds. My curiosity about the note dictated I investigate this next, so I did. All it said was, "Check outside your door."

I did.

There was a box. I opened the box in my office, door shut behind me. The box was the size of a packing crate, and there were holes punched on both sides. Not a bomb. When I opened it, it was apparent why there were holes: there was a cat inside of it, with a red bow around its neck. The cat was gray and a little fat but surprisingly subdued. He looked up at me with sleepy eyes and yawned. Tucked inside the ribbon was another note. Anxiously I opened it up: "*A little pussy for a big dick.*" That was it. The note was typed, like the one on the rock. The cat meowed and climbed out of the box and made itself at home, sniffing around my room, apparently for food. Of course I had no cat food on hand, though I had almost bought some a few weeks before because it was cheap and I was broke. The cat rubbed up against my leg, purring. He seemed lost and lonesome. And hungry. It occurred to me this cat was a gift from The Phone Phantom. I picked the cat up and listened to it for ticking. None. So then I put it down and went to the corner market for some dry cat food and cat litter, which I dumped in the box the cat had arrived in, filling it up to the holes. This was getting weird. But interesting. I was easily entertained. Within a couple of hours I was used to having the cat around for company. We took to each other quickly. I was glad The Phone Phantom had bequeathed me this bizarre token of her affections. Then I thought: What if it's *not* a her? The

66

Phantom, not the cat, whose sex was still a mystery. No, I had to look on the hopeful side. At the end of this trail could be some serious nookie. Once Ma Bell came through I'd track down my stalker and settle this once and for all.

In the meantime I had to call Shiv back. Briefly I wondered if the cat was from him, but that seemed unlikely and ridiculous. He wasn't in at his hotel, and I was glad. I went to the bathroom to take a leak, the cat at my heels, worried I'd vanish on him. Poor little guy. I flipped on the light. Pop. Goddamn it, the light was out again. I looked down at the cat, wondering if this was the answer to my nightly prayer to God to please send me some pussy. God could be a funny guy. Or gal.

Chapter Seven
SINNER SANCTUM

Friday night arrived right on schedule. I pulled up in front of the New Church of Elvis and a throng of believers congregated on the lawn like an outpatient convention at around seven PM. They ran the gamut from hormone-addled teenyboppers to menopause-stricken housewives, from punk rock princesses to suburban sun worshippers. The one constant was the sex of the suckers: decidedly female, sir.

Sweet racket.

As soon as I'd parked, a pair of fortyish femmes decked out in apropos T-shirts and jewelry accosted me, giggling with girlish glee at something beyond my comprehension.

"That's Priscilla's car!" one of them exclaimed. She looked like a telephone operator who played bridge with my old lady back in Brooklyn.

"*Yeah!*" echoed her cohort.

"Come again?" I said, looking around. Obviously they were referring to my Corvair.

"Your car—it's the same car Priscilla had in the sixties!" the phone operator said. "Elvis bought her one just like it. Where'd you get it?"

I kept walking as I talked, my pace quickening along with my words in a somewhat polite attempt at eluding them. "I picked it up from a babe down in Pasadena around five years ago," I explained. "I was there on business and getting around in a rented car when I saw this chick drive by in this thing with a 'For Sale' sign in the window, so I pulled over."

"Was it Priscilla?" squealed the portly one.

"Ah, I think her name was Lynn, actually." She was a looker, too. I'd made a half-assed pass at her and got shot down, but still drove north in the Corvair. Alone.

I ditched the over-aged adolescents and made my way through the congregation on the lawn, just a lot of babes milling around sipping soft drinks and talking about The King. No sign of Lucy yet, but considering the demographics, I was hopeful.

I went inside the church and saw more female fans in the pews and aisles, whispering reverently. I also noticed some lone wolf males, guys in their thirties and forties, licking their chops and drooling, obviously with nothing better to do than stalk confused Elvis fans on a Friday night. Then I thought: here I was, too. Oh boy.

Deacon Rivers was slouching against the neon pulpit up front, chatting with some big-eyed bubble-brained busty babes, held in rapt awe by the deacon's smiling pearls of wisdom. I nearly puked. The pulpit had a glowing visage of The King surrounded by little guitars. I almost tripped over the extension cord and unplugged the neon Messiah as I approached Deacon Rivers and interrupted his private little sermon, obviously a warm-up for tonight's Orientation Meeting, which appeared more and more to be a mere excuse to organize a group of lost women under one hallowed roof, and not for purposes of salvation, either. The few males didn't look lost to me; they knew right where they were, the slime balls.

The deacon grinned in lop-sided Elvis fashion and shook my hand. "Glad you could make it baby!" he intoned. The gals shot me a collective dirty look and dispersed.

"Didn't mean to break up the party," I said with typical insincerity. Mentally I was already composing the synopsis of a screenplay, tentatively titled *Attack of the Killer Teenage Elvis Zombies*. It was part of my subconscious effort to provide my faltering detective gig a safety net.

For all I knew, Deacon Rivers was way ahead of me in the screenplay department. This guy was a prime time player if there ever was one, a bona fide con man and slick huckster bred by desperate times and desperate minds. I think he knew I knew where he was coming from, but if he did, he just played along. Obviously a big fringe benefit of his racket was having just plain fun screwing with peoples' heads, mine included. "The party hasn't even started yet," the deacon said, still grinning. "Can I get you some blood of Elvis?" he then asked, pointing to a keg of Kool-Aid in the corner. At least, I assumed it was fruit punch, judging from the contents of the plastic cups held by the believers.

I passed with a wave of the hand, half-suspecting the deacon had spiked the stuff with hallucinogenic drugs. "No thanks. I had too much liquid today already. I don't want to miss any of the meeting by getting up to take a leak in the middle of it."

The deacon nodded, mentally applauding my dedication, in a sly, subtly patronizing sort of way. "I'm glad you made it—what was your name again?"

"Valentine. Vic Valentine."

"Yeah, I figured it was either that or Doc Holiday. Anyway, there's someone here I want you to meet." My heart leapt and my mind jumped, expecting that older woman Vicki Lee had spoken of. I was curious what her connection to the deacon was. But then after my heart leapt and my mind jumped, my stomach did a little jog of its own. It was Vicki Lee!

"Hey, Vic," she smiled, stepping up from behind the crowd of believers beside the pulpit. "Right after you left, I saw that woman I told you about, and talked to her a bit. If only you had waited, you could have met her too. Although she should be here somewhere."

"What the *hell* are you doing here?" I asked as calmly as possible. "And why didn't you mention this in your message on my machine yesterday?"

"Surprise!" she smiled in Cheshire fashion. "I thought I'd just show up and see you. After talking to Zelda I became interested in this whole thing."

"You two talk while I get ready," the deacon suddenly interrupted. His eyes had been busily scanning the growing crowd. Apparently he had found who he was looking for, and he walked away into the midst of the madness. I raised my own periscope for Lucy while Vicki chattered on.

"I just decided to come and see what it was all about. I figured it could help me out with my thesis." She patted my shoulder appreciatively. "Thanks for bringing me in on this, Vic. It's weird how fate works, huh?"

"Yeah," I said, still searching the flock of fools for my quarry. The deacon had vanished. "Amazing. Who's Zelda? The old lady?"

"Well, she's not old. Late forties, early fifties maybe. Very nice. And *rich*."

"What's her tie-in with the good deacon? You ask?"

"Yeah. She's a sponsor, sort of."

I laughed, then caught myself. "You serious?"

Vicki looked nonplussed. "Sure, why not?"

"Vicki, this guy is a serious rip-off artist. He's probably milking the old broad for all she's worth while he just sits back and laps it up."

"Who's your friend, Vicki?" asked a middle-aged, rather attractive woman wearing a mink coat and too much makeup. I immediately pegged her as old Zelda.

"Vic, meet Zelda. Zelda, this is Vic Valentine. He's a detective!"

The expression on Zelda's fabricated face iced over, and her handshake was limp. "Are you investigating something, Mister Valentine?" she asked in a deep-throated tone.

"No, no, just seeking for truth," I said, putting on my best friendly face.

Zelda didn't really buy it, I could tell, but she was polite just the same. "How nice. Good luck to you." She then waltzed away in a pleasant huff.

It seemed to me the deacon had sent her over to ask me that simple question, and for all I knew, Vicki Lee was a pawn as well. The threads were interwoven a bit too tight for my comfort. This was getting stranger. I had trouble remembering the reason I was there to begin with. Somewhere Shiv was shivering at that very moment, shakily signing my death warrant in illegible script. I was duty bound to just find Lucy and get the hell out of there. Besides, I missed my new cat already.

"Guess what?" I small-talked with Vicki as we mingled with the ever-growing mob. "I got a cat."

"You *did*?" she said, wide-eyed. "Why? When?"

"Yesterday. I, well, it was a gift. Sort of. Someone left it on my doorstep." I searched her reaction for a sign of guilt. Either she was totally innocent or a real sociopath.

She shrugged, still wide-eyed. "Maybe it's from whoever's leaving you weird phone messages." She took another sip of Elvis blood. It suddenly occurred to me that the deacon might have Vicki under some sort of weird-ass mind control, possibly via the drug in the drink. With all these toxic fumes in the air, I decided to pull a Clinton and not inhale. I needed to remain detached and lucid in case I found Lucy. And even if I didn't.

Deacon Rivers had re-emerged on the stage by the pulpit and began speaking in a microphone. Zelda was by his side. She looked at me, pointed, and whispered something in the deacon's ear. Subtlety was not her forte. Vicki was growing more zombie-like by the minute, it seemed. She didn't pursue my cat story, which was odd, considering the fact she loved cats. Maybe her own tragic cat story had rendered the subject off-limits. In any case, we grabbed some seats in the pews closest to the pulpit as Deacon Rivers dictated his disciples to sit their dumb asses down.

"My fellow Elvis dreamers," he began, pacing the stage with

the microphone in his hand like a TV evangelist on a roll, "for that is what we are: dreamers, following that dream, one of the Ten Commandments as given to us by our savior, The King, remember? Number Two, *Follow That Dream*, right after *Don't Be Cruel*, and just before *Treat Me Nice*, for The King puts us *first*. Anyway, what was I sayin'?" He seemed to have a serious buzz on, imbued by the Spirit or maybe some spirits along with a few snorts of white powder. "Oh yes, yes—*dreamers*. That is what we are. Dreamers, sleepwalkin' through life. Following our dreams. And, say, how many here know all Ten Commandments? Would those who know like to recite them along with me, for the benefit of the newcomers in the audience tonight?" There was a wave of acquiescent murmuring, and the deacon launched into a litany of song titles unabated by the hesitance of his flock. "Okay—*Don't Be Cruel* is Number One, of course. Then Follow That Dream, our Commandment of the evening, and then Treat Me Nice, of course. Those are three very basic ones, I think, that lay the foundation for the remaining Commandments. All right, let's say them together now...

"*Number Four: Surrender*." A small portion of the audience repeated it in unison, obviously pre-brainwashed, while the rest, like Vicki and me, just listened, dumbfounded by the sheer stupidity of the whole thing. At least, I was. Vicki Lee seemed to be somehow moved, which I attributed to her drink, hopefully. "Surrender," the deacon continued. "Surrender to The King.

"*Number Five: Now or Never*. Speaks for itself.

"*Number Six: Return To Sender*. That's right! Stick an Elvis stamp on all your grief and worry and pain and fire it right back at whoever sent it to ya!" The audience liked that one, and cheered in response.

He continued, "*Number Seven: Wear My Ring Around Your Neck*. The way I see it is: carry The King's message with you wherever you go. Spread the Word, or The Lyric, and wear your love for Elvis with pride!"

Another uproar from the maddening crowd. Even Vicki let out a whoop. I was getting nervous. Zelda just sat in a chair behind the deacon, beaming and clapping and acting like a geriatric cheerleader on speed.

"*Number Eight: Don't*. That's *it*. Just plain *Don't*. Your heart will tell you what it is Elvis doesn't want you to do." The audience grew strangely silent, probably doing a little soul searching, fearful of screwing up by following the wrong dream. Me? My inner voice said Don't Get Sucked Up Into This Racket, Just Find Lucy And Blow. Thanks for the tip, El.

"*Number Nine: Viva Las Vegas*! Meaning: *live it up*! Take chances! Life is a crapshoot—but be careful not to gamble away your soul. That's where the *Don't* part comes in, and only you can answer that question. And now...

"*Number Ten: Shake, Rattle, and ROLL*! That's right, baby— have *fun* with your life, mix it up, get happy! *That's* The King's message." The audience went wild, and the deacon was already working up a sweat from ranting. I wasn't at all surprised to see Zelda hand him a scarf to wipe off some perspiration, which he then flung into the audience, creating a familiar hysteria as several female disciples fought for its possession. Nausea welled in the pit of my stomach, while Vicki just applauded and yelped with the rest of the congregation. The deacon, high on the audience response, went on: "Thank you very much. All right, thank you. You're a fantastic audience. Thank you." When all the idiots calmed down finally, he said, "All right. Okay. Shake, rattle, and roll. We're to do just that. Shake the *world*, baby! *SHAKE IT*!" The audience went nuts all over again. My patience was wearing as thin as an anorexic pygmy. I scanned the audience again for a sign of Lucy, but there were too many fatheads in the way. The deacon continued: "All right, now. Okay. You have all followed your dreams to this very place tonight, to receive The King and his glory, to listen to his message, to learn and heed his Commandments. Why? Well, Elvis has a song for that question, too. Know what it is? From 'King Creole,' his personal favorite? *Don't, Ask, Me, WHY*." The deacon punctuated each word with a shake of his fist. The audience ate that up too, much the way Elvis once devoured any junk food set in front of him. Maybe that was part of the process—create a feeding frenzy of sugarcoated garbage, get them addicted, then rake in the cash and nookie. At least, this was how I called it at the time. I wasn't sure if I was more flabbergasted by the ignorance of the people around me or by the sheer gall of Deacon Rivers' exploitative profiteering. I wasn't even sure whether I hated or envied him.

Suddenly I felt Vicki Lee slip her hand into mine and squeeze it. My hormones raced through my system like hot rods in a 50s JD flick. Our eyes met, and she appeared to be full of, well, *some*thing.

"Kiss me," she practically implored. "Kiss me, Vic."

I wanted to pinch her, to make sure I wasn't lost in wet

dreamland. "*Kiss* you?" I stammered. "You mean right here in front of Elvis and everybody?"

In response she merely pulled my face into hers and sucked my tongue nearly out of my mouth. That was okay. I let her suck. I sucked back. We remained in this lip lock until the audience had once again died down, and I breathlessly pulled back. Then Vicki Lee whispered in my ear: "Vic, I don't know why, but I am so horny!"

"Can I get you some more Kool-Aid?" I asked.

She giggled, then pointed up to the stage, where Deacon Rivers was resuming his "sermon." Reluctantly I followed her finger, but on the way I noticed that many other couples were disengaging from their own smooch sessions. Whatever this Deacon Rivers was into, it apparently was working. Despite my better instincts I felt myself getting seduced by this whole setup, at least as long as Vicki remained hot and bothered. We continued to hold hands and caress each other as the Orientation progressed.

"I'm happy to see your enthusiasm. Elvis appreciates it. He's with us now, you know. Here in this room now. And you know what he's doing? He's living through all of you! That's right, Mama! He's got a lot of livin' to do, so live a little, love a little for The King!"

I was under Vicki's spell now, not Deacon Rivers', but the point was, I wasn't concentrating on my chief objective for being there in the first place. Vicki's sweaty palm and pouty lips and lingering taste in my mouth were all distracting me. The taste in my mouth was a combination of sweet saliva and Kool-Aid, and I wondered if that spiked soft drink had infected my brain, too. I should have worn a tongue condom. Better yet: a *brain* condom. Mental disease was rampant in that room.

Perhaps it was because of too many bodies crowded together, but I was growing hot and dizzy. I needed some air, quickly. Gently I let go of Vicki's hand, kissed her cheek, and whispered in her ear I'd be right back. Then I went outside and breathed in the foggy night air. The Pacific marine mist and breeze helped to clear my head and soothe my senses. I began to get a grip on reality again. Then I noticed a lone figure leaning against a tree, illuminated by the lights from the church but still a shadow with no obvious identity. I moved a little closer. It was a young girl. As I grew closer and closer the realization crept along side of me, so that even before I was there I knew whom it was.

"Lucy," I said softly, and she turned to look at me.

It was her, all right. I recognized her from the photo, which I'd studied hourly since Shiv had given it to me. Only she didn't know who the hell *I* was. The noise from the church faded into a distant din as Lucy walked away from the trees and towards me. Obviously my intrusion had disrupted some intense contemplation on her part. She looked at me curiously, then suspiciously.

She was even more beautiful than her photograph. Now I forgot all about Vicki. I felt entranced by this teenage princess.

"Who are you?" she asked in her velvety voice.

The fact that this pretty face could actually talk momentarily threw me, since I'd grown accustomed to it being merely a one-dimensional picture. "Ahm, my name is Vic. Vic Valentine."

"How'd you know my name?" she asked, moving closer, trying to recognize me even as she realized I was a complete stranger.

I didn't know what to say. I was unprepared, even though I came to this shindig fully expecting to find her. Just walking out and finding her alone was not only jarring, it was a bit anticlimactic.

Now what?

"Well?" she repeated. She had attitude aplenty. Probably genetic.

"I'm, uh, well, to hell with it. My name is Vic Valentine. I'm uh, y'see, your old man—um..."

"Get away from me," she said coldly, walking away from me, not into the church, but down the dark, mean street, into the shadows.

I followed her, feeling somewhat maniacal, like a stalker, chasing a beautiful teenage girl down the block in the night, but in a way, it was enticing. I was getting sicker with age.

I touched her arm, and she turned and belted me in the solar plexus in such a way that told me instantly she knew how to defend herself, and wasn't simply striking out blindly. I groaned and she kept walking, but not very fast. Slow and cocky, in fact.

"Yo, wait up," I said, as I'd often said to people on the streets of Brooklyn. She was bringing out the old neighborhood in me already.

Suddenly she turned on me, silhouetted eerily beneath a lamppost, the last one on the block. A few more steps and the blackness and mist would have swallowed her.

"What do you want?" she insisted irritably. "I want to be

alone, and if you have anything to do with my father, you can fuck off right now, cause I'm not having any. Got it?"

I had to catch my breath. Even brisk walking these days winded me. I was so out of shape it was pathetic. "*Lucy!*"

"Don't call me that," she snapped.

"That's your name, ain't it? Lucy G-Guisseppe?"

"What's with the stutter? I make you nervous?"

"Well, yea, you do, actually."

"How come? I make my father nervous too. That's why he shakes. Maybe you've noticed."

Briefly the molestation allegations danced across my mind, but I kicked them offstage for now. I'd deal with that later. "Lucy, I won't lie to you. Not much, anyway."

"You call me Lucy again I'll kick you n the nuts. No foolin'. You'll never screw again."

Words of sex from those pouty, luscious lips gave me nasty ideas, but I immediately suppressed them. Especially if she was an incest victim. Notice how she threatened my ability to have intercourse, as if that were a male's most precious and vulnerable asset. And it is. But she was too young to know this, much less use it against me. I had to keep my libido in check for moral purposes. I have this morality problem sometimes. Can't get rid of it. Maybe Lucy would finally cure me, somewhere down the dark lonesome road.

"Okay, *whatever* your god damn name is!"

"Oh, it *is* Lucy. I just don't know you well enough to let you call me that. You may call me *Miss* Guisseppe."

A little princess bitch after all. Figured. "Okay, okay. *Ms.* Guisseppe, the reason I'm here."

"I know already."

"You *do*?"

"Yea, to hit me, why else? Just get it over with, why doncha. Dark, quiet street, no one will notice if you got a silencer or a shiv, unless I scream, which I won't, cause I don't give a shit anymore, and the bay's not too far away, so you can just dump me."

She was crying now, despite her forced bravado. She was only a child, after all. An extremely well developed child, but a child all the same. I held her in my arms as the sobs poured forth. She was trembling, poor thing. I patted her head and back and tried not to notice her voluptuous body pressed against mine. My kindness took her by surprise, but she welcomed it. She clutched at me like a little girl lost, which is exactly what she was.

"Lu—,uh, Miss Guisseppe, I'm not here to bump you off, or else you'd be dead already, right? I mean, ain't that how the Family works? Quick and deadly and mysterious, right? None of those are *me*, I can tell you right now."

"You mean—I thought you said my father sent you. Only the Family could track me down like this, or would."

"Well, actually, I never said your father sent me. But he hired me. I work for myself. I trust nothing organized, especially this scene over here. Why'd you get mixed up in something like this, so obviously fake?"

"I love Elvis," she explained with a sniffle.

"Serious? That's *it*?"

"Well, why *else* would I be here?"

Her naiveté seemed real, and it got to me. "Lu—, uh..."

"Call me Lucy," she said softly, holding me tighter.

"Lucy. Okay. *Lucy*. I need to get you away from here. This guy Rivers is a lunatic and possibly a pervert."

"No shit?"

"No shit? Oh yea? So why are you here?"

"I *told* you."

"Lucy."

"All right. I'm lonesome. I needed a place to stay, and he lets me stay in the mansion for free."

"Mansion? This cat has a friggin' *mansion*?" I thought of my hovel and my honest living and considered how life was so unfair.

"Well, it's really his friend's, but it's kind of his too, now."

"I don't suppose his friend's name is Zelda, by any chance."

"Yeah, you know her?"

"We met, that's all. So where's this mansion?"

"I don't know. Up in Marin County somewhere, near the mountain and the woods."

"Muir Woods?"

"Hm, near there, yeah. I think. Why?"

"Just wondering. What goes on there?"

"More of the same, that's all. Non-stop Elvis worship and, y'know, whatever. So are you going to tell my father where I am?"

"That's what he hired me to do."

"Yeah, but are you *going* to."

I held her closer, then let her go, gently releasing her arms from my waist. "I haven't decided yet. C'mon, let's get back inside, or else they'll get suspicious."

We started walking back toward the church, and I noticed for the first time that the stained glass windows, illuminated by the proceedings, contained configurations not of Jesus and Mary, but of Elvis and Gladys.

"Why were you outside?" I asked Lucy.

"I'm sick of these Orientation meetings. Always the same thing. And all he does is meet new people and ignore me."

My heart flinched. Oh no—not *that* snag. "What do you care?"

"I get sad when he ignores me, reminds me of..." She didn't finish the thought, but she didn't have to.

I didn't know what to say. Deacon Rivers was fulfilling the Daddy gap in Lucy's life. Right idea; wrong guy. *Big* time. And apparently Lucy was hooked, I could tell by her eyes and tone. This Deacon Rivers had to be stopped, and since 007 wasn't around, it was up to me.

"How'd you meet this guy?" I asked her, approaching the church entrance.

"I picked up a flyer in the Haight, some guy was passing them out by Golden Gate Park, you know over there? Lots of weirdos."

"Yeah. And so you hooked up with him and you liked him, huh. Did you always like Elvis, though?"

"Yeah, who doesn't? He's The King."

The way she said it, by rote, was in a spooky monotone, so I couldn't be positive of its veracity. That was becoming more and more of a problem lately.

"There any more churches like this one?" I asked her.

"He's starting one in Miami and one in Europe somewhere and I think in Tokyo, too, I'm not sure. I just overhear stuff. He travels a lot with Zelda."

"Oh yeah?"

"They fly all over the world looking for Elvis."

"*What*?"

"Yeah. Ricky says he heard of an Elvis sighting in Russia or Africa, and the next day they're off."

I rolled my eyes. "Where's he get his expense account, I wonder. Then again—no I don't. Hey, you call him *Ricky*?"

But she didn't get a chance to answer me. When we walked into the church, what I saw silenced both of us. It was a veritable orgy in progress. Everyone was kissing and making out with everyone else, half-dressed or less, all to the tune of Zelda playing what I gradually recognized to be "Can't Help Falling In Love" on the organ behind the pulpit. Zelda was in her underwear, a look of rapturous ecstasy on her painted face as one of the middle-aged males mounted her from behind. Then I saw Deacon Rivers making violent love with someone on stage, fighting off other females as he did so, since the ratio of male to female was way off, explaining, I supposed, why so many women were kissing and fondling each other. Lucy held my hand tightly as we made out way through the throngs. Several women grabbed at Lucy with zombie-like hunger, but she slapped them off. I was too busy noticing whom Deacon Rivers was slobbering all over next to the pulpit.

It was Vicki.

I heard him calling her his "wahine" as he put a Hawaiian flower wreath around her neck while he plugged her doggy style. Vicki's eyes were closed, her face twisted by the same rapture that possessed everyone else. I had to get out of that madhouse.

"We're outta here," I said to Lucy, and I pulled her outside, across the lawn, and into my Corvair. I wasn't even sure where we were headed, so I drove across the bridge and to my apartment, dazed and vaguely horny, but mostly disturbed. I didn't know what to do with Lucy, but I knew I couldn't let her return to that asylum of sin. She went along with me, strangely quiet and pensive as I drove through the night. I had found her, at least, but it couldn't be this easy. It never is.

Chapter Eight
MISERY TRAIN

When I woke up the next morning I was naked and Lucy was gonesville. Panic shook off my sleepiness in a hurry. Mentally I summarized the events that took place following our return to my apartment: I kept telling her not to worry, I wasn't going to just turn her over to her crazy old man, probably wouldn't unless I could determine it would ultimately be for her benefit, but in the meantime I had to keep her on tap, under my auspices, and she told me she understood completely. And then made her, no scratch that, made *myself* a makeshift bed out of extra blankets and a pillow in the outer office, near my desk, so she could have my bed. Hanky-panky was the furthest thing from my mind at that point, as I recalled. Lucy loved my cat, and when she asked its name I didn't have one, so I made one up off the top of my head: Puss. Was it a boy or girl? she asked me, and I wasn't sure of that either, so I just said it didn't matter anymore since the cat had been fixed and was basically sexless, and Lucy laughed and let it go. I put on some Sinatra to lullaby us to dreamland, and she didn't complain, but then why would she, being a wopette? We talked a bit before turning in, me sitting on the edge of her bed and...wait a minute. Something was fuzzy at this point. I remembered talking to Lucy about why she was so afraid her own father would order a hit on her, maybe talking about the old neighborhood or something as well, just to inject some levity into the conversation, and then I got up to take a leak in my black bathroom, and then *WHAM*!

The little Mob princess had cold-cocked me in the dark, as it were. But I had woken up in the office, stretched out nude on the floor with a headache that wasn't a hangover. And that's all I could put together. Had she raped me while I was unconscious? Or did she just want me to think something happened? Or...

The cat, now christened Puss, was hungry, rubbing my legs and licking my feet while I threw on some clothes and made coffee. I wondered what Lucy had hit me with as I fed the cat. I asked him but he played dumb. Typical. Then again, he meowed at me a lot, so perhaps he was trying to communicate some info I was too ignorant to decipher. As I petted the cat while he or she purred and ate, I remembered a strange dream I'd had the night before:

I had to take the cat to the vet for some reason, and when I brought it home, it was human, but androgynous so I couldn't tell whether it was male or female, so when I lay down on my bed and it started cuddling up to me I got very tense and rigid as it displayed its affection, licking my face and nuzzling my neck, so gently I felt around the cat being for a sign of sexual identity, like breasts, but the chest region was inconclusive, soft and lumpy but not necessarily indicative of a male or female, so I just lay there as the cat human climbed all over me, staring at the ceiling and hoping it was a girl after all so I could...

Jesus, I needed to get laid, I thought. The cat seemed to concur, since it suddenly ran away from me and hid in the dark bathroom. No, I needed sex with a female human—sex that I could remember. If I had nailed Lucy, it would have been very unethical, to say the least, but also probably very enjoyable, so at least should be able to remember it as I rotted away in a jail cell on charges of statutory rape. But what if I pleaded unconsciousness, that Lucy had molested me after knocking my lights out? Yeah, right. Explain that to a judge with a straight face. And to her father.

Shit.

Where the hell was she?

The mansion in Marin.

But how could I find it? There were many Victorian palaces in that neck of the woods. Who would know exactly which one it was?

Vicki Lee, that's who. That traitor. I recalled the look of pure joy on her face as Deacon Rivers corn holed her or whatever he was doing. She was his sex slave *wahine* bitch. What had been in that damn Kool-Aid? Obviously it was spiked. But with what? Spanish fly? No, something more elaborate than that—something with a mass mind-controlling drug in it, something I didn't understand, but planned to. Putting aside my feelings of jealous rage, I dialed Vicki's number in Mill Valley. For all I knew she had been in cahoots with Deacon Rivers all along. Hadn't he known that I was acquainted with her at the Orientation Meeting? *"There's someone here I want you to meet!"* he'd said in such a way that implied I already *had* met her at some point. Obviously they had discussed me before I showed up. And Vicki hadn't mentioned she'd be at the Orientation Meeting in her message on my machine. If she was lying about all this, she could've been lying about leaving music on my machine as well. All these thoughts, tangled up in one big ball of confusion, bounced around my throbbing head as her phone rang and rang. Finally her machine picked up, and one of her bimbo roommates breathily requested the caller to leave a message, so I did, politely restraining my anxiety as I told Vicki to call me back ASAP, it was very urgent I speak to her right away. For all I knew she was up at the mansion herself, or still at the church, banging away. Slut. No, that was cruel and judgmental—she couldn't help herself, could she? And what the hell time was it, anyway?

I looked at the clock on the office wall. It was nearly noon. For some people that would've constituted half a day wasted already. But for me, it meant only a loss of an hour or so. I finished my coffee at my desk, casually staring at my autographed pinup photo of Mara Corday, as I often do, then got up to leave, destination unknown, just out of my office, possibly to The Drive-Inn or Rendezvous to think some more, but when I opened the door to exit, someone was standing there, barring my way.

Just whom I needed to see. Shiv. Shaking like a man on a fuzzy tree.

"Hey!" I said with a shit-eating grin I had trouble wiping off. "I was just going to, uh—c-come over to see you. You get the messages I left at your hotel? We seem to keep missing each other."

While I was rambling on, Shiv was walking inside my office, closing the door behind him, and calmly tightening a silencer onto a handgun.

"Shiv, what's up? What are you doing?"

His shakiness made the silencer process somewhat awkward for both of us. He had trouble getting it together. In a moment of stupid fear I nearly offered to help him. He looked so silly, in a way. But then it was on, and he pointed the gun at me, backing me into my desk.

"I have to kill you, Vic," he said matter-of-factly. "Simple as that."

Briefly I mentally flashed on what Raymond Chandler had said to do when a story was getting slow: have someone walk in with a gun. Perhaps Shiv had read the same thing somewhere. Fat chance. He shook so much the words would blur if he tried to read anything at all. "Shiv, this isn't funny," I said, trying to sound detached. "Put the gun down, huh? Obviously there's been a misunderstanding."

"No misunderstanding," he said simply, firing and putting a hole in the desk between my legs. I jumped backward over the desk and was now next to the bay window facing the street below and tricky emancipation.

"*Shiv*! For Chrissake, what *is* it!"

He kept walking toward me, but stopped with the desk between us, taking more careful aim this time. His shivering grasp made even easy targets something of a challenge. There was that to be grateful for, at least.

"Vic, I can't understand why you're so excited," Shiv said with that eerie aloofness in his tone. I wondered if he took Valium whenever he killed someone.

"I don't want to die," I croaked.

"What's the big deal?" he said, firing again and shattering the windowpane just over my left shoulder. I ducked down and was now on my knees, literally pleading for my life.

"Shit," he murmured to himself, trying to steady his aim for his next shot, aligning the long thin barrel with my head, now crouching by the windowsill.

"What do you mean, 'what's the big deal'?" I yelled. "I want to *live*, okay? Now cut it out. *Jesus*!"

"Why, Vic? Look around you. You call this living? I'm doing you a favor. Goodbye, Vic."

I could see his finger trembling on the trigger, ready to squeeze. Then he thought better of it, walked around the desk, and aimed at my head point blank. Even in convulsions, no one could miss at this range.

I did the only thing I could think of. I grabbed Shiv by the shins and begged for mercy. Obviously Lucy had found him and told him I had raped her something outrageous like that. I couldn't figure why else Shiv would be so intent on icing me, without even an explanation from either side of the gun.

"Vic, you're groveling," he said as he pressed the barrel to the top of my head. "Not very becoming."

"Just tell me why, Shiv," I said with a little sob for dramatic effect.

"Does it matter, Vic? I think you know why, anyway. So let's just get this over with, all right? I have somewhere to be at—say, it's noon *now*! I'm late! So long, Vic."

He pulled the trigger and my brains would've made an

embarrassing mess on his tailored pant leg—right around the crotch, too—except I pulled his legs toward me up from the floor and sent him flat on his back. The gun was only tentatively in his grasp anyway, so with this action it went flying. I jumped over Shiv and picked it up and pointed it at him. We both stood up at the same time, slowly, eyeing each other with a mix of distrust and disdain, just as before—except now I had the negotiating tool, not him. This was what I had in mind all along. You think I'd debase my dignity in front of a bum like Shiv? What would Frank Sinatra say? He'd say be a punk, no matter what. So I acted like a bum, but did the punk thing. The situation had now reversed in my favor. I sat down at my desk, the gun still trained on Shiv, who glared at me with hate.

"How could you, Vic," he hissed. "I *trusted* you."

"'Scuse me? You trusted me? And I betrayed you by not letting you decorate my office with my own brains?"

"Don't flatter yourself, Vic. There isn't enough there to cover a roach motel, much less this expansive dump you call an office."

"In any case, what I do have I want to keep where I can get to it easily. Between my ears is perfectly convenient, thanks. Now then, let's you and me have a powwow. Tell me why you wanted to just waltz in here and waste me. Despite what you may think, I can't imagine. I'm such a nice guy and all."

"Where's Lucy?" he asked.

"I have no idea," I said, thinking: that was tarnished truth, at least. Puss the cat had taken off for the murky depths of the black bathroom. Some watchdog he'd make. Or she. I still had to check on that. I made a mental note to myself to do that once I got rid of Shiv for the day.

"You're lying," Shiv said patly. "My brother said she called him this morning, and she told him how she'd escaped from you."

"Escaped?" I swallowed hard. He had me. My famous poker face needed a lift.

"Save it, Vic. My brother of course wouldn't tell me where she was calling from. He merely alerted me to this fact because he wants me off her tail. He wants me to go back to New York City. You know why, Vic? Because of what you told him. That I *harmed* my own daughter. That I did filthy and disgusting and immoral things to my *own daughter*. How could you say those things about my own daughter to my own brother, Vic? You don't even know me. How could you make such accusations and soil my name within my own family? What kind of man *are* you,

Vic?"

"Exactly! I don't even *know* you!" I pointed out, the gun still on him. "So how and why the hell would I know shit like that? Antonio told me about how you mistreated your wife and daughter, pal, and *he* would know."

"He was fucking my wife *and* my daughter!" Shiv exploded.

I massaged my temple with the gun barrel, thinking how easy it would be to end all this. Instead I unscrewed the silencer and tossed it inside my desk drawer, then got up and handed the gun back to Shiv, who just stared at me warily.

"Here," I said. "Even you wouldn't attract attention by blowing me away in broad daylight. People saw you come in. The noise would get the whole neighborhood on your ass. They like me, believe it or not. So take your piece and beat it, if you catch my drift. If I hear from Lucy again, I'll be in touch. You're right, I found her hooked up with some sick cult last night, brought her back here, but when I woke up, she was gone."

"Why didn't you call me, cocksucker?" Shiv said, wondering what to do with the gun. It just hung limp in his hand, aimless.

"I was planning to, once I'd had a chance to ask her about those allegations by her uncle."

"Don't fool yourself I won't use this, bang or no bang," Shiv said, "so watch what you say. Don't insult a man with a gun in your belly."

The muzzle was snuggling with my inner tube, all right, but I didn't let that bother me. Shiv had lost his edge, at least for the time being. I knew then he wouldn't have actually killed me, not before I screamed out Lucy's whereabouts. He was playing me. I had to learn to deal with him from that angle. This was poker.

"It's none of my business," I said coolly. "That stuff is between your brother and you. But Lucy thought I was a button man at first. She actually believed her own father wanted her iced. Why's that, Shiv?"

Shiv slowly removed the gun from my gut and replaced it in his shoulder holster, discreetly hidden beneath his snazzy jacket. "If you don't find her, or if you know where she is and you don't tell me, then you have reneged on our arrangement. Is that how you customarily conduct your business, detective?"

"I won't ask for any more money," I said. "I found her, as our deal dictated. She got away, something I didn't anticipate. She's afraid of you so she's afraid of me, since I told her you hired me. I thought she trusted me but obviously she doesn't. I won't ask for another penny unless I find her and turn her over. In the meantime, I'll track her on my own, no charge." Shiv's eyes were balls of ice. He reached into the other side of his jacket and instead of a gun pulled out a wad of neatly wrapped bills and threw it on the desk behind me. "Take it. Find her. Call me when you do. This is business. If I treat you like a professional, you should act like one. It's a question of honor, isn't it? You have it or not, Vic? This is your moment of truth."

He started to walk out of my office. I didn't even count the cash on my desk, though I was tempted. It had sounded heavy when he dropped it. My chivalrous speech seemed to ring hollow all of a sudden. I picked the cash up and followed him to the door.

"Don't offer me money I can't accept," I said, handing it back to him. "I'm not guaranteeing anything. That's as much honor as I can work up for you. I won't accept this. It smells like a bribe, anyway."

He raised his eyebrows. "A bribe? For what?"

"I dunno. My silence. Lucy's silence. Lucy returned to you no matter what she says."

He still hadn't taken the money from me. He just smiled, put on his shades, and walked out, shutting the door between us and leaving me standing there with a year's worth of rent money in my hands, or that's how it felt.

I stashed the cash in my wall safe—now hidden behind the heart board—and then was ready to leave for some lunch and quiet reflection when the phone rang. I raced over and picked it up before the machine could intercept the caller.

"Yeah?" I said.

"Vic?"

"Yeah?"

"It's *me*. Vicki."

"Oh. Got you before you could leave some mystery music, huh?"

"Vic, I told you *before*."

"Yeah, yeah, you know nothin' about it. Anyway, I didn't call before to talk about that or about that weird shit last night."

"*What* weird shit?"

"Like you don't know. Vicki, you're not my girlfriend or anything, and you don't have to answer to me about your sex life, not that it looked like a secret or anything, up on stage for all to see."

"Vic, will you *please* tell me what you're talking about?"

"Next you'll tell me you don't remember an orgy at all."

"*Orgy*? Vic, you're crazy."

"Sorry, maybe my terminology isn't as hip as it should be. In my day, we referred to massive group sex and indiscriminate fucking with a bunch of strangers in one room as an 'orgy.' Please excuse my quaintness. Call me old-fashioned. You can call it whatever you want. I believe your pal the deacon calls it an 'orientation meeting.' Whatever."

There was real silence on the other end.

"Vicki?"

"You need help, Vic. Either you're hallucinating because you're on something or you have a brain tumor. Either way."

"Wait a minute. Are you telling me the deacon wasn't fucking you and calling you his *wahine* last night, onstage, while the crowd mauled each other to the tune of an Elvis song on the organ? You telling me I imagined all those details in my own sick little *mind*?"

"Yes, Vic, that's *exactly* what I'm telling you," she said emphatically.

"Well, I beg to differ, sweetheart. I wasn't swilling on spiked soda pop, remember. I was a lucid as can be, and I saw what I saw. Like I said, no explanation required, really. You weren't even my date. All I want from you is the deacon's address in Marin. The mansion."

"Vic, you're babbling. I don't understand you."

A few minutes before I was *groveling*. Now I was *babbling*. "Where are you calling from now, sweetheart?"

"Stop calling me 'sweetheart.' I'm calling from home, anyway. I'm returning your call."

"What time did you get home last night?" I knew where I was going with this, but I was hoping Vicki couldn't second guess my destination and throw me a detour.

"Um, from where? The church?"

"Yeah."

"Oh, I don't know. I tried to find you after services were over, but you had left already. You never came back, in fact. What happened to you? Remember? You said you'd be right back."

"Yeah, yeah, I remember. I had a bad case of instant claustrophobia. Needed some air. Then I found who I was looking for and left with her, but now she's vanished. *Again*. Under, shall we say, mysterious circumstances. And her old man took some potshots at me just a few minutes ago. I'm surprised I'm not more shaken up than I am. Guess I'm getting used to spontaneous danger and insanity, especially lately."

"Wait, Vic, just slow down, okay? First you say something about an orgy, and now people are trying to kill you."

"Right. Which part don't you get?"

"Um, Vic, I'm worried about you, really. We should talk. In person."

"Sure. I'll be right over."

"*No*! No, not yet. Later. Tonight, maybe. I need time to get ready."

"What for?"

"Just company. I got back late last night."

"What time?"

"What's the difference? Late."

"You didn't go up to the deacon's mansion for a night cap?"

"*What* mansion? Vic, I told you—nothing you're saying makes *any* sense to me. We sang some songs and I listened to what he had to say and then I drove home after looking all over the place for you. You said you found that girl you're looking for?"

"Yeah, brought her home, woke up, and she split after knocking me cold with I don't know what. Took my clothes, too. Or hid them."

"You mean you woke up naked?"

"Yep. But I never touched her, I swear."

"And you're accusing me of screwing people on stage. Vic, what are you *on*?"

"Vicki, for Chrissake, are you *still* denying what I saw with my own two eyes? I came back in with Lucy and all hell had broken loose. Or heaven, depending on your POV. Vicki, I *saw* you, okay? I saw Deacon Rivers *schtupping* you on stage while everyone else did the Sodom and Gomorrah thing all over the joint, so I left with Lucy and we didn't look back in case we'd turn into fuckin' pillars of *salt*. Got it?"

"Vic, you're insane. Don't *ever* call me again," she said coldly, and she hung up.

And I still didn't know the location of the mansion. On a hunch, I called the phone company and asked them if they'd installed my instant call-back service, and sure enough, they had just hooked it up that morning from their home office. So I hit the appropriate button and the phone rang. And rang. But Vicki didn't answer, nor did her machine pick up. She wasn't home, after all.

She had lied to me. She was calling from someplace else.

The mansion.

I let the phone keep ringing until I was satisfied no one could or would answer. Vicki would've suspected it was I since it rang so soon after she had hung up. So I let it rest around ten minutes, then tried again.

A female voice answered. It wasn't Vicki. "Hello?"

It caught me momentarily off-guard, but then I said, "Um, excuse me, what number did I dial?"

A pause. "You're asking *me*?"

"I think I may have dialed wrong."

"Well, who do you want to talk to?"

I thought quickly. "Zelda."

Big pause. "Speaking."

Bingo. "Zelda, this is Vic Valentine. We met last night, remember?"

"No." She was very reserved and distant now.

"No? Last night. At the party. I mean the meeting. I'm Vicki Lee's friend."

"*Who*? I'm afraid I've never heard of you, Mister Thanksgiving. And don't call again." *Click.*

Bitch. Deacon Rivers had been coaching her on how to be a wiseass, obviously. At least I knew for sure Vicki was lying to me. But I still didn't know where the goddamn mansion was. And what if Lucy hadn't returned there? Why did she call Antonio and tell him she'd escaped from me? Why did Antonio tell Shiv, knowing he'd over-react as usual and inflict bodily harm on me? And why didn't Shiv even bat an eye when I told him I found Lucy in a "sick cult"? A truly concerned father would have jumped all over that. Shiv didn't even seem fazed. Why did he really want Lucy found so badly? And why did Lucy think I was hired by her own father to grease her?

She had something on him, *that's* why.

I went downstairs to The Drive-Inn and told Doc I needed a new windowpane and for the electrician to come back and fix my bathroom light for good this time. Doc wanted details about the windowpane but I hurriedly told him I accidentally fired my .38 while cleaning it and blew my window out by mistake. He said he'd take care of it, and then went on about how he put an ad in the paper for more exotic dancers and how nothing was going to stop him from upgrading—or *downgrading*, depending on your POV—his establishment. I just nodded and told him I had to go, which I did. I needed food and a good fortune before I went to Antonio's bakery for some fresh answers instead of half-baked bullshit.

Louie, the waiter at the chop-suey joint with the mysterious fortune cookies, greeted me in the usual fashion. "Hello, Mister Walentine—or can I call you Mister Wic?"

"Call me stupid, and give me the number four, Louie, pronto."

"Okay, Mister Stupid."

"And give me my fortune cookie first, not with the bill."

Louie nodded and returned shortly with the complimentary tea and a fortune cookie on a tiny tray. I opened it quickly and read: "*Warning to all: There is a minefield around your heart.*"

Say *what*?

I cancelled my lunch from Louie, gave him a buck for the fortune cookie, then drove directly to North Beach, grabbed a few slices of pizza, thinking all the time about that minefield business, afraid it'd go off any second now, then guzzled a latte from Café Trieste before heading up to Guisseppe's Bakery.

Surprise! It was closed. Not temporarily. I mean closed down. I mean out of business. I mean boarded up, empty, no trace of life, *gone*, as if it had never existed. The only thing that greeted me was a real estate "For Lease" sign plastered on the plywood blocking the entrance. I could see around the wood just barely, and the windows were dark, the bakery abandoned, without any signs of people or pastry. I went to a payphone and called the real estate number. When I inquired as to the whereabouts of the former renters of that property, the bitch curtly told me she had no access to that information. All she told me was that the business had closed down hastily and recently, "within the past week or so." h, no kidding. I hung up, figuring whoever had prompted Antonio into closing shop had taken care of the real estate assholes as well. Maybe it was the Feds. Maybe it was the Family. Maybe Elvis had come down from a UFO and kidnapped his own personal baker for endless doughnuts in outer space. At that point, nothing made sense, so anything seemed possible.

I pulled my fortune out of my pocket and sat on a bench in Washington Square, studying it. Was Fate trying to clue me in to something here in its own cryptic way? Or was I only imagining these ethereal connections in my desperate ignorance?

A minefield around my heart. Anyone gets close *KABOOM*! If I try to escape it *BLAM*! I was trapped. Made sense. I've always felt trapped. My own heart was holding me prisoner, rigged with hidden explosives that were detonated either by careless intruders or by my own foolhardy attempts at emancipation, freedom to make immoral choices, thoughtless decisions, inflict pain on others needlessly, just for fun. If I tried any of those things, the secret bombs went off, sending me back into the recesses of my gullible heart, laced with good intentions and noble delusions. I knew I was trapped within my own heart, or else I could've nailed Lucy without even worrying about it, or just dropped this case altogether, or taken Shiv's money and found Lucy and turned her in. I did none of those things, and didn't plan to. I just couldn't. If I tried, I'd get blown to pieces, no matter what my brain or Little Elvis demanded I do.

So I got up off the bench and walked back to my Corvair and drove around, thinking, suddenly scared for my life, since I knew I couldn't just walk away from this even if my heart let me. Shiv was insane. I thought maybe he hadn't really wanted to kill me, that it was just a demented ploy to control me and spill my guts, not my brains, but then I remembered how he had pulled the trigger with the muzzle planted firmly in my skull. There was no way he could have anticipated I'd jerk him from his feet and take the gun. I had saved my own life. Otherwise I'd be dead.

Why? What did Lucy know about him? What did he think I knew, that she told me, possibly? Where was Antonio? Who could tell me? Only one person: whoever was waiting for me at the end of the line. This train was barreling ahead, making unscheduled stops with an unknown destination, and my conductor had just disappeared. Maybe Fate was the engineer, maybe Chance. Hell, maybe Elvis. It didn't matter. I was the passenger, and that's all I knew for now.

I went back to my apartment, and sure enough, there was a mystery musical message. It almost seemed like whoever was doing this was clocking my coming and going, to make sure I wouldn't be around when they called and pick up in person so they couldn't terrorize my machine. This time it was the dreamy instrumental by Santo and Johnny, "Sleepwalk," complete with scratches and pops. *God*, that tune always killed me. But what was the significance of this choice? Mentally I reviewed the litany of song titles so far: "Cry Me A River," "Then You Can Tell Me Goodbye," "Sweet Dreams," "Crazy," "Lover Man," "Surrender," and now "Sleepwalk." No obvious pattern beyond romantic yearning, all sticking to my taste in music. Hm. Then I thought: I can nail The Phone Phantom right now! No one else had called, so I hit Star 69 and a recording informed me that this number had been disconnected.

Chapter Nine
COFFEE SHOP CONFIDENTIAL

Human beings. You can have 'em.

I was sick of *every*body. Well, almost. Except for Doc and Esther Williams. I had just woken up from one of my recurring wet dreams about Esther, which have been happily haunting me ever since I saw *On An Island With You* on TV as a kid. I think she must have been my first hopeless love obsession, but I forgave her since she made up for it in my fantasies, which I won't tell you about on the off-chance she reads this some day, or her macho son Lorenzo. Anyway, everyone else except Doc—who refused to stock her movies, since she was too innocent for his tastes—was on my shit list. Shiv, the deacon, Vicki, Lucy, and especially The Phone Phantom. Humans. To hell with 'em. When I go I just want to wake up on a Technicolor tropical island with Esther in her prime, eternally removed from this race of two-legged rats.

And I'd take Puss with me. He shared my low opinion of my own race, as most cats do, and I knew why. Cats hate rats.

I called the phone company and asked them to check out the so-called callback service, Star 69, and make sure it was working according to Hoyle. They said okay, they'd get back to me, but I decided against holding my breath till they got around to it. No way could The Phone Phantom have pulled the plug on her own phone line that quickly, and anyway how would she know I had this service? She or he, I mean. I only *hoped* it was a she, even though I sort of hated her by now. I was hard up for the attention.

I hoped against hope it was Esther Williams. She was still alive, I thought. Even if she had taken that Big Dive already, I was gladly willing to join her for an eternal dip in that big swimming pool in the sky.

With my luck it was the ghost of Lizzie Borden on the line.

But The Phone Phantom took a temporary back seat to Lucy. I just had to locate that little broad and set the record straight—about her old man, about her, about the deacon, and about me waking up naked in the middle of the floor.

And what the hell *had* happened to my clothes? They were missing along with Lucy. I supposed she had worn them out for her flight, but then what the hell had she done with *her* clothes?

Later that morning I decided to bite the proverbial bullet and relax at Rendezvous, but I didn't stay there long. Someone had the bright idea of playing Elvis on the sound system! Normally they played jazz, lounge, and surf. I asked the little snot-nosed college-age punk behind the counter what was up with the new soundtrack.

"Not my call," he said. "Personally I hate the dead fat slob. I hate the rest of this old shit, too. They never let me play *my* stuff." The kid had an earring and long stringy hair in a ponytail. I didn't like him. I hadn't seen him there before, so he must have been a recent hire.

"So who *does* call the shot?" I asked the kid. His SF State T-shirt was already covered with coffee stains, and a few others I didn't dare guess about. Rendezvous was turning into slacker central lately, and now they were hiring acne-faced grungeheads to make my lattes. This was going too far. "I want to speak to the manager."

"She ain't here."

"Well, when *will* she be here?"

"I dunno," he mumbled with a shrug, avoiding eye contact with me. "I hardly ever see her."

"I didn't even know this joint was run by a woman."

"Not a woman. A girl. She's a TA at school. Maybe twenty-four."

"Oh, yeah? A looker?"

"A *hooker*?"

"*Looker*, junior. Is she cute?"

"Yes, I guess. How come?"

"What's she look like?"

He grinned, revealing yellow fangs. "What're you, a detective or somethin'?"

I pulled out my P.I. license and laid it on the counter next to the two bucks for my latte. He looked at it with raised eyebrows as he finished steaming the milk, then handed me change, which I put in my pocket and not in the tip jar.

"Is she in trouble?" he asked.

"No, not at all. You asked if I was a detective. So happens I am. I just want to talk to her as a customer of her establishment, though."

"Why, you hate Elvis too? I'll tell her you complained. She lets me bring rock sometimes, but only surf music, no new shit, which sucks for me."

"Like what kinda surf music?" I asked. It was one of my favorite musical genres.

"Hold on," he said with a sigh. The kid dug below and came out with CDs by The Trashwomen, The Neptunes, The Aqua-Velvets, The Mermen, The Phantom Surfers, The Ultras, Pollo del Mar, Meshugga Beach Party, and The Deadlies, all local bands, as well as Man…or Astroman? from Alabama and Impala from Memphis.

"Any Ventures or Dick Dale?"

"No, at least we can play *new* surf music. This ain't a *museum*."

"Dick Dale still puts out new stuff."

"Really? Well, she would know. She always catches his shows at Slim's. She's in a female surf band, that's why, like the Trashwomen, only sexier."

"Oh yeah, could I have heard of 'em?"

"Doubt it. She only plays *here* sometimes."

"What's the name?"

"Judy Fagin."

"Okay, I mean the band."

"Um, wait—The She Beams."

"And they play *here*, you said? I didn't know they allowed live music."

"She's the manager. She calls the shots. I got no say."

I took a quarter back out of my pocket and put it in the tip jar, only because I was beginning to think the kid had helped me out far more than he realized. "Here, pour this into a to-go cup," I said to him, and he did so promptly. By the time I walked out the door Elvis had been replaced by The Aqua-Velvets doing "Spy in the House of Love."

I walked back into The Drive-Inn, trying to remember seeing a cute surfer babe bossing people around at the Rendezvous. I did remember surf music playing there frequently, and now I knew why they were so hip. But they'd never played Elvis until now. I just had to meet Judy Fagin. When I got to The Drive-Inn I asked Doc for a phone and a phone book. I looked up Rendezvous and dialed. The kid answered and I hung up. Their line hadn't been disconnected after all.

"What's goin' on?" Doc naturally inquired.

"I'm not sure, but in an insane way it's all coming together," I said, sipping the beer I usually have after my Rendezvous latte.

San Francisco didn't really have many of the classic '50s Googie style coffee shops that made L.A. inhabitable whenever I went down there, so I had to get my atmosphere-and-caffeine-and-nostalgia fix in several different places. Rendezvous had the right colors—purple and green—but the wrong motif, too modern and slick, as opposed to mid-century modern and sleek, though somehow still cozy, because it was so dark and the music so cool, I guess. Anyway, they supplied the coffee, and Doc the atmosphere and nostalgia. I usually only drank his booze, though, since his coffee sucked. "I had one of my Esther Williams wet dreams last night, then I at Rendezvous I found out the manager is a music lover, specifically surf music. She's in all all-girl surf band called the She-Beams."

"I see a theme emerging. Deep water. Time to bail out or drown, Vic. Your head's barely above the surface as it is."

"Yeah yeah, but today when I walked in they were playing Elvis."

"And?"

"Doc, you slow or what? I think maybe she's in on it."

"On what?"

"Jesus Christ, Doc, what do you *think*? The phone messages."

"You still on that kick? I'd think the Mafia shit had taken your mind off that crap already. You got more important things to worry about."

"Doc, somebody's *stalking* me, I mean other than the Mob. And the cat thing really freaked me out."

"Whoa. *What* cat?"

Shit. I'd clean forgotten to tell Doc, my landlord, about my new roommate. I gave him a quick rundown and he just stood there, shaking his head.

"No, Vic."

"Whaddya mean, 'no'? It's only a cat, Doc. I can handle it. It's where it *came* from that bothers me."

"Vic, it so happens I'm allergic to those damn things. So out it goes. Sorry."

"Doc, so *what* you're allergic? It's *my* pad."

"No, Vic, it's *my* pad. You just pay rent. Most of the time. When you eventually move up and out I may need to rent it to someone *else* who's allergic, or I may stay there myself, and I don't need no lingering cat hair and shit, and anyway they always fuck a place up with their claws and shit. Out if goes, Vic."

"Doc, I just can't. C'mon."

He just kept shaking his head.

"All right, give me some time to find it a home at least, okay?"

He held up a finger. "One week, then out it goes to the SPCA or YMCA or some shit. Got it?"

"Yeah, whatever. Listen, you ever meet this Judy babe down at Rendezvous?"

"No, but she don't own it anyways, her mama does."

"What, you know her?"

"Her mother? No, I know *of* her. She's a rich broad, owns a mess of cafes and residential hotels and shit. Tried to buy *me* out, even."

"What's her trip?"

"Just a bored ass widow with nothin' better to do than buy neighborhoods. I only see her once every blue moon. She pulls up in front of Rendezvous in her stretch limo, just to count the receipts, I guess. I was down there one time gettin' my cappuccino and she pulled up and I guess her daughter was there and I didn't even know she was the manager, but anyway they had words about somethin' and everyone felt kinda embarrassed for the little broad."

"Judy?"

"Yeah, I guess. Yeah, *Judy*. I heard her mother call her Judy, now that I think of it. Cute little thing, or really not so little, if you dig me. Blonde, All-American type. She's in a band, you said? Maybe she likes to dance, too."

"Forget it, Doc. Stop corrupting women for your own capitalistic gains."

"I'm American, ain't I? This is the land of opportunists."

"Bullshit. Hey, you catch the old lady's name?"

"Yeah. Somethin' weird. One of the guy's behind the counter called her by it, said, 'Hello Dolly,' or whatever it was."

"What?"

"Uh—Greta. No. Franny. No. Za—Ze—Zelda. Yeah, that was it. *Zelda*."

"A rich bitch named Zelda? Doc, you're positive?"

"Scout's honor. How could I forget a weird moniker like that? Zelda. Yeah. The dude says, 'Hey, Zelda,' and the broad just stares him down and says, 'Where's Judy'? Cold bitch, too."

I was beside myself. This was too much. "Doc, think carefully. How long ago was this exactly?"

"Coupla weeks. What's the difference? What, you think the old lady is harassing you now? Vic, you're either really paranoid or you need to do a serious ego check, my man."

I explained to Doc about all the recent events, waking up naked with Lucy gone, Vicki Lee and the orgy, the mansion I'd heard about—and Deacon Rivers' wealthy sponsor, who had to be this Zelda.

"Shit, all this just happened?" Doc said. "Vic, I never want to hear you complain about how bored you are again. God *damn*!"

"Doc, I need to find Lucy. That baker guy just disappeared, right after Lucy contacted him, and he ratted me to Shiv. I'm afraid for Lucy's life, really. Shiv is desperate, man. He tried to ice me yesterday. I was just lying about me cleaning the gun and it went off."

Doc's face was constipated with consternation. "Well, Vic, I figured that, but, Vic, I'm afraid we need to re-negotiate your lease. Fur balls are one thing, but bullet holes are another. And as much as a pain in the ass you are sometimes, I'd hate to come knockin' on your door one day and find *my* room decorated with *your* blood. That shit is nasty, and it stains like a sumbitch."

"I'm touched by your sentiment, Doc. But I think *your* Zelda and *my* Zelda are the same Zelda."

"Think so? C'mon. How can you be so sure?"

"C'mon yourself, Doc. Only so many rich babes named Zelda who play Elvis music in their shops."

"True. So what's your next move? Want me to go undercover for you?"

"Huh? In what capacity?"

"Whatever. As long as I get to attend one of those orgies. This Zelda sounds like a lotta fun. And Vicki Lee? Shit, Vic. I'd go under them covers *any* ol' time."

"When did you meet Vicki Lee?"

"She came by lookin' for you, didn't I tell you?"

"No, you didn't, Doc. When was this?"

"Uh—Friday, last Friday. Day you went to the Elvis orgy. You'd already left, though. She was with the Zelda bitch, in fact. I saw her leave and climb into Zelda's limo."

"Doc, why didn't you *tell* me all this?"

"It slipped my mind, and I didn't think it was any big deal. I just wasn't putting all this together yet. I mean, why should I? Now that you're telling me this crazy shit, I can see a pattern. A *zigzag* pattern, but a pattern."

I picked the phone up again and dialed Rendezvous. The kid answered and I identified myself as "The Detective" and asked him when Judy Fagin's She Beams were scheduled for another gig there. The kid said there was a flyer he was supposed to hang up but forgot to. There was a gig lined up for 9PM that evening.

"It's all coming together, Doc," I said, polishing off my beer.

"Yeah. That's what you *always* say right before it all falls apart."

"Yeah, yeah. Just get my window and bathroom light fixed, willya?"

"I tell you what—I will as soon as you get rid of that damn cat. Deal?"

"Oh, yeah? Well, I'll lose the cat once you start giving me my messages on time."

"Yeah? Well, I'll start givin' you your messages when I become your personal goddamn secretary."

"And you'll be my secretary when you grow blond hair and big tits and your dick drops off."

"Well, there ya go."

He had me there. I shot my forefinger at him and left.

Music, music, music. Everything had a musical connection. Elvis, torch songs, now Surf. I liked it. My life had a soundtrack. In the old days with Valerie/Rose, my main music was New Wave and West Coast Jazz and Big Band Swing. Now I had grown into a more eclectic music lover, which was good, considering the case I now found myself locked into. The music helped me keep it all together. For instance, jazz, blues and standards made me think of The Phone Phantom. Elvis made me think of Deacon Rivers and Zelda. Surf made me think of Judy Fagin and her unknown but obvious connection. Judy could lead me to Zelda who could lead me to Lucy. Yes, it was all coming together.

So why was I such a goddamn wreck?

I drove down to the Cliff House and watched the waves and the seals and thought about love and life and all that jazz until it made me nauseous. By the time I returned to my apartment the electrician had shown up and was working again on my light fixture, plus the window fixer guy was fixing the windowpane. But where was the cat? The door was open and it was nowhere in sight.

In a panic I ran down to The Drive-Inn to ask Doc where my pussy had gone. But it wasn't there. Monica the exotic dancer was.

"Hey, haven't seen you since your debut as Doc's resident strip-teaser," I said.

She was in a foul mood. "Don't push my buttons, Vic. I'll tell Doc you were lookin' for him."

"So how come you're in such a snit?"

"I'm tired of being treated like an object, that's why."

"What're you talkin' about? Doc *loves* you, Monica."

"You mean he *needs* me. But that's how it is in this fucked-up society. Women are victims of men's power trips. In some ways he's no different than O.J. Simpson."

"Ah, I'd say the differences greatly outweigh the similarities, baby cakes."

"Same difference, though."

"Say what?"

"Men are assholes."

"Me too, Monica?"

"'Fraid so. Baby cakes."

"Hey look, we assholes have it just as rough. Sure, Doc tries to make you a sex object and all. But women objectify themselves by selling themselves to the highest bidder. I was just thinking of this down by the ocean, contemplating how ultimately meaningless everything is. The only meaning there in *any*thing is what we give it. That's why there's such a thing as an Elvis religion. Why not? It's a blanket pat explanation for mysteries we'll never solve and a comment on the absurdity of modern life. But anyway, women, like I said, objectify themselves by selling themselves to the highest bidder. Wait, let me finish. Really good-looking women—like yourself—complain about being objects, but then they won't date men who can't afford the company of their beauty. I'm not saying *you're* this way, I'm just generalizing—like you are when you say men are assholes. Beautiful women turn themselves into prizes to be won, then complain because men only look at them sexually. Don't you see? The poor nice guy loses every time because he doesn't have the material wealth to win the prize. You see it all the time. This makes men *frustrated*."

Monica threw the beer she had poured for me in my face. "I'll give Doc your message, that your pussy is missing. No wonder." Then she walked away.

I went upstairs and washed my face and changed my shirt. The widow guy was just finishing up, and the old electrician dude said he'd really fixed it this time. Whatever. I had to take a leak anyway, so I just whipped it out with the old guy on a ladder behind me, but I was so self-conscious I couldn't go, so I just shook my pecker and flushed anyway. Shy bladder. Then I heard a familiar meow and traced it to a place beneath my bed. There was Puss, looking agonized, all crouched into a tight ball of neurotic fur. Something serious was ailing him, I could tell—I just couldn't tell what.

Just then Monica ran up and inside my bedroom. "Doc's back, I gave him your—oh. Vic, I'm sorry, really. It's that time of month, and—hey, your cat looks like it has urinary tract blockage or something."

"*Huh*?"

"Put it down for a second." I did, and Puss immediately started whining and acting strangely, straining with its back arched in a peculiar pose of would-be waste relief. Monica then reached beneath its stomach and felt around. "I used to work part-time in a vet's office. This is common in cats. Male cats."

"What is?"

"I told you, urinary tract blockage."

"Meaning?"

"Meaning he can't pee. If you don't get him to a vet soon, he might, you know."

"No, I don't know. What?"

"Well, *explode*."

Great. If I'd come home any later my combustible cat would have wallpapered my room with fur, blood and piss. "Is this really an *emergency*?"

"Unless you want him to die a painful death, *yeah*. Want me to take him? It's the least I can do. Just give me a credit card or something. This could be expensive."

I groaned. I was already frying in credit hell, a result of a high credit line and low spirits. Depression costs big bucks, especially when your chief therapy is a massive LP/CD collection. Plus the Corvair had been in the shop a couple of months before, and now this? Why did God or Elvis hate me so much? I gave Lucy a bank VISA and ATM code and told her if they needed me to sign it in person I'd be down later. She told me which vet she was taking Puss to, and I thanked her. All was forgiven. The window and light guys both left, so at least that was all over with. I flipped on the bathroom light just to watch it glow. The joys of electricity had been rediscovered. Then I decided to take a nap before show time at the Rendezvous. I wanted to be alert for The She Beams' gig, since their leader was such a significant if unknowing participant in this tightly woven human mosaic, weaving itself into an unidentifiable pattern I could follow to Lucy Guisseppe, if Shiv didn't figure it out first.

At 9PM sharp (though my senses were dull) I went down to Rendezvous. I saw four cute college age babes setting up with their instruments—a guitar, a bass, drums, and a sax. There was only one blonde in sight, so I figured that was Judy. The others consisted of an Asian, a black chick, and a Latina. Typical San Francisco boiling hot, and full of hot water. Maybe Doc was right about that deep-water theory. All I could do was go with the flow.

Working the counter was a grunge gal dressed in a flannel shirt and torn jeans. The epitome of style, man. I just didn't get it. Nobody had any class anymore, it seemed. The surf babes had a semblance of it, at least, decked out in neon halter-tops and hot Capri pants, sort of nouveau beach party style. They were all in their mid-twenties, it appeared, and perfectly luscious specimens of femininity, a credit to their fashion-bankrupt generation. My impulse was to simply approach Judy and identify myself as a private dick on a case that needed her to put me in touch with her old lady. That would've been the direct approach. But instead I decided to take a seat and enjoy the set first. Like I said, I like surf music. It's the cleanest guitar sound ever, and the astro-twang and unearthly vibes made me feel like a super-spy in outer space. My ego needed the artificial sonic boost.

Judy was obviously the leader of the quartet, and she was the one who introduced The She Beams to the paltry audience. She didn't seem shy at all, but bold and confident. I wondered if her musical abilities would live up to this bravado.

They did.

They rocked through four ethereal numbers before taking a breather. Their sound was full of hooks and original melodies (though variations on classic Surf) and their unit was tight. Judy even sang on a couple of numbers, and her voice was sweet but strong. The She Beams were a class act. I couldn't believe Judy had a mother like Zelda. I wondered if Judy knew where Zelda was last Friday night, and what she was doing. Somehow I doubted it.

I waited for an opportune moment to accost Judy, but just when I thought it was apropos she launched into another number, so I just sat back and enjoyed the music for the duration. When I was certain they had finished, about an hour later, after most of their small but appreciative audience had drifted into the night, I went up to Judy and waxed enthusiastic. Her response was grateful but cool. I didn't know whether it was because she was disappointed by the turnout or she was simply stuck up, but as usual I didn't allow her shield to deflect my advances.

"You guys from around town?" I asked, following her as she went about putting her guitar away in its case and unplugging the mini sound system. "I'd like to check you out again sometime."

"Just here," she said curtly, not looking at me. The other three hurried through their breakdown routine and bellied up to the bar for some wine. I could tell Judy was anxious to ditch me and join them. She must have thought I was hitting on her. Under different circumstances, I might've. But right now I had to find momma. I blocked out thoughts of what Lucy was up to in the mansion, either out of concern or outright jealousy. I couldn't be sure anymore.

"You guys are good enough to record an album," I continued, unabated by Judy's aloofness. "Ever send a tape to Hightone in Oakland? They put Dick Dale back on the map. Or any other local labels doing Surf music."

"What're you, a wolf or an executive?" she suddenly asked, finally giving me direct eye contact and a little shot of sexual voltage along with it.

"Neither. Just a fan that wants to see you get ahead. It's about time real talent got discovered for a change."

I was sincere, and she could see that, so she relented slightly and cut me some slack. "Well, I appreciate your support, um, haven't I seen you in here before?"

"All the time. This is one of my hangouts. I'm Vic Valentine. And you're Judy Fagin, the manager, right?"

"Yeah, how'd you know?"

"I'm a detective by trade. I know stuff. Besides, I've seen you around. I put two and two together, without even using my professional expertise."

"That's pretty good, since I'm hardly ever even here. I devote most of my time to my day job and my music. I just run this place for someone else."

"Your mother, I know. And you're a TA at SF State. One of the kids here told me. What courses?"

"Music, naturally."

"Natch." I followed her over to the bar where she joined her buddies, who were putting it away pretty good now. Judy introduced me as their biggest fan, and I paid for their bottle of wine and ordered a second, while I had a beer. We were lined up at the counter in a cozy way, and I almost felt guilty for having a hidden agenda and secret motives for exploiting their company. But I got over it.

Girls, girls, girls. Fate was supplying me with female companionship via conveyor belt these days, it seemed. Mass production often yielded false results, though, but still, I was complaining as of yet.

I cut it up with the girls for a little while before I could segue in a roundabout way back to the topic of Zelda. I found out the Asian chick was from Japan, the black chick from Jamaica, the Latin chick from Barcelona. Nice mix. They'd all met at school, in a pop music class, and shared a penchant for classic Surf, it turned out, so the group was a natural result. They were one of the few all-girl surf bands in history, much less the current circuit. "So is your mom your manager?" I asked Judy, who was now on her fourth glass of wine courtesy of yours truly, and conveniently tipsy to boot.

Judy laughed long and loud, and her cohorts giggled (they had introduced themselves by first name but none of it registered well enough to stick in my mind.) "No, no, no, Vic. Ma doesn't give a damn about me or my friend or my 'little projects,' as she calls 'em. I just make out the schedule and order the coffee beans and booze here and she pays me and leaves me alone. I only do this so she'll think I'm a responsible young lady." She said that last bit with mock-snooty flourish.

"So the upshot of it is, she stays out of your business and you stay out of hers," I said in a leading way, though she was too bombed to pick up on that.

"Exactly. Vic, you are one ace detective, my man. How 'bout another round on the house?"

"I thought *I* was footing the bill," I said.

She laughed again. "*I'm* the boss when the old bitty ain't around," she said with a cute little hiccup. She was getting pretty tanked, and her thigh was rubbing up warmly against mine. I could sense chemistry ready to explode. I was weakening every time she looked at me. I knew she was a bit attracted to me by now, and I was feeling cocky as a result. "*C'mon, wench, serve us!*" she yelled at the grunge goddess behind the counter, who obviously was getting tired and wanted to go home. She had been busy cleaning and closing up shop while we were having a blast. If she knew how to dress like a lady and not like an eyesore I might've even felt sorry for her. And it wasn't like she wanted to go home and take a bath. That would've been decidedly uncool and out of fashion. To hell with her—I'd stay as long as Judy and company let me. The bar "wench" served up another round and by this time even I was a bit lightheaded, and not only on alcohol.

"So you grew up around here?" I asked Judy.

"Yep. Born down in Santa Barbara, though. I still live there part of the time. My boyfriend goes to school there."

I felt a familiar pang, but ignored it. I think I was building up immunity to disappointment. Judy's eyes were that deep kind of blue one could drown in, so blue they looked fake, and her skin was smooth and soft and tan. Sitting so close to her was torture. I tried keeping my mind on my objective.

"So where around here?" I pressed.

She looked deep into my eyes, and my dizziness increased accordingly. "Guess, detective."

"Ahh, hm. Berkeley?" She shook her head. "No. Santa Cruz?" She jerked her thumb in an upward motion. "North?" She nodded. "Santa Rosa?" Her thumb went back down. "San Francisco?" The thumb went back up. "Ahh—somewhere in Marin?" She pointed at me. "San Rafael?" No. "Sausalito?" No. "Ohhh—Mill Valley?"

Bingo. She pointed at me again and nodded.

"In a big mansion, I bet," I said, and then I felt instantly foolish. She just stared at me, wide-eyed. I just shrugged uncomfortably. "What, you're tryin' to tell me I'm right? Simple girl like you?"

"My real daddy died in a truck crash on 101. He had the San Francisco-L.A. route, and died in a head-on one foggy night. He liked to drink, so I think he was drunk, but they never found out whose fault it was. So then my mother married his boss, a rich asshole who lived up here. I was only like seven or so. I have a sister by this asshole, but we don't talk. She's away at school, back east. But my mom's like a virus, you know? I mean, she was pregnant with my sister before my father even died, so she was fooling around with this asshole for a while at least before she married him, but then two years later he died in a private plane crash up near Seattle where he was at a convention of Japanese businessmen or something. Personally I think he had a mistress up there, out on a lake or something, and he was bound for Canada when the plane went down just by the border, so my mother decided not to get married again, 'cause she was like cursed, right? And anyway, she got all of his business interests, all the cafes and hotels here and in Reno and Tahoe, she's like filthy rich, and she had lots of men. She was real pretty when she was young, a bathing beauty and all that, and she was even in some movies in small parts, and my father wanted to be a writer, and one of his screenplays was just about to be optioned when he died. I think then they just took the basic idea and reworked it with another writer at the studio or something, I don't know. They never had to pay my father, at least. My mother was pushing thirty at the time and wanted out of that whole scene, so she hooked up with the asshole and that was that, a built-in retirement plan. I think she was even relieved when he died. I know I was. So *any*way." She took a big breath then a big swig. I wanted to put my arm around her and console her, but I figured she'd take it wrong, so I simply nodded and sighed compassionately. So many lost little boys and girls out there.

I almost felt bad for continuing this line of conversation, but I was almost there and couldn't stop now. "So you were raised in a mansion in Mill Valley?"

"How did you know I was raised in a mansion, anyway? On first guess."

I winked at her. "I told you, beautiful. I'm a detective. I guess I picked up on class and royalty on your part. Where in Mill Valley?"

"Well, it's not exactly in Mill Valley, it's *near* Mill Valley, by Muir Woods. I never go there anymore, since, y'know."

"Since what?"

"Since my mother met this new guy. He's a psycho, I think, but she says she loves him. He's the only guy she's marry, she said, ever since the asshole bit it. I don't get it. I mean he's *such* a flake. He's obsessed with Elvis Presley, and she used to be, too. She says as a teenager she was in the background in some Elvis movie. So they have that in common, but he's absolutely crazy. He's using her, feeding her obsession for Elvis and getting her to do whatever he tells her to, in the name of The King, as he puts it. It's *insane*. I mean, my mother and I have our differences, but I hate to see her treated like this, y'know? And he's spending *all* her money. I don't even take much money from her anymore. I tell her I'll wait for my inheritance and she thinks I'm waiting for her to *die* or something. I think this guy sort of plays us against each other. He even has her playing Elvis music in *here* now. I mean, I don't care much, I like the guy's music and all, but I'm not one of these *nuts* like *this* guy is, and he's turning my mother into a nut, too." She waved it all off and finished her wine. "Anyway, I'm sick of talking about me. What about you, Vic?" She put her arms around me and leered tipsily in my eyes, then raised her eyebrows suggestively. "I don't think I can drive home in this condition."

"We'll drive you!" the black babe said, and they all laughed. Suddenly I got the impression they had subtly disassociated themselves from Judy and me, moving down the counter a seat apiece and putting distance between them and us, giving us space to be alone.

"I live right down the block," I whispered to Judy, and she nodded and kissed me and me on the tip of my nose.

"Lead the way," she said, and we got up to leave. Judy had told the grunge gal to leave after the last round, so after locking up the shop real quick she bid adieu to her fellow musicians and walked arm in arm with me back to my apartment.

My attitude was this: Whatever it took to get over. Same as any good undercover agent. If I had to sleep with babes from the opposition to win them over to my side, then so be it. I pictured Elvis watching over us all, and thought: I'm on His Majesty's Secret Service.

Chapter Ten
SURF'S UP

Monica had slipped a note under my door from the vet, explaining Puss's predicament, something about crystals forming in his bladder and stopping him up or something, along with the bill. I went through the roof, my internal ceiling, at any rate. Not only had my stalker stuck me with a responsibility I didn't ask for or need, but it was defective to boot. A broken cat. Terrific. Answer to my prayers. And by now I was already much too attached to the little fuck to have him put to sleep, so I had no choice but to let them unplug him at any cost. Judy was drunk and didn't appreciate my sudden foul mood and proceeded to dance around my office and giggle flirtatiously. *Pussy, pussy, pussy. Faster, kill, kill*! I finally understood the title of that Russ Meyer masterpiece. It was killing me in all different forms, from all angles. And I wanted *more*. Just like the Sisters of Mercy song.

Normally I would consider such an expedient seduction (without any effort on my part at that) an incredible boon, but I figured Fate was on a roll anyway, and if I started to think about it Judy would evaporate like a mirage. I was too thirsty to nitpick. I wanted to indulge the moment's opportunity without any of my customary analysis. Later I'd think about it, dream about it, beat off to it—unless, of course, Judy took off her dress and had a dick. Then I'd further eschew analysis and hurry he/she out the door and cuss Fate out and beat off to Bettie Page until I fell asleep, as per usual.

Anyhow, I was fairly convinced Judy was one hundred percent female, and had been born that way. Why this sudden boon in poon tang? Who cared? I instinctively threw on my Juan Garcia Esquivel CD appropriately entitled *Space Age Bachelor Pad Music*, and the wacky way-out rhythms of sci-fi swing set the perfect Cad On the Make With His Stoned Date mood, in classic '50s lonely guy tradition. Judy not only got into it, she recognized the artist, whom I thought to be totally obscure outside certain circles, haunters of record shops for strange outdated easy listening treasures (like me). Judy was just too good to be true. And for all I knew, I'd just scored with Lucy. I was determined to remain alert and sentient for this encore performance with a totally unexpected but welcome partner in passion, so I could recall it fondly in the morning and for many mornings to come.

Judy kept dancing in the middle of my office to the esoteric Esquivel sound waves emanating from my CD stereo, a by-product of loneliness and boredom. I Was A Space Age Bachelor, and this was my music. It was dreamy. The tension about the cat situation evaporated. I almost didn't care about Lucy now. I figured I'd get to it in the morning. In the meantime, I danced a bit with Judy, who was obviously suffering from the spins by this time, and was practically oblivious to my presence in the room, much less my proximity. Her eyes were closed as I leaned over and stole a playful kiss. Her eyes opened wide. She stared at me for a beat, her blue pools of light glistening with surprise and desire. Then she threw her arms around me and planted a wet one right on my kisser. I briefly flashed on Vicki kissing me with similar unbridled intensity a few nights earlier, and I momentarily marveled at the phenomenon of having so recent a reference point. This was indeed rare for me. And then I recalled waking up naked on the floor. God, I wished I could remember whether I slept with Lucy too! Perhaps Judy would reawaken the memory from my tortured subconscious soul. The way we were making out now, slowly then quickly undressing each other right there in the middle of the office, it felt as if Judy would unearth secrets of my soul from past lives. Was I Romeo? Casanova? Don Juan? It only made sense I was the incarnation of this single wandering spirit of love. Me. Vic Valentine. Lover of the Ages, doing it to Esquivel in San Francisco in the new Millennium, before Time erased all traces of the previous two thousand years of raging passions, and I had to start with a clean slate, possibly in a new form, facing ever greater challenges, making conquests on other worlds perhaps, on and on, my soul returning again and again for the sole purpose of bringing worldly pleasures to earthbound beauties— but hell, *someone* had to do it, for the sake of propagation if nothing else. I was a one-man crusade against artificial insemination and virtual pornography. Yes, this was the purpose of my existence in the Cosmos! I *swear* these idiotic delusions of grandeur were banging around my brain as Judy unzipped my pants and fondled my manhood. But then a spontaneous eruption occurred. As soon as Judy touched my throbbing tool I came all over her neck and cleavage. I couldn't help it. Her breasts were hanging over her halter-top and her nipples were so large and round and pink and soft-looking, just like in a Vargas calendar, plus I hadn't jacked off since the orgy because I was stressed out and preoccupied. For all I knew it had been months since my last encounter, with Flora on this very floor, and the prospect of the ultimate pleasure reoccurring in the same year was just too grand. Judy said "ick" and retreated to my bathroom, suddenly sober it seemed.

"Hey, where's the light in here?" she yelled, and I groaned, going to the kitchen sink and washing myself off with a wet paper towel. I suddenly felt degraded and slimy. I didn't deserve a consistently operable bathroom light. Christ, I had just *met* this woman, and now she was wiping my bodily essence from her bosom! Why didn't that thrill me? Instead I felt nasty and depressed. I couldn't look her in the eye as she returned to the living room, her clothes now tightly buttoned up, her face a mask of polite annoyance.

"So how did you come up with the name 'The She Beams'?" I asked, staring at the wall as if contemplating a faraway enigma.

Judy sighed and walked over to my desk and sat down as if very, very weary. She massaged her face and sighed some more, then replied, "Ever see 'Blade Runner'?" I nodded in the affirmative. One of my favorites. "What's-his-name, the blond guy, the big replicant, um, Rutger Hauer, in his last speech in the rain just before he dies or shuts down or whatever, he talks about seeing sea beams on some planet or asteroid or something, and that phrase stuck in my head, so when I decided to start a surf band, She Beams just sorta popped up."

I nodded some more. "Oh," I said, standing there stupidly with my hands in my pockets, staring at the floor. "Cool." Then a strange thing happened. I got another boner. She must have sensed it, because the next thing I knew, she was removing her neon halter-top and her neon Capri hot pants and I was lapping away at her thighs and womanhood. She never even got up from the chair. I just knelt between her thighs and ate her right there until she climaxed. The entire outside world was fuzzy in my peripheral vision, and as I licked her privates I imagined her going about her business that day on a collision course with this moment, with me, and then I went further back and pictured her as a little girl dreaming of future boyfriends and then as an adolescent first overcome by her hormones and fantasizing about future lovers and me across the country with similar reveries and now we were part of each other's litanies forever, and the beauty of it just overwhelmed me as I licked and licked and licked. Then when she had finished, her back arched, her face contorted, her breath short and heavy, she pushed my face away with her foot and put her panties back on.

"I'm still horny," I whined.

"I'm *not*," she snapped.

This had an eerie *deja vu* feeling to it. Last year a similar episode had occurred with Monica, though she had made me beat off in my bathroom. At least with Judy I beat her to it. As it were. But the obvious pattern disturbed me.

So much for the Lover of the Ages.

I wiped her vaginal juice from my face and then went to the bathroom to clean up. She was right—the goddamn bathroom light *was* out again. When I returned to the office, Judy was gone. I ran down the stairs and saw her walking up the street. The night was misty and cold. She was crying. Oh boy. I caught up with her and tried to win her back to my side. James Bond. Right.

"Mon—, I mean Lu—, I mean, *hell*."

"*Judy*," she hissed.

"I'm sorry," I said.

"No, *I'm* sorry," she said sincerely, though still walking at a rapid pace. She was trembling from the cold, since she was still dressed in her nouveau beach outfit. She had left her sweater in my apartment. For some reason she was in a hurry to get away from me. Just like Lucy. Just like *all* of my women.

How come, Fate?

Ah, fuck you.

"I didn't mean for that to happen," she continued as I trotted along beside her. "My mother slept around with all these men, and I feel like I have to prove something, to myself, to her, I don't know, but I just don't want to feel inferior to her, the way she wants me to feel. She wants me to be a nice little virgin, but I'd rather be a slut if it pisses her off. Do you understand?"

WHY? Why did *every* woman I sleep with have to rationalize it with some neurotic psychobabble? Couldn't they just be attracted to me on a base animal level and let it go at that? Why did intimacy with me have to stem from some childhood tragedy? That's what I wanted to know. Little Elvis, he couldn't have cared less. Nookie is nookie, any way you call it, according to him. But after he was satisfied, I'm the one who had to put up with the moral justification and emotional jostling.

"I understand," I lied. What a nice guy. See? I put up with

this crap. That's why they did it. Because I'm too damn nice for my own good. By this point I even felt guilty for jizzing on her. How could I have taken advantage of her vulnerability? What kind of woman goes home with a man she just met? A slut. And was Judy a slut? No. Simply a confused child trying to get back at her mother. Why couldn't I have seen that? Monica was right. Men *are* assholes. But I was right too. Women are *crazy*. Stalemate.

Anyway, I didn't have time to sub for Judy's shrink. I had work to do. I walked Judy back to my apartment, my arm draped around her in brotherly fashion to shield her from the cold. Before she left I had to obtain one key piece of info, the impetus for this whole embarrassing scenario: the location of her mother's mansion in Marin, where Lucy no doubt was hiding out from both me and her wacko father, plus anyone connected with him, including Antonio, wherever the hell he was now. Now that I had experienced an orgasm in the company of a live woman I could concentrate more on the case at hand, so perhaps it was a good thing after all, at least from a business perspective. So I made Judy some tea and we small talked a little bit longer until she felt comfortable enough to look me in the eye sometimes, and vice versa, and our impromptu loneliness-and-alcohol induced interlude didn't seem so nasty anymore. Christ. Sex was more complicated than it was worth. I was better off fantasizing to lingerie layout ads. No fuss, minimal mess, a small tissue bill, but that paled compared to dinner and drinks and therapy. And I'm not even the one night stand type. Really. Normally I wine and dine a chick, lay some Sinatra and candlelight on her for a couple of dates before I make any moves on her. But Judy was so cute and luscious and willing and I was so horny, probably some residual desire still pent-up from witnessing that orgy and then waking up naked after a night with that little Mob Bombshell, that I just felt compelled to seize the moment and Judy's rack along with it. Sue me, sue, shoot bullets through me, as Nathan Detroit once sang to Adelaide. Ah'da laid her sooner, Nate. We live in different times, my friend. Not my choice either, believe me.

"Let me drive you home," I offered after a half hour or so of engaging in the type of conversation we should've had before sharing bodily fluids. "It's the least I can do. It would be my honor. Remember, I'm a *fan*."

"All right," she said with a sniff. Then she gave me a hug and I hugged her back, hoping she wouldn't notice my persistent boner. What a tasteless, selfish prick that little guy is sometimes.

She put on her sweater and I walked her down to the Corvair and revved it up impressively, or so I believed, then peeled out even more impressively, though Judy remained nonplussed, staring out the window into the foggy night, lost in some distant place I wasn't welcome. As I drove she guided me with simple directions, hand signals and mumbles, to a residence on Green Street on the bottom of Telegraph Hill. It dawned on me that I had recently watched her mother engaging in public debauchery, and here I was giving her daughter a pearl necklace. I needed to sublimate my sex drive into something more spiritual, I decided.

"Nice digs," I remarked as we pulled up in front of her pad, and she kissed me on the cheek and climbed out without a word. I got out and scrambled after her. I didn't know how to approach the task of wriggling that address out of her with discretion. If it came down to it, I'd just have to be rude. I could handle it if I had to. Part of my Brooklyn background. It's a gift.

"Aren't you going to ask me in?" I said.

"No. My boyfriend's coming into town tomorrow morning," she said. "You know, from Santa Barbara."

Now I *really* felt like scum. I had completely forgotten about him. Of course, so had she, but that was a moot point, as they say.

"Thanks again," she said, kissing me once more on the cheek, and then she dashed to her tenement door up a flight of stairs and began jiggling the keys. She was obviously uncomfortable and wanted to banish my evening with her into memoryville as soon as possible. I was nervous I'd blow it because of getting sidetracked by pussy. Time was being wasted. I had to find Lucy and rescue her. I felt that in every fiber of my being. Intuitively I sensed she was in danger, and here I was diddling around. I felt ashamed. I had to get to that mansion. *Tonight.*

"Judy. We need to talk," I said firmly. I followed her up the stairs where she was waiting for me.

"What's wrong?" she asked in a tiny voice.

"I haven't been strictly on the level with you," I said.

She opened the door as if to make a quick entrance if warranted. "What?" she asked nervously. "You're HIV positive?"

God, what a paranoid society we lived in, I thought. Too damn sad. "No, no." Then I briefly panicked. Was I? I decided on the spur of the moment to get tested later. The thought hadn't really crossed my mind before, since my sexual encounters were so few and far between. What if Rose, so promiscuous, had infected me? No, she would have contacted me by now. What if Judy herself had it and didn't know? She admitted to sleeping around as a revenge tactic. But then I tossed these thoughts out of my head. Concentrate, damn it. "Judy, it's about your mother. I need to know where she lives. For personal reasons."

"I don't get it," she said, looking frightened and edging her way inside her flat, her eyes trained warily on my every twitch and nuance.

"Simple. I'm a detective, like I told you. And one of my clients has a daughter trapped in that cult up there in your mother's house. Deacon Rivers is brainwashing babes right and left, not just your mother, but lots of *young* ones. It's a veritable god damn commune up there now."

She looked very sad now. "I know," she whispered. "But what can I do about it? I just want to do my own thing and ignore all that. There's nothing *I* can do about it."

"You can tell me where the mansion is," I said.

She nodded, went inside, turned on a light, I followed her, she wrote down the address and directions on a sheet of paper, and handed it to me. Simple. Real simple. That's all I had to do in the first place. I was sidetracked for nothing. Well, not *nothing*. Judy was a dish of which I'd heartily if prematurely partaken. I'd shared an intimate evening with a true babe. Later I'd look back and appreciate it. Maybe when she became famous I could even brag about it. But in the meantime, I had to complete my mission.

"You used me to get that, didn't you," Judy said softly.

My impulse was to hug her, but her wall was up and I didn't have the energy to break it down again. "No, no. I really think you're talented and lovely. What happened just happened. I enjoyed it, and I'll look back on it fondly. I'd love to see you again sometime, I mean outside the cafe, if that's all right with you. I mean, just as friends. Your boyfriend could come along even. Okay?"

She shrugged and said something that sounded like "sure." Then she looked at me and said, "Don't say hello to my mother for me, okay?" I nodded. Then she led me to the door and kissed me on the cheek and I walked to the Corvair and sped toward the Golden Gate Bridge, feeling cooler than I'd felt in ages. I think I handled that pretty stylishly, don't you? Even if I am slightly exaggerating for your benefit in retrospect, that's basically how it went. Slick Vic. Love 'em and leave 'em wanting more. *Ces't moi.*

I didn't actually make it to the mansion near Muir Woods until dawn because my car ran out of gas half way across the Golden Gate Bridge and I had to hitch a ride to a gas station and then take a cab back with some fuel. But I was still cool. I really was.

It was right before the AM rush hour so all was quiet as I followed Judy's directions up Highway One along the dramatic coastline and finally reached the mansion near Muir Woods, right on the outskirts, isolated from the community at large and not really belonging to any particular neighborhood. Unincorporated paradise, at least to some. Me, I'll take a hotel room in The French Quarter of New Orleans or Midtown Manhattan any day. But the air was clean and misty and very invigorating. My adrenalin picked up the slack. When I knocked on the door of the mansion, which was naturally Victorian style and painted in gaudy grays and assorted primary colors, I felt prepared for anything.

Well, almost.

A young doll I'd never seen before answered the door on the fifth long rap session. My knuckles were developing calluses already. The girl was maybe twenty and red-haired and sleepy-faced, but still rather pretty. One of Lucy's playmates, I surmised. It was only then I realized how early it was. The dawn was as gray as the mansion, and the stillness of the new day had failed to remind me not everyone was awake anticipating my arrival into their listless lives. Certainly not the little doll currently rubbing her eyes and trying to figure out whom the hell I was.

"Who the hell are you?" she asked after squinting at me for a few seconds.

"I'm a friend of Zelda's," I lied smoothly. "Zelda Fagin lives here, right?"

"So? It's early as shit, man. What the hell ya want?"

"That's between me and Zelda. Actually, is Lucy around? Lucy Guisseppe?"

Lucy's name was like a bucket of ice-cold water tossed into her sleepy face. "Who *are* you, man?"

Just then another body pushed in from behind the little red-haired doll. It was ol' Zelda. She shoved the little doll behind her and confronted me with a patronizing smirk. "Well if it isn't Dudley Do-Right," she said.

"Actually, it's Vic Valentine. And since everyone here is tired, I'll cut right to the chase: I'm here for Lucy."

"Lucy Ricardo? She doesn't live here, I'm sorry. Try Cuba."

"You know who I mean. The little doll behind you knows her,

and I traced her here, so give her up and I'll be on my way."

"Why the hell should I? You a pervert?"

"Funny, coming from you. I met your daughter, by the way. Judy. She manages my favorite cafe, Rendezvous. Sweet kid. A little mixed up, but surprisingly well-adjusted considering whose loins she sprang from."

Zelda, recently awoken, sans makeup and rather scary looking, was un-amused by my commentary. "I don't have to take this," she said, rolling her eyes in exasperation. "*Ricky*!" she then yelled to someone behind her.

"Ricky Ricardo?" I said, but she didn't hear me, so I stood patiently and waited for Deacon Rivers to show up at the door.

"Whassgoanon?" he intoned. He was wide-awake, too. Been up all night doing "The Clam," no doubt. Then he saw me, and flashed that lop-sided grin. "Hey! It's Christopher Christmas!" He reached out and grabbed my hand for a shake, unwilling as I was. Zelda threw up her arms in disgust and retreated into the mansion, along with the little red-haired doll. That left the Deacon and me. "Say hello to my baby sister, did ya?" the deacon then asked me, jerking a thumb back at the doll.

"That was your *sister*?" I said needlessly. "Same red hair. Only she's actually attractive. Anyway, I'm not looking for her. I'm looking for Lucy."

"Her name's Mandy," the deacon interrupted me, still smiling and trying to sell his sister to me. "I think you two would hit it off. Just intuition, and I'm never wrong. Well, hardly ever. Come in for some breakfast? I was just rustling some up."

"Don't tell me. A pound of burnt bacon, grits and ham hocks."

He looked pleasantly surprised. "Howdja guess? Your E.Q. must be goin' up."

"Say what?"

"E.Q. Same as I.Q. only more important. Elvis Quotient. You left out fried peanut butter and banana sandwiches."

"Well, I'm still learning. Anyway, enough of the bullshit, or *king*shit, as the case may be. I want Lucy Guisseppe to come out here."

He wrinkled up his brow. "*Who*?"

"Don't fuck with me, man. I'm tired and sick of your games. You don't fool me. I was never interested in your racket except strictly as an undercover operative hired to find Lucy." I whipped out my badge and flashed it at him. He retained the same bemused expression throughout my spiel, as if nothing fazed him, except as a source of entertainment. "I don't know what you expect to ultimately accomplish with this setup except unlimited poon tang, and frankly I don't care anymore, as long as Lucy isn't suckered any further into this non-stop harem holiday you got goin'. I have a personal interest in her welfare, beyond the professional, and believe me, you don't want to screw around with my employer in this case. To say he has an itchy trigger finger would be a tragic understatement. *Got* it, slick?"

He rested against the door frame with his arms folded, looking down pensively at the ground with the same smirk frozen on his face, only now it appeared he was contemplating an inside joke I was not privy to, but definitely involved in. Finally he looked up at me and said, "Breakfast is gettin' cold. You comin' in? 'Cause otherwise I have to shut the door in your face, and that would be rude."

I just didn't know how to handle this character, especially with no sleep and a growling belly. So I just nodded and said, "Lead the way," and then I followed Deacon Rivers into Disgraceland.

Chapter Eleven
THE BIG DOLLHOUSE

When I walked into the mansion I saw Vicki Lee sitting in the living room on the sofa in a skimpy fuchsia robe, her long tan beautiful gams stretched out over some huge fluffy throw pillows, her gorgeous face entranced by the antics of Bugs Bunny on the tube. Bugs was doing one of his drag routines and I have to admit I watched for a second or two before surveying the rest of the joint. Not surprisingly, it was all Elvis, Elvis, and more Elvis—like Deacon River's church office, only more elaborate and tacky. Wall hangings, candles, framed portraits, albums, tapes, CDs, DVDs, a veritable library of books, curious collectibles, and a Jolly Elvis flag—his laughing visage over crossbones and a black background—waving over the entrance to the main living room adjacent to the parlor I was now standing in, awestruck by the vastness of the obsession. The furniture was appropriately gaudy, the rooms decorated in an array of royal reds and passion purples and collard greens. Deacon Rivers just watched me walk around in circles into the living room, where Vicki Lee turned her head and finally noticed me. She jumped up from the sofa like a deer surprised by a hunter while grazing, not sure where to run, her eyes full of apprehension. I like her that way, on the defensive.

"Vic, what are you doing here?" she said with a sleepy rasp in her voice.

"Might ask you the same thing, sweetheart," I said. The deacon went into the next room, which I guessed was the kitchen, leaving Vicki and me standing there with Elvis and Bugs and a batch of questions screaming for answers. "What I can't figure is why you wanted me to think you never even heard of this racket before I mentioned it to you. I mean, what do I care?"

"How'd you find this place?" she asked.

"What's the difference? I got connections. I have a secret life, same as you. But you still haven't explained to me why you've hidden this from me. I don't get it."

"I didn't want to let you into our circle until I knew you didn't want to hurt us. You kind of threw me when you happened to ask about it, so I just played kinda dumb until I found out your *real* agenda."

"*Hurt* you? Baby, you *are* paranoid. I got a job to do, that's all. Find the little Mob brat I told you about. *That's* my goddamn agenda. If you really want to play Graceland, that's fine by me. I couldn't care less, Vicki, really."

"I don't think so. I think you want to expose us, turn us over to the authorities and start a media feeding frenzy. Whoever hired you is using this missing runaway child as a ruse for their true purpose. They just needed someone to front for them, snoop around first, then blow the whistle, make us look like a cult of freaks. They needed an inside man. That's what you do, isn't it?"

"*Money.* That's all he cares about," called Zelda's voice from the kitchen, from which emanated the mixed aromas of burning bacon, cinnamon toast, and frying banana with peanut butter. I must say my palate began to tingle as the smell wafted in the room. "He's a muckraker in sheep's clothing," Zelda added, mixing metaphors as arbitrarily as she did her food items, though I hoped with smoother results. I was getting hungrier by the second, and Vicki's loose-fitting bathrobe made me salivate all the more. I was afraid I'd drool on the crimson carpet.

"All I care about is finding Lucy," I said loudly, then added a few octaves higher: "Lucy Guisseppe, that is," as if calling her by name, which in effect I was.

"You don't understand us, Vic," Vicki said, her arms folded over her cleavage in a defensive stance. "You're prying into something innocent and pure and beautiful, the only organized religion in the world today that asks nothing of its devotees but their honest emotions and feelings, and all their needs are met—physical *and* spiritual."

I looked Vicki up and down, thinking of the Deacon corn-holing her from behind on the pulpit last week, and probably spending the previous night on a tour of the islands. "I'll bet," I said after a beat. "How long have you been into this scam?"

"It's no scam, Vic. Leave your preconceptions and prejudices at the door. I first met Ricky in the Book Depot in Mill Valley months ago, and I even invited him to speak to our Philosophy class, and our Popular Culture study group in The City. He's very hip to what people are into, what they respond to, what they really want. He has a sophisticated vision honed by keen observation of modern civilization and a frankly divine gift for interpreting society's signals, finding the hidden truths behind the media and pop culture, and is offering his hard-won epiphanies to those of us who are less observant and sensitive and intelligent as he is. All he asks in return is honesty and freedom of expression from our bodies as well as our minds, so that he can open up new dimensions of thought and experience and broaden our conception of reality in the modern age, which will be mankind's final era unless we listen to what The King is trying to tell us in own inimitable, entertaining fashion."

"Yeah, whatever," I said, watching Daffy Duck set his bill straight after having it shot around his head by Elmer Fudd. Pretty soon every day reality would make the surreal goofiness of cartoons obsolete and unimaginative. "Vicki, this is a run-of-the-mill sex racket, nothing more, nothing less, with unusual trappings, okay, but no place for naïve teenager all the same. If you want to invest your dignity in a set-up so obviously phony as this you're free to do so, you're a grown woman. But Lucy Guisseppe leaves with me this morning."

"I knew you'd take this attitude of moral posturing," Vicki snapped. "You're *such* a self-righteous asshole, Vic. You think you know it *all*, don't you?"

"Less and less every day, actually. But I don't care that life makes no sense anymore. I make up and play by my own rules as I go, answer only to myself, not some kook who raids candles and graves for his own sick purposes and self-satisfaction. You hear this, Deacon?"

"*Come and get it while it's hot!*" the deacon shouted in response, but I knew he'd heard me.

I strolled into the kitchen with Vicki Lee fuming at my heels. "I wish I'd never kissed you," she hissed. "I thought I could win your confidence and understanding with love, but you're such a *stubborn* bastard."

"You're wasting your breath," Zelda sighed, sitting down at the '50s-diner style red and gray Formica kitchen table in one of the plush red booths. The kitchen was literally covered in Elvis stuff—cookbooks, kitchenware, the works. Not to mention lots and lots of food. The deacon was dishing out the grits and bacon with that bemused smirk still resting on his face as he contemplated that private joke he refused to let me in on. Maybe my just being there was it. He knew I knew he was full of shit, and I think he even respected me for voicing my opinions in this bastion of psycho conformity, but he would never admit it was just a game, especially with his disciples around. And I suspected their presence made no difference. Part of him actually believed this was an authentic religious organization, because if he admitted for a minute, even to himself, that it was an epic gag, the infrastructure would collapse around him, and bury him in his own devious defecation.

"Look us up sometime in the religious register," Zelda said haughtily as I sat opposite her in the booth. "We're an official church recognized by the Government. This is no *cult*."

"Meaning cultists can't get tax write-offs," I said. Vicki slid beside me and I smelled sex. A pang of jealousy collided with my hunger pangs, but I was simply too exhausted to care much. I was somewhat numb by then from fatigue and general disgust. Also, some of that residual sex I smelled could have been coming from *me*. And when Zelda stuck her bare painted toenail foot in my crotch under the table just as the deacon joined us, I nearly lost my lunch, and I had hadn't even started breakfast yet.

"Dig in, Dick Tracy," the deacon said, pouring ketchup on his grits in heaping amounts. I wondered how he stayed so skinny. The coffee was peach flavored but tasted good just the same, not that I needed the extra rush at that particular moment. And though I hardly ever eat bacon, I was starving and couldn't help but munch on it savagely as Zelda continued to play my organ out of sight. If she only knew who'd been playing that same organ only hours before. I felt cheap and horny simultaneously. I mean, Zelda was pretty attractive for an older lady. Nonetheless, I found myself squirming and pinching her naughty ankle just the same. The deacon seemed totally oblivious—or was he?

"Ever hear of the Incas, Dick?" the deacon asked me as he guzzled down his bloody grits with chocolate milk. I was going to correct him about my name but figured it would only egg him on, so I let it slide.

"What about 'em? They worship Elvis too?"

"Oh, of course!" he said with an emphatic nod. "They just didn't realize it. Same with ancient Egyptians. Ever notice how Elvis and King Tut are similar? Both called 'the boy king,' both from a city called Memphis—hell, they even *looked* alike, if you check out the face on Tut's tomb. I suspect the Greek god Dionysus, the god of pleasure, was Elvis too. Elvis has been with us forever, in one form or another, and he always will be. Anyway, my point is that the Incas used to practice polygamy, meaning they didn't put a cap on wives. Any powerful leader could have up to thirty women. Same with harems. Many primitive cultures operated under this system. You even see it in nature. Gorillas, for instance, often take more than one mate. The *males* do. But female chimpanzees? Hell, they're the original happy hookers."

"What's your point, shithead?" I asked him, scarfing up a fried peanut butter and banana sandwich from the plateful in the middle of the table. I must admit it was much tastier than it looked. Maybe I was just delirious by then.

"My point is monogamy is against our nature. Elvis knew that. I'm not saying I *don't* believe in love and marriage. The King himself supported that holy institution for the sake of our children's stability." I glanced over and saw Vicki had stopped eating and was now gazing at the deacon with intense devotion. Save me, I thought. "But," the deacon went on, "the courtship ritual should not be limited to a single partner in life, or even for one night. Did you know Elvis recorded two versions of the same song, 'One Night'? One was 'One Night of Sin,' the other 'One Night of Love.' One he's payin' for, the other he's prayin' for. Elvis represented love *and* lust. He's for everybody, and for everybody havin' a good time and not worryin' too much about restrictions on our natural libidos. The Whirling Dervish of Sex, they called him. But even though he was initially condemned, he still got off the first shots in the sexual revolution." The deacon took a deep breath and waited for my witty rejoinder, which by now he had come to expect, maybe even appreciate on some level of repartee. It seemed no one else around ever gave his ego and intellect a run for their money, and he welcomed the challenge to his perverse but apparently well-researched and thought-out convictions.

"Well, call me old-fashioned, but I'm a romantic," I said. "I like to believe our sexual nature can happily coincide with our spiritual nature, but not in the way *you* say. One has to control the other. I'm from the opposite school than you. I think we all have low impulses we can choose to follow or ignore based on the prudence of the situation. We can aspire to something higher and more romantic and idealistic—*un*like an ape. Plus we often choose partners out of sheer loneliness, without regard for propagation of our useless race. I mean, lonely baboons don't sit in hotel rooms knocking back bourbon, calling 1-900 numbers and listening to 'One For My Baby.' Dig?"

The deacon just smiled. "They would if they could, Vic. You see sexual hierarchy in all forms of wildlife. The most desirable female makes the most powerful males compete for her. The losers are lonely. It's natural selection. Powerful males want the most beautiful females, beautiful females want the most powerful males, so that the species can continue to purify itself. So it goes with humans. Elvis was The King. *Is* The King. He has all the wealth, so he has all the women. He's the height of our civilization. He's what we aspire to, the paradigm of humanity. Generous, fun-loving, mother-respecting, sexual, spiritual. He was *it*, man. The King freed us to pursue our natural impulses, but within a controlled, civilized framework. He set the standard for modern life as it could and should be lived. He's the top of the evolutionary scale. He lived life to the fullest, and was duly rewarded."

"You mean by dying on the toilet an overweight junkie?" I said, relishing the friction the remark caused. "I'm sure he was eternally grateful."

The deacon just looked at me for a beat with an expression I can only describe as sympathetic. "Boy, you got a *lot* of livin' to do. By the time I'm through with you, you'll be cryin' in the chapel, begging Elvis to forgive you for such an ignorant outlook. Answer me this, Vic: are you a happy man?"

Zelda was really digging into my goodies now, and I was visibly disturbed by it, but no one seemed to notice, least of all Zelda, who didn't even look up from her meal. The thing is, I have this foot fetish, and Zelda had nice feet, so the distraction was almost impossible to ignore, but I managed to concentrate long enough to answer the deacon's query: "No, but who is?"

"I am," all three said at once, in perfect unrehearsed unison, but also in something of a drone. Then they added, also in a single monotonous chorus, "Thanks to Elvis." I was almost surprised no one crossed themselves.

"Happy people are idiots," I said simply, which is indeed part of my overall philosophy. "How can anyone look around at this fucked-up planet and say they're happy? Anyone *sentient*, that is. Anyone with any intelligence or just plain common *sense*, that is."

They all laughed, then abruptly stopped, like canned laughter on a sitcom. "I'd rather be a happy fool than a miserable genius," the deacon said, and they held up their coffee cups and clinked them together in an impromptu but perfectly orchestrated salute.

"So you can ignore everybody else's pain?" I said. "You can just tune out the world and go around singing Elvis songs like that's all that matters?"

"But it *is* all that matters," the deacon said with sudden

seriousness. Zelda stopped her pedestrian probe of my privates for a moment as if to absorb this ersatz truism, then continued relentlessly. In a moment I was going to have to either give in and enjoy it or ask her to stop in front of our company. Both were equally tempting, so I was still thinking about it.

"You're a serious basket case, fella," I said. "I watch you in this so-called church rutting like a pig in heat, and you try to tell me it's all for a good cause."

"Which is living and living well, the way Elvis would want. Partaking of our sexual menu is certainly more enjoyable than the many other bogus past-times people occupy their time with, such as hurting others either individually or *en masse*. We're anti-pain, anti-violence, anti-despair. We're each following our own dream wherever it leads. Did you know that Anne Helm, the co-star of 'Follow That Dream,' visited our church once and gave us her blessing as Elvis's emissary?"

"Bullshit," I said.

"I'm not lying. I have it in writing. She signed a picture of her and Elvis circa 1962. I met her in Miami at my church there, where she was visiting with her daughter, a beautiful young model that I suspect might be Elvis's love child. On the picture she wrote, 'Follow That Dream Always...With Love, Annie Helm.' I have it upstairs in a frame."

"And that's it?"

"That's what?"

"An autograph means an endorsement?"

"It does to me. See what she wrote? I'll show you later. 'Follow That Dream.' One of the commandments. She was telling me to continue my mission. You have to see beyond the obvious, Mick."

"It's Vi—, forget it. So you have a church in Miami too, huh?" I said, thinking, *stupid people are everywhere, so why not*?

"*And* Honolulu *and* Tokyo *and* Budapest. We're growing, Vic. No one can stop The King."

"Not even Michael Jackson?"

"Michael was married to Lisa Marie, not to Elvis. In his own way, he was doing The King's work, I'm sure. But he still can't touch The King's crown or steal his jewels. No, *sir*."

"Bet he would if he could."

"That doesn't concern me, Mick. None of my business. Just like it's none of my business Priscilla and Lisa Marie won't ditch their Scientology front and join me in speaking out to the world about The King and his message of personal emancipation for all. They have their reasons, their assignment, and I have mine."

I finished my coffee, wiped my eyes, pinched Zelda's foot until she yelped and recoiled, shoved Vicki out of the booth, grabbed the deacon by the shiny green lapels of his white silk *Kid Galahad* robe, and said authoritatively, "I've had my breakfast. Now it's time to talk about my assignment. So cut the crap and hand Lucy over." I then reached behind me and pulled my .38 out of my waistband and stuck it in the deacon's smirking face. "Right *now*."

"Looks like you're following a low impulse," the deacon said, seemingly unaffected by my sudden move, whereas Vicki and Zelda were living tension wires.

"The situation calls for it," I said. "Now c'mon. Where's Lucy?"

"Lucy who?"

"Don't mess with me, man."

The deacon help up his hand and made it tremble. "Look at me. I'm *shakin*'. Help!" he shouted with mock fear.

"You think *you're* shaking, you should get a load of her old man," I said. Then I cocked my pistol and stuck it in his left nostril. "Last chance."

He stared down the barrel, still grinning. "Or what? You'll blow my head off?"

"Yep."

"Go ahead. I *dare* you. Right here in front of witnesses. You'll have to kill them, too. And then everyone who heard the gunshots, and this house is *full* of people, Vic." At least I had him calling me by my right name now.

"He's *crazy*!" Zelda yelled. "Give her up, Ricky! He attacked my foot just now! He's *vicious*!"

"Give *who* up?" the deacon said, his brow wrinkled with mock puzzlement.

I sighed long and loud, uncocked the piece, and sat back down in the booth opposite Deacon Rivers. "I know she's here, dickface," I said to the deacon. "Lucy. Lucy Guisseppe. Her father is not interested in your little cult here. I don't work for any investigative journalists or TV tabloid shows. I was hired by Lucy's father to bring her back to him. If you don't believe me, ask he yourself."

"He's right," Lucy said, walking into the kitchen. Behind her was about a dozen young babes of varying ages and races and sizes—but pretty much all the same *shape*—obviously aroused by the commotion. Jesus, I thought. This place was like a merger between Playboy Mansion and Graceland. Maybe Hugh Hefner and Priscilla Presley were bankrolling this operation along with Zelda. Nothing would have surprised me at this point. I just wanted to get this over with, rescue the little brat, resume my normal boring lifestyle, and pretend this was all just a bad dream. I stood and walked right up to Lucy and took her by the arm with my left hand, the gun still brandished threateningly by my right, and led her past the little throng of groupies into the parlor by the front door. She was acquiescent and didn't struggle. She was wearing a slinky pink nightgown that revealed her voluptuous figure to a distracting degree. *God*, that little babe was stacked. But I was so tired and pissed off I was able to temporarily ignore her natural gifts and get down to the nitty-gritty of the situation.

"Why are you doing this to me?" I asked through gritted teeth.

"You have a persecution complex," she said with annoying maturity. "That's not *my* fault. No one's doing anything *to* you."

I squeezed her arm a little tighter and she grimaced but didn't even let out a squeak. "Why did you cold-cock me and rip off my clothes? What *happened*? I gotta know right *now* before we go any further."

She adopted this sly little grin and looked at me with the expression of a savvy, sexy woman, not a confused, victimized little kid. The little broad knew the score, all right. "Don't you know?" she said eerily.

"No. Tell me. *Now*."

"*Nothing!*" she yelled in my face. Then she twisted her arm free and gave me a long, loud raspberry. The little kid was still present after all. I heard a chorus of laughter and looked to see that her housemates had been eavesdropping, huddled into a cluster in the living room just outside the parlor. Behind them were the deacon, Zelda, and Vicki. They all looked at me as if to say, "Go on, Galahad."

So I went on. Couldn't disappoint the fans. "If nothing happened, why did I wake up (*gulp*) naked? And why did you split on me?"

"I wanted to go home," she said with a precocious pout. "I *hit* you with your gun butt, but I didn't *take* it, did I? Maybe I should've, but then you'd feel emasculated." (*Cheers from the fans.*) "I just wanted to go without you stopping me. I don't want any trouble. I don't want to go back to my father. I took your

126

clothes just so you'd wake up and wonder where they were. I have them upstairs if you want them."

"So, so—nothing *happened*?" God, I sounded so pathetic.

"You mean like sex with a minor" More cheers from the peanut gallery. "Sorry. How could you get it up if you were out cold?"

I never even thought of that. That's who stupid I was. I was thinking with the wrong head, as usual. "I don't think it *ever* goes down. *Especially* when I'm asleep and dreaming of Esther Williams." No one understood that remark, which is why I said it. "Anyway, go upstairs and get my clothes and then let's go. I'm beat." I was a bit disappointed as well.

"Go *where*?" she said, actually batting her eyes. "Back to *your* place?"

"*WOOOOOOOO*!" said the crowd collectively.

I was blushing big time by now. "If you *want* me," she said, "come and *get* me!" Then she ran past the fans and up the staircase. I noticed she was wearing pink high-heeled slippers as well. She looked like a living lingerie ad. Naturally I raced upstairs in hot pursuit, my fans cheering me on.

I saw her go into one of the myriad doorways in the upstairs hall lined with framed portraits of The King, and managed to reach the door before she closed it. But I think she had it planned that way. When I burst into the room she slammed it shut behind her. I whirled around to see her standing with her back against the door, the nightgown down around her ankles. Now she was wearing only her glorious birthday suit, and Little Elvis was already launching into a chorus of "Happy Birthday" as she kicked the nightgown over to me, laughing like a siren, walked toward me, arms outstretched, large firm bosoms with round erect nipples headed straight for me like twin torpedoes.

She stood on tiptoe and kissed me with her tongue deep in my mouth as she backed me up and into the bed. She sat on top of me and began ripping the buttons from my shirt and massaging my chest as she kissed my neck and her breasts rubbed up against me and I didn't want to touch her but did anyway—her thighs, her hips, her breasts which seemed to be coming from everywhere. I kissed her throat and mouth and eyes and cute little ears and her long thick hair fell in my face and she laughed and I remember a drowning sensation just before all went dark.

Chapter Twelve
POP! GOES THE CULTURE

I think the deal with the modern world and me is a classic case of mutual disinterest. I find it lacks taste, style and substance, and it probably sees me the same way. We have to tolerate each other for an undetermined amount of years, however, so I suppose we try to find the best qualities in each other in order to endure. It's a tough task, and gets more so every day. I think the world is hopeless, it thinks I'm a loser. We have no real use for each other anymore. The honeymoon is way over. I delve into the world's past to find tidbits of romanticism to sustain me, and every now and then it tosses me a night of passion to soothe my nerves. But that's about it. Basically what we have to offer each other is pitifully limited.

In any case, I woke up later that day around four or so in the afternoon, according to my watch (the only thing I was wearing), only you couldn't tell from the quality of light in the room. It was pitch black. At first I was worried I'd woken up in a tomb or something, especially when the recollection of recent events broke through my mental fog bank. Not again. The last thing I recalled before once again blacking out under Lucy's suspicious auspices was her enveloping me in her jailbait body. The cops were probably their way now. Yeah, that was it. Deacon Rivers set me up. But no, I was still in the mansion. No way he'd let the cops into this sinful sanctuary. As for me, I'd blown it again. I assumed I'd been drugged by the peach coffee, since I didn't recall anyone else drinking some at the breakfast table. What the hell, I needed the excuse to rest anyway, but I definitely passed out at a crucial moment. Once again the question plagued me: Did I or did I not nail Lucy Guisseppe? She was fucking with my head if nothing else. Why? Because she could? With most natural born mind-fuckers, that was incentive enough. But I don't think Lucy was born this way. She saw me as some sort of authority figure, and it brought out the worst in her. She was constantly turning the tables on me, humiliating me, mainly in a sexual way. My hunch was that her old man had something to do with this psychological aberration. She was too young for this psychosexual power trip crap. And Deacon Rivers was like *Beacon* Rivers for girls like Lucy. I was probably trapped in a house of emotionally imbalanced and mentally and physically abused women. Vicki included. It was slowly dawning on me that *she* was the one who left the cat at my doorstep.

After turning on the light I noticed that no sunlight penetrated the bedroom, which was full of teddy bears of all shapes and colors and sizes. One big bad bear was staring me right in the face when I hit the switch, and I recoiled in terror. Oh, I get it, I thought. The "Teddy Bear Suite." Original Elvis LPs abounded next to an old but perfectly preserved hi-fi stereo system. The teddy bear motif was taken to typical extremes—even the bed sheets and pillowcases were decorated with teddy bears. Then I noticed that the windows were covered with tin foil. I remembered reading somewhere that Elvis used to do this in order to catch up on his sleep during daylight hours. Whatever. I tore down the tin foil and bright light burst into the room so abruptly I thought I'd crumble into dust like Count Dracula. No such luck. I still had to see this nightmare through. Wonderful.

Predictably I couldn't find my clothes. *Or* my gun this time. I was trapped in there as long as I was naked. Or was I? I noticed the bedroom had an adjacent bathroom. I went in to find more cutesy teddy bear crap all over the pink tile and pink towels and toilet seat cover and bathmat and shower curtain and toothbrush and WHATEVER JESUS GOD JUST LET ME OUT OF HERE! I grabbed a teddy bear towel, wrapped it around me, looked at myself for a few moments in the mirror, sucking in my gut and flexing my muscles, then when I felt suitably sexy, I went out into the hallway. No, the door wasn't locked, as I'd feared at first. They wanted me to strut around in the buff, the sick sex maniacs. I marched right downstairs, following the sound of a piano playing an Elvis tune I vaguely recognized as "Young and Beautiful," only when I walked into what can only be described as the Music Room, where the deacon was seated at the grand piano surrounded by a bevy of beauties, he changed the tune to "I Want To Be Free."

"The Reverend Horton Heat, I presume," I said as I walked in, clutching the teddy bear towel tightly around my torso. They all gawked at me and then started giggling. Lucy was not among them.

So you doped me up and stole my duds and now I'm your prisoner," I said as I made my way to the piano, blushing nonchalantly as the assorted groupies cleared a path. The deacon was his usual happy-go-lucky self, only now he had traded in his *Kid Galahad* robe for a gold lame outfit like Presley wore on the cover of "Elvis' Golden Records Volume Two." His wardrobe bill alone would've broken most devotees. This Zelda broad must've been truly loaded, and I don't mean strictly the monetary sense. "I feel a bit groggy, but I could still kick your ass unless you give me back my gun."

"No clothes?" The deacon grinned, still playing the piano. My entrance hadn't even broken his musical stride. He looked like a hippie Liberace.

"I'll take those too," I said. "Where's Lucy?"

He shrugged. "Around. I don't kept anyone on a leash, Sherlock."

One of the girls poked me in the side, and another pinched me on the ass, then they all giggled and ran away en masse, leaving the deacon and me alone. Whatever.

I slammed the lid to the keys shut but the deacon second-guessed my move and avoided getting his fingers smashed. He was smirking as he said, "You just can't intimidate me with that towel wrapped around you, I'm sorry." Then he laughed, and his fans squealed approval from the living room, where they were now congregated around the television watching cartoons.

"Shouldn't those kids be in school?" I asked him, ignoring his comment.

"They are. And not all of them are kids. And school-time is over. You missed it. You were out of it all day. Must have been pretty tired, huh?"

"You telling me you're those kids' legal guardian?"

"No. The *King* is."

I wanted to hit him, but he was right, I felt too silly and vulnerable to act tough. Instead I just said, "I'm getting tired of all this mumbo jumbo which we both know is only an excuse to play doctor with wayward women and lost little girls. Don't yank my chain anymore, Deke. One way or another, even if I'm half-naked, I'm taking Lucy back to her old man. Then I'm dropping the dime on you to the proper authorities. If, like you say, it's all on the level, you got nothin' to worry about, do ya?"

"Did you notice what you called me?" the deacon said rather anxiously.

"Um, dickhead? I don't know. What's the difference what the fuck I called you? A wacko by any other name."

"Deke. You called me *Deke*. As in Deke Rivers, Elvis' name

in 'Loving You.' Sherlock, your E.Q. is improving by the hour. It must have been gaining altitude even while you were asleep."

"You mean *unconscious*. What was that you drugged me with, anyway? And what's this mind control stuff you spiked the Kool-Aid with at the orgy?"

"*What* orgy?"

I sighed and buried my face in my hands. "I don't have time and I certainly don't have the energy for any more of these insipid exchanges, Deke or Dick or whatever the hell your name is. You can't just dope people up and get away with it, *you* know."

"The only drugs I use are prescribed by a doctor my personal physician in Berkeley whose name I don't feel at liberty to disclose, but he's a legitimate community sawbones. All on the up and up. You can check on that later, the prescriptions, I mean. And I *never* spike anyone's drink. You're hallucinating, but that's not my fault. You take a nap and then blame it on me. Next you'll accuse Lucy of knocking you cold again. Not that I wouldn't understand—she *is* a knockout, isn't she? My sister was a little jealous, I think."

I grabbed him by his gold lame lapels and the towel dropped down around my ankles and I was standing there totally nude as Zelda walked in behind me and set a tray of milk shakes on the piano. "Hope I'm not interrupting anything," she said snidely as she glanced at my goodies and shook her head and then walked right back out.

The deacon merely smiled as he took a sip of his milkshake, which had whipped cream and a cherry and looked pretty delicious. There was another one on the tray, but I felt in my compromised position I couldn't really reach for it. I put the towel back on and then just took it and drank it down, wiping the whipped cream from my upper lip as I stared the deacon down.

"Ever lick whipped cream off a woman's tit?" the deacon asked me suddenly. "*Hmmm*, yummy!"

I was pretty tired of being patronized by that point. I was so humiliated I felt I had no place to go but up. I looked around the room. Elvis this, Elvis that, shiny electric guitars, a saxophone, drum set, LPs, CDs, an elaborate sound system, keyboards, shelves of sheet music, on and on. "I guess Zelda lets you lick whipped cream off her tit in exchange for all this," I said.

"That's a dirty remark," the deacon said matter-of-factly. "I'm surprised at you, Charlie."

"*Charlie*?"

"Like Charlie Chan. May I call you Charlie?"

"May I call you one sick sex-crazed motherfucker, and I mean 'motherfucker' in the literal sense."

"Sure, but that's quite a mouthful. How about just calling me Elvis Incarnate for short?"

"I just don't see it. How could you fool so many women into *believing* this shit? You're not particularly handsome, maybe charming in an offbeat way, and you obviously don't have any dough of your own—or *do* you?"

"Charlie, would you believe me if I told you I went to Harvard and majored in Law and then switched to Psychology before dropping out and studying Elvology in the School of Life?"

"No."

"Okay, then I won't tell you that. Doesn't mean it isn't so, though."

"You trying to tell me you're an Ivy League grad?"

"Would've been if I'd kept it up. With honors, too. But like I said, I dropped out in my final year to pursue my true bliss." He slowly lifted the lid back up and kept playing the piano softly as he spoke, a medley of Elvis ballads.

"You left *Harvard* to do this Elvis shit? You're kiddin'."

"Why, that doesn't make sense to you? To follow that dream wherever that dream may lead? Why should I have stayed in a world that didn't interest me any longer, where I couldn't fully exploit my knowledge and passions? I found my calling, and I left the world of my parents behind. I come from a rather prominent Boston family, Charlie. I used to go boating in the Poconos and Martha's Vineyard with the staff of The New Yorker and the Kennedys. But it bored me. Their E.Q. was so low I couldn't stand being around them. And they wouldn't listen to me. I tried to share my enlightenment with them and they scoffed. My mother tried to have me committed, my father virtually disowned me. So I left the East Coast and traveled all over the world in search of truth, and in so doing met other seekers, like Zelda. Zelda had met The King, had a personal experience with him, and introduced me to Larry Geller, Elvis' hairdresser and spiritual guide. Through Larry I discovered more intimate sides of Elvis that fleshed out my perception of him and his place in the Universe, and subsequently my place as one of his disciples. Larry and I had a little falling out which I'm sure we'll resolve somewhere down the road. Larry thinks I'm on a big ego trip, but Zelda understands. So do the girls and all of my followers from Miami to Tokyo.

Sure, my flock is predominantly female, because women are much more open to the truth. Beauty seeks out beauty, I suppose. But they will have children who will be born with this knowledge, and then preach it to the rest of this troubled world, and then maybe one day Utopia will be discovered through Elvis's Word, or Elvis's *Lyric*, as I prefer to call it. Ever hear that Mojo Nixon song 'Elvis is Everywhere'? That's a very spiritual song. It goes somethin' like this…"

I'd had enough, towel or no towel. I slammed the lid back down and threw his milkshake glass against the wall, followed by my own. They both shattered noisily and attracted a crowd, including Lucy and Zelda. This is what I'd been hoping for. The deacon just watched with that same passive expression which was really beginning to grate on my nerves. During my outburst I shouted, "Now you're giving me this *Dr. Strangelove* shit about populating the world with a fourteen women to one man ratio! Start all over and do it right this time! And you're the number one designated sperm donor, right? You think I can't see through that, you scumbag? You think I can't, can't…" The sudden expenditure of energy left me feeling dizzy. I grew faint and collapsed in a heap beside the piano.

This time when I woke up I looked at my watch and saw it was around ten PM. I was in another room this time, a jail cell. The bars were real but the rest of it looked fake, like a movie set. It felt like I was on board a '50s rocket ship, in the brig. At first I thought the cops had finally caught up with me. Then I remembered the milkshake. Drugged again. I felt groggy and disoriented and nauseous. Not only was he doping me but he was doing it in junk food. My system was in serious trouble if I didn't start eating vitamins and veggies right away. I felt so out of sorts I passed right back out again, and didn't wake up until seven the next morning. This time I forced myself to keep my eyes open and my brain active. As I scanned the rather luxurious jail cell, which had posters of Elvis from *Jailhouse Rock* plastered on all four lavender-painted walls, my vision began to focus, and I saw Vicki Lee was kneeling beside me. I had clothes on this time: a black jacket, black pants, and a striped shirt, just like Elvis wore in the big production number from the movie. This *had* to be a dream. It just *had* to be. At that point I half-expected Vicki Lee to turn into Betty Boop or Jessica Rabbit. But she just cradled my tortured head in her soft, slender arms, rocking me like a baby as I gradually came to.

"Why do you keep doing this to me?" I said feebly. "Why. Just tell me *why*."

"*Ssshhhh* now. No one's doing anything to you, Vic. You're just imagining that. You have a persecution complex, like Lucy said. I've always thought that about you. But it's okay, *we'll* take care of it. Healing through Elvis is what we do here, Vic. Everything will be all right."

And then god damns it if I didn't start sobbing in her arms. I was losing it. I was sick and weak and confused. Then when Vicki bent over and started kissing me I grew delirious, slobbering all over her face and then her neck and chest as she held me and hummed "Love Me Tender." Then after a while she laid me down, climbed on top of me, and we began a heavy make out session. As we continued to smooch, I whimpered in Vicki's ear, "Why did you give me that cat?"

She sat upright, though still on top of me, and looked into my eyes and said, "As a token of my affection. I felt I owed you something for finding *my* cat."

"But when I found your cat, it was a mess."

"So's yours," she said, sticking her tongue in my mouth and shutting me up. She was right about that. Puss was in the hospital right now, racking up credit bills. Now Vicki was trying to seduce me into joining her so I'd leave the deacon and Lucy alone. But I wasn't having any more of this, thanks. I was wise to the routine by now. Vicki was just kissing me into submission. Lucy had never had sex with me, either. These dames were into mind-fucking only. I was in a den of control freaks. Their only objective seemed to be dominion over outsiders, luring lost souls into their ranks and then brainwashing them through any means necessary. The deacon needed numbers on his side if he was going to succeed with this demented enterprise. Sex never failed. Except *this* time.

I forced myself to sit upright and topple Vicki in the process. I tore off the black jacket and flung it across the room. "What the hell am I doing in this ridiculous costume?" I shouted to no one in particular.

Vicki picked herself up off the floor. She was in a foul mood now, I could tell. "You're doing the jailhouse rock because you've' been a bad boy," she said.

"Vicki, you need help, sweetheart. Seriously. Now let me out of here so I can take you and Lucy and all the rest of the girls who want to go out of this fuckin' asylum. This place should be burned to the ground. I can't believe an intelligent girl like you got suckered in by this garbage. I mean, Vicki, look around you. You call this *normal*?"

"What's normal, Vic?" she said flatly, but I could tell I was getting to her.

"The opposite of *this*," I said, extending my arms in a sweeping motion. "Whatever this *ain't* is normal."

"You consider other religions *normal*?" she said coldly. "Religions that spread hate and fear instead of love and freedom? Religions that preach prejudice and repression in the name of God? If that's normal, Vic, I'm glad you consider this insane. I really do."

I was dizzy, afraid of passing out again, but I fought for my strength. I was afraid of being imprisoned here indefinitely. Deacon Rivers seemed harmless enough, not a serial killer or Manson type, but nonetheless, I wanted to get out of there as soon as possible. And when dealing with crazies, you never knew their snapping point. I could bring out the Manson in Rivers yet. The Waco massacre probably wasn't in David Koresh's master plan either. Or maybe it was. Who cared. I was no longer interested in the schemes of sickos. I just wanted my lonely obscure life back. And I was worried about my cat.

"Vicki, *please*. Just let me outta here, okay? I mean, what do you want with me ultimately, to sacrifice me to Elvis?"

"Don't be stupid, Vic. All I'm supposed to do is keep you here until you agree to leave and let us alone, for *good*. No outside intervention, no authorities. Just pretend you never met us."

"Lucy included?"

"She's free to come and go as she pleases, Vic. We *all* are. And she obviously wants to stay. Why would she want to go back to that monster of a father, the one who molested her for years until she finally escaped?"

"You know about him?"

"Of course. We all do. There are no secrets here, Vic. We're like a big sorority, only closer, because our bonds are for life. All of us here are damaged goods, Vic. Even me. I've been looking for my father in professors and older men all my life, because I never knew my own. And I know what you're thinking, but it isn't true. Ricky is not my surrogate dad, Vic. He's my guide, my savior, but *not* my father."

"So who is, Vicki? *Elvis*?"

She looked at me and said, straight-faced: "Elvis faked his death for our sins, Vic."

I laughed so hard I doubled over. I just couldn't take any more of this. At that point I would've agreed to sodomy with The Pope just to get the hell out of there.

"Okay, Vicki, okay," I said, tears rolling down my cheeks as I sat on the floor and resumed my composure in the face of her unamused authority. "You win. I promise not to tell anyone about this place. I promise I'll let Lucy stay here of her own free will. But there's one exception: I have to tell her father where she is. It's my duty." The way I saw it, Shiv deserved to deal with this madness. And Antonio, wherever he was, was right about Shiv molesting Lucy, it seemed. Either the Feds or the Mob had put Antonio out of commission now. Lucy had no place to turn except me. My gamble was she'd leave with me rather than stay here and wait for Shiv to come get her.

There was just one little detail I was as yet unaware of, which Vicki revealed haughtily: "Her father has known where's she's been all along. We just won't turn her over, that's all."

I was stunned into silence, but then said, "I don't believe it. Why would he need me then? Why doesn't he just walk in and take her away by force? He's got the muscle to do it, and the gall."

"He doesn't know she's here in the mansion. He knows she's with us, that's all. Her uncle told him a long time ago. That's why he flew out here. He's been to the church in Berkeley, made some threats, but we hid her."

"Aren't you guys afraid he'll blow his top and just *kill* everybody?"

"Not without finding Lucy first. But he's getting close. He came to the church the day after you did. He threatened Ricky and pushed him around, but Ricky wouldn't admit Lucy was with us. He knows it, though. He's been following you to get to us. That's what we're afraid of, that he followed you here."

It made sense. Now I knew why Shiv hadn't been fazed when I'd mentioned Lucy was in a cult. He already knew. Antonio could have relented and told him where Lucy was a long time ago. Antonio just didn't tell me he told Shiv. Why? Who knows. Who cares. Not me, certainly. But then there was Lucy. The Elvisites actually showed some decency in hiding a victim of molestation from her father. But then they were harboring her in a sex cult. None of it made sense. Everybody was to blame. Even me for letting Lucy's charms distract me. She needed real help, and soon, if she was going to survive this onslaught of abuse. No, I had to rescue her from both Shiv and the deacon, or I'd never forgive myself.

"Okay," I said. "Okay. I promise I won't tell Shiv, either. I'll tell him Lucy went to the Tokyo branch, or maybe the Budapest one, throw him off. Chances are he'll shoot me, but what the hell. The world and I won't miss each other much. Okay? Just let me out of here. Keeping me here is no good. What if he followed me here? He's waiting for me to come out, maybe right now. He won't just walk up and knock on the door because Lucy would have too many people on her side. Just like back at the church. Too many witnesses. Lucy will run the second she sees him. He knows that. So why does he want her back? The answer is he *doesn't*. He wants her *dead*. And he wants to do it himself. There's more than incest going on there. I think Lucy threatened to turn some info in to the Feds or something. Or maybe—maybe *not* the Feds. They already got Antonio. Or *do* they? Maybe the Mob, or The Family is behind all this. Maybe Lucy has some dirt on Shiv he doesn't want the Mob to know."

"Just molesting her would break the Italian code," Vicki said. "That would give him the label of a degenerate. If he has any aspirations to greatness within the mob ranks, that could ruin him. Chances are they'd even kill him. Traditionally mobsters despise perverts. Murder and extortion are fine, but child molesters are considered mad dogs to be put down."

"How do you know all this?"

"I go to college, Vic. Remember? I'm not just some flake." She sighed and tapped her foot, arms akimbo, as she considered my situation. "All right, Vic. Now that we've had this little chat, I'll take you upstairs."

"You mean we're in the dungeon?"

"Basement, actually. Don't worry, Vic. We'd never detain you indefinitely. We're just trying to protect our own. Remember your promise. I trust you because I know you don't want Lucy harmed in the long run, and now we all know the score with her sick father. Let's go." She removed some keys from the pocket of her skimpy outfit and led me to the door, and then we walked down a dark hallway and up a creaky flight of stairs and into the light.

We were just in time for the party. The deacon, Zelda and the girls were huddled in front of the bay window facing the lawn. I looked past them and saw Shiv and four men dressed in black and armed with Uzis standing there waiting for Lucy to come out. Lucy ran up behind me and squeezed my waist. She was crying and screaming for me to protect her. The deacon turned and looked at us with an unusually sober expression. It was then I noticed that everyone was armed with the only weapons they had available in a pacifist environment: lots and lots of *food*.

Chapter Thirteen
BITE THIS BULLET

Surreal is not a word that does descriptive justice to the situation I found myself trapped in. Now my sorry life was literally in danger. I had mixed feelings about that, but set them aside selflessly so I could put my priorities in the proper order.

"*It's the devil in disguise!*" Zelda shrieked hysterically.

"Can you hold 'em off?" I asked the deacon, now my *paisan* in peril.

"We can try," the deacon said wearily. "You got any bright ideas, now's the time to light the flare, Charlie. This is all your fault, after all."

"*My* fault?" I said, but then was interrupted by a familiar voice from outside.

Shiv shouted shakily: "Just let me talk to her. Tell her I only want to talk to her, and then she's free to do what she wants." The four goombahs were still standing two apiece on either side of Shiv, Uzis at the ready, like extras in a John Woo shoot-em-up. I also wondered if maybe Quentin Tarantino was off to the side, getting all this on film for his next bloody crime flick. Blood and vegetable juice, that is. Be hard to tell the real thing from tomatoes if the shit hit the fan. The mood was tense in this ridiculous standoff, and apparently I was elected the mediator between madmen. Lucky me. "*This is your final warning,*" I heard Shiv add. Jesus. How could I take such corny dialogue seriously?

Answer: When one of the goons fired a rapid round into the air for effect, it was easy.

"This is all *your* doing," Zelda hissed at me. "*You* talk to him!"

"What can *I* tell him?" I said, looking into Lucy's face, so pallid and frightened. No sex appeal now. Just a scared child with nowhere left to run. "All right, gimme room," I said, nudging through the little crowd and then yelling out the window, "*Yo, Shiv! It's me, Vic!*"

Then a strange thing happened. Shiv lifted a trembling finger and I saw one of the goons point an Uzi in my direction.

"*Holy shit! Get down!*" I yelled just before a round of bullets blew the window open, spraying shards of glass all over the Elvisites and myself. With utmost caution I raised my nose just above the windowsill as the others huddled into a mass of jangled flesh and nerves on the living room floor. Some of the girls were crying, others were silent and stoic. Some were cut by the flying glass. Lucy had run upstairs, and Vicki had followed her. I motioned for the rest of them to follow suit, and everyone except the deacon and four of the older girls complied. Zelda led the retreat. The deacon and the remaining girls readied their weapons, grabbing pineapples and squash and coke bottles and pork rinds and anything else handy. Finally I raised my face all the way over the sill and yelled, "What the *hell* kinda negotiating is *that*, Shiv! Try that again and you'll *never* get Lucy to talk to you!"

"*You cheated me, Vic!*" Shiv yelled. "I paid you to do a job and you took the money and ran! Why, Vic! You screwing my daughter *too*?"

"*You should talk!*" I shouted back reflexively, realizing instantly that was a mistake. Another round of Uzi fire was Shiv's witty rejoinder.

"*I should just walk in there now and wipe out the bunch of you!*" Shiv shouted.

"*Then why don't you!*" the deacon yelled, and I winced. But then it hit me: why *didn't* he? Answer: he wanted Lucy all to himself, no one else. I think he was also worried she'd off herself before he got to her. She was still his flesh and blood, after all. Maybe he wanted to see if he could talk her out of ratting him out to the Family. If not, sayonara, sugar. Sick bastard. One more round was tossed through the window. Set 'em up, Joe. A few more rounds like that and we'd hit the high road for heaven—or hell.

"*I don't like unnecessary casualties!*" Shiv yelled. "*I am not a violent or an unreasonable man! I only want my own daughter to come out here and talk to me! Now!*"

I thought for a moment, then came to this conclusion: "*I'll go talk to her, Shiv,*" I yelled. "*You just sit tight and stop the fireworks until I get back to you. Okay?*"

"*And remember we still have our secret weapons!*" the deacon shouted. I rolled my eyes. But Shiv still hadn't stormed the place because of this idle threat, so maybe the deacon wasn't so stupid after all. Shiv knew the deacon was cracked and probably capable of anything, so he gave him the benefit of the doubt, not even suspecting that the "secret weapons" were groceries.

Shiv yelled at me just as I stood up, "*Hurry the fuck up! I got a plane to catch, but I won't catch it without talking to Lucy first! Move it!*"

"Yeah, yeah," I yelled back, then I shot up the stairs and kept looking in all the rooms for Lucy. Different girls were indifferent rooms, all crouched beside the windows, watching the mad melodrama unfold as if from the balcony of a movie theater. Each room had a different theme relating to The King. There was a "Hound Dog Suite" full of stuffed hound dogs and even a couple of real ones; a "Burning Love Suite" decorated completely in torrid tones of red and full of sexual paraphernalia catering to S&M tastes; and a "Blue Hawaii Suite" lushly furnished Hawaiian style with a mini-waterfall and fake palms and twangy Hawaiian music in the background, like the ultimate tiki lounge. That one got to me. I almost wanted to hole up in there for a week and forget everything, but I had work to do first. Later, maybe. The deacon certainly didn't slouch in the idea department. I finally found Lucy back in the "Teddy Bear Suite," cuddling with a big stuffed bear as Vicki tried to console her. (Zelda had headed straight for the "Burning Love Suite," which didn't surprise me.) Lucy was sobbing, and Vicki was holding her as she held the bear. The bear itself looked totally disinterested and detached. I envied its apathy.

"Leave me alone with her for a few minutes," I said to Vicki, who considered this for a moment and then nodded, giving Lucy kiss on the forehead just before she rose and left.

Lucy clutched at her teddy bear even tighter in Vicki's absence. Me she totally ignored. Too much weird stuff had already happened between us for me to suddenly assume some authoritative posture of respect. All I could do was shoot straight from the hip.

"Lucy. I want to be as gentle as possible about this, but I know what your father did to you. Antonio told me."

She shot me a hateful look that sent a jolt straight through me. "Did my uncle also tell you he was having an affair with my mother?"

So *that* much was true too. No one was totally innocent. Ever. "Actually, your father told me that. But he didn't ever touch you, did he? Your uncle, I mean."

She buried her wet face into the bear, so her words were muffled, but I still made them out. "No, I almost didn't mind him sleeping with my mother when my father was away, though I felt bad for my aunt, who never knew. Mama needed the attention, and I used to like my uncle. Then I told my uncle what my father had been doing to me since I was eight, and he got really mad and told my mother, who totally freaked out. Then my uncle stood up to my father for me, and they had a fight and my uncle just packed up and moved away one day, and wanted me and my mother to go with him. I didn't even know where he was going at first. He just disappeared one day. My mother told me later he'd informed on the Family and the Government sent him away into hiding, and my uncle somehow got in touch with my mother just before she died, because he wanted to send for me, without letting the Government know, and so she gave me his address, and one day I had a fight with my father and just ran away to San Francisco. But I think my father had connections or something, or he found the letters my uncle sent me, but anyway he found out where my uncle was and said if my uncle didn't turn me over he'd tell the Family where he was, and then my uncle told my father if he didn't leave me alone he'd tell the Family about the nasty things my father used to do to me, and, and..." She broke down into another crying jag, but it really was just a breather. I touched her shoulder but she recoiled. Touching her was not a good idea. I just let her get it all off her chest in her own good time, hoping the deacon and his warriors didn't have to resort to a food fight in order to hold the fort. "My father is afraid I'll tell the Family about him, too. That's all he cares about. He wants to be head of the Family in Brooklyn, and he will unless they find out about this, and I told my uncle about you, and he said he knew. I called him from your place after I hit you with your gun. That's when my uncle told me that he told my father I was in this Elvis thing, so my father would give up and go home, but instead he hired you so he could trace you to me and not get the Family involved or scare me away. I hit you with your gun because I still wasn't sure you didn't come from the Family, then my uncle told me you were really a detective, but then I got scared anyway and came back here. I didn't know where else to hide. If I stayed with you he'd find me. I think my father wants to kill me, but of course he can't tell people from the Family this. He has to make it look like an accident. I told Vicki all about this. She's very nice. Did you like your cat?"

"Ah, yeah, it was great. But, *Lucy*."

She laughed slightly, with a sniffle. "That was a stray cat that kept getting his bladder blocked, so we decided to give it to you as a joke! Wasn't that funny? Well, it was her idea, but she told me about it."

"Yeah, yeah, I'm in stitches, but Lucy, where's Antonio now?"

She shrugged. "The Government took him away when they saw Shiv visiting him. My uncle can call me but I can't call him anymore. That night I called him was the last time I talked to him. That's when he told me he was going away again, but he promised to call me later after he was relocated, probably in another country now."

"That's too bad. I guess Shiv never turned Antonio in to the Family because they're brothers, right?"

"No, that's not it. It's like I told you. If my uncle told the Family about what my father did to me, they'd probably kill him, or at least exile him to Italy or something."

"Yeah. Vicki told me about that code of honor thing."

"I told her, that's how she knows. I tell Vicki everything. She's like my sister. Everyone here is. It's my *family*, can't you *understand* that? Not my uncle's family or my father's family— *my* family. Why do you want to take me away, Vic? Why?" Again the tears flowed and I felt like scum. I was tried of feeling like scum. I'm such a good guy, with good intentions. Yet I always feel like I'm fucking everything up. Maybe I'm too hard on myself. Maybe my hard-on itself was the problem. Whatever. Lucy fell into' my arms and I held her as she cried and cried and said into my ear over and over, "I have no place else to go, I have no place else to go."

There was only one thing I could do now. "Lucy, where's my gun?" I asked her. She got up and went to her bureau and removed the gun from a drawer, where it had been stashed beneath some panties. She handed it to me with a sniffle. I took it and checked the chamber. I had four bullets left. One for each goombah, I thought. And they had Uzis. But we had a ton of groceries and The King on our side. There was no way I was turning Lucy over to that scumbag. I also didn't want to leave her in this nuthouse, but it was the lesser of two evils at the moment. Right now I had to deal with the mob, and fight fire with fire and food.

I patted Lucy on the head and gave her chin a little goodbye tap and then went back downstairs.

The deacon looked happy I had my gun back. "I only asked Lucy to take it because I wasn't sure whose side you were on," he said with the lop-sided grin. "Sure wish we had the Memphis Mafia to show these wiseguys how to dance!"

"Look, I got four bullets," I said. "I'm going to put one in a kneecap of each of the gunmen. That means you have to distract them with a barrage of this stuff. I'm a pretty good shot, but I've got to get them off in rapid succession if I'm going to disable each one of them. They can still shoot with a fucked up kneecap, but not as well. Hey, has anyone called the *cops* yet?"

"No cops," the deacon said adamantly.

"You afraid they'll bust you too?"

He looked at me and nodded. "They wouldn't understand. Cops generally have very low E.Q.'s, generally speaking."

"I hear ya. But it's that or we go out in a hail of bullets. All I can do is buy time until the cops get here. If we wait they could bust in here and hold us all hostage when the fuzz finally does show up. We have to hold them out there, and a fight looks like the only way to delay them now. We've wasted too much time already. I know this character; he's nervous and unpredictable. But he can't stop shaking long enough to shoot his own gun, so he hired the gorillas out there. I guess Shiv was counting on you *not* callin the cops, but we gotta do it anyway. Dig?"

"No way," the deacon said.

"Well, fuck it, I'll call 'em myself. Now get ready!"

"Not if you're gonna call the cops," the deacon said. His customary coolness was nowhere in evidence now. He was seriously worried about doing a stretch for statutory rape and fraud and a dirty laundry list a mile long, no doubt.

"Can you think of a better idea?" I said. "Those meatheads mean business."

"*Time's runnin' out!*" I heard Shiv shout. "*Where's Vic and Lucy?* Two *minutes and we come in blazing. Last chance.*"

"What's it gonna be?" I asked the deacon. "Your call."

"Okay," said the deacon, "but give me a chance to escape first. I've got a helicopter on the roof that can take me to the Marin Airport where a private jet can get me to Miami. I'll just lay low there for a while. And I'll take Zelda with me. Deal?"

"Okay, but then Lucy stays behind with me."

The deacon thought and said, "Okay." The other girls were trying to eavesdrop but didn't quite hear us, or else they'd have declared mutiny then and there, I'm sure. Poor lost souls. But it was best they get out from under the deacon's broken wing sooner than later anyway. "Let me go tell Zelda," he whispered, then he ran up to the "Burning Love Suite." Maybe he really cared for the old girl after all. The mother figure that wouldn't reject him on account of his obsession for Elvis, because she shared it too.

God, Oprah would have a field day with this setup. The four girls looked after him and then at me with petulant expressions.

"Went to talk to Lucy again," I lied to them. Then I yelled out the window at Shiv to stall for a little more time. *"She's coming, Shiv! Just hold on a second! She's scared but she wants to set things right between you! Just hang on!"*

"Hurry the fuck up, my plane leaves in an hour!" Shiv shouted. The Four Buttonmen of the Apocalypse just stood frozen. I wondered if they were local talent. They couldn't represent the Family back in Brooklyn, because then Shiv would have to explain all this somehow, why he needed Mob muscle to rescue his daughter from a San Francisco Elvis cult, why she wouldn't talk to him and ran away to begin with. I remembered how Shiv was always out when I called him, always had an appointment. My hunch was that Shiv was out here on the West Coast not only to find Lucy and silence her for good but to cut some deals of his own, expand his horizons in Reno and Tahoe in case things went sour with The Family back East. The four gunmen looked too impassive and burly and healthy to be East Coast boys. No, Shiv was drawing from the local pool, maybe from his new well of business contacts. I wasn't sure, and didn't really care. I was trying to plan my shots. Once I got off the first shot, they'd be alerted and probably spread out, hit the ground and open fire in an all-out assault, military attack style. I could maybe get the first two in the kneecaps, but with the other two I'd have to aim for whatever was open to me, even if it was their heads. I hoped it didn't come to that. I'd never shot anyone dead before, though I often fantasized about it. Thinking about what Shiv had done to Lucy, I almost wished I had one more bullet.

I had planned to call the cops as soon as the deacon returned, but he jumped the gun on me, as it were. He came racing down the stairs yelling "ATTACK!" and the four girls started heaving food and bottles out the window, creating some confusion amongst our adversaries of which I took quick advantage.

I nailed Goombah One in the kneecap or its vicinity anyway, then all hell broke loose. I fired again quickly as a hail of bullets came my way, hitting Goombah Two in the belly, it looked like. The rain of food continued as the girls and the deacon just threw it outside aimlessly while crouching close to the floor to avoid the bullets. I got winged in the left shoulder but fired again, this time hitting Goombah Three in the arm, making him drop his weapon. Shiv had run for cover as soon as the melee commenced, and I neither saw nor heard him amid the chaos. The mansion front exterior was getting shot to hell, and the bullets were starting to penetrate the old wood. I was getting scared. Why hadn't the deacon given me a chance to call the damn cops first? Selfish prick. In fact, when I turned around to locate him, he was gone.

The girls ran upstairs all of a sudden, giving up the fight, and I was left alone, with one bullet, a bleeding shoulder, and a bag of groceries at my disposal. Through the continued gunfire I heard the whirring roar of a helicopter on the roof. Then I just barely heard the deacon shout above the mayhem, "*Ladies and Gentlemen, Deacon Rivers has left the building*!" Sonofabitch was bailing on us. I had the impulse to run up to the roof and use my last bullet on him, but gave it up. I took careful aim during a lull created by the sudden startling sound of the fleeing helicopter and nailed Goombah Four in the groin. Now all four were wounded.

Then I heard what sounded like music, but which was in fact the rapturous melody of sirens. The cops were on their way after all. Either someone nearby had heard the unusual racket and called them, or else someone inside the house had hit the alarm after all. In any case, the Calvary had arrived at last. The cops and the mobsters exchanged fire for a bit, then all was quiet. I sat back and took a deep breath, feeling the pain in my shoulder for the first time. As my adrenalin rush calmed down the numbness disappeared and the wound began to sting. But I was too tired to bitch at that point.

Through the haze of my blurred vision I saw Zelda, Vicki and Lucy running down the stairs, right for me. They surrounded me and did stuff to my shoulder, wrapped it up tight, and then I remember cops storming into the place and lining everyone up against the wall and asking a lot of questions and then I just closed my eyes and tried to pass out. But I couldn't. When I really wanted to be unconscious, I was wide-awake. I kept my eyes closed anyway as paramedics loaded me onto a stretcher and into a waiting ambulance.

When I decided to open my eyes again, Lucy and Vicki were at my side inside the ambulance, each holding one of my hands. Then I noticed that both were cuffed to their own cop. Routine. They'd question everyone down at headquarters then let them go. No harm done. The deacon was long gone by then, winging his way to Miami, but sans Zelda. She had refused to abandon ship. Possibly she'd agreed to join him in Miami or Tokyo or Budapest later. In a way, I hoped she did.

Chapter Fourteen
THE PHONE PHANTOM

When I finally made it home from the hospital a couple of days later, and the old dive never seemed so cozy and appealing. The red light on my answering machine was blinking, and I just had to see who called me before I did anything else, take a shower, a leak, whatever. There was only one message, a musical one. I was almost relieved. I'd almost clean forgotten about my old pal The Phone Phantom. This time the melody was "Beyond the Sea" by Bobby Darin. Or part of it, then *click*.

I dialed Star 69, the callback code. By now the phone company should have looked into my callback service and fixed it, so there was no reason the system shouldn't work. I would now lay this final mystery to rest, and then I would follow. I was exhausted.

But I still got the same annoying sound followed by a recording telling me the number had been disconnected. Whatever. There were no calls from Vicki or Lucy yet. Both were supposed to call me once the cops had let them go, or if they were still detained, they were to call me anyway so I could help them out. I was worried. Also, there was no word from Monica or the vet about poor Puss yet. I decided to go to The Drive-Inn to see my old pal Doc Schlock and fill him in on the recent astounding events, which had gotten some press attention, though my name had been left out on request. That kind of publicity could hurt my reputation and my business. I didn't want to be pegged an as Elvis worshipping sex fiend by the media. Privately, I had no defense that made sense. Only Doc would understand.

When I got down to The Drive-Inn, Monica was there alongside Doc. I guessed they'd made up, which was good. As weird as that place is, it felt refreshingly normal compared to where I'd just been. I looked around at the lonesome losers and the psychotronic videos and thought: It's great to be home.

"*Vic*!" Monica and Doc said in unison as I walked in, like I was Norm on *Cheers*. Doc poured me a beer and Monica came around the counter and gave me a hug, careful not to touch my arm, which was in a sling along with my ass.

"Can I be the first to sign that?" Doc said.

"Sure," I said, sitting down on a stool and stretching my cast out onto the bar. On the TV screen was a documentary on Jim Jones. "Hey, Doc, what else you got to play?" I asked as he autographed the cast.

"Um, new documentary says Elvis is alive I thought you'd like. Says the FBI or CIA or some shit put him into hiding because he knew shit about some conspiracy against somethin'."

"No, no," I said, waving my free right hand. "Somethin' that has nothin' to do with cults and The King and anything strange. Nothing that would attract the attention of Mulder and Scully, let's put it *that* way."

"Well, I knew you'd be comin' in today, so I got *this*." Doc reached under the counter and came up with *Neptune's Daughter*, the Esther Williams flick. "You can watch it here if you want, but you make sure you take it home with you. This shit is too *white* for me, know what I'm sayin'?"

I nodded and gave Doc the high sign to pop that baby in. A little Technicolor fantasy was always a welcome tonic to bitterness. At least it always worked for me.

"Your cat gets his surgery today," Monica said suddenly.

"*Surgery*? For what?"

"Well, it turns out that when a cat gets repeated blockage, something drastic has to be done, or he'll die. I didn't think you wanted him put to sleep."

"Monica, what are you *saying*?"

"Well, he needs an operation if he's going to survive."

"Like what *kind* of operation?"

"Like, well, they cut a hole for him to pee, so he can't get blocked, so the crystals won't plug up his thing."

"I don't get it."

"They cut his dick off."

"*What*?" I spit rum all over the bar. "You mean my cat's getting a sex change operation?" Customers aroused by my outburst turned and stared, but I was oblivious. Doc wasn't.

"Vic, settle down. Why are you so wound up? It's only a few hundred dollars!"

"Few *hundred*?" I was gasping, losing oxygen. Monica came around and gave me an impromptu massage. "Monica, give me the exact figure. *Now*."

"Well—altogether?"

"Monica."

"Altogether, including the catheter and the special diet—oh, yeah, he has to be on a special diet from now on—and hospitalization and the actual operation and some tests on his kidneys and..."

"*Monica.*"

"About a thousand. Give or take."

I nearly fell off the stool. As I said earlier, I was in debt up the wazoo. I just paid the monthly minimum payments and they kept raising my credit limit and shit kept happening. It was a goddamn conspiracy, I just knew it. Puss was in on it, too. Maybe Elvis knew about the credit card conspiracy and was sent underground because of it.

"On the lighter side," Doc said as I downed my beer, "I spent a bundle and had the entire electrical wiring in your bathroom replaced, so the light should work like a charm from now on."

"Wonderful," I said. "Everyone's gettin' their wiring replaced at my expense."

"No, Vic, I told you, the bathroom thing is on me," Doc said. "Just relax. Shit. What's been happenin', anyway? We read about that shootout up in Marin, and I just know you were there, so enough with the suspense. Give it up, cowboy."

So I gave Doc and Monica the lowdown on the whole shebang, from the time I dropped Judy off at her pad to the bullet they took out of my shoulder. Actually, okay, I was only winged, there wasn't a whole bullet in there, just a piece, like shrapnel. I was a veteran of the Elvis Wars. But I still felt a little like Clint Fuckin' Eastwood, I have to tell you. Those wiseguys I popped? In the same hospital, with police escorts, banged up real good, then off to the slammer. And Shiv? In the pokey, Jack. He'd be cooling his shivering heels for a long time. After his sheet was pulled his East Coast lawyers refused to bail him out until they conducted their own investigation into just what the hell Shiv was doing at that mansion anyway, which could land Shiv in even deeper do-do with the Mob. Detectives Shoemaker and Sharp, my old pals on the SFPD, who made their second visit to me in a hospital in less than a year, told me this. They found this highly amusing, I can tell you. Only this time, I wasn't a Victim. I was a Victor.

Doc and Monica just shook their heads as I related the tale. "You're a hero, Vic," Doc said, slapping me on the shoulder. Monica was giving me slinky looks, too. Little Elvis wanted her to dance, but later, I told him. I needed a long rest, especially from sex. For once, that prospect turned me off. Sex meant nothing but trouble. I was getting romantic again. I wanted true love or nothing. And at the time, I preferred nothing.

"Vic, we got one other homecoming surprise for you," Doc said a little later. "Ladies, if you please," he said, and I turned around expecting to see a troupe of exotic dancers traipse in the front door. Instead it was The She Beams, in full regalia, ready to rock. "My new strategy," Doc explained. "Live music. After you disappeared on your secret mission, Judy here was worried about you and stopped by. She was fixin' to go up and see what you were doin' up at her mom's house but I told her it'd be best if she didn't crash the party just yet. Little did I know you were doin' the jailhouse rock with a teddy bear, but I did what I thought you'd want me to do, run interference. Anyway, Judy and me got to talkin' and figured we could help each other out, y'know. Wholesome sex appeal and hot music to boot, and nobody gets offended. Monica here quit her gig on Broadway and hooked up with The She Beams as a go-go dancer!"

"I can sing harmony too," Monica added quickly with a touch of pride and relief. Happy happy, joy joy all around. I gave all the girls a hug and they signed my cast and then set up in the corner of the shop and the rest, as they say, is history. People hearing the music from the street drifted in and bought booze and said, what a unique place. Doc was beaming.

And yet, with all this cathartic celebrating going on, I couldn't help but feel depressed as hell. Maybe it was the cat bill looming over my head. Maybe it was something else.

After a few numbers, Judy sat down next to me and gave me a kiss on the cheek. "I broke up with my boyfriend," she whispered in my ear.

Uh oh. "How come?" I asked, trying to sound disappointed. In fact, the thought of this petrified me. I craved simplicity for a while, not further complications. "Can't you guys work it out?"

She shrugged. "Long distance has its problems. Maybe we'll get together later, but for now, I just want to concentrate on the band and on me. No entanglements. I want my freedom. You understand?"

I raised my beer glass. "Amen to that. Say, you hear from your old lady?"

"Yeah, she's in Miami."

"Figures. How you feel about that?"

"That's one relationship that needs the distance. Maybe the Elvis guy isn't so bad for her after all. She told me he was the one who called the cops and all. The cops tore her place up looking for evidence. No one's sure exactly what that was all about. My mother locked the place up but the police have like yellow ribbons around it anyway. They don't know what they're looking for though. I mean, being an Elvis fanatic isn't against the law, is it?"

"You *kidding*? A hundred years from now, it'll *be* the law. What happened to all the girls up there?"

She shrugged. "Scattered to the four winds, I guess. Some will probably go to Miami, I imagine. I don't know. It's too weird. My mother said calls started coming in from all these tabloid and entertainment shows. The Elvis guy is pissed at all the publicity. He has a rap sheet for some stuff with minors and a few other offenses, nothing major, my mother told me. So I guess you did good, Vic."

"Then why do you look so glum?"

"I don't know," she murmured.

She looked down, and I lifted her chin up and kissed her lightly on the nose. "It'll work out, honey. You miss your mom, huh?"

She shrugged. "She's all I got, good or bad. I said I'd visit her in Miami, maybe on a tour with the band. We've been getting some interest, so—Vic?"

"Yeah, babe?"

"I think you're so cool."

It was my turn to shrug. I was doing the Twist on Cloud Nine. "I do the best I can."

"I wish you didn't come so quick, though."

My ego took a dive back down to earth. "Like I said, I do the best I can."

She kissed me gently on the mouth, arousing the attention of Monica, who decided to join us. I remembered watching *Cat On A Hot Tin Roof* as a kid and wishing I was Paul Newman with Elizabeth Taylor pleading with me to make love to her. He had his leg in a cast and was an alcoholic mourning the death of a football buddy, which he blamed on himself and took out on his long-suffering wife. Liz looked so sexy and gorgeous in that flick I could barely stand watching it all the way through for fear I'd break into hives or explode or something. I always thought, what a sap that Paul is—how could he resist, even if his character *was* gay? But sitting there in The Drive-Inn with two sexy babes on either side, vying for my attention, all I could do was sympathize with poor Paul. Sometimes no matter how good the offer, you're just not in the mood.

I excused myself a short time later complaining of pain in my war-wounded arm. The girls wanted to follow me up and nurse me back to health, but I pulled a Newman on them and made a solitary retreat.

As soon as I got inside, though, the phone rang. I picked up hoping to catch The Phantom off-guard. But it was Lucy. She wanted to meet me somewhere before she left town that night. I told her I'd meet her in Chinatown at my favorite chop-suey joint with the suspicious fortune cookies. I'd been planning on going back there anyhow, wondering what my next fortune could be after that "minefield around your heart" message last time. I cleaned up in my brilliantly illuminated bathroom—it was almost *too* bright—and then headed for Chinatown.

"Wic Walentine!" Louie greeted me as usual, grinning ear to ear. Jesus, didn't that guy ever take a night off?

"Wooie," I said, giving him my trench coat. "I'm here to meet a young lady."

"Yes, I know. She very pretty. Very young. Very nice. Very *young*."

"Louie, how is it you can say the 'v' in 'very' but not in my name?"

"What your name?" he said with a puzzled expression.

"*Vic*," I said, enunciating the lead letter carefully. "Vic Valentine."

"That's what I say. Wic Walentine."

"All right. Whatever. Where's the girl?"

He led me to her. She looked so grown up now. Maybe it was the way she was dressed, like a '40s glamour puss. Maybe it was something else.

I sat down and we small talked a bit about my stay in the hospital and her plans to return to New York and live with her maternal grandmother and finish high school (*gulp*) and then go to college or something. She didn't seem very thrilled about her prospects for the future. So young, so jaded. At least with me it took some time.

"You talk to your father?" I finally asked.

"Yes. He said he's going to get a good lawyer and get out and *kill* you."

"Oh yeah? Oh well."

"Aren't you worried?"

"Me? I kiss danger in the dark, baby."

"In the *dork*?"

"The *dark*, I said. Anyway, what about *you*? He said he still wants to kill you?"

"He said he never wanted to kill me. But he will, though, after I testify."

"*Testify*? You mean because of his mob ties? Sweetheart, think that over first. You want to live like your uncle, constantly on the run, in hiding."

"No, no. I don't mean about racketeering. I couldn't care less about that stuff. I mean about, *you* know."

"You're taking him to court?"

"I think it killed my mother and it almost killed me. He deserves to go down for it, don't you think?"

"I thought your mother had cancer."

"Yeah, of the soul."

"You're growing up fast, kid."

"I'm no kid. Not any more. You know that as well as anybody." I blushed. "I'll hire a lawyer with some money my uncle gave me. My uncle will testify too. When it comes out the Family will cut my father off and he won't be able to order a hit on anybody. He'll be too worried about his own useless life." A tear escaped her big brown beautiful eye, and I reached across our dinner and wiped it off. Suave, so suave. Of course, I also got soy sauce all over my sleeve, but what the hell.

"I have faith in you," I told her sincerely, and I did. She was one tough, brave little broad, as it turned out. Going up against her father the gangster would be ballsy enough, but against her father the child molester? I had new respect for her. "When you get back to New York, you keep in touch, okay? Keep me posted on everything. I plan on making a trip back there myself soon."

"Really? Why?"

"Unfinished business." I didn't want to go into it with her, but I had a lead on who shot my dirty cop father dead in a Brooklyn alley, and I wanted to follow it up personally. More on that later. "Anyway, where's Vicki? Cops let her go too, I imagine."

"Sure. She headed straight for Miami."

"You're kidding! After all *that*?"

"She's only going to visit, then she's leaving for Hawaii after she graduates, she told me. Her thesis is now on Elvis and modern mythology, of course. She might run the new Honolulu branch of the church. Ricky wants her too, but she has to think about it. He isn't a bad guy, Vic, really. This whole Elvis thing is just his way of making sense out of a world that makes no sense at all, and who doesn't do that in their own way? He likes sex, sure, but he never touched me. That's all I care about."

"*Never*?"

"No. He knows what happened with my father, and that I'm a little screwed up because of it. He only has sex with women if they're healthy."

"Well, Vicki's healthy all right. But you sound like you're on your way to a full recovery too, sweetheart."

"I'll be okay. Vicki said she'll call you."

"Yeah, yeah—she ever mention leaving music on my machine before?"

She grimaced. "Huh? What music?"

"Never mind." If Vicki had come clean about the cat, then she would've admitted the phone music by now. No, The Phone Phantom was still on the loose. Then I addressed a subject I'd been skirting, but had to deal with head-on sooner or later. "Lucy, about that night…"

"Which one?" she giggled. "Vic, I'm sorry. But nothing ever happened, either time. I'm just—I don't know. I have some stuff to work out. I might see this shrink that gives the Family free service. That's what my uncle suggested. When these charges come out in court, the Family will want to take extra special care of me."

"And you'll let them, I hope." Family is family.

"I guess. But I want to sort of distance myself, though, y'know?"

"So you plan on going to Miami with the rest?"

She shook her head. "No. Been there, done that. Time to move on."

"You sound so mature."

She looked at me and smiled mischievously. "Maybe it'll rub off on you."

Once a brat, always a brat, I thought. She picked up the tab, though, and I let her, calling it her fee. Then it was my favorite time of the meal: Fortune Cookie Time.

Louie brought them on a little tray with the receipt. Lucy broke hers open first. It said: "*Forget the past but remember the present.*" She looked confused. "But the present will *become* the past," she said.

"Don't look at me, I don't get these little buggers either." Then I tore mine open. It was blank.

155

"I want another one," I said angrily. "*Louie!*"

"Why don't you just write your own?" Lucy said. "Maybe that's what the message is. Your write your own fate from now on. That's what I'm going to do, or try, anyway."

"Yes, Mister Walentine!" Louie said.

"Nothin', Louie. We'll see ya later." We got up to go.

"You make cute couple!" Louie yelled after us. "Come back on Valentine's Day!"

Wise guy.

I drove Lucy back to her hotel and then took her to the airport and waited with her in the bar until her flight was ready. We didn't really talk much. I told her again to keep in touch and that I'd look her up when I went back to Brooklyn. She hugged me and kissed me and told me I had made a big difference in her life. That made me feel good. It almost made up for the blank fortune.

Almost. Story of my life.

The next day Monica dropped Puss off, shaved around the hind legs and groin, wearing a cone around his head to keep him from chewing the stitches out. He could hardly see where he was going. He'd have to keep the cone on for three whole weeks until the incision healed. And it would take months for his gray fur to grow back completely. He looked like a Space Poodle. I just called him Dickless. He looked so pathetic I felt sorry for him and nearly forgot that his sex change had cost me a grand. And I still had my *own* hospital tab to pay, though Shoemaker and Sharp were so grateful to me for rescuing Lucy they said they'd try to help me out. I'm still waiting for their help as the bills keep flowing in. Puss and I were one fucked up couple of celibate bachelors. But it was good to have his company again. Or hers. Whatever.

After a week passed I called Judy, but she had left a message on her machine she would be in Santa Barbara for a few weeks and that she'd check messages from there and get back to you. I didn't leave a message. No point in pursuing that any further. So much for her independence. I guess she really loved the dude after all. A surf band can't replace certain aspects of life, I suppose. Then I called Monica, but she told me she had met some guy in Golden Gate Park and they were going camping for the weekend. Whatever.

I never heard from Vicki Lee again. I think she was embarrassed. Maybe she didn't realize her little joke had cost me a grand. Maybe she did. Whatever.

I tossed darts at my heart board and listened to Sinatra and watched Dickless the Space Poodle bang around my room, wondering what was missing. I told him he was better off without it.

Plunk, plunk, plunk.

Ring!

I let the machine get it. Beep. Elvis sang a few lines from "I'll Remember You." *Click*.

The Phone Phantom returned! I was so happy to hear from her, or him. Whatever. I hit Star 69, my heart pounding. Please, I thought. Please somebody pick up.

Ring, ring, ring.

Then: "Graceland," said a muffled voice, either male or female, I couldn't tell. It sounded disembodied.

Huh? "Hello?" I said. "Who *is* this?"

The connection started to break up. Static interfered with the mysterious androgynous voice that said, "Hello? Graceland. Hello?" Then the connection broke up altogether and the line went dead. I hung up and hit Star 69 again. The number had been disconnected.

No. Couldn't be.

Could it?

Messages from beyond. Maybe Doc was right. I was getting calls from the Age of Romance. Or Elvis Presley was alive inside Graceland and crank calling a lonely private eye in San Francisco, just for kicks. Or maybe something ethereal was going on. Or maybe it was Vicki Lee or Rose or Flora, being incredibly clever. Maybe it was just my desperate imagination. Maybe no calls were coming in at all. In my solitude I was hallucinating. Maybe.

In any case, that was the last call I've received from The Phone Phantom to date. And now after all that excitement, I have no romantic prospects for the future. Not even The Phone Phantom, whoever he or she really was. I was on my own now, writing my own fortune. No more lost crazy women. I planned to visit my mother in the funny farm back East, and find out why I kept attracting these imbalanced babes. I'd forget my past and remember the present and plan for the future. Then I'd be ready for true love.

Yo, Fate. My pimp.

You're fired.

The End of

FATE IS MY PIMP

But

Vic Valentine will return in

ROMANCE TAKES A RAIN CHECK

A Vic Valentine Adventure

Chapter One
SEND A MENTAL JOURNEY

Most people leave their hearts in San Francisco. Me, I left my heart in a can of Crisco. Cryin' in San Francisco, Fryin' in Crisco. I just can't tell the difference anymore.

I told myself—Vic Valentine, Private Eye—to quit whining and order another beer from the waitress. I was sitting alone in the Great American Music Hall on O'Farrell Street in San Francisco, waiting for Deborah Harry and the Jazz Passengers to come on stage. I chose a table in the back on the main floor so as not to be conspicuous. I even resorted to the old lonely guy trick of scribbling notes in a little pad so people would think I was a music critic, purposely solo for the occasion so as to concentrate for my review. It didn't make me feel much better, and neither did the beer. So what. I was there to see Debbie, my old flame from CBGB back in Lower Manhattan, when I was a swingin' stud hipster cat daddy, or something to that effect, at least in my own estimation, and Debbie was performing with a band called Blondie. She had inspired me to take up writing about the new wave scene, and she inspired me even now, though I'm not sure how. Maybe in just a simple, nostalgic way. I mean, the very next morning I was on my way back to the Big Apple to dig up some worms from the past, and watching Debbie here in the present made me feel I had come full circle. Coming any way makes me feel good. In little squares, triangles, whatever. But full circles really turn me on. The thing is, the next day I was starting a whole new circle of events, one I'm not sure I would like as much. It would be a full circle, all right—but full of what, I wasn't sure.

The Jazz Passengers were an avant-garde arty experimental free form improvisational progressive something or other, and Debbie was touring with them out of the goodness of her heart, it seemed. The joint was packed to the rafters, SRO, and I wasn't willing to share my table, either. I kept myself isolated and insulated, intimidating anyone who wanted to sit down with me by acting aloof and intensely engaged with my notepad. Back in the old days I sat in the back of many a club—CBGB, Max's Kansas City—and jotted down one-liners and impressions of

Blondie, Talking Heads, The B-52's, The Cramps, The Ramones, Devo, whoever, and then the article would come out in the local Greenwich Village rag and at a party babes would remark on what a witty wordsmith I was and then I'd take them back to my little studio off Canal and close the deal. Those were the days. Nowadays I still use my racket to get laid, though private eyes aren't quite as seductive as music writers, I've found. Maybe it's because I was younger then, too. I just attracted more action. Then I met Valerie, a.k.a Rose, and my party days came to an abrupt end. Then Valerie disappeared and my happy days came to an end. But what the hell. At least I still had Debbie, as much as I ever had.

When the lame duck opening act finally waddled off stage, it took another half hour for the main attraction to show up, and the natives were getting restless. I kept ordering beer until even my thoughts were beginning to slur. I couldn't figure out whether I looked forward to going back East or not. I hadn't been back in around eight years, since starting this P.I. racket with the aid of one Captain Alfonse Marcus, an old buddy of my old man's who transferred to SFPD from Brooklyn shortly after my father, Vernon Valentine, was found shot dead in an alley when I was only seventeen. My mother, Dorothy Malone Valentine, subsequently lost her mind, since the year before my older brother Johnny had jumped off the Brooklyn Bridge, leaving a note in his bedroom that said simply, "*Went for a dip, Ma, don't wait up.*"

My mother blamed herself for that cryptic suicide, though I suspect it had more to with Johnny's frustrated dreams of being a musician even though my old man was grooming him into a hard-ass cop like himself. Johnny was to report to Brooklyn PD for a physical and mental exam the day after his "dip," but my mother never made that connection. Me, the old man never really noticed much, though I think he wanted to re-invest in me once Johnny took the plunge, something he never talked about (with me) but which must have broken his heart in the same way it broke my mother's. Anyhow, her sister eventually committed my old lady, and then I moved to Manhattan and started hustling my writing to the local rags. My mother had wanted to me to go to college, but I figured where she was going she'd be unable to check up on me, so I blew that off. In one year I lost my whole family, I was on my own at eighteen in the heart of sinville with no supervision, and I tried to make the most of it.

Little could I have suspected during that first flush of freedom that I'd wind up where I was now, a single, mostly celibate private eye in San Francisco, a twisted town I had never given much thought to while ensconced in the bohemian behemoths of Manhattan. For some reason I now, at this late date, wanted to know why my life had followed this unplanned and unwanted path. The tip I'd been given by some friends of the late Captain Marcus was the perfect catalyst to send me on this journey of discovery about the mystery surrounding my father's death—his killer was never found—which may well lead me into some dark alleys of my own mental cityscape, places where secrets of my psyche lay buried beneath years of trash and cobwebs.

And if nothing came up—what the hell, I needed a vacation. Besides looking for my old man's killer, I also had two other little things on the agenda—look up my old lady in the loony bin, something I'd been meaning to do for years (I kept in touch the first few years I came out here, but then gave up after her maniacal, rambling letters in return freaked me out), and pay a visit to my old high school sweetheart, Dolly Duncan, whom I heard had gotten married to some Philly dentist named Donald Dunlap. Last I'd heard they were living in heavenly domestic blissful ignorance somewhere in South Jersey, the perfect place for it, since no one there knew any better. It depended on whether her address was still good—and I suspected it was, because her phone number, which I dialed then disconnected when she answered, planning to surprise her in person, was still the same since the last time she'd contacted me. That was during my first year in San Francisco, when I was lonely and dialed her up for old times sake.

She was just getting ready to move into her Jersey house from the house she grew up in Bayshore, and she gave me the number. She had been pretty excited to hear from me, and we kept in touch off and on for a year until her hubbie got wind of the correspondence and put the kibosh on it. The thing is, Dolly and I had never gotten the chance to consummate our adolescent relationship, and when I moved to Manhattan she stayed behind in Brooklyn for a while, then went to the University of Pennsylvania to study nursing which was really only a pretense to meet a med student, and we only saw each other on her vacations, but by then I was playing the proverbial field and we lost touch, especially when she start dating Donald. I always knew I could never offer her the security she wanted out of life—her old man worked at the racetrack, and was a bookie on the side (I know, because my old man was one of his steadiest customers), and her mother worked as a waitress in the same diner for the past twenty years, but despite this blue collar background, or maybe because of it, Dolly wanted something more out of life, to live comfortably in luxurious suburbia, with a pool and a two car garage and all the trimmings. I not only wasn't in a position to offer her that bogus bourgeois bullshit, I didn't want it myself. So I sort of let us drift apart. It was all for the best, I told myself then. But now, years later and alone, I found myself again dreaming of Dolly Duncan Dunlap, not so much because of what we did do together— bowling, movies, racetrack—but what we didn't do together. My scruples I'd leave behind in San Francisco. When I saw Dolly, my aim was to make up for lost time and opportunity, the dentist be damned. I had to make some dreams come true before I cashed in my chips, even if they were just leftovers. If I only knew then what I know now. I should have that engraved on my tombstone.

Anyway, Debbie Harry finally came out on stage sometime during my reverie, still looking as elegant and cool and beautiful as she had singing "X Offender" back at CBGB. She even sounded the same. It was kind of a time warp, except the music was somewhat out of sync with her style. The sax player had been one of The Lounge Lizards. It was all right, but you could tell everyone was there to see Debbie. They kept requesting Blondie songs and she just shrugged helplessly, but then she came out and did an offbeat, off-key version of "The Tide is High" and the crowd went nuts and gave her a standing ovation. I just sat in the back and applauded, wishing I could have sat closer. I had met her at a party in the Village back in the old days and wondered if she'd remembered me. Probably not. A couple of times I could've sworn she saw me across the dark sea of strangers and made eye contact, but maybe not.

I didn't want to take the chance and embarrass myself, so after she walked off stage following the encore and ovation I slipped out through the throngs and made my way down O'Farrell and then up Powell to Lori's Diner, a '50s retro restaurant that featured a real, nicely preserved Edsel on display inside the joint. My Corvair was parked nearby. I went into Lori's for a late supper, or maybe an early breakfast, staring at the cheesecake magazine covers and the Edsel and into space, listening to Elvis croon on the jukebox. Elvis. Not long before I had wrapped up a case involving a missing Mafia brat named Lucy Guisseppe and traced her to an Elvis-worshipping sex cult in Marin, ran by a wacko called Deacon Rivers. Lucy was back in Long Island now and I was planning to look her up too, maybe, while Deacon Rivers was in Miami, last I'd heard, hiding out in that branch of the New Church of Elvis, banging the local talent in the name of The King. Whatever. Lucy's old man, a mobster called Shiv with a chronic shaking problem was still behind bars, or so I hoped since he threatened to kill me if he was ever free again. He had molested his daughter Lucy and if the Mob ever found out he'd be dead, so he wanted to silence her for good, but instead she was free and he was locked up and awaiting trial for molestation allegations brought by his daughter. Certainly the Mob had caught wind of this already and I didn't have to worry. But who knows? Anyway, I had other fish to fry now. Later, Elvis. I finished my sandwich and coffee and then returned to my Corvair—which my pal Doc Schlock promised to keep an eye on while I was away, along with my cat—and returned to The Drive-Inn, the establishment just beneath me, or my office that is, for a nightcap.

Doc Schlock, originally Curtis Jackson of Oakland before he opened this combo bar and cult video store—and now nightclub thanks to an all-female surf band, The She Beams—was just getting ready for last call when I showed up. The She Beams, led by my lovely friend Judy Fagin, only played on Friday and Saturday nights, so tonight the place was almost empty, which was good. Up on the video screen behind the bar was the latest from Velma Vale, a blonde, busty starlet of B movie fame who fended off everything from aliens to assassins while scantily clad in torn blouses and bikinis. She was my new favorite actress. In her own way, she was a genius. This particular effort was called Jungle Goddess on the Moon. It was an instant classic, I could tell. "Make sure to dub me a copy of this," I told Doc as I sat down. "Give me something to look forward coming home to."

"You got it, my man," Doc said in his usual winning way as he poured me a beer. I loved Doc like a brother, even though, as my landlord, he had initially given me a hard time about keeping my cat, a gift bequeathed me by a girl named Vicki Lee, now in Hawaii running the Honolulu branch of the New Church of Elvis, or so she said in a belated postcard. The cat, which I simply called Puss, was a chubby Russian Blue whom I'd grown quite fond of, especially since I had invested a grand into his sex change operation. When Vicki Lee left him on my doorstep, she neglected to mention he was suffering from chronic urinary tract blockage, and required surgery—namely, getting his dick whacked off to make more room for the pee or something. My friend Monica Ivy, a young pretty thing who worked for Doc and sometimes sang with The She Beams, took care of it for me, getting Puss to a sawbones, or sawboners, I should say, but at my expense. I threw it on my trusty credit card—one of 'em, I forget which, since I collect them—and saved the cash Shiv had given me to find Lucy for my trip East. I had clean forgotten Shiv had given me this wad until days after the case was wrapped. I'd just thrown it in the safe behind my heart-shaped dartboard and didn't give it another thought—until, that is, I planned this trip. It was probably dirty Mob money, but what the hell, I figured as usual. I was too broke to nitpick, and anyway most money changes dirty hands eventually, and also I'd be taking the ill-gotten gains of a criminal and financing a crusade for justice. This was how I justified it, at any rate. Also, I sent a bunch of it to Lucy in Long Island. She wrote back and told me she'd use it for college, if she ever went. Yeah, right.

Anyway, Doc felt sorry for the cat and me and figured we were in a similar predicament so he broke down and let me keep him/her. The only catch was I had to put up with endless jokes about sodomy and castration and bestiality. It was worth it. I missed the little guy already. Or gal. Whatever. "How was the show, anyway?" Doc asked.

"Good," I said. "Debbie's as great as ever."

"You didn't stalk her, did you?"

"Naw. I'm saving my energy for the big trip." I sighed and rubbed my face, my head spinning from the combination of beer and coffee that waged a perpetual war in my bloodstream. "You should've taken Monica with you insteada goin' alone," Doc said.

"She wanted to bring that dude she's dating with her. The musician she met in Golden Gate Park. And anyhow when she found out it wasn't a Blondie reunion she lost interest. Not into jazz. Kids these days, Doc. What's the world coming to?"

Just then the Dolores Vale video said, "The End." I grunted.

Doc rewound the video and popped a CD into the sound system called "Las Vegas Grind," which I let him borrow. It was a collection of obscure sexy saxophone stripper music from the 50s, the stuff I dig the most, and it suited The Drive-Inn perfectly. He also played Martin Denny and Les Baxter stuff I lent him from my collection. While I was away he was free to rummage through my collection and play anything as long as he safeguarded it with his life. Normally I don't lend out my prized music library, but

Doc understood how precious this stuff was to me and the world in general, he appreciated and championed pop culture and was a kindred spirit in this respect, so I let him embellish The Drive-Inn's atmosphere with my mood music. I'm very neurotic about traveling, anyway—I keep worrying about what can go wrong. Will my stuff get stolen? My place burn down? My car ripped off? I was very possessive about what material things I did collect. I had no desire for a home and family and all that crap—but my videos and CDs and albums and cat and Corvair were all I had in this lousy world, and I needed the insulation they provided me to survive. You can't insure sentiment.

"You nervous about leavin', aren't you?" Doc said, putting stuff away and locking up, and I just nodded. The last of the lonely losers reluctantly left the shop, clutching his two Jayne Mansfield videos for the long night ahead. Poor bastard. That was me, in a way. In fact, *The Girl Can't Help It* is one of my favorite movies. I love the part where Julie London sings "Cry Me A River" to Tom Ewell, only he's just hallucinating. This song had been one of many classic love ballads from the Age of Romance left on my answering machine over a two or three week period, and I never found out who The Phone Phantom really was, since he or she had suddenly stopped—just when I was getting addicted to it.

"I wonder if my high school sweetheart is The Phone Phantom," I said finally as Doc locked the front door and pulled down the shade and put up the CLOSED sign, which always depressed me, for some reason. As long as The Drive-Inn was open, the world was an okay place, I thought. When it was dark and empty, so was the universe, it seemed. There was no refuge from reality to seek sanctuary in.

"I thought you said The Phone Phantom was either the Ghost of Romance or Elvis or both," Doc said.

"I'm keeping an open mind," I said.

"Be careful what the fuck might fly in," Doc said. "So you're gonna look up your mama

and old girlfriend and shit, huh?"

"Yup. That's the plan, anyway."

"Well, I guess we all gotta do that kinda thing now and then, but you sure you want to dig up these old skeletons, Vic? I mean, what's the point? Okay, you say you wanna know who 86'd your papa, and I dig that, but I don't know. I just got a weird feeling about this, I gotta tell you."

"Whaddya mean? You're not exactly pumping me with

166

confidence, Doc."

"Well, shit, Vic, look at all we been through together, especially lately. I mean that Rose shit, or Valerie or whatever her name was. Now, you knew her back in New York, am I right? And then she bailed on you and showed up here years later screwing baseball teams."

"Hey, easy there, Doc. That's the woman I loved, remember."

"Yeah, yeah, you and the god damn National League. Bitch was our favorite national pastime's favorite pastime. And I watched you make a fool out of yourself, get beat up and nearly killed cause you just had to set the past right, and then what did you accomplish? Just fucked up your present and some of your future. You were better off never seein' her again at all. Nothin' changed by tryin' to bring back the dead, or even figure out how the dead got that way. What difference does it make, Vic? Forget the past, man. Concentrate on your future. That's all I'm sayin'."

"But, Doc, that *is* what I'm doing. This is nothing like the Valerie thing at all. No one's hiring me to find anyone, like Tommy Dodge did with me to find Rose, who turned out to be Valerie. How could I have known that, anyway? That whole situation just fell in my lap, Doc. This is different. This is just about me now. I can't go on with the present or plan for the future until I solve these mysteries from my past. That sounds trite but I like it anyway. Doc, c'mon, man. I just need to know what my pop was into, who killed him and why, and I need to tell my mother face to face that it's not her fault. Not my brother Johnny jumping off the bridge, not my father screwing around on her, not me turning into whatever the hell it is I am today, which I may be able to define better if I can untangle this whole mess."

"And lookin' up your old girlfriend, who is now married and probably raisin' a pack of brats in New Fuckin' Jersey, what's that about? Let that go, Vic. So you never nailed the bitch. Who cares? You sure ain't gonna get in there now, and why would you want to? She's probably a fat housewife sittin' around on her hemorrhoids watchin' soaps and talk shows and shit."

"And I will probably seem very romantic to her. She's probably dying to have an affair with a swinging single stud like me."

Doc gave me a look.

"All right, but her standards are probably pretty low after wasting her prime with a god damn dentist, Doc. Dentist. Shit. His sexual technique is probably the same as his dental one—make her numb just before he drills her. Anyway, I didn't say I wanted to fuck her, did I? Just say hello, that's all."

"Aw, shit, Vic. Go all the way down to Jersey just to say hi? How dumb you think I am? You want to close an old deal, my friend, which is unlike you, her bein' married and all. I thought that kinda thing went against your code of ethics."

"The code's been updated and revised, Doc. Anyway, that's just a sideline. My main goal is to clear this mystery up about my old man, see my mother, and maybe, y'know, whatever."

"Get laid."

I shrugged, listening to the stripper music. He knew me too damn well.

Chapter Two
DETOUR ON DREAM STREET

I arrived at John F. Kennedy airport in a storm, almost grateful to be alive, but I didn't want to jump to conclusions until I saw how my trip went. The rain was heavy but my luggage was light. I had made reservations in a cheap but cozy hotel I knew about in Bensonhurst, appropriately called The Honeymooner to capitalize on the success of Jackie Gleason's old TV show, which had been set in this very neighborhood. Before the show took off the hotel had been a brothel called The Hot Box. Fact is, the clientele and hourly rates only went up after the switch to a more respectable facade. My father had been one of the more reliable customers.

I first found out about The Hot Box, or The Honeymooner, as it became in 1956 I believe, a few years before I was born, when I went around the neighborhood as an adolescent asking beat cops where my old man was, and no one seemed to know. They just told me to go on home and wait for him there. Then a local wiseguy who lived a few blocks from me and of course hated my old man, who was on the take from the Mob, amongst other local charitable organizations, told me where to find him. I later found out the wiseguy owned the damn Hot Box, and he was sore at my old man for taking the wiseguy's wife and teenage daughter there on occasion. You'd think that would've gotten my father rubbed out by the Mob, but the wiseguy was a rat who got sent away by the Feds and then was found in the trunk of a sedan with a wire around his throat somewhere in Arizona. My old man told me this himself. The Mob liked my old man, played pool with him, went to the track and ballgames with him, exchanged info and favors and poon tang, even drugs from busts in Jersey and elsewhere my old man was connected—like South Florida, where he had a cousin in the DEA—and didn't care who he banged as long as it wasn't nobody's mother. The wiseguy who owned The Hot Box was an exception, because he was a rat, and my old man, being on the inside with the local FBI office, knew this and took advantage of it. Like I said, I heard all this from my old man himself, just before he was found dead in that alley.

My leads told me the Mob was not connected. I first planned

to look up the local boss just to clear my mind of this, but in my heart of hearts, I didn't think it was a hit. Too sloppy and unprofessional, for one thing. It looked like a crime of passion, somebody's enraged husband maybe. My father was found outside of Pop's Pool Hall with forty stab wounds to the head and torso, then eight .44 bullets in his skull, heart, stomach—and crotch. All this happened in an alley around 2AM. Somebody was around when it happened, because Pop's was just closing up and that place is hopping right up until last call. Pop was retired now, and the pool hall was run by his son, Junior, but I still wanted to grill Pop. My leads suggested he knew something he wasn't telling.

Like I said, there was a storm when I got in, so I just hailed a taxi and since I knew exactly where I was going the Iranian driver couldn't take me on an unwanted tour of the eastern seaboard before I got to my destination. It was early autumn so I knew the scenery would be vivid and colorful and beautiful, leaves bursting crimson and gold, especially bright after an early season rain session. And I was right. When I woke up in my compact but comfortable room the next morning, soft slivers of sunshine shot through the dark curtains, which I opened on a scene that took me back to carefree times of youthful splendor. The sidewalks were bustling with people shopping and shooting the breeze. Fall colors made the moving canvas sparkle with nostalgic radiance. It reminded me of going to school and anticipating seeing Dolly Duncan in my first class, then at recess, then after school outside the gym, flirting with her as she waited for her old man to come pick her up. Ancient adolescent feelings of romantic yearning tugged at my jaded heart as I stood and took it in, then hunger tugged at my gut and I remembered my old haunt the Bay Diner was nearby on New Utrecht and 18th Ave., by the old El. I couldn't wait to get there. It was good to be home.

The feeling in the cool, crisp air was resplendent with memories as I walked to the Bay Diner. Unlike California, New York was slow to change, at least outwardly. It was a much safer place to invest sentiment in. Your youthful dreams were preserved, even if they never actually came true in your mature life. I was to find out anyone who remained in this time warp of a neighborhood had their ambition frozen along with the architectural design.

I ordered coffee and a scrambled egg breakfast and then perused the New York Times with a detached eye. I had trouble concentrating on the political unrest and senseless killings adorning the front page for some reason. My own personal sense of complacent nostalgia overwhelmed the conflicting reports of human suffering. Life was beautiful and the world was an interesting place to pass the time, no matter what the goddamn Times said. I turned to the Entertainment section and read about the relatively benign tribulations of movie stars instead. Again, I couldn't concentrate. I didn't care who was sleeping with whom in Hollywood, that far off fantasy world with no seasons, and movies and the people who played in them seemed so dull compared with the adventure of true-life experience. I felt on the verge of an epiphany or something. I finished my breakfast then went for a walk around the old neighborhood, postponing my pending appointments in favor of doing the Stroll down Memory Lane.

As I said, everything and everyone looked the same. I heard Benny Goodman and Nat King Cole and Frank Sinatra and all of their peers performing in my head as I took in the sights and sounds and smells of Bensonhurst, which was one of the cleanest and prettiest parts of Brooklyn, thanks to the fastidiousness of the Mob residents, who wanted their families thriving in safe, decent, old-fashioned environs. It was slightly seedier in certain sections, but for the most part, the Mob's pride in the care taking of its own backyard was meticulous. Elsewhere, the Mob's handiwork wasn't as heartwarming, such as in the Jersey dumping grounds or the Bronx battlegrounds, but here, on their suburban turf, good Catholics went to Church and raised their children and had picnics and went to the movies and in general led exemplary lives with traditional Family values. Same values the Republicans embraced, different Family. Way different.

Anyway, the thing is, I distrust and dislike anything organized, at least when it comes to people. Lions, birds, elephants, seals— that's all right. But people? Forget it. On an individual basis they're petty and insecure and unreasonable enough, but in groups, it's overwhelmingly obnoxious. This is why I despise religions, political parties, any parties except possibly pajama parties, corporations, unions, armies, leagues, clubs, sports teams, families, and even picnics. I believe in the integrity of the individual, making up one's own mind, thinking for oneself, and not relying on the illusion of power in numbers. The so-called competitive spirit people find so healthy is, to me, a pathetic way to increase one's own sense of self-worth by defeating and humiliating someone else. Whenever humans feel inferior and oppressed by the societal majority, they split off into sub-groups, so that they can feel secure in the company of fellow minorities, but in a sub-majority, so they don't feel misunderstood, dejected, and lonely. Face it: feeling misunderstood, dejected, and lonely is the natural state of life, so get used it. Stop whining. Strikes and protests are useless. Be yourself. Any true rebels didn't set out to change anything or anybody—like Elvis Presley. He was just being himself, respected the right of other individuals to be themselves, but did his own thing no matter what anyone else thought. Then millions of alienated young would-be rebels took his lead, and made him an inadvertent leader for their "cause," when all he really wanted to do was be himself, doing his own thing his own way. Then those who made him a leader put him on a pedestal, and when he didn't act like a leader anymore—which he never wanted to be anyway—they tore him down. This is the mob mentality. They want to be individuals with freedom from authority, but in packs, with someone telling them what to do and think, looking out for them. Me? I don't need anyone else's endorsement to substantiate my own opinion. You agree with me or you don't. Doc says I just have a chip on my shoulder because I'm a lonesome bastard and am resigned to this lifestyle, but with bitterness. That's just what he thinks.

But what the hell. Why bitch. People waste too much time bellyaching and fucking each other up as it is. It's like you have a half hour for lunch and you blow it by throwing a food fight. I cleared my mind of all this pointless mental editorializing as I took the N train to Coney Island, then transferred to the B Express into Manhattan. I got off at 34th Street because I was too busy daydreaming and missed my Greenwich Village stop, but that was okay. I just wandered around Macy's, ate at a Broadway pizzeria, thought about how enraged Damon Runyon would be at the price of Lindy's cheesecake these days (I had some anyway, for old times' sake) and even went up the old Empire State Building, like a tourist. It'd been so long since I was in town I felt like one. The day was getting grayer and cooler, the sun obscured by autumn clouds, but I liked it. It made me want to walk up Fifth Avenue to Central Park, so I did. There were still horse drawn carriages, and the little zoo I used to go to as a kid, though of course the Bronx was the real Zoo, or where the real Zoo was, that is. Kids with balloons and cotton candy held their parents' hands, and lovers strolled amongst the colorful foliage, which looked like a

Maxfield Parrish painting. It was beautiful, man. Even the noise and grime felt comforting. And for once seeing so many people didn't bother me. As long as they left me alone, which in the Big Apple is no problem.

I went into the Natural History Museum, my favorite hangout as a kid, to see if the big blue whale was still hanging from the ceiling, and if the awesome dinosaur skeletons were still intact, and if the amazingly realistic stuffed wildlife exhibits behind glass was still there. They were all perfectly preserved, as if frozen by my childhood memory. That museum was a dark, cozy time warp. I had blocked out all the shitty aspects of my rotten childhood and had focused on the fun aspects instead, when I had a sense of awe and wonder at the spectacles of this old world. But as I got bigger (though not much) the world got smaller and less impressive. I'd give anything to feel the adrenaline rush I did as a child looking at this stuff, but all I could do was dimly remember the thrill. I left the Museum slightly depressed.

Next, I took the train back downtown and got off in the Village and walked around my old haunts. CBGB was still there, and I walked in, took a look around, and walked right back out. Max's Kansas City was long gone. I was getting depressed again. It hit me that nothing really raced my engines the way it had when I was younger, as a teenager in the SoHo punk scene, or as a twenty-something writing notes on the underground, dating cute young waitresses who danced uptown or acted in plays off-Broadway or attended Columbia and NYU and thought I was so cool and independent, doing my own thing. I wasn't a rebel to change the world, remember. I did it for nookie. Like Elvis. And it worked, maybe not on the same scale as The King, but I held my own court just the same.

Memories of Valerie, before she became Rose, or maybe after—whatever, it's a long story— haunted me as I walked around and it grew darker and before I knew it I was sitting on a bench in Washington Square alone and realizing the years had passed me by and I had little to show for them. And God only knows where Valerie was. She existed now only in my recollection, which was fading like the sunlight. Sitting there watching the pigeons I felt suddenly overwhelmed by the urge to call Dolly Duncan down in Collingswood, New Jersey, the Philly suburb where she still lived with Donald Dunlap the dentist. It was desperate loneliness dictating my desires as usual, but so what. I belonged to the lonely-hearts club like everyone else. No, wait, I didn't. No clubs for me. I was a loner alone, just how I wanted it. Well, unless Dolly Duncan was home and alone, too.

I took the train back to Brooklyn, ate at the Bay Diner again, and then returned to The Honeymooner to call Dolly. *Ring, ring, ring.* Then:

"Hello?" The familiarity of the voice hit me in the gut like a jilted kick-boxer.

"Um, may I sp-speak to Dolly please?" I was stuttering and breathing so hard she probably thought I was a pervert. "Dolly Madison Square Garden?" That had been my pet name for her. I was young, give me a break.

"Vic?" A pervert she knew personally, at least. "Vic, is that *you*?"

"Yeah, it's me, all right. How ya doin', babe?"

"I don't believe it! Where are you?"

"Brooklyn."

"New York?"

"Yeah, that one. In town on business."

"Still a big detective?"

"Aw, well, big as ever, I guess. Still a big dick, if that's what you mean." She laughed and my knees were so wobbly I had to sit down and stop pacing with nervous energy. "So what's up? Long time."

"Too long. You gonna come visit me?"

"Well, yeah, I had that on the agenda actually. Wanted to check with you first. You still married or what?"

"Oh, yeah, I guess." She sounded encouragingly tentative.

"You sure?"

"Yeah."

"Same dude?"

"Oh yeah."

"The dentist?"

"Yeah. Donald. You remember. How 'bout you? There finally a Mrs. Valentine?"

"Me? Naw. Y'know."

"Not even a secretary?"

"No. I don't even use a computer. I'm old-fashioned. You know me."

"God. Sounds like you haven't changed at all. I can't wait to see you! When are you coming?"

"Well, that's kinda up to you. I have some business to take care of, then I'm a free man."

"*Ooo*, well, let's see. Donald is going on vacation next week, so that would be perfect!"

No way my luck could be *this* good. "Aren't you going with him?"

She laughed. "On a golfing expedition in Chicago? Not me, sweetheart."

"He's going to Chicago to golf?"

"That's where he's from, and what he likes to do. There, here, everywhere."

"Sounds like a fun guy. There, uh, any little golfers puttering around the house yet?"

She laughed yet again. "No, no." There was an uncomfortable pause. The mood seemed to shift abruptly. "Vic?"

"Yeah, babe?"

"I really missed you. Why haven't you kept in touch?"

"Well, I just thought, you know. You have your life, I have mine, different coasts, different goals, different people." I held my breath for her response.

"You'll find I'm not the same little girl you once knew, Vic."

"No? How have you changed, exactly?"

"Oh, you'll see. Next week."

"Donald home now?"

"No, out with the boys. I guess. Who cares?"

"Not me, that's for sure!"

She laughed once more, and I felt absolutely buoyant. "Me neither."

I paused. "You look the same? I mean, will I recognize you?"

"I'm the same, only better. You?"

"Ditto."

"*Ooo*. Well, what business have you got back home, anyway?"

"See you. No, just kidding. Well, no, not just kidding, I planned to see you, surprise you, but I didn't want to come all the way down if you'd moved or died or something, so I called."

"Well, I have some leads on who killed my old man, for one thing, and then I plan to go up and see my mother in the funny farm. And then see *you*."

Silence. Long and loud.

"Dolly?"

"I'm here," she said in a small, rather spooky voice.

"You okay?"

"Yeah, I just—what are your leads, anyway, after all this

time?"

"People I know in San Francisco, on the police force, used to know Al Marcus, remember him?"

"Hm, sorta. Met him once, I think."

"Did you? I thought I just told you about him a few times. So you met?"

"Oh, I guess not. Anyway, so what do they know?"

"They don't know anything, but they said I should talk to Pop at the pool hall and a few other people that Marcus talked about. Y'know, I think that old buzzard knew who iced my old man and took it with him when he croaked, never told me."

"Al's dead?"

"Yeah, heart attack, coupla years ago, maybe more, I lose track. You call him Al?"

"Well, that's his name, right?" She sure was touchy all of a sudden. "Too bad. So. Anyway, Vic, the Mafia did it. Everyone knows that. It's obvious. Let it go."

"Oh yeah? Not what *I've* got."

"Why? What have you got?" she snapped.

"I'll let you know. Don't worry about it. It has nothing to do with me and you, so forget it."

"It doesn't?"

"No. Course not. Should it?"

"No! Stop putting words in my mouth!"

"What? Putting *words* in your mouth?"

"Oh, I'm sorry, Vic. It's just that—maybe I'll tell you someday."

"Problems at home?"

"Well, you could say that."

"Yeah. You seem tense all of a sudden. You sure you're okay?"

"I'll be better when I see you. Let's set a date right now, so I can look forward to it. You want to see you mother first, I guess."

"Yeah. I think I'll do that tomorrow, get it over with."

"Over with? That's kind of cold, Vic."

"Well, Dolly, it's not a pleasant thing to visit one's natural mother in the loony bin. God knows what state she's in by now."

"I thought she was in New York? Sorry, Vic. I'm not as good with jokes as you."

"Yeah, but you got other talents."

"Maybe some you can teach me."

I paused. This was even more bizarre than I anticipated.

"Yeah. Maybe I can at that."

So we arranged to rendezvous the following week in Atlantic City. Dolly liked to gamble. Something told me her dice was loaded, too.

I hung up with an odd mixture of emotions: Anticipation, fear, joy, love, lust, and something that felt suspiciously like guilt. For what? I hadn't done anything yet. Yeah. Not *yet*.

The intervening years crashed in on me like a breaking wave in my brain as I lay back on the bed and stared at the ceiling. Dolly's voice made it all seem so fleeting, like a dream you wake up from barely able to recall. That's what my life out West seemed like now—a weird dream. This was reality. My reality, at least. Like I'd never left. My waking world. Except I was older, a little pudgier, but still solid. A few laugh lines, surprisingly many for someone who hardly ever laughed. I felt lonelier than hell all of a sudden. It ached like an ulcer. I missed Puss. I called my machine in San Francisco and talked to him for a while, mostly baby-poo gibberish normally reserved for retarded lovers and spoiled children of neurotic women. Suddenly it felt so strange to be so far away from home. The one I dreamed.

Chapter Three
BROKEN DOWN ON MEMORY LANE

My mother was a resident, if that's the delicate description, of the Chipper Monks Upper New York State Mental Institution, and had been for nearly twenty years. Their mascot was a smiling chipmunk wearing a robe. Whatever. I have to admit, it was on beautiful territory, somewhere outside the outskirts of Albany, the nearest big town, but far removed from the industrial dreariness of that depressing burg. There were lots of forests and rivers and small mountains, and it being autumn and all, the scenery was especially gorgeous, bursting with crimson and gold and evergreen. The crispiness in the woodsy breeze was chilling and invigorating. I only hoped they let her out now and then to appreciate her naturally bountiful surroundings. I pondered this as I drove my rented Coke-machine red '65 Comet (at a higher rate, but worth it so I wouldn't have to be seen in a recent, stylistically bankrupt vehicle) through the imposing iron gates and up the gravelly driveway to the coldly impressive house where my mother lived. Or resided, that is.

It was the morning after my conversation with Dolly, and I was in a weird enough mood without subjecting myself to this cathartic confrontation, but what the hell, for all I knew it was the last chance I'd ever have to see my old lady alive, or in a semblance of life. God knows what had kept her breathing this long. I'd called the joint early that morning and arranged an "appointment," for one o'clock that afternoon, just in time for lunch. They said they'd arrange a private room, which was nice. I asked how she was doing and they said she was near catatonic, had barely spoken a word in years. They were hopeful my presence might bring her out of her tragic trance, at least for a little while. So was I.

I was going to wait until I'd cleared up the business about my father before I saw her, but then I figured, she probably didn't want to know, or didn't need to, anyway. I had to see what condition she was in before I sprung something like that on her, or even brought up the subject. From what the nurse on the phone told me, I wasn't too encouraged. I thought perhaps the whole mess was best left unresolved and unspoken as far as my mother was concerned. It probably wouldn't affect her in a therapeutic way to know at this point, but it could affect her adversely. I'd be better able to tell when I looked into her eyes.

My mother used to take pride in the fact she had the same maiden name as an old time movie actress, Dorothy Malone, a brunette beauty maybe best known as the bookstore proprietress who gives Humphrey Bogart a rainy day matinee in *The Big Sleep*. I least that's how *I* best remember her. She was also in the Douglas Sirk flick *Written on the Wind.* I think she won an Oscar for that role, whatever *that's* worth. My mother *loved* that movie, but then it was old school melodrama, right up her alley. The strange thing was, my mother even resembled Dorothy Malone, except she was smaller, more petite, not quite as glamorous but could have been had she more to live for. My mother loved old movies, but never wanted to be a movie star. Her dream was to become a concert pianist, and her mother, who passed away when my mother was very young, prodded her to pursue this as a career. I don't think she ever fully recovered from the loss, as they were very close. My mother had lovely ivory smooth hands and was talented I'm told, but by the time I was a teenager she'd long given it up, and the baby grand in our living room, a family heirloom bequeathed by her mother, was perpetually covered with dust and magazines and the residue of a home without a heart. Busted hearts and shattered dreams litter our sad little world, though, and unfortunately my mother wound up just another statistic, a casualty of reality. She became so remote after Johnny's suicide and then after my old man's murder I couldn't tell whether she realized who I was anymore, or even cared. Her letters from the nuthouse were rambling and incoherent, and when the correspondence seemed pointless I cut if off, taking her letters, sometimes three a day, from my San Francisco P.O. Box and putting them directly into a trunk in my closet, where they remain to this day, unread and unanswered. As I opened the door my heart pounded and my eyes stung, and I began to feel guilty for not having been more stalwart in the face of my mother's deterioration. I only hoped she'd remember me so I could apologize.

When I walked into the reception area the icy nurse shook my hand with obligatory politeness and then asked me to take a seat. The atmosphere was akin to an asylum in a '40s B movie, but then maybe that's just my take on it since that's where my head's at.

Still, the sterile but spooky ambience reeked of Universal mad doctor matinees. Hans Salter music could barely be heard in the background, at least in my imagination. The owners or attendants or whoever had attempted to give the joint a homey, Thanksgiving Day festive feeling, hosted by Boris Karloff. There was a fireplace and throw rugs and even a dead deer head on the wood-paneled wall. Here and there were chipmunk emblems, which was tiresome. The selected waiting room magazines consisted of *Life* and *Reader's Digest* and other safe, traditional fare. Yet there persisted an eerie somberness, partially due I suppose to the seriousness of the staff despite the phony decor, so that the overall effect was Norman Rockwell meets Norman Bates. I was relieved when the nurse, who resembled Marie Windsor with a poker up her ass so that she was sort of sexy in an austere, uptight way, like a repressed schoolteacher, finally came in after about twenty minutes and told me my mother was waiting for me in her private dining room.

"Does she realize who I am?"

"We told her she has a guest she'll be happily surprised to see, but it didn't seem to register. She just nodded passively, didn't even blink." Then Nurse Windsor, as I'd mentally dubbed her, gave me a sidelong glance and said with acid in her tone, "I don't suppose you've kept in touch much. I didn't even realize she had a son." I'd had to show proof when I showed up, even, birth certificate and some photos and such. "Though I vaguely recall some letters many years ago."

I felt on the spot, and resented her, but kept my cool. "I used to exchange letters, but it got to me, y'know. I didn't think my writing her was doing her any good."

"Oh?" she said with undisguised disgust. "Feeling lonely and abandoned by your family can't do much good, either."

"I didn't abandon her," I said, straining to maintain my poise, "I just got scared off. But hell, here I am, so quit beefing and let me see her. You're not my mother, so get off my case."

Nurse Windsor went into a snit but didn't say anything else, which was fine. She led me up the stairs past a series of doors I had no desire to ever look behind. I felt like I was on a guided tour of the set of *Dark Shadows.* I half expected Baby Jane to come popping out of a room any second with an axe, or Norma Desmond to tap my shoulder and give me a nightmarish close-up while asking me to write a script for her. It was that Gothic Grand Guignol film noir kind of feeling I can do without. I'm paranoid and imaginative enough without the outside embellishment, thank you. The chiaroscuro intensified as we walked up one more flight of creaky stairs. White walls, dark shadows. My stomach was doing the Watusi by the time Nurse Windsor knocked on a door and two chubby, balding, pasty skinned orderlies who resembled your basic child molester stepped out into the hallway, leaving the door slightly ajar. Nurse Windsor nodded at me and I went in.

"Please close the door and give us some privacy," I said before I even looked at the person waiting for me inside the small, musty room. Nurse Windsor nodded curtly as she slammed the door behind me. I gave the room the visual once-over without looking directly at the person I was there to see. It was just a tiny alcove with hundred-years-old wallpaper and some portraits of dead people hanging around. Cheery.

Then I took a deep breath and turned to face the stranger who had carried me around in her womb thirty odd years ago.

My initial impression was Blanche DuBoise. There was that stoic sense of tragic poetry and fallen beauty right out of Tennessee Williams. Except it was only me, Brooklyn Vic, saying hello to his long lost mother for the first time in nearly a decade.

She appeared wan and her hair had gone shockingly silver, but, amazingly, her eyes were still beautiful, clear and emerald. She had lost weight since the last time I'd seen her, when she ballooned after indulging her depression with gluttony, and her frailness made her look more like a TB victim in a sanitarium than a mental patient. She didn't look up when I came in, or in any way acknowledge my presence when I sat across from her at the little table, which had already been set up with our meal on covered plates. She just stared out the bay window at the courtyard below, which was ringed with an array of beautiful flowers and was quite peaceful to behold. The expression on her weary face was impassive, and could be interpreted as either serene or aloof. Only she knew for sure, and from what I could see, she wasn't telling.

"Ma—?" I said gently after a few patient, tasteful beats. "It's *me*, Ma. Vic. Your son, Vic. All the way out from California to pay you a visit." No response. "C'mon, Ma, don't be like that. I know I haven't kept in touch much. Sorry about that, but I'm here in person to make up for that, okay?" *Nada.* Outside it began to cloud over and drizzle all at once, and as little tiny drops trickled down the windowpane her eyes didn't even flinch. I then noticed how the orderlies must have hastily and sloppily applied makeup and a quick makeover on my mother. She looked like a painted mannequin just sitting there silently, slightly smeared lipstick and eyelash liner and her scraggly hair pulled back into a bun combining for the false effect of self-esteem. I felt tears form in my eyes, but I fought them for her sake. My sniveling wouldn't do wonders for her emotional outlook, that was for sure.

After a few more minutes of watching her stare out the window at the increasingly wet courtyard, I tried to break through her autistic barrier again, as gingerly as I could. "Ma, look, you don't have to say nothin'. That's all right, I understand. But if you could just nod now and then, that would be nice, huh? I mean, I need to know you know me, Ma, otherwise, I mean, I want you to know that out there somewhere, outside your window, beyond that little courtyard, you have a son who *loves* you, Ma. Really. That might help a little, right? And it would help me too to know that, somewhere inside of there, you like me too, think of me sometimes, I mean, y'know?"

No dice. I sighed and removed the lids from our plates. I couldn't tell exactly what it was underneath but steam rose from it so at least it was warm. I picked up my utensils and dug in, since I was pretty hungry. "Aren't you gonna eat, Ma? C'mon. It's not bad. Really. Dig in. Hey, remember all those meals you used to make for Johnny and—" I stopped cold. She seemed to twitch slightly when I said Johnny's name. *Bingo.* I decided to push that button until I elicited some kind of response from her, even a scream, something to snap her out of this daze. I knew she was in there somewhere, listening to me, or at least hearing my familiar voice, and it had to trigger some chords of response sooner or later. For all I knew she was faking it. I wouldn't put it past her. I persisted, feeling hopeful after that twitch. "Yeah, me and Johnny used to love your cooking, Ma. Really. Italian food the most. Man, you could cook." I deleted any references to the old man for fear of sending her on a suicidal plunge out the window, and I wouldn't be able to live with that any better than she would.

I rambled on about sundry family collective memories as I ate and she stared. Of course our happiest times occurred when I was too young to remember them well. Vaguely I recalled a vintage Corvair station wagon loaded with goodies driving through the woods—Appalachian? Poconos? Niagara Falls?—and then a picnic and a rushing river and the smell of evergreen and timber and the sound of Patsy Cline, my mother's favorite singer, as Johnny and I splashed around in the water and played catch with the old man. God, I must've been, what, five? Then I recalled a fishing trip—same trip?—only Ma was nowhere around, it was just Johnny and the old man and me sitting on a pier, and every time the old man and Johnny, who was maybe twelve, would catch a fish I'd toss it back into the water, so after a while the old man and Johnny turned around and saw their day's catch floating beside the pier where I'd attempted to either rejuvenate the poor bastards or else give them a decent burial at sea. The more I verbally remembered the more torrential the flood of recollections became, until it seemed I was just bouncing them off my mother, who was in a world of her own, oblivious to my flashback babbling.

After I'd finished listing my favorite boyhood cartoons—*The Flintstones*, *The Jetsons*, *Spiderman*, *Jonny Quest*, dozens more—I went into a litany of my favorite boyhood songs, most of them sappy stuff my mother listened to, like "Love is Blue," "Scarborough Fair," Henry Mancini, Nat King Cole, Frank Sinatra, Johnny Mathis, "Telstar," Roy Orbison, Bobby Vinton, "King of the Road," Johnny Cash, "Downtown," Elvis, "Those Were the Days." Then I stopped. She was humming. I stood up and stooped over the table to listen.

It was "Those Were the Days," faint and barely audible, but unmistakable. She used to like playing it on the piano when I was a kid. She played all that stuff I mentioned, well, what she could on a piano. Sometimes she played Duke Ellington, only I didn't realize it then. When I wasn't within earshot—or so she believed, late at night when Johnny and I were supposedly asleep, and Pop was out on "assignment"—she'd play classical pieces her mother had forced her to learn, Chopin, Beethoven, Mozart, that whole long-haired crowd which never turned me on much, except when she played "Stranger in Paradise" or, even better, "Swan Lake," because that reminded me of Dracula. I remembered curling up with her watching old movies, Bogart and Cagney and Gable and Grant and Flynn and all her favorite dream lovers, while the old man was off somewhere and Johnny was in his room practicing his music, mainly guitar. He loved The Doors, The Stones and of course The Beatles. Me, I was with Ma. I liked the old movies, too. To this day I watch them thinking of those afternoons and evenings when she'd make popcorn and cookies and we'd stake out the T.V. for hours on end, gangsters and monsters and soldiers and cowboys and spies and lovers parading before us in black and white and Technicolor. We helped each other escape from the real world back then, until the real world came crashing into our fantasy world, and forced a hostile takeover.

And now, all these years later, here we were. I had an idea.

I got up and summoned the nurse by pushing this little button. Nurse Windsor showed up with the two bum orderlies. I whispered that my mother was humming an old tune from my childhood, and requested I accompany her back to her room to watch the AMC channel with her, hoping the experience of watching an old movie together would further coax her out of her shell. At first Nurse Windsor didn't think it was a good idea, but when she couldn't explain why it wasn't, she had to agree it might be after all.

Ma stopped humming when the orderlies walked in, and my spirits sank accordingly. I could barely watch as the orderlies whisked away her cold, untouched meal and then helped her to her feet. It was like leading a sleepwalker. I followed them down the hall to her room.

"This may be hard to take," Nurse Windsor said to me lowly, touching my arm and holding me back as the orderlies led Ma into her quarters.

"Whaddya mean, hard? What could be worse than just how she is?"

"Her room," the nurse said simply, "is where she spends all of her time. She never comes out. It could depress you to think of her in such a claustrophobic space. We try coaxing her to go outside more often, but she shows no interest, only sits in a lawn chair and sleeps."

"Believe me, I've seen enough. If I can handle her like that, I can handle her room. She's a prisoner of her mind anyway."

"All right." Nurse Windsor nodded and I went into Ma's sanctuary. It was a carbon copy of the "private dining room" (which obviously was just a vacancy) except for some significant additions—mementos and medication piled up on little bedside tables. And there was a television, with the American Movie Classics channel already on. One of the orderlies said to me, "Funny—she always turns on that station anyhow, but we can't tell if she knows what's playing, much less enjoys it."

I nodded at them and they left. Ma was lying on her bed, staring at the television screen. It took me a few seconds but I made the picture playing: *Out of the Past,* with Robert Mitchum and Jane Greer. It had just started, with the hood looking for Mitchum, ex-private eye and gas station owner, in the little Tahoe cafe. I didn't think Ma and I had ever seen this one together. I pulled up a chair. "Ooo, this is a good one, Ma," I said. "Remember we used to watch movies together like this, huh?" She was back in her own private movie, with no soundtrack now. I just paid attention to the movie on the screen, and as it progressed, I supplied a running commentary on the action, all the while taking in the incredible supply of bedside pills, and the framed pictures of Johnny and Pop and me at various stages of our old life, which seemed so distant and unreal—like an old movie. I pointed out Kirk Douglas when he came on, talking like a film historian giving a lecture, when in fact I was softly sobbing on the outside and raging with sorrow on the inside.

Outside the rain began to pick up and the howling wind and downpour nearly drowned out the sound of the TV, so I turned up the volume a little. I wanted to grab my mother and shake her into a sentient state, but held back my emotions. Instead I sublimated my frustration into my usual cynical mental discoursing. The fine line between the ephemeral and the ethereal seemed especially thin during such moments, when life felt so pointless and truth so intangible. I wanted to explain to Ma what I did for a living by pointing out Mitchum's profession in the flashback detective scenes in Mexico and San Francisco when he runs off with femme fatale Jane Greer, unbeknownst to gangster Kirk Douglas, who hired Mitch to find her, not fuck her, but now it seemed Ma wasn't even watching the TV anymore, just space and time or maybe a memory. I couldn't even watch the movie without thinking how sad it was that film and video eventually rots and all these special images from the celluloid past will disappear like they never existed, and they were the only legacy of times I spent watching them with Ma, since one day Ma and I would disappear, too. I just wished the films themselves could last forever so some other mother and son could cuddle up on a couch and enjoy them together. Flicks made nowadays just weren't cuddle material. There was no innocence in them, no charm, nothing to cuddle to that wasn't contrived and insincere. I was no different. I'd lost my innocence, too, and couldn't appreciate the old by-gone era of romance as much as I used to. I had lost faith in it, had no reference points in my own life to give it dimension, but struggled to maintain at least a connection to it by going through the motions, hoping deep down the transient beauty of this world meant something in the long run.

I shut off the TV and the room was suddenly dark, so I flipped on a light, sat next to Ma on the bed, and realized it was chilly in the room. Where was the goddamn heat? I asked her if she was cold but she didn't reply, even in song, so I gently pulled the covers down under her as I held her frail body in my arms and then tucked her beneath them. I looked into her eyes, searching in vain for a glimmer of recognition, and then I kissed her forehead and one of my tears trickled onto her face and fell down her cheek as if it were her own.

I held her for a while, just rocking her back and forth in my arms, hoping maybe the motion would shake up something inside of her. I whispered "I love you" in her ear, hoping she'd hum something in response, but no, she was gone again. Maybe that little musical interlude had been a lucky aberration after all, and I was trying to force the impossible. What the hell. Forcing the impossible is what I like to do best. But at that moment, I was wasting our time. No, I wasn't. At least we were together for the first time in a long time. "I'll be back soon," I whispered in her ear. Then I kissed her goodbye on the cheek and made sure she was secure beneath her covers. Her arms fell limply at her side, and her eyes remained open, as if waiting for someone to put pennies on them. But she continued to breath, and as long as she did, there was hope.

I walked out the door and clicked off the light behind me. It was nearly five o'clock anyway. Visiting hours were almost up. I walked downstairs and looked around for Nurse Windsor. I found her in the reception area talking to some other family about an inmate or resident or whatever you call them. I waited tactfully for her to finish her business and then accosted her. "Hey, I have a few suggestions to run by you," I said to her constipated countenance.

"Oh?" she said coldly. She didn't seem very receptive to my ideas. Tough.

"Yeah. First, that place is freezing. Where's the heat in this joint?"

"Well, it takes time to warm up."

"Make it quicker."

"Mister Valentine, we don't need any advice on how to run our facility from an outsider."

"I ain't no outsider, I'm a customer. Or whatever. With a vested interest, no? I mean, it's my mother shivering up there in the dark, not yours."

"But it's her sister who's paying her expenses, not you. And she's perfectly happy with Dorothy's treatment here."

"You mean she condones all those drugs?"

"They're not recreational, I assure you."

"Where is my Aunt Florence these days, anyway?"

"If you don't already know, I don't feel at liberty to tell you, Mister Valentine."

I wasn't too tight with my Aunt Florence. She though I had let my mother down by moving out west and not going to college and making something special of myself, i.e. getting into a lucrative profession respected by polite society. Florence was also an uptight conservative Catholic Republican who didn't condone what she perceived as my "bohemian" lifestyle. She thought all guys my age who weren't married and raising a family were out sucking cock or something. Whatever. We just didn't hit it off, and I didn't trust her when it came to my mother. There had existed a sibling rivalry and even as a kid I had picked up on the tension during holiday get-togethers. My mother was prettier and more talented than Florence, who was married to a banker and had half a dozen kids but no dreams. Ma's dreams didn't come true, but at least she had them to begin with, and might've made something out of them had life been kinder. Still, Florence was footing the bill here. For now. In the meantime, until I eventually tracked her down, I wanted to insure Ma's comfort. That humming episode had proven she still inhabited the same sorry world we did, and the right treatment could bring her out of the darkness and into the light of day, for what that was worth. Sometimes I wondered if the world in your head wasn't better than the one outside. I needed to know Ma was making a conscious choice, at any rate.

"All right, listen then," I said to Nurse Windsor in a new tone of diplomacy, a tack I fell back on when my customary brusqueness failed me. I pulled a twenty spot out of my wallet and handed it to her. "No, this ain't a bribe to turn the heat up and ditch the drugs. For that I'd give hundreds. But all I'm asking you to do is buy a copy of Patsy Cline's greatest hits and play them in her room for her. You got a CD blaster around, I assume? If not, I'll get one for you."

"No, we can arrange music, but why Patsy Cline?"

I winked. "Her favorite. Trust me. At least I had her humming, right? Music. Not movies or pills. Just music. That could be the trigger, the key to unlocking that tomb she's shut herself in. Music. And maybe, just maybe, *me*. Added up, we may find a cure yet."

Nurse Windsor took the money—no one says no to money—

and said, "I'll grant your request, Mister Valentine, but I should inform you—she's well beyond hope, we believe. At least as far as her acute melancholia is concerned. Maybe she will talk again, but she'll never be well enough to live on her own again, I'm afraid."

I rolled my eyes and shrugged. "We'll see. Here, take my card. I wrote my hotel number in Brooklyn on it. Please tell Florence I'll be there indefinitely on business and to give me a buzz, all right? And don't forget the CD. Patsy Cline. 'Greatest Hits' will do. Okay, babe?"

She took the card and snapped, "Fine. But do not refer to me as 'babe,' Mister Valentine."

I shot my forefinger at her and got the hell out of there. The rain had slacked off somewhat but it was dark and the traffic was terrible. I made it into the city by eight or so and went directly to Times Square to let off some steam. Now New York didn't seem so exciting and friendly and postcard perfect. I saw only fear and paranoia and garbage, all with a rap music soundtrack, and it gave me a headache. After parking the Comet in a garage I walked along Broadway and ducked into a few of those peep show joints, just to kill time. It was depressing. I wasn't even horny. For once the sight of bare bouncing boobs didn't float my boat. I felt like I left a trail of slime behind me walking out of the booth. The noise and neon outside didn't seem glamorous, just gaudy and annoying. This wasn't the slick bebop town of Sweet Smell of Success anymore. It was lost soul central, ugly and worn out by its own desperation. I ate in a Howard Johnson's and then went back to the garage and returned to The Honeymooner with one single thought burning in my brain: Whoever killed my father had also killed my mother, and I was deadly determined to find them even if it also killed me.

Chapter Four
A FLEA DOZED IN BROOKLYN

Character assassination in the latter part of the Twentieth Century is rampant, and I don't mean insults to human dignity, either. There is no dignity in this fouled up so-called contemporary culture of ours, or what's left of it is the shrapnel from the fallout of personality genocide. You know what I mean, and if you don't, then you're probably a victim of the same crime against humanity, if our species ever deserved that moniker to begin with. What I mean is, they just don't make people like they used to. Case in point: all the remakes of and sequels to the classic films of yesteryear, cast with bland, boring mannequins culled from the catalogues of corporate studios run by bloodless, gutless yuppies. America today is peopled with conformist nimrods weaned on the comforts of tract homes, fast food, and sitcoms that destroy what brain cells and original ideas are left after a steady diet of drugs and Nintendo games and fascist political rhetoric disguised as "family values." There are no more Jimmy Cagneys or Humphrey Bogarts these days—especially not on the screen. But in real life, there are remnants of the classic tradition of characters that once went about their colorful business in a land still naive enough to believe in ideals like true romance and individual expression. Brooklyn is one of the few holdouts in this respect, only you have to look hard, primarily where the old timers hang out, congregated in stubborn huddles as they prepare to leave behind a legacy of courageous lunacy which may be forever forgotten in our conformist future.

Pop's Pool Hall is one such oasis in this postmodern wasteland of which I speak and pay reluctant rent in. Pop himself is one such rebel. He's an Italian immigrant who married Irish (like my old man) at the age of seventeen and has spent every day since landing on Ellis Island with his brand new bride cultivating the character that is vanishing from our once proud nation. His son, Junior, inherited some of it, but his teenage boy and girl are typical TV brats with no interest in their own history. Anything in mono or black and white is deemed prehistoric by these young hipsters, and their idea of entertainment is whatever makes the Top Ten, whatever everybody else is brainwashed into buying. Anyway, Pop is like eighty now, and Junior is maybe fifty, fifty-five, and both are still as feisty and robust as ever. I never got along too well with Junior, to be honest, since he's got this macho thing going on and always has to prove how much testosterone he has coursing through his vermicelli veins. He's the type who's always conducting arm wrestling contests in the back room when poker or prostitution isn't going on (Pop's lets several of the better looking neighborhood tramps use the cot in the back after hours or during daytime lulls). Pop himself is a baseball fan from way back, and could always be found watching the Yanks or Mets on the big screen TV behind the bar, whether he was on duty or not. But there was a strike this year, and Pop had retired, leaving Junior totally in charge with some new hired hands, or so I'd heard, so I wasn't sure what or who I'd find when I breezed into Pop's the day after visiting Ma. I wasn't surprised at what was waiting for me.

There was Junior behind the bar washing mugs, and Pop sitting at the bar channel surfing across the vapid airwaves of cable TV. Still life, man. Frozen in time, like that famous painting of dogs playing poker. From the back I heard the fast knocking sounds of pool (the twin tables doubled sometimes as whore beds when the cot was already in use). I sat at the bar and nonchalantly ordered a Bud. Junior nodded, did a double take, then loudly announced my arrival.

"Yo! I don't freakin' believe it! *Vic Freakin' Valentine*!" Junior shouted. Several heads in the joint turned, including Pop's. The old guy smiled then coughed from the exertion. Junior reached his hairy beefy arms across the bar and grabbed my head with both hands and awkwardly hugged it. I blushed and expressed salutations in muffled tones. I was glad he didn't kiss me, but then he had a macho reputation to uphold, so I was secure in my safety from slobber.

Pop's last name was Benenito or something, I couldn't really remember because since I'd first heard about him as a little kid everyone just called him Pop. Same with Junior. Even Junior's wife called him Junior and Pop 'Pop.' Pop struggled to get up, ostensibly to offer me a hug as well, but I made it easy on him, went over to him and let him put his feeble arms and musty senior smell all over me. Well, not all over, but enough.

"Where you been, you son of a bitch?" he said, holding my face in his hands, and squeezing my red cheeks.

"San Francisco," I replied simply. "Past eight years or so. Thought you knew. Got my own business and everything."

"Frisco?" Pop said, his wrinkled countenance wrinkling even more. "You ain't a commie cocksucker now, are ya?"

Had to laugh a little. Still ignorant after all these years. "Naw, I ain't takin' it up the wazoo and I still salute the flag when I have to, Pop. Nothin' radical. Just livin' life as it comes—or as it goes, can't figure that out yet."

"Yeah? Married? Kids?"

"Nope."

"Lucky fuck!" Junior exclaimed. "My family's drivin' me to any early grave, and I look it, like a fat freakin' zombie over here. But Vic, you look like a million bucks! Good to see you, *paisan*." I smiled and nodded. None of the other patrons recognized me and vice versa. They went back to watching the TV and talking about whatever they were talking about before I came in. A few wiseguys were in the audience, I could tell, and they might've heard of me but played dumb, and probably kept one ear on my conversation even while engaged in their own privacy. I played it cool. "What business is you in back in fairyland?" Junior asked.

"I'm a private detective," I said with rehearsed flair. I even flashed my P.I. badge for extra effect. Pop and Junior nodded with non-plussed expressions.

"Better than bein' a cop," Pop said, and Junior and he cracked up.

I shrugged and grinned, feeling a tad uncomfortable now. "Place hasn't changed much," I said, looking around at the familiar wood paneling, framed Gil Elvgren pinups and Norman Rockwell Saturday Evening Post covers and a few Edward Hoppers prints. And, yes, in the back room was the "Dogs Playing Poker" painting, also framed. Sinatra crooned on the classic jukebox, which also stocked Tony Bennett and Bobby Darin and all their contemporaries, but nobody else. Nothing had changed. Or so it seemed.

"Except the sign's gonna be changed to 'Junior's'," Junior said proudly. "Pop's retired now. Just hangs out cause he's lonesome."

"Yeah? What about—?" Then I stopped. Mom was old as Pop. Or *would* be.

Pop just nodded, tears forming in glassy eyes. "Last year. Ticker." Pop pounded lightly on his chest.

Junior nodded grimly. "Yeah, so now Pop figures I can handle it alone. Guess you hadn't heard."

"Actually, some pals of Al Marcus heard about it and told me in San Francisco."

"Alfonse Marcus, that *prick*!" Pop exploded, catching me by surprise. "Don't *mention* that cocksucker's name in my place!"

"Or mine," Junior chimed in. "Anyway, how would they know?"

"Right after Pop retired, Al kicked off. He told his pals before he went, they told me."

"We don't know anybody knew Marcus," Junior said. "Best not to bring him up, anyway."

"Didn't realize there were hard feelings there," I said.

"Now you do," Pop said flatly. "Anyway, can you believe these asshole ballplayers went on strike! Give unions a bad name." I sensed several wiseguys perk up behind me, but I ignored them. Pop was okay, could shoot off his mouth anytime he wanted, since he was part of the neighborhood fabric and was a guinea to boot. My old man told me Pop was one of the few local businesses not required to pay protection in the old day, but he made donations anyway as a gesture of respect. This set him in solid with the Mob and he knew it. Pop was a politician in some ways, and people listened when he spoke.

"Baseball belongs to *us*, the people. I ain't got many seasons left, and these overpaid cocksuckers walk out on me. What's the world coming to, Vic? What brings you back home anyways? Just miss the old neighborhood?"

"Yeah, what brings you back?" Junior echoed. The mention of Al Marcus's name had put a strange tinge in the conversation all of a sudden. I never thought Al was a touchy subject. Al was good people, I thought. Maybe not, at least in Pop's estimation, which counted plenty in local circles, so that was something to follow up on. According to Marcus' pals on SFPD, there was no obvious cause for Pop's apparent hostility toward Al, who always spoke of Pop in warm terms.

What gives here?, I had to wonder. Already the plot was thickening, like slow-stirred spaghetti sauce over a low flame, bubbling with mystery ingredients and secret spices.

I took a deep breath and said, "Well, I tell ya, fellas, the same guys that told me Pop had retired told me you knew somethin' about my old man." It just came out. I couldn't help it. I was too antsy for discretion. I wanted to get to the bottom of this and cut the bullshit reunion chitchat. Maybe later, after this was cleared up and I could relax and take a real vacation, we could chum it up. Junior didn't really like me anyway, because he didn't trust any male who didn't watch football as a matter of religion, but he was being nice for Pop's sake. Pop likes everybody from the neighborhood, and hardly anyone out of it. That was fine, but in the meantime, I wanted to get down to the nitty gritty.

Man, that laid a bomb. After several tense moments of heavy silence, emanating from not only Pop and Junior but also the wiseguy patrons nearby, Pop leaned over and said, his cigar breath nearly bowling me over, "Maybe we should take this to the back, Vic." Pop nodded at Junior, who looked like he was ready to heave or hit me, or both, and then Junior walked back to the pool/poker room. I didn't hear any verbal exchanges, but a moment later three young wop studs silently marched out, leaving their cues behind on the table. Then Pop motioned for me to follow him. I tried helping him off his stool but he crankily waved me off. He was pissed all right, and I have to say, my heart was pounding. Already I'd hit two nerves—or maybe the same one twice. I gulped and followed Pop back to the poolroom and Junior closed a curtain behind us. Pop nodded at Junior, who nodded back and returned to the bar. Even Sinatra had stopped singing. All I could hear was my heartbeat and Pop's wheezing breath. Pop sat slowly onto the come-stained cot and I hopped up on the come-stained pool table, and there we sat until Pop caught his breath, looked at me seriously, and said, "You don't want to know what I know, Vic. But tell me first—just who are these friends of Al Marcus, and why did they wait this long to tell you to come talk to me?"

Good question, but I only had half an answer. "Al never said shit to me, Pop, but he did confide in some detectives on the San Francisco police force whom he trusted, with instructions to pass on the info when he was gone. The friends' names were Sharp and Shoemaker. First names aren't important since you don't know them anyway. Al figured he didn't want to be around when I came to see you—plus a few other people. Al was holding out on me—and so are you. How come, Pop? Mafia after all?"

Pop raised a finger to his thin, lizardy lips. "*Sssshhh!*"

"Yeah, yeah, I know the score, but they can't hear us now."

"They hear it all, Vic. You should know that. But they didn't rub out your father. I can tell you that much."

"And what else?"

"You don't want to know."

"But I do. I flew thousands of miles to see you so you could tell me to my face. What do you know?"

"It will hurt you, my boy. You're better off not knowing. Al was right not to tell you. No, he did send you to me, but after he croaked. That figures. Yellow bellied cocksucker!"

"Pop, just what is it with you and Al? He was a good guy and one of my old man's best friends, if not the best. What's your beef with him?"

The old guy sighed and coughed, then coughed some more. I waited patiently for him to regain composure after wiping a pint of phlegm on his green sweater sleeve. Pop was still wearing his brown Fedora, cocked to one side like always. I'd rarely seen him without it. Finally he said, "Vic, I liked your father. Let me say that right off. He was a bastard and treated you and your mother, God rest her, like hell."

"Ma's still alive, Pop. Just saw her yesterday."

"I know, I know. You think I don't know that? But believe me, she's been dead for years, even before they sent her away. May as well be a mausoleum as a crazy house, but—where was I? Oh yeah. Your father. God rest him, though I'm sure the devil has him now. You know that, Vic, well as anyone. But your father, he did have a heart, Vic. He thought with his *cock*, but he had a heart he listened to sometimes as well. I've seen it. Used to go out of his way to help people sometimes, using his authority to clean out bad neighborhoods and going past it when he had to, to make sure people was safe. He gave people on his beat presents at Christmastime. People loved him. But Al Marcus was not his friend. Couldn't be trusted, screwed your father any chance he got. Just jealous, I guess, I don't know what's wrong with people. That's my beef with him. He was a snake, that son of a bitch. May he fry in Hell, for all I care."

Pop coughed as he grew excited, and again I had to wait it out. It was getting tiresome, let me tell you, especially when he started launching projectile snot in my direction, inadvertently I assumed.

"Pop, that's some nasty cough, you get that checked out?" I asked delicately.

"Never mind that, kid, I'll outlive all of youse. Just listen to what I'm sayin' to you, Vic: Go back to California and forget this business about your father. Let it rest, let him rest, let yourself rest. It won't do nobody no good diggin' up his corpse now. I just wanted to tell you he wasn't as bad as you may think. He had a heart, kid. Just remember that. Your mother deserved better, I admit, but don't blame him for what happened to her. All of us are responsible for our own destinies in this rotten world, my boy. Your mother is where she is because he couldn't let go. Don't let that happen to you. Now, that's all I gotta say."

Pop started to get up, but I hopped down off the pool table and stopped him. "Pop, you didn't tell me *nothin'*. Al's pals said you know either who aced my old man or you know somebody who knows. Just point me in the right direction, Pop. C'mon. Let me decide if it's worth knowin'. C'mon."

"Beat it, Vic," I heard Junior say from behind me. He was sticking his fat head through the curtains. "My father is too weak for this shit. Leave him alone and go back to fairyland or whatever you gotta do, but leave my father in peace. I mean it. *Blow*."

"But..."

"*NOW*." Junior was a big guy. I might've been able to cause him some damage under other circumstances, but not without some expense to my own well being, so I let it slide. I handed Pop my card with my hotel number on it.

"Call me if you change your mind," I said.

Pop looked at it and laughed. "The Hot Box? Vic. You got no taste, my boy. No class. And no sense if you don't let this die."

"Yeah. It's buried anyway," Junior added as I passed him, feeling the friction.

I saluted them both and then walked out, feeling the heat from the wiseguys but blowing them off as I stepped into the bright, brisk day. I had a feeling I'd be hearing from Pop before it was over.

I went back to The Honeymooner and called Doc. I didn't want to overdo it since it was expensive complaining long distance, but at that moment I needed his wisdom and reassurance. "Vic, you're an idiot," he said.

"Doc, gimme a break. I'm payin' for this call."

"Call it therapy. Then it's a bargain rate all the same."

"Shit, Doc. That's the best you can do me? I called for support, not a hard time. I got enough of that here."

"What's so bad? Sounds like an interesting change of pace at least, right? Stop bitchin'."

"Change of pace? Goin' to visit my old lady in the loony bin, finding out everyone knows who iced my old man but me and nobody's talkin', you call that a change of pace? Cavalier motherfucker, aren't you? Mister Cool himself."

"Vic, I'm surprised at you. Look at you. You're doin' okay. Your brother is a fossil in Hudson Bay somewhere, your mother is locked up in the fuckin' House of Usher, and your father is probably diggin' ditches for the Devil. You? You're hangin' out in the Big Apple, eating in your favorite coffee shops, jerkin' off, havin' a grand old time by comparison. Now, do I lie?"

Goddamn it. I couldn't even enjoy a simple bout of self-pity with Doc around. I should've known better than to call Doc before I finished wallowing in it. "Doc, you're a pain the ass, but I love you. Thanks for the cold-blooded perspective. But, really, Doc, don't I get just a teeny bit of sympathy?"

"Not from this end. I know you too well. You'll let it soften you. You gotta be a tough motherfucker if you're gonna go the distance with this thing."

"So you do think it's a good idea, then? Me bein' here?"

"Vic, that's beside the point. You're there already. I was against the war to begin with, but now that my troops are already on shore I can't abandon them now. Go for it. Make me proud. Then come home to your new Dolores Vale videos."

"Thanks, Doc. But I'd rather be coming home to Dolores Vale herself."

"That's the spirit. Anyone but that Jersey bimbo. Keep your distance, Vic. Don't let sentiment cloud your judgment. Don't be a damn necrophiliac. Bitch is dead as far as you're concerned. Remember that. That whole part of your life is zombieville. You're like Peter Cushing in those Dracula flicks, looking for the undead so you can drive a stake through their chests and bury 'em for good so they won't bother you no more."

"That's harsh, Doc."

"Truth sucks, my man. Just remember—I tell you this stuff because I love you, too."

"Fag," I said, and hung up.

I lay back on the creaky bed and stared at the framed stills from The Honeymooners lining the wall, over the tacky gold and crimson wallpaper, left over from the bordello days. They just took out the plush king size beds and silk sheets and replaced them with standard cheap queens and twins with covers you'd normally use for painting the house. I missed my cat. I forgot to ask Doc if he was feeding Puss all right, but I didn't call back to make sure. Waste of money. I just called Puss instead and baby-talked on the answering machine, hoping no one was around, like Monica, feeding him while I was doing so. My humiliation quota was already full for the year, and it wasn't over yet.

Doc's admonition about Dolly stung me. I was really horny for that chick all of a sudden. Part of it was just being back in the old neighborhood surrounded by ghosts of our mutual past, but also, it had been a while since I'd seen my old sexual stomping grounds. In New York I'd been a stud. Memories of my own conquests turned me on. Plus I was lonesome as hell. I couldn't wait to see Dolly the following week. I fantasized about her for a while and then went into the bathroom and washed my hands. I looked out the window. Early evening, vivid and brisk. The rain had cleared out the New York haze that used to bring me down, make me feel like I was living under a dome. I decided to go for a walk past my old house, which had been sold long ago, after my mother was committed. I hadn't planned to initially—too depressing—but what the hell. Like Doc said, I was here already. Might as well charge ahead rather than snooze in the trenches.

My old house, the one I grew up in, was around the corner and a few blocks down from The Honeymooner, which posed some geographical dilemmas to my old man when he frequented it. Our home was a typical Brooklyn brownstone with a porch, a screen door, a front door, a back door, a front lawn, rear garden, and the usual in-between furnishings and domestic doldrums. Nothing special, except for the memories still attached to it, which engulfed me as I stood at a discreet distance. It looked like a Jewish family had moved in, because just as I walked up I saw one of those guys wearing those curly sideburns and big hat walk in, with the black robe and everything. Hasidic, I guess they call that routine. Whatever. Made no difference now. My neighborhood had grown progressively Jewish over the past two decades or so, and Ma used to complain about it, while my old man didn't give a damn, since the Jews were there to serve the Mob's interests, like medical and legal needs, or at least the core group was that initially took over our block and the ones nearby. The rest were extended family, which, like the Italians, were legion. Few blacks were around, and I missed that growing up, because I dig their culture. Well, the old school. Hip-hop just doesn't move me like jazz and the blues. My paper route used to take me into some shady neighborhoods, as it were, and I made a few friends over there, but none that lasted. They were intimidated by the Italians, and vice versa. Actually, there was a grudging admiration between the two races, since blacks considered Italians white niggers and Italians considered many blacks, whom they feared more than whites, therefore respected more, as chocolate covered wops. In my locker room at high school they used to brag about which had the bigger schlongs. The white bullies just walked around flexing their muscles and swatting little guys like me on the ass with their towels.

I strolled past my high school, deserted now at night. There had been turf wars there like everywhere else, and the classrooms and playgrounds were divisive—honkies, kikes, wops, pollocks, chinks, niggers, spics, and micks stayed in their cliques, and only mingled secretly on weekends for basketball and even interracial dating on the sly. What a bunch of hypocrites. Learned it from their parents, who learned it from theirs, and so on. Whatever.

Me, I was half wop, half mick, but mostly, I kept to myself, created my own class distinction, my own rules, and stuck by them ever since. I never understood why men of different colors and creeds didn't put aside their petty differences and band together against the common foe: Women. After all, you never see a black cat and a white cat fighting over the color of their fur. They fight over bitches, which is perfectly natural.

I got bored quickly, as I often did when actually living in Bensonhurst, so I ate at the Bay Diner then returned to The Honeymooner. I thought about giving old Dolly a buzz, telling her about walking past my house and our old school. Why not? Fuck Donald the dentist. He probably wasn't even home, the louse. The hotel lobby was eerily quiet and the desk clerk had put up a sign saying he'd be back in five minutes. Didn't matter, I had my key. My room was dark but just as I reached for the light a hand grabbed my wrist so I didn't get a chance to see who pistol-whipped me until it was too late.

Chapter Five
HAVE FUN, WILL UNRAVEL

When I came to I was sitting up, tied to a chair. How original, I thought. I could taste something warm and salty, and I felt sticky and achey all over. It was a vaguely post-coital sensation, at least until the pain set in, which didn't take long. Whoever had worked me over knew what they were doing, and were conscientious about it. A professional. That was a reassuring initial sign - a sloppy, overzealous amateur might've killed or at least crippled me by accident. As far as I could tell, all my vital signs were in order, and nothing felt permanently broken. Not yet. Then my bleary eyes confirmed the fact I was still in my hotel room, because I recognized the tacky wallpaper, so the perpetrator was no doubt close by, just out of my damaged range of vision. I strained my neck around but the agony aborted the attempt at a 180 or even 90-degree angle head turn. "*Shit*!" I said, and then I heard motion behind me. On the bed. Someone had been resting, waiting for me to wake up. My chair was in a corner facing the wall, like I was a dunce or something. Or a bad boy.

The footsteps were surprisingly light, especially since I was expecting a goombah to show his smug mug any second now, slap me around a little more, maybe cut my ear off and whisper sweet nothings into it, telling my good ear he saw that in a movie once. But why? What information did I have anyone would torture me for? I was the one looking for clues. Then that was it. I'd stepped on some shiny Florsheim toes. Mob.

Wrong. *Way* wrong.

It was Dolly.

"Hello. My name is Pussy Galore," she said with a smirk, at least in my battered brain. Everything is a movie with me. In actuality, I don't think she said anything.

"I must be dreaming," I naturally responded anyway. But this wasn't *Goldfinger*. It was real life. So real it hurt.

She leaned over and planted one on me, right on my bruised lips. I tasted the familiar sweetness of those long lost lips, and I pined for more, despite the fact that she was picking pieces of my cracked flesh and dried blood off her chin. "That hurt. Do it again," I said.

"Should I untie you first, or would you prefer I left you that way? The possibilities tempt me, even in your condition."

"Kinky, but there are a few things I want to clear up first. Like why did you beat me and tie me up? Your idea of kicks? You were never that adventurous when we were dating."

"Not with you!" Then she whispered in my ear, "Just kidding," and untied me. The knots were pretty damned tight, but she had been in the girl scouts, so she managed finally. I slumped forward into her arms and she helped me to the bed. From what I could tell, what with my confusion and shock and pain and all, she looked great, her face still pretty and smooth, her pin-up figure still intact, dressed in pink and white like she was going a church social. But at the moment, the inexplicable nature of her sudden appearance, under these circumstances, superseded my appraisal of her sex appeal. Nothing immediately added up, and it was bugging me in a big way, ruining our reunion, at least for me. Dolly herself seemed downright jolly.

I let out a groan as I lay back, rigid muscles relaxing slowly under her ginger massage. She kept running to the bathroom for cold compresses and stuff, and then I noticed she had a medical bag with her, filled with first aid knickknacks, like she was anticipating just such an occasion. "I don't get it," I said. "First you whip me senseless, then you fix me up. Is this like breaking up just to make up, in a perverted kinda way? Please, Dolly, stop for a second and give me some answers. *Please*."

"Well, now just lay back and relax, and I'll tell you what I know. First of all, I showed up here hoping to surprise you. It was dark down in the lobby, no one was around, so I remembered your room number from our phone conversation and snuck upstairs and was going to knock on your door when I saw it was slightly ajar, so then—*careful* now, relax, remember I'm a registered nurse, or would be if I practiced. So anyway, I walked in, turned on the light, and there you were, tied up to that chair, bleeding, so I ran downstairs and got my stuff, which I brought with me because I told Donald I was going to visit my sick sister in Queens and was going to save her a trip to the doctor, and idiot he is, he bought it. But as it turns out, my lie worked out for the best. *Weird*, huh?"

"Understatement of the year, or week, at least. It's been a weird coupla days already. So, you call the cops?"

"No, think I should?"

"Dolly, are you serious? Someone broke in here and

ambushed me and tied me up? Why? What's missing?"

"I don't know what you brought, plus I didn't check. Vic, I just got here, remember."

"You seem to be taking this well enough."

She bent over and kissed me again. "It's so, so good to see you, in any shape. Under the bruises you look as handsome as ever, you devil."

I brushed her aside, now wearing only my pants since she had stripped off my blood-soaked shirt and socks, and took a gander at myself in the mirror. "I look like hell. Who did this, Dolly? And why just leave me tied up? What's the fuckin' point?"

"Vic, you're just upset."

"Goddamn *right* I'm upset! Jesus Christ, Dolly! Look at me! And you—you look *terrific*. A little *blonder* than I remember."

She got up from the bed and walked up to me and put her arms around my sore neck and kissed me again. "Vic, you just don't know how good it is to see you again. I'm just mixed up, I'm sorry. Between you suddenly calling me and then I couldn't wait for our rendezvous so I made up that lie and I drive up to surprise you and now *this*. I'm so sorry. Maybe I should go until you work this out." She was sobbing now. Broads. Nothin' like 'em.

"No, no. It's good to see you too, no matter what." Then I kissed her back, and the missing years meant nothing, including the people in them, like Donald. Hell, pain-racked as I was, I was ready to make love to her right there, but she led me back to the bed, sat me down, and picked up the phone.

"What're you doing?"

"Calling 911. You need an ambulance, I guess. I can only do so much. Your ribs are badly bruised, maybe cracked, and you have a slight concussion, I think. Plus, you're right, we have to call the cops. I wasn't thinking clearly. I just wanted to get you alone for a minute before they took you away from me. It's been so *long*."

"There, there. Stop crying now. *Ssshhh*." I took the phone from her and hung it up. "I don't need no stinking badges," I said, and she giggled slightly, that little girl giggle that always killed me. Then I kissed her again and started unbuttoning her pink blouse, but she stopped me, pointing out the ring on her finger.

"Maybe I should take it off first," she said with a wicked, lascivious grin. "I don't want to hurt you any more than you already are by scratching your back up with it."

I was dumbstruck as much by my boldness as hers. Innocence

lost. Good riddance. The way I figured it, I'd already paid for what I was about to do, sort of a pre-punishment plan. She removed the ring, put it in on the bedside table, then finished unbuttoning her blouse herself while I watched. She stood up, took it off, cast it aside, slipped out of her skirt, kicked it away, sat on the bed beside me, removed her nylons slowly, seductively, kicked off her high-heeled shoes, then the nylons, then she stood up again, unhooked her bra, slid it around my throbbing head like a silk serpent before letting it slither down to my lap, laid me back, gingerly climbed on top of me, kissed my face and neck ever so gently, then my chest which was now washed and shiny, then my belly which I sucked in a bit, partly out of sexual excitement and partly out of embarrassment, whispering, "No washboard stomach, just wash*tub*, maybe," but she was too into what she was doing to acknowledge my humble mumble, too busy unbuttoning my trousers, then slipping them halfway down my legs before taking my man-tool into her mouth and sucking it till I came in a delirious spasm down her throat.

I closed my eyes and sighed, my pain temporarily forgotten. Some nursing school she must've gone to. Bedside manners like that could make hospital stays much more tolerable, even popular. She climbed back up and said, "You're not finished yet, handsome. *My* turn." Then she wiggled out of her pink little panties and sat on my tender face. "*Eat me!*" she demanded. "God, Vic, *please*! I want you *now*!"

My words were a bit muffled as I said, "I want you to, Dolly, but lie down and let me do it to you like I always wanted. This is like high school, and that's good, but I want to finally consummate our, *whatever*."

I could say no more, because her wet, juicy muff was thrust onto my mouth as she balanced herself against the headboard and gyrated her hips, directing, no, demanding my lips and tongue to kiss and lick her starving snatch. I grabbed her luscious thighs and held them firmly as I strained my aching neck and brought her to orgasm in record time, attributable as much to her horniness as my expertise. Then the next thing I knew we were lying side by side, panting, sweating, our bodily fluids mingling, including my blood, since our frenetic erotic activities had reopened a few of the wounds she had dressed. She just kissed my cuts and licked the blood away like a voracious vampire. Good thing I'd tested negative, and at the moment I assumed she was safe, being married and all, plus a nurse. This wasn't the old Dolly, not by a long shot. It was the new Dolly, and I was so glad to meet her.

As she sat up and took a cigarette out of her purse and lit it, I glanced over at the bedside clock. It was nearly 4AM.

"How the hell long was I out?" I said, sitting up and feeling instantly dizzy. "Jesus, it's morning practically."

"Well, I got here around an hour ago, so I don't know. When did you get beat up? Remember?" She leaned back and snuggled her head against my neck. Her tousled hair smelled perfumed and feminine. I was so easily distracted, so weak when it came to women. I hadn't changed at all. "Hey, what are you thinking?" she said, snapping me out of my trance, blowing her smoke in the air above us.

"Hm? Nothin', I dunno. Just—I never did it with a married woman before."

"I'm not just a married woman, I'm your ex-girlfriend. We didn't do anything we haven't done already, anyway. What's the difference? Wasn't it *wonderful*?" She sighed, kissing my neck. "I want some more. I love the *taste* of you."

"Yeah, well, cigarette smoke makes me sick." I forced myself to sit upright. She sat up with me, her small but perky breasts erect and covered with a fine mist of sexual residue. The smell of her made me crave her all the more. It was a mix of perfume and sweat and come. Her toes were painted red, tucked up next to her heart-shaped ass. I grew dizzy with desire, but the pain was making a comeback as well. My head hurt. I needed medical attention. I rose from the bed and paced in agony as she just smoked and watched me. So cool. So casual. I just didn't understand it.

"I got slugged by a gun when I walked in around seven or so," I said as I paced. "I saw it coming at me out of the darkness just before it hit me, then I felt the first few blows before I went out. The shadow in the room was *big*. A dude, definitely."

She smiled. "See? Feel better now? Once it comes back to you you'll be able to go get 'em. And I'll wait right here till you do, tough guy."

I looked at her, illuminated by the weak lamplight, her clothes strewn across the floor, nude except for some covers pulled over a portion of her hips, smoking away. Then I realized smoking was prohibited in the rooms, but I didn't say anything to her. Waylaying patrons was probably against the rules too, but that didn't stop anybody from doing it. And where was the desk clerk, anyway? "You say you didn't see anyone downstairs when you came in?"

"No, but it was like three or so in the morning, so maybe there *isn't* a graveyard shift."

"Yeah, there is. 'Round the clock. Told me when I checked in. I didn't even see anyone when I walked in early this evening. Strange. Maybe somebody told them to take a break. This joint is probably run by the Mob still, so—*damn*. Maybe they are responsible for taking out my old man after all, and my pals in San Francisco just tossed me a red herring for some fucked-up reason. Shit. None of this makes any sense. I hate things that don't make sense—*ouch*."

"Come here," she cooed, patting the mattress with a come-hither pout like I was a cat or something. A cat. God, I missed Puss. I fell back onto the bed with a moan, and she massaged and kissed me from head to toe. I looked at her ring on the bedside table and felt a pang of guilt, so I did the only thing I could under the circumstances: I turned away from the ring and watched Dolly smother my beaten body with TLC. "I'm so happy to see you," she said as she patched me back up with bandages and stinging liquids from her medicine bag. "I've felt so trapped for so long, hoping a handsome stranger would come along and rescue me, and one day the phone rings and here you are."

"Dolly, *ow*, why not just, *ouch,* like, *divorce* the sonovabitch. If I'd known you were *this* miserable I would've come back a long time ago."

"Well, I need to figure out what I'm going to do first. Woman cannot live on alimony alone."

"What d'ya mean? You got a nursing degree, right? Use it. Dump the asshole and break free. We could—" I stopped. What was I saying? Did I love Dolly, or was I just being sentimental and horny as usual? Did I really want to sacrifice my independence and drag Dolly around with me? I looked at her smooth ivory breasts and thighs and tousled dirty blond hair and big brown eyes and painted toenails and did a quick mental comparison test with my lonely lifestyle. *Nolo contendre.*

"We could *what*, Vic? Run away together?"

"Well, let's not get carried away. I don't want you to do anything for me. Do it for yourself. And then, when you're free. We'll see."

She sighed and lay beside me, still smoking despite my claim of disdain for the stuff, but blowing it away from us, toward the cracked ceiling stained with God's urine. "He won't ever set me free, Vic. I don't know what to do, except *this*. Cheat."

My heart stopped for a few panicky seconds, then resumed with staccato enthusiasm. "H-how many guys you do this with, Dolly?"

She glared at me with chilling resentment. "You saying I'm a slut, Vic? Is *that* what you're saying? Well, fuck you. You're the one with my juice all over your chin, Mister Morality." She got up and started getting dressed with indignant urgency, muttering as she went. "I thought you'd understand, of all people. I'm so sick of self-righteous judgmental small-minded bigots I could scream, but you—I thought you'd be *different*, Mister Worldly. Mister Man About Town."

"*Mister Lonely,*" I sang, a la Bobby Vinton, but she didn't crack a smile. Women. "Dolly, what the hell? I just asked you if you sought consolation in other men's arms over the past ten years, that's all. I was a long time coming, sweetheart, remember."

"Not *that* long, Quickdraw McGraw." Now she had her skirt back on. I reached over and grabbed her and pulled her toward me and began kissing her nipples with hungry intensity. She slapped me and continued dressing. I cried out in exaggerated pain and stopped her cold. "*Oohhh*, I'm sorry, honey." She sat on my lap and kissed me. "Just don't *judge* me, all right?" She tweaked my cheek then pinched my chin and stared into my eyes seriously. "*Ever*," she said with emphasis.

"Deal. But, are you gonna answer my question or not?"

She stood back up in a huff. "I'm going to see my sister now. Donald might call there in the morning."

"Doesn't he *trust* you?"

"Yeah, but I told him to call me there just in case. I just wanted to see you first, catch you off-base."

"Congratulations. That you did, baby cakes. You and someone else."

"Vic, I want you to promise me something."

"Maybe. What?"

"I *mean* it now. Don't mess with those guys. The Mafia. They mean *business*. This was just a message to back off. Let's leave stinky old Brooklyn and go someplace else, like Florida. Then maybe San Francisco, after this has blown over and they forget about you. Promise?"

"Wait, promise to which one? That's a lot of requests, sweetheart. For one thing, what makes you so sure this was Mob?"

"Well, I should've shown you sooner, but..." She finished buttoning her pink blouse as she rummaged in her purse and produced a rumpled piece of paper with some writing scrawled on it. She handed it to me with a petulant expression on her face. Then she went to the bathroom to fix her face as I read the words: "*Go back to fairyland, faggot. Daddy doesn't want you to join him yet. Signed, you know who.*"

Junior? No way. But the "fairyland" crack traced it to him. Maybe.

I walked into the bathroom where Dolly was brushing her teeth. She said through the foam, "Maybe I should take a shower, now that I think about it. I smell like I've been having sex all night. Not that my sister cares, she knows it wouldn't be Donald, but still, what if someone *else* shows up, like my *mother*? Yeah, shower for sure. You read your little note?"

"My 'little note'? Yeah, Dolly, I read my little god damn note. Where'd you get this?"

"Well, it was stuck in the ropes they tied you up in. I took it out and, there it is."

"*Why the hell didn't you show me this sooner?*" I exploded, grabbing her wrist and twisting it.

"*Ow!*" She tried to twist free, couldn't, then tried to slap me with her free hand, but I caught it mid-swing and held both arms pat.

"Tell me what you know, damn it. I didn't fly out here just to see you, you know. What the hell's going on, Dolly? What do you know?"

She pulled free because I let her, then she sat on the toilet and sulked. "All I know is someone called me in Jersey and told me, better tell your boyfriend to watch out, or else, then they hung up. They said you were askin' too many questions, said curiosity killed the cat and so you better stop pussyfooting around. This was this afternoon, around three. So I tried calling you but you were out, so I called my sister, arranged this pretense for a visit, and rushed up to warn you in person, but they got to you first."

"*Who*, Dolly? Who got to me? *Mob*?"

She shrugged. "I guess so," she said in a small voice. "They didn't really say. But who else? Teamsters?" Then she started crying again, cradling herself in her arms and rocking back and forth on the toilet. "I'm scared, Vic. Let's get out of here, okay? It's just not worth it. I was scared to untie you until I was sure they were gone. Truth is—truth is, I saw someone coming out of your room, two big guys, never saw them before, didn't really look at their faces though, just as I was coming up the stairs, and they

206

walked right past me, but I didn't look at them, didn't make eye contact, just acted like a tenant minding her own business, going to her own room. Then when I heard them go down the stairs, I snuck back into your room, turned on the light, and sat on the bed for a minute to think about what to do, and the very next instant, you woke up. I had the note in my hand and when I saw you stir I stuck it in my purse so you wouldn't freak out. Now, I don't know what to do. Oh, Vic, hold me. Please hold me..."

I held her. She made me help her undress, and I was still naked, so we both got into the shower and washed off the smell of our sins. We took our time, sponging the other one off, making love—though she still wouldn't let me enter her—without speaking. Then we got out and put towels around us and lay on the bed and watched dawn break through the curtains, silently wondering what to do next.

"Donald won't ever set me free," she whispered finally, in an ominous tone. I didn't know what to say. Then she sighed sadly and said, in a monotone, "I have to go to my sister's now."

I watched her get dressed for a second time. "The postman ain't gonna ring twice at *my* door, Dolly, no matter what, so in case you're thinking along those lines. Forget it."

Her brow was wrinkled as she put on her shoes. "Huh? What are you *talking* about? What postman? You need sleep, dear." She leaned over and kissed me, looking into my eyes with an odd expression of sadness, which I attributed to her own sleepiness and disorientation, then she went into the bathroom to fix her face for real this time.

"Call your sister, tell her to cover for you," I called after her.

"No, she wants to see me too," Dolly called back.

"See her later. I've waited longer, I deserve you more."

"I'll be back, or I'll meet you somewhere. But not here. It's not safe, Vic."

"Well, I'll meet you anywhere, but I'm not leaving till I settle this. Screw the goombahs." I waited for a response but there was none so I went on. "Dolly, I went to visit my mother coupla days ago. She won't even talk. She's like in a waking coma or something. My old man's death did that to her. I have to find out for sure who did it, and why, and my leads tell me the Mob is in the clear for sure. Someone wants me to think it's Mob, so I'll lay off. But no dice. I'm doing this for Ma. I need to go up there and tell her it's over, she can wake up now, nightmare's over. And *then* I can deal with you and me. Ya understand that? Dolly? *Dolly*!"

I got up and went into the bathroom. Dolly had slit one wrist under the faucet and was slumped over the sink, barely conscious.

Chapter Six
ANGEL WITH AN ANGLE

I carried Dolly into the emergency room at Brooklyn Hospital like a monster bearing his bride to (or from) the crypt. I was in bad enough shape, but Dolly had a towel wrapped around her wrist and was hardly breathing, so the doctors and nurses tended to her first. Then they cleaned up and bandaged me again, fed me, and I felt good as new in an hour or so, so I got up out of my bed after a short nap and wandered around, looking for Dolly. A nurse ordered me back to bed but I ignored her. I had to make sure Dolly was all right or else I couldn't relax. Also, I had to know why she had done something so drastic and stupid. Donald? Me? Something she wasn't telling me? I badly needed rest and I was delirious and feverish, but driven by adrenaline and anxiety. Later I'd collapse and sleep for a month, but before I did, I had to speak with Dolly.

None of this made sense. I needed to talk to Doc for an objective viewpoint real soon, but at the moment I was stranded in my own homeland, which never felt so foreign to me as it did that day, wandering the halls of the hospital, calling Dolly's name.

I collapsed in one of those hallways and woke up back in my room. I immediately got up and went to the door but it was locked. I went back to my bed and pushed the nurse button several times before I got a response. A typical overworked, no-nonsense middle-aged type showed up, already sighing at the prospect of dealing with me.

"Am I a prisoner now? Let me outta this joint already," I told her. "I'll be swell. Really. I got important business to tend to on the outside."

"The doctor recommends you spend the night," the nurse said to me in a schoolteacher tone. "Now please lie down and relax. Please."

"Yeah? What if I told you I had no dough or insurance? Bet the ol' doc would recommend I take a hike, right?"

"This is a county hospital, Mister Valentine, don't worry about it."

"How'd you know my name?"

"You wrote it on the admission sheet, remember?"

"No, I don't, matter of fact. What's goin' on here?"

"Well, then maybe your friend did it."

"Friend? What friend?"

"The one visiting Ms. Dunlap now."

That did it. I tore past the nurse and out into the hallway, grabbing anyone with a nametag and demanding to know the whereabouts of Dolly Duncan Dunlap. An eager intern who didn't know any better directed me to her room.

I burst into her room and there was Dolly sitting up laughing and having a good old time. Seated beside her was some well-dressed goombah that reminded me a little of old time actor Steve Cochran, tall, dark, and devilishly handsome, with a killer grin, literally. My mind did some paranoiac acrobatics as I stood there in my gown, attempting to sort out the sordid details of the scene.

"*Vic!*" Dolly exclaimed, reaching out for a hug. Her arm was bandaged and she looked wan, but surprisingly radiant. I didn't approach her, just stood there obviously waiting for a formal introduction to the stranger, who stood up and walked over to me instead, killer grin still on his swarthy kisser, and hugged me tight as a grizzly.

"Meet me outside, we'll talk," he whispered into my ear, giving me an extra squeeze that seemed to mean "or else." The offer sounded more like a threat, so I obliged. I waved weakly at Dolly, who waved back with a bemused look on her face, then I stepped out into the hallway. Surprisingly, no doctors or nurses accosted me and demanded I return to my room. That cinched it. Steve Cochran was Mob, maybe the guy who brained me. And he was Dolly's pal. Whatever.

He stepped out, smiling at Dolly, then shut the door, grabbed me by the lapels, and threw me up against the opposite wall, nearly mowing down a couple of interns, who stepped aside like they were avoiding an out-of-control steamroller pushing a pile of manure. "Just stay out of this, buddy. You got that? What's between Dolly and me is between us. Got it, slick?"

I was blushing and barely breathing, but I managed to mutter, "How about letting me down so we can converse like two civilized adults? I understand now you're quite virile, but really, this whole display was unnecessary. All right, Tarzan?"

Slowly he released me. As I slid down the wall my gown slid up my keester, so when I was on my feet again I had to pull it down like I was adjusting my summer dress in the breeze, Marilyn standing over the subway. How embarrassing. But none of the passers-by, in-house or otherwise, seemed to notice or care. The big ape kept attention at bay rather than attracted it. Mob. Then again, this was New York, famous for people minding their own business. And up close he didn't seem so Italian, just tan.

"First of all, I don't even know who the hell you are," I said. "What's your name, anyway?"

"What's it to you?" he said with gruff snootiness.

"Tell me yours I'll tell you mine."

"I already know your name, Vic Valentine."

"See? Now is that fair? C'mon."

"Fuck you. Beat it."

Now I was getting pissed. "Oh yeah? Well, Fuck You Beat It, if that's what you call yourself, I got business with Dolly, whether you like it or not."

"She doesn't want to see you. Beat it before I get rough."

"Look, just who the hell *are* you anyway?"

He grabbed me by the throat and lifted me back up against the wall, but by now I was fed up and simply kneed him in the groin. He folded like a lawn chair and I ran into Dolly's room.

She hugged me and kissed me and all that, and I asked her how she was and she said much better, thank you, that she was really embarrassed and all but now everything was hunky dory again, then after the preliminaries I cut to the chase. "Who's the big palooka shoving me around and telling me to blow?"

"Who? Petey?"

"Petey? That guy's name is Petey?"

She giggled. "Well, I call him Petey. But everyone else calls him Pete the Meat."

I gulped. "Why? He hung like a horse?"

She grimaced. "How nasty, Vic, I'm surprised at you. No, his last name is Cleaver. So they call him Pete the Meat or something."

"Pete the Meat *Cleaver*. Right. No relation to the Beaver, I take it. So why are you hanging out with mobsters all of a sudden?"

"What? Petey's no mobster, Vic. He's just a guy from a well-off family in Jersey. His father is like a politician or something, owns a lot of businesses in Wildwood and Atlantic City. Petey knows Donald, even. They belong to the same golf club. I met him in college in Philly. We've been friends for years. He's the one who drove me up. Wasn't that nice of him? He lives in Cherry

Hill."

Just then Pete the Meat grabbed me from behind by the straps of my gown and looked ready to slug me when a nurse walked in and screamed. The nurse ran out, and Petey calmed down, walking briskly over to Dolly's bed and holding her hand warmly.

"I tried to get rid of this joker, but he hit me below the belt," Pete the Meat said sweetly. "Wait'll I get him outside, though," he added, manfully glaring my way.

Dolly playfully slapped Pete the Meat on his muscle-bound arm. "Oh, Petey, I wasn't talking about him. He's not the one to worry about."

"He's not?"

"No, no, silly. I said he's the one who got beat up. Vic Valentine is my dear friend from California. We need to protect him. He doesn't want to hurt me, Mister Tough Guy." They were so cuddly I felt as if I were intruding. I pinched myself to make sure I wasn't in a coma or something.

"Pete the Meat, huh," I said. "No wonder you wouldn't tell me your name."

Pete the Meat was all smiles now. He walked over to me and held out his hand, and when I was reluctant to respond he simply grabbed my hand and shook the shit of it. "Sorry about that, Vic. Got you mixed up with somebody else, I guess. Dolly was kind of out of it when she told me about you. I thought youse was the guy I was supposed to *look* out for, not *watch* out for. Fine line."

"Huh? *What* guy?" I said.

"The guys who are looking for you, you know, the ones who beat you up," Dolly whispered, looking at me with a play-along-for-now look. "I was afraid they'd come looking for us here in the hospital. Petey's my bodyguard now, sorta. Yours too. I told the doctor he was our friend. So keep your voice down."

Pete the Meat looked puzzled now too. "Hey, what's goin' on here really, Dolly? Who is this joker to you, anyway?"

"I'm her lover," I said in order to provoke a truthful reaction instead of the charade they were giving me now.

They both froze, then Dolly startled me with a sudden, shrill laugh. "Oh, Vic. You're such a card. Stop it."

Pete the Meat wasn't convinced though. "That right? You fuckin' Dolly, you sick bastard? Your own friggin' flesh and blood?" he said, moving towards me with malice on his mind.

"She's married, pal," I said. "I was just kiddin.' And I don't know what flesh and blood you're talkin' about." He looked at me, then at Dolly, then back at me, very nonplussed. "Um, you mind if I speak to Dolly alone for a minute, Petey? After all, she was with me when this happened."

"When what happened?" Pete the Meat said, his face still twisted with confusion, his deep-sunk dark eyes glassy and dangerous. "You mean in the shower?"

I had no idea what he was talking about, and didn't care. Then Dolly said sweetly, "Petey. Please. Five minutes. Vic saved my life. He's a true friend. C'mon now, Petey. I'll be fine."

She was practically talking putrid baby talk now, coaxing Petey like he was her son. Or lover. I was as confused about him as he was about me, maybe more, but I acted suave to keep the situation from exploding. Pete the Meat was a volatile individual. That aspect of his personality was clear, at least.

Sulking, Pete the Meat nodded and stepped out petulantly. "I'll just be outside the door here," he said, shooting me a cautionary look.

I winked at him and grinned flirtatiously, but he was too mad or dense to appreciate the sarcasm. Then I got cozy with Dolly and said seriously, "Dolly. Maybe I'm still a little dizzy from getting my head bashed in, so pardon me if I'm a little slow on the uptake here, but just who is this asshole, and why is he here?"

"Oh Vic. I do believe you're jealous."

"Damn it, Dolly, don't give me any Scarlett O'Hara southern belle shit, just be straight with me. That guy connected?"

"Connected?"

"Is he, you know. *Mob*."

"Vic, I told you. He's just a guy. A rich boy. Playboy. All he does is drive speedboats and play polo. He's harmless. But his dad is a bigwig who may know people, I don't know. I thought he could help us, maybe get these goons off your back, so I brought him along. He's big, too, knows karate and all, so I thought he could protect you, not that you can't handle yourself, but two's better than one, right? But he was too late, obviously. He dropped me off out front of the hotel then went to his friend's house in Manhattan, or so he told me, but really, he was waiting downstairs in the car the whole night and followed us to the hospital. The big teddy bear. He's so protective over me! Oh, and I told him you were my cousin, so don't blow my cover. Okay?"

"Oh, yeah? Well, something tells me he ain't buying that story anyway, which is good, far as I'm concerned, cause I don't understand why he has to think that to begin with, and why does he have a moniker like Pete the Meat? Tell me that."

"It's from college football. He only got into school on an athletic scholarship, since he is no intellectual, didn't even graduate, the bum. Anyway, he used to block tackle and he cut through the other team like a cleaver, so it stuck. What's the big deal? And Petey doesn't know that I, you know. He couldn't handle that. So I told him I slipped in the bathtub while shaving my legs. Calm down."

"Well, shit, whatever. What about your sister, anyway? You get in touch with her?"

Dolly looked down with a very guilty expression. She was even biting her lower lip.

"Dolly—? What will your sister think if she doesn't hear from you? She'll call *Donald*."

"Vic. *Stop*. I have a small confession to make. I don't know where my sister is. We haven't spoken in years. Last I heard she got married and moved to D.C."

"So, wait. I don't get it. Why would Donald believe that story?"

"Oh Vic." She started sobbing again. "I'm sorry. I should have been more honest with you from the start. I—I *left* Donald. I just left him a letter telling him I needed time to think about our lives and I'd get in touch with him later. I told him I'd call him when he got back from Chicago, so he'd have time to think too. But Vic, I'm just afraid he'll wig out and not give me a divorce and kill me or something. That's why—that's why I tried to end it, just like that. I'm so, so sorry Vic. You shouldn't have been put through this. I just slashed one wrist on a whim sort of, I've tried killing myself a lot of different ways before, but never with a razor, and there it was, your razor I mean, and I never thought of doing it at home because we have such a nice, expensively tiled bathroom and I didn't want to ruin it in case I lived, but there in your dingy little room, I thought, what the hell, but then immediately regretted it and...oh, Vic, I'm just a mess! Hold me, please. Just hold me."

Then she cried and cried in my arms and Pete the Meat and two doctors and a gang of nurses came in and separated us and I was led back to my room, where I was formally discharged and ordered to leave the hospital. Two burly security guards offered to escort me to the closest exit, but I said I'd be nice and cooperative. They wanted to hold Dolly for further observation for at least twenty-four hours, and were considering detaining her in the psycho ward if the mental evaluation warranted it. It was S.O.P. and there was nothing I could do about it. I scouted around in vain for Petey before I walked out of the hospital and climbed into my rented Comet, but then I just returned to The Honeymooner and slept on everything Dolly had told me. I can't remember clearly, but I think I had nightmares of the Alfred Hitchcock variety.

The sun was shining into my room when I heard a persistent knock on the door around noon the next day. I'd slept all night and into the following morning. I felt hung-over and groggy when I opened the door. I wasn't thinking clearly or I would've asked who it was first. After all, it could've been my friends from the other night, back to polish me off. It was Pete the Meat.

"Got a message for you from Dolly," he said flatly. Before I could even reply he went on, "She says to pick her up at the hospital in an hour."

"They're letting her *go*?"

"Dolly said you was smart."

"So what about you?"

"Oh, I'll be around. Don't worry. From now on." Then he turned and walked down the wall. I was too muddle-minded to follow and interrogate him any further. I just shut the door and went into the bathroom to wash up.

Ten minutes later I was in the shower and someone was pounding on the god damn door again. Jesus Fucking Christ. I almost hoped it was my pals back to 86 me. I was tired and yearned for a peaceful prone position. I whipped the door open with an attitude and Dolly jumped into my arms.

"*Surprise!*" she said, kissing me all over. "I couldn't wait so I got a cab. They released me under my own recognizance or whatever. Petey signed some papers for my release, so you don't have to. God, you'd think I was posting bail or something! They make such a big deal out of these things." She was pacing the room now, peppy and full of energy, which wasn't contagious. "Before, whenever I tried to off myself they didn't really give a shit down in Jersey, probably cause my shrink told 'em I was only doing it for attention and after a while they got sick of me I guess. Well, anyway, I'm starving. Wanna eat, hm?"

I was firm but gentle. "Dolly, just sit down and relax for a second, okay? I'm going to get dressed and then we're going to have a nice little pow-wow here and now before we go one step further. Okay?"

She just looked at me and nodded with wide-eyed little girl acquiescence. Our reunion was wearing me out. What the hell had I been thinking? I was paying for our infidelity already, before and after the actual act. Was it worth it? I recalled her sitting on my face and wiggling with delight and decided it was. Heaven help me, I'm so weak. Pussy is like kryptonite to me.

I toweled off and shaved and then got dressed and felt cleaner and better than I'd felt in what seemed ages. My abrasions only bothered me like a workout at the gym would if I ever went, so I ignored it. Besides, my body aches had overwhelming competition for my attention.

"So," I said, sitting beside her on the bed, "you lied to me about lying to Donald about your sister. You say you're leaving Donald for good but you're afraid of him. And out of nowhere comes this palooka whom you claim is your platonic bodyguard, but you tell him I'm your cousin. Now, how do I know what's the truth and what isn't?"

She shrugged. "Believe what you want. Petey's a trusted old friend who helped me get out of Jersey, and I told him I was going to stay with my poor cousin in Brooklyn, who was in the red with some loan sharks. If I hadn't said that, he wouldn't have driven me. Okay?"

"Like that's hard. Leaving New Jersey. People do it everyday, and most would rather not come back."

"Including me. But I don't have any of my stuff because I left so impetuously, before Donald got home from work. I'm going back to the house while Donald's in Chicago so I can get some clothes and things and then, y'know."

"Then what?"

"Well, that depends on you."

"Dolly, I told you—you need to do this for yourself, not me or Petey or anyone else." She hit my arm. "Vic! Petey and I are just friends, I *told* you!"

"Who said otherwise?"

"I can tell what you're thinking. Stop it. Just stop it. I'm mixed up enough. I mean, Petey and I fooled around a little in college, but that was before Donald proposed."

"You've *slept* with that gorilla!"

"A long time ago, forget it! Vic, please, I've had a hard night with all these tests and shit. Please. Let's just go back to New Jersey."

"*Whoa.* You want me to *go* with you?"

"How do you expect me to get there? I told you, Petey drove me. Donald could have me tracked in our car, someone could spot it and identify me. I'm like a fugitive, Vic."

"Well, can't Petey the getaway driver take you back? I'm busy here, Dolly."

"I thought you came back to see me!"

"I did, but not *just*."

"Well, what *else* is there?"

"What else is there? Shit, Dolly, I told you. I need to find out who killed my father. Not just for me, but for my mother's sake, poor thing. I can't just leave her up there like that. I need to help her by giving this thing a sense of closure."

"Vic, are you serious? After the Mafia practically killed you! And you want to go through with that? It's obvious it was the Mafia, Vic. And you can't take them on. It's been tried by like the FBI and all, and who are you? Case closed. But no, you have to play Mister Detective, while my life is falling apart right in front of you. I'm alive, Vic! You can save me, or desert me and then whatever happens will be on your head. See if you can live with that. It's too late for your father and mother and brother, Vic, but you can still help me, someone who is still alive who really loves and needs you, someone who is in deep trouble, who has no one else."

"All *right*! *Fuck*! Just shut *up* for a minute!" I stood up and paced. "What's with the guilt trip here, Dolly? I mean, what would you have done if I'd never called you? *Huh*?"

"Probably kept trying to kill myself till I succeeded, I don't know. All I know is seeing you has given me the strength to finally stand up for myself."

"With my help."

"Well *excuse* me! If that's asking too much, go play 'Green Hornet' till the fucking cows come home for all I care!" She got and was about to storm out. I didn't stop her. She went to the door and then in frustration kicked it savagely. I walked over to her and put a hand on her shoulder. At first she faked a recoil but then she made an about face and put her arms around my neck like a noose. "I'm sorry, Vic. Everything's so mixed up. Now that Petey's left me I'm all alone."

"What? He was just here."

"I know, but I bumped into him in the lobby and we had a fight and he left without me back to Jersey or wherever. His girlfriend is probably pissed at him anyway. She *hates* me."

"Wait, wait, *wait*. He has a *girlfriend*?"

"Several. They *all* hate me, for no apparent reason. I suppose he just goes for insecure women for some reason. Beats me. So now you see why I need you to go back to Jersey with me and pack a suitcase so we can go to Florida."

"Florida? What the hell's in Florida?"

"My sister. She'll help us."

"What? I thought you said you didn't know where your sister was?"

"Well, I meant we haven't spoken in a while. You remember Cecilia, right? Well, Sissy is divorced herself and living in Miami now, so I'll call her and explain the situation and hopefully she'll let us stay with her until we get situated."

"Hey, hey, hey. Slow down and stop a minute here. You're assuming way too god damn much here. First of all, I have no intention of going to Miami. You also said you'd heard Sissy was still married in D.C. now but I'm too fuckin' tired to follow that up, so I'll let it go for now. But my life is in San Francisco, and after I finish my business here, I'm going back. For good. I've decided Thomas Wolfe was right on the money."

"Huh? Who? Tommy Wolf? Who's that? Guy in our math class?"

"No. Forget it. How can we get along if you don't get any of my literary or cinematic references? It'll never work. Now, I'll put you on a train for Jersey, call your sister, and then call me from Miami, okay?"

She looked at me for a tragic moment and then got down on her knees, holding my legs and crying. "Vic, please. Please. Just drive down with me and help me pack. After all, it's your fault Petey left me stranded anyway."

"Huh? How come? Where do get that?"

"We fought because of you. I told him I was in love with you, that you weren't really my cousin, which he suspected anyway, and he got really really mad and said he didn't ever want to see me again and then he left."

I didn't know what to say. This was way more than I bargained for. I let out a deep sigh, then said hoarsely, "Okay, Dolly. I'll be your taxi, but not to Florida. I don't care who's trying to scare me off or why, I'm coming back to finger the person who iced my father, then I'm going back to see my mother and make her talk to me before I head back home. I miss my cat."

She was smiling now. She looked up at me, her cheeks

streaked with tears, and said, "Oh yeah? Does your cat do this to you?" Then she unzipped my pants and took me in her mouth and sucked me till I almost came. At the last second I pulled her upright and held her firmly by the shoulders.

"One little thing," I said. "If I do this for you, you have to do something for me."

"I thought I was."

"You know what I mean. In all the years I've known you, you've never let me put it in you. Why? You're not a virgin anymore. I assume your dentist drilled you, and you already told me about Pete the Meat."

"Petey never put it in me, either. And neither has Donald. That's why we have no children."

I let her go and stood back from her, my mouth wide open like my fly. "Why? Whom are you saving yourself for?"

"I won't know until I meet him," she said softly. "And even after I meet him, I'll need to know I can trust him first. With anything. With my life. Okay?" Then she got back on her knees and finished blowing me and I let her, coming all over her mouth and in her hair and eyes, and she laughed like a child in the rain.

Chapter Seven
OUT OF THE PAST AND INTO THE FRYING PAN

I just could *not* believe what I was about to do.

First, I called the Chipper Monks to make sure they had bought that Patsy Cline CD or tape for my mother. The receptionist or whoever left me on hold for a hundred hours while she checked on it, then returned and said sure they had, but so far my mother wasn't responding. I told her to keep up the musical therapy, around the clock, just let it play, and I'd be back in a few days or so to check up on her. Then I hung up.

Next, leaving Dolly, beaming victoriously, alone in my room, I went downstairs to check out and hand my key in. Some geeky bookwormish desk clerk was there, as usual when people were checking out in the morning and early afternoon. Good. I had a few questions for him.

"Hey, man, where you the other night? I came in early evening and no one was here. I thought this place had round the clock service."

"Um—*oh*. Our man was sick that evening, and we had no one to replace him. I'm terribly sorry if that inconvenienced you in any way. Why, did you need something?"

"No, but, hypothetical, say people came up to see me I didn't want to see, and no one was here to stop them."

"Then how would they know your room number, sir?"

"Don't get snotty, Pomeroy."

"My name isn't *Pomeroy*, sir."

"Well it *should* be Pomeroy. Anyway, yeah, how would people know where to find me if no one was here?"

"A minute ago you were worried they would be able to, now the issue is they wouldn't. I'm not following you I'm afraid. Is this a complaint or a game?"

"Neither, Pomeroy. I just want to know, in case I check back in like a day or two. Either way, if someone wants to see me or I don't want to see them, I need to know someone is *here*."

"Well, I'm afraid we're all booked up for the month anyway,

sir."

"Huh? *This* cheap dive? Get outta here."

"If that's your opinion of the place, why don't you check into the Ritz."

"You tryin' to say this place will be full tomorrow?"

"I'm afraid so, sir. A convention is in town."

"What? Who? The Raccoon Lodge?"

"How'd you know?"

"Well, say I'm a member."

"Then check with your lodge brothers, sir, maybe you can share a room, but as I said, we're full up. Now if you'll *excuse* me."

"I want a deduction for the other night. Some people were looking for me and didn't know my room."

"Then you should have given them your room number, sir. I'm so sorry. Please try us again next year." Then he went off in a huff.

Something was rotten in Brooklyn, all right. Someone definitely wanted me out of the picture. It had all the earmarks of a Mob deal but something was wrong with the picture. Dolly's story just didn't set well with me—none of them, that is—and Pete the Meat bothered me in a big way. I tried remembering the face of the lug who slugged me. It was dark, the shadow was big, and I sensed the presence of a companion, who seemed to be male as well, but maybe not. It was vague and hazy in my memory because my lights went out too quick to illuminate the situation. I hated to think it was Pete the Meat who slugged me. He was big enough. But what would be his motive?

Dolly.

But why would Dolly have him slug me, tie me up, write a phony note, make him leave, then wait till I woke up to patch me right back up? And Petey was obviously jealous of me. I could believe he would wait around for us downstairs all night, then follow us to the hospital. He had the aura of a dupe as well. Dolly was manipulating both of us. But why?

By the time I got back to my room, I was furious in my conviction that Dolly had, for some reason, set this whole thing up.

When I stormed into the room she hopped up to greet me, ready to leave, but instead I shut the door and balefully stared her down to size. She knew I meant business and she stared back with apprehension.

"Dolly, be straight with me right now or I swear to God, I'll *lose* it."

"Vic? What is it, honey? You all right?"

"Shut up. *Now*. The desk clerk told me the place is all booked up and I can't check back in. The other night I was pistol whipped by a big guy. You show up right after with a cockamamie story, then you distract me with your feminine wiles, then you pull that stunt and we take a trip to Emergency, where a big guy shows up all palsy-walsy with you. It doesn't take a detective to figure out he was the one who brained me. You're trying to get me out of here, out of Brooklyn, away from my business here. And I want to know why. *Now*."

She had started crying, of course, during my spiel, but I didn't let it stop me. She just looked at me for a moment like I had just pulled off my outer skin to reveal an alien lizard, then she lunged at me and started beating me around the chest and face, screaming as she did so, cussing me out and biting and scratching me while I tried to calm her down, putting my hand over her mouth, and trying to hold her flailing arms pat. It was like taming a wildcat, and I'm sure we aroused some interest from the neighbors, but I didn't care. Finally I busted the bronco babe and laid on top of her on the bed until she reluctantly succumbed.

Breathing heavily, I said, my face in hers, "Now, how am I supposed to interpret that? A confession? I hit a nerve, baby?"

She tried to bite my nose but I didn't let her. Then she spat at me and said, "*Fuck you, Vic*! *Fuck you*! After all I've told you, all I've been through! Don't take out your shit on me, goddamn it! Obviously you've been hurt but who hasn't, but fuck you if you think I'm going to be the scapegoat for all those other bitches in your life! It's *me*, Vic! *Dolly*! Remember? Not fucking Mata Hari! *Grow up*! This detective shit has ruined your brain! You live in a cartoon fantasy land, a paranoid old movie! If you don't trust me then to hell with you! And you wonder why I don't let you screw me. If you don't trust me why should I trust you? *Huh*? That's all you want from me, anyway, isn't it? You and all the other assholes in my life. But still, I was willing to take a leap of faith with you, because unlike you Vic I'm not hung up on the past. I still dream of a better future, and I thought maybe we could share one, the one we used to talk about when we were kids, but how stupid of me. At least this came out before we actually went through with it, thank God. Now get the fuck *off* of me. I want to leave. I'll take a fucking train after all. Who needs you or Petey or any of you assholes! Fuck *all* of you! Now get off, and not like you want to, either, I mean get off of me. *Now.* I mean it, I'll scream some more. *Now.*"

I didn't know what else to do. I got up and she jumped off the bed and straightened herself out and then marched for the door.

"Dolly," I said hoarsely. "Dolly. Please. Wait a second. I'm sorry."

"Too late," she said, door ajar, not looking at me. "You insulted me, Vic. I trusted you. Shit, I even drove all the way up to warn you, help you if I could, and in a weak moment I lost my head and nearly died, but I didn't go through with it because I knew, I thought, anyway, that I had a friend. Not Petey. He's just company. But you were *special*, Vic. Until just now. My God, how you've changed. You're even putting on weight, I noticed." *Ouch.* "But. you look the same, otherwise. Still handsome, sexy, but on the inside—wow. I guess that's what they call growing up. Getting jaded and cynical. You're just like everyone else after all. Goodbye, Vic." Then she went out the door and closed it behind her. I just stood there for a minute, waiting for her to come back in, then I ran downstairs. She was already climbing into a waiting taxi on the corner. I raced down the street and jumped in just as it was about to pull away.

"Vic, what are you doing?" Dolly gasped.

"Dolly, after all this time, I can't just leave it like this."

"Well, you blew it, not me."

"Give me another chance. Please. There's something I need to explain to you, why I'm this way. A lot's happened, you're right. Maybe I was projecting my own paranoid fears onto you, I don't know."

"Hey, Mac, this ain't friggin' Oprah," the cabbie said. "Meter's running, lady. Call it. Is Donahue going with us or what?"

Dolly considered for a tense moment. Then she gave me a certain look and I said, "Take us to the Bay Diner." So he did, making two bucks for his trouble. Over coffee and sandwiches I told Dolly all about Rose and Tommy Dodge, how this ballplayer (whom Pete the Meat reminded me of) hired me to find someone I had been looking for myself, but had given up on, and how after it had ended with me in the hospital and Rose long gone, I still wasn't sure whether she had set me up to begin with. I explained to Dolly that perhaps some residual bitterness remained, and that I would need time to trust someone I loved again. She lit up when I said that.

"Are you saying you *love* me, Vic?"

"Well, besides Valerie, or Rose or whatever her name is now, no one has touched me like you have. And I lost you just like I lost Valerie, and then got you back, briefly, like I did Valerie. I'm just afraid to lose you again, like I lost Valerie again, and, well, that's why I said the things I said, thought what I thought. That's just how I put things together in my head now. So you see, you're not the only one who needs to escape the past."

"But I believe in the future, Vic." She reached across the table and took my hand in hers and squeezed it. "*Our* future."

She looked at me with such tenderness I didn't know how I could have ever doubted her.

When we went back to the hotel my stuff was in the lobby waiting for me. "Glad you came back before we had to store it or sell it, sir," the geeky desk clerk said to me. I overcame an urge to hit him.

"I can't believe this flea bag is booked up," I told Dolly as we got into the Comet. "And this will cost me, you know, in mileage and all. The guy asked me not to take it out of the state, even, but for you."

"You'll have it back by tomorrow," she said, cuddling up and kissing me. "Then we can fly from New York to Miami and live happily ever after."

I didn't say anything, didn't tell her I had no intention of doing that, but she was obviously unstable and I didn't want to tip the scales against me just yet. Jesus, between her and my mother I was carrying on quite a balancing act.

"Remember, I'm not Rose," she said as we headed south for the Turnpike.

"No, you're not," I said, thinking: Next to you Rose was Rebecca of Sunnybrook Farm.

As we drove the hundred or so miles down the Jersey Turnpike, Dolly lollygagged comfortably, hanging her pink socked feet out the window and gossiping on and on about our lost days of youth. "Remember so and so, remember that time, remember when..." All the while I tried to prevent my paranoia, such as it was, from penetrating my ultra-cool veneer. I was in no mood for nostalgia now. The present situation had cured me of that yearning for my past dreams of the future. I had a new perspective on things now, from the opposite direction. I looked at Dolly, who just stared out the window letting the cool breeze of the autumn day whip her lovely face and hair, talking and reminiscing, and I realized we were in the god damn future already. I marveled how quickly we had gone from there to here, and it filled me with trepidation to think how fast I'd go from here to wherever we were going. Immediately that meant Collingswood, New Jersey, but soon that would be in the past too. Not soon enough, I thought. Not soon enough.

A song was lodged in my head as I drove and Dolly babbled: "Love Will Tear Us Apart Again," by Joy Division, who later became New Order after their leader killed himself on the eve of their first American tour. I used to think that song was so cool, so hip, so modern, so un-1970s, a decade I despised save for the Do It Yourself scene at CBGB, which was likewise composed of disillusioned misfits longing for the sudden violent death of the plastic commercial nightmare engulfing us. That was also my Kraftwerk and Visage period, when moody synthesizer music about rejection and suicide seemed so dramatic and important and—dare I say it?—*deep*. That was also when I began drifting apart from Dolly, who was into Journey and Kiss and that kind of head-banger crap. At least we both pretended to hate disco. Joy Division was the anthem someone with money and settle down. In a way, we'd both realized our respective dreams, even though I was far from content in my current profession. I stuck with it because of the autonomy, which I thought a writing career might afford me in the long run, but I burned out on that long ago. And Dolly met Mr. Right and moved to an affluent neighborhood in the suburbs and didn't have to work. Yet now she couldn't wait to get away from it all and run off with the guy she had left behind in the first place. Talk about irony.

"Dolly, why are you so unhappy with Donald?" I said about midway through the state, the steady stream of houses and trees and diners and little else slowly lulling me to sleep. I needed some interesting dialogue to pep me up, because Dolly's memory-laden monologue was as flat and uninspiring as the landscape. "I mean, you haven't exactly said why, after all these years of staying with him, you're so hot to bolt all of a sudden."

She looked over at me like I had spoiled her private party with an off-color joke. "What's the difference why? We should never have gotten together to begin with, and you and me, well, we should never have broken up to begin with. With you there's *passion.* I *need* that. Now I realize passion is more important than money."

"Dolly, c'mon. You're used to a certain style there's no way I can offer you. Passion can't buy you fancy clothes or finance a weekend in Atlantic City. The most it can do is get you off, but that gets old in and of itself, take my word for it. Love, on the other hand..." I trailed off, still uncertain if that's what was going on here, and she didn't say anything, either, so I just said, "Donald gives you the life you grew up wanting, right?"

"I've had that, Vic. Didn't work. Time to try something else, something adventurous and exciting. That I can get with you, and nobody else I know. Everyone else is so, *I* don't know. They play it nice and safe, like everybody else, like *I* did."

I wasn't sure what to say. In a way, I liked the fact she held this bogus view of me as a globetrotting trouble-shooter. So far it had been to my sexual advantage. But what would happen when she realized that in between sporadic bursts of activity and mystery my life was as dull and commonplace as hers? Well, maybe not commonplace, but uneventful, at least. Then again, I did have those periodical aberrations when my lifestyle almost deserved its reputation. Maybe that would be enough for Dolly to coast on. No, who was I kidding?

"I don't think my life is what you think it is," I said after a pause. "You shouldn't want me because of the dashing facade I present to damsels in distress such as yourself. There are long stretches of waiting for the phone to ring, and when it does, it would be too abrupt a turnaround from shopping malls and garden parties."

"But that's what I mean, Vic! Being with you has all these possibilities of danger and adventure! Just look how much fun we've had already! Gangsters, hot sex in a cheap hotel—it's so *cool*!"

I sighed. "Dolly, if this is your idea of fun, you need help, young lady."

"Then why do you do it? Not the money, obviously."

"The independence. I'm my own boss, call my own shots, make my own hours. That's basically all I've ever wanted. With you along, I'd lose part of that, wouldn't I?"

"Yeah, but think of all the blow-jobs!"

I gave her a look that said it all.

"When I know I can trust you, Vic. You'll just have to wait."

"Are you saying you don't trust your husband?"

"I don't think he'd cheat on me. I just don't trust him in the way I mean, with my life. But I can trust him to a point."

"Then why haven't you consummated your marriage! Jesus! Why does he put up with that?"

She shrugged. "He loves me."

"That's the point! How can he express it?"

"There's other things in life besides sex, Vic."

"Not on your honeymoon, there ain't."

"Donald considers himself lucky to get what he gets when he gets it."

"I don't get it."

"You haven't met Donald."

"He that much of a nerd?"

"Yup."

"So why'd you marry him?"

"He asked."

"So what if I had? You'd have shot me down because of the security issue, right?"

"Hm, probably."

"So you married the first safe, decent guy who proposed? That it?"

"Basically, yeah. I was a kid, Vic. Young and stupid."

"So what are you now? Old and wise?"

"Still pretty young, and pretty horny. You know how women my age are at their peaks, right?" She reached over and started unbuttoning my pants. "Donald never goes down on me. I get no satisfaction from him whatsoever. It's just me pleasing him, then him rolling over. He wants kids someday and I keep putting him off, telling him my religious views won't allow me to let him penetrate me until I'm ready to have a family. Which I don't think I'll ever be. So in the meantime I just keep doing *this*."

"Dolly, no —*Dolly*, please, we'll crack up, a cop'll see us or something. Dolly. *Dolly*..."

We almost crashed when I briefly closed my eyes during climax, but I recovered. A passing motorist saw me swerve and shot me the bird. "*Drunk shithead asshole!*" the old lady yelled as she zipped past us in her Oldsmobile. Jersey. Land of hospitality.

As we got closer to Philly, Dolly turned on her favorite station, which played easy listening and soft rock stuff. Her other favorite played hard rock, and yet another favorite played country. I put the kibosh on those, and let her play the easy listening one when I realized that was the only station left. I was spoiled in San Francisco with its eclectic airwaves and tastes, I supposed. I remembered exactly where I was suddenly, and felt uneasy and out-of-place. "Rocket Man" by Elton John was on, followed by "Don't Go Breakin' My Heart," two songs Dolly was all too happy to hear, since they were popular when we were in school. The Elton John block led into a Diana Ross block, featuring "Do You Know Where You're Going To?" and "Love Hangover." Memories of snow and the schoolyard and a certain little girl in study hall swirled dimly in my head. And sitting next to me was Dolly Duncan, all grown up with my semen in her stomach. It was surreal. Then came a Paul Simon lineup, "50 Ways to Leave Your Lover" and "Slip Slidin' Away," and by this time I was getting seriously depressed.

"Must be another '70s weekend," Dolly said. "Usually they play Michael Bolton and Whitney Houston. You now, modern stuff."

"Any jazz or punk stations?" I asked as if I were begging for mercy.

"Not really. There's a station that plays Kenny G and stuff."

"Terrific." Man, I felt lost. And homesick.

She switched the dial and my heart leaped. It was Frank Sinatra! This was his home state after all. I was happy until I realized it was the sappy Kenny G station and the Frank tune was off one of the recent "Duets" albums, where he sings his classics paired with contemporary whiney dip-shits trying to cash in on Frank's legend.

"Aw, shit," I said. "I *hate* this 'Duets' crap. I mean, why can't they just let Frank sing? Why can't the other person just shut the fuck up? Frank only did this to prove he's still the Chairman, even at eighty or whatever he is, and all these other little pipsqueaks are pathetic imitators. I tell you, pop music is a dead art, man. Not even Springsteen does anything good anymore."

"I *like* this," Dolly said distantly, looking out the window again. "I like 'Duets.' I like Bruce Springsteen singing 'Philadelphia,' too. I like all the new stuff. You always did like old stuff more than me. Hey, remember all those old monster movies you used to make me watch on TV on the weekends?"

I lit up at the thought. "Oh yeah! Zacherle's Creature Features! Man, those were the days. This video store below my office has all that stuff. It's run by Doc Schlock. Well, that's what everyone calls him. His name is like a takeoff on the old monster movie hosts. Yeah, I remember those. 'The Creature From the Black Lagoon,' all the 'Mummy' flicks, 'Teenage Werewolf,' 'Teenage Frankenstein,' giant bugs—yeah. Those were the days."

Dolly was looking at me strangely now. It gave me the creeps.

"What?" I said.

"Nothing. Turn off here."

We finally drove off the damn Turnpike and into the heart of suburbia. They don't call Jersey the Garden State for nothing. Plenty of areas are very nice, with lots of tree-lined streets and grand old houses. Convenience stores abounded. For some reason it reminded me of Long Island, and then it hit me: the little Mob brat I'd rescued from her father Shiv and the Elvis cult back in San Francisco, Lucy Guisseppe, was in Long Island and wanted me to look her up. I'd said I might but didn't promise. Now I realized I had to: Lucy could put me in touch with some Mob brass who might in turn introduce me to the Brooklyn chapter bosses. Lucy might even know them personally. I wanted to confront them face-to-face and have them tell me to leave town. Then I'd know they killed my father, they'd know I knew but couldn't really do anything about it since I was a lone operator with no hard proof, and that would be that. I'd go sit by my mother until we had a conversation, maybe tell her the Mob hit the old man and it had nothing to so with her, as if that would help, but at least she'd know. And then Dolly would be safely in Miami. I didn't want to go to Miami anyway, because that's where Deacon Rivers of the New Church of Elvis was, and I was afraid if I ever saw him again I'd kill him. I'd just drop Dolly a line and go home. Case closed. Simple.

Yeah, right. Whenever I make a definite plan, I know everything is ready to go totally haywire.

She directed me along this freeway and that, down this street and up another one until we reached Collingswood, former hometown of Michael Landon, star of *Bonanza*, but I'll always remember him in *I Was A Teenage Werewolf*. He was great in that, should have died right after, like a lycanthropic James Dean. His career was downhill from the Ponderosa to the *Little Prairie* to the *Highway to Heaven*. Oh well.

Dolly made me park a block or so away, to make sure Donald's car was gone. She got out and crept along the sidewalk, straining her head for a sight of her husband, who right this moment should have been on a plane for Chicago.

But wasn't.

She came running back and jumped in the car and told me to back up in a hurry. "He's still home?" I said. "We came down here for *nothing*?"

"His car's still in the garage. Maybe he postponed his flight. I know he didn't take a cab to the airport because he hates cabs, thinks they're beneath him. We'll just have to wait till he leaves. You can help me so it'll be quicker. Oh shit, Vic! Why won't the jerk just leave? Like for *good*?"

"Like you said, he loves you."

"Back up *quick*!"

"Don't worry. He can't make the car, remember?"

"Oh yeah. Right. Good. Oh, Vic, I'm so glad I have a real live true detective to watch out for me!"

"Ever hear 'Watching the Detectives' by Elvis Costello?" I said.

She hadn't, of course. We made out a little, Dolly keeping one wary eye on her house, which was double storied and sprawling, surrounded by well-tended foliage, big enough for a *Brady Bunch* sized family. It was a *Brady Bunch* kind of block, filled with *Father Knows Best* kind of families, I imagined. Only Dolly's house was almost empty, almost being the operative word.

"Nice digs," I said. "You sure you wanna give that up for me?"

"Not for you," she said.

"For you? Good."

"For *us*."

As she kissed me she turned the ignition and flipped on the radio, and turned the dial. "Love Will Tear Us Apart Again" by Joy Division came leaping out at me. I stopped her finger on the dial.

"What the hell station is this?" I said.

She shrugged. "I don't know. Never heard it. Must be new, alternative rock or something, college station. Why, what's this music? It's *weird*."

"Yeah," I said. "Eerie."

I could almost hear Doc laughing clear across the continent.

Then Dolly shut off the radio, her face white with shock. I followed her gaze and saw Pete the Meat just getting out of a black Camaro in front of her house, and a guy from inside who must have been Donald, tall and lanky with thin brown hair and glasses, was crossing the lawn to greet him.

Chapter Eight
DANGER IN DAISEYLAND

I already knew Donald the dentist and Pete the Meat Cleaver were acquainted through their mutual golfing club because that's what Dolly told me. Then I realized: that meant absolutely nothing. So the look of shock on Dolly's face should not have thrown me like it did. But it did anyway.

"Dolly, *what*? So Petey pays Donny a visit. Big deal. What can it hurt, besides delaying Don a little on his flight to Frank's kind of town? And you're right—he looks like a serious nerd all right. *Jeez*." I was relieved, too, since now that Dolly and I were trysting I was suddenly possessive of her and resentful of any competition. I couldn't help it—I was territorial when it came to sex, especially with someone I cared about, which was usually preferably the case. And God help me, Dolly still meant something to me after all these years. Maybe it was simply sentiment. I'd figure that out as I went.

"Vic, I lied," Dolly said in a whisper. "My last one, I swear. I didn't know Donald and Petey knew one another. I never introduced them in college because I was having an affair with both of them at the same time and—*look* at them! They're going into the house together!"

I sighed. "Yeah, so they are. And Petey's talking up a storm too, and your hubbie looks kinda pissed from where we're sitting. Dolly, when did you become such a chronic sociopath? I never really noticed that aspect of your personality in high school."

"Oh, Vic, shut up and let me think for a second. I don't know what we should do now."

"You keep lying to me there ain't gonna be any 'we,' I'm telling you. I *mean* it, too. Anyway, what's the worst than can happen? They plotting to take over the world? Donald building a robot in his spare time? Petey a spy? Settle *down*, for Chrissake."

"Petey's going to tell Donald where I went in spite. He knows your name. He'll tell Donald I spent the night with you."

"Ooo, I'm shakin'. I'm fucked now! Donald the dentist is putting me on his shit list. I'll be spit and rinsed. My cavities will be left out in the cold. My wisdom tooth hurts just thinking about it. Man, I'm in some serious trouble."

"*Shut up!* Donald knows about us, I mean in the past, so he'll figure I'm running away with you. Lucky he doesn't know where my sister is."

"And you *do*?"

"I told you. Miami. We can still go there."

"Dolly, *no*. This is getting too weird. I said I'd drive you down to pick up some stuff, and here we are. But that's the extent of my obligation."

"That's what you think, buster."

"Huh? What's *that* supposed to mean?"

"Now that Donald knows about you we're both screwed. He'll hunt us down wherever we go! We'll lay low in Miami for a while, see how long we can hide at my sister's before he smokes us out, then maybe we can head for San Francisco. I've always wanted to go there anyway. But no, he'll find out that's where you've been living, and we should just leave the country. I've got some money saved."

"Dolly, *whoa*, stop." I couldn't help but laugh. "We're talking about a dentist, right? Not the CIA, not the Mafia, not the KGB. Not even the FDA or PTA. Just Donald the dentist. Shit. I thought *I* saw too many movies."

"But you don't get it—Donald will hire Petey to find us now. I just *know* it."

"What? Pete already found us, and so what?. He didn't do anything about it then, and anyway, what can some Ivy League dropout jock do anyway? I'm not worried, to put it mildly."

"First of all, that's why I told Petey you were my cousin, because he's jealous and childish and would blow the whistle on me in spite. I should never have told him who you really were, but he was getting so mad anyway, I just let it out so he'd leave me alone. He said he felt used and would get even. Since Donald didn't know I'd kept in touch with him since college I didn't really see why he'd believe anything Petey had to say."

"So then why worry *now*?"

"*Because*! Petey came right here practically! He probably called Donald up and Donald told him to come over for a meeting. Maybe they're waiting for us, setting a trap? You think?"

"Yeah, I think you're nuts. Let's just wait till the Terrible Twosome finish hatching their little chickenshit conspiracy plot, and when they leave I'll go in with you, you can pack, and I'll drive you to the airport. Okay?"

"And you're going with me, right?"

"Dolly, I will find out who killed my father. I hired myself to do it, and I always complete a job. Now that's it. I'm not asking you to go with me, am I? *Why*?"

"Because you don't really love me," she pouted.

"No, I do. Or I think I do. Anyway—stop looking at me like an orphan waif, too—anyway, you were right. My work can be dangerous. I don't want you caught in the crossfire, baby cakes. Because I do care about you. Get it? That's why I won't be *selfish*."

"That's just an excuse. All right, fine, Vic. Then when you read about me killing myself back in California, you'll be sorry, all right!"

I grabbed her arm and squeezed, and she squirmed but shut up. "Damn it, Dolly, don't pull that on me, now! I got *enough* to deal with, with Johnny bailing on me and my mother slowly draining her own brain like a vein, and my father probably had a death wish, too, and set himself up for the big fall—so god damn it, don't you wimp out on me too! I need you. I, yeah. I *need* you. I don't want to lose you, too. All right?"

She wiped away a lone tear and tried to hug me, but I was hard now, and not in the way she liked. "Then please stay with me for a little while. I need you too. I'll help you with your father's thing. I promise. Then you'll help me. We'll be a team. Deal?"

I searched her eyes for sincerity, and found something that looked like it. It could have been a masquerade, at least partially, or I just saw what I wanted to see, as is so often the case, but it was too late now anyway. The gauntlet had been thrown, as the saying goes. I was in it already. All I could do was make the best of it. Doc would gloat when I got back and told him this. And I would deserve it, too. "All right, Dolly. You help me by staying out of my way and letting me settle my situation my own way, and I'll be there for you too. Those are the terms. You stick to 'em and, yeah. Deal."

She hugged me and felt around my waist. "You're either too high or too low," I said.

"And we should be careful about arousing attention."

"I just want to make sure you brought it with you, didn't forget it. Where is it?"

"What? My dick?"

"Your gun, silly. Same difference, I guess. Both for banging. I saw it in your suitcase when you were checking out of the hotel."

"It was hidden under my stuff."

"I know. I'm sorry. I was just curious about what you packed."

"Dolly, what about this *trust* thing? You want to trust *me*, but if I can't trust *you*—!"

"You can, Vic, I *swear*. And what do you have to hide anyway? I'm sorry, I know, that's not the point. It's just part of this tryst, I mean trust problem I have. Ill get over it in time, the more I'm around you. So?"

"So what?"

"You bring it? Your big bad gun, Dirty Harry?"

"Of *course*! Whaddya think I did with it? It's still in my suitcase, where I thought I hid it. At least my pals from the other night didn't take it. But why do you care?"

She just shrugged and said, "You never know." She looked back worriedly at the empty Camaro and the house. It was getting dark and lights were going on up and down the block. Except in her house. People starting passing us on the way home and I got antsy. Not only that, but it suddenly struck me that if Pete the Meat had followed us from my hotel to the hospital in Brooklyn, he could make my car. Plus, I wasn't sure what to expect after that exchange with Dolly about my gun. With Dolly, as she said, you just never knew. She wasn't lying about that, at least.

"We shouldn't just park here, people will get suspicious, think we're casing houses and call the cops," I said as night fell. A light went on in the Dunlap house. "Let's go get something to eat close by, relax a bit, then cruise back and see if the Camaro is gone and the lights are out. Maybe Pete will take Donald to the airport, tell him not to worry. Okay?"

"Okay, but make sure your gun is loaded, okay?"

"Dolly, what are you scared of? I can handle Pete the Meat, gun or not. Guy ain't nothin' but atomic beef jerky anyway."

"He may get ugly though, and he's big and a *killer*. His father used his influence got him off a manslaughter charge in college, a fight in a bar, one reason he dropped out and quit the football team. He could have had a career as a pro and all, but he screwed up. He's crazy, Vic. I just don't want to see you get hurt."

One bomb right after the other. "Don't worry about me, sugar. I've dealt with rougher customers than your rabid frat boy in my time."

She smiled that girlie smile. "God, that turns me on. Maybe we should check into a motel or something."

"Naw, waste of money."

"My treat. I'll charge it. And we can work on that trust thing.

Okay?"

I nodded. For some reason I was more curious and determined than ever to put my penis inside Dolly Duncan. If she really was still a virgin, it would be magical. I don't think I've ever had a virgin before. And something told me once she had it she'd never get enough of it. It could be the wildest passion either of us had ever experienced. Plus we loved each other, in some warped, twisted, sentimental way. I just had to make her trust me, no two ways about it, and I would trust her right back. Oh yeah. One hitch: she was obviously imbalanced. I never even saw this side of her as a teenage kid. She'd hardly been the hard-boiled reform school girl type. She seemed so sweet and innocent, even in bed, when we explored the options to intercourse tenderly and affectionately. Dolly was Protestant or something, and couldn't reconcile her beliefs with fornication in the strict sense, so we just did everything *else*. But now she was practically wanton—except for that one significant detail. Not even with her married partner! Go figure. Me, I just could not escape crazy women to save my life. It began with my mother and just didn't let up. It must have been my destiny. I guess something about me just drives women mad. Oh well.

We ate at a local diner and then found a cheap motel called Tropical Gardens to lose some time in. The joint had phony Hawaiian decor, with a gaudy mural of a tropical island covering one whole wall, and lamps that looked like tiki statues. I guess the proprietors figured you could stay there and forget you were in New Jersey. But only New Jersey would have places this ersatz and tacky. It was more like a reminder of where I was, rather than a tonic. Anyway, at least they had cable. I lay down to relax and channel surf a bit, something I hadn't done in a while, I realized. But Dolly unbuttoned my shirt and then trousers. That woman was insatiable.

We fell asleep in each other's arms, naked and content, watching *True Romance* on HBO, and didn't wake up till the following morning. We both felt refreshed and invigorated as we showered and then had breakfast in the same local dinner we'd had dinner in. In case you haven't noticed, I'm like that. When I find a coffee shop that appeals to me, I like to give it repeat business at varying hours, to see how the mood shifts with the changing light of day and night. Also, I can sample breakfast, lunch, and dinner, not to mention the different waitresses on the separate shifts. Classic coffee shops are like the final outposts of classic Americana, along with certain bowling alleys, train stations, bus depots, drive-ins, tiki lounges, and old motels and hotels. One day they'll be gone to only to be found in history books and videos. Hopefully this won't occur in my lifetime. I just don't know what I'd do without a really cool diner within my reasonable vicinity.

It was a beautiful fall day, too, crisp and clear and bright, the leaves splattered on the dark, wet streets and sidewalks like impressionistic paint drops on a zigzagging canvas. Dolly looked radiant, though she was anxious for a new set of clothes. Her green dress was the last thing she'd brought with her. She'd need a change of wardrobe soon. I promised her we'd take care of it. At that point, I felt the scent of her going to my head again, like it used to—her perfume, her natural musk, her hair. I was falling for her all over again, though the gaps in our interests, always something of a chasm, had only widened over the years. I tried not to let that bother me. Hell, even the idea of spending some time laying out on Miami Beach sounded enticing. Dolly always looked swell in a bikini.

"Purple," I said suddenly over breakfast.

"Come again?"

"Gladly, later. But purple. Definitely. That'd be the color bikini I'd like to see you in."

She smiled. "Oh? Coney Island's a bit chilly this time of year, Vic."

"You know what I mean. In Florida."

"I thought you didn't want to go there with me?" she said, batting her eyelashes.

"After I deal with my thing, why not? I need the vacation. If I'm frugal with my dough, it'll be fine. I'll send Doc next month's rent—but my cat! Shit. He's all alone."

"Your cat's by himself in your apartment?"

"Yeah, most of the time. Monica is watching out for him, or her."

"Don't you know what sex it is?"

"Well, it was born a boy, but things have changed, slightly."

"Vic! What weird, kinky things are you into these days? Anything I should know?"

"Nothing too outrageous, I'm afraid. Never experimented with hallucinogenics or tried corn-holing an animal. I'm pretty straight, I'm afraid."

"I should hope so, with all those fruitcakes out there."

"Whaddya mean?"

"I mean San Francisco. Aren't there a lot of like strange people out there?"

"Oh sure. I fit right in."

"Do *you*?"

"Well, I can do my own thing and nobody hassles me, let's put it that way."

Her face was somewhat contorted with some deep concern. "Vic, have you ever, like, made it with a *guy*?"

"*Me*? You kiddin'? Pussy-whipped sap like me? Oh, sorry. But no, I haven't, and unless I get gang raped doing a stretch in San Quentin, I don't ever plan to. Not even curious. Male bodies are hideous to me. I remember 'em from the locker room at school, and I don't even enjoy looking in the mirror. Though I do spend a lot of time fondling myself in the dark. Babes? Hell, I appreciate 'em even when I'm not horny. I could be laid up on my deathbed and still enjoy a watching a good-looking nurse who fills out her uniform cross the room. I'd even imagine her removing her white uniform, slowly, sensuously, and—hey, you have any uniforms left from your nursing days at the university?"

"Maybe. Want me to bring 'em to Miami?"

"Definitely. Just so I could watch you take 'em off."

"But, Vic, where will we go from there?"

"Like you don't know. Oh, you mean Miami? I don't know about you, but I'm going home."

"You mean Brooklyn?"

"No! Brooklyn hasn't been my home since I was a teenager, Doll. And Manhattan—too many memories. I mean California."

"San Francisco is nice, is it?"

"Yeah. One giant fruit basket. I mean, I get sick of it, the isolated sense of doom I get sometimes on a foggy day, or even a cloudy one, or a hot, dry, sunny one when it feels like an earthquake is gonna destroy my puny life any minute, but I don't know where else to go."

"Why'd you go there to begin with? Oh, right—because you thought that's where Rose went, right?"

"Yeah, when she was still Valerie. Yeah, but that's behind me, too. Now, well, there's Doc, who I told you about, and my business, and my cat, and a few friends, and—my *freedom*."

"Well, that's good for you, but, what I'm trying to say is—I don't know if I'd fit in out there. I don't think I'm weird enough."

I grinned. "Baby, believe me, you'll do fine." The check came, and we got up to leave.

Dolly still seemed concerned about something, though. I knew what was bothering her. She came from a very conservative background, worse than mine, and it still stuck with her, whereas I used mine as an impetus to shake the shackles of conformity and oppression in the name of God and the President and whoever else was trying to tell me what to think and do. Dolly didn't like being judged herself, but I could tell she was pretty hard on everybody else. She'd always been something of a WASP princess, but she was so cute I didn't let it get to me as a kid. She was somewhat prejudiced against minorities, gays, even poor people. I've never been a champion of the P.C. movement—in fact bleeding hearts repulse me, because they're as humorless and uptight and hypocritical and self-centered as their enemies on the right—but I was strongly opposed to the mainstream bigotry and fascism sweeping our country at the time, and Dolly probably voted for it. In a cheap hotel room, pussy was pussy, but in the light of day, these ideological differences could cause irreparable rifts further down the line. Our future didn't seem so rosy as I drove her back to her house to check on our pals. I put these doubts in the back of my mind so I could concentrate on the current situation, which was increasingly unpredictable.

The coast seemed clear. The Camaro was gone, and so was Donald's BMW in the garage. Flashy suburbanites always killed me. It's still Collingswood, New Jersey, pal, not even a pinprick on the national map. We parked a block or so down the street and stealthily sauntered up the street. I noticed a bunch of Halloween decorations in the windows of the houses and realized it was right around the corner. In San Francisco Halloween came several times a day, so I was immune to its charms by now.

Dolly was nervous, clutching my arm as we approached her door. The lawn was well manicured, so they obviously hired help for the upkeep of the place. Dolly's hands were shaking as she pulled her keys out of her purse and opened the door. "Got your gun?" she whispered.

I nodded and rolled my eyes. You'd think we were breaking into the Pentagon.

The interior of the place was about what I'd expect—clean, neat, museum-like in its quiet display of furniture and carefully placed framed pictures and books. I immediately wanted to leave, it was so stuffy and sterile, but I just sat on the sofa and made myself at home, flipping on the big screen TV while Dolly raced around franticly upstairs.

"Are you watching outside?" she yelled. I shouted yes and told her to relax. "Don't you want to see what the upstairs is like?" I shouted *no* and told her to hurry up. In spite of her panic she seemed to be taking her time, though. Even if Petey and Donald showed up, what could they do? I was carrying, as if that were truly necessary. We could hardly be accused of Breaking and Entering. This was still legally Dolly's residence, and I was still legally her friend. Petey was such an arrogant asshole I would've relished cleaning his goddamn clock if he came at me and gave me the excuse. Donald looked like all you had to do was say "boo" and he'd blow away. There was nothing on except soaps and talk shows and other nauseating daytime TV fare, so I shut off the tube and walked around looking at the pictures.

One made me stop cold in my tracks. I could feel the blood draining from my head then flooding back in a heated rush. It was a picture of Donald, Dolly—and Al Marcus, out in the woods on a golfing and fishing trip or something. The picture looked around ten or so years old, before I went out to California, maybe right before Al died. Or *after*? He frequently visited the East Coast even after being promoted to SFPD Captain, took all his vacations there, right up until the end.

I didn't want to confront Dolly with it just yet. I decided I'd just keep the photo discreetly hidden in my overcoat pocket until I could grill her a little more about her secret acquaintances, then spring it on her in the midst of another lie. Why? Why was she doing this? She must be privy to what Al was, that's why. Something told me she knew something about my father's death through Al, and wanted to hide it from me. I still wasn't sure it was her who engineered that ambush in my hotel room, since as I said it was too slick a job, but maybe she knew more about it than she was letting on. I took the photo out of the frame, which I stuck in a drawer, and stuffed the incriminating snapshot in my pocket just as Dolly came running down the stairs with two huge suitcases.

"Aren't you going to help?" she said shrilly. "Some gentleman *you* are."

"I'm from Brooklyn, remember?" I said, then I met her halfway and helped her carry her stuff out the door and down the street into the Comet.

"We have to stop in Philly real quick," she said breathlessly. "I won't be long, I promise. Then we'll head straight for New

York, okay?"

"What the hell's in Philly? You have a sudden urge for cheese steak?"

"Just beefcake, honey," she said, blowing me a kiss. "And in return all the cheesecake you can eat. Really, I have to stop by my apartment there. I left some medicine and things there that I really need."

"Wait. Whoa. You have your own apartment?"

"Sure. Right on Chestnut. Donald got it for me so I could shop late in the city and not have to drive all the way home. He doesn't even have a key, the dope. At least I don't *think* he does."

"This guy's just a dentist? He lives pretty well for a dentist, wouldn't you say?"

"Well, his family in Chicago is well off, too. His father died while he was still in college and he inherited a bunch of money, too, which he invested well. He'll probably retire early, like when he's fifty. But by then I'll be long gone, collecting those checks every month."

"I thought you said he wouldn't give you a divorce? And didn't you sign any prenuptial agreements regarding the inheritance?"

"Nope. That was a condition of our marriage. I suck him off and he takes care of me for life."

"I think he wanted to be sucked for life too, sweetheart," I said, disgusted by the image of her going to town with Donald's little wee-wee.

"He did. He does. But we'll find a way. Right now I just want to get as far away from him as possible. C'mon, let's go. I think he must be in Chicago by now. I called the office from upstairs and he wasn't in, they said he'd left for vacation, so *good*."

"What about Petey?"

"Screw Petey."

I spread my palms and took off, heading west and over the murky Delaware River via the Walt Whitman Bridge, or maybe it was to the Ben Franklin. Whatever. As I looked at the hazy river and Philly skyline, I ached for the sight of San Francisco Bay and its two glorious bridges. I thought of the picture in my pocket and wondered why I'd ever left to begin with. Doc was right. So was Pop. I was better off not knowing the. truth. But it was too late now. I had to see this through.

And another thing: I was falling in love with Dolly all over again.

It wasn't far from the bridge to Dolly's digs on Chestnut, but first she made me detour through South Street, because of a certain boutique she wanted to stop in real quick. I waited in the car. I'd only been to Philly a couple of times in my early twenties for concerts, and it always struck me as a pretty quiet town compared to its cousin across Jersey, their mutual neighbor in between, trying so hard to maintain respect and dignity, like Oakland does with San Francisco. I wouldn't exactly say it lives up to it's nickname The City of Brotherly Love—read David Goodis—but it has some swell museums and parks, and is less nerve-racking than Manhattan. Not nearly as exciting though, which was why I never went back more often.

While Dolly was in the boutique for close to half an hour the sky turned gray and began to coat the town with a silvery sheen that made it look all the better. I kept looking at my watch and sighing, then getting out to put another nickel in the meter. Finally she ran out with a bag full of junk, all smiles. She kissed me on the cheek, partly out of guilt, and I just gave her a sidelong glance and put the Comet in gear and flew.

"This is where I lived when I was finishing school," she said, meaning the University of Pennsylvania, "cause that was in such a shitty neighborhood." We pulled up in front of a rather elegant townhouse on a shady block rife with Cadillacs and mink coats.

"Donnie pay your rent then too?" I asked her snidely, getting out of the car.

She was way ahead of me already, pretending not to hear me. I caught up with her in a courtyard, apparently right in front of her tenement. "You hear me?" I said.

"Yeah. I'm looking for my key, hope I have it."

"You sure there aren't any duplicates that Donald may have you don't know about?"

"I never gave him any, and the lease is in my name, and I pay the rent."

"From your joint bank account, I take it."

"Why are you being so snotty?" she snapped, still rummaging through her purse for the keys.

"How's your mother these days, anyway?" I asked suddenly, for no reason other than I just thought of it.

"She, uh, died. Year after my father." Her old man croaked from a coronary at age fifty or so, during Dolly's freshman year, right around the time I began drifting away from her myself. I always thought she resented me for pulling away from her during such a critical crisis—she was very close to her old man, who was a loud-mouthed louse in my opinion—but in truth, she grew distant from me during that period of mourning, and I understood. She was protecting herself from intimacy, which meant vulnerability. After that untimely demise she was a little harder each time I saw her.

"How come you never told me your mother passed away during our correspondence?" I wanted to know.

"You never asked how she was, so I figured you didn't care."

"Aw, shit. What from did she die?"

She gave a blasé shrug—*too* blasé. "Broken heart, I guess." She murmured something else I couldn't make out. We were standing in front of her door now. "Damn it, what did I do with those stupid *keys*?"

Abruptly the door swung open and there was Pete the Meat Cleaver, wearing a leather jacket and turtleneck sweater, looking like a preppy hood. "Looking for these?" he asked, jingling a set of keys dangling from the end of an open switchblade.

Chapter Nine
TRUE DEFECTIVE

I made a quick, impulsive grab for the keys rather than the knife itself for some reason and wound up with a sliced palm for my trouble—my *good* palm, too, the one I need when I'm all alone, which is more than often the case. Shit, a paper cut on a forefinger or thumb on that hand was bad enough, but a deep cut clear across my palm? Man, was I pissed! With my left hand knotted into a fist I took an awkward swing at Petey's elevated kisser, which seemed to throw him, but not nearly as far as I wanted it to. I caught him on the chin and he stumbled backward. The keys slipped off the blade but he retained control of the handle. He swung the knife out wide and ripped some buttons off my overcoat. He was hitting every spot on me that was the most precious. I had to stop him before he emasculated me or something. I didn't notice till later he'd scratched a thin bloody swath across my chest, too. I already had a mess of claw-marks on my hands and arms from wrestling around with Puss. If this kept up I'd look like I fell into a thicket of thorny roses—no pun intended.

Dolly wasn't just standing idly by in the stands, either. After retrieving her keys from the ground, she assaulted Pete on all fronts, kicking and scratching and biting, until she finally made solid contact with his recreation center. You'd think big guys would realize anyone smaller than them would go for their most vulnerable spot and that they'd take better care defending the jewels. While Pete was doubled over in agony I took advantage and caught him with an uppercut that sent him reeling back into the apartment and into a table or something. Dolly and I heard the crash and ran in to investigate.

There was Donald, standing with his arms folded, leaning against the opposite wall, shaking his head. "You just can't get good help these days," he said. I didn't like the looks of this and instinctively drew my gun, a police issue .38 bequeathed to me by my old man, then whipped out my P.I. badge for extra effect.

"Start explaining quick, and make it realistic," I said through heavy breathing, keeping a wary on eye Pete, who picked himself up rubbing his jaw with one hand and his nuts with the other. His lip and gums were bleeding and I was glad.

"Aren't you the ones who should be explaining?" Donald asked in his whiney, nasal voice, trying laughably hard to sound authoritative. "After all, she's married. To *me*."

"*Fuck you, Donald*!" Dolly lashed out, giving Petey another kick as she walked by him, this time in the gut. He groaned and cussed and sank to his knees in a prayerful position. This wasn't his day to play tough guy. I trained my gun on him, but I don't think in his humiliated state he even noticed. Then I saw the blood dripping from my gun hand to the floor, felt the butt getting slippery in my grasp, pocketed the badge now in my left palm, and shifted the .38 over to my good hand, wishing I was ambidextrous and hoping they wouldn't notice that I wasn't.

"You have no right to be here, this place is *mine*!" Dolly said, getting in Donald's face. The dentist was surprisingly aloof. I supposed he was just used to her by now. Donald shook his head and said, "It's in your name, but it's my money you use for the rent, don't forget. And tell your, ah, friend to put his gun away. There's no need for that. We're all rational adults, are we not?"

Donald was dressed casually, in gray sweats and sneakers, and a fine film of sweat covered his white, white skin. He looked so much like a yuppie dentist—or an accountant—it was frightening. He reminded me of Dennis the Menace's dad, and looked about as capable of achieving a hard-on as, well, my cat. No wonder Dolly wanted to dump him, but how much money did he have in that inheritance to make her his love slave to begin with? A doll like Dolly could've landed a better catch than this—at least Petey was handsome, in a smarmy way, and obviously loaded as well. There was something going on Dolly wasn't telling me, but then so what else was new?

"Fuck you, Donald," Dolly repeated, but quieter this time, as if the dentist had some unknown power over her which was slowly draining away her resolve.

"Dolly, tell your friend to put his gun away now. Or *else*."

Or else what?, I wondered. He'd commit first-degree route canal? Dolly turned and looked at me with an odd expression. She was verging on tears. Petey began to stir now, and finally pulled himself back up to his shaky feet. "Tell your boy Pete here to take an enema, and we'll all be civil," I said. "Otherwise I keep the gun out, as long as I detect this hostility on your part. It makes me feel more secure. Call it a complex. Nobody—not even Dolly—tells me what to do with my gun, Donny boy. Got it?" Donald let out a pathetic little laugh but I switched the aim of the gun in his direction and he sobered up right quick. "You gonna be cool, Petey?" I asked, still watching Donald. No answer. "Hey! I'm talkin' to you, butt-head! You wanna hit something, beat your own meat, Pete, but me and the lady are out of bounds. Now, you cool or what?"

"Yeah, yeah," Pete the Beat Meat grumbled.

"Where's that knife?" I then demanded. I'd lost track of it in the shuffle.

"Over there," Dolly said, running over to the open door, closing it, then picking up the sticky blade like it was dog shit and holding it up triumphantly in the air. "My God, Vic, you're *bleeding*!"

"I'll be all right, baby," I said, though the sting was getting to me, and I was leaking crimson all over my overcoat, and that shit stains like a motherfucker, let me tell you. I'd make Dolly buy me a new one. "Give me the knife," I then said, putting my gun in my pocket, followed by the bloody knife. "Now that all the weapons are in one safe place, who wants to start the peace process?"

"But she's *my* piece," Donald said, which sort of stunned me. "And you can't have her. My, ah, spy here told me all about your little all night tryst in a dive in Brooklyn. I've heard a lot about you over the years, Vic. Nice, no, *interesting* meeting you. Now get out of our lives. For *good*."

"Dolly says she's through with you, and asked for my assistance," I said. "You'll have to ask her what she wants to do now. I'll go along with whatever the lady says."

Donald smiled wickedly and produced a small but full bottle of capsules. A prescription? After a fashion. He walked over boldly to Dolly and teasingly held them up in front of her face and rattled the contents. "Come back for these? I thought you would."

"What the hell are those, Dolly?" I asked ingenuously.

"Oh. My *nerve* pills. I have high blood pressure and that's my medicine." Her hand was actually trembling as she reached out to snatch the little bottle from Donald's grasp, but predictably he pulled them back safely into his custody. Dolly and Donald struggled a little and it got boring quickly.

"All right, I don't have time for this crap," I said finally. "Either give her the bottle or I'll shoot you, Donald. Clear?" I pulled out my gun again, then realized the photo with Al Marcus was in the pocket I'd stuck the knife in. Now the shot was no doubt gooey with gore. Oh well. I'd whip it out later and make sure it was still identifiable before springing it on Dolly. She had more and more explaining to do as time went merrily on. But I wanted her to do her explaining elsewhere, anywhere away from these goofs. Donald was actually slimier than I had imagined, trying so hard to talk the talk and walk the walk it was laughable, and something told me this dentist routine was nothing more than a front for another racket—something still in the medicinal field, but far more lucrative. Inheritance, my ass. Donald was a pusher, and Dolly was a puller.

Donald sighed at the sight of the gun and let Dolly have her "nerve pills." That was a good one. Petey was just glowering off in the corner, looking lonesome and fed up with the whole scene.

I waved the gun at him and said, "Beat it, tough guy. Go out for a long, long pass." Then I added: "Loser."

He slowly walked out the door, pointing a threatening finger at me but saying nothing. His expression said it all: "See you later sometime." But he had the finger, and I had the gun. For now, anyway. Then he was gone.

I thought of something. Why wait to bring out the photo? After locking the door behind Pete, I put the gun away and then pulled out the photo and handed it to Dolly. It was pretty sticky but the visages weren't obscured. While she gawked at it I went into the kitchen and grabbed a hand-towel and wrapped it around my cut hand. Donald just stood there looking at the picture with an insipid look of smugness on his WASPy kisser. Just for fun I shoved him out of the way and onto his ass to get to Dolly so I could look at it with her. His glasses went flying. Donald regained his composure and then sat on the sofa to sulk, but he said nothing. He still had a hand to play, I could tell, and he was biding his time. Whatever. I planned to be back in Brooklyn by the time he played it. Hoped he got off on Solitaire. I always did.

"Well well well, Lil' Alex," I said in a limey accent, a la *Clockwork Orange*. No one got it, which was fine. I kept doing it just to annoy them. "Well well well well well well *WELL*!"

"*Shut up*!" Dolly screamed, tearing the photo in two and chucking it aimlessly. "So we knew Al Marcus. Big deal. What's your point, Vic?" She was dying to get into that bottle of pills, but not in front of me, I could tell.

I decided to let her squirm a bit. She deserved it for deceiving me, the one man who had ever been in that room probably who truly cared for her and wanted to try to understand her, try to help her out whatever mess she'd made for herself. Donald was simply your basic Republican white bread dope dealing slime-ball from the suburbs. No one told me but I bet he was from the suburbs of Chicago, too, not the city itself. If he was from Chicago. I'd received that information from Dolly, remember, who told more fables than Mother Fuckin' Goose.

"So what's the scoop with you guys?" I asked good-naturedly. "Looked pretty chummy there, Doll, with a guy you say you can't remember meeting."

"We bumped into him in the Poconos once, and he had a picture taken. So what?"

"And you had it framed just for the hell of it, to take up space." I looked over at Donald, who as just staring into space, smirking at whatever he thought he saw. "What about it, Donald? Al recognized the lady here from the old neighborhood and decided to crash your party? Or what? *Huh*? Hey, whitey, I'm asking you a question."

"Whose side are you on, anyways?" Dolly exploded. "Stop being an asshole, Vic. Where do you expect to go with this?"

"To the end, now," I said. "I want some solid answers about what's going on here, and I don't mean your little dental dope ring either, Don. Or is that 'ether?' How long you been running this racket?"

"I don't see why I should tell you anything," Donald said. "That tiny toy badge doesn't permit you to bust in here and boss us around. Who do you think you are, Sergeant Friday*? Dum, da dum dum*. You're just a little fish in a big pond, buddy. The wrong pond. You don't know what you're mixing with. Pete was nothing. I got connections that won't be scared of a puny little cop cap pistol and cheap bravado borrowed from a TV show. You screwed my wife, mister, and each breath you take is a lucky one. You're swilling on gravy."

I looked over at Dolly and said for the hell of it, "From what the lady tells me, not even you are screwing your wife, much less me."

A faint smile flickered across Donald's bland face. "You believe everything Dolly tells you, you're dumber than I thought. If you believe anything she tells you, you're nuts."

I went over and slapped him to shut him up. His whiney voice grated on me, and so did his words. *He* was the phony, like those suburban white kids who think all they have to is turn their baseball cap around and say "yo" and listen to rap and that makes them brothers from the school of cool. *God*, I hate that. I'd rather listen to Ray Charles sing country western any day. I let out a big sigh, looking at Dolly.

"Take your pills, Dolly. I'm not nearly as dumb as Donnie would like me to be." I turned back around at Donald, who was shielding his face from further assault. "I don't plan to bust you, dude. I'm not a narc or DEA. I'm on a totally unrelated case, and I got no time for this horseshit. At least. I *think* my case is totally unrelated." I glanced over at Dolly, who avoided my gaze. "Now, I'm leaving with the lady here, and after I square things with her, that's the last you'll hear of me. Whether you ever hear from her again ain't got nothin' to do with me. *Capisce*? Best of luck to you. *Geek*." I motioned for Dolly to follow me out the door, and she nodded obediently. Before I left I looked at Donald and said, "Oh, and you're the one who better watch his back, white bread. You yuppie players never realize that you're the ones being played until it's too late." I wanted him to stew in that admonition while Dolly and I booked. I wasn't lying, either. I knew Donald's type. He was a dilettante dealing with some cutthroat customers who were only using him for his respectable facade. Maybe I was calling it all wrong, but I didn't think so. In any case, I didn't really care—as long as Dolly didn't get caught in the crossfire. Her sins I forgave, for no other reason than I loved her, even if we had no future as a couple. In spite of everything, though, I still hadn't given up completely on that scenario. I'd see how Dolly was far away from this crowd, on her own turf, clean and honest, and then decide. In the meantime, I wouldn't ask Doc for advice. I already knew what he'd say.

"I hope you trust me about that photo, Vic," Dolly said after we'd climbed into the Comet and sped off. I kept an eye out for Petey, and I'm pretty good at spotting a tail, since I've had so much practice doing it myself. He wasn't around. Yet. His bruised ego might force another confrontation somewhere down the road, but it would have to be on my time, on *my* territory. "Vic—?" Dolly repeated. "You *do* trust me, right?" I could tell the "nerve pills" had a relaxing affect on her. Downers. Bush league. I just hoped she had no aspirations for The Show.

"Be quiet, Dolly, I'm watching for a tail by Petey," I said, gently deflecting her affections.

"You mean Peter Cottontail?" she smiled, but I didn't so she dropped it fast. "You're mad at me, I can tell. You don't believe anything I ever tell you. And you want me to trust you. That's not how it works, Vic. It's a two way street, trust."

"So far it's been a two-lane highway with lots of head-ons and fatalities due to sloppiness," I said.

"Don't get cute with me."

"Don't get cute with me either, sister. I've had it with lying dames. I thought Rose was the champion but congratulations, sweetheart, you're the new heavyweight queen."

"Oh, is that what you think? And stop comparing me with women who burned you. I love you, Vic, that's the important difference—and they didn't. I haven't lied about anything important. I've only twisted the truth a little to keep you from getting hurt. Is that wrong?"

I stopped for gas and let her sit and stew for a while. While the car was getting cleaned up and filled I went into the restroom and tried to wash up, wrapping my wounded hand in gobs of towels. It wasn't too bad, really. The attendant had looked at my fucked up appearance funny but didn't say anything. He knew better. I knew Dolly wouldn't make a run for it. Now I really was her only chance of emancipation. Once that sunk in completely, she'd have to come clean with me. All I had to do was wait.

We drove back across the Ben Franklin or Walt Whitman or whichever damn bridge it was and headed north. I didn't say much. Dolly flipped on the radio but I adamantly flipped it back off. No chickenshit Kenny G to the rescue. I was trying to smoke her out with silence.

"Vic, where are we going?"

"Back to Brooklyn. Wasn't that the bargain? I help you, you help me? Well, it's *my* turn."

"Are you going to trust me from now on?"

"We'll see. What's in that bottle Donald gave you."

"I told you. *Nerve* pills."

"And you say you only knew Al casually, ran into him once in the woods. That *it*?"

"*Yes*! Yes. I told you already. What's the big deal about that, anyway?" I sighed. Night was falling. Again. It began to rain. Again. And Dolly was lying to me. Again. Some vacation. "All right, Dolly. When you're ready to be straight with me about simple things like this, then maybe we'll move on to the big things."

"Fuck you, Vic. This is no help to me at *all*."

"Oh? Want me to let you off at the nearest bus station, so you can go back to the doper dentist?"

"What makes you think he's a doper?"

"Dolly, this is getting us nowhere. Maybe we should just call it quits now."

"*All right*! All right. I'm sorry. I'm sorry. Just don't *abandon* me, please. I don't know what I'd do then." She turned on the waterworks. I told her to stop it and she did. "The pills are medication to calm me down. I've been taking them ever since the time I first tried to kill myself in college, after my father died. My life hasn't been the same since he left me. And then we drifted apart. Donald got me hooked on this stuff when my prescriptions just weren't cutting it. I was always suicidally depressed. And then my mother moved away."

"I thought you said she croaked?"

"Let me finish? You want the whole truth, right? She may as well have died. She moved away and didn't tell me where to until years later. She was always closer to Sissy than me. Then both went down to Florida and contacted me later. I was hurt for a long time but then I got married to Donald and they came up for the wedding and everything seemed okay again, but then they went back to Miami and I hardly ever heard from him. I think my mother thinks I let her down or something."

"How come? She doesn't know Donald's true nature, right? On the outside you got it made."

"I don't know, Vic, I think she feels I sort of sold out. She was raised blue collar and so was I, then when I went to college on the money they saved for me she thought I became a snot, while Sissy just stayed behind in Bayshore and got married and my mother moved in with them."

"Sissy still married?"

"No. She is divorced, from a guy from D.C. In the military somehow, I don't know exactly. But the point is my sister looked out for my mother and I didn't. Plus Sissy told Mother I was wild, and she believed it."

"*Wild*? In what respect? You always seemed pretty straight when we were going out. A little dingy and disoriented, but I chalked that up to routine adolescent angst."

"Well, *I* was. Straight, I mean. Mostly. It was a sibling rivalry thing that really heated up when Daddy got sick. Sissy just made up stuff about me and my mother believed it, and I always resented her for believing it, and I felt alone in the world. Only Daddy understood. And *you*."

"Wait, what stuff did Sissy make up?"

"Well, drugs, for one thing. I admit, I experimented a little, pot, nothing crazy or heavy."

"You mean in high school?"

"Well, yeah. A little. Nothing major."

"I never knew that."

"Well, you were so straight, the little policeman's son, and I didn't want to alienate you, so I did it when you weren't around. Pajama parties and all, you know."

"I can't believe I never noticed you being high."

"Well, I was careful, and remember, we had our rocky periods. That was usually when I did it, because I was depressed."

"Shit, Dolly. I never even noticed your being that depressed."

She was looking out the window now, speaking in a confessional whispery monotone. The rain beat down softly on the Comet. I felt spooked, but at least we were getting somewhere now. She seemed genuine for the first time since our reunion, and I wanted to take it all the way down the field. "There's a *lot* you didn't notice, Vic," she said in a small voice. "But that's not your fault. I was pretty crafty."

"So, what else? You sleep around?"

She turned and shot me a malicious look. "That's unfair, Vic."

"Well, Donald seemed to hint, y'know."

"What are you asking me, Vic? *What*?"

"Well, are you a virgin or not?"

She looked back out the window and finally answered curtly, "No."

"When'd you lose your cherry?"

"None of your fucking business."

"Before or after me?"

"Does it matter?"

"To me it does, Dolly! Jesus Christ! We dated off and on for over three years and you never let me go there, and you know I was aching to, going out of my mind, *begging* you."

"You ever cheat on *me*?" she said, snapping her head back around at me. Uh oh. "*Well*?" she repeated, tears in her eyes, her tone tense, her expression accusatory and defensive simultaneously.

I sighed. "Yeah."

"Well then. So. There it is."

I hadn't counted on the tables being turned on me like that. I forgot how good Dolly was at strip poker. And there I was, stark naked and shivering in the cold.

"How many times?" she demanded, not looking at me.

"Does it matter?"

"Does it matter who I lost my cherry to?"

I looked over at her and tried to take her hand, but she pulled it away. "Stalemate. Okay. Truce. Forget it. The past is past. This is now, and we're dealing with a whole different situation. Just tell me one thing, Dolly, if you would. Please. And I didn't cheat on you with anyone you knew or liked, and not often. Maybe three, four times. But I was a kid, Dolly. A horny kid who needed to get laid, all the way, and since my own girlfriend was holding out on me."

"Holding *out* on you? Ugh, *men*! The truth was, Vic, *you* were the special one, the one I wanted to wait for. All right?"

"Wait for *what*? You'd have never married me. I was too poor, remember?"

"*Don't you get it*?" she shouted, weeping in a torrent like the rainfall. "It wasn't that I thought you weren't good enough for me. I thought I wasn't good enough for *you*. So one day I just gave it away to some loser, some stranger, and then I couldn't stop. I knew you didn't want to hear this, especially after how promiscuous you said Rose was, but with me, it's different. I didn't do it because I liked it, or as some sick power trip. I did it because I didn't care about myself anymore. My sister and mother made me feel cheap and unwanted, so I started acting that way. My father was sick for years before he died, but he was always there for me. And so were you. But I just didn't think I deserved your love anymore, so I started acting cheap, and the cheaper I acted, the less deserving I felt. It was a bitter circle. Then I met Donald and my mother was pissed at me for not marrying you instead. That's a fact. She loved you, Vic. But you're partly right. I thought I could buy into this rich world and maybe win my mother's respect again, and leave behind this blue collar loser image I grew up with, and—oh, Vic, I'm so, so sorry. Please forgive me. Please."

She was sobbing heavily now, and I reached over and touched her shoulder and she let me. She scooted over and we held each other as Manhattan finally came into view. We went through the Holland Tunnel silently. On the other side I said, "Your father was blue collar, and he was no loser, Dolly. He knew a good thing when he saw it." She smiled and kissed me and squeezed my hand so tightly I thought I'd scream. After all, it was my wounded hand. But I let her squeeze anyway. It felt kind of good.

I didn't want to pump her any further for the evening, as it were. I decided not to grill her about the ambush in the hotel room, see if she was still holding out on any other pertinent information there. I didn't believe she was now. For all I knew, Pete the Meat set that whole thing up, with Donald's help. Maybe Dolly had been set-up, too. There was that phone call she said she'd received telling her to warn me to back off. Who could that have been? Donald's pusher pals, tapping her phone line? Or someone from my own backyard in Bensonhurst? Everyone knew we were attached. For all I know my phone at The Honeymooner was bugged. Maybe that geeky desk clerk was just following his boss's orders after all, telling me there were no future vacancies. There were several wiseguys eavesdropping on me when I went into Pop's Pool Hall. Maybe even Junior blew the whistle on me—that note was a lot like something he'd say. No, Dolly had nothing to do with that, I decided to myself. I let it go. Part of the new deal, helping each other no matter what.

It felt so good not to be lonely anymore.

We checked into a hotel in Manhattan this time under assumed names—"Mr. and Mrs. Jackson" —and then spent the night in each other's arms, kissing, but nothing sexual. "You're right," I whispered in her little ear, just before she drifted off to sleep. "It's better we wait, and make it special. We've waited this long, but at last we're back on track."

She looked into my eyes and said, "I trust you, Vic."

"I trust you too, sweetheart."

"So, Miami?"

"Yeah. Miami."

"Great place for a honeymoon," she smiled, and I agreed.

Chapter Ten
ZOMBIE LOVE

Away from the corruptive influences of her stolid existence in New Jersey, Dolly was as sweet and innocent as I'd always remembered her. I even bought her line about Al Marcus, and decided the link that interested me was between Donald and Al, and she was an innocent pawn in the middle.

Her surprise at discovering her old pal Pete the Meat was on Donald the doper dentist's payroll seemed sincere, and that's what sold me on her overall veracity from that point onward. That, and the feel of her lithe, warm body in my arms, the sensation of her kissing my neck in the morning, just as we were awakening, and the look in her big brown beautiful eyes when she told me she loved me. This is what I'd been after all my life, and as it turned out, I'd found it a long time ago, let it go, and now had rediscovered it after a painful detour through the mirage in my mind. This was reality at last. I had no further use for dreams I couldn't touch. I'd come full circle at last, and I felt so complete, so happy, so fulfilled I couldn't stand it.

At least, this is what I told Doc on the phone from our Greenwich Village hotel near NYU the next morning, as Dolly was singing in the shower, some Top 40 tune I didn't recognize. So we had little in common when it came to music. Or movies. Or anything remotely cultural, political, or spiritual. Bottom line, we were kindred spirits in more significant respects—both of us had lost our parents and sought their replacements in the wrong places, and both of us achieved a cathartic rebirth via our reunion, putting us back in touch with the fundamental elements that make life worth living, and—

"What a load of bullshit," Doc said. I could hear him shaking his head and rolling his eyes. "Vic, you're whipped, my man. The single most pussy-whipped sad sorry motherfucker on the face of the planet, and maybe the whole damn galaxy."

"Doc, please. You don't understand. You don't even *know* this girl."

"Yeah, but I know you. And from what you've told me, she fits right into the pattern of every other psycho bimbo who ripped your heart out, and frankly, I'm sick of watching it. Find yourself a nice, decent, simple girl and settle down. Not every bitch in the world is a neurotic space case. Most aren't. But whatever percentage of them are, you seem hell-bent determined on tracking down each and every one of them and giving them an open target, while all you get in return is some nookie, which I bet ain't worth the price of admission. Healthy in mind means healthy in body, and that goes double for sick in mind and sick in body, know what I'm sayin'?"

I was hearing but not listening. He just didn't understand. "Doc, look, you'll feel differently when you meet her, I swear. She *is* a nice young lady, the one who's been waiting for me and vice versa, with a few problems, okay sure, but that just makes her more interesting, right? I'm bringing her back with me after a brief stopover in Miami, and, well, we plan to elope, to be honest, Doc. Can't do much legally until she's free of the dentist, who's really a yuppie drug pusher, small time from4 surmise, and then maybe she'll finish her nursing degree and maybe I'll, I dunno, get a *real* job."

"Hold it, Vic. Now just chill for a second here. Now, I'm assuming this is jet lag or something in the water that's talkin', or just a sex hangover, because nothing you just said makes any sense at all. Vic, please, promise me you won't throw your life away on this bimbo, please? You're cheating yourself and the real true nice young lady who's out there right now waiting for you to show up and sweep her off her feet. What is it with you, anyway? Still trying to find your young mama and save her? *Wake up, Vic*!"

"No, Doc, you're the one who's stuck in a dream out there. You're just jealous cause I found my true love and you haven't." I was out of line and realized it instantly, but I was so frustrated with his lack of endorsement I couldn't help it.

There was a pause on the other end and I held my breath, about to apologize when Doc said, "All right, Vic. Fine. What have you. It's your life, my man, and you're not really hurting anyone except yourself, so good luck. You're cat's in good shape, Monica's taking good care of him, so don't worry about that. I'll look for your rent check in the mail, and then drop me a postcard from Miami. All the best to the Mrs. Now, I got work to do, so if you'll excuse me."

"Doc—!"

Too late. Dial tone.

I didn't have time to mope, though. I put Doc's negative

assessment on the back-burner, justifying it as blind, cold prejudice due in part to my history, believing Doc would change his tune once he met Dolly, and then I'd have his approval. Not that I really needed it. You know me—I don't need anyone's approval but my own. Except it would make things easier if Doc and Dolly got along, since they were the two most important people in my life. Anyway, no time for this now, I thought. I heard Dolly wrapping up her shower and hurriedly called SFPD headquarters and asked for Captain Sharp, recently promoted from detective. His former partner Shoemaker had been passed over and was pissed, blaming it on sexism since she was a broad, but I didn't really care about that. I just wanted to know one thing:

"Who's lying to whom, Sharp?"

"What do you want, Valentine? I'm a busy man. I did all I could do for you, told you just what Al Marcus made me promise to tell you once some time had passed after he was gone, and now that's all I can offer you. Really."

"Wait a second, please. I'm still out of the loop on some things and I need them cleared up before I can continue."

"Where are you calling from, anyway?"

"New York, where else?"

"Are you *serious*? You are one obsessive s.o.b., Valentine. I didn't think you'd take it this far and turn it into an outright investigation."

"Well, what did you expect me to do? Just sit on it?"

"But there's not much you can do *now*, is there? Christ, I shouldn't have said anything, but Al made me promise, and he knew you better than I do. You talk to that guy at the pool hall?"

"Pop? Yeah. Said I'm better off not knowing the truth."

"Well, maybe Al thought so too, and just wanted you to hear it from someone else. You talk to anyone else?"

"Like Mob?"

"I told you, Al told me the Mob was not tied into this. Your father was small potatoes. And you know how messy the hit was, right? Not their signature, kid. More like a random hatchet job by some serial wacko, or a personal vendetta by some small time bookie or pissed off stoned lover."

"Save the conjecture, man, that I got plenty of. Pop also said Al was an A-1 asshole, and no friend of my old man's."

"I know nothing about that. According to Al, Pop was okay, so that's something personal. All I know is what Al told me to pass on to you—that Pop was there that night, and so was Junior, and so was that list of names I gave you. Al himself closed the investigation because he had nothing solid, no hard proof or talkative witnesses, or so went the report, but in truth, he thinks these guys were hiding something."

"And Al knew too and didn't want to tell me himself, is that it?"

"Who knows? He's gone now, too. Maybe, like I said, he just wanted you to hear it from the source. Or maybe he thought they'd tell you something they wouldn't tell a cop, especially since, as you say, Pop had a hard-on for Al, for some personal reason."

"So maybe these guys were covering up for the Mob, ever think of that?"

"Look, believe what you want, kid. I got work to do in the land of the living."

"Wait, one last thing. Al ever mention a Donald Dunlap to you? Dealer out of Jersey? Uses a dentist office as a front?"

"Nope. Why?"

"Al have his hand in the drug trade, Sharp?"

"That's it, kid. I won't listen to you besmirch Al's good name. He took care of you, kid, just remember that, out of the goodness of his heart and in deference to your father's memory, whom he loved like a brother and forgave all his sins, which he had no part of, I assure you, and you have no right to drag his name through the mud like that, so can it. He loved you like a son, too, after your father was killed, which was why he wanted this info, pointless as it may be now, passed on to you."

"Yeah. Or maybe he felt guilty about something."

Big sigh. "Invent your own truth then, kid. I'm out of it now. Get back to me if you get something solid. Otherwise, don't bother me anymore." *Click*.

When I hung up I sensed Dolly behind me and turned to see her in the doorway of the bathroom, towels wrapped around her hair and torso. She'd heard part of the latter conversation, her face told me. I hadn't wanted her to at first, didn't want her to think I was snooping around behind her back, but now it was too late, and it didn't really matter anyway. "Hey. Talking to a friend of Al's in San Francisco, the one I told you about, who sent me on this wild goose chase out here. The more I delve into this, the more it seems Al was into some unsavory shit, along with my old man, and— shit, Dolly, I'm wondering if Al himself took out the old man. Deal gone down bad, a rip-off, a silence job—that's how it's beginning to add up, anyway. And Al wanted to clean his conscience and maybe his memory too, by having me dig this up posthumously. Hell, it was Al's idea I become a P.I. to begin with. Maybe in a way he wanted to be found out, because it was nagging him. But that doesn't explain why the Mob wants me off their backs, unless—hm. Maybe Al was working for them, did it for them, or was in cahoots with them, purposely making it sloppy to throw everyone off, and maybe Pop and Junior saw something they shouldn't have, and are sworn to secrecy, but if I came out here and confronted them personally, me being a crack detective and all, I'd be able to deduce that, and—*shit*. I don't know. I just don't know what to make of this, Doll."

I put my face in my hands and rubbed my eyes and temples, suddenly weary and fed up. Maybe it was time to pack this in after all, like everyone kept telling me, and concentrate on my own happiness, which walked over and sat beside me on the bed, massaging my shoulders, kissing my neck and ears and then lips, holding me, letting the towel fall away from her soft, curvaceous body, so sweet-smelling and feminine and tender after the shower, and I sucked on her nipples like a nursing baby while she held my head in her arms and hummed "There's Always Tomorrow" from *Annie*. That sort of ruined the moment, unfortunately, so I sat back up and sighed, and then Dolly turned me around to face her, looked deeply into my eyes, and said: "Vic, I know for a fact it was Al who killed your father."

Naturally I was incredulous. "What—? Spill it, Dolly. All of it, right now, no matter what you're afraid of. I need to clear this up completely before I can concentrate on you and me."

"I realize that now. I should have said something a long time ago, when I first talked to you, but then I got that phone call, and drove up to warn you, and after that everything just sort of spiraled out of control, but things started coming out into the open anyway, and I just didn't have the guts to come right out and tell you, Vic, I wanted you to see that picture of Al and Donald. Donald used to do business with Al and your father for years. A lot of Donald's customers were in Brooklyn, and Al and your father got paid for protection, plus a piece of the action, but your father didn't like Donald, wanted to double cross him on a deal, then kill him, and so Al, who was loyal to Donald cause he had the loot, right, pretended to go along with it, and they set up a meeting one night at Pop's pool hall, where your father would feel safe, and then Al told him to come out into the alley where Donald had stashed some stuff, only Donald wasn't even in town, he was back in

Philly, waiting for the word, and Al killed him, made it real messy to confuse everyone, and he had help, too, I don't know who, but Donald thinks it was Mob, and then after that phone call, I *know* it was. Donald used Al as a go-between for the Mob because Donald is scared of those guys, which he should be, he's such a wimp, and I knew this for years, Vic, but didn't see the point in telling you. I really didn't. And then when you showed up out of the blue like this, with all these hot leads. I just didn't want to see you hurt, Vic. In any way. I was afraid you'd get too close to something dangerous, trace this back to Al and then the Mob and even to Donald, which meant you'd suspect me of covering up, which I wasn't really, I was just protecting you." She let out a long, heavy sigh and lay back on the bed, as if this was a big load off her mind.

I lay back beside her, staring at the ceiling, feeling dazed and confused, like I had throughout the '70s. "Dolly, are you telling me the truth?"

"I *swear*, Vic. You figured it out anyway, so I didn't see the point in holding out any longer. I wanted to tell you before you traced it all to Donald and then—I'm sorry, Vic. Donald's a monster, but he never killed anyone, or gave the order to. The real reason Al went back west was because things got hot after that, and the Mob used its connections to pull strings and have Al transferred by his bogus request, all on the up and up, so he'd be far away, out of sight, out of mind, above suspicion. And then it died down and everyone forgot about it until you showed up."

"But I wouldn't have if Al hadn't passed on these tips to Sharp to give to me! I *still* don't get it."

"Oh, Vic, isn't it *obvious*? Al was afraid you'd eventually find out on your own, he didn't want that screwing up his posterity, so he sent you out here hoping you'd ask the wrong people the wrong questions and wind up like your father. Now that I think about it, maybe Donald was worried, too, and made Al do that, so you'd be on unsafe ground, sort of, and then Donald could make some calls, plus he was always jealous of you, Vic. He knew how much I loved you, and still do."

"But, Dolly, then who was it who ambushed me at The Honeymooner? From what you say it could've been Pete the Meat, right? Sent by Donald to scare me off, think it was Mob?"

"But Petey was with me, remember? Spying on me, the bastard. But if I'd agreed to run away with him like he wanted, he would've blown Donald off, I bet. That's how Petey is. He's weak, blows with the breeze, which was pretty cold from my direction, so he went back to Donald and now you know everything. You going to tell your mother?"

"Huh? Naw, it'd only confuse her. Hell, I think I might join her up there. Three squares a day, cable TV." I picked up the phone impulsively, dialed the Chipper Monk's number, then hung up. Not in the mood. "This just doesn't feel like a resolution, Dolly."

"You mean it's not the one you wanted, right?"

"What? Whaddya mean?"

"Well, who did *you* think the culprit was?"

"Oh, I don't know. I always thought it was a jilted lover or jealous husband myself. It was too passionate, too intense, too premeditated."

"*Premeditated*? All those bullets and knife stabs, all over his body? Sounds pretty spontaneous to me, or made to look like it, anyway."

"Right, which would make it premeditated, or, or really spontaneously executed, so to speak, but long considered. And hey, how did you know about the way he died, anyway? All the bullets and knife wounds?"

"Didn't you tell me?"

"Don't think so."

"Well, must've been Donald then. Vic, this doesn't change anything between us, right? I mean, you said to tell you everything, the whole truth, no matter what I was afraid of, which was alienating you. I don't want you to think I was covering for Donald, though I was sometimes scared he'd hurt me if I said anything."

"Really? He threaten you?"

"Sure. All the time. Made him feel he was in control. He only told me about Al because then he'd have something to threaten me with, said if you ever found out he'd have me killed, too."

"But, Dolly, I *have* found out."

"He doesn't know that."

"He must've figured that was an inevitability, though, if we were hanging out. It was more than just jealousy motivating him, Doll. Remember, Pete had a switchblade when you showed up at your apartment, right? Donald second-guessed you'd go back there, stole your keys or had copies made before you left for Brooklyn, knowing you'd think he was in Chicago, then baited the trap and waited like a spider."

"Vic, oh my god. You're right. Petey would've killed me, stabbed me to death, to shut me up, and you too."

"Make it look like a routine B&E which you or we walked into and interrupted. Yeah, you're marked, Doll, just like me, for sure. We're still out there, scot-free, and Donald must assume I know it all by now, and that I'm stealing his woman and alibi to boot. Dolly, just what are his connections? And Pete's? We talking major league here or what?"

"Donald never really told me much about his business. I really don't know. Like I said, Al was Donald's Mob connection, and he's dead, and Petey's dad is a politico, so anything goes there. I really don't know, Vic. I just sort of zoned out when I was down there, didn't really pay attention, just blew Donald and a few lines of coke, but not ever again, Vic. I realize now I deserve better. You make me feel worthy of something better in life."

I kissed the tip of her nose. "Only the best, sweetheart. And Donald loses out, cause he don't deserve nothin' as good as you. He really even a dentist?"

"Sure. Like you said, it's a respectable front."

"And you? What were you?"

A tear fell down her face as she said, "A customer. A *whore*."

I held her and kissed her and we made love but not all the way. We were still saving that for our honeymoon. I never wanted any woman more in my life than I wanted Dolly. She was so different from Valerie, so much more vulnerable and needy and delicate I just wanted to take care of her. Plus she had an actual conscience, and I could feel her love me and me alone, whereas with Valerie/Rose I was just part of the assembly line. Dolly needed me and me alone, and the feeling was mutual.

I was sick of hotel rooms, so after I showered we checked out and went for a drive northward, through the country. It was a perfect autumn day, the gray sky offset by the explosion of earthbound colors, the wind chilling but refreshing. It was very romantic. We had a picnic somewhere off the road and kissed so much I was afraid we'd have to have our lip-lock surgically detached. Fat chance. There was no place else I'd rather have been stuck for life. We didn't talk so much about old times anymore, even though it was hard to disassociate the past from the present, difficult not to notice the way the threads weaved winding patterns in the barren interim of our separation, though it was apparent now the path was not random at all, but deliberate. We told each other the absence and distance was necessary because of what had happened in Brooklyn that night, but now, after all these years, I knew that hadn't been the purpose for my return at all. The *raison d'etre* was in my arms, rolling on the cold ground in the colorful bed of leaves fallen from dying trees. We rolled and rolled and rolled until we hit something hard and solid and unmovable. At first we thought it was a tree trunk, but it wasn't.

It was a tombstone. We'd been frolicking in a graveyard.

"They're coming to get you, Barbara," I said to Dolly with a bad Karloff accent, a la *Night of the Living Dead*, but she didn't get it.

"Let's get out of here, Vic," she said. "It's a bad omen."

"Huh? Ah, c'mon. All it means is, they're gone, and we're still here, and should make the most of it. Al, my father, my brother, your father. Sorry, Doll. Yeah, let's go."

It began to drizzle when we got back to the Comet, which was going to cost me a fortune in mileage, I realized. I'd probably just wind up buying it, adding it to my classic collection. Next would be my dream: a '57 T-Bird. How sleek that would look gliding through the Art Deco of Miami Beach, I thought. Then I realized that while I was pipe-dreaming Dolly was visibly upset.

"What's the matter, sweetheart?" I asked her as we drove back to Manhattan, probably just to check into another hotel.

"Oh, Vic, can't we just go straight to Miami? What's holding us here now? The case is solved, right? I helped you like I said, now it's your turn. I just have a bad feeling if we stay here, that it'll all come apart somehow."

"That's ridiculous, Dolly. I should turn the Comet back in soon, though. I don't know, I just—I have to see mother before I leave, you know. Want to come with me?"

"Oh, all right. Can we just do it now? She's upstate, right?"

"Well, it's too late now, we wouldn't make it before visiting hours were over. Y'know, seeing you might help snap her out her trance. Yeah. She always liked you, you know."

"Really?"

"Oh sure. Why not?"

"I don't know. I'd think she'd want the best for you."

"Dolly, where did this inferiority complex of yours come from, anyway?"

"I told you, my sister and mother. I guess. But then I always felt that way, and that just made it *worse*."

"Well, I think you're the greatest thing that ever happened, and I won't stop telling you until you realize it, too." She smiled wanly. "Tell you what. Tomorrow we'll go see my mother, then the next day, Miami. Then we'll go see *your* mother, and settle thing once and for all. Time to bury all the old hatchets, wouldn't you say?"

She looked at me fearfully. "What a way to put it," she said cryptically.

"You know what I mean."

"Yeah. Vic?"

"Yeah, babe?"

"I love you. No matter what. I really do, and always have, and always will. No matter what. Promise you'll never forget that, okay?"

"Well, I'll do what I can, but I think I'll need you to remind me on a daily basis for the next fifty or so years anyway. Deal?"

She looked at me and smiled that sad smile, and nodded, but didn't say anything then or for the rest of the way back into town. She just stared out the window into the dark misty night, and I couldn't tell if the drops running down her reflection in the window were of rain or tears.

Chapter Eleven
THE POSTMAN SINGS NICE

The next morning the alarm on the midtown Manhattan hotel clock radio went off at 9:00AM, and I was greeted with the old New Wave tune "Teenage Enema Nurses in Bondage," by Killer Pussy. Perfect. Took me right back to the old days here in the heart of my merrily misspent youth. With a big grin on my face I rolled over to see if Dolly caught the irony of the song lyrics and then noticed she was gone.

I didn't panic at first. I got up, checked the bathroom. No trace. In fact, her suitcases were gone too. She's taken a powder on me.

Frantically I searched for clues to the reason and time of her abrupt departure. Damn it, just when I was beginning to trust her, to believe in true love again, to have faith in my own future. Why couldn't Doc ever be wrong? I just couldn't bear going back home and facing his "I told you so" look.

Then I saw the letter, taped to the lampshade. I grabbed it and read:

"Dearest Vic—by now I'll be in Miami, or on my way. I want you to think very, very carefully about everything I told you yesterday, not just about us, but about your father and Al and Donald, too, and then decide if I'm really, really what you want. If so, there's a ticket waiting for you at the airport. It leaves tomorrow, so you have time to think about it and see your mother. I'll be waiting for you at the airport in Miami, but if you're not on the flight, I'll understand. I can't say whether I'd go back to California with you, so I'm asking you to make a decision I can't. I'm sorry to make you choose like this, Vic, but what can I say, I'm insecure. You're so cool and brave and independent, and I admire you so much. I just want you to be happy. If you're sure I'm what it would take to be make you happy, if you absolutely can't live without me, then I'll see you tomorrow. If not, that's fine. I'll always think fondly of you, and you'll never be replaced in my heart, but I think I'll have the strength to move on by myself. I've learned that these past few days, being with you. Your strength inspires me, always has, always will. God bless you, my darling. Love always and forever, Dolly."

Down at the bottom of the letter were flight details, but no address or phone number in Miami to contact her. If I wanted to see her again, I'd have to be on that plane, and I very definitely planned to be.

I felt a little better after reading the letter. At first I was deadly afraid this would turn into a faithful remake of the Rose story—promise to love me, then vanish. That would really give Doc reason to gloat. Not that he would. Doc was into this tough love trip, but I never doubted his friendship and understanding. I'd really miss him. The way things looked then, San Francisco was slipping further and further into the quicksand of my past, while Miami beckoned. I'd have Monica ship my cat and CDs and videos, and then I'd relocate to South Florida, set up shop in Little Havana or something. Had to be plenty of work for a P.I. there. After all, look at all the action on *Miami Vice*. Few people realize it, but that was a fact based show. New York? Been there, done that. The knowledge—or alleged suspicion, with some corroborative witnesses and no circumstantial evidence after all these years—that Al Marcus had indeed been the trigger-happy knife-crazy wacko who'd turned my old man into a barely identifiable heap of hamburger in a dark, dirty alley, leaving my mother a mentally challenged widow, was somewhat anticlimactic for some strange reason. The fact that Al Marcus wasn't the man he pretended to be didn't faze me. Hell, who was? So what was missing from this picture? Had I been expecting something more romantic? More glamorous? It certainly was devious enough to satisfy the tabloid mentality lurking in the outer fringes of my sophisticated psyche. But for some reason, it just didn't gel with the initial facts. Or maybe I didn't like having Dolly just flat out tell me—belatedly, that is. Maybe I *did* want to play *Green Hornet* till the fucking cows came home. Well, it seemed they were home now. Time to send Black Beauty to the garage and Kato back to Hong Kong. I was hanging up my mask for good. In Miami, I'd resurface in a new guise, a new man. A happy man. What a concept. Let's roll, Kato.

I called the Chipper Monks and made an appointment to see my mother later that afternoon. Then I made one more call, on the spur of the moment, not even fully realizing why. I called Lucy Guisseppe. Some old woman with a heavy wop accent—her grandmother, I assumed—answered the phone. Lucy was still asleep, but I pressed Grandma Guinea to summon her my little charge from the depths of slumberland. This was of utmost urgency, I told her, though I don't think she fully grasped my words. Just my tone. Good enough.

"H-hello?" a thick, sweet voice said huskily.

"Yo, Lucy! It's me! Your old pal Vic!"

She woke right up. "Holy shhh—wow! Vic Valentine! My hero! Why haven't you called sooner? How *are* you?"

"Well, I wanted to wait until I went back East like I said I was gonna do, remember?"

"Yeah, okay, so, so *wait*. So that means—don't tell me you're in New York?"

"You got it, babe."

I heard a long, loud scream. Slow times in Long Island, I supposed. Easily excitable.

"*Ohmygod*! I told *all* my friends about you! You have to come meet them! And Gramma, too! *Grammy, it's Vic! Vic Valentine*! Hey, you hear about the trial? Well, maybe not, since it's in New York, but I think it was national news, sort of. My father's been convicted after a like a record trial, rushed through by the Family's lawyers and judges and people, and so he's been put away for life, unless something happens on the inside, y'know? But I don't keep up with Family business, so I don't know about that. In a way, I'd rather he lived to suffer."

"Actually, baby doll, I need to ask a favor of you."

"Anything!" The sensual tinge to her voice momentarily distracted me. She had just turned seventeen, so I still had a year to go before I could even consider following my impulses in that direction. Only by then I'd be in the throes of marital bliss. Oh well.

"Well, actually, I need some inside dope on The Family, maybe not yours directly. I was thinking more of Brooklyn. You know anybody there?"

"Jeez, only about six uncles and fourteen cousins and nine aunts. Why, what's up?"

"Well, ahm, it's kind of a long story." So I filled her in as briefly as possible, sticking mainly to headlines and abbreviating the full stories as best as I could for time's sake. I gave her the lowdown on my old man in the alley, but omitted any references to Al Marcus, Donald, or Dolly. I wanted her to give me an unadulterated report on what she knew about my standing with the Brooklyn Family. I told her just to drop my name casually to a cousin she could trust, maybe tell about our adventure with her father and Deacon Rivers back in California (it turned out she'd already told the whole extended Family), then slyly segue into the topic of my investigation into my father's murder. Then the cousin could ask an uncle about "Lucy's friend Vic Valentine" and his little local private murder case and see if it triggered some kind of response. Any response at all could mean they were behind the whole deal and knew who I was and what I wanted and definitely wanted me out of their hair. They'd probably get a "message" to me right away, and then I'd know for sure it was them all along. Lucy seemed a bit perplexed but she owed me one because of her father, so she promised to get back to me by the end of the day.

"Then you're coming to visit me, right?"

"Sure," I lied. No time for that, though. I was gone early the next morning, Paradise-Bound.

I called downstairs and booked the room an extra night, showered, shaved, got dressed, and headed out the door to go see Ma. But when I opened the door, there was Pete the Meat Cleaver, who didn't waste any time. He had a sap wrapped around his huge paw and took a massive swing in my direction. I managed to tilt back far enough so that he only grazed my jaw, but that was enough to send me backward into the bed. He jumped on top of me and I told him to control his lust, which only pissed him off more. And he was already plenty pissed.

"You're not getting the jump on me this time, Valentine," he said in my face. I strained and shoved him off of me and hit him with a one-two combo that did little more than slow him down. I dove for my overcoat with my gun in the pocket, which I'd dropped when Petey swung at me, but he was all over me. He was a big guy, and I was a not so big guy. I was in trouble unless I cheated quickly.

"*Run, Dolly!*" I yelled suddenly, and when he sat up and turned around to look at the empty doorway, I kicked him full force in the gut, then in the face. This bought me the time to get my gat and press the muzzle against his temple. I stood him up and sat him down in a chair, kicked the door shut behind me, and then said, "Start talkin'."

"'Bout what? This is between you and me."

"Oh, a macho ego thing? I'm surprised at you, college boy and all. Thought you intellectuals were above that kind of thing."

"Fuck you."

"Sorry, but you don't appeal to me that way. Dolly says you barely escaped a manslaughter beef, that right?"

"Friggin' A!"

"*Tsk, tsk*. Obviously you haven't learned your lesson, young man. Maybe I should call the proper authorities."

"G'head, frickin' coward. My dad'll get me out in five minutes and then I'll find you and show you who's better for Dolly. She wants a real man, Valentine. Know what I mean? A *big* man. Follow?"

I nodded, then hit him in the head once with the gun butt. He swore but then I pressed the muzzle to his temple again and he behaved. "That how you hit me that night in The Honeymooner, tough guy?"

"Huh? Don't know what you're talkin' about. You're crazy. Put the gun down and we'll settle this like real men, or don't you know how, you frickin' faggot?"

I raised my eyebrows, let out a little puff of air, then brained him again. "Y'know, just because I don't get off wearing tight trunks chasing a ball down a field and slapping my robust team-mates on the ass in the locker room doesn't mean I wanna suck their dicks, either, big fella. Just to set the record straight, as it were. And ask Dolly if you don't believe me."

He grinned the killer grin. "I know what Dolly likes, faggot, and you ain't got it. G'head. Hit me again. I'm addin' it all up, and one day I'll come collectin'."

"COD, huh?"

"COD, what's that?"

"What college did you go to again? Must mean Confederacy of Dunces."

"You're a funny guy, Valentine. *Real* funny. I had a funny friend once. Made everybody laugh. Hardy har har. Now he's tellin' worm jokes with a mouthful of dirt, got it, slick?"

"Your pal in the bar?"

"That's right. When I kill you, I'll walk away from that, too. I might even get a reward."

"Oh yeah? Who from? Jesse Helms?"

"Who?"

"Your idol, I thought. Or is that O.J. Simpson?"

"Funny, funny, funny. Hardy har har. So what now, Valentine? You gonna use that gun on me or what? I gotta take a leak. And unless you pull the trigger, you can count on me comin' back. Where the fuck's Dolly, too?"

"I was wondering when you'd mention her. That's why you really dropped by, am I right? Try to win her back? Or did Donnie boy send you?"

"I don't take orders from nobody."

"From anybody, college boy."

"Fuck you."

"F.U. must be your alma mater, am I right?"

"Huh?"

"Never mind. But, hm. If I put this gun down, you'll try to beat me up."

"Worse. I'll frickin' kill ya, man. *Count* on it."

"So, then I either have to take my chances mano y mano, or just blow your brains out here and now. That'd be the quick, easy way. But then I'd have to leave a buck for the maid. Or in your case—only a quarter. She'll probably just think I had a small case of diarrhea."

"Hardy har har."

I pulled the trigger.

But the chamber was empty. I knew that. He didn't—he flinched with frenzied fear. The gun wasn't loaded, and hadn't been since I'd left San Francisco. I had a permit to carry a firearm while traveling, courtesy of Al Marcus and the SFPD, but I had to carry the bullets separately. I was bluffing back in Philly, and I was bluffing now. I decided to play some Rushin' Roulette since I was in a hurry and had no time for this shit. I pulled again, and noticed a dark wet splotch around Petey's crotch was getting larger and was beginning to stink up the joint. "*Damn*," I said. "Where is that bullet?"

"*Fuck*!" Petey exploded at last as I pulled the trigger once more. "All right! I'll go and you won't hear from me again, you sick frickin' maniac!"

"Oh, bullshit. I know you got somethin' to prove and you won't be happy till you prove it. So I may as well put us both out of your misery now, right? I'll just say you broke in to rob me and I was defending myself when the gun went off accidentally."

"*Okay already*!"

"And with your record I'll make it stick easy. Okay, this could be it, Johnny Urinitis. Time for that big field goal in the sky, the last dropkick, toots. Here it comes."

I shielded my face from the impending would-be gore and squeezed the trigger again. Petey suddenly jumped up, shoved me out of the way, and tore out the door and down the hall. He left a stain on the bed, too. I tossed a buck for the maid next to it and left.

I felt great. Petey's little visit helped clear my mind of any lingering doubts he had been the one who jumped me at The Honeymooner. He had nothing to lose at that point for confessing it but he still claimed ignorance, and someone as ignorant as Pete just can't fake true ignorance. I almost didn't need Lucy's subterfuge any longer, but I'd already sent her on her mission, and I had mine.

Then I got sidetracked again. I was in the downstairs garage about to get into the Comet—which I'd promised to have to the owner by that evening, planning to take a cab to the airport—when who should confront me but Donald the doper dentist. Pete the Meat was next to him, but standing in the background now, sulking. "I ain't got time for this crap," I said, getting into the car. Right then I saw two more goons standing on the other side of me, like they'd appeared out of nowhere, instant henchmen. They gave me threatening looks and flexed their muscles inside their designer jackets and I just idly jiggled the car keys, waiting for their next move. I didn't have the chance to jump inside and peel away. They had me, for the time being.

"Where is she?" Donald asked coolly. He had on designer shades but still looked scrawny and non-intimidating.

"Who?"

"You have less time than you think, Valentine. Tell me where Dolly is and it'll all be over."

"Don't know, Donnie. She amscrayed on me."

"Come again?"

"Skedaddled, boogied, went on the lam. I have no idea where she is. Now back off. I have an appointment."

"Fine," he said to my surprise. "But if you meet with her in Miami, you'll suffer the same punishment she does. It's your choice. Is she worth it?"

I tried to looked nonchalant, but since I could only see things from my perspective, I don't know if I was successful. "Miami, huh. Well, that's a long commute from San Francisco, ain't it? So, don't worry about it, Scarface. Anyway, she's not worth it." I only said that so he'd leave me alone. If I saw him later, I'd deal with him then, prove just how much she really was worth it.

"You're so right. Little tramp. You're such a naive fool, Valentine. You have no idea how she's using you."

I swallowed. Now he was getting to me. "Huh? Like how?"

He smiled in a reptilian fashion. "Oh, don't you know? I suppose by now she's fed you that tired old story about Al Marcus and me conspiring against your dear departed daddy?"

I saw no reason not to concur. "Yeah so? Al's dead. The Mob wants me out, so I'm out. And you? Shit. Now that Al's gone, the Mob will make breadcrumbs out of a slice of Wonder like you, goons or no goons. These ain't true-blue goombahs you got here. Just hired muscle from the local gym. You don't fool me with these two-bit Vikings and you don't scare me, Donnie Osmond. If I thought you were either directly or indirectly to blame for my old man, I'd have let you know by now. It was Al all along, with the Mob. You're nothin' but a two-bit player, with no say in anything. You got nothin' to worry about from me, shitspine. And whether I see Dolly again anywhere ain't none of your god damn business."

I stooped to get in the car and one of the goons took hold of my shoulder. I whipped out my gun and stuck it in his face.

Donald laughed arrogantly. "Pete told me about your little game. It's not loaded, is it?"

"Wanna try me?" I said, cocking the piece and placing the muzzle square between the goon's eyes, which were surrounded by newly formed beads of sweat.

"Sure," he said. "Plenty more where he came from. Like you said, down at the gym."

I sighed and uncocked the piece and got into the driver's seat. "My car's red but his blood's yellow. Wouldn't match."

"See you in Miami," Donald said as I shut my door. Then he walked up and leaned his slimy head inside the window at me. "And she's lying about Al, Vic. I met him through her. Once. In that picture. Then I never saw or heard from him again."

"Yeah? So how do you know about that story she told me?"

"Because. That's the one she made up a long time ago, to tell *everybody*. Her cover story. Also, she concocted this lie to hurt me, but it didn't. I find her fantasies harmless and amusing. But you won't, not when you find out what she's trying so desperately to hide. She knows I know it, too, the real truth, the whole sordid story, and that one day, I'll tell the right people. Unless she comes back to me."

He had my full attention again. My gut felt queasy, my skin clammy. "You're full of shit." I tried to start the engine, but it wouldn't turn over. I tried again and again, then noticed Pete was grinning with the fuel pump dangling from his hand. "You sonovabitch," I said with no effect. Then they were all laughing.

All I could do was sit and stew. No way I'd get that fuel pump back. I'd have to track down a brand new one before I brought the car back, and that would take valuable time and expense and effort. They knew that. Now they knew I knew they knew that, and they were loving it.

"So shoot me!" Pete the Meat said. I took out my gun and aimed it at him and he took off out of the garage, but with the fuel pump, like he was charging for the goal line with the prize pigskin in tow. Kiss my ass, the boy really could run after all. Then I deposited my empty gun in my overcoat and looked at Donald, beaming arrogantly with his hired help like a trio of Caucasian cannibals. The goons were as offensively white as their boss, only of the albino orangutan variety, and obviously had nothing directly to do with the traffickers he did business with, who would one day slice him and dump him in the Atlantic for fish food, but not soon enough. No, this loser had no Mob ties. Why would the Mob need a wimp like him? He was dealing with small-time Latins or Blacks in Philly, maybe even the Chinese gangs. Kid stuff. It was clear to me he had nothing to do with my father's death, even indirectly. I ixnayed any possible revenge plans. Could've been he only told me Dolly was lying to avoid just such an agenda, but I doubted it. My gut told me he was nothing more than a penny-ante middle man with a beautiful wife who hated him, but over whom he held some deep, dark secret in an effort to control her.

What was that secret?

I got out of the car and went back upstairs without even saying goodbye to Donald and the boys. I made some calls around to several garages, but everyone said that parts for a classic had to be special ordered and shipped in, and that would take weeks. I had no choice but to tell the rental guy to come tow the car at my expense, order the pump at my expense, and install it at my expense. He was pretty unhappy over the phone but I told him it happened in a shitty neighborhood and I had no idea why they'd heist a fuel pump and nothing else, but I was glad that was all. So was he. But then he asked about the police report, and I had to admit I made that all up. So what happened to the pump? I told him it was a long story and I had a short schedule, then hung up in his ear. He was so pissed he'd probably charge the whole car to my credit card. I didn't care. What really bothered me was that I had no transportation to go see Ma now, unless I cabbed it. I checked my wallet. Cash was low, and my credit cards were maxed out, or would be I'd spent most of Shiv's money on hanging out with Dolly and plane tickets and hotels. All I knew for certain was that I was going to make that plane for Miami no matter what. Then I'd come back and see Ma somehow, then head home. The honeymoon was over. Around five the phone rang, waking me from a nap. I half hoped it was Dolly, but it was Lucy.

"Hey, Vic? Guess what? You're a big celebrity in Brooklyn!"

"Oh yeah, why's that?" I mumbled sleepily.

"Cause of what you did for me! The Family is grateful to you for exposing my father's sickness and everything. The whole Family knows about it! I had no idea it was so spread around. And you know what else?"

"No, what?"

"They're not going to kill my father in the joint while I'm still alive, out of respect. He'll have to live and suffer! Isn't that *great*?"

"Hm-hm. But, Lucy, what about my murder case? My old man? Anyone comment on that?"

"Yeah! Word is, you want their help, just ask for it! They loved your father too, it turns out."

I felt suddenly ill, like I had food poisoning. I left Lucy hanging and ran to the bathroom to throw up. When I returned, she was still rambling on like I'd never left.

"And all my cousins want to meet you, and I said you're real cute and half Italian, too, but I said I won't share you with them, so when you come visit—"

"Lucy, wait. I can't come visit. Not now. I have business. About my father."

Long pause.

"Lucy? You hear me?"

"Yes, but when can you come, then?"

"I don't know. When I get back from Miami, maybe."

"Why? What's in Miami?"

"That's what I plan to find out."

"Your dad's killer?"

"Someone who knows the killer maybe, yea."

"You going to hunt the killer down and arrest him after all this time?"

"No, can't do that. I'm not a cop."

"So are you gonna kill them?"

"No, can't do that. I'm not a criminal, either."

"My uncle will do it! He said so! And they can find anyone!"

"No. I just want to know, that's all." I felt really ill now. "Lucy, I gotta go. I don't feel well."

"Aw, want me to come over and take care of you?"

"No, that's okay. I'll be leaving soon."

"But you promise to come to my birthday party, right?"

"What? *Which* birthday?"

"My eighteenth, silly!"

Suddenly I felt better. "But I thought you just had your seventeenth?"

"I did! So you have to come to my eighteenth because you missed my seventeenth. But that's okay—eighteen's even better, know what I mean?"

"Yeah!"

"Vic, weren't you listening to anything I said a minute ago?"

"Oh, yeah, I was listening all right. So you're sure, you're positive the Mob doesn't want me gone, right?"

"You mean the Family?"

"Yeah, whatever."

"No, Vic! They love you! You're a hero! They'd kill anyone who hurt you!"

I was sick again. "Okay, gotta go, Lucy. I'll call you, okay? Yeah, when I get back. Postcard, yeah, yeah, sure. I love you too. 'kay, bye."

After I finally got off the phone with Lucy I realized I never called and cancelled my visit to see Ma. It was about a half hour after visiting hours ended, too. I called and got Nurse Windsor on the line, who gave me a speech about letting my mother down and I surprised her by agreeing with her, I was a shit-heel, but I'd make it up when I got back from Miami, and I asked her to please continue the Patsy Cline music, even though it had had no apparent effect so far. Then Nurse Windsor told me my Aunt Florence had tried calling my Brooklyn hotel but had been told I'd checked out. I told Nurse Windsor to tell Aunt Florence I'd leave word with Chipper Monks where I could be reached in the near future, but for the time being I was in transit, incommunicado. Nurse Windsor wanted to launch into another lecture but I just hung up on her, went into the bathroom, and threw up again.

I didn't sleep much and before I knew it morning arrived and it was time to go the airport. I got cleaned up and checked out and noticed the Comet was gone, either picked up by the rental agency or stolen, I didn't care which, then I hailed a taxi for La Guardia, where hopefully my reservation was waiting. It was. Dolly really did want me to come to Miami and be with her.

During the flight I convinced myself Donald was lying to save face, Lucy was misled by her elders to throw me off course, and that true love lasts through anything. It was a bumpy flight, but I made it. And there she was, waiting for me, just like she said.

Chapter Twelve
RED PALMS

We embraced as if we hadn't seen each other in years, and I was a long lost lover, home for the holidays. In a way, it felt like that. I was afraid I'd never see the real Dolly again, worried I was being escorted out of Miami International by an evil imposter. Still, I wanted to give her the benefit of the doubt. After all, what could she possibly be hiding from me? So what if she knew the real killer and was holding out? She must've had her reasons. Whatever Donald was using to blackmail her into staying with him had to be inconsequential as far as Dolly and I were concerned. I'd promised never to judge her, anyway. I already knew she was a junior junkie and not a vestal virgin, so what else was left?

She was squeezing my arm as we walked through for the airport and out toward the parking lot. I just had my one carry on piece of luggage—like I said, I always travel light—so we could just get going.

"I can't tell you how glad I am you came," she said, a tear escaping her control.

"Yeah, me too," I said, and in a way I meant it. "Though this little test was totally unnecessary." She clutched me even tighter now. "We going to meet the folks?"

"Oh, sure. But I just got in myself, remember. I haven't really had the chance to look them up yet. I'm staying in Miami Beach until I get it all together. Also, I want to make sure I wasn't followed, y'know?"

I nodded, but didn't mention the little visit that had already been paid me in New York. Not yet. I was still wondering how they tracked me down. I was almost positive Pete couldn't have tailed me himself. He's not that smart to be so invisible and elusive, and I've dealt with pros. Maybe Donnie did have Manhattan connections that kept tabs on me. Whatever.

We got into her rented car, an old bronze Impala, and drove toward Miami Beach. I turned on the radio and Culture Club was doing their old hit "Do You Really Want To Hurt Me?" The Euro-calypso rhythms nicely complemented the scenery, and the lyrics fit the mood I was in. I keep telling Doc there's a radio conspiracy against me but he just laughs. Maybe The Phone Phantom moonlighted as a celestial DJ.

I'd been to Florida once on a sojourn with my family when I was about eight or nine, but only remembered Sea World and a picnic on Key Biscayne, feeding raccoons. As an adult I appreciated the decadent Third World ambience, the palm trees swaying trance-like in the warm breeze, stark and sinister against the clear azure sky, as if voodoo dancing to a beat only insiders and spirits could hear. I was an outsider, but not for long. I was determined to learn that secret tune and hum it to Dolly one sultry night, find out if she knew it too. Maybe she could teach me the words.

It was pretty hot by mid-afternoon, when we arrived at her hotel in Miami Beach, a typical pastel seashell with rooms called The Surfcomber. The humidity was oddly titillating, probably because it'd been so long since I felt it, being used to bone dry California, and long removed from summertime in the Northeast. The colors here were so much more vivid than in California or New York, and I don't just mean the pastel art deco architecture, much of it newly renovated after the runaway success of *Miami Vice*. The ocean was aqua-blue, the sky powder blue, and together they looked like a brilliant backdrop on the horizon. Everything had an airbrush feeling to it, like Vargas doing Edward Hopper. The rows of pastel buildings along the strip looked like something out of a Tahitian Toyland, especially when you added in the tourists dressed in flower shirts, but then you noticed some dark-skinned homeboys giving you the evil eye and the cartoon beauty was tainted with the foreboding feeling of imminent danger. Just how I liked it.

"Doesn't even feel like America," I said as we went up to her room.

"It isn't," she said. "That's why I like it. It's so different than home, from anything I know up north."

"Been here before?"

"Never. But I feel like I've been here forever already."

"San Francisco had that effect on me too, first time I went there," I said.

"You'll get used it here and like it better," she assured me, pulling into her room and on top of her on the bed.

"Too hot," I said, kissing her.

"Hot can be good," she said, kissing me back. "Hot and

steamy. Anyway, everything is air-conditioned, see?"

The room was cool, and walking in had the effect of stepping out of a hot tub into a walk-in freezer. "Surprised people don't get pneumonia with these sudden temperature changes," I said.

"My arms will always be warm, you can count on that," she said, and then she added with a whisper in my ear, "and the rest of me will be hot. Hot, and wet..."

An hour later we took a shower and got dressed and then walked down Collins Ave. to Wolfie's Deli, on what was known as Celebrity Corner. My hand, the one that Pete the Meat had sliced back in Philly, was beginning to really bother me. My palm was all red and swollen, and the wound itself looked nasty. Dolly told me she would go to the local drugstore and bring me some appropriate medicinal aids and she would personally take care of it after dinner. She was my private nurse. I trusted her.

At Wolfie's we ate well and small talked, dodging the big issues so as not to spoil the mood, the sensation of being in a faraway place together, away from anything or anyone we knew, surrounded by exotic experiences to explore at our leisure. After dinner we walked down to Ocean Drive and strolled along the beach at sunset, the sky a violent red, holding hands like those stupid lovers on late night commercials for easy listening compilations. Then we walked back up to the strip as the lavender dusk was ending and the dark blue night beginning and sipped *cafe con leche* at a place called the Palace Bar & Grill, which had a sidewalk patio facing the sea and the stars.

That was when I broke the spell, because until I exorcised all demons from our past, I wouldn't be able to enjoy our future, or even the present. I took a deep breath during a lull in conversation and said: "Donald paid me a visit in New York." She looked away and I went on. "He told me you were lying about Al, and implied he was blackmailing you into returning to him, because he knows something about you that he'll broadcast unless you go back to Jersey. I get the idea that's what's prevented you from leaving a long time ago, maybe even has something to do with your selling yourself into marriage with him to begin with. Now, Dolly, before you get all iced over, I'm not saying I believe any of this. I'm just running it by you so you know he's still out there and still playing hardball. And, by the way, he knows you're in Miami."

She was icing over anyway. Either it was a standard fabricated reaction when she was on the spot, or else she was really offended. I had to take that chance. "Vic, you just aren't *ever* going to trust me, are you? You take that asshole's word over mine? What could I possibly be lying to you about by now, Vic? I've bared my fucking *so*ul to you!" Heads turned, but that never stopped Dolly. I think it encouraged her. She liked the security of a large audience. The waterworks leaked right on cue, but not gushing, just subtly dripping, like a broken faucet. "What else do you want from me? An affidavit? Photographic evidence? Character witnesses? When are you going to let your past go, Vic? It bogs me down in my own, because we share so much, and I need to leave it all behind more than you do. If you can't trust me then forget it. I gave you a chance to think this over, and you showed up, and I thought that was that, this was the start of our future, a clean slate. But just when I'm getting comfortable, when I think tonight could be the night we finally go all the way, because there's real trust now, you pull this. It's never going to *end*, is it? How can we be happy if somewhere in the back of your mind you'll be constantly doubting me, looking for some slip-up that will reveal my true nature? What do you think it is Donald could have on me, Vic? *What*?" I shrugged. "Right. *He's* the criminal. *He's* the liar. For all I know there's something he thinks I know I shouldn't. He's probably afraid I'll just call the cops on him from here and they'll take him down. I could, you know."

"So why don't you? Sounds like a good idea to me."

"I might. But he could take me with him. After all, I was his best customer, remember." I winced. "I just married the asshole for his money, and for his access. I was a lost kid, Vic. Lonely, confused. I don't even really want to look up my sister and mother, now that I'm here with you. But if you want to believe Donald's desperate lies, go ahead. Him or me, Vic. It's that simple. You have to take that leap of faith this minute, or else just go right back to the airport. I just can't take anyone putting me down anymore. Especially not you."

I sighed. I often sigh. "All right, Dolly, you're right. But you have to look at it from my viewpoint, too. All these conflicting stories!"

"Choose one, then, and then take it from there. *Now*, Vic."

Her firmness startled me. I thought about Lucy telling me how admired I was within Mob ranks in Brooklyn, how they offered to help me. I tried to find a hole in that, and did. Lucy had a little crush on me, would tell me anything she thought I wanted to hear, just to get me to come see her. Also, maybe there were internal factions that were involved with Al, and those were the one that threatened me off their turf. Maybe those same factions didn't want the bosses to know they'd helped murder one of the Mob's prized payroll policemen. My new reputation as a child saver and pervert-buster might not be enough to earn me some straight answers about my father. That alleged offer of help to find the killer could've been just another ruse to throw me off, too. No, there wasn't enough there to confirm anything, I decided. Dolly was right. I had to choose whom I was going to believe. "Invent your own truth," Sharp had told me from San Francisco. I looked at Dolly and nodded. "Let's get married," I said.

She squeezed my wounded hand and it hurt. So did the scratch on my chest from the tip of Petey's switchblade. She cooed and kissed my palm, leaving lipstick on it, and then took me back to the hotel and tended to it with professional aplomb. We made love but not all the way. We weren't married yet.

"But we can't get married legally until you're divorced," I said as we lay in bed in the dark, listening to the soothing hum of the air conditioner.

"True. We may have to resort to bigamy."

"I'm game. We can always deal with Donald later, right? If ever. Maybe we can move further away. Hawaii, maybe." She liked that idea. "I gather you dig tropical climates, baby. I like it cool, but...anyplace is paradise when I'm with you."

"I know of a 24 hour chapel right near here, you know. No blood tests, no questions. It's made for people like us, on the fly, in a romantic haze."

I looked over at the clock. 2AM. I wasn't sleepy. I was too happy, wanted to be awake to enjoy it. It was such a new, unique sensation. And once we were married, I could finally, at long last, consummate my love for Dolly Duncan. We could zip right down, buy the ring, say the words, then zip right back to bed and do the deed. I hadn't seen Dolly's ring from Donald on her finger since that first night in The Honeymooner. In her heart, she was free now. That's all that counted. "Let's do it," I said.

Like two kids eloping we ran downstairs and into the Impala. This was it. Finally. Happiness. The drive was maybe five minutes. On the way I popped one last question.

"Dolly, don't get mad, especially not now, but how do you think Donald knows you're in Miami?"

"Where else would I go? He could be staking out my mother's house right now."

"Right! Right. You'll make a good detective, babe. Maybe we

should avoid that area for a while, then. Where's she live?"

"Coral Cables. Nice area, I'm told. But maybe I can call Sissy, meet over her in Coconut Grove, near where she goes to school, I hear. She's studying computers or something, last I heard, about six months ago. She probably still is. Anyway, we could meet them in a cafe in the Grove, unless you think they'll be followed."

"Could be, we'll see. First we'll take a long awaited honeymoon, just the two of us. Okay?" I kissed her and then the next thing I knew we were there.

It was a modest chapel, with a neon sign that said "Open 24 Hours," like it was a doughnut shop. It was tucked away on a side street, I don't know where, somewhere near Indian Creek, though, because I could hear the water lapping restlessly in the background. There was something in the air tonight, all right. The neighborhood was decidedly shady. In fact, right next door was a bar with a rowdy clientele, motorcycles lined up out front, loud rock music and stoned voices blaring from the dim interior. Then as we got closer to the chapel, I realized it was emanating its own soundtrack. Elvis was singing "Crying in the Chapel" on a speaker system.

Oh no.

"Dolly, what do you know about this place?" I asked just before we went in. I noticed there was no cross. Non-denominational?

"Not much. Actually, I asked downstairs at the desk of our hotel, and they recommended it. I couldn't wait, wanted to get married as soon as you got here, before either of us could chicken out. So here we are."

I gulped. "Yep. Here we are, all right."

Inside was a small reception area with a few chairs and flower arrangements and Elvis' voice a few octaves louder. The interior was painted bright pink and lavender and green. Blinking Christmas lights were strung around the room with festive gaudiness. Framed portraits of Elvis and Priscilla Presley at their Las Vegas wedding mingled with smaller Polaroid snapshots of other couples, ostensibly hitched on the premises. "Crying in the Chapel" ended, and "Love Me Tender" began, apparently on a continuous tape loop, and before I could say or do anything Dolly had pressed the buzzer and then Deacon Richard Rivers of the New Church of Elvis appeared from behind a sliding panel, rubbing his puffy little eyes, wearing his gold lame robe, his hair still long and red and braided, his grin still dopey and lopsided.

When he recognized me he was instantly awake. At first he kept grinning his lopsided grin, then he lost it when he saw I was not amused.

"Gary Groundhog Day, right?" he said, pretending to struggle placing my name. "Or was it Vinnie Veteran's Day?"

"Vic Valentine!" Dolly volunteered cheerfully. "Vic, you're famous!"

"Let's get outta here," I said to Dolly.

"What's the hurry, Vinnie?" the deacon said. "Hey, I should wake Zelda up. She'd be glad to see you."

"I'll bet, but don't bother," I said. "C'mon, Dolly," I said, taking her by the hand.

"What's going on?" Dolly demanded, breaking my grip and putting her foot down.

"I'll explain later, dear," I said through gritted teeth.

"Y'know, I shouldn't be happy to see you—and I'm *not*," the deacon said. "Thanks to all that publicity from the brouhaha in California, my churches have been systematically dismantled by the Feds. They claim income tax evasion, that my church wasn't legit, but I say it's plain old denial on a grand scale. The religious right wants me silenced, because I preach Truth and they're just spreading the same old ancient hypocrisies, and people were starting to wake up and smell The King."

"I really don't care, dickface. You're still the same old phony creep to me. I'm glad you leaving your precious flock behind to fend off the bad guys."

"Unlike you, Gary, I have faith. In The King, that is. I just left him in charge, that's all. I'm not the man he is, and neither are you. He helped you take care of it, and I appreciate that. But truth is, you did it for selfish reasons. To be a big hero, impress your little teenage girlfriend."

Dolly looked at me but I just shook my head.

The deacon went on, "Not for me or Zelda or even The King. The upshot of the whole deal was the leveling of my empire. So I'm starting over, after greasing a few palms, and with Zelda's help we'll be right back where we were before the anti-Elvis rears his ugly head. He's out there now, Vinnie, you better believe it. Could be Michael J. Fox, could be Newt Gingrich, could be Eddie Vedder. Hell—it could be you, for all I know. What are you doing here now, anyway? Followed me all the way across country to get in my shit again?"

"We're just here to get married," Dolly said, confused but

stalwart. "I had no idea you knew each other."

"We don't," I said.

"So let's *do* it!" Dolly exclaimed, unabated by the tension. "I was told you sell rings here, and then we can go right into the ceremony!" Now Elvis was crooning "Can't Help Falling in Love." Last time I heard that was at an orgy in the deacon's Berkeley church, during an "orientation meeting."

"This guy's a fake, Dolly," I said. "And a pervert."

"No way," the deacon said. "This is a registered wedding chapel. One of many all over the world, I'm proud to say. Vicki Lee is High Priestess of the Honolulu chapel. We have chapels from Reno to Rwanda. We're starting over small, with the wedding chapels, so people won't think I'm a sex maniac as has been wrongfully and maliciously reported. I believe in the sanctity of marriage, contrary to vicious rumors, and even Zelda and I are on our way down the aisle soon maybe. I'm no pervert, Miss. Your boyfriend's been misled by bigots with an agenda, and I'm frankly surprised at him. That kind of slander is the religious right's greatest weapon, but it won't work now. Anyway, Vinnie, if you and your woman-friend want to tie the knot under the holy auspices of The King, just say the word. I'm man enough to let bygones be bygones. Are *you*?"

"C'mon, Vic," Dolly pleaded. "Neither one of us is religious anyway. This is the only place like it around, and I just don't want to wait any longer. It'll just be our little secret, but it'll be enough. Then we can start our honeymoon. Right away."

Little Elvis was in cahoots with Big Elvis, it seemed. "Well..."

"Ready?" the deacon said. "Time's a tickin' by, and I gotta be movin' on soon. Marriage might do you good, Gary. It won't make you a puppet on a string, but king of the whole wide world! Your world, anyway, which you're welcome to. We can't go on with suspicious minds, though."

"All right," I said, throwing my arms up into the air. "Whatever. Let's just go in and buy the damn certificate and say the words and get it over with. This place is as good as any, I guess, for our purposes. All these joints are shams, anyway, so what's the difference. Where're the rings?"

"Sorry, sold out," said the deacon. "And we're closed. Your twenty-four hours is up. I just wanted to make you bow down to The King just once. But come back when you have a little more respect for the man you'll be saying your vows to. There may be hope for you yet, Vinnie." Then he added, "Sucker," and simply walked back behind the sliding panel and disappeared.

Dolly rang the buzzer desperately but I told her to forget it, telling her I'd explain everything later. On the way out I "accidentally" knocked over a candle on a table of brochures and a small fire started. Then I grabbed Dolly by the hand and we raced for the car, smoke billowing behind us, the fire alarm ringing up and down the block and sending people scrambling out of the bar and into the street, causing a near riot. Back at our hotel I heard fire engine sirens in the distance and fell asleep with a smile on my face.

The following morning we had breakfast at Wolfie's and I related to Dolly the whole sick stupid story of Deacon Rivers and his sex cult of Elvis worshippers, or Elvis cult of sex worshippers. Whatever.

"Maybe it just isn't meant to be," Dolly said sadly. "Us, I mean. What are the odds that of all the chapels we walk into *this* one?"

"Aw, c'mon, Dolly. Getting married is just a formality, right? In my heart I'm married to you already."

"Oh, Vic, you're right, you're right. You're so strong and sweet and smart. What should we do now, though?"

"Well, since we're married in our hearts, anyway."

"Sorry, Vic. The time isn't right. I'm not in the mood."

"Why? What's wrong?"

"I'm just worried I'll get over it. Forget it. Maybe tonight, if it feels right. We're getting close, Vic, hang in there. Just promise me you trust me and won't ever listen to anyone else ever again, okay?"

"Yeah, yeah," I said, prodded by Little Elvis, who would agree to anything to finally get inside Dolly Duncan. "I told you that. What say we just wing it, like tourists or real honeymooners? Okay?"

"Okay," she agreed. "Sounds like fun. Where to first?"

First we took a quick drive past the Elvis chapel. Damage looked minimal but annoying enough. The sight of it made my day, and I was sure Deacon Rivers and Zelda got out alive, with the alarm and commotion and all. Then we headed over the Rickenbacker Causeway to Key Biscayne after picking up some materials for a picnic. I wanted to return to the densely wooded wonderland I'd been to with my family as a kid, feed the raccoons, check out the lighthouse, do the full circle thing. Dolly was quiet and I let her be. I showed her the Houses on Stilts out in the middle of Biscayne Bay, and we both agreed they'd make wonderful hideaways, only accessible by boat. Except they'd be scary in a storm, and speaking of which, the winds were picking up and the sky was getting cloudy, so we decided to get through the picnic on the beach before the storm hit. The raccoons showed up, descendants of the ones my brother and I had given bread to way back when. I told Dolly about my murky memories of that trip.

"Sounds like you and your family took a lot of trips," Dolly said. "And you always make it sound so bleak and tragic, growing up."

"Not really, not till I was a teenager. Then everything went suddenly haywire. As a little kid it was kind of idyllic. I had my paper route and spending money for movies, and Johnny and I played catch with the kids from the block, only Johnny was more athletic than I was. My old man liked traveling every vacation he had, and he always brought us with him, until I was about thirteen or so. That's when he and Ma started having a lot of fights, and he was never around, and then Johnny and the old man started going at it, cause Johnny was more and more into his music, and he got moodier and more distant with me even, so I turned to Ma, who turned to me too. My old man and me got along okay, y'know? But he always kept me at arm's length. We didn't talk much when I was growing up. It wasn't till Johnny died that my old man started talking to me about being a cop like him, but that was only cause now there was no way Johnny could. He'd gotten out of that destiny, but permanent. But my old man wasn't gung-ho about it with me like he was with Johnny. Me, I was leftovers, really, and I had an artistic bent too that my old man thought was a sign of weakness. That's what he said about Johnny's death—it was weakness, he pussied out, like any other chicken-shit musician. But Johnny's suicide still just took the spirit out of everybody, or what was left. My old man gave me the gun I still carry to this day, and taught me how to shoot it, and I thought it was cool, like in a movie, and it really pissed off Ma, but by then they hardly ever talked anymore anyway. I thought maybe now that Johnny was gone my old man and I could finally be close." I shrugged and sighed. "Then he was gone, too. Oh well."

Dolly was going into another crying jag but I held her. The storm kicked up and the raccoons scattered and it was time to go. The imposing lighthouse looked majestic and eerie against the dark, disturbed sky, like a rocket ready to take off into another dimension. If only it was, I'd hop right in, and take Dolly with me.

Since this was Florida, the storm was tropical, therefore more powerful than the autumn rain showers up North. At first it drizzled as we drove across the causeway, then by the time we got back into Miami Beach it was a deluge. Out of nowhere, like the sudden summer storms of my youth, which I always got a kick out of, really. Lightning flared and thunder boomed, and back in our hotel I felt like Edward G. Robinson holed up in the hotel during the hurricane in *Key Largo*, sweating and pacing frenetically. Dolly was oddly distant now. She watched TV idly for a little while, then suddenly got up and said she was going for a walk.

"What? In this weather?"

"Just down to the lobby, silly. I want some cigarettes."

"Oh yeah, I forgot you smoke, even."

"I just do it when I'm nervous now. I gave it up entirely for a while."

"Well, what are you so nervous about now?"

"I don't know. The storm, I guess." Just then there was a brilliant flash followed by a pulsating explosion. The firmament was on fire.

"Shit, I might start smoking myself," I said. "You can't smoke in the rooms anyway, Doll. This ain't a dive, either, like in Brooklyn. See? Smoke detectors."

"That's why I'm going down to the lobby, silly. Be right back."

I noticed her checking her watch, twice before she even left the room. Before she went touched her arm then embraced and kissed her.

"I'll be right back," she laughed as I nuzzled her neck. "You'd think I was going away forever."

"Don't ever," I said seriously. "I couldn't take it. I love you, Doll. We're really together now. Promise?"

She looked pensively into my eyes, squeezed my lower face with her hand, kissed me delicately on the lips, whispered, "Promise," and then walked out, shutting the door behind her.

Thunder boomed and I felt suddenly so lonely, here in this strange town with this strange woman. missed her madly after about five minutes. In a paranoid min-fit I checked her luggage. All there. She wasn't going anywhere. Damn, I had to learn to trust her if this was ever going to work. I had to let my love for Dolly eclipse all those bad memories of Rose from my mind. Our love.

Time passed.

I watched TV. The wind rattled the windows and it felt like

the hotel was going to come apart any second. This was scarier than an earthquake, because it just went on and on. An earthquake was just like BOOM, then it was over. I wondered if this really was a hurricane. I turned on the news and they said it was just a strong storm system. What was the difference? A half hour had gone by. What was she doing, smoking the whole goddamn convenience counter? But if I went down to check on her, it would seem like a lack of trust. Couldn't afford the setback. This could be the night after all, I hoped. Stormy weather outside, nice and snug and cozy inside, confessions of undying mutual love, married in our hearts, far from anyone who could harm us—

Donald.

Had she been kidnapped?

I waited ten more minutes then called down to the lobby and asked the clerk if she was around. He told me she'd been there, bought some cigarettes, stepped outside under the awning to smoke, and then a gentleman showed up and she got into a car with him, about twenty minutes ago.

I slammed the phone down and raced downstairs. I asked the desk clerk what kind of car it was that my "wife" had left in, and he just pointed outside, where it was still parked. She'd gotten in, but it never left. It was too dark to make the car out clearly, so I just walked outside to get a closer look.

Dolly was in the car with another man, and they weren't just talking. From what I could see, she was bent over his lap. I ran through the rain and pounded on the window, expecting the lightning flashes to illuminate the face of Donald or Pete the Meat.

But it was neither.

It was Junior.

Chapter Thirteen
LOVE ON THE ROCKS, WITH A TWIST

"*Rape!*" Dolly cried when she saw me, wiping her mouth and pushing the car door open—right into my crotch. I doubled over with pain but she tried pushing me back into the hotel anyway. She kept licking her lips and wiping her face with rainwater. We were both soaked in no time, and so was Junior, who jumped out of the other side of the car screaming:

"*You little lying whore, you get back here and finish what you started!*" Junior was adjusting his pants and pulling up his zipper as he lumbered toward us, following us through the lobby of the Surfcomber past appalled bystanders and into the elevator. Dolly tried desperately to close the elevator doors before Junior made it in, but she was too late. He squeezed his bulk through the closing doors at the last second and tried to slap Dolly, but I punched him roundhouse style in the side of the head. He just cursed and then hit me back, square in the nose. I felt blood gush out of my nostrils but I still had to get him off Dolly. Junior had her cornered now and was pounding away at her furiously. He was going to kill her. Had to think fast. My gun. With no bullets. He didn't know that. But it was upstairs. In our room. Had to get him there.

"Junior, hold it," I said in a funny voice because of my busted nose. "Let's take her to my room so we don't get the cops in on this, okay? Believe me, I want my share of whacks, too."

"*Vic!*" Dolly screamed, but Junior covered her mouth with one big hairy hand. Man, this would need some *serious* explanations. Dolly kicked and struggled to little avail. Junior was out of shape but beefy and overbearing. He could kill Pete the Meat with one punch, I bet. Couldn't catch him, though.

The elevator stopped at our floor and Junior dragged Dolly into our room. I'd left the door wide open, and I left a trail of blood all the way from the elevator. We went in and I shut the door and locked it, went into my overcoat, and stuck the gun in Junior's nonplussed puss.

"See this?" I said, then I hit him as hard as I could in his nose with the gun butt. Now blood spurted from his fat wop snoz and we were even. He cussed and crouched over and I brought the gun down savagely on the back of his head. Now he was on his knees. Dolly was sobbing hysterically on the bed, but I barely noticed her now. I got a chair from the dresser set and ordered Junior at point blank gunpoint to sit his fat ass down. He complied, holding his geyser nose and giving me a hard look of menace.

"You're *both* dead," he said.

I cocked the empty gun and said, "You first. Unless I get some straight answers, but quick."

"What the hell can't you figure out? Big time detective you are. Dolly was blowin' me and you showed up out of nowhere."

"*That's a fuckin' lie, Vic! He forced me! Rape!*" Dolly screamed.

"*You lyin' little whore!*" yelled Junior. "Fuckin' bitch! I'll *kill* ya! You almost bit my prick off!"

"Both of you shut up," I said vehemently. "We don't want any publicity on this, do we?"

"What the hell are you doin' down here anyways, Vic?" Junior said. "I thought you'd be back in Fairyland by now."

There was that word again. "*Fairyland.* You leave me that note back at The Honeymooner, Junior?"

"Who else?"

Bingo. "You mean you cold-cocked me with a gun?"

"No, no gun. Friggin' tire iron. Wanted to make sure you went right out."

"Really?" I whistled, then told Dolly to pipe down, I'd get to her in a minute. I was finally on to something that resembled truth here, and I wouldn't let it go for anything, my insanely jealous and betrayed heartbeat notwithstanding. "A tire iron. Wow. Nice working over. Real pro. Must've taken lessons from your patrons at Pop's. Someone was with you."

"So?"

"Who?"

"You mean you haven't figured it out yet, after all this time? You must be starving to death, detective as lame as you. Peter Gunn you *ain't.*"

"Clue me in then, and I promise to go back and finish my detective correspondence course."

Junior just shook his head and laughed. "Jeez Louise, put the gun down, Vic. You may want to save the bullets for yourself. *And* Dolly."

My blood ran cold. Thunder cracked. I was about to. I looked at Dolly, who was very quiet now, her face a mask of ice. Her eyes looked small and puffy, not just from tears, either.

"Dolly—?" I said. I dropped the gun, but Junior didn't go for it. I sank to the floor, blood all over my shirt and pants and the carpet, mixing now with Junior's. "Dolly, *why?*"

Junior actually seemed to feel sorry for me now. "Everyone knew, kiddo. I thought you did, too, by now. Remember that pool table we let the hookers use? Well, Dolly here was a regular."

"Customer?"

Junior shook his head. "No, not a customer, moron," he said, and Dolly didn't even protest this time, just sat watching us with that wan expression as the storm wailed outside, nearly drowned out by the pounding of my heart. "Dolly's been selling it to guys since she was fifteen, Vic. Me, she gave it to. And not just me, neither. But I'll let her tell you that part."

"Al Marcus?" I said.

"Sure," said Junior. "There was Al's piece. Gratis, so he'd leave her alone. They even got high together. All three of us, more sometimes. Until Al screwed me over on a deal, your father too. Pop told Al not to come into his place no more. Your father got pissed at Al, too, for ripping us off, and since Al was a cop there wasn't nothin' we could do about it. Al was taking my junk, not paying for it, then selling it for a one hundred percent profit to some joker in Jersey."

"Donald Dunlap?"

"Who? Oh. Naw, some Cubans with a Miami hotline. Me an' Dolly came down here all the time in the old days. She came down with a lot of people. *Went* down on 'em, too. Sorry, Vic, that's how it was."

I was feeling oddly resilient and impervious now that all this was finally coming out. I wanted more. I wanted it all. It was cathartic. "So did Al kill my old man, Junior?"

He shook his head. "No way. Al and your father had their differences, but no way. Al loved Vern, and vice versa."

"So it was Mob?"

"Fuck no. Vern never fucked with the dons, he knew better. He couldn't keep his dick in his pants but he never nailed nobody that would get him in trouble. He had respect where it was due, and was treated that way in return. There was a contract for a while on the person who knocked off your father, you know that? *Everyone* loved your Vern, Vic. Well, *almost* everyone."

"So why'd you leave that note, like it was Mob?"

"That note said nothin' about Mob. I just wanted you to leave before you found out the ugly truth. So did Dolly. That's why she called from Jersey and we set that whole deal up, to scare you. But then it looks like she hung around and God knows what. What are you doing with her down here, Vic? She's the devil's mistress, but she gives great head."

"That's enough," Dolly said in a voice that did sound possessed. In one swift motion she had jumped off the bed and grabbed my gun. She trained it on Junior, who looked unfazed. "Get lost," she told him. "You've done enough damage for one night."

"You'd have been dead a long time ago if it weren't for me, slut," he said. "You've been followed everywhere by some people ever since you left New York last week. All those hotels, everywhere. By our man Pete the Meat Cleaver and his pals. Yeah, Pete knows some people down in Cherry Hill who know people in Brooklyn, know what I'm sayin'? He's cuttin' your hubbie out and takin' his action any day now, selling it to the people in Cherry Hill. Their people got in touch with the New York people I know and they've been keeping tabs on you for Petey, who kept your hubbie informed as a cover, until he made his move and then took you, too. Petey wants you for himself, though. I told him you're a pill-poppin' slut but he won't buy it. Blinded by love. Like you are, Vic." That's why I couldn't make Pete's tail, I thought. He had Cherry Hill and New York on our asses the whole time. "He's no genius, Pete, but he ain't as dumb as he acts. And you thought you were just introducing me and Petey that night for the first time, huh slut? What Petey doesn't know about though is the old contract, which never really expired. The only thing keeping the New York people from filling it is me and the Cherry Hill deal. Once that's done, they'll just cut Petey out, then they'll be free to do it. Me, I just don't give a shit anymore."

He looked at Dolly and made a cutthroat gesture with his bloody hand.

"What contract?" I said, my voice shaking.

Junior looked at me sadly, but with a slight smile. "The one for your father's killer, Vic."

No.

Dolly pulled the trigger. *Click.* She pulled it again and again, bangless, all the time aiming at Junior's head, but he didn't even flinch. She screamed with frustration and began beat Junior in the brain until he collapsed in a heap on the floor, blood billowing from his cranium. He was still breathing, though. Unlike my old man.

I looked at Dolly, who had let the gun fall to the floor. She wouldn't look back at me, though. Not for a long time. Finally I said hoarsely, "Dolly, tell me he was lying too. Please, *God*."

The room was very dark now, except for the sudden flashes from outside, but finally I heard Dolly, a silhouette in the lightning, say in a voice that sounded disembodied, "I can't lie anymore, Vic. I just don't have the energy. Junior called me right when I checked in here, said he was coming down to see me tonight, he had some time off coming, and maybe we could cut a deal. He didn't know you were coming here so I didn't know what he meant. I guess the people he was talking about traced me here, and told him. So I went down to the lobby, knowing he'd be knocking any time, and waited. Then when I got in the car with him, he said if I didn't do what he wanted, he'd get word to you about stuff. He already sent Donald an anonymous letter because I refused to stop sleeping with him, with Junior and his friends. Vic, you asked me who took my cherry, remember? And I didn't want to tell you because, well—it was your *father,* Vic. He was my first customer on that pool table at Pop's. Actually, I didn't charge him because he was a cop, and I was new, and he got to break in the new talent, and I don't know. I stopped hooking for money after a few months, because it was too dangerous, but by then I had my rep and I felt like dirt and so I just did it with whoever, you know. Including your father. In The Honeymooner. Right in the same room we were, in fact. All the time. Over and over and over. Then Al, then Junior. Pop tried, couldn't get it up. I was always stoned so I couldn't remember any of it, or much of it, anyway. But then one day, one day I decided I couldn't do it anymore. You and me were getting close and I wanted to be clean again, so I told your father no more, and he threatened to tell you everything if I stopped, so I kept it up, and he even pimped me out to his pals for money in his own pocket, and he got me hooked on more junk so I'd be weak, but only powder and pills, Vic, I never shot up in my life, I swear, it's too dirty. And so this went on and on until one night after a gang-bang at Pop's. I waited for your father in the alley with a knife I stole off a john and jumped him and stabbed and stabbed until he stopped moving but I just kept stabbing because I was so enraged at him but really at me and then to make sure he was dead I shot him with his own gun, again and again. Then when I stopped there was Junior standing there looking at me, plus a few other people. Junior just told me to get out of there quick, he'd take care of it, and I thought he was being really nice for covering for me, because Al Marcus knew Junior knew something, and I don't know if he ever told or not, but in the meantime, I had to keep being Junior's sex slave, and everyone else who saw me that night, too. Then I let you go, because I knew then it was over, no matter what. Ever since I've just wanted to die, because I killed a man to save myself, the father of the boy I loved, but instead I just got in deeper. And *deeper.* And then you came back home and called me and I freaked out, afraid you'd find out, why'd you ever call me?, so I called Junior for one last favor, hoping to throw you off with this Mafia story, but I was still afraid you'd find out one day, because too many people knew, and Donald still has that anonymous note from Junior, hanging it over my head, and now you know why I wanted you to think about us, Vic. I was hoping in a way you'd change your mind and go back to San Francisco without me, but I loved you so much, Vic. You're the only good thing that's ever happened to me."

I waited for her to pause, then said, "Your father loved you, didn't he? You had that."

"Sure—in about the same way yours did."

"What?"

"My father started molesting me when I was seven, Vic. I finally told my mother and my sister but they said I was sick and demented and a whore, so I felt like one, and then acted like one. My father finally stopped when I pulled a knife on him one day. No, Vic. I've never had anyone love me like you. And I don't deserve it. Now you know that. I never let you put it in me because you were *special,* Vic. I know that sounds weird, but I wanted you to think I was virtuous, and in spite of everything I hoped one day you'd come to my rescue, and it'd be like none of this ever happened. And you did, but too late. Instead I married Donald, who had the pretense of decency, but had maggots crawling inside him, just like me. I used Donald's money to buy Junior off, so I wouldn't have to screw him anymore, he's so disgusting, but he still wanted the sex, so what could I do except kill myself, which I tried to do? That's probably why that contract was never filled. Junior never told them who killed your father, because he wanted me alive to—y'know. It's all about control, isn't it Vic? That's all it's ever about. People who can't control themselves wanting to control everybody else instead."

I just didn't know what to say. Shock. Horror. Revulsion. Pity. Mere words. I was feeling a combination of these, but a lot more. There was no word for it, no description for the mixture of emotions that churned within me violently until they abruptly sputtered out and then I was left feeling numb and empty. I was shell-shocked into apathy, practically.

What now?

I heard sirens through the storm just outside the window, probably a response to the ruckus.

"Now's your chance to turn in your father's killer, Vic," Dolly said lowly. "Justice will finally be done. You'll be able to sleep nights now. Case closed. I have no place to go now anyway. I called my mother and sister but they don't want to see me. Ever. I used Petey to get their address to begin with, since they cut me off years ago. They hate me. And Junior will surely make that contract good when he wakes up. If he wakes up. So I guess it only makes sense to turn me in. Go ahead, Vic. We're even now."

I just looked at her. "*Are* we, Dolly? Are we? You took more than my father away from me, and away from my mother—you took your love out of my life. A part of me is dead now, too. And what have you lost?"

"My soul," she said softly. "And you. Which means everything. You still have your life, Vic. *Live* it. Forget me and Rose and go see your mother and tell her you love her. Don't tell her the truth though. I'm afraid it'd kill her."

"Dolly, I don't blame you for what you did, if it's like you said. You killed my father because you thought if he told me about you it'd kill me, and he was abusing you horribly. And my father was fucking his own son's girlfriend, so I can't say he didn't have it coming, can I?"

"But now I've killed you too, haven't I?"

"No. I still have my life. My puny little pathetic loser life. For what that's worth."

"I've never had mine at all," she said, and then the room was swarming with cops.

They told us to put up our hands and we did and then they confiscated my gun and I showed them my P.I. license as they were bent over Junior's unconscious body and I said, "That guy tried to rape my fiancée in the elevator. She tried to fight him off, but he dragged her in here, then I came in and beat him senseless.

294

We were just about to call you."

They took Junior away in an ambulance and us in a separate one and then after they fixed my nose up we were brought down to the station-house to make statements and all, and early the next morning Dolly and I were back at The Surfcomber, just to check out. We'd hardly spoken all night in the presence of the police. Dolly kept a wary eye on me but I never said anything about what she told me. I was too busy absorbing everything, thinking, wondering how to handle it.

While she checked out I called a cab for the airport. It showed up just as Dolly came out to join me. Both of our bags were packed and on the sidewalk but I shook my head and didn't let her get in the cab. Instead I handed her a wad of Shiv's money and said, "Here. Get lost. Forever. Leave the country. That contract is still on your head, but I'll make some calls and within no time it'll be gone. I guarantee it. Then you can do whatever you want. You heard Junior. Pete will take out Donald, then Cherry Hill will take out Pete. Fuck 'em. You're free, Dolly. You're alive. Make the most of it while you can. And don't throw it away. Promise me that."

"I promise. But I don't know what to do with it, without you in it."

"Finish your nursing degree, learn to take care of yourself. But I, we—I'm sorry. I just can't. I just *can't*."

"I understand. Thanks for not turning me in, I guess."

"You've paid enough, sweetheart. We're even."

She nodded and looked away at nothing, then looked back at me, her face unbearably sad and pitiful, but still beautiful. "What will you do now, though?"

"Go back to New York first, see my mother, tell her I love her, then just go back to San Francisco and pet my cat and listen to Frank Sinatra and watch weird cult movies and beat off to Bettie Page and maybe solve a few cases. The usual, y'know."

"That's so sad," she said.

"No, it's not so bad. I have friends."

"More than I've got."

"You've got me."

"Not like I want to," she said, a lone tear falling down her face. "But I know there just can't be any redemption for me now. I tried to force it, but at least you don't hate me, right?" I nodded, of course not. I pitied her, even loved her, though I couldn't say that to her now or ever.

The storm had blown over in the night and now it was just gray and muggy. Appropriate for the mood I was in. I kissed her tear away, but it was followed by a flood. "I love you," she said in a sob.

"Clean slate," I whispered in her ear just before I kissed it lightly, as if that were some from of absolution. Then I got into the cab and didn't look back. I just wiped her teardrops from my cheek and kissed them off my fingers forever.

Chapter Fourteen
RETURN TO SPLENDOR

I went right from La Guardia airport into a taxi and straight across Hudson River to Long Island to pay a surprise visit to Lucy Guisseppe, another survivor of child abuse. I wanted to get that contract on Dolly cancelled—if there really was one—and make damn sure Lucy was as well adjusted as she seemed. I knew now firsthand what that kind of abuse can do to a kid, and how they can hide it from even those close to them. I was going to look very closely, though.

When she saw the cab pull up in front of her Stony Brook home and me climbing out of it with my bag she ran out down the lawn and jumped into my arms. "Vic! You came to visit, and to stay a while too, it looks like!"

"Actually, not too long. I'm in transit, so I got all my stuff with me. I need to talk to you alone, though."

She said fine, whatever, as long as later she could throw a welcoming party for me and invite all her cousins. I said sure—as long as she invited her uncles from Brooklyn, too. She said no problem. Grandma made us coffee and assorted treats on a platter and Lucy and I sat outside on her backyard patio, which was very pleasant. I was burned out, exhausted beyond endurance, but I also felt propelled by the desire to turn my trip into something meaningful, something useful, so I wouldn't return to San Francisco a complete wreck. Lucy was one way of doing that. My mother was the other. As for the revelation about Dolly, I'd deal with that later. When I was alone. Right now, I had work to do.

First I told Lucy all about running into Deacon Rivers down in Miami. "What a weird coincidence!" she said. "You have the weirdest life of anyone I've ever known, and I've known some weird people."

"Baby, you don't know the *half* of it."

"So why'd you burn his chapel down? That seems *mean*. He wasn't *that* bad."

"He exploits girls in trouble, lost girls, hurt girls, like *you*. That pisses me off. Anyway, it didn't burn down. He's got money. Too much."

"Zelda?"

"For one. Anyway, to hell with him. I came to talk about you. What are your plans now?"

"Oh, I don't know. I was thinking of going to college next year, there's one right near here, y'know, that's pretty good, but I'm sort of losing enthusiasm. Right now I have a private tutor and all, from The Family, and I'll earn a high school equivalent thing, and then I just don't know. I'm sort of mixed up these days, y'know?"

"You hate your father?"

"Yup."

"Good. But don't ever blame yourself."

"Huh? Why would I do that?"

"I'm not saying you would, but I knew, I know a girl, a woman, a *lady* like you, and that's what she did. She felt worthless and ashamed and then brought down anyone who got close to her, because she didn't feel she deserved their love, their closeness. That's bullshit. Take it where you can get it, and hold on to it."

She smirked. "Coming back for my eighteenth birthday?"

I smiled back, but nodded in the negative. "Doubt it. I live a long way off, and I've blown most of the money your father gave me to find you."

"He gave you all that money just to wind up in the joint. Talk about a bad investment."

"You're getting wise, kid. Stay that way."

"I could give you some money back from what you sent me."

"No. No, keep it. Go to college."

"*You* never went, right?"

"Right. And look at me."

"What? You turned out okay."

"Think so?"

"Oh yeah. You're my hero. My cousins will be here in less than two hours, by the way."

"And your uncles?"

"One or two. Why?"

"I got some business to clear up."

"Your father?"

"Yep."

"Find the killer yet?"

"Yep."

"Who?"

"Friend of mine."

"*Friend*? Some friend."

"She did it for altruistic reasons."

"Huh? What's that mean?"

"Go to college, kid."

"Don't patronize me. So why do you need to talk shop with my uncles?"

"Just to clear some stuff up. They'll talk to me, right?"

"Sure. They owe you one. But now what can they do?"

I looked out at the yard, at the dead leaves being blown across the dying grass. "To save one more life, maybe, before it's too late."

Lucy shrugged and sipped her coffee in a grown up manner that was sort of cute. I'd lost my lust for her, especially now. I was afraid I'd lost my lust for anything—including life.

Her umpteen cousins showed up and all were younger than her and ran around and asked me a lot of questions about detective work—like I would know—and California and a bunch of other stuff, while two old goombahs and their wives sat inside with Grandma watching a TV special and talking in low tones. I ditched the kiddies in the back yard, where loud pop music was blaring and everyone but me was dancing, and took Lucy aside to give me an introduction to her uncles, tell them I needed a brief sit-down. They'd already shaken my hand and thanked me for Lucy when they arrived, but then I was left with the kiddies. I wanted to sit at the grown up table now. Lucy went into the house for a minute and then said yeah, sure, go inside and talk, no problem.

Grandma and the wives got lost in the back room while Mike and Sonny—no fooling—asked me to take a seat. A football game was on but they turned the sound down so we could talk. They thanked me again and said their brother-in-law Shiv was a louse and a pervert and I asked them if they'd heard from Shiv's brother Antonio and they said I was better off forgetting about Antonio. They blamed both of them for their sister's, Lucy's mother, death from cancer. So I said sure, whatever, I perfectly related to that, because of my own mother's deterioration at the hands of a sick man, and then I told them I knew who killed my father.

"Vern?" said Mike, thin and oily, but handsome. "The cop?"

"Yeah. It was, *whew*, my high school sweetheart."

Sonny, bigger, fatter, more virile than his brother, looked over at Mike, who looked back, and both tried not to laugh, but gave up guffawing after a moment and then just busted out. "Sorry, kid, sorry," Sonny said. "I just—that's pretty sick, ain't it? You sure 'bout dat?"

"Junior told me."

They got somber in a hurry. "Pop's kid?" Mike said.

"Yep."

They looked at each other again. "Sonofabitch been holding out on us!" Sonny said, his face getting red. "We should be the contract out on him!"

"So it's true," I said. "There *was* a contract."

"Yeah," Sonny said. "Long time ago, cause whoever popped your old man cost us a valuable connection, but we couldn't get no straight answers from Junior. Or Pop neither, or nobody. Junior said it was some hooker he never saw before and never saw again, and we couldn't get a line on her."

"It *was* a hooker," I said, letting out a weary breath.

"Your goilfriend was a *hooker*?" Mike said. He looked at Sonny with a bemused beam.

"Banging your own father? So she's on the rag one night and sends him straight to Hell by Federal Express like so much pizza? *Maron*, that's some cold shit to swallow!" And they both laughed again. Then apologized profusely, like it made a big difference. Whatever.

"Kid, you really take Junior's woid for this?" Sonny asked me.

"Can't take that mug's woid for nothin'. He's just a junior mobster, is what he is. Or he'd *like* to be, but we only use him as a go-between, and it rubs him the wrong way. Could be he's just sore at the world and wants to foul things up out of spite. People are fucked up in this fucked up woild, kid, don't forget that—well, I guess I ain't gotta remind ya no more *now*."

"No, it wasn't Junior. She told me herself. Finally, when she was cornered. I let her go, though" They looked at me like I was the crazy one. "All I want to know from you is, can you cancel that contract?"

Mike looked at Sonny, Sonny at Mike. They were old school, knew the ways of the world, didn't have to ask why I'd forego free vengeance, or why I'd have the nerve to come here and ask them to forget a business deal because of something personal. They both just looked at me and nodded in the affirmative simultaneously. Then we all stood up and they hugged me and kissed my cheek then slapped it like I was a long lost nephew.

I returned to the backyard and discovered Lucy had been eavesdropping. She hugged me too. I felt a little better now. Just a little. The Family was like a surrogate family to me now. I called the airport and booked a flight for San Francisco leaving very early the next morning, which meant I was on a tight schedule. But I was anxious to leave New York and the past behind as soon as I could. My nostalgia bug was cured for good. If I hadn't gone back my memories would've remained pristine. Now they were tainted by this tragic knowledge. Oh well.

Later that night after some strained, polite socializing I called another cab and said arrivederci to all. Mike and Sonny told me "don't worry 'bout nothin' no more," and said I was welcome in Brooklyn anytime. I said thanks but I planned to stay away from there a long time to come, and they understood. Lucy promised to go to college, I promised to come out for her eighteenth birthday. We both knew we were lying, though. I told her I'd always be there for her, that she was special to me, and she believed that, which was all that counted. I took stock of my dwindling cash supply and told the cabbie, an Indian guy with a turban, I had to go all the way upstate. I didn't have an appointment and it was late, but I didn't care.

I arrived at the Chipper Monks joint around 10:30 that evening under a full, luminous, ominous moon in a cold, clear sky. I gave the cabbie his next vacation to New Delhi money, and asked him if he'd go to a local pub and have a drink and come back in an hour. The nearest pub was in Albany, he told me, and he didn't drink. So how did he know where the nearest pub was? I peeled off a few more bills and asked him just to hang out for a while. He was on a roll with me and since he was all the way up here anyway, why not? Then I went up to the dark door and pounded away until someone answered: Nurse Windsor, in her civies, looking none too pleased by the nocturnal disturbance.

"I gotta see my mother," I said, breathing heavily, which didn't help in making myself a favorable impression. "Right away. It's an emergency. I'm going back west tonight and I *have* to see her."

She was her typically bitchy self, enhanced by the rudeness of my timing. "Visiting hours are between the hours of 10AM and—"

"Can it, lady, I'm in no mood. Do I have to pull a gun on you or are you going to let me in to see my own mother? This is her house, and I'm her son, so cut the crap."

She looked at me, my busted nose, sliced hand, bloodshot eyes, and said, "Your Aunt Florence was right about you. You're a menace. If you don't leave the premises at once I'll call the police." She was going to shut the door on me but I stuck my foot in the crack and forced my way in, past her, and up the stairs. Two orderlies came after me but I turned on them and kicked one in the nuts and belted the other one in the face and then showed them my gun. They backed off for more help and I ran to my mother's door and knocked then went in.

First I barricaded the door with every piece of furniture that wasn't nailed down, except Ma's bed. She was asleep, but I sat beside her on the bed and gently stroked her face until she opened her eyes. I heard commotion outside but they wouldn't want to bust in and freak my mother out, right? So I relaxed. I looked around the room and didn't see any music player or hear any Patsy Cline. Bastards took my money and lied. Big surprise. So instead I sang "Crazy" to her myself, continuously, as she just stared into the space beyond me. I can barely carry a tune but at least I could fake it, and I knew all the words. Red lights flared outside the window and I got up briefly to notice a cop car, but it was empty already. They were inside now. I also saw my cab was still waiting at the far end of the grounds. He was probably just taking a nap. He was awake now, though, I bet. I had to hurry. More cops would be on the way from Albany because of my gun, like I was going to hold my mother hostage, kidnap her or something. Hm. No heat, no music, screw Aunt Florence. Could I—?

Naw. My gun wasn't loaded, and unlike wiseguys, many cops had no honor and would go for the shootout and then waste a virtually unarmed man. Couldn't use my Ma as a shield, that was for damn sure. I left my bullets in the cab with my luggage. I had the weapon and the target, but not the ammo. Story of my life. So I lifted my mother up and held her and kissed her, humming "Crazy" in her ear as the cops knocked on the locked door and ordered me to open it or else blah blah blah. I squeezed my mother tightly, realizing this was probably the last time I'd ever see her, thanks to Aunt Florence and my little escapade here tonight, and then I slowly released her.

She was smiling. "That's my favorite song," she whispered. Her trembling hand reached up and touched my tears and then I kissed her hand and her lips and told her, "I love you, Dorothy Violet Malone."

"I love you too, Vic Valentine," she said. "Vic, you're home. My boy." Her eyes looked alive now, but still distant. "Your father will be home soon, Vic. And tell Johnny to turn his amplifier down, I'm getting a headache. I'd rather listen to Patsy. You know me best, Vic. You always did."

Then she patted me on the top of the head, like she was shooing me out the door to go play so she could finish cooking dinner. So she was living in her own virtual reality after all. I figured she was better off there than here. Sounded like a neat trick to me. Maybe I'd try it sometime.

The cops were ready to break the door down, my mother's delicate condition be damned, and so I kissed Ma one last time on the forehead like I was just going out to play, which I was, in a way, and then I went to the window, saw it was only two stories, shimmied down some ivy, fell about half a story down, twisted my ankle, then limped across the lawn and past the flashing squad car to the cab. In the distance I heard more sirens.

"Get me to La Guardia and I'll make you rich," I told the cabbie, and we were out of there.

"I love this country!" he said as we flew.

I slept in the airport, waiting for my flight. I was a mess. My ankle was swollen but fortunately I was still in New York and no one asked me any questions. I could've died and no one would've caught on for hours, till I began to stink up the joint and scare people away and they started losing money. I was a fugitive on the lam and no one cared. No SWAT teams surrounded the airport and sealed off the runways, though. The cowboys up north probably just forgot about me. Ma was all right—better than before I got there, that was for sure—and nothing was stolen. All I left in my wake was some bruised orderly egos and bodies, but big deal. Anyway, dawn finally came and the sunlight shot into my face and woke me up just in time for my flight and I was on my way back home.

The Drive-Inn was in the afternoon doldrums but a welcome sight when I walked in and sat at the bar, direct from SF International, my luggage by my side, my nose pulsating with pain, my hand throbbing with irritation, my ankle swollen with agony, my heart broken into about six million pieces. Doc and Monica had their back to me, doing inventory or something. So I just spoke up and said:

"Set 'em up, Joe. I got a story to tell, that you oughta know."

"*Vic*!" More hugging. I was such a loveable guy, it seemed. Everyone wanted to hug me, which would be fine if it didn't hurt so much.

"So how was your trip?" Monica asked. Then she looked at me and I looked back at her and Doc just shook his head and put his hand on my shoulder sympathetically.

"Let's hear it," Doc said. "Or if you're too tired, I bet I could tell you."

"Shut up, Doc," Monica said. "What happened now, sweetie?"

I gave them the whole lowdown, at least the headlines, and with my by-line, they could fill in the details themselves. Doc didn't say, "I told you so." He didn't have to. Instead he said, "Vic, you've been through what no man should go through. Betrayed from all sides, in the worst way. And you never even got to close the deal with that crazy bitch, either! Daddy did it for you! That's *gotta* smart. I can't even imagine itself, but it's just gotta be the worst feeling in the world, or close to it."

"I wouldn't recommend sticking it in a bottle and opening shop," I said.

"You just haven't met anyone who deserves you, that's all," Monica said.

"Yeah, that must be it, huh? Must be. I should stay away from Vegas, gambler with my luck. What kills me is that I had it all figured out almost right away, only I thought it was Pete who jumped me, not Junior, though I thought of Junior first when I read the note, so had I not been sidetracked by Dolly, I might've saved myself a lot of grief."

"Just physically," Doc said. "The truth woulda hurt no matter when it came out. You just woulda gotten it over with quicker."

"Some detective I am," I sighed.

Monica kissed my cheek. "But a helluva guy."

I was feeling dizzy so after a few stiff shots—which I hardly ever take, being strictly a beer and coffee man—Doc and Monica practically carried me upstairs. They wanted me to go the hospital to have my ankle looked at but I said I'd twisted it before and it'd twist back.

"Sounds like your *life*," Doc said. "But you're home now, my man. With people you can trust, who love you. Forget everybody else. New York is a done deal now. You gave it a decent burial. And I gotta say, Vic, I'm damn proud of you, my man. Let that bitch go cause you knew she was too fucked up to think straight, and had a heart of gold and all that shit. You did the right thing, Vic—not what I or most *other* people woulda done, but the right thing for you. Yeah, damn proud. So let me slightly amend my former statement: You're the most *honorable* pussy-whipped idiot on the face of the earth. I'm proud to know you."

"Gee, thanks, Doc. That makes it all worth while."

They laid me in bed and Doc set up Sinatra's Capitol

Collection on the CD stereo to play continuously and Monica brought me my Bettie Page books for my bedside in case I got the urge later, but I really didn't have the energy to even think about that sort of thing. Then Puss hopped up on the bed and I was never so glad to see anyone in my life. I hugged the little dickless wonder and it felt so good to be back with my true pals again. They left me alone for a while, and I fell asleep and then woke up early in the evening and got up and took a shower. My ankle and other wounds felt a little better now. I went to the fridge and noticed Doc or Monica had stocked it well sometime that day. Puss rubbed up against my shins and I picked him up and we watched a little TV in my bedroom with the sound down, so Frank could sing.

Then it hit me. Like a belated avalanche, all at once. I cried and cried till my gut hurt and my eyes were swollen. Not for me. For Ma. I hadn't really helped her after all, as long as she was imprisoned in that nuthouse, and in her own fantasy world. And for Dolly. Where the hell was she? Would I ever see her again? Did I want to? Would she despair in her isolation and kill herself? Should I have run away with her anyway, despite everything, let bygones be bygones, realize our present loneliness superseded the mistakes of our past?

The answers to all of these was "I don't know." Except for the last one. I thought about it a while and came up with: "No." Loneliness was the price we paid. For what, I don't know. But that's the way the dice tumbled. I was lying in bed when I heard someone unlock the front door of the outer office and walk in. It was Monica. And she already had a brand new hairdo—long and black with bangs, a la Bettie Page, her new obsession, thanks to my educating her. She also knew what I liked.

She sat beside me and we watched TV for a while but didn't say much. She and Doc wouldn't want to talk about it in any more detail until I did, and that could take a while. So we just watched TV, switching channels, since I couldn't concentrate on any one thing for long, and then we drank this bottle of wine she brought up. I got pretty buzzed in no time, since I hardly ever drink wine. Then I even shared some of Monica's joint, and she got more comfortable on the bed next to me, wearing only a skimpy leather skirt and halter top. She'd shed her fishnet stockings and leather jacket by now. I was beginning to feel more and more like myself by the minute. I wasn't watching the TV now—I was watching *her*.

"Do you want to come over for Thanksgiving?" she asked me, turning suddenly.

"Huh? Oh, sure. Why not. I guess. I have so much to be thankful for. Who else will be there?"

"Judy and The She Beams, who may do a number for us, and Doc and my friend."

"What friend?"

"You know. That musician I met in Golden Gate Park?"

"Oh. Right. You still seeing him?"

"Yeah."

"How's it going?"

"Fine."

"Serious?"

"No, not yet. Still early, gimme a break, but he's, y'know. Nice. Not as cool as you though, but who is?" She stretched and I saw her cleavage and I momentarily forgot all my other problems. I was recuperating splendidly. Then she leaned over and kissed me full on the lips, and I kissed her back. "He's out of town, though," she whispered in my ear. "Doc was going to come over with me but we thought maybe tonight it should just be you and me. We could finish what we started that one night, remember? And I promise—this time, I won't make you beat off in the bathroom."

We made out for a while and I kissed her face and throat and she let the straps of her halter slip over her smooth shoulders and I kissed her breasts until her nipples were hard and she moaned and climbed on top of me and we were just about to get down and dirty when I abruptly stopped.

"I'm sorry," I said. "I just can't. Not tonight. The flesh is willing but the spirit is weak."

"*That's* a twist," she said, sitting back, still on top of me.

"Yeah, I've been doing The Twist a lot lately."

"You want me to leave?"

"Yea, I need to be alone for a while. Tell Doc I'll call him tomorrow and we'll go hang out somewhere. You too. I'm sorry. You got my blood boiling again, which is a healthy sign, I guess."

"Dolly?"

"Yeah. I think so."

"I understand." She kissed me on the lips lightly just once and then got up and slowly put on her fishnet stockings like a teasing cheesecake flick and then her leather jacket and she was ready to leave when I grabbed her by the wrist and looked into her pouty young face and pretty bedroom eyes and asked: "Take a rain check?"

The End of

ROMANCE RAKES A RAIN CHECK

But

Vic Valentine will return in

I LOST MY HEART IN HOLLYWOOD

A Vic Valentine Adventure

Chapter One
STAR SUCKER

Leave it to cleavage.

I was entranced by the voluptuous vision of luscious loveliness slouching seductively before me, larger than life. She was everything I had ever dreamed of and more. So soft, so curvaceous, so vulnerable—yet also witty, cultured, intelligent. At least, that was my impression of her when she wasn't being pursued by slimy bug-eyed monsters or notorious desperate gangsters hungry for her body. Me, I appreciated her mind, her heart, her soul—as well as her breasts, which, no doubt about it, were twin works of living art. Her name was Velma Vale, and she was known as Queen of the B's amongst connoisseurs of cinematic trash, underground gems that popped up routinely at booze-and-vomit infested movie palaces on Market Street for a week or a day or two hours before landing on video in some obscure cult collector's shop—like The Drive-Inn. In fact, it was my old pal Doc Schlock who had first turned me on to Velma Vale, who already had her first cheesecake calendar on the market, and was a regular at memorabilia shows even though she was only 26 (according to her official fan club bio, which I'd looked up under the guise of detective work). Velma was a glorious throwback to the halcyon days of Mamie Van Doren, Bettie Page, Mara Corday, Marla English, Fay Spain and of course the Fifty Foot Woman herself, Allison Hayes: the drive-in goddesses of the '50s who still haunted the wet dreams of many an outmoded postmodern bachelor—like me, Vic Valentine, Private Eye, looking for love and finding it in the most unusual places, such as the silver screen of The Strand on Market Street in downtown San Francisco.

I had just returned from a disastrous trip back East, initially to New York to find the true culprit in the murder of my dirty cop dad, only to discover it had been my high school sweetheart. She had been conducting a clandestine affair with my old Pop and resented him for stringing her out on drugs and then pimping her out for petty cash. She informed me of this shortly (but not soon enough) after I'd already stolen her away from her dental hubbie in Philly and was ready to elope with her in Miami. Needless to say, I was in a lousy frame of mind upon my less-than-triumphant return to San Francisco, desperate, dateless, and disillusioned, and needed all the fantasy I could lay my eyes on, if not my hands. The Velma Vale triple feature at The Strand filled the bill nicely that rainy afternoon: *Sex Killers from Space*, *Poison Prison Pussycat*, and my all-time favorite Velma Vale opus, *Curse of the Voodoo Love Queen*, in which Velma plays a hooker/waitress/lounge singer fending off zombie mobsters in New Orleans. Actually, she's really a *witch*, but a *good* one, and her lover, a private eye/mystery writer (!) is a werewolf, and later she turns into a vampire and they team up against the Underworld, as the "Mafia of the Undead" is so deftly described. It's a masterpiece of the macabre, largely unheralded and under-appreciated outside certain circles of squares, though the few drunks sharing the experience with me seemed to genuinely enjoy the nudity and violence scenes, especially when they were combined. Me, I saw the *real* Velma Vale, beneath the G-string, and I don't mean what you think I mean. Velma had a heart, as proven when a zombie ripped it out of her heaving, sweaty, naked chest, but Velma just grabbed it back and stuck it back in. It was hers to keep. I liked that about her. She didn't let anyone steal her heart. It was hers to give, if and when she decided to. Sitting there alone in that drunk tank dive with a movie screen on that wet afternoon, I just hoped she would one day give it to me, at least for a little while.

From where I sit now, I wish I *hadn't* seen the heart beneath the G-string. I should've settled for the fantasy. When it became actual flesh, it was one long skid down into troubleville. But I must admit, I had more fun than usual getting there.

It really began when I returned to The Drive-Inn that wet, misty, mysterious evening after the triple feature to ask Doc if he could obtain some more video copies of Velma's flicks, maybe even bootlegs of the really rare stuff. Rumor had it she had started out in porn flicks and those early efforts were still floating around somewhere. I didn't want those, necessarily—though I wouldn't say no to a peek. Especially now that's she's hotter than ever and permanently retired. It's my fault she was forced into early retirement too. Little could I have known that night what a fatal catalyst I'd be in her brilliant career, which now seems so long ago but persists in my memory like a strange dream.

I was already on my third beer/bourbon shot combo. It was a

Saturday night and the place was boppin'. The resident surf band, The She Beams, sort of a latter day version of the Go-Go's, was scheduled to perform in less than an hour, and their presence attracted a somewhat more eclectic crowd than usual. The She Beams, featuring my friend and would-be lover Judy Fagin (now engaged to a Santa Barbara engineer), had a pending record deal with a local label and were touring the West Coast as a result. They had just returned from Seattle and Portland—I hope to eventually wind up living in either of those misty towns myself— and were pretty beat, but kept their promise to play their usual gig at Doc's, since The Drive-Inn had offered Judy and her band mates their first regular exposure outside the Rendezvous, the cafe I frequented and that Judy managed for her errant mother, Zelda. I was feeling better than I'd felt in the few weeks since the Miami debacle (which I really don't want to discuss anymore, sorry), thanks to the booze and Doc and most of all, Velma Vale.

"I can get you some of her blue movies," Doc had been telling me, "but they may cost you plenty of *green*, red eyes. Maybe you should consider going out on an actual date with a real live person." Doc got around himself, though he never told me much about it; he was a black dude and many of his women were white and it bothered him, I think, that he had a weakness for vanilla, so he didn't like to admit it unless I pumped him. He had stopped banging his sometimes employee and part time She Beam performer Monica Ivy now that Monica was seriously seeing some musician in the Haight-Ashbury whom neither Doc nor I cared for. I had been intimate with Monica myself once, and I guess I was just a bit jealous. Doc wanted me to settle down and kept nagging me about it, like he was my old lady or something. My crazy old lady wasting away in a New York asylum. I wish I had never looked her up to begin with. No, it helped her. I *think*.

"C'mon, Doc, after all I've just been through? Finding out my true love iced my old man cause he was banging her and getting her stoned and selling her body to every scumbag on the block? Jesus, I'm surprised I didn't lose it like my poor old mother. We should be rubber room mates."

"Aw, shit, Vic," Doc said with his typical detachment laced with cool compassion, "you call *every* woman you bang more than twice your 'true love.' I thought Rose was your 'true love.' Then Dolly, Miss Psycho New Fuckin' Jersey. And then the next one will be your 'true love,' right? You just need to meet the right one, and she ain't some skin flick starlet, my man, hate to blow your bubble up. Grow up, Vic. Get wise to yourself. You're gettin' older now. Time to get real, not buried deeper into that fantasy world you call a brain. Come out of it, my friend. Forget this Velma obsession, it's plain ridiculous. I mean, okay, shit, at least she's alive and under seventy, unlike all the other cheesecake dolls you jerk off to, but this ain't 1957, Vic. It's wake up time. End of the century almost. Play time' over, party's been cancelled. Now just listen to me and settle down, maybe even give up this detective shit and find a *real* job."

That hurt. "Like what, Doc? Come work for you as a bartender? Or turn into Ralph Kramden, live in a little dump with a wiseass wife and waste away dreaming of winning the lottery? Or is that 'loitery' for those deadbeats? Not my idea of upwardly mobile, Doc. I don't want the albatross of a whole family—a steady gal with her own income will do. And Velma definitely makes her own living."

"Wait. Are you actually *serious* about this?"

"Well, yes and no. I mean, I did write her a few fan letters that she responded to, or her publicist did anyway. I have her signed photo hanging up and framed and all, so she knows I *exist* at least."

"Vic. Vic, Vic, Vic. You're *scarin'* me, man. That little Brooklyn bimbo has really done a number on you, and I can understand why, but what you need is professional help, not an autographed picture of a blonde with big hooters, hear what I'm sayin'?"

"Well, it's a start, anyhow." I sipped my beer and Doc shook his head. Up on the video screen a silent marathon was in progress—an Ed Wood fest. *Plan 9 From Outer Space* was the current feature. Doc often turned the sound down these days while weird Vegas stripper music or other obscure '50s-'60s exotic instrumentals blared from the stereo. Most of the musical selections came from my collection, since I was an avid aficionado of incredibly strange music from that magical era. Judy Fagin also supplied Doc some twisted tunes to whet the appetites of the clientele for The She Beams' Friday and Saturday night gigs, classic surf and hot rod and all. Anyway, also on the Ed Wood agenda were *Jail Bait* and *Glen or Glenda*, and I was totally content to just sit there and watch them all while getting drunk on booze and music and then going upstairs and jerking off—a typical Saturday night when off-duty—but Fate, my ex-pimp, slipped me a mickey. Persistent s.o.b., that Fate. I guess he wanted to get back in my good graces by laying a bombshell right in my lap. It blew me away, all right.

The She Beams showed up and Judy Fagin came up to me and gave me a big hug and wet kiss and life felt worth living again. I think Doc had filled her in on my travails back East and I was hoping for a mercy fuck later on in the evening, but then Judy introduced me to her big blond Nazi Viking Football hero boyfriend from Santa Barbara, who broke bones all over my body just by shaking my hand. Then Judy flashed the big rock on her finger, crassly announcing her recent engagement in Seattle, and that was that, I thought. Next Judy excitedly told me how The She Beams had some jazzed up Martin Denny and Arthur Lyman Exotica tunes added to their homespun repertoire and she couldn't wait for me to hear them. I acted as thrilled as I could and then the big blond behemoth sat next to me and tried acting buddy-buddy, but I coolly blew him off and dense as he was he took the hint and moved to one of the few tables set up for the occasion. Monica then showed up with her creepy looking musician squeeze, both decked out in black—even Monica's hair was dyed black now, with bangs a la Bettie Page, someone I had turned her on to—and Monica waited tables while singing harmony with Judy on the few vocal numbers. Mostly it was instrumental. The two boyfriends sat together and compared notes, and I don't mean the musical kind. To hell with 'em. I was better off alone, I figured. I tried blocking out all thoughts of Dolly Duncan Dunlap—who was probably screwing Deacon Rivers in the Miami Church of Elvis at this very moment, or maybe the Miami Dolphins in the locker room, or *real* dolphins in Sea World, scot-free after belatedly confessing her crime to me. Even though she promised she had kicked drug and dick addiction for the final time, I didn't trust her, for some reason. I wondered why I just didn't bust her. Sentiment? Sympathy? Stupidity? All three alliterative words? Whatever. I had let her get away with gunning down my old man and indirectly sending my old lady into mental exile, and it bothered me. Too late now. I doubt she would drop me a postcard as she'd promised. And I never even slept with her, as I'd dreamed of doing since I was a teenager. I had thought she was so chaste and pure for wanting to wait, when in reality she couldn't reconcile with screwing her lover's son. And since my old man was dead I couldn't even pump him for the details. I suppose she was good or he couldn't have gotten so much money for her. No, that sounds terrible. But true, damn it! I shouldn't be dwelling on this, I thought as I kept drinking and drowning out the outside world and my own tormented inner tomb.

I was almost ready to go upstairs and miss The She Beams' encore when I felt a tap on my shoulder from behind the bar. It was Doc. He pointed at the video screen. Another Velma Vale flick was showing.

"So what?" I said. "Why'd you send Ed Wood to the bleachers already?"

Then he pointed again, to the person sitting next to me at the bar.

Sure enough, it was Velma Vale herself. In the flesh. Somehow she had walked in and sat right beside me and struck up a conversation with Doc while I just sat and brooded on my ineptitude as a human being. The adrenaline rush flushed out the booze in my brain and I was as lucid as a layman's term as I stared in disbelief, gaping like a beached guppy at the dimensional doll on the stool beside me.

"Are you *really* Velma Vale, the one and only?" I stammered. She nodded and smiled politely. I looked at her video image then back at the real thing in triple double takes and I could tell she felt a bit embarrassed. Everyone else was absorbed in The She Beams so I was her only audience, along with Doc.

"I was wondering when you'd notice," Doc said. "And I swear I didn't set this up. Miss Vale just happened to be in town and just happened to be staying nearby, walked around the 'hood, heard the music, and in she came. As soon as I saw her I popped in one of her movies to let her know she was in the right place."

"At the right time," I added. My unabashed adoration seemed to make her slightly uncomfortable, so I toned it down a few notches, or tried to, anyway. I hadn't been this thrilled to meet someone since the old days as a music writer in New York, hobnobbing at shindigs with new wave celebrities like Debbie Harry and The Cramps and interviewing underground heroes like Ray Dennis Steckler and Bunny Yeager, but this was so much more. It had something to do with how pathetic and vulnerable I was feeling those days after my ordeal, but the ethereal nature of the setting combined with the tangible beauty of the person finally sharing the same oxygen with me would have been overwhelming under any emotional circumstances. As it was, she was like an angel sent from heaven, compensation for my hard luck in the romance arena, once and for all making it all right. I felt things were finally going my way. Instinctively I realized it had to be a set-up. It was just too good to be true, but I wanted to enjoy the dream for as long as it lasted.

And then Velma Vale began weeping uncontrollably, sobbing into a steady stream of cocktail napkins supplied by Doc, who was as perplexed as I was.

"Is—is it the movie?" Doc asked gingerly. "You—you want me to stop it?"

"No, no—I'm sorry," she whimpered in that velvety voice. Her mascara was running now but her beauty remained intact, at least to me. She could do no wrong as far as I was concerned. "You're very sweet—I'm flattered you even know who I am. It's just that I don't want to go into it with strangers, I mean, not that I don't want to talk to you, but I don't want to bore anyone with my personal problems."

"Oh no—I *love* personal problems!" I said perhaps a bit too cheerfully. "I'm Vic Valentine, private eye, that's why."

She looked at me and stopped sobbing. "You're joking, right?"

"Ah, no, I'm not. And this, whom you've apparently already met, is Doc Schlock, or Curtis Jackson, whichever he prefers. Either way he's my buddy and we've been fans for years. Do you remember signing a picture for me a few months ago? Probably not. Never mind. You're probably not in the mood to think about that stuff now."

"I'm sorry, I sign so many I don't even have the chance to see who they're for. I'm sorry. Thank you, Vic. Nice to meet you." She reached out for a shake and sniffled. I responded accordingly. Seeing her in such a sad state made her seem more real and accessible, adding to her appeal. I felt a weird chemistry with her that may have been imagined, but I didn't think so. Especially when she said: "Vic, how would you like to take me somewhere else for a private nightcap?" Doc's eyes bugged out of his head. We were out of The Drive-Inn and in my Corvair so fast it was like a fast-forward on the VCR remote control. It was all very quick and surreal, as if I was truly was only dreaming, but as long as I could still touch her, I didn't mind. I just prayed I'd never wake up. The wake up call was as rude, unsettling and untimely as ever, though.

Chapter Two
REEL GONE, CAT

"Let me see your pussy."

No, dear, demented reader—*I* didn't say that. Velma Vale, the Voodoo Love Queen said it. To *me*. If she *was* Velma Vale. I was beginning to have my doubts as we sat in Lori's Diner on Powell downtown, eating burgers and shakes (her idea of a "drink") like a couple of crazy kids on a date. It was just too much, I'm telling you. I felt so numb I could barely taste my damn food, but gazing across the table at her flawless creamy skin, perfect figure, pouty lips, and large, deep emerald eyes, all framed by a thick mass of beautiful natural blond hair, I lost my appetite. For food, at least. She asked me about myself since I told her I already knew about her from the official fan club bio (she just laughed and said that was all I needed to know, even if it wasn't true, which bothered me), and all I could think of telling her was the tale of my dickless cat. She seemed genuinely touched by the fact I'd spent a grand to have him emasculated because of chronic urinary tract blockage, and for the first time I felt my just desserts were due, and I'm not talkin' banana split.

"Really," she said, not even blushing, "I want to meet your cat."

"Well, I don't have it, I mean him, I mean her, with me," I said. "He-she-it's at home."

"Where's home?"

"Back where we just were. I live above The Drive-Inn."

"That's a great place. Funny I should just walk by like that, huh?"

"Yeah. Velma—I assume I can call you Velma, right? Okay, so, you don't live around here, am I right? I mean your home is in L.A., no?"

"Right. I'm just up for the weekend."

"Why? Was there a premiere for that triple feature I just saw today I didn't know about, or what?"

"What? Don't be silly, Vic. *My* movies? C'mon. The only place they premiere is in some pervert's living room. Oh, sorry. I don't mean you. I mean, I'm just getting away from it all, y'know?

That's all. Pass the ketchup." She looked down at her food and avoided eye contact with me for the first time since I'd met her. And then, also for the first time since I'd met her, I really saw her, beyond my veiled perceptions. I noticed the wrinkles around her eyes, the dark roots in her scalp, the liposuction lips, and then I wondered if even her boobs were real. Just like that, I saw the *true* Velma Vale. And God, how I wanted to fuck her. Without all the glitz and dream angel bullshit, she seemed all too accessible. But then my dizzying desire was disturbed by the expression on her flawed but still naturally gorgeous face. I thought she was going to bust out crying all over again.

"Why did you come alone?" I asked her, pretending not to notice her emotional state as I nonchalantly munched on my fries. Beside our booth was the perfectly preserved real live Edsel, and lining the walls were framed covers from 1950s cheesecake magazines. I should have felt as if I were in heaven, sitting there with a living slice of cheesecake right out of my wildest fantasies, but Velma's mood was casting a dark pall over the proceedings. By that time I was sure she was the real Velma Vale and not a cheap imitator. Her demeanor and forthrightness were too genuine to be faked. Anyway, Velma Vale wasn't famous enough to elicit illicit clones. It was beginning to hit me just how weird and wonderful this situation really was. If only Velma would stop crying, I would be able to enjoy myself without feeling lousy, I thought. I was being selfish, I know, but damn it, I *deserved* this dream date after all the crap I'd been through. Her problems couldn't have been more traumatic than mine, I figured. Perhaps the gods sent us to each other for a night of sweet consolation and passionate compensation. I had to elevate the conversation if that was going to happen though, and also clear up a few minor details, such as where was the inevitable boyfriend? I'd been caught with my pants down before by a jealous suitor and no sex is worth a trip to intensive care, let me tell you. I repeated my query, since she didn't answer right away, seemingly lost in thought, fighting back tears.

"Velma? Why are you alone?"

"I'm *not* alone. I'm with *you*, Vic. C'mon. Let's eat and go meet your cat," she snapped, lighting up a cigarette suddenly, even though we were in the no-smoking section. I noticed then for the first time what she was wearing—tight jeans, a fuchsia silk blouse not tucked in with a leather belt around her hour-glass waist, and her shoes were those silver slippers worn by B movie starlets in the old days. The way she smoked that cigarette conjured thousands of images of *film noir femme fatales* from my mental video library, but then when I thought about it, she was more like a sex kitten from a drive-in '50s JD flick. She wasn't classy, or even mysterious. Just lost, lonely and voluptuous.

"Okay," said, stuffing the last fry in my mouth and washing it down with a mighty slurp of my shake. "Let's go meet my cat."

I hastily paid the check and we skedaddled out of the diner and to my Corvair. It was around 11PM by this time, but neither of us exhibited any signs of sleepiness. The adrenaline flow was rushing us downstream with torrential passion. In layman's terms: we were both horny as hell. At least *I* was, and Velma's body language was not open to a multitude of interpretations. Up for the weekend, obviously just broken up with her boyfriend or in the midst of an argument, in any case rebounding right into my lap, giving me signals right and left, eye contact, foot contact under the table, and now in the Corvair, *thigh* contact. I even noticed her casually unbuttoning her blouse to reveal her burgundy bra, which was already visible beneath the flimsy outer garment, but now her magnificent cleavage was revealed in all its pristine glory. Those babies were real, all right. Real and ready for rapture. Vic Valentine, your night has come, I told myself. Live it up, bucko—tomorrow could find you right back in palookaville with the rest of the coulda-beens. It was serious memory making time.

On the way we chatted, and her mood seemed to perk up considerably as the night breeze made wondrous waves out of her ersatz golden locks of hair. "It's so nice of you to show me around like this," she said. "I really haven't seen much of the city."

"Show you around?" I gulped. "I haven't really shown you anything yet."

She looked at me and arched her eyebrows suggestively. "*Ooo*, what's on the agenda?"

"Well, after my cat?"

She sidled over and cuddled up to me, with my stick shift the only barrier between us. She stroked it playfully, and I nearly wiped out and turned us into James Dean and Jayne Mansfield then and there, but recovered just in time. She just laughed, undaunted by the reckless ride, tickling my ribs and giggling. Then she—God help me—licked my ear. That was it. I slammed by feet on the clutch and brake simultaneously and we screeched to a halt in the middle of Geary Boulevard traffic. Horns honked and people flipped us the bird, but I was oblivious. I just put on the blinking emergency lights and threw the stick in neutral and turned to her and demanded, "Why me? Who put you up to this?"

She just blinked at me, nonplussed. She buttoned her blouse back up and tried hard to act indignant. "What's your problem? Don't you know how to have fun?"

"Yeah, but when something is *this* much fun, I get suspicious. I mean, shit like this just doesn't *happen* everyday. One's dream girl does not just show up and start flirting with him without there being a major hitch somewhere down the line. All I need to know at right this very second is what that snag *is*, so I can prepare for it. I'm not saying this isn't worth it—hell, if you want to hire me to ice your boyfriend, just say so, I'll do it first thing in the morning—but just don't play games with me. I don't like it."

She giggled again and batted her eyes and said, "Am I *really* your dream girl, Vic? C'mon. You're lonely, I'm lonely, we're free people, at least for tonight, what's that song? 'Strangers in the Night'? Just let it go at that, Vic. Two ships passing in the night. C'mon now." She leaned over and kissed my cheek and put her hand on my thigh. How could I doubt a chick that quoted Frank Sinatra at me?

A cop on a bike pulled up along side us. "What's the problem? Engine fail?"

"It's okay, officer," Velma said. "I think it'll turn over once he tries it one more time. You know how it is sometimes with these classics—unpredictable. But worth it, right honey?"

She pinched my arm and I very noticeably flinched. The engine had been idling the whole time, anyway. I just put her in gear, shrugged helplessly at the cop, then took off. He followed me for a bit then turned off the main drag into a side street once the flow of Saturday night traffic resumed its normal tide. I was so, *so* tired of mind-fucking dames I couldn't take it any more. For once I just wanted to turn the tables on one, be the one in control. I was at the wheel but she was driving. She hadn't done anything wrong, really. Maybe I was being too paranoid, I thought. She was right. I had to relax. Enjoy myself. Consequences be damned. Stop analyzing, Vic. What could she possibly do to you that wouldn't enhance your life? And what were the odds of this happening once in a lifetime, much less ever again? And the odds were even greater that once more I was being set up by some neurotic babe. Chill out, man. Go with it. Let loose.

When I parked the Corvair in front of my building I shut off the motor, turned to Velma, and planted one right on her mouth. Long and lascivious and lingering, my tongue probing the furthest reaches of that fabled mouth. Her lips reciprocated warmly and deeply. The next thing I knew my hands were on her breasts, fondling, exploring. She bit my ear and nearly drew blood, then unzipped my pants and grabbed my throbbing man-tool. "Race you upstairs," she whispered. *Race with the devil*, I thought as I beat her to the door, then to the bed.

I realize none of this sounds credible, and perhaps you suspect I'm embellishing these events for your vicarious pleasure. Unless my memory is rewriting history subconsciously, this is not the case. I'm relating everything as it happened in reality, though I must admit, I couldn't have imagined it any better if I tried, and believe me, before this, I had plenty of practice. Even with all of these events so atypical of my average lifestyle, I was still totally in character. After undressing, and watching as she did so, I threw three CDs onto the changer: Martin Denny, Arthur Lyman, Juan Garcia Esquivel, the big three when it comes to classic Space Age Bachelor Pad Music. If this was going to happen—and as she unhooked her bra and tossed it at my feet, the prospects looked better than average—it had to be *perfect*. This was a once-in-a-lifetime shot, I could tell. I wanted to make love to my dream love goddess on a tropical island, a la Esther Williams movies, but since my pathetic office/studio apartment was the only thing available on short notice, I had to create the perfect mood. I dimmed the light in the office and then shut off the bedroom light, so we could see each other but still had the cloak of romantic darkness under which we could do our business. Looking back, I wished I could have taken her out to a classy supper joint and then dancing, like Bimbo's in North Beach, maybe going to see the Brian Setzer Orchestra or something, instead of just listening to the jukebox at a diner over burgers and shakes and then rushing back to my place for unbridled animal sex. But hell, that was like complaining about sailing to Paradise in a rowboat instead of taking a luxury ocean liner. Once you were there, what difference did it make? And baby, I was there.

The lovemaking was magical—passionate, fulfilling, steamy, tender. Flesh, lips, sweat, hair, limbs, breasts, genitals, hard, soft, wet. There was nothing she would not and did not do, and vice versa. We stayed up all night. I had to keep changing CDs every few hours, but other than that, it was unadulterated bliss, the closest thing I've had to a religious experience since witnessing an orgy in the New Church of Elvis. Every now and then it would dawn on me just who this person was, whom I was exploring every nook and cranny of, who kissed me from head to toe and back again, and the surreal ecstasy made me dizzy. It was transcendent. It was acrobatic. It was life affirming. It was—ah, mere words fail me. Just picture your greatest fantasy made flesh, and take it from there. My whole life seemed to have been leading up to this single night. As dawn broke and the sun's rays peeked through the blinds at the residue of our joyous sins, and she gently kissed my lips and closed my eyes then kissed my eyelids and massaged my chest and kissed my neck and cooed what a magnificent lover I was, all I could think was, *Who cares what happens next*?

What *did* happen next remains fuzzy in my mind, since I must have dozed off for no more than twenty minutes. All I remember lucidly is waking up and realizing she was no longer in the bedroom. I called her name. No response. I checked the bathroom. Clean and empty. The office was likewise barren of her presence or evidence of her whereabouts. Then I noticed the note stuck to my heart shaped dartboard with a dart, of course. Shaking in the raw, I reached out and plucked it away and read:

"Sorry I had to go like this, Vic. I had a lovely time. You helped me forget my problems for a night, and I guess I supplied you with a dream come true (hope you weren't disappointed!). I'm leaving for L.A. this morning, right away. I can't run any longer. I'd tell you my personal address but it's best this remain our little secret. Oh, I don't care if you tell your friend downstairs, but no one I know must ever know—for your own good, believe me. Contact me through the fan club, if you wish. You've made a fan of me, that's for sure. Take care, Vic. Sweet dreams. Love, Velma."

There was even a date on the note, like she was autographing a collector's item. Which, in effect, it was, one every Velma Vale fan in the Universe would kill for. All I had to do for it was fulfill my own fantasies with her body. But only for a single night. Now she was gone and I wondered if it had ever really happened. There was no other evidence other than this note and her smell still lingering on my skin. I caressed myself and returned to my bed and beat off thinking of the previous night even though I was raw and sore from the real thing. So was she, I bet. I hadn't heard the shower so my smell was still on her as well, I figured. People on the plane would smell it, realize this beautiful creature had just been made love to by some lucky guy. And that lucky guy was *moi*. Vic Valentine. Lover extraordinaire.

I fed the cat—who had never even been formally introduced to Velma throughout that erotic maelstrom, even after that flimsy pretense of taking her home to meet him—and as I did, I realized how little we had actually talked. Not the cat and me. Velma and me. The cat and I speak frequently, though we never understand a word the other is saying. He's probably still looking for his missing pecker, poor thing, perpetually nagging me as to its whereabouts, wondering what he had done to deserve emasculation. I'd shown him what could be done with one when one knows how to use it. With Velma, I mean, not the cat. He meowed at me more than ever as a result of this new knowledge, but that day I was too high to notice Puss's usual yakkity-yak. In retrospect, perhaps he was warning me, knew something I didn't, and I should've paid attention. But all I could do was think of Velma, of how much she meant to me now.

I admit it, I had it bad. I was one obsessed, pathetic fool.

I didn't even tell Doc what had happened before I made up my mind to drive to L.A. immediately. I just called him up and asked him to keep an eye on Puss for a couple of days. He asked me if I scored and I just laughed and said, "Whaddya think?"

"What do I *think*?" he said. "I think an act of God occurred right here in this very store and now you're holding out the details on me," he said, flustered. He wasn't minding the store today, Monica was, since it was Sunday and he took every other one off to get private shit done. "Stop on by before you hit the road and give me some details, Vic. Come on, now."

"No time, Doc, sorry. I'll phone Monica and tell her to watch Puss until you get back to The Drive-Inn tomorrow, but then I'm outta here. I'll call you from L.A., okay?"

"Well, what the hell you gonna do down there, Vic? Fuckin' *elope*?"

"We'll see, Doc. We'll see."

What I didn't reveal to Doc or Velma was that via my contacts in L.A. and in the fan club, I already had Velma's personal residence in my little black book. I just never sent her a letter there because I didn't want to invade her privacy or alarm her and make her think I was stalking her. Now it was different. I was no longer just a fan. I was a lover. Hot damn right.

"Vic, is she there? Can you speak freely?"

"She left ahead of me. I'm going to meet her."

"She know that?"

"She will. Doc, I'm in love, so naturally I'm impetuous. You can't expect logic in this sort of situation, can you?"

"Well, bless my black ass. Fuck me till I can't sit down. I'll be damned. You *nailed* her, didn't you?"

"No Mr. Kiss-Kiss-Bang-Bang gossip now, Doc, I still gotta pack."

"Well, don't you have like *work* to do?"

"It's Sunday, Doc. Well, okay, detectives work all the time, but don't worry, rent's paid, so relax, willya? You gotta get some fun outta life, Doc, you're too serious. I'm worried about you. Stop and smell the roses sometimes."

"Smell some poon tang is more like it. God *damn*. I just can't believe this shit you're tellin' me, Vic. She in love too or are you just assuming as usual?"

"*Assuming*? You should read the note she left me! I can tell when a woman's got it, Doc, and this broad's hooked."

"What'd you do to her—note? You say note? She wrote you a damn note than split?"

"Doc, don't worry. We rendezvous tonight. I'll call you from her place, okay? Just calm down."

"Me? You're the one's goin' off half-cocked—you don't know this woman, Vic. These Hollywood bimbos chew guys like you up and spit 'em out."

"She swallows, Doc. And believe me, I'm going *full*-cocked. Gotta fly, babe. Don't forget Puss. Call ya soon. *Ciao*." I actually said "ciao," already sounding like a SoCal jet-setting asshole. That's not who Velma fell in love with. Well, became infatuated with. Well, just met and boned all night with. Whatever. And if she was really happy with her "problems" she wouldn't be running away and seducing the first guy she meets, either. *Would* she?

Luckily I'd had the Corvair tuned up upon my return from Miami, just to feel something in my life was in smooth working order, since it felt the rest was falling apart. But now that was different. God had rewarded me for surviving my travails. He sent me an angel to cure my heartaches through intensive physical therapy, make life worth living again. It was like getting a soul transfusion. Velma obviously had a few kinks to work out in her own personal life, so maybe I was sent to her as well. I speculated on what those troubles might entail as I made the drive down the 5 in less than five. Whatever it was, I could handle it, I thought. I was invincible, her knight in shining armor to the rescue, dragon or no dragon.

I refueled for gas and grabbed a bite and coffee to go at some roadside joint, but by early evening I was knocking on Velma Vale's door. She lived in a courtyard tenement situation a lot like *Melrose Place* up in the Hollywood Hills. There was even a pool. The apartments were stucco or something like that out, straight out of Nathanael West. It was rather upscale, but then she deserved it. I knocked again as I stood around taking in the cozy setting. Darkness was beginning to fall, but no lights came on yet. Palm and hibiscus trees took on eerie shapes in the gathering gloom. And it was so quiet, as if no one else was home. I began to feel that peculiar L.A. distinction in the air, and I don't just mean the smog. The whole ambience is different here than in the Bay Area. Up there it's a melancholy feeling. Down here it's desperate. This has a lot to do with the differences in the weather, architecture, and light, but also some intangible variables that go beyond geography.

I knocked some more. No answer. It grew suddenly darker. I was getting tired all of a sudden, the breakneck cross-state pussy trek and the previous night's exertion catching up to me all at once. What the hell was I doing there? Abruptly the ridiculousness of this situation hit me like a locomotive for the loony bin. My motives were loco, all right. Jesus Christ. I'd done some stupid, impulsive things in my time, but this took the proverbial cake. It was a blessing she wasn't home to receive me. She probably would've screamed, slammed the door in my face, and called the cops. So we balled. Big deal. A chick like that probably slept around all over the world. I was no more than a vacation spot on her expedient itinerary. Slut. No, I shouldn't think that. Where's all the people in this dolled up cesspool? Everyone out on a Sunday night? It was best I just turn tail and head home. But God, I was tired. All I wanted to do was sleep. I'd go down into Santa Monica, check into a motel, wake up refreshed, get some breakfast at Rae's, drive around, see some sights, then return to reality. Yeah. Good plan.

Only next thing I knew there were screeching tires and wailing sirens and mean guys with guns racing all around me, kicking Velma's door open and then while I was still in a daze from this frenetic activity I felt some cold steel slapped on my wrists and my rights read to me as I was dragged into a waiting squad car. Naturally I demanded to know the meaning of this.

That's when a beefy, clean-cut L.A. cop got in my face and snarled, "You're under arrest for the murder of Velma Vale, buddy." Then he smacked me in the back of the head and spit on me, called me scum. "Sickest thing I've ever seen," I heard another one mutter in contempt as they hauled my sorry ass away to the station house for booking. I'd use my one phone call to tell Doc what a swell time I was having.

Chapter Three
A BUMMER PLACE

In my dream, Dolly Duncan and I were free together on a tropical island paradise, nearly deserted except for us and Esther Williams, who was swimming in a sparkling pond and waving at us, and Percy Faith's sweetly sweeping theme from *A Summer Place* was soaring over the scene. We made love on the beach and she let me put it in—hell, she *insisted*. Then we went to the Island Diner, where Marilyn Monroe was the hostess, James Dean the soda jerk, Marlon Brando the manager, and Elvis the bouncer. No waiters, though. So for service, all we had to do was think of what we wanted, and it would materialize right in front of us. We simultaneously imagined two root beer floats and they appeared before us like magic. There was a jukebox in the corner, but no need for coins or selections, since the music was likewise summoned by telepathy. "A Summer Place" by Percy Faith segued into Bill Doggett's "Honky Tonk." Dolly and I looked into each other's eyes, and realized this would be our life *forever*. None of the past mattered. It was all erased. Elvis, Marilyn, and Jimmy had never died, Brando never got fat and old and wrote a memoir nobody cared about. Dolly never turned tricks and popped pills and brutally murdered my father in a Brooklyn alley. I never had my heart broken. I was never questioned in connection with the murder of Velma Vale, starlet.

"You mean *harlot*," Dolly said, disturbing the reverie.

"*What*? Dolly, what are you talking about?"

"You slept with her, didn't you?"

"Who—?"

"*You* know who, Mister Studly. That Z grade so-called actress you butchered."

"Wait—are you mad at me for sleeping with her, or killing her?"

"So you're *admitting* it!"

"What? I swear, I didn't kill anybody!"

"Ah-*HA*! So you *did* sleep with her, didn't you?"

"Okay, sure, but that doesn't mean—"

Dolly threw the root beer float in my face and ran outside.

Now the music had turned ugly— Kenny G ruining "A Summer Place" in his inimitable fashion. The sky grew dark and foreboding, the soothing breeze mutated into a hurricane. I looked over on my way out the door chasing Dolly and saw that Brando was fat and old, in a wheelchair, Marilyn was emaciated and corpse-like, Elvis also fat like Brando but decaying like Marilyn, James Dean mangled beyond recognition practically, like he'd been in a, well, a bad car wreck. All a bunch of zombies. Outside the Kenny G music grew louder, and the hurricane accelerated rapidly in one deafening maelstrom of chaotic sound and fury. I raced by the pond where Esther Williams had been swimming and noticed she was screaming because she was being eaten alive by sharks and piranhas. I stopped and watched for a moment as the Creature From the Black Lagoon rose from the pond and grabbed her and started raping her. At least she wasn't being eaten alive anymore, though she still seemed distressed. Couldn't help her, though. Lashed by the storm and tortured by the Muzak from Hell, I cried out, "*Dolly*! How dare you ruin our paradise with that shit! You accuse *me* of being a murderous lying whore? That takes some nerve after what *you* did!" I couldn't even believe I said that. But she was nowhere in sight. Then I heard her laughing, louder and louder, drowning out the other abrasive noises, until I ran smack dab into *Rose.*

I screamed and turned around and there was Velma Vale, a mere shell of her former self, since now she was a naked zombie, ripped from head to toe with gory gashes, her rotting flesh and blood and guts spilling all over me as she grabbed me and embraced me and kissed me and begged me to make love to her just once more: "Vic, oh Vic, you kill me in bed, baby, you just tear me up, Vic, oh Vic oh Vic, fuck me, fuck me anywhere, it doesn't matter now, I have gashes all over, thanks to you—you ripped me new vaginas because my old one just wasn't enough for a man like you—but that's good, Vic, because now you don't need all those other women—you have hundreds of different places to screw all in one girl! Now, Vic. *please.*"

She slobbered all over me, body parts dropping and dripping off, and when she stuck her tongue in my mouth it tore out while she was frenching me, and I chewed on it a bit before swallowing it, and started choking and I fell and saw Dolly and Rose laughing and laughing as Velma climbed on top of me and made me fondle her breasts which peeled off her chest in my hands, and then her jaw fell off her face into mine and her eyes popped out and I screamed and screamed and...

I woke up.

But I hadn't slept through all of that. No, the first part, the idyllic tropical island scene, was a waking dream, a daydream. Then I must have dozed off and had one hell of a nightmare. I *think*. Reality was getting so surreal I could barely discern the difference from fantasies anymore.

Only the nightmare wasn't over. I was in a cramped holding cell at the Hollywood Precinct. I tried not to gag on the putrid, pervasive stench of human urine. Earlier that day I'd appeared before a judge who informed me of the charge against me of first-degree homicide and posted bail. I recalled making my one phone call to Doc and him saying he was flying down personally with the bail money, leaving Monica in charge of The Drive-Inn. I glanced at my wrist but noticed they'd taken it, my watch, I mean. I looked around and saw a clock on the wall outside the cell. It was mid-afternoon, the day after my arrest on suspicion of murdering Velma Vale. Doc should've been here by now to post the amount I'd quoted him, which would come out of his retirement fund, he told me, so I owed him big time. I swore I'd pay it back. I just had to get out of there at any cost, to anyone.

Then I heard a booming baritone voice nearby singing The Mills Brothers' "Paper Doll." Doll. Dolly. "*Shut up!*" I yelled at the unseen vocalist, probably in the cell next to mine. He only increased the volume a few decibels. He was pretty good, actually, especially considering he was doing it solo, *a Capella.* It was just the word "doll" that got to me. Really, that's one of my favorite tunes, too. The lyrics hit a little close to home, though, especially now. My neighbor the minstrel continued, and I tried drowning it out in my brain, blasting "This Corrosion" by Sisters of Mercy out the speakers in my skull. No go. But I didn't have long to suffer, at least not in there. A few minutes later a cop showed up outside my cell, Doc right behind him, looking none too pleased.

"Next time you take a walk on the wild side, make sure there's a cliff at the end of it," Doc said to me. I hugged him anyway. He just said yeah, yeah, let's get the fuck outta here, and I whole-heartedly concurred. As I passed the neighboring cell I saw a huge fat black guy with dreadlocks giving me the evil eye from a prone position on his comparatively tiny cot. He had a makeshift paper doll in one hand, his giant fudge cock in the other. I didn't maintain eye contact with him for more than a few seconds, but I could feel his hateful gaze on my neck like the Sahara sun.

"I just can't *believe* this shit," Doc was mumbling as we walked down the corridor. "There's no end to the ways you invent for gettin' into fucked up shit, man."

"Ever hear of the expression 'seize the day,' Doc?" I said, trying desperately to put a happy face on a grim situation, like a graffiti artist in a cancer ward.

Doc just looked at me. "Ever hear the expression 'seize my dick'?" That shut me up for a while. Doc signed my release papers and the sergeant, last name Bruno, a typical militant uptight redneck with the complexion of sandpaper, warned me not to leave town until I heard from them it was okay.

"What? I don't even live around here."

"We know all about you, Valentine. We called SFPD and a Captain Sharp gave us a little character profile on you, vouched for your morality but stopped short of endorsing your sanity. Said you're prone to rash acts and impulsive behavior, though he didn't know you to be violent or hostile."

"So?"

"So shut up. That's the only reason we're letting you walk out of here under your own recognizance without so much as an interrogation. For now. You were the only person on the scene, so our officers took you into custody, read your rights, but we have no circumstantial to tie you in, no witnesses, nothing but your untimely presence. So far. We have some connections we plan to follow up on, and if you skip town we'll assume you're guilty and come after you. The FBI is in on this, and Sharp said he'd let us know if you turned up back North before we sanctioned it. So keep that in mind, Valentine. Now get outta here, you bother me."

"Wait. This is *bullshit*. My old man was a cop, and this just isn't S.O.P., pal. I know my *rights*."

"We know all about your father and his illicit career, and how your girlfriend murdered him and you let her go. That's another reason I have not to like you or let you go, but I do things by the book. At least when I got people over my shoulder watching. Now get *outta* here."

I was beyond exasperation. Doc kept tugging at my sleeve but I blew him off, told him to wait outside, but he just stood there, gaping at me, desperately signaling me to play along and beat it. But I wasn't having any, not until I got a few more answers, especially after that last little bit about my old man and Dolly. "I wanna know who's telling you this crap, man. And why I was even dragged down here to begin with when you admit you got nothin' but my presence at the scene, but no weapon, no motive, no...how was she killed, anyway?"

"I'm not telling you *anything*, Valentine. Like you don't know, anyway. We already have a file on you, have copies of letters you sent her fan club, and already the FBI has you on their stalker suspect list. They're the ones who mentioned your father and girlfriend to me, and I ran it by Sharp, who corroborated."

"But I didn't tell him shit!"

"Beat it, Valentine. Mister Jackson here has promised to keep us abreast of your whereabouts. He'll call us just as soon as you check into a motel or whatever you're going to do."

"What? I don't have money for that shit!"

"Not our problem. Mister Jackson, I'll be hearing from you. Now if you'll excuse me." Then he walked away and left me standing there feeling grimy and manipulated, not an altogether new sensation, granted, but uncomfortable all the same. I walked out into the smoggy glare of daylight in Hollywood, Doc by my side, shaking his head. My precious Corvair had been impounded at the crime scene and I wouldn't get it back until this was resolved, they'd told me—one more way to keep me in town. I didn't think that was even legal but of course my opinion was disregarded with the rudeness I've come to expect from figures of authority.

"I ain't got time or energy for this shit no more," Doc said as we just stood on the sidewalk, unsure of our next step and direction. "I'm checking you into a motel the Sarge recommended, the Bowl Motel, it's called, on Cahuenga, I think it is, and then I'm outta here. You're on your own, my man."

"Doc, you can't just leave me here to fend off these jackals and jackasses on my own. C'mon."

"I have a life to live and business to run, remember?"

"Call Monica, let her run things for a few days till I clear this up. C'mon. It'll be fun, an adventure. We'll be a team, like Spenser and Hawk."

"Shit. Huck and Jim. And y'know where they went? Up the fuckin' river, which I ain't doin', no way."

"*Down* the river, Doc. Together."

"No fuckin' way. C'mon, we can just walk to the damn motel from here. I'm sick of cabs. Spent my god damn motherfuckin' life savings on this shit!"

"Doc, I'm sorry, I'll pay you back, but what did you want me to do? Rot in jail? This is a set-up. I was *framed*."

"Vic, I'm *tired* of this shit, man. So tired of you and your whacked out broads I can't see straight. What is it with you? Just one after the other, an assembly line of crazy cunts. I figured after that Dolly shit you'd be cured for good!"

"Yeah, but then Velma Vale just comes in outta nowhere, sits beside me, seduces me, bails on me, and you know the rest."

"Yeah, you follow her trail of pussy juice down to Tinsel Town, knock on her fuckin' door!"

"Knock-knock-knockin' on Heaven's Door, I thought."

"Yeah, right. And the Devil opens up laughin' his ass off and you're fooled again. Man, it's not even *funny* anymore."

"Doc, what could I have done differently? *What*? *You* tell *me*. Jesus, *look* at me. I'm such a god damn mess." I just sat on the curb and sucked in bus and car exhaust to clear out the smog in my eyes and lungs, which was filtered through the cool January sea breeze, at least, then I buried my head in my hands and almost started bawling. "I'm just mixed-up, man, and you're my only friend in the world, Doc. I'm sorry I dragged you into this, but—aw, hell, you're right. You've done enough. Go back home, I'll straighten this out, just like I straightened everything out on my last trip."

Doc let out a big sigh and put his hand on my shoulder. "That's what worries me. First you let a murderer go and now you're accused of being one yourself."

"You really think I'm guilty, Doc?"

"Of *course* not, man. C'mon. Let's go eat at the Howard Johnson's on Hollywood and Vine and then check you into that motel. C'mon. C'mon, Vic. Get up. Ain't so bad. Hell, you're the last fuck Velma Vale ever got. Think of it that way."

I perked up at the thought. God, how sick. "Yeah, you're right. Even if they fry me, they can't take that away from me. I'll tell the world! Now that she's gone, I have no reason to respect her privacy anymore!"

"But she was also the only person who could back up your story, too, remember that."

"Oh. Right." I stood up. "Fuck Howard Johnson's. Let's walk down the Boulevard to Musso and Frank's. A class joint. I'll spring."

"Big of you, considering the bail money I just forked out."

"How much did it come to, exactly'?"

"Forget it. It's considered bad taste to leave the price tag on a present, y'know."

"Doc. I swear. I'll pay you back every cent."

"Yeah, yeah, sure. Let's eat, you're starting to sound delirious."

So we walked all the way to Musso & Frank's in the heart of Hollywood, what heart was left. This was still the biggest tourist delusional rip-off in the world. Those poor saps come all the way here from Iowa and Indonesia and Istanbul expecting glitter and glamour and all they get for their trouble is garbage and gossip. The Walk of Fame was more like the Crawl of Obscurity. All those stars covered with spit and vomit and footprints of junkies and hookers and tourists. A celestial sewer. And yet, for some perverse reason, I kind of loved it here. Maybe it was the broken dreams and hearts littering the dusty landscape like so much confetti that got to me, made me think of my mother and her forgotten fantasies as she wasted away in her room at the Chipper Monks mental home and pretended her life had taken the course she'd planned. Or my own reveries rotting in the cemetery of reality. Anyway, this was where many of my favorite dreamers came to die, and I felt in good company ghost-wise, with Doc to boot. Since we both loved movies, we had to admit a grudging affection for this town at the very least, even under these conditions.

Take Musso & Frank's, a legendary landmark and former watering hold for such literary exiles as Faulkner, West, Chandler, Hammett, and Saroyan. This was one of my favorite spots in L.A., along with Norm's and Ship's and Rae's and Dolores's and Dinah's and all the other cool coffee shops, or ships, since they all kind of reminded me of '50s rocket ships. I could pretend I was marooned on the *Forbidden Planet*. Me and Doc. No, I love Doc, but, well, pussy is pussy. He understood, deep down, why I kept getting into this trouble. Nothing can replace the feel of soft feminine flesh. Not even friendship. What you had to do was make them compatible, because flesh couldn't replace friendship, either. Both were essential ingredients for a healthy, successful life, I believed. The bitch was when you had to make a choice between the two. If you were really lucky, you'd fall in love with your lover, and she (or he) with you, and you'd have it all in one nifty package, no conflicts. But life doesn't always work that simply. Hell, *never*.

We took a booth amid the dimly lit classic '40s decor of Musso & Frank's and perused the menu. Then it hit me for the first time, really. My idol and dream lover, Velma Vale, was gone from this world forever. I lost my appetite and just ordered a coffee and a beer, while Doc shot the works, reminding me I had promised to pick up the check. Whatever. Suddenly things like food and money seemed so insignificant. I kept losing all the women in my life, one way or another. At least with Rose and Dolly I could always hang onto the hope I'd run into them again someday, and I did, despite my better sense. My mother was still alive, in her own mind at any rate, and her body existed on the same plane I did, at least for now. But Velma was truly an angel recalled by heaven. I was sure of that. Porno or no porno. Velma Vale was in heaven.

Wasn't she?

"You think Velma is in heaven, Doc?"

"Where?"

"You know." I pointed upward.

"You mean on a plane to Costa Rica?"

"No. You know what I mean."

"Aw, shit, Vic, I just run a bar and a video shop. I don't know shit about nothin', 'cept I'm hungry and I need some food quick. Velma is in a better place even if she's nowhere, hear what I'm sayin'? Just worry 'bout yourself, here and now, in this life, on *this* world. That's all you got to worry about. Let Velma worry about herself, if she has to. Change the subject. Hey, what's the biggest difference you think between down here in L.A. and back East in New York? I mean, I done L.A. before for movie conventions and shit, but New York, I've only been there once with my mama when I was a kid, tourist crap, you know. But you know the insides of both cities, right? So what's the difference, would you say, since they're both the big towns in the U S of A?"

I thought about it and replied, "Well, here, it's like, *'Look at me! Look at me*!' In New York, they're like, *'What the fuck are you lookin' at*?'"

Doc laughed. "Yeah, I gotcha. So what about where we live? Bay Area? How would you sum up people there?"

"I dunno, Doc. Fucked up."

"C'mon."

"Ahm, it's more like, I dunno. 'Look within.'"

I had just tossed that off, but I could tell Doc was actually thinking about it, like it was some sagacious remark. He just needed food. "Vic, for an idiot, you can be pretty insightful. That's why I just don't understand why you keep gettin' into these fucked up predicaments. I love you, you're my bro, but it's the woman thang, my man. They use your brain and heart like they use tampons. Soak it up, toss it out and flush the fucker."

I sighed, sipping my coffee, then my beer. High, low, up, down. Doc was right, as usual. What was it with me? "Could it be my mother, Doc?"

"Huh? Your mother *what*?"

"I mean, am I still attracting these neurotic women because, deep down, I'm looking for my mother? You've said as much sometimes."

"Vic, *I* don't know, man, I mean, yeah, could be, but now that you see that, what're you gonna do about it? I mean, goin' out to see your mother in the nuthouse didn't seem to change nothin', did it? You didn't have a, whatchacallit, y'know, when somethin' dawns on you all of a sudden, y'know, starts with an 'e', an enigma or elephant or egg sandwich or someshit."

"Epiphany?"

"Right, that. The way you were talkin' when you got back from back East, I thought you had one of those. Guess not, or else the wrong motherfuckin' thing dawned on your dumb ass, or you wouldn't be in the mess you're in now."

"Yeah, true. I thought so, too. I even thought I'd lost all interest in sex, even, 'cause I even turned Monica down, though it's just as well since she's tight with this new dude now, but then I just increased my fixation on Velma, and then like magic, she shows up outta nowhere, seduces me, then next thing you know, I got her blood on my hands, insteada my own jizz like usual."

"But you don't. Ain't no blood on your hands, Vic. You said you wrote this bitch alla time, right? Her fan club?"

"Yeah, so?"

"Ever send a picture?"

"Of who?"

"*You*, stupid ass. So she'd know you existed outside your own little world. See, I been watchin' this shit for years now in The Drive-Inn, how people get obsessed with famous fuckers, right, and they figure, if this famous person I idolize knows I exist, then in a way, that makes me famous by proxy. You get me?"

"Yeah."

"So, *did* you?"

"Did I what?"

"Cut the bull. You send her a photo of you or what?"

I sighed. "Yea, I did, Doctor Schlock, or has that been changed to Doctor *Spock* now?"

"With your address?"

"Yeah, so?"

"You ever invite her to come see you?"

"Of course not! Well, not directly."

"So the bitch knew what you looked like, where you lived. Right?"

"If she ever got her mail, yeah."

"So, conceivably, Velma Vale could have picked *you* out."

"Meaning set me up?"

"Looks that way. Whole thing is just too coincidental for my tastes. Maybe you wanna believe Fate is pimping for your sorry white ass, but me, I think we're responsible for our *own* shit down here in the cesspool."

"Doc, you sayin' that—" His food showed up, I paused, then went on as he wolfed it down. "You sayin' Velma Vale *framed* me?"

"Think about it, get back to me. I'm eatin'."

I thought about it. I got back to him shortly thereafter, as he was chewing the last bite of his sandwich. "Doc, you're right. I've never seen the body, not even a picture. She flew up to San Francisco, looked me up, pretended to be escaping her life down here, pretending to find me attractive and all."

"Vic, she saw your picture, figured she could do worse patsy-wise, and fucked your brains out. Literally. But give yourself some credit, my man. She could've landed *any* sap, *any*time, body like that. Shit, even *me*."

"But you didn't profess undying love in a fan letter."

"*Exactly*. She knew I'd just fuck her and that would be that. She needed a sap, made to order, pre-brain-washed, who'd follow her straight to Hell if need be."

"Me."

Doc pointed his finger at me, making a little blasting noise as he pulled the imaginary trigger. "Bingo," he said.

Chapter Four
IDLE WORSHIP

I missed my room up in San Francisco. I missed all my stuff, my cult flick videos, my cheesecake magazines, my vast music library, my dickless cat. Monica was spending so much time watching him for me I was afraid Puss would think she was his rightful owner. I was actually jealous. I wanted to clear this business up as soon as possible so I could return to my little puny wonderful insular womb of a world.

In the meantime, no reason I couldn't fit in a little fun.

Doc and I checked out the Bowl Motel on Cahuenga, right down from the Hollywood Bowl, and I realized it was the same cheap sleazy dive I had stayed in on a case years before. Hookers kept calling me and waking me up at like four in the morning, so I put the old kibosh on that joint with no deliberation whatsoever. I was really pissed the cops had copped my wheels, along with my gun. It wasn't like this was San Francisco, where one could get around by foot or train. The bus system here sucked big time, and anyway I was feeling claustrophobic enough without being transported around La La Land like a wheel-borne sardine.

"Let me go talk to the Sarge," Doc said as we walked back toward the precinct. "Stay outside, and out of trouble. I'll have him sign the car over to me, for the time being, and I'll tell him you're under my, y'know, custody or jurisdiction or whatever. Deal?"

"So you plan on staying a while?"

"Till I get bored. This new theory of mine intrigues me. When I get bored, I'll just drive up North."

"Without me?"

"Up to you. If we can prove this was a set-up, you're home free."

"How we gonna do that?"

"You're the detective, remember? I'm like Watson to your Holmes, or maybe that's Watts to your Homes."

"Oh, yeah. Whatever. Why don't we just go in the station and tell the Sarge what we think is up?"

"You idiot, they *booked* you already! If there ain't no body, they would be the first to know. It was them who said there was one in the first place. Could be they're in on it."

"Oh yeah. I'm not thinking straight, I guess."

"Just let me go get the damn car, then we'll drive around and find something to do, dig?"

"Deep, man. I dig deep, daddy-o."

"Your own grave, you mean. Be right back."

Doc went into the station and came back out around five minutes later while I just stood on the sidewalk and watched the parade of punkers and prostitutes and perverts and pretty people in front of the Hollywood Precinct. Look at me, look at me. What the fuck are you lookin' at? Look within. Look out.

Doc had the keys with him, and he directed me to the garage around the corner where confiscated vehicles were parked. He had a signed piece of paper with him, so we could just drive right off into the sunset, or Sunset Boulevard, that is.

"Doc, you're a diplomatic wonder," I said. He drove, one of the conditions, but that was fine with me.

"And you're the dip I wonder about," he said.

We drove west on Sunset and stopped at an exotic little hole in the wall called The Tiki Room. Inside Martin Denny music was playing and we sat at the tiny bar and ordered some colorful exotic drinks, I don't remember what, something green and red and fruity, and in no time we both had a buzz on. Then I noticed a flyer tacked up on the wall near the entrance. It glared at me like neon: THIS SUNDAY NIGHT AT The Viper Room: THE SHE BEAMS WITH THE NAUGHTY ONES. Then there was a time, 9PM, and some other little details. I pointed it out to Doc and he went ballistic.

"Holy shit, she never *never* said nothin' to me about this!" he said in a slurred tone, staggering off his stool and ripping the flyer off the wall. "She's all over the damn place!"

"Maybe since she's down her a lot, 'cause of her fiancé, she booked some gigs," I said passively, though somewhere inside I was excited. Seeing The She Beams would make me feel like I was even more at home while away from home. "I guess Monica can't make it if she's mindin' the store. And my cat."

"Yeah, shit. But Monica thought I was comin' right back up. I better call her and let her know I'm on a case with you."

"That's so good to hear, Doc."

"So you say. Monica might not be so overjoyed, though, 'specially if she planned on makin' this gig in a few days. I'm gonna go call her. Be right back."

While Doc was on the payphone I ordered another green drink and felt reanimated. It dawned on me The Viper Room was owned by actor Johnny Depp, who played Ed Wood in the film bio, and that River Phoenix, Generation X poster boy, had croaked right out front. I wondered if Judy was making it with Johnny Depp, even though she was engaged to that stud from Santa Barbara. I sat there and recalled the night Judy and I had fooled around, only I blew it right after she blew me by prematurely ejaculating on her wondrous cleavage. Next to poor dead Velma, Judy had the best boobs I'd ever laid hands on, much less eyes. Large but not *too* large. Mamie Van Doren knockers. And Judy always dressed up in gold shimmering low-cut wide-collar jump-suit tights and silver pumps and other clothes like that while performing. I was still hoping for that pity fuck, fiancé or no fiancé. He was a loser, anyway. Judy, Judy, Judy. I became fixated on her all over again while sitting there stoned. Sex in exile. Sexile. I had designs on Judy, all right. Thinking about them took my mind off of Velma, and my own impending trial if Velma's body didn't pop up, preferably still breathing. At this point the O.J. Simpson trial was still dragging on, and I kind of knew how he felt, only I was totally innocent. Of course, he claimed the same thing, but there he sat in a jail cell anyway. That was why I related to him. Other than that, I had no million-dollar defense team, no football trophy, no film career. Just my word of honor, worth less than a nickel in this town.

As I was sitting there daydreaming of Judy playing the surf guitar nude on my bed, I noticed some *yutz* next to me was giving me the visual once-over. We were in West Hollywood so I assumed he was as fruity as my drink and moved one seat down from him. He just kept staring, though. I caught a glance of him while feigning to look around for Doc, and noticed he looked straight enough, not gay but happily hetero, even macho, tan and muscular and dark and burly, but then you never could tell about those things. I moved one more seat over, still dreaming of Judy, even harder now. He didn't budge, just kept staring. I was about to say something cute like "Take a picture, it'll last longer," but decided that wasn't original enough. He broke the silence for me.

"Excuse me, but may I say you have a good look for films?" he said.

Talk about a tired line. "What do I look like to you, Lana Turner?" I said, and he cracked up, but misinterpreted my witty rejoinder as an invitation to get cozy. He moved one seat closer to me and extended his hand, ostensibly for a shake. I obliged without eye contact or even turning in my seat.

"My name's Tony Ray," he said, taking off his sunglasses and smiling like a matinee idol signing autographs. "I used to be an actor, now I'm a producer and director. Writer, too."

"Your modesty has won me over," I said. "But why are you eyeballing me, chief? Where I come from that could be read the wrong way."

"And where do you come from?"

"Most recently, San Francisco."

"Ah, yes, of course. And originally?"

"New York. Brooklyn."

"Great!"

"What's so great about that?"

"I'm from around there, too. Well, Ohio. Cleveland. But I moved around a lot before I settled here."

"Golly."

"What do you do?"

"The best I can."

"Haven't I heard that line in a movie once?"

"You've heard *every* line in a movie once. Or twice. Where do you think lines in the movies come from?"

"Are you always like this or are you just in a bad mood?"

"Hell. I thought I was in a *good* mood."

"Glad I didn't meet you when you were down. But really, what do you do up in San Francisco?"

"This and that."

"Struggling, huh."

"Who isn't?"

"I don't know. Jimmy Stewart, maybe."

"You kidding? He struggles just to breathe these days."

"Guess you're right. Everyone has problems. Have you ever tried any acting?"

"Everyone acts," I said patly.

"Marlon Brando says that."

"'Cause it's true."

"Only he gets paid millions to do it. Most people do it for free. So he's smart."

I shrugged. I wanted Doc to come back so we could go. These kinds of conversations always bore the hell out of me. "No argument there. But I doubt I could join the millionaire's club on the basis of my modest thespian talents."

"You won't know till you try."

"Are you offering me a screen test, pal?"

"Not yet. But I'm working on something you might be perfect for."

"All right, what's your angle? Why are you working me like this?"

"I told you. I have my own script, a neo-noir kinda thing, that Tarantino was gonna do at one point, only he wants to re-write it his way, so I'm going to direct it myself, my way. If he can do it, so can I."

"That's the spirit. You and Orson Welles. Go for it. But really, pal, me, I'm not interested."

"In movies?"

"No, I *love* movies—as a hobby. Not a willing participant. Maybe if this conversation were taking place forty years ago."

"Neither of us would be here."

"Exactly. We're both way too late. Hollywood just ain't the same anymore. All the great flicks have been made, even all the great bad ones. Sorry."

"So am I. But I plan to change that," Tony Ray said with confidence.

"Pretty ambitious, I'd say. Impossible, too."

"I don't think so. Read my script, at least. I want to use a cast of unknowns."

"Who'd bankroll a movie with a cast of unknowns? You need at least one quasi-bankable semi-star. Even I know that. Tarantino would never have gotten 'Reservoir Dogs' out of the gate without Harvey Keitel."

"You have show biz savvy. I like you more and more as we talk."

"Yeah? I generally like people less and less," I confessed.

"You don't have to like me personally. Just read my script."

"Why should I?"

"What have you got to lose?"

Good question. "All right. I have some time to kill. I'll humor you, pal. You got a copy on you?"

He was radiant. "In the car. Be right back."

Just then Doc walked up. "Who's Mister Hollywood?"

"Name's Tony Ray," I told him. "Used to be an actor. Ever hear of him?"

Doc started laughing. "*The* Tony Ray?"

"I guess. Why?"

"Shit, man, the Tony Ray I know of used to do *porn* flicks. Guy's hung like a donkey on steroids. This was a few years back. I got some of his stuff in my porno section at The Drive-Inn."

I should've guessed. "You recognize him?"

"Not with his clothes on. You know, come to think of it, word is those bootleg Velma Vale X flicks?"

"Yeah?"

"He's *in* some."

"Shit! You *sure*?"

"That's what I heard. Never seen 'em myself yet. But he retired from that scene after directing a few himself, wanted to go legit, make art and all that jazz. Should've stuck with all that jizz. He was doing okay."

"Jesus Christ. That dude wants me for his next picture!"

"No way."

"Yup. He's goin' out now to get the script."

Just then Tony Ray came bouncing back in. You could tell he jogged a lot. "Here it is." I looked at the front cover. It was called *Neon Knights*. Oh brother. Doc didn't say anything, just sat down and sipped his drink, but I could sense him smirking. "Say, what's this rated, Tony?" I asked. Doc let out a little laugh despite himself.

He seemed nonplused. "Rated? I don't know! Too raw for cable, I tried that already, but you'll see. Nothing hardcore, but, you know. *Adult* entertainment."

"Uh-huh." I nodded and flipped through the pages. "So what movies were you in before you wrote this, Tony? Anything I might've seen?"

"Hm? Oh. Probably not. Pretty obscure. Nothing major. That's why I quit, to do my own thing. My address and number in Malibu are on the front there. Try contacting me by, say, next week. Sooner the better, though. Where are you staying, anyway? Be in town that long?"

"I'll be around. I'm staying with friends, though, and I don't feel at liberty to give out their number without their permission."

"That's all right. Just get in touch with me, then. I really have to fly, I'm meeting an actress at The Source for lunch." He looked at his gold watch. It was around four. "Or I suppose it's dinner. In fact, she's already committed."

"Where?"

"To the script."

341

"Oh. So I'm flattered, Tony, that'd you'd not only offer me this but also trust me with it."

"I'm not offering it *yet*, Mister—hey, what the heck's your name anyway?"

"Valentine. Vic Valentine."

"Really! *Wow*! That's *great*! Perfect! Sounds like a detective or something. Or a porn star." Doc laughed again. Tony ignored him, if he even noticed. "Vic Valentine—I can see that on a marquee *now*!"

"Where? The Pussycat Theater?" Doc said.

Tony laughed, but uncomfortably. "No, I was thinking more of the Chinese Theater. Up in lights - 'Neon Knights.' That's my dream. After you read it, you'll see why."

"I'm sure."

"Sorry I have to run, Vic, but—may I call you Vic?—I really have to go. Tina's waiting."

"Tina Louise?"

"I *wish*. But it's funny, she *does* look like her, in a way. She almost played the part of Ginger in one of those 'Gilligan's Island' reunion TV movies, but it didn't pan out. She's too young. Her name's Tina Hartman."

"I'll have to remember that, if she's gonna be my co-star."

Tony rapped on the wooden bar. "We'll see. Call me soon, Vic."

"I'll do that, Tony."

He actually said, "*Ciao*!"

"Yeah, whatever."

Then Tony Ray ran outside and drove off in his sleek, shiny Jaguar. I turned toward Doc and he was just shaking his head, laughing.

"Poor dude is desperate as they come," he chuckled.

"You're just jealous."

"Yeah, I'm as green as your drink, man."

"Anyway, you talk to Monica?"

"Yeah. She's goin' crazy up there. I might have to go back."

"But you told Sergeant Bruno you'd keep an eye on me."

"I'm not your keeper, brother. I got a business to keep an eye on, too."

"Monica plan on comin' down for the gig at The Viper Room?"

"Yep. I'm spoilin' her plans. She says she's comin' whether I'm back or not. She'll just close the store."

"But what about my cat?"

"*Fuck* your cat, what about my *store*?"

"I guess Monica is sayin' fuck 'em *both*."

"She might cool off. I'll see how she is tomorrow. Told her I'd see how it went down here before I decided if I'd come back tomorrow night. She is worried about you, though, so we got that in our favor. I told her you need me."

"I do, Doc. That's no lie."

"But now you got Tony Ray, big shot movie producer. Lemme see that." Doc grabbed the script and started thumbing through it. "'Neon Knights.' Shit. Looks like there's lots of dialogue, though, which is pretty avant-garde for a porn flick."

I grabbed it back from him. "It ain't porn, Doc, it's straight cinema."

"With an 's.' Sin-e-ma. Or may it's sin-*enema*. The shit flows out of the theater and gets flushed down your brain." He really cracked himself up.

"Let's go to Ben Frank's up the road for java and get our heads clear. Jesus. Loaded in the middle of the day."

"Lemme finish my drink first, Mister Coffee Shop," Doc said. "Shit, you should write a damn *guide* to those things."

"I'm the only person who'd buy it, though. C'mon, hurry up. I'm sick of this place."

"You're just afraid more washed-up porn stars are gonna hit on you."

"Got that right. Let's go."

We hit Ben Frank's and had coffee at the counter. I was reading through *Neon Knights* when something horrifying and shocking occurred to me. "Doc...this story...it's about *me*. It's about Velma Vale. It's about me *and* Velma Vale."

"Huh? Gimme that."

"I'm still reading it, wait, but from what I can tell, it's about a loner type who meets an actress in a movie theater, at one of her own movies, and he idolizes her, this guy, and she takes him home with her, and"—I read a few pages on—"and he wakes up the next morning and she's *dead*. And her blood is all over him, and he's the prime suspect, but he escapes the cops, so let's see, that's just the beginning. So he becomes a detective, sort of, with the help of his friend, an ex-cop—who's *black*! And they try to find her real killer before—"

Doc grabbed the script from me and started reading through it himself. "This is *eerie*, man. I mean 'Twilight Zone' time. This

Tony Ray didn't just sit next to you by accident. He was in those porn flicks with Velma. He *knows* her. And my hunch is he still *does*."

I got a chill. "What's this all about, Doc? Why me? What's the *point*?"

"Beats me, man. But I'm callin' Monica and tellin' her to keep her cute little heart-shaped ass right where it is. We got work to do down here. This is gettin' *good*."

As dusk fell Doc and I sat at the counter drinking gallons of coffee and taking turns reading the script, cover to cover, every page, every line, searching for parallels with reality, clues to the truth of what was going on, why I was being framed for the murder of Velma Vale. The loner in the script only had superficial similarities to me—though Doc disagreed, obviously viewing me as a pathetic loser stuck in a dead end job with no romantic prospects whatsoever—but the starlet in the script, to be played by this Tina Hartman, was a lot like Velma, almost to a tee. It was apparent Tony Ray had based the part on his old porno partner. I tried picturing Tony and Velma sliming all over each other for the camera, and felt nauseous as a result. It also made me feel that much more meaningless in her litany of lovers. Hell, they probably sold I FUCKED VELMA VALE T-shirts down at Venice Beach at two bucks a pop. At least her tryst with Tony and scores of other hunks had been recorded for posterity, whereas our magical union was concealed within the hazy memory of that strange, distant night, dissolving in the dawn. For all I knew Velma was somewhere getting laid right now, on a cruise to the tropics, telling her lover what a fool she'd made of me. Could have been anybody she ran off with. Anywhere. Could have been Tony Ray in Malibu.

The script turned fairly routine as it progressed, with the loner and the ex-cop interrogating various Hollywood lowlifes who knew the starlet (obviously the "neon knights" of the title), coming up with leads that went nowhere. It ended with the loner going to the gas chamber, and just before the pellets dropped, he saw the laughing face of the starlet just outside the chamber, embracing the ex-cop, who was also smiling and waving. Then the screen faded to black from the loner's POV. The End.

"Runaway hit," Doc deadpanned. "Lots of gratuitous sex and violence. Twenty-eight breasts. Gratuitous Velma Vale. Vic Valentine set-up Fu. Fuck Fu. Five stars, off the scale, one louder. Doc Bob says check it out."

"Even this scenario confirms our suspicions, Doc. Velma is still alive. Maybe this is supposed to tell us *that*."

"Doesn't help you out any. Cops won't buy it."

"Yeah, but it points me in the right direction."

"Which is where?"

I looked at him. "You settin' me up, Doc?"

"Shit. You got me. I might as well go call Velma now and tell her our rendezvous in the Caribbean if off, you blew it wide open. Take me away, officer."

"You didn't answer my question."

Doc gave me a look. "Are you *seriously* asking me?"

I sighed. "Naw—course not. But the dude *is* black."

"But I'm not an ex-cop, Vic. He just made the guy black 'cause the chick likes dark meat. You saw all those brothers she was supposedly bangin'. And the chick is an ex-porn queen, too, before goin' into all those monster movies and shit. Only chocolate éclairs were big and filling enough after nibbling on those vanilla wafers all day."

I leafed back through the script. "So the chick sets up this fan—whom she was stalking, a neat twist, I must say—so she could fake her own murder and pin it on this guy. That was her sister in the bed next to him, but since her face was all chopped up the bonehead couldn't tell."

"So who killed the sister and planted her there?" Doc asked.

I was stumped. "The ex-cop, right?"

"I think so. It gets confusing. I must've been reading it too fast."

I thought some more. "Also, it doesn't explain *why* she wanted her death faked."

"Simple, man. To disappear from the life, get away from all the attention. Escape her past. Start over."

"*Hmmm*. But why did she need a patsy? Couldn't she have just had the cops find her sister mutilated?"

"The cops were *in* on it!" Doc practically shouted. "Like I said before. The ex-cop fixed it so the morgue I.D. would check out, the record would show it was Velma's, I mean, the *starlet's* body. The chick had all the angles covered, and having a suspect go down for it made it all the more credible for the media. A frustrated stalker fan took her out after raping her. Simple."

"And he goes down for it and she gets away with it. And that's it."

"That's *film noir*, my man." Doc polished off his coffee. "But in our case...there ain't an ex-cop involved. And to pull this off, Velma would need an inside connection to make it all fly as far as the record goes."

"You saying she does have somebody on the inside?"

"Gotta be. If we're on the right track. The only other possibility is, of course, she really *is* dead, murdered by her enraged, estranged lover, and you were just in the wrong place at the wrong time."

"But then what about this script? Coincidence again? You said you didn't believe in that stuff."

"I don't," said the Doc.

"And another difference—I still haven't seen a body, stand-in or otherwise, not even a picture."

"You know who might have some interesting pictures of Velma, before and after her 'death', don't you?"

I nodded. "Let's got to Malibu tonight," I said.

"Something tells me we'll be expected, too," Doc said, and I agreed.

Chapter Five
ONCE IN A BLUE MOVIE

The address Tony Ray had written down was located just off Pacific Coast Highway, a modest but exquisitely built house jutting off a cliff, facing the sea. It was nighttime when Doc and I arrived, the sky black and clear, the moon pearly and full, the sea glistening and restless. A fairly strong breeze whipped us as we got out of the Corvair and headed toward the house. The lights were off and apparently nobody was home, but we walked up the little wooden landing and knocked anyway. Maybe someone was hiding in the dark.

As we stood there waiting for a response, I looked around and thought how the placid, windswept surroundings contrasted with the television images of wildfires and mudslides and earthquake damage. It hit me why people might still want to live here despite the onslaught of natural disasters. It also hit me how stupid these people were. Stupid but *rich*.

"I can't believe the FBI is actually building a case against me as a stalker and a slasher," I said to Doc, who was leaning over, trying to peek into the bay window facing the ocean. "Innocent sweetheart like me. Man, I regret the day I ever laid eyes on Velma Vale, much less laid her. Leave it to beavers."

"Maybe they're *not*," he said, straining to see through into the shadowy living room. The curtains were open and everything inside would be visible if illuminated. "That could just be bunk Sergeant Bilko or Bruno or whatever was giving you to make you sweat. Don't worry about that now."

I nodded and shrugged and then scouted around for Tony's Jaguar, a vintage classic, impossible to forget or fail to spot. "Don't see his wheels. Could be he's still out with Tina."

"Who?"

"Tina. Tina Hartman, the actress slated for the part of the scheming starlet."

Just then I was temporarily blinded by the glare of headlights pulling up in front of the house. When the spots cleared from my eyes and I was certain I wasn't going to get a migraine attack I expected to see Tony and Tina walking up to greet us. But it wasn't. It was two tall characters in suits and sunglasses. At night. And they're weren't CHP, not with *that* tailor.

They got in our faces and produced badges that I couldn't make out in the dark, and with lingering spots in my vision, but I heard Doc say out loud, "Shit. Feds. What the hell is this?"

"You the same dudes John and Bobby K. sent to take out Marilyn?" I said.

"Very funny, Valentine," one guy said. Both had slicked back dark hair and both were built solid. Conformists, practically indistinguishable from the other.

"You're right," I said. "You guys were probably still in grade school at the time. Great alibi."

"What do you want here?" the other goon asked anyone who'd answer.

"What's it to ya?" Doc said with typical attitude.

"We ask the questions," the other goon said.

Doc looked at me, and we both cracked up and then high-fived. "It's happened," Doc said. "We've crossed over into one of my videos."

"Should I tap my heels together three times so we can go home?" I said.

"Naw, this is too much fun," Doc said. "Let's see what happens first. I'm hooked, even though I've seen this a million times already."

"Hope the dialogue gets better," I said.

"All right, drop it," Fed One said. "We have a file on you Valentine, and your subversive friend here, too. You're only making it thicker and harder for yourself."

"I didn't mean to turn you on," I said, and Doc and I giggled like schoolboys.

"Yuck it up, laughing boy," Fed Two said, incredibly. Dialogue like that wouldn't even fly on the straight-to-video market these days.

"Must have the same manual from the Hoover days," Doc said.

"Shut up," Fed One snapped. "We're watching you, *both* of you. We know you killed that girl, and she had some very important friends, and they want to make sure you go down fast and ugly, Valentine. Hanging around people's houses when the lights are out isn't doing you any good—not that anything will at this point. We'll be pulling you in any day now, maybe tomorrow, soon as we've compiled enough evidence. Miss that court date and we'll find you and *bury* you."

"Just take me in now, you're so surefire about it," I said, getting pissed. "It's none of your business if I knock on anyone's door. You don't even know whose house this is, I bet."

Fed Two produced a little notepad and read from it in a monotone. "Anthony Philip Raymond, acted under the abbreviated name Tony Ray in a series of pornographic and underground films, currently living off residual checks and attempting to jumpstart a career as a director-producer but is having difficulty getting financial backing from major studios because of his perverse track record. And, oh yeah—was engaged to Velma Vale, the girl you *murdered*. And you expect us to believe you're paying a social call on an old friend. You're a pathetic lying twisted dirt bag, Valentine. Your file makes me puke. Your file is like *bile*. Letting the whore who brutally killed your own father go scot-free—but we'll find her."

"Hey, you keep away from Dolly! She's—"

"She's *what*? Innocent? Apparently she skipped the country, but we have a line on her in a country we have no extradition treaty with. Your testimony could help us, but not you, so we won't even ask for it. Don't need it. We have a friend of hers, and yours, from Brooklyn who's in a Witness Protection Program, and he witnessed the whole thing."

"Junior Benenito," I said with a sigh, leaning back against the door, feeling dizzy.

Fed One checked his notes. "That's him. But that doesn't concern us now, Valentine. Other people are dealing with that. We're on you. You may wonder why this particular little murder is a Federal case."

"Crossed my mind, yeah."

"Well, none of your goddamn business. We just want you to know we're on your ass, Valentine, and should you wish to silence Tony Ray we'll be right there to pin the rap on you before the blood on your hands has a chance to dry."

"You dudes are so full of shit your hair is brown," Doc said. "Bet your eyes are too."

Fed Two took off his shades to reveal cold gray pupils. He got right in Doc's face, nose to nose, and stared him down, or tried to. "My eyes look brown to you, boy?"

"*Boy*?" Doc said. "They call me *Mister* Tibbs, cracker. Back off."

Doc and Fed Two continued the staring contest for a minute

or so like it was a chickie run. Fed Two finally put his shades back on, grinning slightly like a crocodile digesting his dinner. He backed arrogantly away from Doc and then looked at me. His partner never removed his shades or cracked a smile. Fed Two stuck his finger in my face and said, "Watch your ass."

"*You* watch it, sweetie," I said.

Fed Two stood there like a statue for a few seconds, then slowly put his finger away and the two backed away and drove off in their black sedan.

"Tony's fiancée," I said. "Poor Dolly, too. God damn that Junior. The Mob was gonna take him out probably for holding out on them all those years, but they promised me they'd cancel the contract on Dolly. But now the torch has been passed to the Feds, who won't listen to reason or cut any deals."

"They're full of it, man," Doc said, a little shaken up and breathing heavily. He wiped sweat off his brow and then said, "Let's get outta here, check into a motel."

"You gotta tell the Sarge where we are anyway, right?"

"I ain't gotta do nothin'," Doc said as we walked down toward the Corvair. "Fuck the Sarge. Fuck the Feds. And Fuck Tony Ray. Shit, maybe the bitch is dead and *he* killed her and set you up."

"Damn—you're right! That script could be a ruse to confuse me, make me think Velma is still alive, and no one's guilty of anything, except maybe her, of fraud, but that would deflect suspicion off of Tony."

I got behind the wheel and Doc let me. He lay back in the passenger seat and let out a big, tired sigh. We took off back up PCH as we considered the options and possibilities.

"Maybe," Doc said with his eyes closed as I headed toward Santa Monica, "maybe Velma is alive, and Tony is still helping her, and that script is so coincidental he can claim we're imagining the whole connection, and hopefully we'd turn tail and head home."

"Or I'd just fry for her murder. But why me? That's the question."

"Well, the script has the reason, somewhere. Maybe you're just the fall guy because that makes it look like a crime was committed and someone was responsible and someone took the rap for it. Case closed, unlike Marilyn or Sal Mineo, for instance. No one would come snooping around later, and Velma and Tony could cruise the world anonymously, secure in the popular conviction that she is gone forever."

"Yeah—but why *me*?"

Doc slapped me on the shoulder. "You just fit the profile they were looking for, my man."

"C'mon, Doc. There's *plenty* of obsessed stalker fans right here in L.A. Why go to the trouble of plucking some sap from four hundred miles away?"

"*Hmmm*. Maybe all that shit the Fed was telling us convinced Tony and Velma you were the perfect patsy—history of mental instability, covering up for a confessed killer, and befriending a crooked cop on the Frisco force."

"Marcus?"

"Yup. Feds probably had his number all along, and you were his little pal."

"But how would Tony and Velma know this shit?"

"Inside informer—like the ex-cop in the script. Someone on the LA force with a direct hookup to the Feds and their files. Or maybe a Fed himself. Maybe our friends we just met."

"Shit," I said with a whistle, pulling up the hill toward Ocean Ave. in Santa Monica. "You got a sick mind to think of all this, Doc."

"It don't make sense to you?" he said.

"Yeah," I said, "but I got a sick mind, too. C'mon, I know a good motel along here I stayed in last time I was down here."

"Looking for Rose?"

"Yeah."

"I almost miss that bitch, compared to Velma Vale. This one really did a number on you. Hope the sex was worth fryin' for."

I flash-backed on Velma's dreamy creamy dish of a body, the sensual smorgasbord of that night, which I recalled like the sweetest of wet dreams. "You know something? I think it was."

"Damn," Doc said. "In that case, to hell with pity. I *envy* you."

"Wanna change places then?"

"*I* didn't get to fuck her."

"Maybe you will yet."

"If she's still alive."

"Even if she isn't."

"Naw. Ain't into that kinky necro shit. C'mon, I'm tired. Let's hit the sack."

I pulled into the motel on Ocean Ave. and we got two separate rooms. I would've gone for a single with double beds but Doc snored like a hibernating grizzly and I needed some serious shuteye. Besides, I wasn't sleepy yet. The noose tightening around my neck kept my eyes bulging open.

I drove up Santa Monica Boulevard to Dolores's coffee shop, right near my favorite theater in L.A., the Nuart, so I could quietly contemplate my next move. I ordered the eggplant Florentine with coffee and sat there trying to wonder what it would feel like to be dead. Sometimes I thought it would be better if I no longer existed, because if I did live on in some conscious form, chances are I couldn't go to Dolores's anymore, and then why would consciousness be worthwhile? No sex, either. Being a gaseous spirit would get old much sooner than eternity itself. And then the other theory, reincarnation, was equally unappealing. As hard as I was on myself, and as conscious as I was of my many flaws and shortcomings, I didn't want to wake up and be somebody else one day. The idea of reincarnation grates on me—imagine having to go through school all over again! Puberty! First day on the job jitters! And what if I came back as a dwarf or hunchback or a Republican? Or what if I was a native in the jungle, far from the civilization of movies and coffee shops? Or as a woman? If so, I'd want to be a lesbian, so I wouldn't miss out on any pussy. No, it was better to just lose consciousness, to disappear, to merge with the infinite. Otherwise I'd miss Dolores's coffee shop too much. And hooters and B movies. All the things that made existence on this otherwise banal and brutal plane worthwhile. Death was inevitable, but I wanted to stave it off as long as possible, and my pending execution didn't exactly ease my mind on matters of mortality.

I ordered more coffee and sat there for two hours, brooding on the beyond. If Velma was dead, maybe I'd meet her on a cloud somewhere, and our spirits could make celestial whoopee. Maybe the spirit form was even more sensually sensitive and seductive than the physical!

Naw. Sex is mainly for propagation. Cheesecake magazines are merely advertisements for reproduction of our useless species. Tantalizing, artful—but ultimately confined to the continuation of life on this earth. Once I left it behind, no more cheesecake. I ordered cheesecake from the waitress just so I could savor the taste as I thought of Velma Vale in my bed, possibly my greatest single night of livin' and lovin' ever in this rotten, temporal world.

I left Dolores's around midnight, having reached no conclusions other than life was meaningless but great tits on a beautiful broad were wonderful compensation for this sad fact. I figured Feds One and Two were on my tail but I didn't let it bother me. I planned to go see Tony Ray the next morning whether they liked it or not. Especially now, after that revelation about his engagement to our mutual friend. Obviously he was the boyfriend Velma claimed to be running away from. I wondered if he ever really abused her in any way. Then I would kill him. No, I had to wait to see whether she set this whole thing up, with his help, or she did it solo and he was just a patsy like me, or if he set it up and I was a victim just like her. It was too coincidental that he would just walk into The Tiki Room and give me this script. He's been tailing me, for who knows how long. That was one thing I planned to ask him the following morning.

I slept like a rock, exhausted from thinking, and woke up around nine or so the next day. I went to Doc's room and woke him up. He grumbled he'd be out after a shower, so I walked across the street and sat on a bench looking at the Pacific and the girls. It was fairly warm, in the 70s, and very clear and pleasant, with a cool breeze wafting onshore. I liked Santa Monica. It was the most inhabitable section of Southern California, as far as I was concerned. But I doubted I could live here. Too many people like Tony Ray around. And Velma Vale, too, but none of them would sleep with me, I bet, unless I had a pending movie deal, so it wasn't worth it.

Wait a minute, I thought. I *do* have a pending movie deal. What if Tony was on the level after all? I could be a star! I'd never even dreamed of being an actor. A movie star, sure, as a kid, but never an *actor*. Then I figured, no, Tony was too enthusiastic for nothing. My "look" wasn't so hot. Not to me. But then I was being subjective. I went back to my room and studied myself in the mirror, making tough guy poses. Finally I convinced myself that Tony Ray was right. I had "it," man. I was going to be famous and impregnate Michelle Pfeiffer.

"Hey, Doc, I'm gonna be a *star*!" I said to him when I met him outside his door.

"You mean a constellation?" he said, rubbing his bleary eyes.

"No, man, like a matinee idol."

"How the fuck you figure *that*? See, O.J. was famous *before* he was arrested, otherwise nobody would give a shit. You're a nobody. Too late to start now."

"Aw, forget you, Doc. I'm gonna be in Tony Ray's movie."

"From what we read, you already are."

"No, I mean for real."

"So do I." Doc pointed to the ground and the sky and the

motel. "This is *real*, Vic. The movies are fake. Try to keep that straight."

"Doc, I didn't kill Velma. I'll be proven innocent, and then I'll be free. The publicity might even help promote the film."

"What film?"

"'Neon Knights.' Doc, what else? We left the script in the car, I think. C'mon, let's go to breakfast at Rae's and read it again. You can run lines with me."

"I can what? Vic, did you sleep at all last night? You sound delirious."

"Doc, my head's never been clearer in my life. This is destiny, Doc. Not coincidence. *Destiny*. You're witnessing Hollywood history in the making."

"You'll be history, all right." Doc just sighed and shook his head. We walked over to where the Corvair was parked on the street and saw Feds One and Two leaning against it, sipping coffee from paper cups and casually reading the L.A. *Times*. When they noticed us they slowly moved away from the car and loitered on the sidewalk, not looking at us directly, but obviously acknowledging us. Doc and I ignored them as we got into the Corvair. I raced the engine and then peeled off with the pedal to the floor, zipping around the corner and out of sight, turning a few corners before heading up Pico to Rae's coffee shop.

I thought of something I hadn't thought of before in my muddled mental state. Of course, I hadn't looked yet, but I hadn't noticed any mention of Velma's demise in the *Times*. I mentioned this to Doc and bought that day's copy out front of Rae's, though it rightfully should have been in the previous morning's edition. Maybe not—too late for the press run, perhaps. So inside at the counter I looked through the latest edition of the *Times* for a mention of Velma and came up with zilch, which further aroused our suspicions that the whole thing was a cruel hoax at my expense. However, I did run across some other pertinent Velma-related news in the Calendar, or entertainment section. The Pussycat Theater was advertising a triple X triple bill of "Velma Vale's long lost lust loops," just recently rediscovered and now showing in mint condition. Another coincidence?

"Gotta be there," Doc said. "Is there a matinee?"

There was. The triple feature started at one that same afternoon and continued non-stop around the clock until further notice, a porn-a-thon featuring Velma Vale. The ad *didn't* specify the "late," i.e. *deceased* Velma Vale, either. Just the fact that these movies had never been shown before except on bootleg videos. Now they were being released in pristine form on the big screen just for her slobbering legions of raincoat wearing fans. And Doc and I would be first in line.

"We can go visit Tony after the movies," I suggested over our eggs and coffee. "Maybe he'll even be in 'em."

"Yeah, that's right. We can tell him what big fans we are. Converts."

"Perverts, you mean."

"Or pervert convicts if we don't get the skinny on what's goin' on before that court date. Well, *you'll* be a convict. I'll be a resident of San Francisco."

"Some would say that's the same thing. C'mon, let's boogie." We polished off our breakfasts and then headed into Hollywood to get in line.

Guess what? There *was* no line. In fact, we were almost the only ones there, except for three other middle-aged losers with scraggly hair and bleary eyes and pallid complexions. Each of the trio kept their hands thrust deep into their grimy, questionably stained overcoats. One guy wasn't wearing any pants, just hole-ridden socks and beat up shoes. Collectively they emitted the stench of human waste. I felt nauseous just inhaling in the vicinity of these poor slobs. And yet, there we were as well, right along side them. No one would believe we were just there working on a case, so I didn't bother to broadcast it. Instead, I started saying stuff out loud to Doc, like, "I HOPE OUR REPORT ON THE CORRUPTION OF OUR CITIZENRY VIA THE VILE EXPLOITATION OF INNOCENT WAYWARD WOMEN MAKES THE NEXT EDITION OF THE NEW REPUBLIC."

To which Doc replied loudly, "I HOPE THESE WOMEN HAVE HUGE HOOTERS WITH BIG ROUND NIPPLES AND THEY SUCK BIG THROBBING COCKS AND THEN SPIT THE DUDE'S JISM BACK IN HIS FACE AND LICK IT OFF."

"Thanks, Doc," I said, blushing and turning toward the wall and trying to hide my face from the general public. Our three fellow Velma Vale muff buffs didn't even seemed fazed.

"One thing that's lower than a pervert is a hypocrite," Doc said. "So I'm embarrassed to even be standing next to you." Then he moved away from me, toward the box office.

"I wouldn't be here if Velma Vale wasn't in these things," I said, scooting over closer to him, still hiding my face.

"Yeah. You wanna see her naked and humping. What's the

saving grace here?"

"Because. I'm on a case."

Doc laughed. "Yeah, right, undercover as a horn dog. *Shee-it.* Vic, you know if I had these same flicks on video you'd buy copies and jerk off till you were a giant prune."

"Yeah, in the privacy of my own room."

"So your complaint is that you can't jerk off in public, Pee Wee?"

"You got it. I'm a moral guy, Doc. And no, I wouldn't buy them from you. Just rent them out of curiosity. I'd rather jerk off to her monster movies where there's more left to the imagination. Porn doesn't turn me on, Doc. It's too *clinical.* I'd rather look at lingerie ads or a Vargas calendar any day. Or Bettie Page."

"So your problem is an *aesthetic* one."

"You could say that."

"Well, try to enjoy yourself anyway. We ain't here on a case, though, Vic. At least *I* ain't. What can we find out watchin' skin flicks?"

"You never know, Doc. You just never know."

The bored, tired ticket taker, who resembled the Crypt Keeper of *Tales from the Crypt,* finally opened the box office a few minutes after one and we all shuffled in like zombies raiding a shopping mall. By then a half dozen other creeps had joined our ranks, the privileged few to view these notorious underground classics in their rightful domain. I must admit, I was excited.

Six hours later Doc and I walked out of the theater bent on suicide. "Well, I'm depressed," I sighed, wanting to go directly to the nearest cliff and dive off, or the nearest dive and get loaded, so we did, ending up at The Ivy, which had Frank on the jukebox. I needed Frank's life-affirming Voice more than ever.

"Man, I haven't felt this depressed since Sammy Davis Junior died," Doc said sadly into his shot glass, ordering another.

I stuck to beer but was just as morose. "I haven't been this depressed since Jimmy Cagney died."

"I haven't been this depressed since JFK got shot," Doc then added, amending his former statement.

Had to one-up him. "I haven't been this depressed since 'Miami Vice' was cancelled." Doc gave me a look.

"Mine's longer," he countered.

"You mean your dick?"

"That too, along with the length of time since I've been this depressed."

I slapped him on the shoulder. "You're a big man, Doc."

"So was Tony Ray. I told you he was strappin' it to his ankle, didn't I?"

I let out a big sigh. "Those movies were what, five, six years old, you figure?"

"At least."

"Velma looked so young and innocent."

"Young, anyway," Doc said, and I winced.

"Tony was just a kid, too. Skinnier, longer hair."

"Same dick, I bet."

"Velma was beautiful, man. Even wet and grungy with sex. Lousy hairdo, though. Too long and straight, not styled like it is now. Or was or whatever."

"Yeah, I just noticed her pubic hair myself. Remember that one scene in the second movie when those three guys gang-banged her in the barn and then she climbed under that mule and *wow*."

"Shut up, Doc."

"Man, I mean that girl is *insatiable*! You think she was faking all those orgasms? If so, she should get some kinda actin' award for porn flicks. She's the damn Meryl Streep of screaming orgasms! She must have gotten off, what, three hundred times in each movie! Screamin', yellin', takin' it up the ass, in the snatch, in her mouth, her *ears*, cum all muckin' up her hair an' *brain* an' shit!"

I grabbed Doc by the lapels with true menace. "Doc, I *mean* it. That's *enough*."

Doc gently put my arms down for me and nodded sympathetically. "Okay, Vic, okay. I'd be worried if I was you, too. Better get checked out at the nearest clinic first thing in the morning."

"I used rubbers, Doc." At least at first.

"Only a quadruple strength full body condom would've been safe with *that* broad."

That did it. I hit him. Not too hard, just a quick jab to the side of the head, but enough to knock him off his stool. I immediately got up and apologized profusely, but once he was on his feet with the help of the bartender and another patron, he slugged me right back, decking me in the chin, sending me back into the jukebox. Instinctively I lunged back at him Elvis-style but was held back by the bartender and next thing we knew we were tossed out on our keesters and were sitting drunk on the curb, a few yards apart, indignant, refusing to look at each other.

We remained like that for about twenty minutes. Then Doc stood up, wiped off the dust, straightened his clothes out, and I did the same. Then we looked at each other tentatively for a moment. Doc walked toward me and I walked toward him and we met in the middle and embraced. "Sorry, man," he said sincerely.

"Me too," I mumbled.

"I didn't realize she meant anything more to you than a piece of ass," Doc said.

I shrugged. "Who knows? Maybe it's just residual over-sensitive shit from the Dolly thing. And you know me—once I'm intimate with a babe, I get territorial. Can't help it."

"Velma covered one large territory, Vic."

"She *was* the large territory," I corrected him. "The final fuckin' frontier."

"C'mon, let's get somethin' to eat," Doc suggested.

"Norm's?"

"Why not?"

We walked back to the Corvair and there were the Feds, loitering nearby, reading magazines. I was tempted to flip them off but resisted. We tore out of there and to Norm's on La Cienega. We ate dinner and talked about things other than sex and then returned to the motel in Santa Monica. We decided to save Tony Ray for the next day. I told Doc I was anxious to get to bed and sleep, but really, I was horny as hell and needed to beat off as soon and as much as possible. Later that night I came and cried at the same time, springing leaks all over, and sinking fast.

Chapter Six
CASTING COUCH POTATOES

I awoke the following morning reeking of tears and semen. At least they were all mine. I lay in bed for a while trying to distinguish between my inner dream world and my outer one. That ever happen to you? Me, all the time. You know, when you're first coming out of a deep sleep, your waking world seems so odd, so intangible, blurred in your brain. Things and thoughts that normally excite or titillate or amuse you seem remote and strange and insubstantial. What scares me is the idea that the true reality, the eternal residence of the soul is in the inner dream world, the one that envelops us at night, lurking in our subconscious like a stalker in the shadows. Since my nocturnal world is unpleasant, fog-shrouded and eerie and dark in a way that I can't fully explain since it has no real counterpart in our collective waking world, it terrifies me to think that the relatively benign existence of my ephemeral form, pathetic as it may seem to you, is the real reverie that I will one day wake up from forever, only to be banished into the fog world within.

What I usually need to get over this morbid morning contemplation is some strong coffee and music. Normally, back home, I just brew a pot while selecting my wake-up tunes for the day, generally something like bop or swing or stripper sax to get my adrenaline flowing. If it's a rainy day I might play something moody just to keep in touch with the romance of my surroundings, like Vangelis or Tangerine Dream, but if I'm already depressed I'll skip the synthesizers and queue up the saxophones, which always bring me up even if the tune is slow and sad and sultry. Then I'll segue into something harder as I gradually rejoin the waking world, almost always a new wave rocker like "Rock the Casbah" or "Rock Lobster" or "Pump It Up." I think this is because they remind me of a brighter youthful era, when I had daydreams which I believed at the time would eventually come true. Oh well. Anyway, by this point the caffeine is kicking in and my sense of reality does likewise and the murky realm of my subconscious feels distant and non-threatening, at least until I sink back into it like some sap drowning in the quicksand of his own mind.

Unfortunately, most motels don't cater to these idiosyncratic needs, just supplying the simple basics such as soap and towels and a phone. No java or jazz. So I just got out of bed, splashed cold water in my face, took a quick shower, and went next door to wake Doc up at around eight AM, a good three hours be-fore my average wake-up time, except when I was working. And I was working.

As usual, Doc resented my intrusion and grumbled, but I reminded him we had a tight agenda and he told me I had a tight ass and I asked him how did he know and he said because I was so uptight all the time. "Relaxed people have loose assholes," he said, getting washed up in the bathroom as I waited at the dresser.

"That's what my father always told me."

"I guess he was an authority on assholes," I said.

"Like they say, takes one to know one." Doc never really knew his old man, and didn't talk about him much, and I didn't ask. Didn't really care. "What's on the agenda for today, my man?"

"All I can think of is go try Tony Ray again," I called to him. As I sat there, it hit me how bizarre and surreal this situation was, Doc and me on a vigilante hunt in L.A.'s netherworld. I was used to just going out on my own and then returning to the sanctuary of The Drive-Inn for Doc's armchair coaching. Now he was an active participant—and I was the case. Memories of Velma in my bed seemed part of my inner dream world, but so did the memory of getting charged with her murder. Nothing seemed real, awake or asleep. The drawback with being awake was that other people were awake too, and would probably fuck with you if they got the chance. I've never understood why. Any interaction with the human race at all puts you at risk for trouble. That's just human nature. Don't ask me why.

Doc came out of the bathroom with a towel around his shoulders. He had another towel around his waist. He looked to be in good shape for a middle-aged dude who sat around watching movies all the time. I told him so.

He replied, "You're forgetting something—unlike you and the poor slobs who waste away at the bar of The Drive-Inn. I ain't sittin' around whining all the time. I'm runnin' my ass off workin'."

"Good point. I guess I'm too sedentary, except when I'm working on a case that requires a lot of walking, which will never happen in L.A. San Francisco is always good for a workout. All those hills. Speaking of hills, Velma said she liked the way my body felt on top of hers, though, so maybe I shouldn't worry."

"That's 'cause your tits are almost as big as hers, and together they made a comfy cushion. C'mon, let's go see that well endowed boyfriend of hers. Didn't notice *his* titties jigglin' yesterday at the movies."

As we walked out the door I found myself feeling my own pecs. They felt solid to me, at least when I flexed them, but I didn't want to ask Doc to feel them, so I let it go. He was trying to fuck with me, like everybody else. At least he did because he was my friend. Or so he always says.

It was a nice day. There was the threat of rain on the horizon but in L.A. that's always good news. The incoming breezes kept the air fresh and breathable and the sky clean and bright. Santa Monica is almost always a better place to be than L.A. proper, because of its ocean side setting. Doc and I strolled up to the Third Street Promenade for espresso and pastries at a cafe, and once the sugar rush hit my system I felt like living again. *Too* much like living. The threat of being executed hung over my head like a portable storm cloud, no matter how nice the weather was. By the time we hit Malibu I was getting pissed off that I was being put through this. Doc and I looked around for our friends with the shades and badges, but didn't notice them, which didn't mean they weren't there, camouflaged somehow. Feds or no Feds, Tony Ray was going to give me some straight answers. I had the script with me just to point out the striking similarities in front of his tan stupid face, and then Doc and I would tell him about seeing those movies the previous day. There was no way he could lie to us about knowing Velma. And since he knew her then, chances are he'd know her now.

"*Dead*? I just can't accept that," Tony Ray was saying to us in his living room fifteen minutes later. "My God, I had no idea. No idea at all." He sat down slowly on his zebra pattern sofa with a ghastly expression on his face, the tan draining from his complexion. He had on a silk tiger pattern robe and leather slippers. A nearby lounge chair was covered with a leopard pattern. A regular Jungle Jim, or a jungle *gym*, Malibu style. His place was immaculate and tastelessly decorated with gaudy but expensive paintings and sculptures, mostly erotic in nature. In fact, I recognized one right away to be the handiwork of Luke Brandon, one of Rose's old lovers and my old pal from Venice. But I'd follow that up later, if there were time, if it mattered. Something told me it did. There was no coincidence in my life, no matter what Doc said. The tapestry was woven tight enough to choke me, and it would if I didn't second guess the pattern quick enough and break the threads weaving around my neck.

"You really mean to say you hadn't heard?" Doc said just like a cop. He was digging this, I could tell.

"N-no, of course not. God, I *loved* that woman. How did it happen? O.D.?"

I looked at Doc, then back at Tony and said, "She was *murdered*, Tony. And I'm the number one suspect."

He looked at me for a few beats as if the doctor had just told him the tests were positive. Then he lunged at me, but Doc interceded and calmed him down. If Tony was acting, he should've been a star, and really was wasting his talents on the underground market. He had me convinced he was on the level, at any rate. Well, almost. I'd been too trusting in the past, swayed by a brilliant performance. Marlon Brando was right on the money when he said *everyone* is an actor. Most of the best ones go unrecognized. Until it's too late.

Doc eased Tony back down and tried to console him without actually touching him much. Doc didn't like touching guys, especially ones who had been where Tony had been. Cootie central, man. And Tony and I had been in the same hole. The thought made my heart flutter. "Take it easy, B'wana." I said. "I'm as innocent as Bambi. I need to find out who killed her as much as you do—*more*, because my life is at stake, pal." I took the script out of my trench-coat pocket and tossed it on his lap. "I read your movie. It'd make a lousy flick and an even worse newspaper article. What's up, Tony? We already know you starred with Velma in some sleazy porn flicks—we saw 'em yesterday—and that you parlayed that intimate contact into a formal engagement that didn't have a chance to blossom into full-scale wedlock. Now, the question is, does her death, such as it is, cancel those marsupials or was that already a done deal?"

Tony looked perplexed. "Marsupials?"

"The illiterate fool means nuptials," Doc said acidly. "At least I assume."

"Yeah, whatever," I said, shrugging off embarrassment. I needed more coffee, is what it was. Also, my thoughts were racing way ahead of my speech, as usual. "You know what the fuck we're getting at, right Tony?"

"What was between Velma and me is my business, no matter what," Tony snapped. "Why do cops think you did it?"

"Because I came down to visit her, knocked on her door, and next thing you know the cops were all over my ass. I never even saw the corpse, if there is one."

"What do you mean, *if*?"

Doc laughed. "Read your own script lately, Tony?"

"So?"

I looked at him, moving closer with intimidation. "You picked me out and gave me that fuckin' screenplay, which I'm already starring in, as you god damn well know. So can the histrionics, donkey dick. The connection is obvious. I know you wanna play puppet master, but the strings have been cut. Now spill it before I lose my patience. Time's a wastin'. My breathing privileges are about to be revoked by the D.A."

"How'd you know her?"

"Same as you. I fucked her."

Tony jumped back up but Doc pushed him back down and kept him in check. "Why would she fuck a little squirt like you?" Tony snarled.

"Ever hear what Ava Gardner said about Frank Sinatra?"

"Huh?"

"Somebody asked her why she went out with a scrawny guy like Frank and she said, 'Maybe he only weighs a hundred pounds, but ninety pounds of it is cock.'"

Tony was about to get up again but looked at Doc and settled down. It wasn't that Doc was so tough. Tony Ray was just a pussy. He still looked like he was in great shape. I guess all that loss of bodily essence had caught up with him, though. Lancelot he wasn't.

"You're lying," he said. "I doubt your name is even what you said it was, whatever it was."

All right! The moment I'd been waiting for—the chance to whip out my P.I. license. Doc rolled his eyes as I did so. Tony looked at it and then he rolled his eyes, too. Not the effect I was hoping for, so I pocketed the license and went on. "Why'd you give me that script, Tony?"

"Why'd you fuck my fiancée?"

"She had no ring when I saw her."

"When was this?"

I had to think about that. "Not long. Three days ago. Up in San Francisco. She showed up next to me in a bar, totally out of the blue, asked me out, and then asked me in. I woke up in love, drove down to see her, and was promptly arrested."

"She didn't say anything about me to you?"

"Nope. Oh, wait—she *did* happen to mention someone she was running away from, someone who was hurting her in some way, but she didn't want to talk about it."

Tony ran his fingers through his scalp and massaged his hairy chest despondently. "Oh, no—and you say you never saw her body?"

"You mean *dead*?"

"What else? Oh."

I shook my head in the negative.

"A *lot* of people saw her body," Doc said. "When it was *alive*. But we haven't even seen pictures of her yet as a carcass."

"Not even in the paper?" Tony asked.

"Not today or yesterday," I said. "We checked. Coulda been an item the morning after, but I was in the clink and missed that edition. You sayin' you heard nothin' at all from any source, not even personal?"

"No, I swear. Nothing."

"When's the last time you spoke to Velma?" Doc asked Tony.

"Urn, let's see, must have been about a week or so ago. Before she left town."

"You guys have a fight?" I asked him.

"Yeah, but nothing major."

"What about?"

He paused, then said flatly, "None of your damn business." He got up and walked into the kitchen and came back out with some orange juice. "Want somethin' to drink?" We declined. Didn't want to drink out of his glasses, either. It was then I noticed that, although obviously distraught, Tony had shed no tears yet. Was that because of masculine ego or pride or the drainage of all bodily fluids through excessive orgasm? No, that couldn't have been it—I know because I've shed almost as many tears as semen in my time, both usually in private, all alone. Maybe Tony would weep uncontrollably once we were gone. Maybe not. But most human beings shed tears at the loss of a near dear one. It's only natural, no matter how hard-boiled you are. Tony was just shaken up, but not in mourning. My hunch was he knew more than he was letting on, that he wasn't hearing this for the first time from us, but for the time being, I had to go along with his claims of ignorance until something more substantial popped up. Like a body, a curvaceous one, warm or cold.

"Nothing you've said explains this script," I said. "Why'd you give it to me, and why the parallels?"

"I swear I don't know," Tony said, sitting down on the lounge chair, facing the expansive window on the sea, which was growing restless like me. "I just saw you in the Tiki Room and you had the look I envisioned for the lead, so I gave it to you. I'm in no position to court Pacino. I thought I'd take a shot with a nobody. I had no idea you *met* Velma. She didn't tell me she was flying to San Francisco to pick up strangers in bars. Usually she does it here in town. She didn't tell me where she was going. I assumed home to Missoula, Montana. This is just as weird to me as it is to you."

"I doubt that," Doc said. "There's even a brother in the movie. But it turns out he's against the hero, set him up, helped the starlet fake her own murder, and that ain't the case here."

Tony shrugged. "Don't ask me."

"Then who the fuck *should* we ask?" I exploded at last.

"Maybe the person who wrote it," Tony said simply.

I was dumbstruck, but smartened up in a hurry. "You mean *you* didn't write this, Tony?"

"You see my name on it? As the author, I mean."

I checked the script on the sofa. Tony's name and address were printed neatly on the bottom right cover, but there was no by-line at all.

"Who's the genius, then?" Doc said.

Tony didn't answer right away. He just sat looking at the sea and the incoming storm clouds. "Velma," he whispered finally.

Doc whistled. "The plot thickens," he said.

"Yea, well, Tony's lip is gonna thicken if he's jerking us around," I said.

"You really think you could take me on?" Tony asked, as if he were genuinely curious.

"I'm in the mood where I could flatten Mike Tyson," I said. "Of course, I doubt I'll ever have to prove that." I paced the living room, scanning the pastels and paintings, and then my eyes focused on the sculpture by Luke Brandon, the one I recognized from his Venice pad when I paid him a visit a year and half or so before, when Tommy Dodge hired me to find Rose, who was really Valerie, my long lost love. Rose was fucking around a lot and had an illegitimate baby and didn't know who the father was. Luke thought he was the one because that's what she told him so she could leave the baby, Sammy, with him while she tomcatted around the planet. I kidnapped Rose's baby from Luke and had to shoot him in the leg to do so, along with a few of his sculptures, and I'm sure he still held a grudge because of that. I still resented him just for existing, for screwing Valerie when she became Rose again. I was never really in love with Velma, so my jealousy of Tony Ray was purely a matter of pride. Rose had been my true love, and Luke had banged the hell out of her. I still hated him, because she probably enjoyed it. "You get that piece from a dude in Venice, fifty-something, kind of looks like Kirk Douglas? Name Luke Brandon?"

Tony had trouble following my train of thought. But he caught up. "Yeah—why?"

I shrugged, and Doc made the name. "You mean the asswipe who beat the hell out of you and you shot him to steal that bitch's baby?"

"The same. Coincidence, Doc?"

Doc got the heebie-jeebies. "That's *your* thing, man. Leave me *out* of it. I just want to play Shaft for a little while and then boogie on home."

"You a personal friend of Luke's?" I asked Tony.

"We are acquainted, yes."

"Did he know Velma?"

"Through me. We went out together a few times."

"He ever fuck her?"

"What?"

"You heard me, lover boy. Did Luke ever *fuck* your fiancée?"

"What kinda question is that?"

"What Vic is really asking," Doc said, "is did Luke ever poke *another* of his girlfriends."

I looked at Doc, then nodded. "Yeah. Jesus Christ. Rose, Velma—you think he ever nailed Dolly, Doc?"

"Chances are, if he ever visited New York. *He's* a ho, *she's* a ho!"

"Cool it, Doc."

"Sorry, man. Anyway, I don't see how this Luke shit is important. What we gotta find out, fellas, is whether Velma is even actually dead. When did she write that script, Tony?"

"Um, she's been working on it for years. I helped her a little, but it was her thing, really."

"So why'd you tell me it was yours?" I asked him.

"She thought a woman would have trouble getting financing in this town, and she's right. It was her bid to go legit, to do something she could be proud of. I said I'd direct it, and she said okay, because I understood and would stay true to her vision. The whole project was going to be done by a small circle of friends, once we got the money. In fact..."

"What?" I pressed.

"Luke Brandon."

"Yeah?"

"Luke was going to help *produce* it."

I shook my head. "Sonofabitch." I plopped down on the zebra sofa and rubbed my face. "What do you make of this, Doc?"

"Beats me, man. Fate is fuckin' with you again. Who knows? But I'm gettin' the creeps, myself. If Tony here is straight up, then it looks like Velma did this, maybe with some help from your old pal, who wanted some serious payback. She could disappear and he could get even at the same time."

"But why the script?" I said.

"To fuck with you. Who knows?"

I looked at Tony, who was still staring out at the sea. The storm was really kicking up now, the wild wind rocking the little house, huge raindrops pelting the windows. "You got any ideas, bright boy? She ever say anything about where the idea for this opus came from?"

He shook his head. "It was just a movie, man. That's all I know. She's really gone, isn't she?"

"One way or the other. But tell her if you see her the script has a new director now. Me. C'mon, Doc. Let's make like the wind and blow."

"Where to?"

"Venice."

"If that rain stays that heavy we're gonna need gondolas, all right."

"We'll be seeing you, Tony."

He didn't say anything, just stared out the window at the rain. We just left.

It was pouring like hell. Pensively I revved up the Corvair and took off. "Hey, Doc, I was wondering something," I said as we drove toward Venice. "You know the Hideous Sun Demon, that Fifties monster, right? Dude turned into a lizard man when the sun was out, right? So what about a day like today? It's daylight, but the sun's rays are obscured by the clouds, right?"

"Shit, Vic! Who *gives* a damn? Ain't you got other things to worry about?"

"You gonna answer me or what?"

"I just did." We drove in silence for a while, and I could tell he was thinking about it. Then he said finally, as I drove up PCH to Ocean Avenue, towards Venice, "No, man, it's like night-time out now. But that ain't the point. He wasn't the Hideous *Daytime* Demon. The operative word is 'sun.' Hideous *Sun* Demon. So no, in the rain, he'd be okay. The lizard shit didn't run on no clock, like the alarm went off and boom, it's time to go to work attacking people and shit. It was the effects of the sunlight, directly on his radiated skin, see? What a dumb-ass question."

I kept thinking. "So he could be out in the rain, and the rain would protect him from the sun, but then what if there was like a sudden lull, a partial clearing, and a few rays of sunlight got through the clouds, right, he'd turn, right? But then the clouds would come back in suddenly a few seconds later, so would he just develop like a few scales, or make the full-on transformation, and then just shed the lizard skin as soon as the clouds rolled back in?"

Doc sighed. "Shit. As long as Luke Brandon ain't no lizard man, I don't really give a shit, Vic. Shut up and drive, man. Let's concentrate on the issues at hand, in real life, dig?"

Then he was quiet for a while. We were in Venice, looking for a place to park near the Pier, Luke's neighborhood, when Doc said, "I think when the Sun Demon changes, he goes the full nine yards, man, and then he stays that way for a while, he don't just change back soon as the damn clouds roll back in, so if he's got a date with some chick and it's raining and then the sun comes out for a few seconds and they're outdoors having a picnic, she's *fucked*."

"A picnic? In the *rain*, Doc?"

"Well, there ya go. Why the fuck would Sun Demon be hangin' out in the goddamn rain anyway? He'd be inside with the chick, humpin' her, and who knows, maybe the bitch likes scales on her dicks. Let's just move on."

We parked near the one story house where Luke lived, unless he'd moved since last time I saw him. The cops had taken my gun so I didn't have that for protection this time. All I had was Doc, and my anger.

"You think Tony Ray is on the level?" I asked Doc as we approached the house.

"Truthfully? No. This shit's just too *weird*."

"Can't get much weirder, *that's* for sure." I knocked on the door, bracing myself. I clenched my fists, ready to cold-cock him if I felt that would be the safest thing to do, to gain the initial advantage. No answer. I knocked again. I wondered if that Filipino woman was still living with him now that the baby was gone. Probably not. She just hung around for the kid, since she was barren. Why would any woman live with an asshole like Luke Brandon, the muscle-bound middle-aged mad sculptor? He'd nailed Rose, though, and probably nailed Velma and Dolly, too. He had something I couldn't see, like a huge *schlong*. I knocked again and someone finally answered. It wasn't the Filipino woman or Luke or Rose or Velma or even Dolly, but Doc and I were stunned just the same.

It was Judy Fagin of The She Beams.

Chapter Seven
SWING SESSION

It took a few seconds for the shock of Judy's appearance to register, and I'm sure she was equally astonished to see *us* show up at this particular doorstep. Well, not equally, but *close*. Her big blue eyes were even wider and more luminescent than usual. "What are *you* guys doing here?" she said finally after we had all completed quick reality checks.

"Looking for Luke Brandon," I said. "Obviously a friend of yours. What are *you* doing here?"

"Just crashing with The She Beams. The guy who sublet this place to us is out of town."

"Say *what*?"

"Yeah. We put an ad in the paper for a small place to rent for five girls for a couple of weeks for the gig—we have a gig at The Viper Room this weekend—and then we want to talk to some producers for our next album."

"I thought you had a deal with some people up north?" Doc said.

"Well, a bigger label has showed interest, and we haven't signed with anybody yet, so, we'll see. Ever since my mother sold her San Francisco businesses I've been out of work and low on dough—but how did you know we were here? Monica tell you?"

"No," I said. "We're looking for the guy who owns this place. You met him?"

"Yeah, real quick, yesterday. He was on his way out the door."

"Alone?"

"No, there was a girl with him."

"What'd she look like?" I asked.

"Big tits, big hair, the usual. Sexy, I guess."

Doc and I looked at each other, then Doc said to Judy, "Honey, was it the girl who picked up Vic the other night in The Drive-Inn? You remember? He left with some lady and didn't come back, well, not to The Drive-Inn, anyway."

"Yeah! That was her. I think. No, wait, I'm not sure. All those bimbos look alike to me."

I was beyond shock now. I was approaching something that

hadn't been discovered yet by modern science, so I don't know what to call it. But euphoria was definitely in the mix.

"Judy, this was yesterday?" I asked.

"Um, no, wait—day before maybe. Yeah."

"Good enough. And this Luke guy answered your ad in the paper for a house to sublet?"

"Yea, first call. It sounded so good, on the beach and all, we just jumped at it."

"He called you in San Francisco?"

"Yeah, saw our ad in the Times down here, and called right away. What's up, you guys? This is getting, like, strange."

"No shit," Doc said. "Can we come in?"

"Be my guest," Judy said, and we went in. It was surreal to be in that place again, the scene of my twin crimes of shooting and kidnapping, and now here were The She Beams, congregated in the front room like a sorority meeting. There was Nikki, the Jamaican babe, who played the drums; Suzy, the Japanese babe, who played sax; and Esmeralda, the Spanish babe, who played bass. Judy was on lead guitar and vocals, along with Monica, who was still up at The Drive-Inn. Or so Doc and I believed until we saw her walking out of the back room wearing an SF State T-shirt and nothing else.

Doc went ballistic, and I was in orbit right behind him. Monica actually screamed when she saw us. "Hey, what about my *place*?" Doc yelled.

"What about my *cat*?" I shouted simultaneously.

"*Screw* you guys, I'm not responsible for everything in your lives!" Monica yelled back. "What the hell are you doing here, anyway?"

"They're looking for the guy who sublet this place to us," Judy explained.

"Who's minding my goddamn store?" Doc wanted to know.

"And my *cat*!" I added.

Monica sighed. Despite my fury and fear, I couldn't help noticing her shapely gams and the way that T-shirt fit snugly around her torso, barely covering her nookie jar. In fact, all of The She Beams including Judy were casually attired. It was like crashing a pajama party.

But still—"*Who's watching my cat*?"

Monica wearily rolled her pretty eyes. "Doc, your store is closed for the weekend. Sorry. But I had no choice, and it's not my problem. You want it reopened, go reopen it. And Vic, sorry, but your cat is *gone*."

I gulped. "Say *what*?"

"It ran away. I went in to feed it and it just took off. I'm sorry, Vic. But he'll be all right."

"No he won't! He's practically an invalid!"

"Vic, that cat was stray when they gave it to you, remember? It's used to surviving on its own. She probably just misses you and is trying to find you. When you go home, she'll be waiting at your office door. *Trust* me."

I just let my shoulders droop as I tried to block out mental images of Puss in sundry scenarios of distress and danger. "She's a *he*," I muttered to no effect.

"Monica," Doc said lowly, "I'm going to *strangle* you." He ran toward her but she ducked into the back room and locked the door. Doc pounded on it and I just sat down sadly in the middle of the floor. The She Beams surrounded me and tried to console me. Their fleshy feminine company was an amazing tonic, especially at such affectionate proximity. Doc, however, had to be calmed down with a shot of whisky supplied by Judy. Monica yelled from the other side of the locked door she wouldn't come out till Doc promised he'd behave himself. Doc yelled "*Good*!" and added he hoped she suffocated. Jesus, you'd think they were married.

"Judy," I said, "this Luke Brandon has framed me for the murder of that woman I met in The Drive-Inn."

Her blue eyes stared into mine and I felt dizzy with desire. She was more concerned with what I'd just said to her. "Vic, but I saw him with her. I think. I didn't really get a good look at the woman you left with. I was too jealous."

"What? Jealous? *Really*?" I felt myself blush.

"Well, y'know. A *little*." She blushed now, too. It was so cute I nearly puked.

"Hey, why didn't you guys crash in Santa Barbara at your fiancé's house?" I asked her. Judy looked tentatively at the other She Beams, then at me.

"That's off, Vic. I don't want to talk about it now."

I looked at her finger. The rock was gone. "But I thought you guys set the date while you were up in Seattle?"

"We did, but that same night at The Drive-Inn when you met that woman, I realized something."

"Oh yeah? What?"

"I don't love him," she sighed, then she fought back tears.

Women. "That's why I wanted to get out of town. He's going to Acapulco on business and wanted me to go with him but then we fought and I told him I had this gig lined up and—oh forget it. What I want to hear about is this thing about this guy and that girl. I don't understand what you're saying, Vic. Are you in trouble? If so, we want to help."

The other She Beams concurred and voiced similar sentiments. Doc just sat scowling in the corner, knocking back shots of whiskey and belching. Monica was still locked up defiantly in the back room. I looked around at the sculptures and fought a sudden impulse to break every one of them. Unsuccessfully.

The girls tried holding me back, but not before I had busted four works into little pieces of useless plaster. "*Vic, he'll kill us!*" they shrieked, nearly in unison. "*Stop it!*"

Doc just kept drinking obliviously.

"He didn't leave town," I said, panting, sitting back down on the floor amid the debris.

"That bastard is fucking with me again, with Velma Vale's help. Why, I wish I knew. I just can't take it anymore. Doc, let's get outta here for a while. I need a drink, too."

"What are we supposed to do about this mess?" Judy asked.

"Clean it up. No, don't. Leave it. And leave this house, too."

"And go where?"

"Anywhere. This guy is bad news."

A quick vote was taken and the tallies came out unanimously against me. "Screw you, Vic," Judy said, summing it up. "I don't know anything about this. Just leave, damn it. You too, Doc. Go back to your store."

"I plan to," Doc said.

"Doc, you can't just leave me here!" I whined. "Not alone."

"You got the girls. I got a business to run, Vic. Drop me off at the airport."

"But what about Sergeant Bruno and the Feds?"

"What about 'em? Not my problem. The Sarge is probably on the take and the Feds probably ain't even Feds. You can handle it, Vic. Or you could just leave town. They won't do anything about it, especially if there really isn't a case against you. Fuck 'em all."

"I need to know what's what, Doc. It's my nature."

"Well, my nature is to keep my store open and not lose any fuckin' money because of *STUPID ASS BIMBOS WHO GOT NO GOD DAMN SENSE!*" He pounded on the back room door as he said, no, *shouted* those last few words.

"A few drinks for the road, Doc. Please. And Judy, fine, stay here. I'll stay here with you."

"Like hell."

"I'll tell Luke to his face I smashed his place up. Deal?"

Judy shrugged. "Okay, fine. He said he'd be gone till next week anyway."

"No he won't. Not if he's hiring those so-called Feds to tail me. They'll tell him I showed up here. That's why they didn't want us talking to Tony, Doc, cause Tony would blow the whistle on the Luke connection."

"Why would Luke do all this to you, Vic?" Judy asked.

"It's a long story, dollface. Tell you later. Right now I need a drink. C'mon, Doc." I kissed Judy on the cheek and Doc banged on the back room door a few more times and then we left.

The rain hadn't slackened, it had only grown more dense and Biblical. It was a regular deluge. We just walked around a bit before settling on the first bar we came to, called The Cock of the Block. The logo was a well-endowed rooster in silhouette. That should've clued in anyone, much less a professional dick, to what sort of crowd this joint catered to, but at the time it got by me.

We sat at the bar and I ordered beer and Doc ordered some more shots. He was antsy and I was shell-shocked, so we didn't talk much. It took a while for us to realize that this was really a gay bar. The realization hit me when I surveyed the clientele and saw nothing but flamers in hot pants groping each other and dancing to the awful disco music blaring from the juke. Whatever. A beer's a beer. The mustachioed bartender seemed to really go for Doc, though. He kept giving Doc free rim, I mean rum shots with a smile. I wasn't sure Doc even realized it. He always said he wasn't homophobic, but I think he was. I know *I* am, going strictly by the popular definition. Not that I care what people do in the privacy of their bedrooms, but if it's two guys corn-holing each other, I just don't want to hear about it. Male bodies disgust me, though I'm glad I have one because many women actually find them attractive, even mine. See, gay guys are as horny as straight guys and can fuck whenever they want and not worry about emotional hang-ups or pregnancy like straight guys do, so that accounted for their promiscuity, I surmised. The freedom. Of course, here in the age of AIDS that freedom had a terrible price more often than not. And if the number of women who came on to me equaled or was even half the number of guys who did I'd be

James Fuckin' Bond. I just drank my beer and tuned out my surroundings, but then I do that most everywhere.

Doc and I sat there silently for about twenty minutes before I noticed the knuckles of the man sitting on the other side of me at the bar. On one hand he had tattooed, a letter on each knuckle, the word "karma." On the other hand was the word "destiny," though in that case he had put two letters on each knuckle. Karma. Destiny. A one-two punch, all right. The guy was ruggedly handsome with a chiseled face, a mass of dark curly hair and a thick mustache, the latter two both flecked with gray. He was dressed like a '70s biker in worn jeans, a beat up leather jacket, ragged boots, and a leather belt with a huge buckle over his left hip. He looked like if you came on to him he'd beat the shit out of you. Luckily for me he wasn't my type.

Then all of a sudden I felt a sharp slap on my shoulder. I knew it wasn't Doc. Startled, I swerved to see the grizzled face of my old pal Luke Brandon. I followed my first impulse and took a swing at him, but he leaned back and I just barely clipped his chin. Then he countered with a swing of his own which connected. The bartender was yelling in his shrill voice for us to settle down and stop acting "so butch," but I was just getting started. Luke was just finishing, though. He hit me once more and I sank to my knees next to the bar, nursing my sore jaw. I missed my gun almost as much as I missed my cat at that moment.

"Don't tell me," Doc said to no one in particular. "Luke Brandon."

I looked up and Luke was grinning. He extended his hand for a shake and said jovially, "That's me, brother. And you are—?"

"Call me Doc," Doc said, shaking the same hand that slugged me.

The guy with the tattooed knuckles was watching impassively, while the rest of the crowd was gathered around us whispering and *oo-ing* and *ah-ing* like a bunch of schoolgirls. I was in no position to assert my hetero macho ego and tell them to mind their own pansy business, so I ignored them.

"Why don't you just buy him a fuckin' drink?" I said to Doc in a muffled voice. Doc helped me back up to my stool and I sat down and the crowd began to thin out and return to their cruising.

Luke just kept grinning. "Why is your friend so hostile and impulsive?" Luke asked Doc.

"I simply give him a friendly tap and he picks a fight, just like that, fully realizing I'm bigger than he is. What's his story?"

"I thought you knew him," Doc said simply.

"Yes, I do. Vic Valentine, Private Eye." Then he roared with laughter. "Same old pathetic loser, huh Vic? Can't pull a gun in public, either, so you had to resort to fisticuffs. Dumb fuck. Anyhow, I just stopped by my place, Vic, and the girls said you'd been there and decided to go on a rampage. You never learn, do you, Vic? Never gonna grow up."

"You been tailing me, shithead?"

"No, of course not. I have better things to do, believe it or not. I'm just staying up the road with my girlfriend so the girls will have a place to stay. That's the kind of guy I am. Turns out you're pals with them. Imagine that. It's a shrinking world we live in, Vic. So anyhow, I stopped by to check in on them and they told me you'd been there and tore my place up and then you went to the nearest bar, which is here."

I shook my head in disgust. "Who's your girlfriend? Velma Vale?"

Luke laughed some more. "That *tramp*? She's *everybody's* girlfriend, except mine. Well, on occasion she has been, but I go with Tina Hartman, the actress. Maybe you've heard of her."

I banged my head on the bar and Doc patted me on the shoulder. "You'll have to forgive Vic. He's under a lot of stress lately."

"*Lately*?" Luke said, laughing again. "That poor sucker was *born* a nervous wreck! You really should get laid more often, Vic. Or once, at least, the right way, real good. Hey, this Velma, she your latest flame? It seems I have a go at all your women, huh Vic? Imagine that. Well, you don't have to, it's true. Velma is a great lay, great body, but Rose was the queen, Vic. You agree? Think about it and get back to me so we can compare notes. Anyway, I have a bill for the sculptures you destroyed, unless you want the cops in on this. I still have a scar from our last little run-in, Vic, and if I weren't such a mature, forgiving soul I'd take you out into the alley and beat you into fuckin' *pulp*, but I figure Rose did that for me, in her own fashion. I never wanted that damn kid anyway. You did me a favor, Vic, inadvertently, of course. Got rid of April, too. You remember April. Fuckin' bitch. Nice piece of ass while it lasted, but Tina, she's the real thing. She keeps me calm, so I don't overreact in situations like this. The cops still have a file on you, I imagine, from the last time I reported you. I should've pressed charges but hey, you know me, Mister Nice Guy, Mister Mature, right? But breaking into my place and destroying valuable, no, make that invaluable property won't set well with the fuzz, I'm afraid. But then again, if you pay for them, it's like you bought them, and we're even. Okay, Vic? Just looking out for your best interests, as always, because you're like a fuckin' orphan, so lost and sad. Oh, cash only, no checks or charge." He handed me an itemized tally written in a hurry with a pencil that came to a grand total of twenty five hundred dollars and change.

I looked at the paper, then at him, and tore it into around twenty five hundred pieces, and change. Then I let the confetti snow on his feet. "Your work *sucks*. I did you *another* favor by sparing you and the world the bother of putting it on display. I'll put it on your tab, how's that?"

He was not amused, but the guy with the tattooed knuckles was. He laughed out loud.

"Somethin' amusing you, mister?" Luke said, tapping the guy on the shoulder.

Knuckles turned slowly and stared at Luke. "Just because I drink here doesn't mean I want anyone touching me," he said lowly and slowly.

"I ain't touching you cause I like you, fairy," Luke said. Then he faced me again. "Outside, Vic. We need to talk. Let's go, move it. I'm tired of playing with you, you stupid jerk-off."

"Kiss my ass," I said, turning around in my stool with my back to him.

"*Ooo, baby baby!*" I heard someone yell in the background. "*Kiss it, honey!*"

"What did you call me, friend?" Knuckles said to Luke.

Luke acted like a fly was pestering him. "I called you a fairy. Why else would you be drinkin' here, fairy?"

"You mean fairy as in Tinkerbell, or fairy as in homosexual?" Knuckles said coolly, distracting Luke from pounding on Me. "And I might ask you the same question. *Friend.*"

"I mean fairy as in a boat that better fuckin' set sail or I'm gonna sink it," Luke said gruffly. "And by the way, you ain't my friend. mister."

"Meet you outside," Doc whispered in my ear, getting off his stool.

"I'll go with," I said, rising, but Luke gripped my collarbone and slammed me back down.

Knuckles stood up and said to Luke's nose, "Why don't you pick on someone your own size, Goliath?"

"That ain't you sweetie," Luke laughed. Then the next thing I knew, Luke was apparently jerked backward by some violent force and landed on top of a table of onlookers at ringside. The customers disbanded in a panic, fleeing outside, shrieking. But Luke wasn't pulled from behind—he was socked from the front by Karma and Destiny.

Luke stood up groggily, but was instantly put down again by Knuckles. Luke tried getting up a third time and was assailed by Destiny, with a follow-up from Karma. Knuckles just stood over the heaving body on the floor to make sure it wouldn't move again in the near future and molest someone else. The patrons all got on their knees and started bowing like worshipping devotees praying to a god in a temple. Knuckles took out a cigarette, struck a match against a wooden post, lit up, and walked out, satisfied his work here was finished, leaving behind a stunned assemblage of fans and a barely conscious would-be rival.

I ran after Knuckles and caught up with him outside inhaling smoke next to Doc. "Who *are* you, man?" I asked him. "That's one tough customer you just put to bed."

"It's my job, kid," he said, taking a long drag, staring off at something in the rain. "It's what I do. My name's Zach. I help out little guys like you in trouble. Anyway, you take care now, huh? I won't always be there to help."

Doc slapped him on the shoulder. "Nice work, Zach. What's your last name?"

Zach just looked at Doc for a beat, but didn't say anything. "That's all you need to know, buddy," he said. Then he climbed onto the vintage Harley parked out front of the bar, put on his gloves and helmet, winked at us, and took off, disappearing in the mist.

"Damn," Doc said. "Zach. Zachary Kane."

"Who?" I said.

"Remember that bootleg video I got of a flick called 'Bare Knuckles?'"

"You mean the Seventies thing about a modern day bounty hunter taking on a kung fu serial killer?"

"Yeah. That's *him*, man. The real article. They must've based the movie on his secret exploits. Dude's a *legend*, man."

"Fights mean for a queen, too."

"He ain't no fruit, man. He's undercover. He was working in a gay bar in 'Bare Knuckles', too."

"Yeah? He works in gay bars undercover a lot. Kind of makes you wonder."

"Don't matter none to me, if he was who I think he was. He's either the real thing or a real good imitation."

"Maybe he saw the same movie."

"Shit, maybe he's the dude who played him in the movie. Robert something. Looks like him. Could be the role went to his head, like that guy who played the Lone Ranger, and Bela Lugosi, buried in his Dracula cape. Anyway, let's go talk to Luke, now that he's been all subdued and humiliated."

"You were pretty damn friendly with him there, Doc," I said before we went back in.

"Aw, c'mon, I was *playin'* him, man. Hopin' he'd talk to me 'bout what's goin' on, cause your tactic of just startin' a brawl wasn't gonna get us nowhere, that was for damn sure. Good thing ol' Zach, whoever he was, was sittin' there."

"Karma and destiny, Doc."

"Luck, my man."

"No, you didn't see what his knuckles said. C'mon."

By the time we went back into The Cock of the Block the patrons had gone back to their business and Luke was sitting up in the middle of the floor, fighting for consciousness. I heard sirens in the distance.

"I know you set me up," I said to him. "Cops are comin'. You can tell me or tell them. Your call."

Luke looked at me quizzically and then put out his hand. I didn't budge but Doc helped him up and we went out the back. "Let's go to Tina's, it's right down the way here," Luke said, massaging his sore face and neck. Blood trickled from his nose and mouth. It was a beautiful sight.

Chapter Eight
SHOOTING SCRIPT

When Luke opened the door of his girlfriend's apartment, which was only a block away from the beach, I fell instantly in love with Tina Hartman. I recognized her right away as a co-star in several of Velma's monster movies, but either she had used an alias or I just never bothered to check for her name in the credits, since, entrancing as she was, her allure had been overshadowed by Velma's mythical figure. But here in person, Tina Hartman was the rising star of my faltering life.

Contrary to what Tony Ray had told me, Tina did not resemble Tina Louise so much as she did Marla English, perhaps best known for her role in *The She Creature*, an AIP classic from 1956. In that flick, one of my favorites, a beautiful bosomy babe is put under hypnosis and her spirit summons from the depths of time and the ocean her past incarnation as a sea monster (designed by Paul Blaisdell). It was sort of inspired by the Bridey Murphy reincarnation craze of the period. I just liked it because it was moody and the monster looked cool and Marla was one of the sexiest mamas I'd ever laid my prepubescent eyes on. Tina's hair was a little lighter than Marla's, but she had the same full figure and smooth ivory skin and pouty lips and dreamy bedroom peepers. She was more petite and compact than Velma, who was more like Anna Nicole Smith's kid sister. No doubt about it, Tina was one dreamy dish. And here she was, shacked up with Luke Brandon. Go figure.

"Tina, these are the guys I was telling you about," Luke said as he closed the door behind us. Tina looked at Doc and me like we were a couple of Tupperware salesmen she had no interest in talking to. The place was a mess—Tina was obviously no housekeeping whiz—and movie memorabilia was scattered randomly amongst the normal household junk. Mostly there were mounds of old movie magazines and some stills taped to the walls like newspaper clippings in the abode of a serial killer. Many of the stills were black and white glossies of Mamie Van Doren, Marilyn, Jayne Mansfield, and their contemporaries. In fact, one still was of Marla English in *Voodoo Woman*, from 1957. My kind of girl, Tina, as long as she owned a vacuum and some cleaning products somewhere. The place smelled like road-kill. And dirty sex.

"Nice to meet you, Tina," I said, removing my overcoat. She seemed cold and unfriendly, totally indifferent to us and whatever our purpose for invading her privacy happened to be. I handed her my overcoat and she took it and threw it on top of her dirty laundry in the middle of the floor. I turned to see what Doc was up to and noticed he was looking behind him, at the doorway. I turned a little more and saw that Luke was standing there with a .45 pointed at us. He was grinning.

"Sit down, Vic," he invited us in a demanding tone. "Anywhere."

I couldn't place where the furniture was beneath all the shirts and socks and bras and panties and magazines and cigarette trays and dirty dishes, so I just picked a heap and sat on it. Doc just stood pat, looking at Luke, shaking his head.

"Man, I ain't got time for this shit no more," Doc said. "Just let me go, man, all right? I got no quarrel with you. I got a business to tend to. I'm losing money by the minute."

"Shut up," Luke said. The .45 was nickel-plated and gleaming. It was a bad looking piece. I wondered where and when he got it. Probably bought it after I shot him that last time. I asked him. "That's right," he said with a nod. "Can't be too careful these days. Between psychos like you and the ones carjacking people in broad daylight, a man needs to arm himself in this town these days. I had it on me in the bar but I wanted to get you guys somewhere private. That maniac decked me before I had a chance to defend myself. Cheap shot, but I'll catch up with him some day. I knew you wouldn't pay that fucking bill, Vic. It was a joke, stupid. Fact, I've been following you ever since you knocked on my door. The girls still think I'm out of town. I saw through the window how you were smashing up my stuff, but I had to do a slow burn or else blow my cover. You may be wondering why I was on your ass, huh?"

I shrugged. The gun no longer fazed me. "Don't really care, Luke. Put the gun down unless you plan on using it. You know I ain't packin' or else you'd be limping all over again."

"How about Tubbs over here?" Luke said.

"I'm clean," said Doc. "And the name's Tibbs. *MISTER* Tibbs."

I rolled my eyes. Jesus. Everything was a movie. Luke put his gun down. I glanced over at Tina. She was sitting in her flimsy silk robe and slippers on a heap of stuff watching a little color TV set in the kitchen while sipping a beverage and smoking. Some lame game show was on. Whatever. She had tuned us out completely, it seemed. I'd try her wavelength again later, though.

I went into the pocket of the trench coat on the floor and Luke reached for his gun again. "Take it easy, I just want to show you the script, okay?"

"I read it already," he said. He pulled off his sweaty shirt and flung it aimlessly. He was still buffed out and looked pretty good for an older guy, like a geriatric Hercules. I kept comparing my body to other guys' bodies and felt like I never measured up. No wonder Luke got all the pussy. He trained for it.

"So you know why we knocked on your door," Doc said.

"This ain't between me and you, Tonto," Luke snapped. "It's between me and the Lone Ranger here. We got an old score to settle, him and me."

"Where's Velma Vale?" I asked him simply.

"How the fuck should *I* know? You're always asking me where your broads are, Vic."

"That's 'cause you keep fuckin' 'em. She wrote the script, right?"

"No."

"No? Not what Tony Ray told us."

"Fuck Tony Ray. Fuckin' *pussy*."

"So who wrote it? You?"

Luke laughed and massaged his slimy pecs. He was till sore from the beating in the bar, but he was bouncing back nicely, regaining his self-esteem. Funny, Tina hadn't even remarked on his beat up appearance. True love. "I can't write," he said. "I can do everything else, but not write. I'm a man of action."

"So, who, then?"

He shrugged. "I don't know, really."

"But you were going to produce it?"

"Maybe. I had friends who wanted to start an independent production company. I was going to be a junior partner, and this was going to be our first feature."

"So? What happened?"

"What always happens? Money fell through. We tried everything, even laundered Mob money, but we couldn't get arrested."

"What was the production company called?" I asked him.

"Oh, uh—Big."

"Big? Big *what*?"

Luke grimaced. "Just plain *Big*. Big Productions. Get it?"

"Yeah. Catchy."

"I always thought so. Anyway, Velma Vale was another partner in the company. The others were Tony and some guys I never even met. Friends of Velma's. She's the one who got this script, which she said a friend of hers wrote."

"She told Tony *she* wrote it."

"Not what she told *me*. She had no writing ability. Didn't need it. She wanted to star in it, though, but Tony wanted Tina, and so did I and the other partners, 'cause Velma may be a nice piece of ass but can't act her way out of a wet condom, so Velma got pissed and left town and that's the last I saw of her. Now you show up giving me grief again, Vic. Why?"

"Why were you following me?"

"I was tipped off. Anonymous phone call said you were in town gunning for me, so I sublet my place to the girls."

"That's bullshit. I didn't even know you knew Velma until I saw one of your pieces at Tony's house. And what is this with Judy and the girls, anyway? You saw their ad just when you wanted to hide out? Friends of mine? Convenient."

"No, I don't know those girls and I didn't realize they knew you until I saw you hugging them in my house. And I never even set that deal up. So fuck off."

"So who did?"

Luke nodded toward the kitchen. "Tina."

Just when I turned to ask Tina about it and break her away from her stupid game show, there was a knock on the door. Everybody froze. The knock persisted and so Luke went to answer it. No sooner had he cracked the door slightly ajar and peered out than two bullets came ripping through part of the doorframe and his shoulder and chest. He cussed and went down. I grabbed his .45 off a pile of garbage and ran to the door and flung it wide open, but the shooter had vanished down the street already, into the rain.

I checked on Luke, whom Doc was kneeling over. I yelled for Tina, who was barely aroused by the action, to call 911. She shrugged and picked up the phone, and I raced around the corner brandishing the gun, but found no trace of anyone or anything suspicious.

When I returned to Tina's apartment, Luke was lying bleeding and gasping amid the debris of his little life. Tina stood over him passively while Doc wrapped dirty laundry around his wounded shoulder, ostensibly to stop the bleeding. Luke was shivering with shock and so I tossed a dirty blanket from a heap of laundry and threw it over him. But one slug had hit the big guy in the upper chest, and he looked pale and weak. His eyelids fluttered and he was muttering. I asked Doc what he was saying.

Doc leaned over Luke's lips and then looked up at me and recited, "I'm gonna kill you for this, asshole."

"He mean *me*?"

"Think so. Anyway, ambulance is on the way. I think we should boogie and take Tina with us. Dude or dudette who plugged Rocky here may be back for her."

"Good idea." I reached over and grabbed Tina's arm. She resisted but I stuck the gun in her face and she relented, finally speaking up for herself:

"Look, I don't know who you are or what this is about, but you can't just bully me around like this. Put that thing away. You won't use it."

"You see your boyfriend lying there?" I shouted at her.

"He ain't my boyfriend."

"*Whoever* the fuck he is, he's bleeding on your rug, or will be when it seeps through the crud, and you could be next, baby doll. We'll help you but you gotta leave with us. *Now*."

"Why should I trust you? You're a total stranger and a total nutcase, from what I can see."

I had no time for this. "Because if you don't, I'll shoot you and make this look like a domestic spat. C'mon, put some pants on and let's get outta here and figure something out."

"For how long?" she wanted to know. Throughout this whole ordeal her facial expression had never lost its ennui. She was one tough cookie to impress. She took off the robe and was wearing nothing underneath. Nothing but heaven. My heart nearly stopped, and I momentarily forgot anything in the Universe existed besides the voluptuous body before me. While Doc and I gawked she ran into the bedroom and emerged a minute later in a short snug dress, carrying her shoes. Luke started mumbling something louder but I could make no sense of his warbling and ignored it. Probably nothing I wanted to hear anyway. If he bled to death so be it. I led Tina out into the rain and to my Corvair, Doc right behind us, and we drove off just as the ambulance and a police car were arriving.

As I drove I said to Doc, "So if Velma didn't write that script, who did? Luke said she had no writing ability, even, and I kinda tend to believe that, for some reason. Not that one would need writing ability to write that trash anyway."

"Exactly. But we can count Luke out as a player now, at least. He didn't write it. Maybe whoever shot him did."

"With my luck they'll think I did it," I said to Doc.

"Luke knows who did it. He saw 'em."

"This could be Luke's way of getting even, though, saying I did it and this time he presses charges. Last time I saw him he got shot, too—by me. It seems I'm bad luck for him."

"Who the hell *are* you fuckin' guys, anyways?" Tina asked at last from the back seat. "And where the hell are we *going*?"

Doc and I introduced ourselves cordially to her, then Doc said, "I don't know about the Kid here, but I'm goin' *home*."

"Doc!" I said. "You can't bail on me now!"

"Now seems like the perfect time to me. I'm losing money, Vic."

"I'm losing my life!"

"It's a tough call, I admit, but what about Tina here?"

"Yeah, what *about* me?" Tina said. She was still bored, I could tell. And the car was beginning to stink like *essence of unwashed female in heat* was the nearest I could place it.

"I'll take you back to my motel," I said off-handedly.

"What do you think I am, a *hooker*?"

"*Are* you?" Doc said, looking at her seriously.

"Screw you, I'm an actress."

Doc and I both said, "What's the difference?" Then laughed.

"To hell with this," I said, heading for Santa Monica, "do you know who shot your old man back there, Tina?"

"Didn't *you*?"

"*No!*"

"Sorry, I wasn't paying attention. I was watching TV."

"Great witness," Doc said.

"Luke have any enemies you know of?" I asked her.

"Just me," she said. "And everyone else."

"That narrows it down," Doc said.

"Doc, before you book, just do me one favor. I want you to call our pal Bruno like you're just giving him an update on my situation. Wait a while, though, till they have a chance to investigate. Like till late tonight or tomorrow, okay?"

"Aw, shit, man. Why I gotta do that? Why don't *you*?"

"I thought *you* were designated for that honor?"

"Vic, I told you, I'm out of it. Playtime's over. People are using real guns now, and I'm *losin'* it."

"Yeah, yeah, losing *mone*y, you mean, a mint a minute. I just want to know if they think I did this, so I'll know how freely I can move around. C'mon. One phone call then you're outta here."

Doc sighed and said fine, whatever. Back at the motel, Tina slouched seductively on my bed watching a soap opera while I took a dump and Doc waited for me. When I came out Doc was looking at me with an expression of pity and disgust. Since that's his normal expression when looking at me, I asked him what was up.

"Vic, the gun that was used to shoot Luke Brandon, who is in critical condition?"

"Yeah?"

"It was *yours*, cowboy."

"How the hell do you know?"

"I just got off the line with Bruno. Didn't want to wait, wanted to make it seem all was copacetic. But he was goddamn *angry*. There's a dragnet out for your ass, or will be."

"Doc, that's impossible and you know it. There's no way they had time to pull the bullets out of Luke, run them through ballistics, and post an APB in half a fuckin' hour."

"No shit. All the Sarge said was that it was your gun and they were out for you."

"But they confiscated it!"

"Yup."

"Yup? Fuck *yup*, Doc. What the hell's going on here?"

"It's a set-up of epic proportions, Vic. Somebody wants you to go down in a big way, and obviously it ain't Luke. He's just a cog in the machine, man. Whoever wants you had the balls to plug Luke with your gun. Hopefully he won't die, but still, considering you were out on bail after already being charged with a murder, it don't look good, Vic. Makes you look like fuckin' Mad Dog Earl or some shit."

I was pacing like a caged panther now. "So who, Doc? Why? Who would have the power to make cops frame me? Little old me? What's their beef?"

Doc shrugged and we both looked over at Tina, who was immersed in what appeared to be a commercial for tampons. She looked incredibly sexy lying there, and the room was filled with her sensuously pungent odor.

"Ask *her*," Doc said. She didn't even acknowledge us.

I walked over and grabbed her foot. She'd kicked her shoes off and her toes were painted red. Wow, I liked that. When she turned over to face me her shirt fell open and revealed much of her awesome breasts. She just snarled, "Leave me alone, I don't know nothin', and as soon as I think it's okay, I'm goin' home. I don't know who shot Luke and I don't care. Hope he *dies*, the bastard. All he was to me was a lay, and a lousy one at that. So don't ask me nothin', 'cause I don't know and I sure as hell don't give a flying fuck." Then she rolled back over and continued her surveillance of the tube. I didn't know whether I wanted to strangle her or what. I imagined my jism flooding her lying tonsils. It was an entrancing mental image, but I quickly dispelled it in favor of more prudent meditation.

I sat in a chair and put my head in my hands. "Now what, Doc? You still goin' home?"

"Oh, yeah. You bet. Tonight, cowboy. And if you were smart, you'd come with me. You're a sittin' duck in this cesspool, man. *You* know you're innocent, and *I* know it, and *God* knows it, but whoever listens to Him? Tina ain't gonna vouch for nothin', so count her out. Just cut her loose now, she ain't our responsibility. This is too fucked up, Vic. Those Fed motherfuckers know all this shit about you, cops are plantin' your gun on bloody bodies, and if you give Tina here a second thought, she may wind up dead or disappeared, too, and it'll be on *your* credit card, Mad Dog. Let's get the fuck outta here, Vic. *Now*. Watchin' bimbos fuck with your head, that's entertainment, but this is different and dangerous, and I'm in it *with* you this time. Fuck that, man. I'm jumpin' out of the sidecar before it goes over the cliff. This is JFK type conspiracy shit, and I want out now. I'll wait for the video, dig? Now, you comin' or not? 'Cause we ain't got any more time to ponder the situation."

I sat there and pondered anyway. On top of everything, my cat was missing, running around loose on the mean streets of San Francisco. I didn't think running away would help my situation. I got the image of a white Bronco on a freeway, surrounded by cops and fans. Except I had a Corvair, and no fans. "I gotta find out who's behind this, Doc. and why. You're right, go back home, and just do me one favor?"

"What now?"

"Look for my cat."

Doc shot his forefinger at me. "A cat scan, huh? You need one. You got it, Mad Dog."

"And don't call me Mad Dog."

"How about Crazy Cat?"

"How about just callin' a cab for the airport? Quick, before they decide to pull you in as an accomplice."

Doc whistled. "Hey, never thought of that. You're right, I'm outta here yesterday. I just hope they don't sic Zachary Kane, Modern Day Bounty Hunter on your ass."

"Who?"

"Your Guardian Angel in the bar, man." Doc looked over at Tina. "Nice meeting you, Miss," he said to no response whatsoever. Doc gave me a hug and then went back to his room to pack and call the airport to book the next Bay Area shuttle and then a taxi. I stayed in my room with Tina and brooded on my situation, staring alternately into space and at her shapely ass on the bed. Compensation. God, even at a time like this, I couldn't take my mind off of pussy, the main source of my grief in general and my current predicament in particular.

"I'll take you home in the morning," I said to her comely ass, since that was all she'd face me with. "That okay? I'm just looking out for you, you know."

I saw her shrug slightly. "Okay," she said after a few beats. Then she casually added, to my surprise, "Thanks."

"Sure," I said. Then I picked up the phone and called information and got Luke Brandon's house in Venice. I wanted to talk to Judy, but I had a feeling I was too late. I hung up when a male voice answered. Probably a cop, tracing the line. The home was probably cordoned off, too, The She Beams relocated until the gig. Which I planned to attend incognito, to make sure Judy was all right. I also had to find out why Tina had sublet Luke's pad to friends of mine. If she had.

I was about to ask her when she turned around and said to me, pointing at the TV screen, "Hey, isn't that *you*?"

I looked at the tube and saw to my horror that a news bulletin was broadcasting the LAPD police file photo of me, with instructions to call 911 and report my appearance immediately. Oh, I was also labeled "armed and dangerous."

"*Wow*!" said Tina, impressed. "They really think you did it, all right. Did you really kill Velma, too? Not that I'd care if you did."

I felt sick, and sat on the bed beside her. "No," I mumbled. "I didn't kill anybody. It's a frame-up. And there's nowhere to run, no one to turn to, because they're all in on it." I felt like I was trapped in *Invasion of the Body Snatchers*.

"I know," she said casually. "Hey, I wonder if you'll be on 'America's Most Wanted' or 'Hard Copy'! We'll have to see tonight, okay?"

"Okay, great, whatever, but we'll have to switch motels, this place is probably pretty hot, so—hey, you said you know it's a set-up?"

"I know you didn't kill Luke, and I know you didn't kill Velma."

"How?"

"Because. I talked to her this morning and she told me."

I stared at her, wide-eyed, incredulous, almost in tears, and she rolled over toward me and took off her shirt and her sexy scent overwhelmed me as she gently placed my face in her bosom and said, "There, there. Mama will make it all better."

Chapter Nine
TALES FROM THE CRYPTIC

When Doc knocked on the unlocked door of my motel room and then walked in to say goodbye, he was flabbergasted to find Tina and me frolicking freely on the bed in advanced stages of nudity.

"*Vic*!" he yelled. "For Chrissake, man, what's *wrong* with you? You got LAPD and the FBI on your ass, and you're diddlin' *this* bimbo? Man, what is your *problem*?"

"Who you callin' a bimbo, fudge bar?" Tina snapped at Doc.

"Hey, watch it," I said to her, unraveling our limbs, pulling my pants back on and throwing on my shirt. Little Elvis had been ready to launch into his first number, but the concert was abruptly called on account of audience unrest. I was glad Doc showed, actually. It was true—there was no time for this type of distraction. I just kept my eyes off of Tina's mostly nude body as I continued dressing. Doc waited for me outside.

"You got a *serious* disorder," Doc said to me as I joined him, closing the door behind me. "And you hear what that bitch called me, right? Shoulda slapped her, man. What's with you, anyway?"

"I'm w-weak," I stammered. "She made a play for me. Anyway, my picture was on a newsflash. Everyone is town will be after me now. There's a reward, I didn't see how much."

"Oh yeah? So what was this about, then? Last request of a condemned man? Seems to me Tina wanted to keep you in one place until they closed in on you."

"Shit, you're right. You better go, Doc."

"What about you, lover boy?"

"I got unfinished business to tend to."

"You mean you still gonna let that bitch screw you?"

"There's no place to hide if the Feds got a file on me, Doc. I'd rather stand and fight."

"Looks to me like you'd rather lay and love."

"I'll take care of it, Doc. Thanks, man. I'll be in touch." I gave him an awkward hug.

"All right. Vic. Lemme know where I can reach you. But if anyone starts taking potshots at you, might as well come home. If they gonna get you, let it be on your own turf."

"You got a point there. Now beat it before you get involved any further. All right? I'll call you. And find Puss. Promise."

"I'll find your pussy up *there* if you promise to keep away from the pussy down *here*, particularly that nympho in there. Damn, Vic, you even *smell* like her now."

I sniffed my arm. "Aw, hell, you're right. I better take a shower."

"You better take a powder, my man. But quick. A'right now." Doc's cab pulled up and we hugged again and then he was gone. I felt sad and empty after he'd left, like I'd never see him again. He waved to me from the cab and I nearly busted out crying. Instead I went inside the room and confronted Tina. She was stark naked now, and when I opened the door she spread her arms and legs and beckoned me to enter her dark domain.

I just looked at her. Then I took my clothes off and dove in. Last request of a condemned man.

The sex was hot but over rather quickly, perhaps rushed by the urgency of the circumstances. Her scent permeated my senses so completely I felt like even my soul needed a shower. She was very loud, too. Hormones and whore moans. No, that's not nice. But accurate. Probably signaling the cops to come get me. I didn't care, almost. Next to Velma, it was the best sex I'd ever had. Her body was softer than Velma's, and her fleshiness seemed to absorb me. I was glad she didn't exercise. Obviously Luke hadn't influenced her lifestyle, which was a promising sign. Muscles on a woman turn me off. She wasn't as into kissing as I normally like, but she made up for it by giving me the most outrageously sensuous head I've ever received. I flooded her lying tonsils with my jism, just like I'd imagined. Then she rode me and I got it up again and came inside her. Burning the dick at both ends. I didn't have any rubbers and didn't care. I was condemned anyway. When I penetrated her and smothered my face in her redolent breasts I recalled my fantasies of making love to Marla English and all the other scream queens I creamed over in youthful wet dreams. Then as she rocked on top of me I saw "The She Creature" attacking me while I was in my most vulnerable position, and I nearly lost my hard-on, but "Marla" made a comeback just in time. Afterwards we slept into the evening. I fully expected to wake up in the slammer, wet from my dream. But when I did wake up, Tina was watching TV and it was around 7 pm and all was quiet.

"Any more news about me?" I asked her, almost eagerly. Something about being famous in L.A. appealed to me, even if it was as a degenerate psychopath on the loose. It's that fame thing, man. I had the bug that had been going around this town for the past hundred years. I wondered who was watching T.V. and saw the newsflash with my kisser filling the screen—Ann-Margret? Priscilla Presley? Liz Taylor? Brando? Pacino? Newman? I wondered if they thought I was cute and felt sorry for me. The women, that is. Hell, the guys too! Maybe Brando wanted to adopt me, protect me from the law like he had his own son.

"Not that I noticed," Tina answered, and I was slightly disappointed. "You register under your own name here?"

Wait a minute. Actually I hadn't. "No, I used an alias. So did Doc, just in case. I checked in as 'Chumpy Walnut.'"

"*Who*?"

"Nobody. Just the name I use when I want an alias on a hotel register. It's a kooky name but nobody ever beefs about it. If they ask I just say it's a nickname from my childhood that stuck."

"So what do we do now?"

"Wanna go home? Cops're probably looking for you, too, since it was your place Luke was shot."

She grimaced. Her face wasn't as pretty up close, after screwing and sleeping, but it was still very appealing and almost innocent in its appeal, like a cheesecake pin-up from the '40s. "That's right. Maybe they think I'm involved with you. We should stick together, big boy."

I raised my eyebrows and kissed her eyes and nose and lips, puffy with passion.She kissed my ears and neck and chest and stroked me in sensitive places. "Well—*aren't* you?"

"You're a much better lover than Luke," she said, looking me in the eyes with insipid adoration I didn't trust.

I winced. "God, don't say that. Luke ever do Velma?"

She rolled her eyes at me. "*Everyone* did Velma. Even me."

Whoa. "What? You and Velma were lovers?"

She looked up at the ceiling as she spoke. "Yeah, we were."

The image of that drove me mad, but I had bigger things to worry about than my cock, but then who didn't. "And you swear you spoke to her yesterday?"

"Yes," she whispered.

"So she framed me for her murder."

"No."

"No? How can you say that?"

"Because. She's a prisoner."

"*What*?"

"Someone is holding her hostage, won't let her go. She escaped and made one call, to me, because I was the only person who would believe her, but she was cut off. Maybe by now she *is* dead."

"Who? Who the fuck is holding her *hostage*?"

She sighed. "I can't say. He'd kill me. That's what she called to tell me. I don't think she knows about you being charged with her fake murder and all that. I started to tell her, but I think maybe he was the one who shot Luke, or he had it done. He has a lot of connections. I don't know why he'd shoot Luke, except maybe to shut him up. Maybe if you hadn't been there, I'd have gotten it too. I just figured that out, lying here, while you were sleeping. I think it first hit me when I came, actually. My head tends to clear up during an orgasm. The rest of the time it's all murky and muddled. That's why I like to fuck as often as possible, or at least masturbate, to keep my head clear."

I sat up in bed, mentally pacing. "Tina, who? *Who* is doing this?"

"I told you, I can't say. He'd kill me."

"Just tell me how you know him, then."

"You know that production company Luke told you about? Big? Well, *he's* Mister Big. That's the only name I'll give you."

"Mister *Big*? Jesus, sounds like a Seventies blaxploitation flick. Mister Big. Gimme a break. So wait—did Mister Big write that script?"

"You mean 'Neon Knights'?"

"Yeah, yeah."

"*I* don't know. Maybe. He was the one who gave it to Velma, but none of us wanted her to be in it, because she can't act. I'm classically trained, as an actress, I mean, I have a degree and everything, plus I give better head than Velma, so Mister Big said I could do it, be the lead, I mean, which was great because I was used to Velma stealing all my parts from me because her boobs are bigger, but we couldn't get the money, even though Mister Big himself is loaded. I don't think he wanted to be directly involved. He was a silent partner."

"Mister Big was rich?"

"*Is* rich."

"And he's holding Velma captive?"

"He was the past few days. He was obsessed with her. Used to be just a fan, but then he started going to conventions, following her around, making lewd phone calls and harassing her at all hours, and she was going to get a restraining order against him, but then she found out she couldn't."

"Why not?"

"'Cause. He's friends with all these politicos who have influence, and he's above the law."

I got out of bed and paced for real, still in the raw. "Tina, we have to tell someone about this. For *my* sake, at least."

"We can't. There's no one to tell, that's the thing. He has his hand in everybody's pockets, I'm telling you. He'll have us both killed, I'm not kidding you. Or at least he'll ruin my career, which is close enough for me."

"Tina, with all due respect, *fuck* your career. Your Mister Big is making me the fall guy, for some weird fucked up reason. Why me?" The eternal question.

"Why not? You ever write Velma's fan club?"

"Well, yeah. So?"

"He bought influence there, too. Paid the president of the fan club to supply him with names of other fans, for correspondence, he said. I know because I was fucking the president and he told me."

I should've worn a condom. Too late now. "I thought that info was supposed to be classified?"

"It is. But he paid for it. Everything has a price, big boy."

"So, wait. Let me figure this out. Mister Big set me up for Velma's murder so she could disappear and he could hold her captive so he could—what?"

She gave me an *isn't-it-obvious?* look. "What else? So he could own her, like a possession. She wouldn't marry him, wouldn't even sleep with him, and she just got engaged to Tony to ward him off, but if didn't work, and then she and Tony broke it off, I think because Mister Big threatened him. And I think he promised me the part because I sucked him off right in front of her and he wanted to hurt her, so did I, I was so competitive with her, which was I seduced Tony, too, but she didn't care about that, she just wanted the part, because it wasn't like a B movie or anything, it was classy, well, no monsters or shit like that, anyway. But he wanted to control her career, her body, her life, everything. He's a real sicko." Tina yawned. When she wasn't screwing, her ennui set right back in.

"So you think Mister Big got my name and address from the fan club, ran a background check on me, and the Feds."

"Who?"

"These suits following me around. Hey, where *are* they, anyway? They know I'm staying here. I forgot all about them. Haven't seen 'em since Doc and I left the Pussycat Theater yesterday."

"You mean G-men?"

"Yeah, babe. G-men. At least that's what they called themselves. They had all this dirt on me, too, about, well, that's another story. But Mister Big could've gotten that stuff somewhere else. Captain Sharp in San Francisco, for one. Political pull could grease any palm around and my secrets aren't really buried all *that* deep."

"You're losing me. What were you doing at the Pussycat Theater, anyway, you horny devil?"

"Huh? Oh. Velma's X-rated flicks were having their world premiere."

"Really? Mister Big owned them, you know."

"No shit? How? Just bought the negatives?"

"No, he *produced* them. That's how me met her. That's where he made his money. Well, a *lot* of it. He was born rich. His brother is in politics."

"Yeah? Who is he? Anyone I heard of?"

"Can't say, but yeah, you've heard of him. So that's all I know, big boy. You fucked it out of me. Just like James Bond."

My ego swelled like it had a boner. It was funny—amid all this personal turmoil, I was not only getting laid, but it was the greatest physical sensation I'd ever experienced. Literally dreams come true, in the middle of a nightmare. I wasn't sure whether it was the stress of my impending peril or something more complex, but my heart just wasn't in it. Not that I needed it. I enjoyed the sex, sure, but something told me I'd appreciate it more in retrospect, as a pair of macho back-to-back (and every other which way) conquests. Tina had just called me James Bond, my idol. But I didn't feel like James Bond, oddly enough, despite my similar sexual prowess. Instead I felt empty—and alone. Like I said, it may have just been the circumstances, but the new notches on my belt were not emblems of fulfillment and triumph, only meaningless tokens of time wasted.

"Doc's right—I have a problem," I said more to myself than to Tina.

"No problem here," she said slyly. "Should we be on our way, Chunky Chestnut?"

"'Chumpy Walnut.' Actually, the name's Valentine. Vic

Valentine."

"Yeah? I remember you said your name in the car but I forgot it. Vic Valentine. How cute."

Jesus. I'd just been intimate with a starlet who didn't even know my name. How weird was this going to get? Was I turning into a bitter promiscuous flake on the romantic rebound from reality? I needed to get a grip on something besides rotating female hips. "Let's get outta here, Tina," I said with a new worldly tone of authority in my voice, which sounded deeper even to me.

"And go where?"

"I'm open to suggestions." Amongst other things.

"Well, it so happens I have a little cottage in Topanga Canyon we could hole up in for a little while. Nobody knows about it. It's where I go to get away from it all."

"How about Mister Big? He know about it?"

"No one. You're the first man I've even told about it."

"Yeah? Why me?" There was that question again.

Tina scooted over the bed on her knees, embraced my neck, and kissed me, long and wet and deep. Scratch my spiel on feeling empty. I felt something, all right. Maybe it wasn't spiritual, but it was good. "I like you," she said. "You seem sincere. I can tell by the way you make love. You're *aware*. You want to give pleasure as much as receive it. Maybe more. You try to find out what turns me on and then you do it. Most men just shoot their wad and roll over. But you, you're *affectionate*. That kiss? I hardly ever kiss men like that. Kissing is so much more intimate to me than fucking."

I kissed her back, thinking of what Doc said, and of Dolly Duncan distracting me with blow-jobs so I wouldn't realize she was guilty of killing my own father after sleeping with him and dozens of others. Was I a sex addict? I didn't usually get it enough to be considered addicted. If my present pace continued I'd find out. Or was I just looking for love in all the wrong places? Did I really have a problem? I was finally having all my sexual fantasies fulfilled, and I felt miserable. There *must* have been something wrong with me.

"I'm not James Bond," I whispered as I kissed her again.

"You're better," she said, kissing me back. "You're real. Okay, let's go to Topanga."

"Now?"

"Think of a better time?"

"No, but shouldn't you shower first?" Then I gulped, hoping

she wouldn't take offense. My fluids and hers had dried all over her, and she was sticky, and that was just one layer on top of her old one, and frankly, it wasn't such a turn-on anymore.

She just replied with a twinkle in her eye, "I have a hot tub in Topanga. We'll both get wet together."

"Swell. Let's rock, or roll, or whatever."

I got my things together and since Tina had nothing but her scanty clothing we were ready to leave in no time. I could hear a new storm bearing down upon us. We'd get wet long before we reached the hot tub, but that was good, especially for me, since Tina was used to her own odor, obviously.

Just as I opened up, a bullet ripped a hole in the motel door. I still had Luke's .45 tucked behind my waistband. I knocked Tina back into the room and returned fire toward the direction the report had originated. As I thought, my pals the Feds were parked out front with their guns trained on me. I was in a shootout with the F.B.I.—*another* dream come true. Only this wasn't a dream. They had me outgunned, so I did what any fugitive worth his salt would do. I took a hostage.

"*Tina*," I whispered as I ducked back into our room. "Just go along with me, all right? I'm going to stick my gun in your back and we're going to walk out of here. Once I'm on the road I'll lose them, long before I get to your place in Topanga. Trust me. I'm a pro."

"Well, okay," Tina said like a real sport. Then she added, "James Bond."

"More like Pretty Boy Freud," I said, meaning Pretty Boy Floyd. Talk about a Freudian slip. "All right, here goes." I grabbed Tina harshly, stuck the .45 to her temple, and showcased her to the Feds, who held their fire long enough for me to get to the Corvair.

"*You're just making it easier for us, Valentine,*" Fed One yelled. "*By the time you're through it'll be a cake walk down death row.*"

"*I'm just buying time until I can prove how phony this shit is,*" I shouted back. "*I know it's a set-up and I'll prove it, asshole. Tell that to your boss.*" Then Tina slapped my arm, at first I thought for show, but then I realized she didn't want Mister Big to know she'd told me anything, so I added, "*And tell your boss if he tries anything this tramp here gets it. And oh yeah—tell him to say hello to Velma for me.*"

I pushed Tina into the Corvair and took off, practically doing a wheelie as I skidded onto Ocean Avenue and around the corner, weaving in and out of traffic on the slippery streets. Before long I heard sirens, but that didn't worry me. I was used to being in a perpetual state of uneasiness and precarious disaster. Complacency was not my forte. I doubled back toward PCH and disappeared into the darkness. The heavy rain helped camouflage us in the night. I sped toward Malibu, half wondering whether to pick up Tony Ray on the way, but then I realized they'd be looking for me there, too, so I followed Tina's frantic directions and within an hour we were somewhere in the wilderness of Topanga Canyon, ensconced within her little cottage, soaking in the hot tub as the rain beat down on us relentlessly, and Tina finally smelled like a rose. We made love as the storm grew more intense and fierce. I had learned nothing from my past experiences. I wanted the passion, the intimacy, transient and shallow as it was, more than I wanted anything—even my freedom. Or so I believed as Tina enveloped me in her sweet-smelling flesh and told me how great I was. I'd never had anything quite like it. Except for Velma Vale.

After the hot tub session we ate and retired to her waterbed in the little one room shack, decorated much like her Venice apartment, but not quite as sloppy. Close, though. Despite everything, I felt better than I had in ages. I'd shot it out with the Feds and escaped then made love to a beautiful mysterious stranger right off the movie screen all in the same night. If this wasn't living, I didn't know what was. I was finally beginning to feel like the genuine article. Forget 007. I was Vic Valentine, P.I. Pretty Invincible. Passion Incarnate. Partly Insane.

"Tell me about yourself," I whispered manfully into Tina's ear, just before she began drifting off to sleep.

"What do you want to know? Besides that I like sex."

"Well, where are from?"

"Oh, please. Missoula, Montana. I grew up with Velma. We came out here to be actresses and worked as waitresses and then she got into porno but I just couldn't, because I was afraid I'd get sick of sex and that's too important to me, but then Velma started making these monster and gangster things and she got me some bit roles even though I studied acting and she didn't, but then there was always a rivalry between us, even in Missoula, because everything we competed for, she won, like Homecoming Queen or head cheerleader, everything, except the smart stuff, because I got better grades, but who cares about that?"

"So you want to be a famous movie star now, huh, and show 'em all?"

"Uh-hm," she mumbled, eyes droopy.

"I've seen you in Velma's movies, you know."

She perked up a little. "Really? Oh no. Like what?"

"Well, you were a witch in 'Curse of the Voodoo Love Queen,' and you took it all off for that voodoo ceremony and drove me nuts. And now, here you are."

"But you went to see Velma, not me, I'll bet."

"Well, yeah. But I wound up with you instead, in real life."

"Sounds like a movie, doesn't it?"

"Yeah. How'd you meet Luke Brandon?"

"Through Velma. I liked stealing her boyfriends, even if they were slime like Luke, just so I wouldn't feel so *beaten* all the time. That's why I sucked off Mister Big in front of her."

I blocked that out immediately. "So you called Judy Fagin to stay at Luke's?"

"Yeah, but Mister Big told me about the ad. Luke wanted a place to crash and didn't need his place, so Mister Big sublet his place for him. But I made the arrangement. This was before I knew Velma was even missing, though."

"Wait a minute—then it was Mister Big who told Luke I was in town gunning for him."

"Probably. Why would he believe that, though?"

"Ahm, long story. Forget it."

"Okay," she said with a yawn. "I'm *so* tired, Vic. I need to sleep now."

"Yeah, sure, in a minute, I'm thinking. That *script*. It's weird how it mirrored my thing with Velma. You know, how the starlet sets up the fan for her fake murder and all?"

"Yeah, that *is* strange." She was drifting off. Now that we weren't humping, she was getting bored again.

"Worse than that. I think your Mister Big wrote it, had it all planned, and then had Tony Ray give it to me. But then that would make Tony Ray an accomplice, right? Unless—*hm*. I need to meet this Mister Big for all the answers. Can you just point me in the right direction?"

"Not without him tracing it to me."

"You that afraid of him?"

"You've seen what he's done to you."

"Yeah, but I'm still alive, sweetheart."

"That's because he needs you to go down for Velma. She

knows about the plot, I just don't know if she knows she led you into the trap or not. When I talked to her, she seemed pretty scared. It freaked me out, too. She told me to keep my mouth shut, and the next thing you know, Luke's shot down in my house. Coulda been me."

"Shot with my gun."

"Makes you look like a killer."

I sighed. "We're in a spot, baby."

"Um-hm." She closed her eyes, but I was wide awake now.

I let her fall asleep in my arms as I kept rambling to myself. "So if the authorities are on the take, which is a given no matter where I go, it seems, can't trust nobody, then. But not *all* of them are. Just a few LA boys in Hollywood, and those Feds, who may be phonies—they just opened fire on me without warning, which is out of character—and then they waited, though, to close in on me, knowing right where I was the whole time, but not telling the cops, hm. It's a game, sweetheart. But your secret agent super-spy is on the case, dollface, so don't you worry. Tomorrow I'll go find this Mister Big, rescue Velma, prove she's still alive, and then it'll all come out and I'll wind up a hero. All I need you to do is give me an idea of where I can find him. I'll stash you someplace safe, don't worry, until I rescue Velma. I'm *good* at rescuing damsels in distress. That's my *specialty*." I went droned on until I finally put myself to sleep.

I awoke late the next morning after the best sleep I'd had in ages. Man, I felt so virile and alive! I jumped out of bed with a feeling of self-esteem and life-affirmation I rarely experience at all, and never this early in the day. I jiggled Tina to wake up but she wouldn't budge. I kept dancing around as I got dressed, singing to myself. The rain had cleared up and sunshine poured into the little messy room. I went over to Tina and jiggled her again. She was either in a deep, deep sleep or—I felt her cold skin and then her wrist, which had no pulse...

Dead.

Chapter Ten
LIMP, LONELY, AND LISTLESS

I decided hysteria would only hurt my situation, so instead I settled for just plain panic. I tried everything short of sticking Tina's finger in an electrical socket to revive her, but no question about it, she was in James Dean's passenger seat. Her lips were bluish-purple and her swollen eyes were partly open, the pupils rolled toward the back of her head, and saliva or something slimier dribbled from her mouth and down her chin, like she'd been frothing. There was not a mark on her, at least none I could find after a cursory, unprofessional exam. Poison? Frantically my mind raced backwards, reviewing the previous day's menu. The only time she ate or drank was at her house here. I had some coffee and she had—

Some *wine.*

I ran into the kitchen and pulled the near empty bottle of suspect burgundy out of the fridge. I sniffed it but all I came up with was sour grapes. What did I know about poison? Obviously if someone poisoned a bottle of wine they wouldn't choose something aromatic to tip off the swilling victim. I went back to check on Tina. Still dead. Deader, in fact. *Rigor mortis* was setting in, and she was beginning to stink again, worse than ever, and there was nothing sexy about it.

I didn't know what to do. Call 911? No, too late. They'd find her eventually anyway. The people who poisoned her would be by to check on her at the very least. I had to get out of there in a hurry before they did. The authorities would pin this on me, too, if the Feds told the cops that the dead girl had been my ticket to freedom while in flight. If it was yet another set-up they'd invent a way to trace it to me. I had to remain in transit indefinitely, but my Corvair was too easy a mark. I decided I'd hide it nearby in the woods. I couldn't leave it at Tina's, since that would only place me at the scene of the latest crime. And there was a beat up old early '60s model Porsche parked out back by the hot tub. I went through Tina's things and found a set of keys, then I went outside and tried them all until I hit pay dirt. I had a new car. Next I drove the Corvair deep into a thicket and covered it with some dead branches and anything I could find, even dirt, to camouflage it. I hated the thought of just leaving it behind, but I had no choice. Then I walked back to Tina's, climbed into the Porsche, and sped off.

I glanced at my watch. Almost noon. I wondered how long I'd been sleeping next to a corpse. But what the hell, I figured, I'd done worse in my time. At least this one put out first.

The thing with Velma and Luke was, the cops could pin dual motives on me—obsession *and* revenge. But with Tina, how could they connect me with her poisoned body? Just out on a mindless serial rampage? Or maybe the idea wasn't to pin another murder on me, but just to shut Tina up. About what?

Mister Big and his captive love slave Velma Vale, *that's* what. I just wished I had more to go on than a stupid phony moniker like Mister Big. How trite and silly. Not only that, but it was a big city, full of big shots. Only this one had a big shot brother in politics, and he was wacko to boot. Still, that didn't really narrow it down. I wondered what I would do first, besides get gas and eat in some out of the way place. The day was beautiful, weather-wise, and I desperately wanted to live all the way through it and many more like it in the years and decades ahead. All I had to do was elude the cops and Feds and Mister Big and find Velma and prove I was innocent. That's all. No big deal.

I wondered if Custer ever thought that about going up against Geronimo: no big deal. Be home in time for supper, dear. Then *wham*!, arrow through the noggin. I decided I'd search for more inspiring historical parallels to my predicament.

I kept my shades on as I sat in a tiny roadside cafe somewhere in Topanga that had a gas pump out front. I refueled both my body and the Porsche in about fifteen minutes, and then took off. No one looked at me funny, no more than usual, anyway, so I wasn't worried just yet. No sign of the Feds either. What to do? Where to go? I wasn't hungry any more and I sure wasn't horny. I had managed to block out any depressing reflections on mortality because of the urgency of my own situation, but the image of Tina—alive then dead—kept creeping into my consciousness and haunting me. In all my years as a P.I. I'd had very little experience with real live corpses. I'd never actually seen one outside of a morgue, while I was on missing person cases. I never even saw my father's mutilated carcass, and I never killed anybody. I'd shot a few people in the kneecaps and thereabouts, but I never took a life. And though that was still true, I felt somehow responsible for

Tina's death. Lay and pay, that seemed to be the rule. I choked up as her ghastly image kept seeping into my brain. I thought of her lying in her little bungalow rotting away amid all her pictures and clothes and magazines, my life-giving semen still wet inside her decomposing shell, and I started crying. Little did she know her night with me would be her last on Earth. No dreams would come true for Tina Hartman from Missoula, Montana. No movie stardom, no true love, not even the chance to enjoy another day like this one. It wasn't fair.

I decided if I ever *were* going to kill anyone, it would be Mister Big.

As I kept driving aimlessly around Topanga in a virtual circle, it dawned on me that my two greatest lays had resulted in their deaths, at least in Tina's case and maybe in Velma's. Hell, maybe even *mine*, the rate I was going. Was it a curse? The Curse of the Voodoo Love Queen? It would have been better for all concerned if I'd remained celibate, content with my fantasies and flashlight under the covers. Talk about comeuppance. Excuse me, God, for appreciating your handiwork up close and personal. Maybe You should think about making women uglier and sex less pleasurable. No, scratch that. Never mind. Leave it. I'll deal with it somehow, don't worry. (I was worried about possibly praying myself out of future ecstasy, no matter what the price.) But the bottom line was, the whole experience had tainted the best nights of sex I may ever have. The memories were tarnished forever. Oh well. I'd still think about them once in a while, anyway. Had to.

Then I realized something else: Judy Fagin and The She Beams were scheduled to appear that night at The Viper Room. One way or another, I was going to see them. For one thing, I love surf music, but there were other reasons. First I'd need a disguise. That was my project for the day. I wanted to make sure Judy was all right, and I also wanted to ask her if this Mister Big ever contacted her directly, either about subletting Luke's place or about me. Tina had set it up but at Mister Big's behest, and Mister Big must have known Judy was acquainted with me. That was the first thread I'd follow in this tattered little tapestry of treachery.

Various possibilities presented themselves to me as I drove down around Pacific Palisades and its environs, sticking to side streets and mountain terrain. There was always the old standby, going in drag, but some like it hot and some don't. I don't. There was the Groucho Marx fake nose and mustache and huge glasses routine, but somehow I didn't think that would work. I wondered again for the three millionth time in my life how the hell Clark Kent had fooled people into thinking he wasn't Superman simply by donning glasses. What a crock. If only it were that easy. I needed something off-the-wall but on-the-square. I wanted Judy to be able to make me but no one else. Chances are the Feds would be out front, but probably not in the audience. Maybe I could sneak through the back, into The She Beams' dressing room. Then what? Appear onstage as a guest musician? A rockabilly rebel? Naw, I had no musical talent whatsoever. Of course, neither did most musicians making it big these days, but I didn't want to join their unqualified ranks. No, I needed an entirely new angle.

Just then, as I was cruising somewhere in the mountains above the Palisades, a familiar figure on a Harley appeared seemingly out of nowhere and pulled up alongside me. It was my old pal Knuckles, or Zach Karma and Destiny, or whatever. He had on a colorful bandana and a big smile as he motioned for me to pull over with friendly gestures. Cautiously I obliged him. I doubted he was in cahoots with the Feds and Mister Big, or else he wouldn't have decked Luke and left me behind. No, he was his own player, all right. I just didn't know what his angle here was. *Yet.*

"What can I do for you?" I asked him, hearing Davie Allan's theme from *The Wild Angels* in my head. "Zach, right? Fancy meeting you way out here."

"I've been following you, buddy boy. I hear you're in a heap of trouble, that right?"

"You could say that. But what's your interest? I mean, you don't even know me, right?"

"I told you. I help little guys like you in trouble. It's what I *do.*"

"I ain't so little, and trouble I can handle. But thanks." I was letting the Porsche's engine idle, and I kept my foot on the clutch, ready to rip out of there at the first sign of danger. "You live around here or something?"

Zach looked off into the horizon, his eyes squinting through his '70s biker shades. Then he lifted his arm and moved it suddenly in a sweeping motion that made me flinch. "This is my home. However far you can see, and beyond that, too. I was raised by the Indians in the desert. Their name for me is Rutting Wolf. But most people just call me Zach." He said "rutting" though I wondered if he meant "running." He kept staring off into space and time and infinity, contemplating the grandeur of it. Or something. Maybe he was just having a manic episode. Whatever. It was time to leave. I nodded in polite accord with a forced smile and revved up the engine, ready to rock, when Zach got off the motorcycle and walked towards me. "Hey, wait a minute, little buddy. You've got some heavy karma comin' down. Word is the evil empire is out to get you, and I just can't let that happen."

Evil empire? "Who do you mean exactly by that, Mac?"

He looked at me, and I got a chill. "The name's *Zach*."

"Not Zachary Kane, Modern Day Bounty Hunter?"

The look continued, and it got even chillier. "Just Zach."

"Well, I'm Vic. Valentine."

"I know who you are. You'd think I'd be offering to help if I didn't?"

I shrugged. "Beats me. But who's after me—Mister Big?"

"Mister Big? What's that, a comic book character? Grow up, buddy. This is the real world. It's the evil empire, the society of white men that dominates nature's kingdom and destroys her people and resources, that's all that matters. I know you're an innocent man for a *fact*."

"You do? Why, you talk to Velma?"

"Please stop interrupting," he said with restraint, making me feel like Larry King.

"Sorry." I murmured feebly. "Go on. Please continue."

He paused before he did, still stealing deep thoughtful glances at something in the firmament, way above my head, in every sense of the phrase. "I know that the people looking for you are bad, members of the empire, and they've targeted you because you are an individual, someone with few ties to society, someone who will not be missed, someone they can use and discard like a broken toy. This cannot be allowed to happen. When I see it, things like this, I squash them. It's that simple. It's my thing, my mission. Whether or not you want my help is unimportant. It's my job to help you. Now, what are your plans, first of all?"

I let out a repressed sigh and said with resignation in my tone, "Well, my agenda calls for me going to The Viper Room in West Hollywood tonight. There's someone there I need to see and talk to. But the problem is this APB thing, which it seems you know all about already. I need a disguise, a cover."

"Meet me there ten minutes before the first show."

"That would be The Naughty Ones, then, since they open."

"I'll meet you in the alley."

"Which one?"

"The *closest* one. You'll see my cycle parked out front. It'll be pointed toward the alley."

"You know where The Viper Room is?"

He gave me another patient yet chilling look. "How else could I meet you there, friend?"

"Good point."

"I'll get you in and out, no problems, no hassle. Then we'll take it from there."

"Wait, what if I refuse? I generally work solo."

"It doesn't matter. I'll be there when you need me, and only I can and will decide when that is. Okay, friend?" He went back and climbed onto his cycle. He waved once and then sped off, leaving skid-marks on my brain.

Nonetheless, since I had no better options, I was there at ten minutes before nine o'clock that night after a day of aimless driving in the mountains, burning up gas and time. I hadn't been able to come up with a suitable disguise so I was praying for Zach to come through. Doc had called him my Guardian Angel. Maybe he was. At any rate, he was saving my ass, and I was grateful. So far. His resourcefulness had yet to be proven.

I saw the Harley and, looking around for the Feds, parked the Porsche right across the street from it, then dashed into the alley near The Viper Room. There was Zach, leaning against the wall, his fingers in his jeans. He was wearing a leather vest and no shirt, so his hairy round chest was exposed to the brisk night air. I was shivering in my trench coat, which he told me to remove.

"Why?"

"Because. You need to put this on." He handed me a sleek leather jacket with studs, and then a long, shaggy heavy metal-type wig.

"What the hell is this all about?"

"You're walking in there with me as my lover."

"*What*?"

"The Strip is loaded with hustlers, it will work. Trust me."

"No way, man. Forget it."

"You have a better idea, friend?"

I had to admit, at the moment, I didn't, besides forgetting the whole thing and turning myself in, in which case I'd wind up somebody's bitch anyway, maybe the big bad brother who would make *me* his "Paper Doll."

"Well, shit, let me *try* it, at least." I shed my coat and shirt and put on the leather jacket, leaving my chest bare like Zach's, only my stomach wasn't quite as drum-like as his. I felt self-conscious and sucked it in. Then I put on the wig. I'd always hated Van Halen and Guns 'n' Roses and that whole head-banger cock rock crowd, and here I was, undercover as a heavy metal hustler. As long as Judy saw my face it would be okay, though. I'd simply signal for her to meet me backstage, and that would be that. "Let's go," Zach said. "I don't want to miss anything." Then he put his arm around me.

"*Yo!*" I said, pulling away. "No touchy feely stuff, man. That's *out*." I was really starting to wonder about this guy, but I was so desperate, I still went along with him. No choice now.

"I just wanted to hide your face from anyone who might be looking for you. At least till we go inside. Trust me."

"I still don't understand why you're knocking yourself out for my benefit. Look, maybe we should just forget this whole thing."

"Let's *go*," he repeated firmly, putting his arm around me again and walking me to the door. He'd already bought two tickets for the show and gave them to the door guy, who didn't even seem fazed by us. Why would he? Not here in West Hollywood. I kept my trench coat and shirt wrapped like a papoose under my arm. Then, as soon as we were inside, I broke away from Zach and mingled with the crowd.

I realized then how much we stood out. The Naughty Ones were a retro lounge jazz and R&B act from Austin, Texas, and most of the crowd was dressed either neo-rockabilly or '40s supper club style. The She Beams would attract a similar element. This was not a cock rock assemblage. I couldn't stop blushing, even though it seemed no one noticed us as yet. It was also extremely cramped and dark inside. I made my way for the men's room just as The Naughty Ones were introduced and broke into their first number, "I Dig Your Voodoo," a very cool little tune.

On the way to the men's room I felt someone staring at me, paranoid it was my old pals the Feds. But it wasn't. It was actor Mickey Rourke, sitting with a few biker buddies in the corner. I thought I saw Johnny Depp among them as well. Rourke's eyes seemed to follow me to the men's room. Maybe he thought he knew me from somewhere. Didn't matter—this disguise was getting flushed. *Now*.

In the men's room I locked myself in a stall, peeled off the leather jacket and wig, leaving them next to the toilet where they belonged, then put on my shirt and trench coat, hiked up the collar, put on my shades, and walked back out my old self again. My natural gumshoe style perfectly suited the crowd anyway, and if Zach didn't like it, to hell with him. I'd tell him where the jacket and wig were, and he could retrieve them himself. After all, he had appointed himself to this detail. Wasn't my idea, or responsibility. I was taking a chance he'd beat me up, but that was preferable to having him put his arm around me again. I could still smell his cologne, and I nearly puked.

When I went back outside it was even more cramped and had grown darker, so much so I could barely see. Then I remembered I had my shades on. I left them on anyway as I mingled. It was so packed no cop could make me anyway. I stared to relax. I looked around for Zach and didn't see him. Maybe he left. Oh well. Didn't need him now anyway. I was in.

The Naughty Ones' set lasted about forty minutes, and I dug it the most, able to lose myself in the swingin', swoonin' songs and forget I was in the worst jam of my lousy life. I wanted to just go backstage and contact Judy right away, but a big bad black bouncer wouldn't let me. I asked him to just tell her Vic was in the audience and I'd need to see her after the show. He said he'd give her the message but I doubted. People always say they're going to do something and then don't. It's part of being human, I guess. I decided I'd have to contact her directly from the audience.

I didn't see Zach in the audience all during The Naughty Ones' set. When the lights went up slightly during intermission, I got nervous and sort of wished he was still around. I scouted for my pals the Feds but didn't notice them. I got a few beers at the bar and did my best to pretend Mickey Rourke wasn't still leering at me. What *was* it with that guy? I wanted to go up to him and ask, but was afraid he'd take offense and hit me. I did like him a lot in a few of his better movies, particularly *Angel Heart* and *Johnny Handsome*, but I doubt he knew me from somewhere. I supposed he just thought he did, and let it go at that, trying to hide amongst the throngs. I didn't like the looks of his biker buddies, either. And where had Johnny Depp gone to? Backstage banging Judy? I'd kill him if he took advantage of that sweet young doll! No wonder the bozo bouncer wouldn't let me back there. As with most things, there was nothing I could do about it, so I just drank my beer and waited for the lights to go back down. When they did, the crowd went wild, to my surprise. It seemed Judy and The She Beams had attracted quite a following with their few L.A. gigs. A demo tape of theirs had received some local airplay on a college station, and I think even KROQ late at night a few times, so maybe their star was rising more rapidly than Doc and I realized. I was jealous as hell when the dudes whooped it up, howling, even, obviously hungry like wolves, and The She Beams were like lambs in their den, ready to be devoured. I hated the while audience by then, but then I probably wouldn't have liked them anyway if I'd met them individually. People are people, and that's the problem.

The She Beams performed for a little over an hour, proving they deserved the attention and more. They were at the forefront of the neo-surf scene coming out of the Bay Area, along with The Mermen, The Aqua-Velvets, The Phantom Surfers, and The Ultras. In Seattle and Portland The She Beams had played with the incredible Man...or Astro Man?, from Alabama, and the equally awesome Impala, from Memphis. The She Beams' winning distinction was that they were four (sometimes five) gorgeous females, the cutest band since The Go-Go's, and they had something for the guys (sex appeal) as well as the gals (feminism). I was completely in love with Judy by the end of the set, when they came out for an encore, and I managed to work my way through the SRO crowd up to the stage and shout at her.

Judy looked stunned when she noticed me. I took off my shades and she screamed. "Vic! My God!" She got the attention of the other girls. "Look, you guys! It's Vic! He's still alive! *Vic, run!*"

"What?"

Judy pointed to the back of the club and they were three cops shoving their way towards me. I yelped and ran up onto the stage with Judy, who had inadvertently made me part of the act, arousing the attention of not only the fans but also the cops, who obviously had not been able to see me in the darkness of the club. I hadn't noticed them before, during intermission; they'd probably just shown up after The She Beams went on. I grabbed Judy by the arms and for some strange reason laid a huge kiss on her. I guess I was just happy to see her. Plus she looked sexy as hell in her glittering neon bikini and shimmering high heels. The crowd went crazy, thinking I was an overzealous fan, but the bouncer didn't like it and jumped up onto the stage toward me. Without thinking I whipped out my .45 and he backed off, bug-eyed.

"*Hold it!*" a cop shouted from the middle of the crowd, which wasn't exactly parting like the Red Sea to accommodate them. They were obviously on my side. The cops wouldn't shoot with all these accidental targets in the way. I fleetingly considered taking Judy hostage but thought better of it. Look how the last one had wound up. So instead I said: "Where can I contact you later? Quick!"

She was practically crying, and so were all the girls. Monica was standing beside me, her hand on my shoulder.

"Vic, Doc wants you to call him," Monica said in a pleading tone. "Go home *tonight*! *Hurry*!"

"Where are you guys staying? We need to *talk*!" I repeated frantically as the cops moved closer, brandishing their guns. The bouncer was still eyeballing but I kept my new .45 out and held him at bay. Johnny Depp was probably loving this. I *knew* Mickey Rourke was.

Judy gave me a hug, whispered an address in my ear—not the hotel where they were staying, since the cops had it staked out—and I told her I'd meet her contact her there sometime the following day. Then I dashed backstage, shoved some attendants out of the way, forced one at gunpoint to direct me to the exit, and then I ran out into the alley. I heard a piercing whistle and saw Zach was leaning on his cycle on the street. I ran over to him.

"Where the hell you been, man?"

"You didn't dig my disguise, and obviously wanted to play your own hand, so I let you. And look what it got you." I heard a siren suddenly flare up within a few yards of us, and my heart nearly stopped. We'd been spotted. "Hop on," he said, and after a moment's homophobic pause I jumped on the back of his cycle, holding on for dear life as he peeled out. The cops ordered us from the street and from the squad car to halt, and when they didn't, they fired a few warning shots over our heads. Stupidly, overtaken by the heat of the moment, I returned fire aimlessly into the air, but within seconds they were out of range and I was out of sight.

Chapter Eleven
THE ASSHOLE JUNGLE

My Guardian Hell's Angel delivered me to a safe haven somewhere in the wilderness of Laurel Canyon. It was a small shack with no electricity and handmade wooden furniture that was illuminated once Zach lit a few candles. Indian artifacts and artwork adorned the interior. He hadn't been kidding when he told me he had been raised by a tribe in the desert. Paul Revere and the Raiders performed "Indian Reservation" in my head. The *"we will return"* refrain echoed eerily in my brain.

"Who *are* you, man?" I asked Zach as he sat cross-legged in the center of the dusty floor, on top of a hand-woven Indian blanket.

"I am Navajo. I am Apache. I am Rutting Wolf," he said in measured tones. "I am the keeper of the flame, the guardian of the truth."

"You mean *Running* Wolf?"

"I mean what I say, and I say what I mean."

"*Ohhhhhkay.* So, are you like my Guardian Angel?"

"If you are sincere, and you are innocent, and you are in danger, then yes, you may think of me as such."

"I guess I have all the prerequisite qualifications, but do *you*? I mean, what's your stake in this, Billy Jack?"

"Zach."

"I know, I was being colloquial."

"Don't be. It bugs me."

"*Ohhhh*kay. Anyway, Zach, what now? What do you propose we do? Rain dance?"

He was doing strange things with his breathing when he said, "I do not understand how more rain could be of benefit. I have summoned the rain gods enough in the past week, and I do not wish to anger them by being overly demanding."

"Wait. You sayin' *you* are responsible for all the storms and shit?"

"Just the storms. The shit is not my doing. However, since you are in a pile of it, I am trying to help dig you out."

"Why?"

"If I don't, who will?"

"Good point. But what do *you* get out of it?"

He shrugged, twisting his head around in an aerobic motion. "Justice, friend. Justice."

"That's it?"

"That's not enough?"

"Well, yeah, I guess. So what now, then?"

"You must confront the one responsible, and make him face the truth, then force him to show it to the world." He punctured his cryptic words with grand sweeping motions of his arms. "Then the truth, once it is revealed, will set you free, my friend."

"Okay, wait. You said 'I' should. Aren't we like a team, now?"

"No. You don't want my help."

"Who says? Guy like could come in handy in a tight spot. You already have."

"Because. In the nightclub, you took off your disguise and ruined everything, exposed our plan, put you and myself at risk. You have your own way of doing things, and you are very stubborn in this respect. You've survived this long, so perhaps your way is best, at least for you. Besides, I am here to guide you, not hold your hand and fight your battles."

"I don't get you, man."

He shrugged again, continuing his aerobics by candlelight. I couldn't tell if he was exercising or relaxing. Maybe both. "You don't have to understand my part in things, my friend. Just accept, and move on."

"So who's the asshole responsible?"

"Hard to say. It's a jungle you hunt in, and where you are hunted. Be careful."

"Thanks, but that doesn't really tell me much."

"The one responsible is very close, but hidden."

"Not you, right?"

He gave me an odd, slightly patronizing look. "You are very confused, my friend. My faith in you is beginning to diminish."

"Sorry to hear that, Zach. That really your name?"

"To you it is."

"May I call you Rutting Wolf?"

"Not unless you are Indian."

"What's with this Indian jazz, anyway? You don't look Indian to me."

He stopped his aerobics and stared at me, or through me. Not coldly, just objectively, as if addressing a student. "My soul is with my people at all times. I did not know who my natural parents were while growing up, but that does not matter. I was left alone in the desert, at an abandoned campsite, by whoever raised me until I was two years old, and then I was found by Indians and taken to a reservation in the desert, not far from the Joshua Tree, and my people cared for me like I was one of their own until I became one of their own. Then I was sent into the white man's world to find my natural parents, and when I did, I was disgusted. They were part of the disease ravaging our land, so I turned my backs on them after hurting them, but my own people, they said I was banished into the white man's world until I could pay penance for my sins, atone for hurting my parents, who after all did bring me into this world, and so I said I would uphold the law, not the white man's law, but the law of the land. This was, as the saying goes, many moons ago. And I am still paying for what I did, for my lack of honor."

I gulped. "What did you *do*, exactly, Zach, if I may ask?"

He seemed to be searching his internal landscape for the answer. Then he said, staring off into the mystery of space, the candlelight casting pale ghostly patterns on his entranced face, "I scalped them."

I felt sick. "You scalped your own *parents*?"

"I thought they deserved it."

"For what'?"

"For polluting the land, contributing to the *disease*." Then he hung his head in shame. "But now I realize that was *wrong*. I threw away my bowie knife, and now I fight with *these*." He held up his clenched fists. and the words "Karma" and "Destiny" shone in the candlelight. "A woman-friend of mine, whom I met long ago on a spiritual and sexual quest, introduced me to her philosophy, from the Indians of the Far East, took me to her place of worship, her ashram, and taught me the Law of Karma." He showed me his Karma knuckles. "And my chief had long ago taught me of the Law of Destiny." Then he showed me his Destiny knuckles. "I realized they were the same Law, and I decided I would be the upholder of this Law. This would be my *atonement*."

We were silent for a while. Why wasn't this guy in the movies? Oliver Stone would *love* him. Then I said, "Zach, that's a very touching story, really, but why me? How and where do *I* fit in? I mean, apparently you have no radio or TV. so how do you know there's an APB out for me? Where do you get your info? How do you even know there's a Mister Big pulling the strings?"

"There *always* is, my friend. But Mister Big is in truth Mister Small. He conceals his true nature with lies, pretending he is something he is not, abusing the public trust. And my ways of knowing are known to me only, my friend."

"Hm. Karma and Destiny. Funny, a girlfriend of mine used to be into that. Rose."

"Rose was her name?"

"Yeah, why?"

"That is strange. The name of the woman who taught me was also Rose."

My heart slammed into a brick wall and collapsed into a barely pulsating heap of meat. "You're kidding. Long dark hair? Face and figure like a Gil Elvgren pin-up?"

"I don't understand that reference, but yes. Very beautiful. She taught me much in the short time we were together. About the limitations of physical love, and the eternity of spiritual love. I still think of her often. Now I see her only in my dreams."

No, no, *no*. "Rose? You *sure*? How long ago was this?"

"A few years. I've lost track. She lived up North, she would not tell me where. I wanted to follow her, but she made me promise not to. It is strange both of our woman-friends have the same name, no? Karma."

I nodded and sighed. "And Destiny." I decided there was no way Zach could have plucked and fucked my Rose. Not *my* Rose. It was a big garden out there. It had to be a coincidence. It had to be because I *said* it had to be. Zach fit the profile—older, muscular, spiritual, psychotic—of someone Rose would be involved with almost to a tee, but how could it be I would continue running into her lovers? "You ever meet a girl from New Jersey named Dolly Duncan?" I asked abruptly.

He seemed taken aback by the non sequitur. "No, why?"

"Just checking. Anyway, Zach, I better hit the old jungle trail. You wouldn't happen to have any machetes on ya?"

"I told you—just *these.*" Again he showed me his fists. Then he tapped his temple and added, "And *this*. That's all you need, my friend."

"Well, a car would be nice. I left mine back at the club, remember?"

"Then I'll take you back to it. Let's go. You are right, a man needs his horse."

"*Porsche*. It's not a *horse*."

"I know what it is, my friend. Lighten up." He got up and

stood erect and stretched his joints. "You are welcome to sleep here tonight, little buddy. This may be the last bit of help I can offer you. I have much to do elsewhere. There are many people to save in this city. Everyday, someone new. I may not be able to come to your aid again."

"No offense, Zach, but I don't think I could fall asleep here. It feels like an Indian burial ground or something, haunted or something. But, hey, that's just me. I really appreciate you stepping in, but I can handle it from here. But if you *do* know anything about the particular Mister Big in question here. I wish you'd spill it."

He shrugged. "I don't know, my friend. All I know is, he is close, or else he would not be able to track you so easily. He is giving others orders to follow you, and I believe if he wanted you dead, you'd be dead. It's a game, my friend. It is *always* a game. A game in the jungle. You are the hunted. But if you begin hunting him, the tables will turn, and he will panic, and then he will reveal himself. That's how you gain advantage. Think of it as chess."

"I prefer the ol' poker analogy myself. But how can I turn the tables when he has all the cards?"

"Ask your friend."

"Who?"

"The one in the nightclub. The beautiful blond lady on stage."

"Oh. Judy? Hm. Yeah. Say, uh, you didn't happen to learn anything from her about anything, by any chance? I mean about Karma and Destiny?" My paranoia was having a field day.

"No. What a strange question. I have problems following your line of reasoning. You are very odd, my friend. But you have a good heart. Let's go. It's almost time for my meditation."

So Zach Karma and Destiny Rutting Wolf or whatever the hell his name was drove me back into town on the back of his cycle. I was holding my breath all the way. I didn't like being on the back on his cycle, it was uncomfortable for a variety of reasons. I didn't like clinging to a male body, plus he drove like a renegade tornado. It was after midnight when we got down to Sunset. There was no one around The Viper Room because the cops figured I wouldn't come back anywhere near there. Luckily, Tina's Porsche was still parked right where I'd left it.

I didn't know whether to hug Zach or what, so instead I just sort of socked him lightly on the shoulder as a gesture of gratitude. "Thanks, man, whatever your motives are."

He grinned. "That's okay, little buddy. I'll be around if I can, but don't count on it. I have lots of work to." Again the sweeping motion, the stare into the horizon. "All over. Just remember—it is a jungle, and you're the hunted, but in the jungle, anything can happen."

"Call me Mowgli," I said. "I'll keep that in mind." I didn't have the heart to tell him how lame his metaphors were, because he was too sincere about them. Besides, we can't all be creative.

Then he revved up his Harley, nodded at me grinning, and tore out of there, leaving me alone in the middle of the street, in the middle of the night, in the middle of a nightmare.

I felt a few raindrops, courtesy of Zach's pals the rain gods, and climbed into the Porsche. Henry Mancini's "Experiment in Terror" seemed to reverberate from out of the darkness. I got the hell out of there, drove into the Hollywood Hills, parked in the woods on a cliff overlooking the twinkling town, and fell asleep in the cramped car.

I had disturbing dreams of Indian ceremonies and pagan rituals with Velma dancing naked by a fire, surrounded by howling natives writhing with erotic fervor, and then I saw Zach having wild sex with Rose, and Velma joined them, and so did Tina, and Luke, and Tony Ray, and before long the ceremony had descended into a veritable orgy, presided over by Deacon Rivers of the New Church of Elvis. It was utter chaos, and there was nothing I could do to stop it. I was a paralyzed bystander. Then there was a massive thunderstorm that poured down on the wicked proceedings, and I suddenly awoke inside the Porsche, engulfed by a real thunderstorm that exploded around me like a war zone.

All in all, Zach hadn't really helped me at all, except to escape the cops, which was something, but that didn't answer the key questions: Who and where was Mister Big, and why was he orchestrating this maze of madness? Zach did tell me to ask Judy and I intended to, later that day at the address she had given me in Westwood. But first, I wanted to talk to Doc.

I called him collect from a payphone out in Studio City. He was just opening The Drive-Inn for business that day, and he was harried, but glad to hear from me. "You find Puss?" I asked him right off.

"No, man, but I'm on it. Hell with that, what's up with you, man? I've been watching the news and haven't heard nothin' up here."

"There's not a nationwide manhunt for me, Doc, relax." Or *was* there? Whatever. "Hey, guess who hailed me out of a spot?

416

Zachary Kane. Modern Day Bounty Hunter. Or whoever the hell he is."

"Yeah? He didn't try to pinch you, huh? I mean in the judicial sense."

I told Doc all about it, then said, "So I'm going to talk to Judy today. You talk to her?"

"Yeah, man, she called last night at my house, and I'd talked to Monica earlier in the day, to tell her no hard feelings and to apologize for goin' off on her. I told her I'd *fuck* her if it'd make us even, and she said maybe!"

"Doc, skip the soap opera crap. What did Judy say?"

"My dime, man. Anyway, Judy just said she's stayin' at a friend's apartment by UCLA, some chick she went to school with or somethin'. She's anxious to talk to you. There's somethin' she knows that may help you."

"Yeah, what?"

"She wouldn't tell me over the phone. Too scared. In fact, she sort of talked in code."

"In *code*?"

"Y'know, just called you 'our mutual friend' and shit like that, wouldn't say your name out loud, over the phone, like it might be tapped or some shit, talked about having a lead on where your cat was, but I knew what she really meant. Sort of. I think. Anyhow, it's all too weird for me, but I gotta say, I feel kinda bad for bailing out on you just for economic reasons. If you need me. just call, man. 'Course you do got Zachary Kane in your corner, so you're ahead of the game, far as I can see."

"Forget it, Doc. You posted bail, you didn't bail out on me, it's cool, man."

"If you say so. Hey, how was the show, by the way?"

"Show? Oh, great. I almost got nailed, though."

"Good thing Zach was there."

"Yeah. I wish I could figure his angle."

"Just lookin' out for you 'cause I can't."

"Something else—I think he met Rose and had an affair with her."

"Vic, now you're losing me. I hear the connection breaking up—static—*Hello?—Hello?*"

"Doc, c'mon, man. I'm serious."

"*Hello*? You're fading. Vic. Call me back when you're line is clear. I'll be here." *Click.*

I stood out in the rain, wondering whether it was worth going forward with this. With everything, including breathing. Zach's self-appointed crusade for justice sounded like an excuse to be a social outcast with a personal agenda, a vendetta against the status quo. Which is a perfectly honorable objective. I even relate to it, though my goals are somewhat less altruistic and selfless. I admit it. I also think disguising blatant individual non-conformity as a quest for widespread justice is bunk. I remain an independent operator because I don't want anyone telling me what to do and how to think, not because I want to save anybody else *per se*. People need to make up their own minds, save themselves. However, this latest misadventure was starting to obliterate my feeling of autonomy. It seemed no matter how privately I wanted to live, someone was looking over my shoulder, taking notes, creating a file, passing judgment, and casting me in their own megalomaniacal design, for their own selfish gain. What personal freedom did anyone have in this society these days? Maybe the rain knew, but either it wasn't talking, or I just had too much water in my ears to hear it.

Then I saw a homeless dude getting his dirty rags soaked as he pushed his shopping cart full of junk along the wet pavement. He was smiling as he mumbled to himself. When he passed me, I heard him grumble, "*there ain't no justice, there's just us.*" Amen, brother.

Of course, whenever you see someone worse off than you, it puts a different spin on things. That homeless guy was definitely worse off, as far as I could see. So was Tina Hartman, as far as I knew. And so was anyone with a fatal disease or handicap. But that was it. I felt the urge to upgrade my lifestyle. First, I had to ensure I retained a life to stylize. That entailed tracking down Velma, whether or not she was still alive herself.

I spent the rest of that morning coffee shop hopping between the Valley and Westwood, re-reading the fateful (or is that coincidental?) script, finally winding up on Glendon Avenue, at the address Judy had whispered to me. The rain was clearing up and the sun shone intermittently through the remaining clouds. I guess Zach had taken a break from rain dancing. I was glad. I was sick of that sinking, soggy feeling. Hopefully if the weather cleared up it would go away. If it didn't, I'd know it had been something else all along. Probably was, anyway.

I kept my shades on despite the cloudy conditions and turned up the collar of my undercoat, which, incidentally, still sported bloodstains from an encounter a few months prior in Philadelphia, the City of Brotherly Love. They wouldn't come out at the cleaners, and I figured, what the hell, they were like medals of valor. Doc said they just looked like I made a pig of myself eating a chocolate sundae. It's all a matter of perspective.

I rang the buzzer outside the locked lobby door and waited. The building was rather new and bland and very upscale. Obviously Judy's pal was well-to-do. Deep down I wanted to believe Judy was a proletariat heroine, but the fact that she had ever even considered marrying some asshole engineer from Santa Barbara ruined this perception. Judy liked affluence as much as the next pretty girl who could attract it. It was survival in the big city, or big jungle, according to Zach, Master of Metaphors. Jesus. Mister Big. The Asphalt Jungle. Make that *Asshole* Jungle. My life was even more clichéd than the noirish world capsulated on my B movie collection. I liked it that way. It was like things were finally catching up with me, rather than I had to catch up with them.

A sweetly familiar female voice answered the buzzer. I said it was "the guy looking for the cat" There was a pause, then I was buzzed into the spacious hallowed lobby. Judy must've recognized my voice if not the code. I went up in the elevator and then knocked on the appropriate apartment door, per Judy's instructions. I was apprehensive, I must say. It seems whenever I open a door someone on the other side is standing there with a surprise. Or the person them-self is a surprise. Think about it. It's a pattern. I'd be safer if I never opened any doors, just stayed in my room. But then I'd get bored. Had to chance it.

The door opened and there was—

My pals the Feds.

Damn it, they'd used Judy for bait. I said "*whoa!*" and took off running. They yelled for me to halt or they'd shoot, and when I didn't halt, they shot. I returned fire, ducking behind a cleaning lady's cart for cover. Pretty flimsy. I didn't hit anything but the wall, because I was afraid to tip my nose over the edge of the cart. I managed to fend them off until I reached the staircase though. I raced down the stairs, my heart pounding. It's that door thing, man. Never fails. The lady or the tiger? I always get the lady tiger.

I made it to the lobby and the coast looked clear. I ran out to my Porsche and there was yet another surprise, but not as big. It was Zach, leaning against his Harley.

"*Let's get outta here, they used Judy to trap me!*" I yelled at him. "Whaddya waiting for, you imbecile, divine intervention?

I'm not kidding, they got guns, man! *C'mon*!" But he didn't budge. I was ready to hop into my Porsche but then stopped. Zach wasn't even twitching. I ran over to him, panting. "Zach, they got guns, man, which Karma and Destiny are no match for, I promise you. We gotta get movin', *pronto*!"

He looked first at Karma, then at Destiny, then at me. Next thing I knew, Karma was in my face, Destiny in my gut, and Coincidence was nowhere in sight.

Chapter Twelve
THE SAD AND THE PITIFUL

When I opened my eyes, there was Velma Vale, standing over me, wearing a leopard skin halter-top, tight black Capri pants, and no shoes, but her toenails were painted bright red. I noticed this because I was in a prone position on the hardwood floor, so her sweet feet were the first things I saw. I vaguely noticed the pastel, mid-century modernism of the furniture and Googie architecture of the room around me. Then my eyes worked my way up her lovely body and to her wonderfully familiar face. For a second I thought I'd died and gone to pussy heaven. She looked beautiful, even sans makeup, though somewhat tired and disheveled. I thought I was either dead or dreaming until I heard Torn Jones singing "She's A Lady" from a stereo system close by. Remember, snappy tunes help me wake up to the real world and leave dreamland in the dust.

"Velma," I murmured. "Where the *hell*—?"

She bent down over me and stroked my face. "Hello, Vic. I'm so sorry you had to go through all this. I wish there was something I could do."

I bolted to a sitting position, startling her. "Where are we?" I repeated.

"Palm Springs. Can I get you something to drink? You look absolutely dehydrated."

"Wait a minute. Just wait." My jaw and gut ached, but other than that, I seemed to be all right. I staggered to a vertical stance, grabbing onto Velma for support. "How'd I get in fucking Palm Springs?" I noticed the room had no windows, only central air conditioning.

"Some man brought you here on a motorcycle."

"Zach?"

"He didn't say who he was. He said he was hired to bring you in, that he was a *bounty hunter*."

"But he was supposed to be on my side!"

"Well, I guess they made a better offer."

"Who?"

"I can't say. They might be listening."

"Mister Big?"

"*Who*?"

"Tina told me you'd been kidnapped and held prisoner by some lunatic she called Mister Big."

"Tina told you that?" Velma said in a panic, looking around as if someone might be watching.

"Yeah. Before she died."

"Tina's *dead*?"

"Yeah. For real. Poisoned."

Velma put her hand over her mouth. and tears welled in her big beautiful eyes. "Oh my *god*." She ran into an adjoining room, the bedroom, I assumed, and shut the door. Tom Jones was singing "Delilah."

I ran after her, banging on the door, which she'd locked. After a few moments of pleading she opened up. She lay on the bed, sobbing. "Velma, what the hell's going on here?"

"Vic, I'm so sorry. The man responsible—what did Tina tell you about him?"

"Just that his brother was a political bigwig and he had a lot of dough and, oh yeah, he was a silent partner in Big Productions."

"That's almost all true, except his brother isn't the big-shot. *He* is. That's why I can't say anything. He had the CIA on this, Vic! We're powerless!"

"Who the hell is he, Velma?"

"All I can say is he's Republican."

"*I* coulda told you that. At least that rules out the President. Is it a Federal official? A senator? Governor? What?"

She shook her head, still sobbing into the pillow. "I can't tell you, Vic. I'm afraid. My God, they killed *Tina*! Oh my *god*." She was inconsolable. I knew the feeling. "Yeah, and probably they'll pin that on me, and Luke Brandon, too."

"Luke's dead too?" she gasped, wide-eyed.

"No. Well, maybe. Somebody blasted him with my gun. Why me, Velma?"

"Because he knows all about you, your background, and you were the perfect patsy. I guess that's why. He's in the Government. Vic, he can access anything, anybody, anytime. We're *nothing*. Little people. They can manipulate anyone they want, and if you don't cooperate, or if you know too much about something—just look at Marilyn Monroe!"

"You think she was murdered?"

"*Yes*!"

"By Kennedy?"

"How do I know, I'm not Oliver Stone! *Any*one in the Government could do it. They have connections *everywhere*— foreign, Mob, CIA, FBI, you *name* it."

"Yeah, I got two Feds tailing me. Or did. But Zach brought me to you. Why? Why didn't he just take me to police headquarters?"

"I don't know. Vic. It's a game to these people. It's about control, and whomever they can't control, they destroy. Like me. Like *you*."

Brother. I was used to small potatoes, but this was major league. The Government vs. Vic Valentine. Not only did they know my vulnerable spots and my secrets, they knew just how to use them against me. My history with women, my weakness for pussy, my gullibility, my quest for independence, my need for freedom, my contempt for authority, covering up for Dolly Duncan, my Mob ties, everything was an open book to these people. I was no Private Eye. I was a Public Toilet, just like everyone else under the system. And everyone had a price. Even Karma and Destiny could be bought for the right amount. Nice world.

I noticed I'd been strip-searched and left nothing but my pants, with no underwear. My trench coat, my shades, my shirt, my wallet with my P.I. license, the .45, all gone. And I'd left the script in the Porsche. No use trying to escape at the moment—I knew we had to be securely locked in. Anyway, at least Velma could scratch a few of my itches while we waited for Mister Big to play his next card. "Velma, that screenplay, the one Tony Ray gave me, it was called 'Neon Knights'."

"What about it?" she said with a sniffle into the bedspread.

"You know what it's about, right'?"

"Of course. Tony gave it to you?"

"Yeah."

"How do you know Tony?"

"I don't, really. He saw me in a bar on Sunset and just gave it to me, out of the blue. Anyway, did you write it?"

"No."

"So who did?"

"I don't know. The Man, I guess."

"The Man? Mister Big?"

"Stop calling him that, it would only inflate his ego."

"So 'The Man,' or whoever the fuck he is, *he* wrote it?"

"Or had it commissioned. His idea, though, I believe."

"Hm. You say we're in Palm Springs?"

"Yes. I escaped once after The Man had come in here to have his way with me, and I called Tina down in the lobby and saw a newspaper stand. But then he woke up and called downstairs and they grabbed me and beat me and threw me back in here."

"What *is* this? A hotel?"

"Yup. He owns it."

"At least you got music. There a TV in here?"

"Yes, but they cut the cable and antenna. No radio, either, just albums and CDs. And there's a VCR. They just give me whatever movies and records I want. I just sit around watching movies, listening to music, then they bring me food, gourmet, anything I want, and The Man comes in once in a while to rape me at knifepoint, and says if I marry him, he'll free me, but if I don't, eventually he'll..." She made a cutthroat gesture with her hand.

"Did you know you're supposed to be dead?"

"Not until Tina told me. Then she told me you'd been set-up— oh, Vic, *how*? They frame you in San Francisco or what?"

"No, no. Your apartment. I came down to see you, after reading your note. I figured the man you were running away from was Tony Ray, but it wasn't, was it?" She shook her head. "Yea. The Man. Shit, why can't you give me his name? He from California at least?"

She shook her head again, then flinched. "Oops!"

"So he's from out of state. Or maybe just a high-level official, of national standing. *Hm*. So what if I know? He'll probably just hand me over to the cops any time now anyway."

"No. If Tina told you that much, he's afraid now you'll tell someone, and they might believe you. Not all the cops and agents are under his thumb. Just enough. But now you know too much."

"But why did Tony give me that script? That fits into the frame-up. Could Tony be in on it?"

"I doubt it. The Man *hated* Tony. Is Tony all right?"

"Last time I saw him. Except he thinks you're dead. He took it kinda hard. He in love with you?"

She nodded. "Yes."

"You in love with him?"

She shook her head. "No."

"You ever have an affair with Luke Brandon?"

"*No*! That *pig*! He tell you that?"

"Yeah. Tina said she slept with him just to get back at you."

"That may be so, Tina and I had our rivalry, but Luke lied. To *both* of you. She debased herself for nothing."

I just sat there. feeling dizzy. "There something to eat around here?"

"Oh, I'm sorry. I was going to get you something to drink, but when you told me about Tina. The icebox is kept fully stocked."

"By who?"

"His boys, who else?"

"He visit you often? The Man?"

"Whenever he wants to fuck."

"How often is that?"

"Sometimes once a day, sometimes ten."

"And he rapes you?"

"Petty much, yup."

"At knifepoint?"

She looked at me then showed me a scar on her neck, then another on her waist, then another on her arm before I told her to stop. I went into the kitchen, grabbed some random food items and a Coke, and came back and sat beside her on the bed.

"This is one sick motherfucker," I said with a mouth full of food. I was dehydrated and famished. "He can't be allowed to get away with this, no matter *who* he is."

"I *told* you, Vic. He has everything on his side—even the law. He's big, not the President, but close enough. And he's cold. And he's evil. And he's ugly. When he slobbers on me and sticks his thing in me my flesh crawls."

It made me sick just imagining it. "Tina said he produced your, y'know. *Early* films."

She looked at me, startled and embarrassed. "How'd you know about those?"

"I saw 'em, few days ago, in Hollywood."

"You're *kidding*? That bastard! He promised—well, that would be worthless, anyway. His word. He lies to the public all the time. Everything about him is a lie."

"Well, it seems no one is what they seem. Not even Zach. Or Doc, or Judy, maybe. Doc, my friend. you remember him from The Drive-Inn. He told me to go see my friend Judy for some info. So did Zach. And of course she was just bait. Maybe the Feds found her and forced her to lure me in, and Doc knew nothing about it, but it's best not to trust anyone. Anywhere. Any time."

"Vic, that's awful. You trust me, don't you?"

"Honestly? No."

"Vic, *please.* You're my only hope." Slowly, seductively, she began removing her halter-top.

"Now, Velma, what if he came in here and caught us?"

"Who cares? Vic, please, make love to me, like you did that night. I want to feel the skin of someone sincere, someone I can trust, and not some sick animal that just wants to possess me. *Please*, Vic. *Please.*"

As I stammered with weak resistance that didn't even convince me, Velma peeled off her Capri pants and was lying before me in all her glory. She sat up and began kissing me and smothering my face in her perfumed breasts, still the most perfect knockers in the Universe, and then she put her hands down my pants and stroked my boner, unzipping my pants and pulling them down my legs. I lay back whimpering as she took control, climbing on top of me, kissing me, her Amazonian body dominating my every impulse and desire. We made love for hours, just like that night. And this time, the sex had a different subtext, an urgency, a true tenderness. Again, I wore a rubber for Round One, which she supplied, but she only had one, and we did it more than once, so it was a pretty weak attempt at "safe sex." It broke, anyway. I didn't care. In any case, it was a magical encore, and soon I forgot that anyone could walk in at any time and catch us and kill us on the spot, erase us like spots, make it look like we'd never existed.

Suddenly, as we were lost in the throes of erotic bliss, I sensed a presence, and glanced over to see that someone had been watching us from the bedroom doorway, for who knew how long. In shock I screamed and scared the hell out of Velma. The voyeuristic interloper ran out of the apartment and locked the door behind him. I just stood there in the buff, looking at the locked door, wondering if it had indeed been The Man, spying on us, maybe jerking off, sick bastard. I hated him with a purple passion, whoever he was. If nothing else, he was a politician. The pervert shit just came with the territory.

I went back into the bedroom, where Velma was kneeling on the bed, the covers around her breasts and torso, her hair tousled, her face puffy with passion.

"What was it?"

"Someone was watching us," I said.

"*Oh* my god."

"You think it was him?"

"No, he'd have said something. Probably a lackey, going back to report right now. Oh, Vic, what are we going to do? He'll *kill* us."

"Maybe not. Maybe he wanted this to happen. Why else would he have locked us up together? He must know we spent a night together in San Francisco, right? And what else would we do in a hotel room with no cable TV? Relax, lover doll. I'll handle the creep." I talked cool, but inside, I was oatmeal. Tom Jones was singing "I'll Never Fall in Love Again," and I echoed the sentiment. I held Velma in my arms as I asked, "Velma, tell me. When did he bring you here? How long ago?"

"As soon as I stepped off the plane from San Francisco," she explained. "He had some men waiting for me who forced me into a black limo that had tinted windows so I couldn't see out, and it was soundproof, because no one heard me screaming, then they drugged me and knocked me out and I woke up here. I haven't been out except for that one time I called Tina. She knows what a maniac he is, even though she gave him blowjobs to keep him satisfied. Tina wanted a career more than anything. She wanted to star in this movie, took it away from me. But The Man said he'd give it to me and lots more if I married him. I said no way, I won't be a star because of blackmail, I want to make it on my own, so he withheld financing, trying to change my mind, making promises to Tina he'd never keep, because then he'd lose a bargaining chip trying to win me over."

"Tony and Luke said the problem was there was no money to make the fuckin' flick."

"You kiddin'? The Man is *loaded*. He could bankroll an *epic*. But he didn't want to be directly associated with the movie, so even the porn things, he produced them under an alias. He's very sneaky, very perverted, very *sick*. I just don't think I'll get away from him ever. Not alive. And he must think Tina told you something, and if he thinks you know his identity, he'll kill you too, won't wait for the gas chamber to shut you up."

"Maybe we could cut a deal."

"Like what? What do you have he could want? He has everything. Well, except *me*."

"This is like one of your movies. You realize that? I feel like I'm trapped in one of your movies, Velma."

"You sound like you almost like it."

"I *do*. Almost. We'll see how it ends. In your movies, you always come out ahead."

"This is *not* one of my movies, Vic. Try to keep that in mind."

"Yeah, you're right. But I can't help thinking if I treated this as if it were a movie, I'd figure out what to do. The way it's unfolding, it's like it was pre-scripted, like 'Neon Knights.' If I could just second-guess the next scene, I could beat The Man at his own game. Maybe he thinks of this as a movie, too, Velma. Ever think of that? And we're his pawns, his actors, and he's directing his own script."

"So what can we do then'? Can't just walk off the set."

"No, but we can ad-lib."

"He'll just make us do it over till we get it right, stick to the script."

"Fuck the script, and fuck him."

Velma seemed to be getting uncomfortable for some reason, more so than before. "Vic, be careful with these people. They're dangerous, they don't care about *anything*."

"You said it's a game to them."

"It *is*! But the stakes are our lives. and they could care less if we lose. They got it rigged so we lose anyway. no matter what. It's a game they automatically win."

"Then that ain't no game. There's something goin' on you're not telling me, Velma."

"What, what do you mean'? I told you everything I know. Vic, I swear!"

"Yeah, maybe so. Then there's somethin' goin' on you don't know about, either."

"You could say that about anybody anywhere. There's always something going on you don't know about."

"C'mon. Velma. Get real. This whole thing, it's too phony. The script was the tip-off, and it was meant to tip me off that this is just a *movie*."

"Then why can't we leave?" she shrieked.

"We can. I'll show you."

I took her by the hand, led her naked to the door, and tried to open it. Locked. I kicked it and beat it and pounded on it as she stood watching. Then I said, "Okay. So we can't leave. But that doesn't disprove my theory."

Exasperated. Velma went into the bedroom and put on a silk pale blue robe and slippers. She looked like Mamie Van Doren at home. Then she went into the kitchen and made something to eat, silently. I went over to the VCR and scanned the movie titles: *Dragstrip Girl, Reform School Girl, Sorority Girl, Hot Rod Girl, Beat Girl, Girls Town*. Then way underneath, beneath the stack of '50s J.D. drive-in flicks with "girl" in the title, there was a

428

videotape with a handwritten label that said "Neon Knights."

I grabbed it, pulled it out of the box, and popped it into the VCR.

"What are you doing?" Velma called from the kitchen.

"Watching a movie. Come join me."

Velma came in with her dinner and sat beside me on the floor in front of the big screen TV. She looked at the pile of J.D. flicks and remarked, "Hey, where did all those come from? I didn't notice them before. There's some great stuff here, which one did you put in?"

"It's a surprise." I said. Then the images began to flow in a crudely edited but very effective montage of extremely vivid sequences:

First, there was an aerial ceiling shot of Velma and me romping in bed. *My* bed, in San Francisco. This went on for a few minutes, and I hated how out of shape I looked, though I did have a cute butt. Nice technique, too. One of Velma's orgasms was captured for posterity—with me as the perpetrator. *That* I liked. I just didn't realize there was a hidden camera in my bedroom, and that disturbed me. But this was merely the pre-credit sequence. The title sequence itself was brief, with slow sexy sax music over a black background and white letters that read: *Neon Knights* starring Vic Valentine, Velma Vale, Tina Hartman, Tony Ray, Luke Brandon, Rutting Wolf, and special surprise guest stars produced, written, and directed by "???".

I didn't even look at Velma. I didn't even want to blink for fear I'd miss something. For the first time in my life, I was a movie star. Maybe I'd been one longer than I realized. The next scene was of Velma being kidnapped at the airport. It only went on for a few seconds and was very jerky. I hate the hand held camera technique, too sloppy, draws too much attention to the camera and away from the action. Next were a few more jumpy shots of me being tossed into a police car outside Velma's Hollywood Hills tenement. The sound was garbled. This was obviously a rough cut. Next was a shot of me sleeping in my cell, dreaming of paradise, found and lost. Then came a few shots of Velma being mauled by her benefactor, only his face and body were obscured, like they do with hidden witnesses on TV, or crime suspects on that show *Cops*. She didn't look too unhappy. In fact, she seemed to be enjoying it. Maybe it was just an act. Did she know she was on film? I'd think about it later. Next was a real long shot of Tony Ray giving me the script in The Tiki Room, taken with a zoom lens from across the street or something, through the window. It was very brief. Then there was another long shot of the Feds approaching Doc and me at Tony Ray's house in Malibu. Doe's cameo had gone unaccredited. Then there was a series of shots of Doc and me around town, in front of The Pussycat Theater, outside The Burgundy Room, then the motel in Santa Monica.

Next came the most startling shot yet: a very, very quick close up of Luke Brandon opening a door, a look of shock on his face, then the sickening sounds of two gunshots. Afterwards the camera tilted around and shut off. I played that scene back a few times. The camera had been real tight on Luke, so there was no way to see who was doing the shooting, either from the camera or the gun. I still refused to look at Velma for her reaction. I wanted to go on, to the end. I was hooked. This was a hit. In more ways than one.

Next came more shots of me talking to Doc outside the hotel, hugging, him going off in his cab. All of these seemed to be taken from one of the motel rooms, through the window. Then came another surprise: A direct shot, from inside the wall, apparently, of Tina and I making love. As usual the dialogue was garbled, but the riveting action spoke for itself. I could sense Velma' tension, but ignored it.

After that came the chase. What got me was that it seemed to have been filmed by the person or people chasing us. The Feds? The chase scene cut off after I lost them on PCH. Or *thought* I lost them.

The next scene was of me waking up next to Tina and finding her dead. The camera must have been hidden somewhere amid the mess of her room, and ran all night. This video had been edited from all the others. This scene was horrific and depressing, but I heard no response from Velma. I could tell she was into it, though.

Then there were various long shots of me driving around in the Porsche, some apparently taken from the air. There was even a shot of Zach stopping me on his cycle, but it was brief and too far away to hear anything. The filmmakers obviously were graduates of the Roger Corman Let's Just Shoot the Damn Scene and Move On School.

There was a very dark sequence inside The Viper Room, with The Naughty Ones in the background, and then a cut to The She Beams and me running on stage. It was hard to tell what was going on in the murkiness but since I had been there that was okay, though a general audience might disapprove of the lack of clarity and continuity. Then came one of my favorite scenes, next to the sex: the shootout with the cons outside the club. If you could call it that. There was just a grainy shot of me driving away on Zach's bike, firing aimlessly into the air. Actually it looked even more fake than a real movie, but what the hell, they didn't give me any retakes.

There were no scenes of Zach and me in his Indian shack, but they did capture him dropping me off back at the Porsche. Then the movie jumped abruptly from night to day as the camera caught me running out of the Westwood high-rise where Judy was staying, then there was a shot from across the street of Zach knocking me cold. That part was humiliating.

Then the screen went black and a title card read: *To Be Continued...*

Finally I looked over at Velma. She tried hard not to laugh. But she did anyway.

"I don't think this was meant as a comedy," I said flatly.

Tears formed in her eyes, either from amusement or terror, it was hard to tell. "Vic, it's just so amazing. It really is a *movie*. This is so *crazy*."

"And you had no idea."

"*No*! Vic, I *mean* it! I just don't believe it! They must have left this tape for us before they left just now."

"But *why*?"

There came a sound from the door. Keys jangling, the lock tumbling. Someone was coming in. I grabbed Velma and the tape and ran over to the door, wearing only my pants. I stood behind it with Velma and when the intruder entered, I cold-cocked him. It was just a kid dressed as a bellboy.

"That ain't Mister Big," I said. The door was wide open, and no one else was in sight.

"No, it's his son."

I noticed the kid had been carrying a .45. *My* .45. I picked it up out of his limp hand as he rolled on the floor, moaning. I'd hit him as hard as I could in the back of the head, and then his face. He was only about twenty, but healthy. Good thing I'd had the jump on him. "C'mon, let's leave during intermission, this movie sucks," I said, handing her the tape, then leading her out into the hallway, the .45 in one hand, the babe in the other. If only I had a shirt and shoes. Some *schmuck* was going into his room and at gunpoint I ordered him to remove his shirt and shoes and then I put them on after he locked himself in his room. The dude was obviously a hot shot, and his clothes felt good on me, though a little loose. Velma seemed dazed, clutching onto the video, but silently cooperated. Just how I like 'em. We went down an elevator to the lobby, and I kept the .45 out of sight until we made it outside into the cool, dry desert air.

Chapter Thirteen
DROP DEAD, GORGEOUS

Velma and I decided to skip the tour and went directly to the bus depot, which happened to be nearby. No guys in designer suits appeared to be following us so far, but something told me the cameras were rolling somewhere. I didn't feel like a star, however. I felt more like an insect under glass in a lab. My privacy had been rudely invaded, the sanctity of my personal life seriously violated. But at least I had that tape, which proved at least one thing: there really *was* a high level conspiracy against me, and my life really *was* a movie, both long-held theories of mine. I couldn't wait to play it for Doc back at The Drive-Inn, proving once and for all that my longtime suspicions were correct, and that I wasn't simply being paranoid. Doc could even dub it. It'd make a hot rental item. If I made it that far. Hopefully I wouldn't be posthumously glorified, my dramatic on-camera assassination providing the perfect pathos for the finale. But that would be rather anti-climactic, even in cinematic terms. I still had a chance to change that ending, make it a happy one. Audiences like happy endings. I owed it to them, as well as to me.

The next bus for L.A. was leaving in twenty minutes, the next bus for San Francisco in five. I wanted to be on the latter, but Velma panicked, said I couldn't leave her for the wolves. Not only that, but she was the one with the cash—just enough for two tickets, it turned out. She'd rolled The Man during one of his little visits.

"I got the money. I say where we're going," she said firmly.

"But why L.A?"

"Because. I want to go with you to the police station, just walk in and freak them out, and scream at the top of my lungs what that bastard did to me. I'll just stand in the middle of the station and scream my head off, and then the guys under his thumb won't be able to shut me up. Someone not involved will hear me and listen. We'll go right to the President if we have to!"

"You really think that'll be enough, our word against his?"

"No—we have that tape, too, remember."

"But who's to say who shot it?"

"I don't know, Vic! What do you suggest?"

I had to admit. I had no better ideas. "But if this guy really has the FBI and CIA running interference for him, nothing we say or do can bring him clown. Shit. Velma—he *is* the damn law! He *is* the damn justice system.

"But we have the tape. That must prove something to someone."

"If it would—why would they leave it for us, and let us escape?"

"They didn't *let* us, you *made* it happen. You're my hero."

"Velma, they sent some kid up with my gun, which they knew I could take away from him, and then we just waltzed out of the hotel. No goons in the lobby, nobody to stop us. C'mon. They're still playing with us."

"So what, then? What do we do? According to you, no matter what we do, they're still calling the shots."

I could hear "Experiment in Terror" in my head again. Long before our pals with the camcorder showed up, my life had been a movie, replete with soundtrack. That's just how I looked at it, as one long B movie. Somehow it wasn't as painful that way. But someone had taken this concept way too literally, and they were taking control of my living movie to boot. It was bad enough that Karma and Destiny had their say in things without some bozo on a power trip pulling on the strings as well. No one could tell me what to do. That had been the credo I'd always lived by. No one. No one on this Earth, anyway. I just hoped Karma and Destiny would pull rank on them, and I don't mean in the form of Zach's traitorous knuckles, either.

Velma and I got on the bus for L.A., arriving around midnight, broke but not broken. Not yet, boss. Cool Hand Luke. *Ces't moi.* No, no, stop with the movie reference, I kept telling myself. At least for now. That only added to the unreality of the situation. I had to come out of my cinematic trance until I could put things in proper perspective again. What we had here was a failure to communicate. No! Stop it! If I only could. How do you reverse a lifelong trend overnight? You just *do*, that's all. You just do when you have to, and I definitely had to.

Inside the bus station was a box for donating clothes to the Salvation Army. Rather than donate, we stole two dirty coats, full of holes, but free.

Velma was sleepy and wanted to rest, but where? We had no money. We were homeless. And then the drizzle turned into a downpour. I thought of all the times I'd passed homeless people sleeping on the sidewalk in a storm, huddled under makeshift blankets, shivering in the cold as I hurried back to my cozy warm abode, and I figured, this was my comeuppance for not helping them out, though I doubt Doc would have appreciated my turning his tenement into a homeless shelter. Although, in effect, it was— but only for me. And Puss, who was homeless all over again. Wherever he was. I tried hard not to think of my poor little dickless baby out in the freezing dark urban wilderness of San Francisco, alone, howling for his daddy to come rescue him. No, no. I couldn't think about Puss now. I'd just abandon Velma and go back home and find him. One pussy in peril at a time was all I could handle.

So Velma and I just walked the streets of downtown L.A. in the rain in the middle of the night, continuing until almost dawn, looking in vain for a police station, afraid to flag down a squad car for fear it might be one of the Man's minions on patrol. Velma kept the video tucked inside her cleavage, covering it with her coat. Finally we sat down on benches at a bus stop and cuddled together, trying to stay warm and alert despite our chilling wetness. We fell asleep in each other's arms. It must have made a touching scene.

When I opened my eyes, the sun was shining except for two shadows eclipsing some rays. It was Fed One and Fed Two, and I was too tired to run anymore. I gently nudged Velma awake. She didn't even say anything, much less struggle. She just nodded stoically and stood up with me.

"Take us in already," I said. "Me and my murder victim here, or don't you recognize her? Looks pretty good for a cadaver, wouldn't you say? She can walk and talk, too."

They just smugly smirked and led us into their waiting sedan at gunpoint. Taking us to The Man, I figured. Whatever.

"Surprised you didn't hire Rutting Wolf to track us down again," I said from the backseat through the bulletproof shield.

Fed One was driving. Fed Two turned around to me and said, "Who?"

"Zach. The bounty hunter. Raised by Indians."

"That guy wasn't raised by Indians, Valentine. He was raised by the State. Been in and out of psycho wards all his life. His parents were murdered by drug dealers who had the wrong address when he was a kid, and he never got over it, feels responsible somehow. So he found a way to make a living and get revenge at the same time, concocting this whole fabrication about his background to add to his personal myth. But he always gets his man if the price is right, so we use him from time to time. Luckily for us he was already following you. But don't place any value on anything he tells you. Raised by Indians. Last week it was wolves. You social outcasts have such vivid imaginations."

"So does your boss."

Fed Two didn't bite that bait, just turned back around and faced frontward. Velma put her head on my shoulder and sighed.

"I guess this is the end of the movie," she said sadly. "My last one. And you were in it, Vic. My leading man."

I couldn't help but grin at the irony, which was better than having irony grinning at me for a change. What a way to go.

I looked down Velma's cleavage at the tape. It looked like it had weathered the storm better than we had, but I wondered what good it would do us wherever we were going.

They drove us into Beverly Hills and then Bel Air, up the winding tree-lined streets past the gaudy mansions of movie stars and moguls. They went up one secluded driveway and through a private security gate, then stopped before a colorful Tudor style home with a fairyland fountain and bountiful flower garden in front of it. The Feds got out first, opened the door for us, their guns drawn needlessly, and led us up to the door, which opened as soon as we hit the front stoop. We were expected.

There was a small reception area and then a living room, both lushly decorated and furnished with expensive brand names I didn't recognize. It was a showpiece kind of joint, the kind most people would consider a dream house, but to me, it was just another ostentatious example of how lopsided our society is, and how warped its values are. The spoils go to the spoiled, the rest wait out in the gutter. This was the kind of joint often featured on *Lifestyles of the Rich and Famous*. I was more familiar and comfortable with Lifestyles of the Poor and Anonymous. Most people would not agree with me—just how I liked it—but as far as I was concerned, it was merely a massive study in neat, shiny dullness, wealthy American style. I noticed Velma' eyes were wide open with awe, however. I wish mine had been.

No sooner had we entered the bright living room than the Feds grabbed me and relieved me of the .45. I was wondering when they'd get around to that. Next Fed One pressed the muzzle of his piece to Velma's head while the other ripped open her ratty coat, then her blouse, then her bra, and the videotape fell into his hands.

He grinned lustfully at her exposed breasts, and she slapped him. I followed that up with a punch to his abdomen and was rewarded with swift retaliation from both of the Feds, who began pistol-whipping me into submission as Velma screamed.

"*That's enough!*" boomed a voice that emanated from nowhere and everywhere at once. Apparently it was from an omniscient observer with a hidden camera and an intercom at his disposal.

Mister Big. The Man. The Asshole of the Jungle.

"Sit them down," said The Voice. God, it was just like Blofeld of SPECTRE ordering his goons to restrain James Bond and his latest lady companion, won over from their side to his via Bond's usual persuasively amorous methods. The Feds held guns on Velma and me as they led us further into the main room and onto on of the several soft sofas. Then a wall painting that was probably very famous in Europe slid open like a panel and revealed a viewing screen. The lights went down, and then the screen legend said: NEON KNIGHTS Part Two. Naturally.

The video picked up right where the one they'd just confiscated left off. There were shots within the Palm Springs hideaway of Velma and me talking, then making love, then escaping, then running outside of the hotel, then waiting at the bus station. Then there was a quick jump to L.A., Velma and me getting off the bus, scrounging around the Salvation Army box for coats, then a series of fuzzy images of us wandering around in the night rain. Next was an awkward segue to the present. We were being filmed watching the film, as the screen revealed, the images being recorded and projected simultaneously.

Then the screen went abruptly blank, the lights went up, and The Voice said: "That's nearly the end of my movie, Mister Valentine. This is my first screening of it, too, with some of the cast attending the premiere. How do you like it?"

I stood up while everyone, including Velma, remained seated. "*What's this all about?*" I shouted, pacing, looking around in vain for the source of the Voice. "*What kind of sick perverted bastard are you? Why the hell are you doing this?*"

There was an audible pause permeating the room, then The Voice replied, "Because I *can*, Mister Valentine. Because I can. I like movies. I wanted to make my own, but I wanted to try an unusual experiment I thought of one day on the golf course." As The Voice went on I tried placing it and recording it in my mind, but it sounded like your basic overeducated hick, from the

California Delta or the Bible Belt or the Midwest. All of those redneck politicos sound the same to me, partly because I never pay much attention to them. The Voice continued, "Why not do a dry run, a *real* movie, like one of those real life police or rescue or highway patrol programs so popular nowadays? It seems real life is giving the movies and television a run for their money! So after I commissioned this screenplay I told Tony Ray to give you—Tony knows he either takes orders or both he and his career are dead—after it was written by some friends of mine in the motion picture community, I decided to have a little fun, experiment. I made some calls and greased some palms, you know how it is in with your profession, Mister Valentine, and I elected you to be the star of my new real live movie. The background info I assembled on you over the past year or so was incredible! You were the perfect candidate! I had Velma befriend Luke Brandon—who will recover, but probably won't ever make another sculpture, thank the Lord—I had Velma befriend him, and then I weaved my little web from there. My contacts told me you were a movie buff yourself, were obsessed with Velma, fancied yourself an outsider which made you expendable should something go wrong, were easily lured by sex into any trap, even let your girlfriend go free after finding out she murdered your own father, who was a police officer! A dirty one, granted, but still and all, Mister Valentine, your own flesh and blood and an officer of the law! You are one fool for love, Mister Valentine, to put it politely."

"*Hey, fuck you, whoever you are!*" I yelled. "*Who do you think you are—God?*"

"As far as you're concerned, I may as well be. You see, Mister Valentine, God is making a movie right now, with *all* of us. The Universe is his set. I learned that a long time ago. But we can choose our own roles, up to a point. I decided early on I'd use my wealth and influence to ensure I remained at the head of the cast. I didn't want to waste away as a bit player in a thankless role like the majority of you poor nobodies."

"*Hey! I got your big part right here! A leading roll!*"

"Your crude language only reveals your crass nature and meager origins, Mister Valentine. Anyway, my experiment is practically complete, though I'm not sure how to end it. Any suggestions?"

"How about I rip your head off and piss down your neck!"

"Hmmm, no, no, too graphic. Besides, I'm the director here, not an actor."

"Hitchcock always did a cameo. I'll do it while you're walking through the frame, real quick. It'll be great."

"I'm afraid that won't do, Mister Valentine. It's *my* movie, and I have the final cut."

"What do you think you're going to do with this fuckin' thing, anyway? Sell it?"

"No. Play it at parties. Just for laughs. I also wanted to show Velma just how powerful a producer I can be, how I can make people do what I want, anybody, so that eventually she'll come around and marry me, be the star of my life. But I'm afraid you make for a boring hero, Mister Valentine. No surprises. You haven't helped me very much in learning about the moviemaking process, but you have a certain presence, which comes across rather nicely. There may be hope for you yet."

"What about Tina? Any hope for her?"

Another pregnant pause. I looked at Velma, who was staring down at the floor, her head bowed in shame. She'd known what was going on all along, at least to a certain extent. She helped pick me out and set me up. Maybe she had no choice, maybe she hadn't known it would go this far, maybe she didn't know she'd wind up a prisoner once she'd lured me into the web, and maybe her life had been at stake, but still, I felt I couldn't trust her anymore.

"Well?" I repeated. "I'm waitin'. And I don't think God likes people stealing his thunder. He has a big show biz ego that way, I've heard, so you should be careful about stealing His scenes and second guessing His plot-lines."

"Tina talked too much," The Voice replied matter-of-factly. "I warned her not to. She knows all about me. I made an example of Luke, who also had a big mouth and was asking too many questions from the wrong people, but she still didn't take me seriously. Besides, she was a terrible actress. She won't be missed. But her death did make a very effective scene for my little project, probably her finest work ever. It'll make some interesting cocktail party discussions. Philosophical and all that. But you needn't worry about her now, Mister Valentine. You're in the clear. It's over now. The police are no longer looking for you. Velma's so-called murder was never reported. The APB will be quickly forgotten by anyone who happened to see it, because fugitives are a dime a dozen these days. It was all just a game of chess, Mister Valentine—and you were just a pawn. But isn't that life? My people didn't know exactly what was going on, but they didn't have to. Just like we as God's people don't really know what's going on, we just go through the motions, hoping it'll come out right in the editing room. That's how I was with my people. I took His lead. It's like when a filmmaker only gives his actors the parts of the script that pertain to them. Everyone memorized their own scenes and didn't ask about the big picture. This goes on all the time, Mister Valentine. It's real life. I just play my part like everyone else. I'm not omnipotent, quite, but my part just happens to be bigger than yours."

"That's not what Velma told me, shrimp dick."

"Your childish insults don't faze me, Mister Valentine. Now, what about that ending?"

I let out a sigh, paced like I was in deep contemplation, which I was, then suddenly I lunged for the .45 on the coffee table and stuck it in Velma' throat. The Feds were already standing with their guns drawn, aimed at my head, but that didn't matter. One fact remained in my favor: This wacko was obviously obsessed with Velma, and didn't want to lose her. It was a bold move, maybe even stupid, but it was the only hand I had left to play, so I played it.

"What do you think you're doing now, Mister Valentine?" The Voice said nonchalantly, seemingly unmoved by my move.

"I'll exchange Velma for those tapes. The originals."

The Voice chuckled. The Feds just kept their guns on me, intensely. Velma didn't say a word, just breathed heavily, her exposed bosoms going up and down as she inhaled and exhaled. But this time it didn't distract me. I'd lost interest in her as anything but a bargaining chip. I was disgusted with everyone in that room, even myself for falling into such an insane ploy that cost at least one poor innocent person her life. For absolutely nothing. I was the star of a snuff film, and I wanted it destroyed at any cost. I didn't want this psycho showing it at any cocktail parties. He didn't deserve the smug satisfaction.

Finally the Voice said, "Mister Valentine, I tipped you off early in the game with that screenplay. You're a detective, remember? Or so my sources informed me. Not a very good one, but then I didn't want my project to backfire on me. I needed someone gullible but not stupid. But I'm afraid you're just that, Mister Valentine. Stupid. Now put that gun down, or *else.*"

I suddenly aimed at the video of Part One on the coffee table next to where the .45 had been and blasted it to bits. Before the Feds could respond I had the gun back at Velma's throat.

"*Hold your fire!*" The Voice called out desperately, letting me know I owned the moment. "Mister Valentine, you're out of control. Please settle *down*."

"What's the matter? Don't you like my ending? I think it's a goddamn *winner*!" My eyes darted around the room and then I pinpointed the source of the projector twinkling out of a painting on the opposite wall. I aimed for that and blasted it to bits before the Feds could or would fire back.

"Next time he does that—*kill him*!" said The Voice. But I'd made my point.

"Then she gets it first!" I yelled.

"What do I care?" said the disembodied Voice. "She's a *whore*. I let you do a love scene with her, didn't I? Of course, that does turn me on, watching my whore get it on with other men, and women, like Tina—yes, dear, that is on tape—and I feel it enhances my feelings for her, in some odd way. I suppose some people may find that slightly strange."

"*My God, I hate you*!" Velma screamed, startling all of us. "Just run, Vic! Kill me, I want to die! Then you *run*!"

What happened next is like a murky, fuzzy rough cut in my head, badly choreographed and edited with poor sound, but basically, it went like this:

Velma grabbed the gun from me, shot one of the Feds in the face, so he was out of commission right away. Then the other one reflexively shot her in the shoulder, ignoring orders, and she fired back and hit him in the chest, so what we had was two dead Feds and one wounded angel. I took the gun from her and she fainted. The Voice was oddly silent, as far as I could remember, though perhaps his words were drowned out by the screaming and the gunfire. Then I took the gun from Velma's feeble grasp, and she brought my face down to hers and kissed me lightly on the lips, whispering, "I'm sorry." Then she said in a louder tone, broken and obviously in pain, "Listen to me. Not you, Vic. *You.* The Man. I promise I will marry you, on the condition you give Vic the tapes. *All* of them. And you let him go and never bother him again. Then I'm all yours. I promise." She coughed up a little blood during that spiel, but her vital signs appeared to be working so far. She would need medical attention soon, though.

"You can't do this," I whispered to her, cradling her head in my lap, gently massaging her face and neck. Blood leaked on the expensive carpet and on my lap. I wondered if she were making a deal she wouldn't live to fulfill. "You can't sell yourself to this maniac like that."

"He'll make me a star with his connections. That's all I've ever wanted. And I'll know he'll never hurt you. It's the only way, Vic. Otherwise, we're both dead. You *know* it." She pulled my head down and whispered in my ear, "Anyway, there's no reason we couldn't rendezvous now and then. Think of it as payback, giving The Man's wife the best sex she ever had!"

"It's a deal," The Voice said triumphantly. "Mister Valentine, if you'll wait in the parlor, I'll phone for some medical aid for my fiancée and then my servant will be down with the film."

"*All* of it, or no dice," Velma hissed.

"Agreed. My love. Oh, and Mister Valentine?"

"Yeah, what, fuckface?"

"You haven't even seen my face, Mister Valentine."

"Call it a hunch."

"If you intend on coming back to this home and ambushing me in my sleep, don't. For one thing, it isn't my home. For another, if I ever find out you've told anyone that matters about this, I'll divorce Velma and have you killed. Even your friends in the Mafia wouldn't be able to help you."

"I don't even know who you are, man, so relax." For a few seconds I considered doing a check of the house with my .45, but decided it would be a waste of time. For all I knew, he wasn't even on the premises, but was pulling strings by remote control.

The Voice was still worried, however. "But one day, should Velma become the First Lady, you will know. Just keep in mind that you are an ant, Valentine, and I am an elephant."

"Yeah, Tina told me you were Republican, but even though I never vote anyway, there's no chance I'd ever vote for you even if I *did*, even by accident. I'd know your kind anywhere. I can smell you a mile away."

"It's a good thing I'm not staking my political fortunes on you then, isn't it?"

"The First Lady is bleeding to death, Mister President. Cut the chitchat and get her some help. I'll wait with her till it arrives."

"No, please go, Vic," Velma said, touching my face. "I'll mail the video to you or something. I want you to have the scenes of us making love. I'll make copies of those scenes myself, and watch them and think of you. Okay? And one more thing." She hugged my face close to hers now. "One of these days, I'll give that bastard the kiss of death, long before he ever gets the chance to run for President. I'll hump him till he has a heart attack. And I'll think of you as I'm doing it. I promise you this. Now, Please,

Vic. Please *go*."

I kissed her once more and said, "See you in the movies, sweetheart." Then I stood up, pocketed the .45, raised my right middle finger high in the air, made several complete circles as I stepped over the dead Feds, keeping the finger visibly extended so The Man wouldn't miss it, blew Velma one last kiss, and walked outside.

I walked all the way down into downtown Beverly Hills before I realized I had no money to eat or call a cab so I could pick up my Corvair. But then who should show up as I was trudging down Beverly Drive but my old pal Zach the bounty hunter, a.k.a. Rutting Wolf.

"Need a lift somewhere, buddy boy?" he asked affably.

"Your boss send you?" I said, still walking as he glided beside me on the cycle.

"I'm sorry for knocking you cold, friend. Couldn't be avoided."

"Hey, what the hell happened to all that talk about fighting the great white enemy and atoning and all that crap? By the way, I got the skinny on you—you weren't raised by Indians. Or wolves. You're an orphan with an attitude and a warped imagination."

"I blow with the breeze, my friend," he said.

"Blow *this*. Friend." I kept walking, and he kept following me, obviously feeling guilt-ridden and hypocritical.

"Look, little buddy, it's like this: I am a catalyst in the destiny of other people. That is my function. I have adopted the ways of my Indian brothers, and my wolf friends, so in my heart, I am one with them. And do not lie. We all create our own myths, my friend. You have decided you are Sam Spade, am I wrong?" I gave him a look and he went on. "I took you to Velma not because they paid me to, and paid me well, as well as threatened to kill me if I did not comply, but I did it because I knew you were the only one who could save her."

"But I didn't. She belongs to *him* now."

"On her terms, though. Yes, I talked to her. I was waiting outside, and when you left without her, I went in to see what had happened, and she told me. She wants me to give you a lift to wherever you want to go. And she also wanted me to give you *this*."

I stopped walking. Zach opened a pouch behind his seat and removed a large manila envelope. I took it and opened it. Inside were two cassettes, both marked "Neon Knights—original," a note that read, "Copies destroyed," and a C-note that had a lipstick imprint on it. I pocketed the C-note and said, "This will cover lunch and cab fare, so I don't need you, Rutting Wolf. Or whoever the hell you are. Just tell me one thing, man—are you or are you not Zachary Kane, Modern Day Bounty Hunter?"

He grinned as he said, "It's your movie, kid, whatever you say," then he sped off and disappeared out of frame.

I walked further into downtown Beverly Hills and ate at the Brighton coffee shop, then called a taxi that took me to Topanga and my beloved Corvair. After the cabbie had left and I started up the Corvair to make sure it was okay, and it was, I walked over to Tina's house and looked inside the window.

The place had been cleaned out and was totally abandoned. Tina Hartman had been erased like she had never existed, a casualty of one sick mind's power trip. And there was nothing I could do about it. It was up to Velma to keep her promise, to give The Man the kiss of death. And think of me as she was doing it. I only hoped she didn't wait too long, maybe on their honeymoon, after she was already in the will. I couldn't wait for the headlines.

I drove back home without stopping, thinking of that and three other things: Puss's whereabouts, Judy Fagin, and the hidden camera in my bedroom.

Chapter Fourteen
WHERE MY CAT IS HUNG

When I walked into The Drive-Inn later that evening, *The Blue Dahlia* was playing and Doc was still arguing with Monica. I looked up at Alan Ladd, who had been falsely accused of killing his philandering wife, talking to Veronica Lake in the rain, and realized as great a flick as that was, mine was better.

"Shut up and pop this baby in," I said to Doc and Monica, who looked at me, stunned.

"*Vic*!" Monica said, coming around and giving me a hug. "What the hell's going on, we were so worried!"

"What's up, my man?" Doc said with a wide smile. "Catch the one-armed man?"

"Didn't catch anybody, as usual, but check this out. Here, play this, and I'll provide running commentary. C'mon." The place was practically deserted, so I felt free to show it. It was a weeknight.

"Judy needs to talk to you," Monica said urgently. "The She Beams are back in town, have a gig day after tomorrow night at Bimbo's."

"*Sssshhhh*!" Doc said, and Monica stuck her tongue out at him. I don't know why they just don't get married already.

"Find my cat?" I asked Monica. She shook her head sadly in the negative. I sighed and looked up at the TV screen as *Neon Knights* began. I wanted to fast forward through the pre-credit sex sequence in my apartment, but Doc grabbed the remote control from me. He turned the sound down, but watched with rapt attention. So did Monica. I was blushing but proud in a twisted kind of way.

"What the hell is this, Vic?" Doc asked. "An *un*dress rehearsal?"

"More like a *distress* rehearse, Doc. Keep watching."

"Who filmed this?" Monica asked.

"Just keep watching," I said. "It gets better."

So we all kept watching, and a couple of losers stopped browsing through the shelves of videos to watch. "Hey, isn't that you?" one regular bozo asked. "You're a star!"

"Now I have proof," I said. "Even Doc has a cameo comin'

up."

The video went on and on, Doc and Monica and the pair of extras watching with wide eyes. "You think I look fat?" Doc asked. Nobody answered. Too into the movie maybe. The sex scene with Tina made me cringe. I was on a veritable boning binge, with an audience to boot. I knew Monica was looking at me, with either awe or disgust, but I didn't return her stare. "Way to go!" one of the patrons said, slapping me on the shoulder, still thinking it was a real movie. Whatever.

Everyone cheered during the chase and shootout scenes. Then I popped in Part Two, which began with another sex scene involving Velma and which I thought had ended with Velma and me and the Feds facing the camera, being filmed watching ourselves on the screen. But The Man in his perverse manner had kept the cameras rolling, and the tape Velma gave me really did have a bang-up finish, literally, with her blowing away the Feds and me bending over as she slumped to the floor, apparently dying. The video ended with us kissing. How *apropos*. How very Hollywood.

Fade to black.

"Vic, I thought the Rose business was the weirdest thing I ever heard of," Doc said. "And then the Elvis cult with the teenage Mob brat. And then you goin' back East to find out your high school squeeze humped and bumped off your papa. But *this* is the new champ, Vic. You've outdone yourself. Congratulations."

"I still want to know who did this," Monica insisted. "This is the trippiest thing I've ever seen. Mental home videos of the Vic Valentine nutcase files. You sayin' you had no idea?"

"None," I insisted. "Not till Part Two, anyway. All in all, it's not a bad little flick, though I'm not a fan of the *cinema verite* approach myself. I'd have preferred something in the style of Sam Fuller's 'Naked Kiss' or something, black and white and stylistically shot. Oh well. I was just an actor, had no creative control. Until the end, when we sort of winged it, but Velma gets the credit for the finale."

"Can I rent it?" one of the slobbering slimy patrons asked. I told him to beat it. When he didn't, I showed him my .45, then both of the extras ran out of the store. Doc chastised me for literally scaring away business, but I said I was too beat to argue, and he dropped it.

Then I told Doc and Monica all about The Man and his sick experiment, his tabloid technique of filmmaking, his manipulation of innocent peoples' lives for his own twisted amusement, and the fact that Tina's death had not been faked like Velma's. Neither had the Feds', left for dead in the middle of the floor, to be disposed of like so much garbage, no doubt, probably officially listed as MIA or something to cover for the truth. Then there was Luke Brandon. Whatever. Doc and Monica absorbed it all silently, somberly. The massive proportions of what was basically an epic, tragic gag staggered them. Me, I was used to it. I only wished I could have dished out a little justice, but all I had to aim at was a disembodied Voice. I told them about Velma's promise to one day give The Man the kiss of death, but they didn't buy it.

"Vic, she got you into this, man, why believe anything she says?" Doc said with his customary cynicism. "She was the bait, man."

"Yeah, but see her expression when they kidnapped her at LAX? She's not that good an actress, Doc. I think The Man used her to set me up so he could set her up, hold her prisoner until she succumbed. And he won. As usual, I was worthless, useless, no help at all. Now she's this monster's love slave forever."

"I think she'll kill him," Monica said flatly. "Call it woman's intuition. I think Vic is right. Velma got him into this, not fully understanding the rules of the game, maybe thinking it would be just for fun, like 'Candid Camera' or something, not taking it seriously until people started getting hurt, maybe she was coerced into it, who knows? But I think she is really afraid of this guy, because he's proven his power over her, and she will take the opportunity to kill him when the time is right, when he trusts her, when she can make it look like an accident."

"And she has all his money," Doc said.

"Why not?" said Monica.

Yeah. Why not. "Guys, I think this may be it for me, detective-wise," I said slowly, seriously. "My heart just isn't in it anymore. I'm obviously inept. I just get sucked into things

and hope Fate or luck will bail me out. I don't deserve the license of my profession. The fact I solve *anything* is a miracle. Hey, speaking of bailing out, what about that bail money, Doc?"

"Got it back in the mail this morning," Doc said. "Unmarked envelope, L.A. stamped, but no return address. No check. No note. Just cash. Same amount I forked over. That's when I knew you were on your way home, it was all a mistake. Well, a deliberate one. But what an adventure, right? I still feel bad for just leaving you down there to fend for yourself, plus I missed out on more screen time, but, business is business, and I done all I thought I could do down there. Anyway, you came through, like I knew you would. And you had all that great sex! Forget it, man, it's over, no harm done."

"Except for Tina," I said.

"That wasn't your fault," Monica said, rubbing my shoulders. "That sicko would have killed her anyway, if she was talking too much. She was involved with trouble and she knew it."

"You *can't* quit," Doc said. "You've helped a lot of people in your career, man. Me, for one, remember? You found my mother wandering the streets in a daze? And how about the Mob brat you rescued from her sick old man and that Elvis sex cult? And at least you didn't come back from New York totally destitute. In your own special way, you found out the truth. You just made the choice of not doing anything about it, but you could have. Don't give up now, Vic, you're on a roll! I mean, give up and do *what*?"

"Work for you?"

"Ah, shit."

"No, really. Monica is here all the time, missing gigs. I could gain valuable experience, build up the old resume, or start one, anyway."

"Vic, you're not the nine to five type," Doc said, obviously petrified by the idea. "You'd drive us *both* crazy."

Monica kissed my cheek. "You'll get over it. We women need sensitive dicks like you."

"It's not just Tina," I said. "It's everything. Rose. Dolly. Lucy. My mother. Even my cat. I bet I couldn't even find Puss if I tried."

Then right at that moment, I swear, who should hop up onto the bar but Puss. I grabbed him and kissed and hugged him and then felt something warm and wet trickling down the front of me. He was peeing all over me, as well as the bar. Doc cussed and Monica grabbed some towels and tried to clean it all up. The Drive-Inn stunk like a litter box in no time. Then Puss freaked out at the commotion he caused and ran back outside. I chased him up to my apartment, which was a welcome sight. See? I didn't even find Puss. Puss found *me*. Definitely, I was a defective detective.

I got cleaned up and went directly to bed, slept into the next day, and then went right back to sleep, into the inner dream world, which suddenly seemed more appealing than the waking one. I ordered out for pizza, didn't answer the phone, watched television, cuddled with Puss, who seemed very listless and feeble and was acting strangely. He wasn't eating or drinking much, plus he was pissing constantly everywhere except in his litter box, like in the middle of my office and even on my bed. Hell, when I first got him, he couldn't pee at all, and now he couldn't stop. I called The Drive-Inn and asked Monica to come up and look at him. She did, and concluded he had either a kidney or bladder infection and required immediate medical attention. She felt so bad for letting him run away in the first place she volunteered to take him to the vet, where I now had a charge account, and I was so beat I let her.

I cleaned up the cat pee. Outside it began to rain. I was all wet either indoors or out. I spent most of the rest of that day searching in vain for the hidden camera in my bedroom, but came up with zilch. A real detective would have found out. Or a fictional one, even. James Bond for sure, within seconds. Me? I just went to bed and jerked off for the camera, if it was there, and fell asleep and slept well into the next morning.

The next day, after calling the vet, who told me Puss had to be kept for more tests, plus he was on an I.V. because he had dehydrated, I played "Obsession" by Animotion and "Relax" by Frankie Goes To Hollywood for my wake up tunes, then headed out to Rendezvous, my old hang-out, for some real strong coffee. I was tired of being cooped up. It was time to rejoin the living.

Judy Fagin, who sometimes filled in at Rendezvous for friends even though her mother had sold it off months before, was working the counter. She'd left a message on my machine the day before while I was asleep, asking me to look her up. She went white with shock when she saw me, which practically turned her into an albino, since she was so white already, since the winter rains had let her tan fade. Then she turned red as neon. She came around and gave me a big hug, then kissed me, all of which I receive tentatively, and she knew why.

"Vic, before I explain what happened down there, which I promise was not my fault, I was threatened into cooperating—did you hear the news?"

"About what? What could I have possibly missed? *You're* the one who needs some catching up."

"I mean about Velma."

"Yeah—she's still alive."

"Um, not any more."

My heart dropped out through my stomach.

Judy picked up that morning's *Chronicle* off the counter, and opened up to the second page, where there was a small item about the suicide of Velma Vale, starlet, from an overdose of barbiturates mixed with alcohol. A maid found her nude in a Bel Air mansion belonging to a film producer whose name was withheld by request. The journalist pointed out the striking similarities to the discovery of Marilyn Monroe's body in similar circumstances. It was an AP wire report. But, suspiciously, there was no mention of the gunshot wound in her shoulder, and I saw no evidence the lady had a habit. Of course, Dolly Duncan was totally strung out and that got by me too, but the suddenness of this bothered me. Plus it was so well prepared. There was a very small sidebar about her aborted film career, with no mention of her start in porn flicks, and some quotes from people who knew her, including Tony Ray, who took the opportunity to announce his upcoming film *Neon Knights*, in which she was slated to star and which would have undoubtedly given her credibility in the industry and taken her career in an entirely different direction. Yeah, right. It already had. There was also a blurb from Peter Bogdanovich comparing her to Dorothy Stratten, the slain Playboy model turned actress.

Nothing from or about The Man, though.

Had Velma really been so despondent, so soon? Or was this just the sequel to our little movie, Plan B? It was the same mystery all over again, but this time. I wasn't involved, at least not directly.

I sat at a table and slowly read the two articles over and over. It wasn't until the fifth or so time that I began to cry. Just a little, in case she really was dead. Judy sat beside me and held my hand. I wondered if the suicide was real or had been faked, like her ersatz murder. No photos of the body. Or maybe real murder disguised as suicide, to keep her quiet, as many theories contended happened with Marilyn. And like Marilyn, we'd probably never know the real truth. All we had left was her beautiful image preserved on film.

"You think she's really gone this time?" Judy asked me as I dried my bleary eyes.

"Who knows? Maybe I'll hire a detective to find out."

"Monica told me you're thinking of quitting."

"Yeah, well, this pretty much clinches it."

Judy didn't reply, at a loss for words, apparently. She just looked down sadly.

I said, "Judy, about Westwood."

"Oh, Vic, I'm so sorry."

"Forget it, babe. Forget it. I already know. Guys in suits with badges and guns tapped your line, knocked on your door, forced their way in, and made you keep quiet when I showed up."

"How you know?"

"I'll tell you later. I don't feel much like talking now. Actually, the tape. Doc still has them. You can watch if you'd like."

"I did. Late the other night. Monica had them, actually. I saw them after she got back from the vet. More cat trouble, too, huh? The year's getting off to a rocky start. Wish there was something I could do."

The light bulb over my head must have been a thousand watts, because she felt the heat and saw the light the same time I did. Judy told the other counter person she had to leave and then we went back to my apartment and began making out then making love, and it was nothing like the last time. It was sweet and tender and warm, the way it should be between lovers who are friends, not strangers. It wasn't a fantasy. It was real, and it gave me something I didn't get from my last two encounters: fulfillment, fleeting as it was. Judy helped me forget about Velma, at least for a while.

Later on, early in the evening, as Judy slept in my bed and Frank crooned on the CD player, I sat at my desk, tossing darts at my heart board, wondering what to do now. With Velma gone there was nothing to prevent The Man from invading my fortress of solitude once again, either to film me or frame me or fry me. It seemed to be his prerogative. God, I hated that. My single greatest possession, my autonomy, had been taken away from me. I felt between Fate and the Government I had no control over my own life, one of the main reasons I wanted to become a private detective. I had no secrets. My mother in the booby hatch was locked inside her own damaged head, creating her own reality that no one on the outside could touch, and in a strange way, I envied that refuge. It was, next to death, the ultimate escape, the perfect freedom.

What was even more disheartening was that The Man was now free to pursue that presidential agenda, which didn't bode well for life on this planet in general. Oh well. Nothing I could do about it now, short of pulling a Lee Harvey Oswald. I was small fry. He'd probably forget all about me. And there was still the remote possibility that Velma's reported suicide was a ruse so she could submerge from public view, either for her sake or his. Maybe he didn't want millions of men lusting after her in movies anymore, or having a career that took the limelight away from him. In that case, she'd make good on her promise, and kiss him deadly one dark night. I'd just have to wait and see. In the meantime, I had my own life to live, camera or no camera.

Judy suddenly ran into the living room pulling on her clothes and broke my contemplation. "Vic, I forgot The She Beams have a gig at Bimbo's in like two hours! C'mon! They're probably there already, rehearsing!"

"Moving up fast, aren't you, babe? Bimbo's is a step-up from The Drive-Inn." Bimbo's 365 Club was a '40s style supper club on Columbus in North Beach, with red table clothes and portraits of naked mermaids its main motifs. It was my favorite club in The City, though I hardly ever went, since I was usually alone. But tonight, my date would be right there on stage. Seeing The She Beams at Bimbo's would be a welcome tonic after that morning's devastating news, and would buy me more time to brood sullenly on the meaning of life and the Universe and my place in it.

"Yeah, it's a great gig but we have to hurry or I'll blow it," Judy said frantically, but I kept kissing her anyway as she finished dressing and then put on makeup out of her purse. I was trying to decide whether we were in love or just being neighborly. She was a living doll, but something was missing somewhere. Maybe it was just me and my state of mind. Didn't matter at the moment, though. I needed someone just like her, and she was there for me.

I called the vet emergency hotline one more time to check up on Puss's progress, but the results were so far inconclusive, and the credit bill was racking up substantial numbers. Whether I continued being a detective or not, I'd need some serious income flow right away to cover the costs of living, or at least surviving.

The evening was exciting and invigorating. The She Beams played beautifully and announced their new record deal with a local independent label (Judy's L.A. experiences had soured her on anything corporate), and the crowd went wild. Also on the bill were The Mermen and The Aqua-Velvets. The following week they had a gig at Slim's with The Ultras opening up, and then another at The Stone in two more weeks with The Phantom Surfers. The She Beams had arrived on a big wave.

Afterwards I escorted Judy, the new sensation, in my Corvair to Mel's Diner on Lombard in the Marina District. We didn't talk about L.A. or her ex-fiancé or her crazy mother Zelda or anything heavy. Just her future. Then she wanted to hear about mine, and I didn't know what to tell her.

I took her home to her Telegraph Hill flat and dropped her off with a kiss. She invited me in but I politely declined, saying I was still pretty worn out from my trip. She understood and said she'd be very busy for a while but she'd make time for us to get together. I said that would be swell, but we both realized her blossoming career would be her steady date for a long time, and if it was going to work she'd have to remain faithful.

When I got back home there was a message on my machine from Monica, whom I'd just seen at Bimbo's, wondering where Judy and I had gone. I'd deal with that later. Monica's musician boyfriend had been waiting for her after the show and so I hadn't talked to her much, since I didn't like the looks of him, and she knew it.

Then there was a message from the vet that made my heart freeze:

Puss was *gone*. I was to pick his body up in the morning, or just sign something to have him cremated, but he didn't make it. Kidney failure with complications, possibly leukemia. And he'd obviously been deteriorating while out and about on the streets. Maybe he'd picked up an infection that exacerbated a pre-existing condition, but it didn't matter now. They really didn't know anything except that he had simply stopped breathing. He was pretty old anyway, they said. But they offered their condolences along with a bill, and that was it.

I was in shock for a long time, just sitting at my desk in the dark, closing my eyes and hoping when I opened them Puss would be sitting on my lap, purring. I tried it. Didn't work. I played "Old Shep" by Elvis on a continuous loop, sobbing. First Velma, and now Puss. What a day death was having. Maybe Tina would adopt Puss and take care of him for me. I wondered if Puss's soul had a penis. If so, he'd be a lot happier wherever he was, a stud again in pussy heaven.

The Drive-Inn was closed, so I went down to the corner liquor store and bought a pint of Scotch and came back and knocked back some shots chased by beer. I couldn't stop crying. I'd just lost my best little buddy in the world, the most loyal friend I've ever had. I'd found a real companion in that little animal, one who didn't care what I did for a living, or what shape I was in, who cuddled with me every night no matter what. No arguments, no petty mind games, just pure, unconditional love. Well, one condition: it died with him, and cats weren't made to last very long. I wondered why. People are the ones wasting too much oxygen around here. Only Puss would understand and agree with my low opinion of my own species. He shared my contempt for humanity. Now I had no one to commiserate with. If I hadn't lost my heart in Hollywood, it was surely missing now.

As I was sitting there getting plastered, tossing darts at my heart board, I realized there was still one message on the answering machine left. I sat there wondering what more dreadful news awaited me. A mistake on an old AIDS test, I was really positive. My mother was dead. Dolly was in police custody, facing the death penalty. Rose inviting me to her marriage to Zach. I imagined all sorts of horrors before finally playing it. It was from Doc:

"Hey, my man, I left those video tapes in your mailbox, along with something special that was sent to The Drive-Inn today, addressed to you. I was going to drop it off in person today but I was too busy and I dig you've been wantin' time to yourself, then maybe I'd drop it at Bimbo's but, well, I had a date, what can I tell you. Nothing special, but, y'know, she's a sister and not into surf music, so we dug some jazz at Kimball's. Anyway, anyway, my man, it's good to have you home, and I didn't dupe those tapes, won't unless you give me permission, but I'd like to. You were right all along, Vic. Your life is a fuckin' movie, man. Let me know what that special delivery was all about. It looks *weird*. But I'm sure you can handle All right now." *Click.*

I staggered down to my mailbox and got the tapes, which I brought up with me and popped into the VCR. I couldn't watch them, though. The special delivery envelope remained unopened on my desk for a while, as I sat and wondered what to do with the videos, Velma's final flick. I thought about destroying them but couldn't bring myself to do it. If she really was gone, they were the last record of her beauty on this plane, and I would keep the archives alive. I wondered if the envelope might have been from her, but it was postmarked New Orleans. No, it couldn't have been—could it? I was afraid to open it, to be honest.

I put the videos away in my closet with the trunk of still-unopened letters from my mother and then sat at my desk looking at the envelope for a long time. Finally I just slit it open and tore out the contents all at once, like quickly removing a bandage you know will tear your skin, but you want the pain over with in a hurry.

Inside was a round trip ticket to New Orleans, a money order for reservations at any hotel in the French Quarter I chose, and instructions to be at Cafe Du Monde the morning after the flight, which left in two weeks, giving me time to think about it, at least. The paper with the instructions was typed, as was the signature at the bottom, which simply said: *Signed, Your True, Lasting, One and Only Love.*

Rose had sent me her last missive from New Orleans about a year before. But it could have been anybody. Flora. Lucy. Vicki. Dolly. The Phone Phantom, maybe. Even Velma. Or a whole new player. If I had my choice, I'd want it to be from Puss, but somehow I doubted it.

It occurred to me it could also have been another set-up by The Man, but I didn't think so. The ticket was round-trip. I had a built-in escape clause. Besides, even he gave more credit than to fall for him again so soon, and why would he bother at this point? I was an old movie already. And if he wanted me dead, the special delivery would have exploded in my face. No, this was something different. I could just sense it. Another challenge beckoned from beyond. And now when I traveled out of town I wouldn't have to worry about Puss anymore, which was not a plus, just a cold, new fact. One that made me feel lonelier that night than I'd ever felt in my life, I believe. That mysterious special delivery couldn't have arrived at a more vulnerable moment. Talk about timing.

My true, lasting, one and only love. What I'd been looking for my entire life, the main reason I'd become a detective to begin with.

But who had found my lost heart at last and mailed it to me special delivery? Only one way to find out.

The End of

I LOST MY HEART IN HOLLYWOOD

But

Vic Valentine will return in

DIARY OF A DICK

A Vic Valentine Adventure

Chapter One
MASTER BAIT

It's hard to be happy, and I'm happy to be hard.

There I was, Vic Valentine, former San Francisco P.I. and current world class chump, sitting alone in Cafe Du Monde in the French Quarter of New Orleans on Valentine's Day, far from home and sanity, dribbling my *cafe au lait*, nibbling my *beignet*, waiting for my True Love to waltz in any second and rescue me from my pathetic life of solitude and frustration. Well, one out of two wouldn't be bad. Dames are generally the main cause of my frustration, but also the one cure for my loneliness, except for my cat, but since Puss had recently passed on, I had to start scouting around for fresh pussy, if you catch my drift and I think you do.

To begin explaining for you latecomers what I was doing in this place at this time, it has to do with a mysterious special delivery I had recently received from an anonymous source who typed their signature *as Your True, Lasting, One and Only Love*. The package included a round trip ticket to 'Nawlins, unlimited free accommodations at the hotel of my choosing (I chose the French Market Inn on Decatur, near Jackson Square and the Mississippi), and all I had to do was promise to meet them in this cafe. Talk about a grand prize. I thought I hit the jackpot, though it could yet turn out to be one of those bogus sweepstakes deals suckers get in the mail all the time, promising millions because they were specially chosen at random. That was the opinion of my best pal Curtis Jackson, better known as Doc Schlock, proprietor of The Drive-Inn, San Francisco's only combination bar and video store and sometimes nightclub. I think it's the only one of its kind in the world. So is Doc. Anyway, that's Doc's function, to cast doubt and common sense my way, but it's also my duty to be reckless and follow my romantic impulses wherever they lead—especially if someone else was footing the bill. Doc had to agree I needed an all-expenses paid vacation now more than ever, so he just told me to look at it that way and not get involved in anything. I needed to get away. I said I'd call him and let him know how it goes. In his heart of hearts, he wanted to know who my benefactor was almost as much as I did.

Which one of my women deemed themselves my savior? Rose? Dolly? Velma? The Phone Phantom? Bettie Page? A secret admirer? This is what I had to know, even if it was just a hoax. I was too damn lonely to take any chances, miss any opportunities, even with women I never wanted to see again. I was nearly forty, single, and chronically celibate for the foreseeable future, unless my crystallized balls had their fortunes abruptly changed.

So there I was, despite the heartfelt admonitions of all who knew and loved me, which roughly amounted to the same number of fingers I need to masturbate, ironically enough. Besides Doc there was Monica Ivy and Judy Fagin, both delectable young members of the all girl astro-surf band The She Beams, who were up and coming while I was typically down and out. There had been Puss, my best friend next to Doc, but his demise was a "cat"-alyst in my decision to accept this offer, since I needed to get away from my lonesome office for a while. I had to go claim Puss's disease-ravaged body at the vet and have it cremated, probably the single worst moment in my life, which topped a long list that was getting longer all the time. I was painfully aware of his absence at all times. My loneliness was getting acute. What it needed to get was a cute babe for company. I felt fragile and faithless. I just hoped this unexpected New Orleans rendezvous would put me in touch with something or someone to live for again. At that point in my life, I was ready to throw in the towel, which included my so-called profession as a private detective, a real washout if there ever was one.

What *really* scared me was that in my desperation I'd go down an old dark road and hope for a bright new destination. None of the women I'd been involved with qualified as my true love. Take Rose Myers, known as Valerie way back in New York when we'd been a hot item. The love of my life, I had thought at one point. But she vanished on me twice, once in New York and again after I had finally found her years later, by "accident," hired to track her down by her own husband, a baseball player with an I.Q. that paled next to his batting average. She disappeared after the dumb palooka found us together and put me in the hospital, taking with her an illegitimate kid, the product of any one of a number of unions, all with the kind of men who are living arguments in favor of the total extinction of the human species. My last postcard from her over a year ago had been from the Crescent City, written in this very cafe. But I just couldn't believe she'd come to some epiphany and realized I was what she wanted all along. She was probably too busy having more babies by macho men who were intellectually challenged by Barney the Purple Dinosaur. But who else then?

Dolly Duncan Dunlap, the doper dentist's dame? If the Feds hadn't caught up with her and charged her with murdering my dirty cop father in a Brooklyn alley, all because he was doping, pimping, and boffing her, she was probably turning tricks in some remote corner of the world, guilt-ridden but under heavy sedation. Either that, or she'd totally reversed her personal trends and was a nun in some isolated convent. I had let her go scot-free after discovering the ugly long-hidden truth, and even arranged to have a Mob contract on her cancelled, all because I pitied her, but I don't think I really loved her in a true love soul mate kind of way. At least Rose and I had a lot of common interests. Dolly and I had history, most of it bad as it turned out, and little else, but my sentimental instincts had influenced my judgment once again. My hope was that she was a well-adjusted housewife with a new identity and purpose in life, but somehow I doubted it.

The third most possible suspect was Velma Vale, starlet. But she was either dead by O.D. or still alive but hidden under the evil auspices of a famous politician, a warped manipulator of men who had lured me into a series of traps that he arranged then secretly shot on video, just to make a private home movie. I was framed for Velma's fake murder and later, out on bail, woke up next to her truly dead best friend Tina Hartman, poisoned by the filmmaker to keep her quiet. I guess she wasn't sticking to the script, and the penalty for ad-libbing was severe. I was in shootouts with Feds and on the lam from the LAPD with an APB on my ass. And it was all being secretly recorded, a test print for a flick called *Neon Knights.* At the finale in Beverly Hills, Velma promised to marry the wacko, who remained out of my sight, in exchange for my freedom and the original copies of the film. Since forcing her to be his had been his objective all along, he agreed. Two days later I read she had Marilyn Monroe'd herself. Now, all this could have meant this New Orleans set-up was merely a sequel, but I didn't think so. My gut instinct informed me there was something else going on here, and since Puss had bought the feline farm and I had nothing better to do, there I was.

My head was pounding with anticipation as I sat there slurping and waiting, waiting and slurping, hoping it was who I believed it was, the person who could cure my broken heart forever, even if she was the one responsible for putting it into a cast in the first place. I checked my wallet and counted the cash again. Velma's suitor had confiscated my wallet and P.I. license at one point, but a week later Captain Sharp of SFPD called me up and said he had them and I could drop by and pick them up. But by that point, after all that had happened, not only with Velma but also Rose and Dolly, I had come to the conclusion I was wasting my life in this detective racket. I decided I'd try my hand at freelance writing again, as I had done in New York long ago, reporting on the new wave music scene. Sharp just said I could do whatever I wanted with the damn license, and wished me luck with my literary endeavors, hoping I was better with words than people. I told him I already had a few choice words for him, the bastard, since he had cooperated with the Federal and L.A. authorities on the movie-making politico's payroll. He claimed not to know what I was talking about, then hung up. I went by and collected my wallet, and he was conveniently out of the office. Whatever. Then I put the license in the safe behind my heart-shaped dartboard, and that was that. I was free.

Or so I thought.

Cafe Du Monde turned out to be one of my favorite spots on Earth, which is not saying much considering I deem this planet to be merely a giant dung ball in pointless orbit around an apathetic fireball, but the sultry ambience of the French Quarter made the trip here worthwhile, even if nothing else came of it. I'd always wanted to come to New Orleans, ever since I saw *King Creole*, Elvis Presley's fourth and best flick, when I was a kid. It was a noirish thriller with great music shot in black and white and directed by Michael Curtiz, who also did another of my all-time favorites, *Angels With Dirty Faces*, James Cagney's best flick. Anyway, *King Creole* was set here in 'Nawlins, and ever since then, every time I saw this town in a movie, whether it was Jim Jarmusch's *Down By Law* or the '82 remake of *Cat People* or *The Cincinnati Kid* with Steve McQueen and Ann-Margret, I dreamed of coming here. Now here I was, sitting pretty, courtesy of my mysterious travel agent, my admirer from afar. I was spoiled already. Obviously it was someone I had ruined for anybody else, but that was okay, I knew the feeling—I'd ruined myself for anyone else, too.

I sat dreamily staring at the fans whirring on the ceiling, then out at the people and carriages and old buildings on Decatur Street. Since my arrival I'd managed to sneak in a little sight seeing around the Quarter, which was smaller than I thought, but even more sultry and sensual than it appeared on the screen. No one had ever captured on celluloid its esoteric, almost eerie, otherworldly quality. For one thing, unless someone developed aroma-rama, you couldn't inhale in a movie theater the sundry scents of the Quarter, from gumbo to rotting wood to river mist to stripper sweat. Then there was the booze, like "Hurricanes," fruit juice that snuck up and stoned you, which people walked around with in paper cups on Bourbon Street. And you could record the sounds of the Quarter, but you couldn't duplicate the intensity of personally witnessing live jazz on the street corner, or blues in an ancient saloon, one of the original birthplaces of popular rhythm. Then there was the unique climate, which I can only describe as voodoo tropical. Even in February it was steamy and humid, overcast and muggy, and for some reason it made me homier than hell, but there was a feint cool breeze wafting in off the nearby Mississippi, and every establishment you entered was air-conditioned, like Miami, where I had nearly eloped with Dolly Duncan. What a fool I used to be, only weeks before. This time, after a headlong rush into belated maturity, I promised myself I'd be careful, and not just jump into bed and the fire with whoever was scheduled to join me here. Hopefully it was a beautiful dame, either from my past or future, but if not, what the hell—I might move down here anyway. The change, something I'd been desperately pursuing the past year or so, would do my soul and body good, as well as give me the literary inspiration I needed. A muse in the flesh would be nice, but if the person meeting me here wasn't her, there looked to be plenty of other voluptuous volunteers decorating the vibrant vicinity.

I tried to picture the perfect physical mate, the kind I'd order from a catalogue. All of my recent romantic entanglements had been with beautiful women (I am as superficial in my tastes as the next hetero male), but different types. Rose was *nouveau beatnik*, with a touch of Gil Elvgren, slender but soft and fleshy, not bony and anemic like most models these days. Dolly was Donna Reed on dope, the Girl Next Door—Next Door to Hell, as it turned out. Velma Vale was like a postmodern Anita Ekberg, the voluptuous vision of my wildest fantasies. Monica was a sexy, petite Bettie Page wanna-be, and Judy was a beautiful blond nymphet straight out of Bikini Beach. Yes sir, I'd been fairly lucky lately as far as actually meeting women went, but none of them worked out, for one reason or another. For one thing, I'm rating these women on a physical scale, not very P.C., but to hell with that. I know I had to look for more enduring endearing qualities than a cheesecake figure and a photogenic face. After all, I was no prize hunk. Good-looking, fairly solid, but barely average in height, slightly above average in weight. I think any woman who goes for me is succumbing to her maternal instincts more than her drive to procreate as soon as possible. That's okay—I need all the breast-feeding I can get. So the point is, if the person who met me here turned out to be less than an eye-full, I still had to give her a chance. Any woman who deemed herself my true love was obviously compromising anyway, since I'm hardly what most babes would order out of a catalogue. At least, that's my humble opinion. In effect, I was in New Orleans by special order. All the customer had to do was come pick up their package, and see if it measured up to their expectations before sending it back.

I sighed and looked at my watch. The letter hadn't specified the exact time, just sometime during the morning hours of Valentine's Day. Cafe Du Monde was open around the clock, and I'd been sitting there since five AM. It was now eleven, and I was beginning to get the idea I was once again the butt of some cosmic joke. Oh well. At least this time it wasn't entirely at my expense, at least not monetarily. Mentally, well, I'm used to that.

Another hour went by and I had read and re-read the *Times-Picayune* from cover to cover for the final time. I was getting double vision from the caffeine and sugar rush. The busboys were getting suspicious. Actually, one busboy was a girl, a pretty young Creole chick, with whom I exchanged suggestive eye contact. She was maybe eighteen, trouble on a hook, but I didn't bite the bait. Fleetingly I wondered if she was The One, and was just toying with me, but as time went by and she didn't even speak to me other than to ask if I wanted a refill of coffee, I ditched that notion. Finally, at twelve thirty, I got up, stretched, and was ready to head out, maybe leave a note at the counter where I could be contacted, explaining I'd waited all morning and now it was afternoon and I had to take a walk. But just as I stood up, I saw a woman standing outside the window at Decatur, peering inside, apparently at me.

She was average height, with long, thick, wavy reddish blond hair, smooth pale skin, and sunglasses hiding her eyes. She had an hourglass figure I wanted to make time with, and she was wearing a tight-fitting black dress with a slit up the right thigh, nylons, and high heels. She saw me and smiled, and my heart beat like jungle drums at a mating ceremony. She had a tiny mole on her cheek, like Marilyn Monroe, and her lips were full and red with carefully applied lipstick. Too good to be true, much less true love.

Then she suddenly waved at someone behind me, and I turned to see a big darkly handsome stud in a sailor's outfit running out to greet her. Figured.

I stood there and watched them embrace. Then he gave her something and she smiled and kissed him and put the gift in her cleavage. Even from where I was I could see she was wearing a black lacy bra. Wait a minute—a hooker? Didn't matter. She wasn't there to see me.

I sighed and walked outside, then remembered to leave a note. I jotted down my name and the address of the French Market Inn with my room number, and left it with the cashier, asking her to give it to anyone who might ask for it. I slipped the cashier a few bucks with the napkin to ensure her conscientiousness, and then I walked outside. I saw the strawberry blond stranger and the sailor walking up toward Jackson Square, and then she suddenly turned around at me and smiled, as if acknowledging me and encouraging me to follow her. I did.

The strawberry blonde and the sailor sat down on a bench near the big church in the midst of Jackson Square and I sat on one nearby. The babe wasn't just smiling at me—she was sending me a message. Somehow, I knew it was her, The One, even though I didn't recognize her from anywhere other than my dreams. Something told me she was the black widow in the web, even when she started making out with the sailor. It was a game, and since I had come all the way here to play, I stuck around for the next move, which apparently was mine to make.

I hung back and followed them as they walked deeper into the Quarter, and onto Bourbon Street. They went inside a tavern called The Gilded Cage. At least, I thought it was just a tavern, but once I followed them into the darkness, I realized it was something more, or less, depending on what you were looking for. It was a strip joint. I lost them inside, so I just sat at the bar and ordered a beer and scouted around. I saw the sailor alone sitting up by the stripper stage in the center of the room, square and well lit like a boxing ring. Maybe the strawberry blonde had ditched him, because I didn't see her around. Loud saxophone music was playing, and not contemporary crap, either—classic early '60s Vegas stuff that went with a clientele steeped in martinis and sharkskin suits. Which this crowd wasn't—just a conglomeration of rowdy rednecks and naughty businessmen. And me. The sailor was sipping something tall and wet while a babe gyrated in front of him. He seemed to hardly notice her, though. The sailor was a kid, maybe twenty-three, clean cut and rosy cheeked, and his former companion, the strawberry blonde, looked to be around thirty or so. She still wasn't around after five minutes. In the powder room, probably, trying to take a few years off for her Valentine's date. Whoever that turned out to be.

Finally, I saw her, and she wasn't wearing the tight black dress anymore. Or the nylons or the high heels or the shades. She was wearing a G-string and a glittering bra, and when she made her entrance, the lights dimmed even more and a spotlight hit the stage and the crowd went wild. She was the star of the show.

I got up to leave, but just before I reached the door, I couldn't resist turning around once more to look at her. She was looking right back at me as she waved and blew me a kiss. Heads turned to see the object of her affections, including the sailor, but I just grinned and shook my head and walked out into the noisy daylight world parading down Bourbon Street.

I went back to my hotel room and tried to take a nap but I'd drank too much coffee. I went back to the Cafe Du Monde to see if anyone had picked up my note. Not yet. I walked down to the Moonwalk on the riverbank and watched steamboats chug along the Mississippi, feeling not only lonelier than ever, but stupider. I ate in a place called The Gumbo Shop and then went back to my hotel room, wondering whether or not to leave the following morning. My return ticket was open-ended, so I could leave anytime. I wanted to call Doc for advice but I already knew what he'd say. Instead I stayed in my room and jerked off thinking of the strawberry blonde stripper and then stayed up watching late night movies on TV: *The Brain That Wouldn't Die* and *Screaming Mimi*, two sleazy classics from the '50s, my decade of choice. The former was an old favorite, the latter a low budget noir with Anita Ekberg I'd never seen before. She played a stripper accused of murder, but what was really weird was that *Screaming Mimi* lifted the entire musical score from *On the Waterfront*, which is indelibly recorded in my head and forever associated with Marlon Brando and the Jersey dock rackets and all that. At first, when the flick opened up with that familiar music over images of Anita's glorious figure in a bathing suit running along the Santa Rosa shore with her Great Dane, I thought the TV station had the wrong soundtrack in place or something. Then I realized that wasn't the case, Columbia Studios was apparently just cutting a few costs, but I thought I was losing my mind! I could imagine how Leonard Bernstein, the composer, must have felt. I was also worried maybe I'd seen so many movies in my life they had merged together in what was left of my mind. This just added to the overall bizarreness of my situation, being alone in New Orleans and all— same tune, different setting.

Finally, I fell asleep and awoke around ten the next morning.

I felt oddly excited, partly due to awakening in a strange town far from all I knew, but that could easily turn into depression for the same reason, so I quickly showered and shaved and then went down to Cafe Du Monde to see if anyone had picked up my note. Fortunately the same cashier was there.

Yes, it had been picked up.

By whom?

A woman.

Who looked like what?

Pretty, around thirty, reddish blonde hair.

Whoa. What time?

Just a few minutes ago.

A few minutes ago and a day late? What day was today?

I picked up a paper off a nearby table. February 14th. Valentine's Day. She wasn't a day late—I was a day early! I had read all through yesterday's paper and didn't even notice the date. I supposed I was so anxious I had simply spaced out. I had totally blown it. I had missed the date in both senses of the word. Weren't New Orleans and San Francisco on the same calendar if not clock? How could I have been such a screw-up? I arrived in town, checked into the hotel, waited a day, then *whoa*. My flight had left on the twelfth, not the thirteenth, so Valentine's Day would have been two days after my arrival. What a flake I was. But anyway, at least now she knew where I was staying.

I took a deep breath. This was it.

I raced back to the hotel and there she was, apparently waiting for me in the lobby, still dressed in black, but it wasn't a tight sexy dress with a slit up the thigh. It was a nun's gown and habit.

Chapter Two
VENUS ENVY

The ensuing conversation went like this, dialogue out of a dizzy dream:

"Hello, I'm Vic Valentine."

"Yes, I know." Her beatific smile never wavered.

"And you are—?"

"Sister Sue."

"Uh-huh. You're a nun."

"Yes."

"And you sent me that plane ticket."

"Yes."

"Why?"

"You know why. To meet your True, One and Only, Everlasting Love."

"So is that you?"

"No."

"No. Then maybe it's your *other* self. The one I saw in that strip joint on Bourbon yesterday."

"No, that wasn't me."

"No? But you know who I'm talkin' about, Sister Sue?"

"Yes, I think so. You must mean my twin sister, Betty Lou."

"Excuse me? Your twin sister?"

"Betty Lou."

"And you're Sister Sue."

"Yes."

"So *your* sister, Sister Sue, is Betty Lou, the stripper."

"I'm afraid so."

"Twin sister."

"That is correct."

"And you're a nun."

"I serve the Lord, yes."

"And you made me come down here to meet my true love."

"*I* didn't make you. The Lord did. He works in mysterious ways."

"Yeah, tell me about it." I let out a big sigh and sat in the vacant seat beside her. Otherwise the lobby was empty, save for the oblivious desk clerk. "I'm already confused, Sister."

"Yes, I know."

"I mean about this whole set-up. I mean so who's my true love if not you, Sister? Your sister?"

She laughed. "Better not be."

"Yeah? So who, then?"

"The Lord Jesus Christ."

"*What*?"

"Our Lord in Heaven, Your Savior. I am here to convert you back to your rightful faith, Catholicism, before the End arrives. That is my mission, Vic Valentine—to save your soul. The End is near, Armageddon approaches. The signs are everywhere. We have so little time, and so much work to do. The Church needs you, Vic Valentine." She clutched my arm as she looked fervently into my disbelieving eyes. "*I need you.*"

I stood up with a tired groan. "Let me get this straight. You spent all this cash just to recruit me for your side in the Apocalypse?"

"Something like that."

"Why, Sister? Why me?"

"Because you are the Chosen One."

"Chosen for what?"

"You will see. The Answer has always been before you, but you have been blinded by lust."

"Lust? For what?"

"The female form, of course."

"Oh. That. Yeah, well, you got me there. But if I'm such a certified sinner, then why—hey, hey, hey, how do you *know* all this?"

"We have our sources."

"Oh, no. Not again. You mean The Man, right?"

"The Man?"

"You know, the politico who yanked my strings back in L.A. I'm on to you, Sister. Sorry. Now, if you'll excuse me, I have a plane to catch."

She bolted upright and gripped my arm again. "Vic, please. Wait. I do not take orders from The Man you speak of. Only the *Son* of Man."

I sighed and rolled my eyes. "Jesus," I said.

"Exactly."

"Huh? Oh. Yeah, right. So Jesus has been keeping tabs on me, right?"

"On everyone."

"Between him, Big Brother, and Santa Claus, a guy can't get any privacy anymore."

"You better come with me. People are coming here to kill you. You may have sanctuary in the Church."

"Whoa. Say what?"

"Let's go. My sister Betty Lou keeps the company of evil men. Yesterday she was luring you into a trap. She belongs to a very bad man, a gangster in appearance, but someone who is really a much worse than that."

"Who?"

"No less than Satan's ambassador in New Orleans."

"Oh, of course. So you and Betty Lou split the cost of the airfare?"

"No, but she knows about you. There are eyes and ears everywhere in the Quarter, Vic. C'mon, we have to hurry, or the Devil's men will find you here and kill you."

"Why, for Christ's sake? Oh, sorry."

"Because they know you are the Chosen One."

"Aw, shit. Sorry, Sister, but I can't buy this. I gotta get goin'."

"Where to?"

"Back home to San Francisco, where else?" Another aborted vacation.

"But they will follow you."

"You mean the Devil's goons?"

"They are everywhere."

"No kidding. But they got bigger fish to fry than little old me."

"You are Chosen, Vic."

"Now you *do* sound like one of those junk mail sweepstakes rip-offs. Leave me alone, Sister. My cat died recently and I'm not in the mood for games."

"This is not a game, Vic."

"Let go of my arm, please. Thank you. Now, if you'll excuse me, I'm going to check out now."

"They won't let you leave New Orleans."

"Who? The Chamber of Commerce?"

"I'm only here to protect you. No need to be flip, Vic."

"Look, you sent me a round trip ticket, right?"

"Yes. We can't force you to stay and hold you prisoner. Only show you the Truth. The decision must be yours, though. Every man must choose the direction of his own soul."

"Good. Mine's goin' North by Northwest, courtesy of the

Friendly Skies. If you were The Flying Nun, you could join me, but otherwise, have a nice life, Sister." Actually, I wouldn't have minded if her sister wanted to come with me. A westward "ho."

"Vic, why do you think your cat died?"

"Because I saw the body and had it cremated. Next you'll tell me he faked his death, like Elvis. Or Jesus."

"No, I meant, the purpose, the reason, the cause?"

"Um, kidney failure, basically."

"No. Because it's The End, Vic. The Death of all we love, unless you make a stand."

I stood there in the lobby, looking at nothing, feeling numb, trying not to picture Sister Sue as her stripper sister Betty Lou. What a knockout figure there must have been under that black gown. But it was under wraps for keeps. Her twin sister was the one I needed, or wanted, to offer me everlasting salvation. It struck me how this was just like *Angels With Dirty Faces*, wherein James Cagney plays a hood and Pat O'Brien plays his best friend, a priest. They grew up stealing together but Cagney got caught and sent to Reform School, whereas O'Brien got away and went to Bible School. So now one was a gangster and the other a clergyman. I always liked Cagney better. And I bet I'd like Betty Lou better, too. "I want to meet your sister," I told the Sister.

"Betty Lou? But why? She is evil, a seductress, a temptress. She will only lead you to your doom."

"Yeah, well, I'd rather hear it from her, first. Your story sounds a little shaky to me, to say the least. C'mon, let's go to The Gilded Cage and have a chat. I'll buy you a Shirley Temple."

"No, no, no, I can't go into such a wicked place. You'll have to go alone, but at your own risk."

"All right, I'll do that then. I'll meet you later somewhere, this afternoon."

"All right. In front of the cathedral in Jackson Square at six o'clock this evening."

"Fine."

"God be with you, Vic. Please be careful. We need you." She leaned over and kissed me on the cheek, squeezing my arm as she did so.

"Yeah, same to you, Sister."

Then she walked out into the Quarter. I went out after a couple of seconds to see which way she went, but she was gone already. Vanished.

I went up to my room thinking, *Am I ever going to have just a simple, relaxing vacation*?

So the Lord was looking over me. All this time I thought He'd just overlooked me. I figured I'd go catch the matinee show at the Gilded Cage, sit at ringside, slip a note into Betty Lou's G-string that I needed to see her backstage pronto. First, I had to call Doc, but not for advice. I thought for once I'd give him a positive report from the field, even if I had to make one up.

"Doc! It's Vic! I'm in love, man! I met her! The love of my life! The one and only!"

"Dreaming again, huh Vic?" Doc knew me too well. "It's like they say: Waking up is hard to do. You still down in the bayou, I take it?"

"Doc, listen, it's on the level this time. There isn't one but *two* delicious babes mad about yours truly. Twin sisters! I got my choice."

"You're so screwed up you're seein' double. Twin hallucinations."

"C'mon, Doc, why would I lie?"

"Because you know the truth would only piss me off. Just tell me this: when you comin' back, Super Casanova?"

"As soon as I make a decision."

"You mean about where to get your head examined?"

"Doc, I'm not lying, I swear. I got not one but two women after me down here."

"You know these broads?"

"So you believe me?"

"Didn't say that. I'm just tryin' to trip you up with logic. Works every time."

"Aw, shit. I ain't got time for this. My true love is waitin'."

"So you don't know them."

"Not before now, no."

"But they know you."

"Apparently."

"How? They stalking you or what?"

"Could be. One's a nun, the other a *stripper*."

"Say *what*?"

"Gotta go, Doc. Tell Monica Happy Valentine's Day, give her a kiss for me. Judy, too, if you see her."

"Vic, wait a minute, don't hang up!"

"Gotta fly, Doc. I'll drop you a postcard from heaven. Sayonara, sucker." Then I hung up. Served him right. Besides, he was getting too close to breaking me. I figured I'd get back to him when I had some solid info, real or imagined. In the meantime, he'd have something to wonder about.

Valentine's Day. Cripes. Worst god damn day of the year. Usually. But here I was, in New Orleans, pursued by two beautiful, mysterious strangers. I've done a lot worse, believe me.

I killed a little time just wandering around like a tourist, taking in the sights and sounds and smells of the Quarter. I was wearing my Ray-Ban wayfarers and new trench coat, a gift from Monica, who thought I should stick to being a private eye. I'd told her I'd leave my options open, but really, I wanted to write about my life and put it into some marketable format, like a journal or a diary, slightly embellished for commercial purposes, but basically the truth. I'd been chronicling my misadventures for the past year or so, but wasn't sure what to do with them. Maybe shop them around to small presses, publish them under a pseudonym. I used to write for underground rags back in New York in the early '80s, reporting on the punk and new wave music scene, as well as cult cinema and *avant garde* literature and all that jazz. I gave it up in San Francisco when the competition got too fierce, plus I had just burned out on journalism. I wanted to do something, to *live*, not write about other people doing and living, so through a police captain I knew on the SF force, who was once pals with my old man, I got a P.I. license and then basically trained myself, on the job, in the gentle art of detection. Five years later I was still a novice. But no more. I'd decided to retire after my latest fiasco in L.A., which resulted in at least one innocent death and no justice, and then my cat died, and I felt like my life was out of control, it had to change. Then I get this thing in the mail. I was once again embroiled in a mystery, but not as a hired hand. I didn't have my license with me, anyway. Though I did have my new .45 and phony cop badge, in case I ran into trouble. I kept the rod tucked inside my trench coat as I walked around the Quarter and finally wound up at the Gilded Cage on Bourbon around three in the afternoon of the most interesting Valentine's Day of my life so far.

I walked along the stage and noticed the same sailor that had been there the day before was here again. I kept my distance, maintaining discretion in the dark, and selected a seat where I could keep an eye on him. The same sexy sax music was playing, but there was no sign of Betty Lou. So far. I ordered a beer from the waitress, who was a hot little number herself, and sat there contemplating the Infinite, as is my wont, along with the gyrating thighs and torsos in front of me, as is also my wont.

I had to wonder where this Sister Sue got her info. And why she was interested in the Fallen Catholic angle, trying to win a lost cause like me back after all these years. Actually, I'd never been a devout Catholic. I just went to see my mother play the piano at the service every Sunday. It was beautiful, though not her dream come true by a long shot. She was locked up in a mental home called the Chipper Monks in upstate New York, isolated within her own mind, and she'd been that way ever since my father was gunned down, shortly after my brother Johnny committed suicide by jumping off the Brooklyn Bridge. When I'd gone to visit her a few months before this, she was unable to come out of her trance until the very end, when I was leaving, the cops on my tail for some reason, and she hugged me and told me to run out and play so she could make dinner or something. In her head, things had never changed from our family days in Brooklyn. My old man and Johnny were still alive, I was still her innocent little son, she still had her dreams of being a concert pianist some day. I really wished I could join her in that world sometimes, but then the Dolly Duncan debacle made me realize my life had never been that swell and idyllic, even then, as much as I wanted to pretend it was, so at least I'd have some dreams, even defunct ones, to dip into now and then. But I had outgrown that finally, put it behind me. It was time to move on. That's why I was here in New Orleans, to meet the future head on. But first, I had to decide if it was a future worth pursuing. So far, it was too damn much like the past I was trying so hard to escape.

As I sat there working on my second beer, waiting for Betty Lou, something else struck me as a remote possibility. The previous year I'd rescued the teenage daughter of a mobster from a sex cult that worshipped Elvis Presley, run by a slick amoral head-case who called himself Deacon Rivers. He was merely taking advantage of runaways and lost women, like Lucy, the Mob brat, but as it turned out, so was the man who hired me to find her—her father. Now she was back home in Long Island, her father was in prison on molestation charges brought by his daughter, and word was the Mob was going to let him rot in prison as punishment for his perversion. Deacon Rivers was in Miami, last I saw of him, while trying to elope with Dolly Duncan Dunlap the doper dentist's dame. Dolly was still married to the doper dentist but I figured that didn't matter since the only way she'd consummate our long lost love was in the throes of holy matrimony. Nice girl, Dolly. Decent. Except when she was stoned or whoring her body or murdering somebody. Anyway, so Dolly and I walked into the nearest wedding chapel and there was Deacon Rivers, who was somewhat on the run thanks to my busting up his racket, but he vowed to make a Second Comeback. Was this it? I was always wondering if some wacko from my past was setting me up. If you knew my history, you'd understand why I'm not simply paranoid. This Sister Sue was a religious nut, all right, but fallen from what tree? She didn't throw Elvis at me, but still, that could be merely a ruse. I didn't think it was my nemesis from L.A., the politico behind the Velma Vale scam, once again getting his rocks off at my expense, but you never know with some people. All I wanted to do then was get this Betty Lou someplace private, and see what she had to say about it, if she had anything to say at all. Someplace private. Yeah, right. What I needed was a private eye-land all my own. Otherwise, it was almost show time.

Finally, the lights dimmed reverently and the spotlight hit center stage and from the murky depths of the back room emerged Betty Lou, twin sister of Sister Sue. The crowd went wild. Since Sister Sue had been wearing a habit, I didn't have the chance to see what color hair she had, but even if it wasn't strawberry blonde, the resemblance to her slinky sibling was uncanny. Doppelganger dolls? Was I being doppelgang-banged by these babes? I'd find out before the day was through, then I'd decide whether I approved.

I couldn't help noticing as Betty Lou did her thing that sailor boy was eyeballing me across the bar with the proverbial daggers flung my way. I dodged the daggers but he still made his point. He didn't like me. That was all right. I had no particular reason to like him either. But a problem could arise if he tried to stand between Betty and me after the show. I'd deal with it then.

Actually, Betty Lou ignored the sailor and kept sashaying around my corner of the stage, avoiding eye contact, but keeping well within communication range. I scribbled the following words on a cocktail napkin: "*Meet me for a drink at the bar after this set, I have a message from your sister,*" and stuck in her G-string along with a fin. Her skin was silky and smooth, her fleshy beauty warm and inviting, not like the other girls, who appeared to have been chiseled out of out ice. Little Elvis came out of his coma. No time for that now, though. Later, maybe.

At last Betty Lou returned my gaze as she slid her fingers along the length of her loins and removed the napkin and bill. She kept dancing around as she read the napkin, leered at me with a cryptic expression of bemusement, and nodded, then she blew me a kiss and went on to the other suckers, all of whom were somewhat jealous of this exchange. Including sailor boy, who shot out of his seat and over to my side, a chip on his shoulder the size of the Rock of Gibraltar.

"You stay away from my girl, bucko!" he snarled.

I had to laugh at that line, without apology. "Run along, sonny, you're cramping my style," I said with a smirk, but I doubted he appreciated the calculated corniness of that comeback.

"Hey, I'm *talkin'* to you!" he said, steam practically shooting out of his ears, his face red and overheated. I felt like I was trapped in a Popeye cartoon, fresh out of spinach.

"Kid, she's a *stripper*, and I'm a paying customer, so what's your beef? It ain't like I busted into your honeymoon suite and carried her off. Settle down, you're making a spectacle."

I looked at Betty Lou, who pretended to be oblivious as she continued dancing. Everyone else noticed, though, and whip-lashed between the action off stage and on.

"*Hey!*" sailor boy repeated. "Outside, bucko!"

"Let me finish my drink first, kid. Wait for me, I'll be out directly." My tone was dry but I must say I was a little nervous. After all, he was a well-built specimen. But I had a piece, which I'd stick in his face once we were somewhere in private, should this go that far. It seemed like sailor boy wanted to go the distance, but all I wanted to do was talk to Betty Lou, who I doubted very seriously was as attached to sailor boy as he was to her. Probably yesterday was an isolated fling he took too seriously, wanting to parlay a shore leave sojourn into a binding contract, and Betty Lou didn't look like the type to be tied down. Tied up, maybe. But no, she would do the tying, if there was any. Betty Lou struck me as the kind who likes to be in control. Sailor boy was out of control, but in my face. It was a tiresome obstacle, but one that had to be dealt with immediately.

Sailor boy shoved me out of my seat, and the crowd went wild. The girls had competition for the audience's attention now with this little sideshow. I was waiting for a bouncer to save the day, but no one outside of the ringside patrons appeared interested. So I just got up and then sailor boy slugged me, knocking me on my ass, but I got right back up, rushed the sailor, toppled him into a table, and then discreetly pulled out the .45 and pressed it in his gut.

"Go get yourself another gal," I growled in his ear, punctuating each syllable with the nozzle of the gun in his groin. As far as I could tell, it was too dark for anyone to see the gun, but sailor boy knew it was there, all right. Pale and shaken, he nodded with wide eyes and then I let him get up and he ran out of the bar. Belatedly a big bad hillbilly bouncer showed up, looking me up and down after the sailor split. I told him everything was copacetic now and he nodded and that was it. I was a stud.

Then I saw Betty Lou by the bar. Her set was over. She waved at me and I went to the bar and sat next to her.

"We can't drink with the customers," she said in her sweetly feminine voice, which contrasted sharply with the hard-bitten decadence of the atmosphere, "but I'll meet you somewhere later, if you want."

"That your boyfriend?" I asked her, nodding toward the door and the sailor's wake. "Never saw him before in my life," she said flatly, but with a wry grin. I let that pass. "I'd offer you a penny for your thoughts but all I got is a quarter."

"I don't make change. Buy me a drink sometime and my whole mind is all yours, that sound like a bargain?"

Who cared about her mind? That was bargain basement stuff. I wondered what her whole body cost—a six-pack? "Actually, I don't want a drink, exactly. I just want to know why your sister told me you're out to get me."

"My sister? You *met* her?"

"Yeah. Sue. Sister Sue, the sister. *Your* sister. Sent me a plane ticket, told me I'd meet the love of my life. And hey, you saw me yesterday and made eyes at me, so you must be in on it, too."

She was laughing now.

"What the hell's so funny?" I asked her indignantly.

"*You*. What a *sap*! You fell for that? I can't *believe* it."

I hoped the darkness concealed my blushing. "The ticket was legit, free airfare and accommodations, what the hell?"

"But, your true love, you really thought it was a *woman*?"

"Well, yea, why not?"

"But she told you it was Jesus."

"Well, yea, in effect. But, hell, a free trip's a free trip. I can't complain, really."

"You're Vic Valentine, right? The detective from California?"

"Yea, that's right. You know me, too."

"I know about you. She told me. Vic, she's not a nun in a convent, you know. Not a real one."

"No? She does a pretty good impression."

"That's because she's insane. Her convent is a nuthouse, and she's an outpatient with delusions. She thinks she's a nun, wants to atone for her sins, and wants to save me, too, but in reality, she envies me, but can't bring herself to be like me. It's always been like that with us. Now it's just gotten weird. Don't listen to anything she says. Go back home, Vic."

"But, I don't get it. Why? Where'd she get the money?"

"Trust fund. Our daddy was a rich oil baron in Houston who passed on recently."

"You don't have much of an accent."

"We were educated in Europe. I lost it there. My accent, my cherry. My sister just lost her mind. She's convinced we're in the end times and she wants to save people, practically at random. Your name she picked out of a phone book, practically. To her San Francisco is Sodom and Gomorrah in one. She wants to set you straight and then send you back to preach the Gospel. Or something. I don't know, Vic. Just forget her. Anyway, I have to go. My next set is coming up."

"Well, you've certainly cleared up a few things how about that drink later?"

"Well, actually I don't drink."

"Not even coffee?"

"Well, okay. Cafe du Monde. Tonight, midnight. Date?"

"You got it."

"And remember—my sister is crazy. Keep away from her."

"I'll keep that in mind."

I winked at her and walked outside into the fading daylight, though Bourbon Street was getting brighter, neon signs and people all lit up together. I didn't see sailor boy. I had a little more time to waste until my appointment with Sister Sue in Jackson Square at six, and I definitely planned to be there.

You see, Sister Sue had a tiny mole on her cheek in the exact same spot as "sister" Betty Lou.

Chapter Three
WHAM-BAMBOOZLED

Dusk was falling as my suspicions were rising. I paced in front of the cathedral in Jackson Square, alternately looking at my watch and everywhere around me, scouting for my rendezvous partner, growing increasingly perturbed as time ticked by and I remained alone. I don't mean solitude and celibacy, I just mean getting stood up, though I guess time was leaving the other two in the dust as well.

Finally, at a quarter past six, Sister Sue walked briskly through the center of the park. I figured she'd be coming from inside the Quarter, but she was approaching from the opposite direction, the riverbank. Quite the quick-change artist. She wasn't even out of breath or sweating or anything. She just walked up to me with that same serenely insipid expression of beatitude on her admittedly lovely face. The face with the telltale mole, right where it should be.

"You're late," I snapped. "Flakes bug me, so we're already off on the wrong foot."

"I'm sorry, it couldn't be avoided."

"You got a watch?"

"No, but the convent has a clock."

"Fix it. This kind of crap is a serious pet peeve of mine."

"I told you, it couldn't be avoided. You wouldn't understand the demands made upon me in my vocation, so I won't bother to go into it. Did you talk to my sister?" She obviously wasn't in the mood to spar, had no time to spare. Double ditto for me.

"I talked to Betty Lou, yeah."

"What did she say?"

"She said you're crazy. Which makes her doubly crazy, if you catch my drift."

"I'm afraid not."

"What you need, Sister Sue, is a change of habit. That one's old already. You don't fool me—Betty Lou."

She gave me a mock-offended look. "Are you under the impression we're the same person?"

"Oh, it's a little more than a wild guess, Sister." I reached out and touched her cheek where the mole was. She flinched and pulled back, but she knew what I was referring to.

"Birthmarks run in the family?"

"We're twins, I told you."

"Can it. Twins don't have identical skin markings like moles. I guess you both get zits in the same spot, too."

"Vic, if you really think I'm Betty Lou, why am I lying to you?"

"'Cause. You're nuts. Schizo. And you know what? I must be too, for even standing here talking to you. I just wanted to satisfy my curiosity that you and Betty Lou were one and the same, and now that I have, I have a life to get back to. Nice meeting you—*both* of you. And say hello to the other twenty-six 'sisters' you got locked up in that pretty little head."

"But—"

"Don't bother," I said, holding my hand up. I just walked away from her at a rapid pace through the park and up Decatur to the French Market Inn, never looking back. I told the desk clerk I was checking out that night—I'd pay for it anyway, since it wasn't coming out of my pocket—and then I went upstairs to book a flight home and pack.

There was a knock on my door a few minutes later. I had just finished shaving and was only half dressed, but since Sister Sue was a phony, I didn't feel inclined toward modesty. The knock was persistent so finally I answered it, flinging the door wide open. It wasn't Sister Sue. It was Betty Lou, wearing a long dark coat which she casually removed as she walked into the room, flinging the coat on the bed. Underneath she had on a short black satin dress, leather gloves, high-heeled pumps, and glistening nylons. So the Black Widow wasn't waiting for me to fall into her web. She made house calls. How sweet. But as tempting as she was, I wasn't in the mood to have my precious fluids sucked out of me. For once in my life. I was learning. I was growing, and I don't mean somewhere in the pelvic region. Doc would be so proud. If he believed me.

She lay back on the bed with a sigh and kicked off her pumps and cooed, "Did you think I'd wait till midnight, bad boy?"

"I could ask you how you found me, but then, I guess Sister Sue told you. Left brain talking to the right brain. Convenient, but what a breach of confidence."

"I don't know what you mean, Vic. I haven't seen my sister since you left this afternoon, have you?"

"No mirror in your dressing room, huh?"

"What? I really don't know what you mean."

"What I mean is, you're free to help me pack, you wanna be a pal, or you can just watch. Both of you. I'm easy. I don't ask for much."

"Pack? Why, are you going somewhere?"

"Sexy and smart, too. What a package deal."

She rolled around playfully, and I felt my resolve draining fast. "Want to unwrap the package, bad boy?"

"I can hear the bomb ticking from here. No thanks." I was in the bathroom, going through the pretense of washing up. I only had on a wife-beater T-shirt and my boxers. Little Elvis was suffocating. I couldn't hold out much longer. Restraint in sexual situations is not my strongpoint. Not yet. I kept stealing glances at her lounging on my bed in provocative poses, and I was asking myself, why not? But no, I had to grow up sometime. She was clinically crazy, like so many of the others. In fact she was two in one, at least, and I had to make up my mind to concentrate on myself from now on, and stop falling into these teasing temptress traps of trouble. This was a test, and I was determined to pass it for once, then graduate finally, become a solid individual, and then maybe I'd really find my true, everlasting, one and only love. Even if it only turned out to be my right palm.

I walked out of the bathroom with a towel around my neck that felt like a noose. Now she was doing a striptease right there on my bed, removing the nylons ever so slowly, then the gloves, flinging them my way as I went through the motions of packing. I tried very, very hard to ignore her. I really did.

"This won't work," I said. "Playtime's over. Go back to the convent and repent or something."

"I don't believe you don't want me, Vic."

"Well, I'll prove it to you."

"Looks like you've got some hard proof already, but to the contrary."

I was standing there in my boxer shorts, and Little Elvis was peeking between the shirt I had just put on. How could I win? I was outnumbered. I tucked him back in despite his muffled protests and turned my back on Betty Lou as I pulled on my trousers. She slithered up behind me and put her slinky arms around my neck and licked my ear. Beat red, I turned on her and shoved her onto the bed. Now she was only wearing her black bra and panties, and as I stood there gaping she began removing these.

"C'mon, Vic, I know what you like," she said as she unhooked her bra and swung it around before flinging it at me. I caught it and tossed it back at her. "My sister told me all about you. Oh, and by the way—your true love? It isn't Jesus."

"That'll break His heart. Go on, beat it."

"I thought you liked doing that yourself. But since I'm *here*."

"Hey, hey, c'mon, what's with you, huh? You don't even know me."

"In the biblical sense? In a minute I will." She got up and moved towards me, skillfully slipping off her panties as she did so. My pants fell down around my ankles and Little Elvis stuck his head back out for some fresh air. Betty Lou got on her knees and took hold of Little Elvis and he launched into an aria. "Please stay, Vic. *Please,* I *need* you." She continued stroking my pecker as she talked. I just held my breath and pretended it had no effect on me, though my red face and heavy breathing probably betrayed me. "My sister is a certifiable loony. She sends for guys all the time, pretends she wants to save them, then she makes for a play for them, and when they tumble, she, well, you don't want to know."

"Tell me," I whispered, eyes closed.

"She slices them up and dumps them in the bayou. I'm here to protect you, Vic. She's a serial killer, but most of the men she kills deserve it. Rednecks, wife beaters, lowlifes, macho morons, but *you* Vic, you're special. I can't let that happen to you. So I'm going to have you first, and then she won't want you. She doesn't want anyone I've had, she'd feel like she was secondary."

"But why?" It was all I could do not to shoot all over talkative mouth. I was still making up my mind whether I was going to succumb to her. I wanted her to talk me into it, give me a good, solid reason so I wouldn't feel stupid and weak as usual. So far her case was far fetched, but I was still listening. Only fair.

"*Because.*" She gently kissed the head of my throbbing penis, gave it a tender lick, then teasingly stopped to talk, though she still kept one soft hand on the shaft, delicately massaging it. It was like she was speaking into a phallic microphone. "She says she was raped by a priest as a little girl, a priest I seduced, a priest who thought she was me, and didn't understand why she resisted. I don't know if that's true, though the priest did hang himself in the rectory not long after she told our mother this story, which my mother made her swear not to tell anyone. This mole? The one I'm rubbing with the head of your dick? It's real, but hers is *fake*. If you had really looked closely, you'd see it's on the opposite cheek from mine. Don't ask me why she wears it. Like I said, she's crazy, a killer. Stay with me, Vic, before you go. Please. And then I'll take you to your true love."

"Which is who?"

"She's my room mate. I told her you were in town, and she wants to see you."

"Who is she?" I whispered, near the breaking point.

"Her name is Rose."

I opened my eyes wide, picked Betty Lou up by her shoulders, then picked up all her clothes, opened the door, and threw her out with her clothes behind her. Then I slammed the door and yelled through it, "I might've let you fuck my body but not my *mind*! Now get out of here! I'm on the next plane out and I never want to see you *again*!"

She was pounding on the door, screaming for me to let her back in, creating quite a ruckus, but I had more urgent things to attend to. First on the agenda, I went into the bathroom, gave my pulsating pecker two quick strokes, shot my wad into the sink, washed up, then pulled my pants back on and finished getting dressed. My face was flushed, but not just from the expedient orgasm. I was shaking all over, too. Betty Lou kept pounding on the door.

I froze when I heard her yell, "She was going to come with me tonight to Cafe du Monde, but wanted me to tell you first, so you wouldn't be shocked!"

I went to the door and said through it loudly, "*Bullshit*!"

"Oh, *yeah*? Then why do I even know her *name*, huh?"

Good point. "But you said your sister sent me that ticket, not Rose."

"How do you think my sister knows all about you, Vic? It was all part of her scheme to get you down here, so she could seduce and murder you!"

Briefly I wondered who else was listening to this. "Well, why me? Why go through all this trouble just for me, Betty Lou? Rose, if it is Rose, broke a lot of hearts besides mine."

"There's something else, Vic. I told you my sister is crazy, right?"

"A moot point. So what?"

"Well, she's been in and out of psycho wards all her life, committed by me or my parents, but she keeps escaping. The last one she was in was in Upstate New York."

Oh boy.

"Yea?" I said, heart pounding. "So?"

"She met your mother there. Vic, she knows all about you. She made your mother convert to Catholicism on Christmas Day just to prove she could, even though it's all a scam. She has this sick fixation on you. When she escaped and showed up on my doorstep I wasn't home, but Rose was. Rose let her in and they talked and when I came home I freaked out and threw my sister out of the house on her habit and told Rose all about her fake nun trip and where she had just come from. Then Rose told me her old lover's mother was a resident there, too. Then my sister kept coming back to the house, and Rose pitied her and they got to talking and— Vic, can I please come in now? I'm getting cold out here."

After a yarn like that, it was the least I could do. Slowly I opened the door and Betty Lou, dressed again, though disheveled and shivering, came in. Her mascara was runny from crying. I held her in my arms and kissed her and she kissed me back and before I knew it we were on the bed in a heavy make-out session.

Then I stopped and sat up. We were both still dressed, though ready to remedy that, and Little Elvis was all set for his second show the night, especially since the last one was such a bust, but this was too weird, even for me.

"Wait," I said. "If you're Rose's room mate, then why are you seducing me?"

"I find you attractive. Plus I've heard so much about you, I feel I know you already."

"But what if Rose wants a reconciliation?"

Betty Lou looked at me with a bemused expression, and then she busted out laughing. She laughed and laughed until finally I had to shake her into silence. "Vic, I didn't finish what I was saying. You see, Rose took my sister's preaching to heart, and, well, Rose really *is* a nun now, Vic. A *real* one." Then she started laughing all over again. In a way, I wanted to join her, but I was too stunned to emote at that point. I just sat on the bed massaging my aching cranium. My hard-on had subsided, at least.

When Betty Lou had calmed down some, she began rubbing my tense shoulders and neck as she said sweetly, "Don't take it so bad, Vic. When I met her, she was a stripper. At The Gilded Cage. That's where I met her. She was lost, trying to find herself. She just went from one extreme to the other, I guess. Now she's trying to convert me. She won't believe me when I tell her my sister is only a serial killer masquerading as a nun. They go to the same convent and do work, even."

"Well, how can your sister belong to a convent if she isn't straight up?"

"She talked them into it, said she was a wandering spirit who had thought of giving up the life somewhere else, but now wanted to make amends. She had the outfit so they let her in."

"But if she's such a fraud, Betty Lou, why not turn her in?"

"I did. But she beat the rap. Plus she threatened to kill me if I ever did it again."

"Well, how do you know she's doing this?"

"Because. She showed me the bodies rotting in the swamp."

"And did you take the cops there?"

"Told them about it, yeah."

"So?"

"So what?"

"Betty Lou, what did the cops do about it?"

"Nothing, obviously. She's still out there, isn't she? She told the cops I was the crazy one, that I stumbled on these corpses in the swamp and tried to say she did it just to hurt her. And they bought it, since she's a nun. All I can do now is warn her suitors and would-be victims. Like you, Vic. Vic the Victim."

"Not anymore." I stood up and paced. I looked at my watch. It was nearly ten. Two hours till we were to meet Rose. But why wait? "Can you call Rose and tell her we'll meet her now?"

"No."

"Why the hell not, Betty Lou?"

"Because she's out of touch. Working late at the convent, scrubbing toilets full of holy water."

"So call her there."

"No chance. They're not allowed outside contact while on duty."

"You said Rose is your room-mate, right?"

"*Was*. Now she lives at the convent. With my sister."

"What about her kid?"

"Who?"

"Sammy. Must be a couple or so years old by now. Her kid. You know."

"I don't know of any kid, Vic."

"What?"

"She never mentioned a kid to me."

This didn't make sense. Again. "Betty Lou, the Rose I knew had a little boy named Sammy."

"Well, if she does, she's done a good job of hiding him. She hasn't even mentioned him to me. And this has to be your Rose, Vic. How else would she know you? I mean, you're her *Vic*, anyway."

"Shit. Where's her god damn kid?"

Betty Lou shrugged and lay back lazily, staring up at the ceiling. "Not my problem. Maybe that's why she joined a convent. She feels bad about something."

"Hey—you could be right. I thought maybe it was for fucking me over, but...when did she show up at The Gilded Cage?"

"Hmmm, a few months ago. Five, maybe."

"And when did your sister show up?"

"Only about two months ago, direct from the funny farm. She was rooming with your mother and I was rooming with Rose. Small world, huh?"

"So wait. Hm. Rose showed up five months ago. Last I heard from her was from here, though, just over a year ago."

"She said she'd done some traveling. Miami, to see her folks, then Europe. She just likes it here, she said."

I'd forgotten Rose's parents lived in Miami now. Miami was where I'd left Dolly Duncan at the altar, too—the sacrificial one. I wondered if Rose had ever run into Dolly in Miami. They knew about each other through me, but what were the odds of their encountering each other without me as a liaison? Odds mean nothing in my life, though. Anyway, the fact that Betty Lou knew this stuff confirmed her story about Rose. My Rose. The one and only. I was going to see her again, something I thought would never happen again in my lifetime. I got excited despite my anxiety. This was turning into a hell of a trip after all. Wait till Doc heard about it! But I'd wait to make my report after all the facts were in.

Then something else hit me, and hit me hard. I had to sit down. "Betty Lou, you said your sister converted my mother to Catholicism?"

"That's what Sue told me. Your mother's name is don't tell me. Dorothy, right?"

"Yep. Holy shit. But Ma was always Catholic."

"Well, she renewed her vows. But that's just what my sister says."

"Betty Lou, I just saw my mother a few months ago, and she was autistic, not communicating, in a dream world of her own making inside her head."

"Well, either Sue is lying, or your mother snapped out of it."

"I have to talk to Sue about my mother, Betty Lou. I have to know what happened up there, if she really is recuperating, even as a Catholic."

"But Vic, she'll *kill* you! Sue is not what she seems, I keep telling you. She has one plan for you, to get revenge on all man through random selections, with God as bait. It's part of her sickness, ever since that priest raped her. If he did, which I think is probably true."

"But I thought that was only if I let her seduce me?"

Betty Lou's expression lost its glow, like she had just struck out in the bottom of the ninth. "Oh yeah...but Vic, if we make love, then my sister won't bother you anymore."

"How will she know?"

"I'll tell her!"

"Can't you just lie?"

"She'll know I'm lying. We're twins, Vic. We have this sixth sense about each other. There's only one way to make absolutely certain she won't seduce you and hack you up and let your remains rot in the swamp."

"What if I don't *let* her seduce me?"

"She'll kill you for scorning her. Trust me, Vic. It's too late. She's already made up her mind about you. You won't be able to talk your way out of it. All you have to do is let me take you, and then she'll move on."

"Well, I do have to talk to her if I want to know about my mother."

"I suppose that's true. I didn't even think of that."

"But I don't want to dodge axe blades, either."

"Follow your basic instincts and you won't have to, lover doll."

I smiled at her. God, she was a dish. Ann-Margret on a plate. Much too pretty to waste herself in a stripper club, even as the feature attraction. But then her sister was too pretty to waste herself in a convent. So was Rose. And my mother was too pretty to waste away in a mental home. It was a wasteful world. "Do you offer yourself to *al*l her victims?" I asked Betty Lou with a sly grin.

She lay back and lowered her eyelids. "You're the first, Vic. And probably the last. The rest deserved what they got."

"And what do *I* deserve?"

Betty Lou reached over and planted a juicy kiss on my

quivering lips and whispered, "*This*." Then she kissed me again and I kissed her back and then we began undressing each other as I looked at my watched and figured, what the hell, we still had plenty of time to kill.

Chapter Four
BLUE BALLROOM

You'd think after a horizontal tango with Betty Lou my carnal inclinations would have been at least temporarily curbed, but this was not the case. The idea of Rose in a nun's get-up turned me on unendurably. In fact, the whole time I was making love to Betty Lou, my thoughts were on Rose. I don't know if it was the ex-Catholic bad boy rebel in me, tempting divine retribution by mentally desecrating a living temple, or if it was simply residual desire mixed with lingering bitterness. After all, if Rose was a nun, I'd have the upper hand in certain ways. (Because of our history, I could only consider any future contact in adversarial terms.) For one thing, it would be sexually advantageous for me if her libido were effectively decommissioned. In the past, her promiscuity and allure posed a deadly double whammy for anyone—namely *me*—contemplating a monogamous relationship with her. Now it seemed at last that God was on my side.

Betty Lou was a memory maker in her own right, though. Next to Velma Vale and her late pal Tina Hartman, caught in the crossfire of conspiring circumstances, Betty Lou was the greatest fantasy fulfiller I'd ever come upon, as it were. Since she was obviously somewhat wanton, as were many of the women who broke down and slept with me—which rather depreciated the value of these would-be conquests, I might add—I used protection, giving the phrase "burning rubber" a whole new and exciting meaning, especially since they kept breaking in the heat of intercourse, and I gushed my hot loads inside of her anyway. However, once the deed was done and then re-done and finally well done, I was anxious to shower and go meet Rose. I gathered Betty Lou picked up on this, and was a little ticked off by my enthusiasm.

As we showered together to save time and also to have one more chance to revel in each other's nakedness, she said, rather pointedly, "So now you're safe from my sister."

"That *is* a relief. Now I can talk to her without worrying about winding up another statistic, corpse-wise. Thanks a lot, babe."

"No trouble at all, but you know, this doesn't protect you from other women, Vic."

"Good."

"What do you mean, 'good'?"

"I mean, should another woman ever deign to let me defile her, I'm glad your influence won't turn her off."

"Another woman—like Rose, perhaps?"

"She's a *nu*n, for Christ's sake! I can't beat up her boyfriend, you know. Jesus was pretty tough for a carpenter, I understand."

"Maybe seeing her will give her bad thoughts."

"Well, then I'll tell her to get down and give me fifty Hail Mary's, and that'll be that."

"Down where? On her knees?"

"Hey, what do you care? Whaddya wanna do, pee on me like a cat? You're not like in *love* with me, are you?"

That pissed her off more than anything. She abruptly shut off the hot water, and the cold spray turned my skin blue. By that time she was already out of the shower and drying off. Quickly I turned the water all the way off and jumped out beside her, shivering, goose bumps breaking all over me like hives.

"What the hell's *wrong* with you?" I wanted to know.

"Your romantic etiquette needs some work, Romeo," she snapped without looking at me. Then she went into the bedroom to finish dressing.

I followed her with a towel around me, stealing a furtive glance at the bedside clock. It was a quarter to midnight, we had no time to waste on a petty squabble now. So I was willing to let bygones be bygones. Desperation dictated diplomacy, as is so often the case. "You're right, Betty Lou. I'm sorry, really. I shouldn't have said that. I mean, I know you're not in love with me, because why would a class act like you fall for a *schmoe* like me—?"

"Get dressed in the bathroom, please," she said with sudden shocking modesty. "And shut the door." Her icy demeanor left no opportunity for further negotiating. Anyway, I no longer cared what she thought of me. Maybe that seems callous to you, that I used her and discarded her, which was not the case, but hey, she wanted to bake the clams as much as I did. And I knew she wasn't in love with me, because that was scientifically as well as logistically impossible. We'd simply engaged in a lustful encounter, which in this day and age was not such a healthy proposition, though for some reason, these opportunities kept presenting themselves to me lately. And despite my innate gallant instincts of romantic nobility, I kept succumbing to them. Maybe it was because I was in my late thirties and felt I had barely tasted life, and couldn't afford any missed chances. I chalked it all up to experience, a cavalier new attitude I wish I'd always had. Of course, this latest episode was veiled under the pretense of saving my life from a serial killer, and while I didn't embrace this as gospel truth, so to speak, I coasted under the assumption it might be, in some twisted guise. In any case, it was over now, our bodily fluids had mingled over latex, and I had to move on. If Sister Sue still had an axe to grind, I'd deal with it then. In the immortal words of my spiritual mentor, James Bond, as personified by Sean Connery, "You can't win them all."

So I just went back into the bathroom, closed the door as she requested, dried off, got as dressed as I could with the clothes available to me in there, and then I knocked on the door with mock gentility and opened it.

The bedside lamp had been turned off, but I could still make out a figure in the illumination from the bathroom. Betty Lou was dressed, but not in the sexy duds she had walked in with. She was dressed as her sister, Sister Sue, in full holy regalia. And in her hand was a gleaming hatchet, which she immediately swung my way, accompanied by a banshee-like shriek.

For a brief second I wondered where the nun get-up came from, but then I realized I'd best ponder that later. I dodged the hatchet and it was buried in the door instead of my skull. While Betty Lou hastened to loosen it and cause further mayhem, I dealt her two swift blows to her solar plexus. It felt kind of strange and cathartic, belting a nun, and maybe this sick sensation even aided me in my moment of need, but in any case, Betty Lou doubled over with pain. I then lunged in the dark for my overcoat with the .45, but since it I had trouble seeing anything, precious seconds were lost in the quest, and Sister Sue or Betty Lou or whoever she was recovered and yanked the hatchet from the door. She began swinging randomly in the dark, and my gut felt queasy and I felt pee dripping down my leg. Finally I found the overcoat draped on a chair and began fumbling for the gun, but the commotion succeeded in alerting her to my exact whereabouts. She stood over me, eerily silhouetted like the dark angel of doom in the bathroom light, and just before she brought the hatchet down on my skull I gained control of the gun and blew a hole in her death-wielding wrist. She fell back with a weak cry that almost made me feel guilty. After all, I had just shot a nun. Not a defenseless one, though, a significant point. I looked at the clock. Two minutes till midnight. I had to go.

I threw on the light and finished getting dressed as Sister Sue rolled on the floor in agony, thinking it over. She was muttering maledictions, but I ignored her. After her rather rude outburst I didn't feel inclined toward phony politeness anyway. The hatchet had flown out of her grasp and was imbedded in the bureau. I then saw the duffle bag on her long black coat, obviously what she had used to smuggle in her nun outfit. I guess she'd tossed them it the bed and covered it with the coat so I didn't notice. Some detective I was. See? But I was right about one thing: Sister Sue and her stripper sister Betty Lou were the same lame dame after all. What a case. But I'd think about it later. I was certain someone had been aroused by the ruckus and the cops were on their way. They'd probably want me to go to the station and make out a report and blah blah blah, but fuck all that for now. I didn't want to take a chance on missing Rose. I had no idea where she lived or worked or anything, so making that appointment at Cafe Du Monde was my only chance of seeing her again. And obviously, as insane as she was, Sister Betty Lou knew Rose, and knew Rose knew me. That part wasn't a lie, at least. Actually, nothing she told me was a lie, except for the part about there being two of her instead of one. And in her twisted mind, that probably wasn't a lie, either.

By the time I was ready to go meet Rose it was one minute past twelve. I was a nervous wreck with dried pee on my leg, but I hoped Rose would overlook these details with sanctimonious sentiment. Sister Betty Lou was cradling her wounded hand, sobbing, but I just stepped blithely over her prone form on my way out the door.

In the lobby a horde of cops were just coming in the door. I wanted to just breeze past them but the desk clerk blew the whistle on me. "*That's him*! That's the guy that lives in the room the sounds came from!" the old guy yelled hysterically.

I tried feigning ignorance, but it was no use. The cops surrounded me and began bombarding questions my way, and then I heard authoritative voices from upstairs, saying there was something to see up there in my room, and so I was forcefully escorted back there, politely protesting all the way, and my reticence I'm sure was misinterpreted as guilt. I looked at my watch. Five after twelve. Damn. If I missed Rose now, I might miss her forever. I just didn't have time for this psycho shit right now. I planned to from now on hang a figurative sign around my neck that said, "*No time for psychos or bimbos*."

In my room, the cops were all over the poor nun bleeding on the floor, and at first it didn't look too good for me, considering my urgency to book with this wounded lady of God left in my savage wake. Of course, I could easily plead self-defense with the hatchet in the door, which I did, desperately.

Naturally, the good sister had another version to tell. "He *raped* me! Go ahead, I'll take a medical exam to prove it! His wicked semen is still dripping down my thigh—you can test it for DNA! Then the sick man wanted to butcher me, but when I screamed and tried to escape, he shot me instead!"

Oh boy. I looked at my watch. Ten after midnight. My chances of rendezvousing with Rose looked increasingly grim. As did my chances of living a normal, peaceful life. Of course, her fingerprints were all over the hatchet, not mine. My story would hold up after a lengthy investigation, but who had time for that?

Sister Betty Lou was delicately led downstairs with a towel around her bleeding wrist and I was left standing there with egg frying on my flush face. "Officers, this woman is obviously imbalanced. She's a stripper, I picked her up in The Gilded Cage on Bourbon. Check with them to verify her employment there. When she knocked on my door I was ready to check out. Ask the desk clerk. But then she took off her clothes and one thing led to another and we fooled around, sure. But she told *me* she *wasn't* a nun."

"Didn't the habit give you a clue, son?" the redneck cop asked me.

"She wasn't wearing one when she came in. See that duffel bag? She tricked me."

"This nun seduced you, is *that* your story?"

I sighed loudly. "She's not a real *nun*, man. She's a *stripper, I told* you. She's sick. *Very* sick. In fact, you don't know the half of it. She confessed to me that she's killed many men under these circumstances and dumped their bodies in the swamp."

"Did she tell you this before or after you had sex with her, boy?"

"Before, does it matter?"

"And you slept with her anyway."

"She *made* me!"

"You better come down to the station with us, son. You can explain the rest there. Think hard on the way."

"But I have a date!"

"Your dance card for the evening has been revoked, lover boy. Let's go."

Like I said, it didn't look good.

So I was taken downtown and put into a tiny musty room and interrogated for a few hours, well into the wee small hours of the evening. I'd blown my shot with Rose, detained because of this wacko broad, and I had only myself to blame, really. If I'd never let her seduce me, chances are she would've waited to pull the slasher shit on me, and I would've been able to see Rose. As it was, I was worried for Rose's safety, if the nutso nun ever got out of this. As far as the cops went, I just repeated my story, the true, one and only, everlasting story, over and over. Meanwhile, the poor nun I'd allegedly terrorized was being treated in a nearby hospital. I hit some serious trouble when they found out I had no license for the .45 I'd used to defend myself from the holy hatchet. All I had was a phony cop badge, which really didn't set well with the good old boys, let me tell you. My P.I. license, which would've corroborated the background character info I was laying on them, was back in San Francisco. So I used my one phone call to once again call my reliable pal Doc Schlock in San Francisco. Since it was two hours earlier Pacific Coast time, it was only midnight when I rang him up at home. He was just getting home from a Valentine's date he wouldn't tell me about, with the new mystery lady in his life. All he told me was they'd seen the Johnny Nocturne Band at Pearl's. Doc liked secrets, no matter whose they were. The rest of the conversation went like this:

"Doc. Do me a favor. Go up to my safe behind the heart-shaped dartboard you gave me and get out my P.I. license and send it to me, pronto. Special overnight service. I'll pay you back."

"*What*—? Vic! It's *late* here, man, and even later *there*. What's the big rush?"

"I'll explain later. But I need that badge ASAP, pal. Don't let me down. Just send it in care of the hotel I'm staying at, the address I already gave you." Then I gave him the combo to the safe. What the hell, if I couldn't trust Doc, I couldn't trust anybody. I didn't want him to send it right to the police station because I didn't feel like putting up with all the shit he'd give me when he found out. Not yet. I was just too tired to deal with that now.

"Okay, sure, my man, but what's goin' on? How's that stripper and nun doin'?"

"Forget all that, that was just kind of a joke. There's a new angle now. You remember Rose, right?"

Big pause. "Oh no, Vic."

"Yep."

"No, no, no. Please tell me you're not gonna get mixed up with that crazy broad again. *Please*."

"I haven't actually seen her yet, but in case I do, that badge may come in handy, right?"

"Shit. Just come home, Vic. By the way, while we're on the subject of crazy women."

"Am I ever off it?"

"You got a letter today from a certain Dolly Duncan? I saw it today when I was collecting your mail for you like you asked. Didn't open it, though."

Too much. Just too damn much. "All right. Maybe I'll have you open it for me later and read it to me, depending on how long I'm stuck here. Jesus Christ. Just tell me where it's postmarked."

"That's the weird thing."

"What? *What's* weird?"

"It wasn't mailed. It was dropped off, just stuck in your mailbox. The envelope just says, 'To Vic Valentine, Confidential, Dolly Duncan.'"

"Holy shit! You mean she's in San Francisco?"

"Looks that way, unless she sent it to somebody here who dropped it off for her. Now that I think about it—maybe you shouldn't come home, Vic."

"So where should I go then?"

"Hell, that's a good one. Ain't no place safe. You got a crazy broad in every port! Fly a rocket to the moon, but then you'd probably run into the cat-women, with your luck. Shit, try your luck again with Rose, then. At least she ain't no killer like Dolly. I mean, you ain't hangin' with psycho killer chicks no more, at least not on purpose, am I right?"

Brother, talk about a leading question. "Doc, I can't talk now. Gotta go. Just mail that badge to me right away, right now, please. Trust me, it's important. I'll explain it all later, all right? Say hello to your lady for me, and make sure you do a thorough background check on her before making any commitments. Okay? You know what I mean. Gotta go now. Thanks again, bye." And I hung up in his ear.

The cops told me to stick around town until this was cleared up. Since it was my word against hers before forensics results were in on that hatchet handle, they let me go back to the hotel. I told them I'd be back with my P.I. license once I received it. They wanted to know why I didn't have it with me anyway, and I explained I was supposed to be on vacation. But it seemed my vocation didn't allow for vacations, however. That's one more reason why I wanted to quit.

Before I left, though, I asked a cop if I could get in touch with the nun's roommate.

"You know her?" he asked me.

"Yeah, I do. In fact, she could vouch for my character and history, and maybe tell you a few things about our friend the stripper slasher nun."

"She a stripper too, this room mate?"

"Was. Now she's a nun, too. Well, that's what *this* dame told me, don't look at *me*. See, the stripper told me she had a twin sister who was a nun, who knew my mother in the loony bin, and I don't want to go into this all over again. You have my statement, and that's what I'll stick to no matter what she says, she's out of her fuckin' mind."

"Watch your language, boy, this ain't no pool hall."

"Sorry, officer. Anyway, the thing is, the reason I was rushing off? I was supposed to meet this room mate of hers at a cafe at midnight, but then I was distracted with this hatchet attack, and I missed her."

"If you know her so well, just call her yourself."

"But I don't have the number. I haven't seen her in a while, lost touch, and now I'm afraid I'll never find her again. She'll probably come down for questioning anyway, right?"

"If we find her, she probably will, especially with that story you told us. A schizo serial killer, and a woman at that, dressed as a nun but she's really a stripper, leaving dismembered bodies in the bayou. That's a hot one. You've seen too many horror movies, son."

"Yeah, well, whatever. Just please have this roommate get in touch with me at my hotel, okay? Her name's Rose Myers. I think. Well, she's prone to name changes without notice."

The redneck cop just looked at me like I was a typical Californian polluting his pure Southern air with my Left Coast amorality. "You just run along now, son. We'll find you when we need you, don't you worry. And you can pick up the gun when we establish your innocence, or guilt."

"Thanks, officer." Asshole.

I got back to my hotel around dawn, only to be told my room had been cleaned and rented out to someone else. I was no longer welcome.

"Where am I supposed to stay?" I asked the old desk clerk.

"Not my concern, sir. The bill reflects the repair estimate for the damage. Please sign here."

"Hey, I ain't signing nothin' till the verdict is in. I'm an innocent victim in all this, just remember that. The cops are expecting me to stay here so they can find me later, when I'm cleared of all charges. You wouldn't want to tell them you let me go, right?"

"If you say so, sir. I'll wait until I hear from the police, then. You may have your old room back, if you wish."

"I thought you said it was rented out?"

"I was hasty. I apologize. But if there is any further commotion, I'm afraid you'll be asked to leave."

"Whatever." I took my key and ran up to my room and went straight to sleep. For once I didn't have to worry about having nightmares. Nothing in my sleep could compare with the one I'd just lived through.

There was a knock on the door some hours later, I wasn't sure how many. It was the bellhop with my Fed Ex package. I ripped it open and there was my license. Vic Valentine was back in action.

I took a shower and got dressed and tried not to notice the hatchet slice in the door as I left. I went down to Cafe Du Monde for some *cafe au lait* and *beignets.* It was early afternoon, a nice, breezy day. I tried to relax.

So Dolly Duncan was back in town. Terrific. All of the loony ladies from my past were converging on me at once, it seemed. But I must say, that was the most exciting Valentine's Day I'd experienced in many moon. Hell, ever! It had it all—sex, violence, mystery, intrigue. The more high I got on caffeine and sugar, the better I began to feel about my overall situation. But then I considered the fact that there seemed to be no escape for me from these crazy women. I got depressed again. Then, when I thought about my mother doing rosaries up in the Chipper Monks mental home, I got even more depressed. I wanted to call them to check up on her, but the last time I was there, I'd sort of worn out my welcome. It's a long story. Suffice to say they'd hang up on me if I ever called. And sending Ma letters was out of the question. They'd just be torn up. Maybe I'd read the letters Ma had sent me that I'd never opened. Those and the one from Dolly. Was Dolly seeking asylum from the Feds? Probably. I just didn't have room in my brain for all this, much less my life. What could possibly happen next?

Then who should waltz into the cafe but Rose. And she wasn't dressed as a nun, either.

Chapter Five
MERMAIDS LOVE SEAMEN

It was like hearing an old song on the radio that you haven't heard in a long, long, time, one with indelible associations in your memory, like "King of the Road," which always reminds me of a certain road trip into the Poconos with my family. My mother loved that tune, and turned it up loud when it came on the radio, and I remember looking outside the window as we glided through the darkly emerald and rustic beauty in our Corvair station wagon. I can still hear the river rushing, smell the pines and burning wood of the campfire, whenever I hear that song to this day. But the nostalgia is tainted with this knowledge: that time and place, that woman who was my mother, are long gone, intangible outside of my recollection. They only exist as a dream in my head, inspired by timeless music.

So it was seeing Rose. The sudden sight of her triggered sundry emotional responses in my psyche, and in my mind I heard Al Martino singing the old standard "Painted Tainted Rose," about a guy shunned by his true love, only to run into her years later when she is a mess, but he doesn't feel vindicated, he feels sorry for her. Rose wasn't in a nun suit, but she didn't look so hot. She'd put on weight, which actually looked good on her naturally curvaceous frame, but her face looked worn and puffy, her sexy green eyes lifeless, and she had on too much makeup, which for her was an anomaly. She was wearing tight jeans and an even tighter lavender tank top. No bra. Her naturally graceful gait was now a slutty, come-hither sashay. And her hair, dyed jet black last time I'd seen her, was back to its original auburn, but was still long and thick and wavy. Rose was still beautiful, but somehow cheaper, or maybe just older. It'd been a little over a year since I'd seen her last, but she looked like she'd aged much more in that time. She didn't seem to notice me yet. She just went up to the counter to order something. I stood up, took a deep breath, sucked in my gut, straightened my shoulders, and accosted her.

I tapped her delicately on the shoulder and she turned abruptly as if I'd startled her. Her tired eyes, nearly buried in mascara, widened when she saw me. I noticed the huge crucifix dangling in her cleavage just before she gave me a big hug. "Oh Vic! I don't believe it! *Vic.*" She hugged me very tightly, and I hugged her right back, and the emotionalism of the scene was obviously attracting some attention, but she didn't seem to want to let go. I felt embarrassed and self-conscious, and must have been beat red, but she just kept holding me, whispering in my ear: "Vic, you came. You came. Oh Vic. Hold me. I have so much to tell you, to show you, my darling." Then she kissed my face, but not my lips. Just my cheeks and all. I couldn't decide if it was like running into a long lost lover or long lost sister. Or both. And that crucifix was cutting into my chest. Gently I made her release me as I smiled and kissed her lightly on the lips.

"Let's get our coffee to go and take a walk," I said with surprising coolness, as if none of this had much effect on me.

"All right," she said with a radiant smile. Her eyes had a spark of life now. Our reunion had rejuvenated her, it seemed. What a switch, an odd twist. Last time I was the one who felt needy and vulnerable, and she was the one who was in control, pulling the strings. Life, man. Fucking life.

"This must have been the single weirdest twenty four hours of my entire life," I said as we walked out of the cafe with our coffee in to-go cups. We kept looking at each other, then looking away coyly. It was a strange combination of discomfort and excitement, like we were just meeting for the first time, after all we'd been through over the years.

"What do you mean, seeing me?" she said. "You knew I was here, right?"

"You knew I was here, too. Betty Lou?"

"Uh-huh. I had no idea you two knew each other."

"We don't, not before I came down here."

"That's not what she told me."

"I'm not surprised."

We strolled along the Moonwalk, on the bank of the Mississippi, sometimes inadvertently touching each other's arms and shoulders and hips, then drawing away discreetly. We didn't know what boundaries existed, had to start all over again. But in a way, I didn't want to start all over again, or even take up where we left off. I didn't even want to be here anymore.

"You know where she is now, right?" I asked.

"Who, Betty Lou?"

"Yea."

"Well, last I saw of her, she went to work, and said to meet you guys at that cafe last night, but you never showed up."

"Uh-huh. Know why?"

"No. But from your tone, it sounds bad."

"You could say that."

"I get the impression something happened between you."

"Oh, yeah."

Rose took a deep breath, like she was getting ready for someone to belt her. Her coffee was getting cold, but she wasn't drinking it anyway. I was trying to figure out why I felt so blase about seeing her again. I had to work at giving a damn.

"So, what happened?" she asked finally.

I told her. Everything. The sex, the hatchet, the story about the sister. Rose took it all in almost passively, attentive but distant, like I was recounting the plot of a Douglas Sirk movie. It was so melodramatic it was comical. But neither of us laughed. I guess we were both numb by now.

"That's a hell of a story," Rose said as we stood watching the river.

"You don't seem overly fazed," I told her.

"I knew Betty Lou was crazy, a religious fanatic, but the rest of it. I had no idea I was rooming with a psycho."

"You never met Sister Sue, I take it?"

"Oh yeah. But I never saw them together."

"That never made you suspicious?"

"No. I have my own problems to deal with."

"Sammy?"

"How'd you know?"

"Well, I had a conversation with Betty Lou before, y'know."

"Before you fucked her?"

"That piss you off?"

"No. I'm celibate now, anyway. And you don't *owe* me anything. Besides, you paid the price anyway, right?"

"Like always. Rose, did you send that plane ticket?"

Long pause. "Yes."

"So why'd you have Betty Lou meet me?"

"I was scared. I wanted to see if you'd actually show up first, but she took it into a whole new direction, didn't she?"

"I can't believe you didn't know she was a split personality."

"Well, maybe because I am too, in a way."

"So why, Rose? Why'd you fly me down here after all this time? Especially since you've sworn off, y'know."

"I don't need you to get laid, Vic."

"Never did. Sorry."

"Still bitter, I see."

"Can you blame me?"

She shrugged. "I guess not. I have a lot of atonement on my agenda. I'm starting with you."

"So why'd you sign the letter my true love and all that crap?"

"What? That must have been Betty Lou's doing."

"So you're *not* still in love with me."

She looked at me hard. "Part of me is, may be. I don't know, Vic. I just don't know. But of all I've been with, and there's been many, I can't seem to shake you. I feel I *do* owe you something."

"You don't owe me anything, Rose. I've been through so much shit this past year, you'll never know."

"On the rebound from me?"

I had to think about that one. On the rebound from Rose. That explained a *lot*, actually. Dolly, Velma—I never loved them, not the way I loved Rose. Dolly was sentiment. Velma was sex. Rose was the love of my life, and I thought I'd lost her forever. Could that have influenced my subsequent series of screw-ups? "Hell, no," I said anyway. But I was still thinking about it.

"Your tone gives you away," she smiled. Then she reached over and laid a maternal kiss on my cheek. "That's okay, Vic. I'll make it up to you somehow."

"You're taking too much for granted," I said. "That episode with your room mate typifies, no, epitomizes my experiences ever since, y'know."

"Since I left you?"

"Let's change the subject."

She laughed. "To what? Sports?"

"Speaking of which, how's Tommy?"

"Don't know, don't give a damn, Vic."

"Hard to believe."

"I don't give a damn about that, either."

I nodded at the crucifix. "Tough talk with that necklace and all."

She fondled the shiny gold sacred ornament thoughtfully, smiling softly. "I guess I still have a way to go. I always had a mouth on me, not sure what all Betty told you."

"She said you were a nun now, for one thing."

"God willing, I will be. I plan on joining a convent, if I'm deemed worthy. That's why I wanted to see you before I retreated from the world. My conscience wouldn't let me go on with my life until I'd squared things with you."

I just shook my head. "What happened to all that Far East philosophy?"

"I don't know. I still embrace some of it, but I need something *more*. After some bad wild nights at The Gilded Cage and then some guy's room, coming home feeling like hell, wanting to die, and there was Betty Lou's Bible. I started reading it, and I'd talk to Sister Sue about it when I saw her."

"And you never realized Sister Sue *was* Betty Lou? C'mon!"

"I didn't care, Vic! Shut up and listen, will you? You may think this is all very amusing, but I'm very serious. It gave me something I needed, this Bible, this book I'd always made fun of. That's all that mattered. I started going straight from some loser's bed to Church, and then I cut out the sex altogether. After I lost Sammy, I thought I'd lose my mind, too."

"What? You lost him? He's dead?"

"I thought Betty Lou told you?"

"Just that he wasn't around. I asked about Sammy, and she had no idea what I was talking about."

"Oh, Vic." She started crying, first lightly, then in a torrent. "I gave him up. I gave my son away. I gave him away."

I held her and we sank to the ground together and she cried in my arms, repeating that declaration over and over. That explained it, or some of it. She was racked with guilt for giving her son up for adoption, for not coming through as the mother she always dreamed of being, for being selfish and scared. Things I could relate to. Hell, I'd never want the responsibility of a kid. The difference was, I didn't have to make that decision. Rose made it, then reneged on it, after the kid was already here. Now she regretted it, and had a painful gap to fill somehow. Maybe with religion. Maybe with old friends. Like me.

We just sat there and I held her for a long time. Twilight descended on the Crescent City. It was placid and soothing. She told me Sammy was living with some well-to-do family here in town, actually, and his new father was a professor at Tulane. They lived in a big old house in the Garden District. She wanted Sammy to have the best, and he did. She figured he was young enough to forget her, but she wasn't going to be able to forget him. The new family adopted him on the condition she wouldn't try to contact him and confuse him. When she gave him up she was at the bottom of the pit she'd dug for herself. She'd gone from man to man, looking for love and all that. She wasn't a fit mother for

Sammy, she concluded. She wasn't going to be able to change in time, to turn her life around, to settle down. Holding her as she whimpered in my arms, she was so pathetic I couldn't believe it. Once she'd seemed so together, so sure of herself, so self-righteous in her convictions. Now, here she was, one foot in a convent, the other in Hell. The opposing forces were tugging at her like a wishbone. And her one wish was to die, unless something or someone came along to convince her life was worth living. And who would that be?

Vic. Good old reliable Vic.

But that whole Betty Lou thing had been the final straw, I think. I just didn't have it in me anymore to go down this road. I had to think of myself, my future, and stop succumbing to the dictates of my dick. I had my writing career to pursue now instead of skirts. Soon it would be a new millennium, and I'd be forty, still trying to figure out what the hell I wanted to do with my life, straddling two centuries, hell, two millennia, an in-betweener who didn't really fit in either. I had no more time for fin de siècle flings. I didn't want to waste any more of it helping other people help themselves.

"Rose, if it's absolution you want from me, not sure I can oblige."

"No, Vic. I just need to know you still care. That's all. You're the most sincere man I've ever known. The only one. All the rest were just stepping stones to nowhere."

"Welcome to nowhere, sweetheart."

"And you came. You came all the way down here, because you knew it was me, right?"

"I wasn't sure who it was, actually. But my curiosity was piqued, that's for sure. Plus, a free trip to New Orleans, how could I pass that up?"

"But who else could it have been?"

"Well, let's see." So I told her all about Dolly and Velma and all the others in between. She listened patiently and with real interest, trying hard not to laugh most of the time. The more I went on, the more convinced she was that all of this happened because I was on the rebound. Talk about ego. I told her she was grossly overestimating her influence on my life. I told her the Dolly thing would have happened anyway eventually, because I always felt compelled to go back East and track down the killer of my father, who just happened to be my high school sweetheart.

"Yes, but, Vic, really—eloping in Miami? You were going to

actually *marry* that sick woman?" Rose was beside herself with mirth.

"I don't know if I'd have actually gone through with it, but, y'know, I was just sort of winging it. That seems crazier than me putting myself through hell over you?"

"*Yes*! You loved me, Vic, and I loved you. That was never resolved, really. There was actually something real going on there, but this story you're telling me is ridiculous. I remember you talking about Dolly when we were together in New York. You told me way back then you two never belonged together. Nothing in common, different goals, all that."

"Okay, okay, so maybe I was being overly-sentimental. But she made me feel sorry for her, and I was lonely, and I wanted to make this connection with my past, y'know? Re-live it, re-do it, make it right this time, and Dolly was my link, I thought."

"And all the time she was dropping you clues that she never was the person you wanted her to be, not even in high school, but you were too blind and dumb to see it. Even in high school, she was a fucking junkie, and a ho, and you refused to see it! *God*, Vic! How could you be so *stupid*?"

"Hey, *you're* the one who was boarding with Lizzie Borden and didn't have a clue! And I'm not joining a convent! I'm not the desperate, disillusioned one here, remember."

"I'm not doing this out of desperation."

"Oh *no*? Rose, if someone had told you a year ago you'd be applying for nunhood, you'd have laughed in their face, and you know it. Anyway, you just don't look religious, even now."

"What are you talking about?"

"Well, look how you're dressed, for instance. Not exactly like you're on your way to Sunday school."

"Fuck you, I mean, forget you! I still have to work, don't I?"

"You mean you're still a stripper?"

"Uh-uh. Bartender. Not at the Gilded Cage. Just some tourist bar. But they want me to dress like a homegirl. I still have bills to pay, you know, rent until I move into the convent, if they have me."

"Hey, we need to go down to the police station."

"Me? Why?"

"Jesus Christ, your room-mate just tried slashing me to death!"

"Don't say the Lord's name in vain in front of me."

"Yeah, yeah, sorry."

"Vic, I *mean* it!"

"Okay! Didn't any cops show up at your door last night?"

"I don't know, I haven't been home."

"Where have you been?"

"At a friend's."

I stood up. Our coffee cups were lying empty on the ground. It was getting dark now, and even a bit chilly, at least for this town. Maybe it was just the company and the circumstances. Suddenly I just wanted to leave town. "A *friend's*, huh. I thought you were celibate now?"

"Well, mostly. I'm still trying, Vic. He's someone I've been seeing, and he's leaving soon, anyway. Betty Lou was seeing him too so we didn't stay at my place. I ran into him here at Cafe Du Monde last night waiting for you to show up and then we just went to his hotel. He's in the Navy."

"Holy shit. I wonder if he's the same guy I saw Betty Lou with."

"He is, probably. She dumped him and then we started a little thing but that has to end now. He's not happy about it, first getting the shaft from Betty, now me."

Funny, I was hardly jealous. "He's the one giving out the big *shaft*, babe. But you did him a favor in a way. If I hadn't have shown up, he might have been her next victim instead of me."

"Damn, you're right. Poor Betty Lou. She really *is* lost."

"Lost? Rose, c'mon. This broad was hacking guys up and you never noticed something was a little off about her?"

"We didn't talk much. I talked more to her sister."

"Who was the same person."

Rose shivered. "I guess I should go down to the station and clear things up with them, huh?"

"Good idea. You gotta date tonight?"

"No. I told the sailor last night was our last. I just wanted one for the road, I guess. I thought I was supposed to see you last night and when you weren't there I figured you didn't want to see me and I got depressed. Let's just go, Vic, and get his over with, okay? I have to be at work soon, in like an hour."

"Call in sick."

She just looked at me and said, "Okay."

Then we went down to the police station and I waited as they grilled Rose for a long time. Betty Lou was in a psycho ward. The cops had been to her apartment and found incriminating stuff, they wouldn't tell me what, and in the hospital she had freaked out and had to be put into a straightjacket, and so my story checked out. I showed them my P.I. badge and my gun license, but they no longer cared about that stuff. I got my .45 back and they said they were sorry I was put through this and I said yeah, yeah, yeah. When Rose came out of the interrogation room she was sobbing and all, and she told the cops she didn't want to see Betty Lou now or ever again. She also said she was moving out of the place she shared with Betty soon anyway. She didn't tell them it was hopefully into a convent.

We left the police station and went back to her apartment, near the Faubourg Marigny. It was a flat inside one of those ancient ambient courtyards. There was a cop by the door who asked for I.D. and all before they let us in. The place was a mess, ransacked by the cops, so she gathered up a few things and we headed back for my hotel. That old room with the hatchet marks gave me the creeps now so we switched to a different one where neither of us had to be reminded of our close calls with catastrophe. She dropped her stuff off and then we went out to eat, going whole hog at Galatoire's restaurant. We deserved it.

Over dinner, we tried to figure out what to do next.

"You're going back soon?" she asked me.

"To San Francisco? Sure. Tomorrow."

"What? Why so soon?"

"I have a *life*, Rose."

"But what about *us*?"

"I thought you were hooking up with the sisters soon?"

"Well, you're not going to try to talk me out of it?"

"You kidding? Why? Whatever works, I always say."

"Don't you still love me?"

I rolled my eyes. "Oh, so *that's* it."

"What?" she said.

"You were hoping for a reconciliation?"

"No, not exactly. I'm not sure I'm doing the right thing. I need a different perspective."

"Rose, *look*. You heard what all I've been through this past year. But it wasn't as fun as it sounded. I've changed, somehow. I'm not the man I was in the hospital a year ago. I don't even want to be a detective anymore."

"Well, what do you want to do, then? What are you qualified for?"

"Well, I've thought a lot about it, and I want to start writing again."

"Really? That doesn't sound so far fetched, really. You were always good. That's part of what initially won me over about you, your wit. So what do you want to write now? About music again?"

"Naw, *me. Mi vida loca.* My crazy fuckin' life. Maybe fictionalize it, but I figure all this weird crazy shit I've been through lately has to be worth something, right?"

"Yeah." A teardrop escaped her control and rolled down her cheek. I reached over and wiped it away.

"What's wrong?" I asked her.

"I just feel like I'll never see you again, after tonight."

"Well, if you're locked away in a convent down here, not much chance we'll run into each other."

"But don't you care? Won't you miss me?"

"Sure. I've spent most of my life missing you, Rose. I guess I'm just used to it by now."

"Do you think I should join that convent?"

"Not my call, babe."

"Vic?"

"Yeah?"

"I really do love you, you know."

"I love you to, Rose."

We held hands across the table. The waiter left us alone for a while.

After dinner we walked along Bourbon Street and Rose told me she was quitting her job the next day and would ask the sisters if she could move into the convent full time. She said it like it was an ultimatum, but I didn't let it bother me. I just nodded and said whatever she thought was best was fine with me.

Since this was her last night in the secular world, though, we decided to go all the way. We had Hurricanes at Pat O'Brien's and watched some traditional jazz bands cooking at Preservation Hall. Every now and then she'd kiss me on the cheek, then as the booze kicked in, the lips. We held hands and she squeezed mine so tightly it almost made me cry, because I knew in my heart this really was our last night together.

We were walking back to my hotel around midnight when a drunken shadow lurched out at us. It was Sailor Boy.

"You want *all* my women, asshole?" he blurted with a belch.

"I thought your ship had sailed by now," Rose said to him simply.

"Beat it," I said, brushing past him. But he reached out and grabbed Rose by the hair. I went into my trench coat for my .45

and stuck it in his face and cocked it. Drunk as he was, he backed off, cussing, swearing he'd get even one day, but in the morning I'd be long gone, and so would Rose, and so would he, probably. This night was only a dream, after all.

In our room Rose removed all her clothes and climbed into the bed while I was in the shower. When I came out, I just looked at her and said, "Rose, you belong to God now and all that kinda shit. We can't. He'll kick my ass worse than Tommy Dodge."

"It's our last night together, Vic. Please."

"I thought you got that out of your system with Sailor Boy."

"Tomorrow you'll be gone, Vic, and I'll be out of touch for who knows how long. This isn't about sex, like with the sailor. It's about me and you and the love of my life. You see, Vic, I did sign that letter your true, everlasting love, hoping you'd think it was me, because I wanted to be thought of like that by you, because *you* are the love of my life, too, Vic Valentine. But we can't be together, can we? You don't want to, not forever. You don't think it would work. And I *know* it wouldn't. I gave up Sammy, whom I adored more than you, in some ways, because I can't commit myself to anyone. I'm hoping the sisters will teach me how, and I'll learn to one day forgive myself. But tonight, I want to make a memory, Vic. Think of me as a mermaid or something, who wants to spend one last night on land with her lover before she returns to the depths of the ocean forever, where she belongs. Please, Vic? Please."

So I got beneath the covers with Rose for the final time and we made love all night and into the morning, without sleeping or talking.

Early the next morning I quietly packed and then kissed her once lightly on the forehead before I left.

Chapter Six
ATTACK OF THE LOVE LEECHES

Later that same day I was back home in San Francisco, sitting at the bar of The Drive-Inn as Doc Schlock and Monica Ivy went about their business. By now I'd recounted my New Orleans adventure, and they were still shifting through the details, incredible as they were. Me, I just took the whole thing in stride. I was changing, growing, and they could see it.

"And it's about goddamn time," Doc said, washing glasses. Monica didn't do glasses. She was busy pouring drinks for the losers beside me. Up on the giant TV screen behind the bar the old classic *Attack of the Giant Leeches* was playing. Sexy Yvette Vickers was tormenting her rotund hubby Bruno Ve Sota as she got dressed to go see another man.

"I agree, Doc," I said. "You gotta finally give me some credit."

"Shit, I've been giving you credit for years, Vic. Which reminds me—if you ain't doin' the detective thing no more, what about that back rent you owe me? What about *future* rent?"

"Doc, *relax*. I ain't gonna just go cold turkey. I got my license back in my wallet. I'm not closing up shop just yet. I gotta wait till I get established as a writer before I just quit the day job. And night job and every time in between."

Monica came over and put her hand on mine and squeezed it. Her hair was still dyed black, but shorter, and she didn't have bangs anymore, it was parted. Her Bettie Page phase was fading, but she wasn't sure what her next look would be yet. She was still young—like twenty-three or so—so she had time. Me, I had time too, but not as much. I felt I'd wasted my youth trying to figure out what to do with it. "I'm proud of you, Vic," she said.

"Yeah?"

"Sure. You finally were the one to leave. I know how you felt about Rose. That was strong of you."

I sighed with worldly wisdom. "Yeah, it was tough to go. But I knew if I stayed, it would just be the same shit all over again. Rose ain't gonna last in no convent, I tell you that much. But she needs to try something new and different, on her own. The solitude will do her good, if nothing else. And maybe she'll get

Sammy back somehow. In a few years. They're in the same town, and she probably won't want to leave Nawlins without seeing him again, if *I* know her."

"Think you'll hear from her again?" Monica asked me.

I shrugged. "Probably. I mean, I didn't think I'd see again the last time she bailed on me, and look."

"But this time *you* left," Monica said. "Doesn't that feel better than being the one who gets left?"

"I don't know. Neither feels too great."

"I know. I just broke it off with my boyfriend."

"Really? The musician dude?"

"About time for that too," Doc chimed in. "I never did like that little punk."

"He was a *bum*," I said. "Frank Sinatra would call him a bum. He wasn't a punk, Doc. *Monica* is a punk."

"And so are you," Monica said to me.

"Yeah, for once," Doc said. "I'm glad you left that bitch behind too, Vic. But you just had to sleep with her one more time, didn't you?"

"Doc, how could I say no? I may never see her again."

"That's so romantic," Monica said dreamily.

"Thanks," I said to her.

"Bullshit," Doc said typically. "You just can't resist pussy, Vic. Face it. Never could. I mean, I'm proud of you and all, but c'mon, that thing with the slasher bitch shows you still got a ways to go, my man."

"Whaddya mean?" I said defensively.

"What do I *mean*? Vic, she was so obviously fucked up from the beginning, and you fell for that absolutely lame ass story about her twin sister the serial killer nun, and that if you didn't sleep with her, you'd be her next victim, and then of course, as any idiot would figure out, there *was* no twin sister, and so she tricked you into pushing her wacko button, and you nearly paid the ultimate price. I mean, if that hadn't have happened to shake you up, I think you might've stayed in New Orleans and tried to talk Rose out of joining the convent. And not only that, it could be Rose set you up—*again*—and had that crazy broad meet you first, knowing she'd pull this shit and kill you. Don't ask me why, Rose is just as crazy in her own way, but that's just how you like 'em, Vic. I still think your next woman will be whistling loony tunes as well. You attract 'em, Vic, and then you give 'em just what they want. Rose is history, but you still got this magnet for manic muffs inside of you. That's just what *I* think."

"Thanks for the vote of confidence, Doc."

"Don't listen to him, he's just cocky these days, cause he's got a girl himself," Monica said with a sly smile.

I looked at Doc pointedly. "Yeah! Here I am, spilling my guts as usual, and you still haven't given us any details on your new mystery lady."

"I won't either."

"Doc! C'mon! Is that fair?"

"Fuck fair, I want my *privacy*. See, Vic, you like all the attention, face it. But I like keeping my secrets in the bedroom where they belong. That's just me."

"But you told me when you were boffing Monica here!" As soon as I said that, I knew it was a mistake.

"I gotta work, Vic," Monica said icily, walking away.

"Fuck you," Doc said, and he walked away too.

I just finished my beer then went upstairs to my one bedroom apartment/office to relax. They'd get over it. They always do. Anyway, I wanted to get to that letter from Dolly Duncan sitting on my desk, waiting for me ominously like a notice from the draft board. One reason I had gone down to The Drive-Inn to begin with was so I could get juiced up for the experience. Because after I read the letter from Dolly, I planned to finally read the unopened letters from my mother, sent over the years from the Chipper Monks mental home. The major regret I had in leaving New Orleans was that I didn't have a chance to grill Betty Lou about my mother. If only I had known Sister Sue was inside Betty Lou the whole time, I could've asked her to come out and answer a few questions about my mother before she buried the hatchet in my head. Now, since the people who ran the Chipper Monks had officially put me on their shit list, I didn't know when I would ever be able to hear about my mother again. But maybe through her old letters I'd learn something valuable, get to know her better, find out what makes her tick, tick like a god damn bomb. This was it. I was taking stock of my entire lousy life and cleaning house, once and for all.

First, though, just to warm up, I tossed some darts at my heart shaped dartboard. I put on some Sinatra, the Capitol collection. I leafed through my prized collection of '50s cheesecake magazines. I gazed at my personally autographed pin-up of Mara Corday, one of my most cherished possessions. The one thing missing in my pad was Puss. God, I missed that little fur-ball. I had felt a lot less lonely with him around. It didn't seem fair he was gone. Maybe his life as a dickless pussy cat wasn't so hot, and I was being selfish in wanting to keep him around forever, or at least until I met a nice girl, but I couldn't help but curse the heavens for taking him from me. I was too damn lonesome, man. The Space Age Bachelor Lifestyle was getting old. I was a failure both as a cad and as a romantic. What was left?

Fuck it. I opened the letter from Dolly, which was not postmarked. She was somewhere close by, or had been when she dropped this in my mailbox. That creeped me out more than the slasher sister almost. My hand was shaking as I pulled out the letter and read:

"Dear Vic—I know this must really surprise you and I'm sorry if I caught you off-guard or something but I just have to let you know that I still think about you all the time. You are the only one who ever meant anything to me. I've left Donald for good and am free but now there are some people after me I don't know who - Mafia? Cops? But I am on the run and I didn't know where else to go so I am here now in San Francisco to ask you, to beg you for help, any kind you want to give. What I really need is a place to stay for a while until I can decide where to go next. I know this is asking a lot but you are really my only friend in the world. I don't deserve you, and I understand if you want nothing more to do with me, but if you have any feeling for me left in your heart from the old times, please contact me as soon as you read this. I'll stay here until I hear from you or for a week or so, whichever comes first. Thank you just for reading this far. Love always, Dolly."

Oh man.

At the bottom of the letter written in the scrawl of despair was a hotel and room number. It was a cheap joint in the Tenderloin with no phone. I'd have to go down and knock on the door. But would I?

No telling when she had dropped this in my mailbox. I'd been in New Orleans for a few days, so her week was almost up, if it wasn't already. Why was all this happening at once? What did it mean? Was Fate just bored and mixing everything up to pass the time? As usual, I had no say in the matter. I just went along for the ride.

Those letters from my mother would have to wait a little longer. I couldn't deal with it right now, with all this other stuff going on. I put the letter from Dolly in my pocket, put on my trench coat, and went down to my trusty sky blue '63 Corvair. Night had fallen, and the fog was drifting in.

In fifteen minutes I was on O'Farrell Street in the heart of the Tenderloin, or maybe it was the pancreas or the bowels. Whatever. The crumbling dive where Dolly said she was staying seemed to be inhabited by your basic junkies, pushers, pimps and prostitutes. Dolly should right at home.

The lobby smelled like cheap perfume blended with puke and a dash of piss. No one was around except for a few tenants rotting away in the lobby chairs, waiting for a fix or death, whichever came first. I went up the creaky elevator to the fourth floor. I got out and walked a long the dimly lit hallways half-expecting the Minotaur to come barreling around the dark corner. Finally I located Dolly's room number in the flickering light and knocked.

She opened almost right away, as if expecting me. She had on a pink negligee and a carnal smile. She jumped into my arms and smothered me with kisses. I carried her into the room and kicked the door shut behind me and set her down on the bed.

"You look great," I lied to her. Actually, she still looked pretty, but puffy and painted. Like Rose. Jesus, did every woman who screwed me over wind up like this? It was too good to be true. No, on reflection, it was too depressing, especially when you considered the fact that I wasn't in such great shape myself. We were all locked away in solitaire, it seemed, trying to find the guard with the key so we could plea bargain for our release.

The lamplight in the tiny room was dim, too. It was hardly furnished, and only had a sink with a small dirty mirror in the corner. There was a communal restroom down the hall. It was your typical residential hellhole. I hated to see Dolly in a place like this. I only hoped she wasn't paying for her room the way most women here did.

"You look wonderful," she said. Her eyes were glazed and when she sat up on the bed and reached up to embrace me again I could tell she was high, and not on life, either.

"Dolly, c'mon," I said, delicately putting her arms back down to her sides. "Let's talk. What's up with you? Why are you in a dump like this?"

"It's all I can afford. Anyway, the people looking for me won't come around a place this, I hope."

"Who? Who's looking for you?"

Her head wobbled on her shoulders like those little dogs from a rear view mirror. Her words were slurred. Her tousled blond hair was showing its dark roots. Her nightie straps had fallen down her smooth white shoulders and her perky breasts were popping out. I fought the urge to touch them. Come on, Vic. New man. Strong. You can do it. Don't give in. You've had enough pussy to last a lifetime just in the past few months. Time to grow some ethics now. "I don't know who the people are looking for me," she said, sounding like a lush.

"Well, how do you know anyone's looking for you?"

"B-because I was in Havana! After Miami? And men in suits came looking for me, and roughed me up, but I talked to one of them, in a room, and he sort of fell asleep and I escaped and then left Havana and went to Mexico, Cabo San Lucas, and I was okay for a few weeks when more men came around, and—what do they want, Vic? Are they Mafia?"

"Honey, if they were Mob, you'd be dead. I got that contract on you cancelled, but Junior, he's in the Witness Protection Program now, and I think he spilled some beans about you and my old man, but see, I was in L.A. recently, it's a long story, but the gist of it is, there was this politico who knew all this crap about me, had connections, and one of the things he knew was all about *you*. His goons told me that Junior had told some of their people about how you killed my father and I knew it and let you go. But since you were in foreign countries, they couldn't extradite you, right?"

"That's what I thought, but they were pretty rough."

"What did they say they wanted?"

"Just that they were taking me back, whether I wanted to or not, whether or not it was legal, to face charges. I thought maybe you narced on me."

"Not me, babe. No way. I told you—clean slate."

She hugged me and held on so tight I had to let her. She kissed my neck and whispered in my ear, "Vic, I think they want to kill me. I've been *bad*, Vic. Again. I went back to being, you know. A whore. That's what I was doing in Cuba and Mexico, and these men only let me go if I did stuff to 'em. But they practically *raped* me, Vic! And then they said they were taking me back anyway! But they didn't say to whom, or for what or anything. I got back on junk, I was so depressed, and I just didn't know where to turn except to you. Please help me, Vic. *Please*."

I just held her and she kept kissing my neck and then my face and before I knew it we were rolling around on the flea-ridden mattress as roaches watched and mice listened.

"I want you to put it in me, Vic," she whispered passionately. "Please. I won't make you wait any more..."

She had my pants half way down my legs and was gently stroking Little Elvis when I mentally flashed on her getting gang-banged by a mariachi band and a bunch of horny renegade Feds and then Castro himself and I just couldn't go through with it. Little Elvis got serious stage fright and went back into hiding.

I abruptly stopped making out with her, sat up, pulled my pants back on, and then put on my shirt.

"Vic, what's wrong?" she whimpered in a little girl voice. "Don't you like me anymore?"

"Dolly, you need *help*. That's for *damn* sure. But I'm not the one to help you. Not any more. I just can't. I mean, Jesus Christ, Dolly, you iced my own *father*! You're lucky I even speak to you, much less kiss you! I just have to start saying no, Dolly. I'm sorry it has to start with you, but it's just timing, that's all. I've been through a lot lately, in L.A. and New Orleans, not to mention my thing with you back East, and I just can't do it anymore, Dolly. I'm sorry. Really. You'll just have to learn to fend for yourself. Sorry. Really. I just, I gotta go." I stood up resolutely.

Predictably, she started crying. I ignored it as I walked toward the door, my trench coat over my arm. Then she said in a sob-choked voice: "I'll kill myself in you leave, Vic. I mean it. I really will."

I froze with my hand on the doorknob. "That's not my problem anymore, Doll," I forced myself to say.

"You don't care about me, or *any*one, do you? I thought you were the one who was different, who didn't just want to use me, but now I see, since I'm just a broken down slut now, you're tired of me, huh? Well fine, Vic. Let it be on *your* head, then."

I whirled around and ran over to her and grabbed her by the shoulders and shook her into stunned silence. "God *damn* it, Dolly! What else do you want from me? *You killed my father*, and that nearly killed my mother, and all I want is to let you go free, so you can start over! Why can't that be enough? Why are you laying all this guilt trip crap on me, huh? Why? Because in the past I was stupid enough to fall for it, that's why! But not anymore, Doll. Not anymore. The fuck stops here."

"Oh that's cute," she snapped spitefully. "What happened to you in New Orleans, Vic? Get burned again? Blaming it on me?"

"That's got nothin' to do with it," I said. "But down there I saw someone else I need to forget. Rose. Remember Rose, Dolly?

Yeah. I told her the same thing I'm telling you, basically. That I can't help her. I have to live my own life without her now, and she has to do the same thing. And so do you. You don't love me, Dolly. Not in a real way. You've just known me longer than anyone else. Look at you—you're still young enough to get it together, go back to nursing school or something, meet a doctor, settle down, all that jazz."

"I tried that already, remember? Donald? That life nearly *suffocated* me!"

"So what the hell do you want then?"

"I don't know! I just don't *know*." Then she turned the waterworks back on. I just couldn't resist her in such a sorry state. I sat back down beside her and held her in my arms, trying not to think of Dolly as she was now, but when she was a kid, and we listened to the same songs on the radio, and talked about our future. She had been molested by her father and felt worthless, and then she started turning tricks and my old man was one of them. Then she was so guilt-ridden she started popping pills that he supplied. When she wanted to stop he threatened to tell me about their affair and her extracurricular activities. In a demented delirious rage she shot him with his own gun and stabbed him repeatedly as Junior Benenito and a few others watched outside Pop's Pool Hall. Then began the blackmail, the lies, the deceit, all of which I wasn't privy too until I caught her with Junior in Miami and it all came spilling out in one horrendous torrent, like projectile vomit. The Mafia had a contract out on whoever iced my old man, because he was a valuable asset with inside dope, as it were, but I managed to get them to cancel that. But then Junior was running scared for not handing her over to the Mob years ago, instead forcing her to pay for his silence with sex. So he turned himself into the Feds, and now Dolly was back in hot water, with no place to turn. I just didn't want to abandon her, but what else could I do for her now?

I asked her.

"First, tell me one thing, Vic."

"Yeah, sure, anything."

"Did you sleep with Rose before you left her?"

My hesitance told her everything.

"So why not *me*, Vic? Please? Remember how you always wanted to put it in me, in high school, in Miami? Well, I want to do that for you, Vic. I want you inside me. Don't worry, I carry protection. Just please, put it in me, just once, and then I promise,

I'll go away. I have a little money saved from, you know, and I'll go to Canada or somewhere, and become a nurse, help people until I feel better, feel like I've given something back, made up for everything. I promise I'll be a nurse and help people and myself from now on, Vic, only please don't turn me away, not this one night. Let's finish what we started so long ago, and then it'll feel complete. I'll feel complete. We both will. Please, Vic? *Please*?"

She kissed me and unzipped my pants and an hour later I left Dolly Duncan behind forever.

Man, if this kept up, I'd shrivel up and blow away. I'd spent so much time in my solitary life fantasizing about sex, and now my fantasies had invaded my reality, and I had no place to run. I was exhausted, emotionally, mentally, and especially physically. Three different women in three days. A new record for me. You'd think I'd feel like a stud, but I didn't. I'd finally consummated my affair with Dolly, and there was no sense of completion, of joy, of triumph. I told her as I put it in that I loved her, and I meant it, in a way, and she told me loved me, but the words felt hollow. The sex was okay, but then Dolly always turned me on. Afterwards she reiterated her promise to get herself together, and told me this night had inspired her to live. That made me feel good, that I wasn't just getting my rocks off, but helping out another human being the best way I could. But still, when I got back to my room, I felt empty and alone.

Except my room wasn't empty, and I wasn't alone.

At first the figure sitting up in my bed startled the hell out of me. Who the hell was this now? Rose? Dolly? The slasher sister? I flipped on the light.

It was Monica. The covers fell down around her waist and her big beautiful bosoms were totally bare.

"Vic, I told you I broke up with my boyfriend, but I didn't tell you *why*."

"Why?" I gulped, weak-kneed.

"Because I'm in love with someone else."

"Oh yeah? Who?"

"You know who, Vic."

"Doc?"

"*No*, silly. C'mon, you're a big time dick. Figure it out." She stretched out her soft arms and beckoned me into bed with her.

Chapter Seven
BELOW THE BIBLE BELT

Fortunately, I was already drained, both fluid and emotion-wise, from the brief, frenetic encounter with Dolly, so it was easy to come to a quick decision about Monica. I just smiled at her and walked right into the bathroom, locked the door behind me, and turned on the shower.

"*Hey*!" I heard her yelling from the bedroom. "I think you're missing a few clues, detective!"

"No, I got 'em," I yelled back, stripping down and stepping into the cold, bracing shower. "*Ah*!" I screamed in initial shock.

"Don't tell me you're taking a fuckin' *cold shower*!" Monica yelled, jiggling the locked doorknob furiously. "I take personal offense at that!"

"It ain't personal, babe!" I yelled back. "Believe me—you got one of the best set of hooters in San Francisco!"

"So here they are—what's the problem?"

"No problem. I just can't let myself look at 'em, or else."

"Or else what?"

"You know god damn well what!"

"So? I'm offering it to you, Vic! Remember those close calls we've had?"

"Yeah, I remember once you made me beat off in the bathroom after I satisfied you. A thing like that tends to stick in one's craw."

"Oh! So what is this—revenge?"

"No! It ain't that. No, no, no."

"Then what—? Vic? *Vic*!"

"*What*?"

"Open the damn door and come out here!"

"Not till you leave."

"What are you so afraid of? I don't get it!"

"Yeah you do."

"Not from you. And I want you, Vic. You have a naked woman on your doorstep, begging you to make love to her, and you're takin' a cold shower? This isn't like you at all, Vic. I'm worried about you."

"Monica, believe me, under other circumstances, in another time, when I was younger, I would be all over you, but you happened to pull this when I'm about to start making some major life changes, and being more selective about who I get involved with is *numero uno*."

"Vic! This is *Monica*, Vic! Your bosom buddy! Not some floozy, some tramp, some stranger, it's *me*! I'm not doing Doc anymore, haven't for, heck, months and months, and anyway that was only like two or three times, and I dumped my boyfriend because I've thought about it a lot, and I just want *you*, Vic. I've been here for you through Rose, through Lucy, through Dolly, through Velma, even *Judy*."

"Hey! How the hell you know about Judy?"

"She *told* me, duh!"

"What?"

"You obviously don't know women as much as you wish you did, Vic."

"Yeah, no shit. That's why I need to chill out and settle down. I mean, okay, I'll tell you. I just got back from a cheap hotel in the Tenderloin. And you know who was there?"

"Mamie Van Doren?"

"Yeah, right. No. *Dolly*."

"*Your* Dolly?"

Now I had her. "Yup."

Big pause. "You do her?"

"Yup."

"Vic! How *could* you?"

"It was the only way to get rid of her."

"Well, making love to me is the only way you're gonna get rid of *me*!"

"Monica, c'mon! Gimme a break! What do you want from me?"

"You know."

"But why me? Why *now*?"

"Because if I wait any longer some other neurotic spaced out bimbo will show up and steal you away. I'm not crazy like the others, Vic."

I didn't say anything to that.

"Vic?"

"Yeah?"

"You hear what I said?"

"About what?"

"Fuck you, Vic!"

"Not me, babe."

I could hear her pouting. "Vic, remember after you got back from New York, and I dressed up as Bettie Page, and came up to see you, and you said you were still getting over the Dolly shit, but you asked if I'd take a rain check?"

"Yeah, so?"

"Well, what did I say?"

"You said yes."

"Well, time to cash in, bub. Get your butt out here. I mean it, Vic. I'm not leaving until you do."

I turned off the shower, toweled myself down, and opened the door. Monica was standing there with a triumphant grin on her angel food face. Her body was pure devil's food, though. She was only wearing her purple panties and a garter belt. God, she knew what I liked. She walked up to me and enveloped me in her arms and began kissing me passionately. My towel dropped down to my knees, and Little Elvis broke into his opening number.

"Doesn't it bother you I've just been with someone else?" I asked her as she led me by the pecker to the bed.

"Does it bother *you*?"

"A little."

"Well, get over it."

This time, she didn't make me beat off in the bathroom.

A couple of hours later, we were lying entwined in each others limbs, surrounded by empty Chinese fast food cartons, listening to Russ Garcia's '50s ambient outer space album *Fantastic*a. Monica felt good in my arms. I was one hell of a stud all of damn sudden, I was thinking. What was the sudden attraction? You'd think I just won the lottery or a guest star stint on *Melrose Place*. Had I inherited some money everyone but me knew about? Won a contest? Never in my life had I experienced anything like this. It had started in L.A. with Velma Vale and Tina Hartman, and ever since New Orleans had escalated rapidly into something out of James Bond's wildest dreams. I made Mike Hammer look like Pee Wee Herman. What the hell was it? I was using the same after shave, wearing the same wrinkled outdated clothes bought at the neighborhood thrift shop, had the same cynical outlook and antisocial demeanor, the same slight thirty-something inner tube hugging my mid-section because of my lack of real exercise. What had changed about me? Nothing, that's what. It was the world around me that had suddenly changed, or else gradually, but I just wasn't paying attention, too inside my head to notice or care.

"Why, Monica?" I asked her as she lay content and sleepy in my arms. I'd made her come four times to my two, and so her conversational skills were somewhat nullified.

"Huh?"

"Why am I suddenly stud central? Rose, Dolly, Sister Psycho, you. And before them Velma and Tina. After years of begging girls to look twice at me. Of course, in my early twenties in the early eighties I was hot shit, back in New York, when I was writing, and, *hmmmm*. Maybe *that's* it? Just deciding to be a writer has turned my romantic clock back!"

"Writers don't get laid that easy unless they're famous," she mumbled, eyes closed.

"But maybe you smell fame *comin'*, right? Could be a good barometer of impending success."

"What, your dick?"

"Well, yea."

"Vic, do you really think I wanted you because of royalties on stuff you haven't even written yet, much less sold?"

"Well, what then?"

"Just because you're you, Vic. Just because you're *you*."

"That was never enough before. Remember Flora, the nurse at the blood bank? The one I kept going down and donating all my blood to see, so much I was gettin' fuckin' dizzy?"

She laughed. "Yeah?"

"And she wouldn't go out with me because she was dating that bonehead sax player, so I went around with my camera and took pictures of The Date That Never Was and gave it to her in a folder?"

She laughed some more. "Yeah, you nut, I remember The Date That Never Was. But she wasn't right for you, Vic, that's why you had to go to all that extreme length for nothing."

"Well, actually, a couple of months later—"

"I know, I know, you guys made it, but after she hired you to find her fiancé who skipped out on her, and then she just went back to him when you found him. You *sap*."

"Closed the deal, anyway."

"That's not you, Vic. Don't talk like that."

"Monica, I gotta admit, all this attention—it's going to my head. *Both* of 'em."

She opened her eyes and smacked my face rather harshly.

"Don't let it, or I won't love you anymore. I love you for the romantic idiot you are."

"Monica, you're not *really* in love with me, are you?"

"Yes, I am."

"But, what if I'm not in love with you?"

"Well, I'll give you time to come around."

"Monica, you're too young for me. I mean, I'm too old for *you*. And you're right, going from one bed to another, both with women in them, is not like me. Or the old me. It's the me I always dreamed of being. But, I dunno. Something feels *off*."

"Vic, I keep telling you. Those women weren't right for you. It's like, once you start getting it, the women smell it on you, and want you. The more you're wanted, the more attractive you become. See how mature I am? So shut up and go to sleep, and in the morning I'll make you breakfast."

"Monica, could it be you're just on the rebound from that dude?"

"*Sssshhhhh!*" she said, putting first her finger on my mouth, then her lips, kissing me into acquiescence. I relented and piped down, but didn't close my eyes. She did, and was soon fast asleep. I just lay there trying to figure out what to do, and with whom. What Monica said made sense—the more women who wanted me, the more I'd be wanted by women. It was a dream come true. I finally deserved the title Space Age Bachelor. No more entries in the Loser's Log. I didn't think Monica was truly in love with me, but I'd let her pretend until she got over it, and she would. In the meantime, could I really keep this up, so to speak? I wasn't the same age I was in New York, over a decade earlier, when I cut a similar sexual swath through Lower Manhattan. Then I met Valerie, who was really Rose being schizo, and then she left me one day and it was downhill after that. Now I had left Rose, and it was uphill all the way, it seemed. I didn't even miss Rose anymore. She'd be okay. She was a survivor if nothing else. I still felt sorry for Dolly, but knew her well enough to realize that whole story about Cuba and guys in suits chasing her was at least partly a fabrication. She just wanted to see how far she could manipulate me again. I gave into her sexual advances, partly for old times sake, partly for new times sake, but then I refused to spend the night or ever see her again. I was not only getting laid, but I was doing it on my terms, for once. No longer was I the patsy, the fool, the loser in love. I had firm hold of the reins for the first time in my life.

Or so I thought until the next day.

When I woke up, Monica had Billy Idol on the CD player, and I was greeted with "White Wedding" along with the inspiring aroma of coffee that wafted in from the kitchenette by the outer office. I also picked up the scent of frying eggs and toast. Then as my senses readjusted to this sweet reality, she came in wearing only a slinky purple robe that matched her purple panties. She sat the tray on my lap, embraced my neck, smothered me with kisses, and said, "If you go back to Dolly or Rose after all this, I'll kill you."

"*Whoa.* Take it easy," I said with an awkward laugh. "This is all very cool, but this ain't like our honeymoon or anything."

She licked my ear and said, "Not yet."

Now I was getting nervous.

"Monica, c'mon. You know me. I'm a confirmed bachelor."

"Oh, I don't want a *ring*, silly. That's not my style, either. I just want you to be my boyfriend, and I'll be your girlfriend, and when I go on the road with The She Beams, you'll go with me."

The She Beams were Judy Fagin's all-girl surf band, which Monica sang harmony with sometimes when she wasn't tied down to The Drive-Inn and school.

"What? What if I'm working?"

"Detectives go everywhere. Hey, that should be a bumper sticker on your car."

"No, my bumper sticker should say, *gumshoes get stuck.*"

"How about, *private eyes need contacts!*"

"How about telling me what this is all about, Monica? Why the sudden change of heart?" I sipped the coffee and bit a piece of toast. Perfect. She could cook, too.

She pouted, but that only made her cuter and more kissable. "It's not so sudden, Vic. We've never been just friends."

"Yeah, but you never seemed to want me in a monogamous kinda way. What's up? Just on the rebound from the musician?"

"Oh, fuck that asshole, Vic!"

"No thanks, I got my hands full."

She seemed agitated now. I'd hit the wrong button, or the right one, depending on how the conversation turned out. "I just don't know. I'm just afraid, I guess."

"Of being alone?"

"Well, yeah. You know how my parents died, right? Murder-suicide?"

"Down in Woodside. Yeah. Tragic stuff."

"Well, you're kinda like me. A mess. I mean, with a screwed up background and all. We're both kinda funky and weird and misfits. I just think we could make each other's lives a little easier, help us forget the past. Doesn't that make sense?"

"Sure, but why the dog-tags? I mean, you always seemed like such a free spirit. Now you're June Cleaver, for Christ's sake. Or June *Cleavage*, at least."

"I'm just trying to make you happy, that's all. Wasn't last night wonderful?""

"The best."

"Don't you *like* me?"

"Sure, you know I do."

"I mean, in a special way."

"Monica, c'mon."

"All right, I won't be pushy anymore. But today is my day off. You know what I'd like to do?"

"Fuck?"

"*After* that. Go to Grace Cathedral."

"What? Up on Nob Hill? How come?"

"I've always wanted to go inside and walk the Labyrinth, but not alone. And then we can go get plastered at The Top of the Mark. That sound like fun?"

"Well, sure, but Grace Cathedral? You getting religious on me, too, Monica? I mean, the last religious chick I met didn't turn out so hot."

"I'm not going to chop you up and dump you in the bay, Vic. I just want to have a special day with you. You never know when, y'know. It'll all end."

"When what will all end?"

"*Everything*. You, me, the world. Life is short. I want to do everything I want as soon as I think of it."

"Monica, what the hell is bringing all this on with you? With *everyone*? There's this urgency, this desperation. What the hell's going *on*?"

She just shrugged, looking melancholy. "I just want to live and love while I can," she whispered.

I thought of Puss, and my mother, and Velma Vale, and Tina Hartman. Made sense to me. Monica already had the day off from work, and we both decided not to spring our little tryst on Doc just yet, though Monica figured he'd find out sooner or later anyway. My hope was that Monica would have her love bug exterminated before it got any further than my bedroom. In the meantime—what the hell? So far she hadn't exhibited any homicidal traits or overly neurotic tendencies. She was crazy, sure, but in a garden-variety young, insecure and oversexed kind of way, and didn't seem as dangerous as the others. Not yet. I was lonely, she was lonely, so unless and until she pulled any particularly nasty stunts, I had nothing to lose by keeping her company. Unadulterated feminine affection is the best tonic I've found for those lonesome-sad-mortal-broken dream blues.

We hit Nob Hill and Grace cathedral around one in the afternoon. It was one of those postcard perfect days in San Francisco, with a view of Alcatraz and the Bay so obscenely scenic I nearly retched on a cable car. The clouds were white and fleecy, the air brisk and clean from the recent rains, the breeze bracing and cool. We even held hands as we strolled along. Man, I was almost happy, or as close as I ever get.

The Cathedral itself was very old time San Francisco, and had a cozy, warm, inviting atmosphere that almost made me feel guilty for my lapse in faith, Catholic faith, at least. The ceiling was high and curved like a dome, the stain glass windows strangely inspiring with their configurations depicting better times and people, or at least simpler. I was in awe as I stood there taking in the stone temple of modern worship. Too bad I had so little respect for the people who attended services. I didn't know them personally but I had a feeling they were all a bunch of phony hypocrites. Well, a lot of them, anyway. Take my word for it. That's one reason I'm not religious in the conventional sense, besides the politics and abuse of power and reliance on ancient hearsay that could be heresy: Just too damn many people involved.

Nonetheless, as I stood there watching Monica solemnly walk the Labyrinth, this maze on a rug between the entrance and pews, which led to a center where you stopped to meditate before walking the same way back, I couldn't get Sister Sue out of my mind. Or rather, her initial spiel to me about the Apocalypse and my role in it and all that. It occurred to me that maybe all this was happening to me as part of an end of the century, end of the world clearance sale, we've lost our lease, everyone must go, or come, as it turned out. Was I wasting my time diddling around when I should be busy saving my soul and others somehow? I mean, Bible prophecy aside, the world isn't getting any better, had pretty much always sucked except for a brief shining interlude in the '40s and '50s, and it sucked then too but just looked prettier doing it, in my opinion, and I did believe in an afterlife. Those Nature programs on PBS convinced me that something grand is going on we can't really figure out, because that would be like the puppet second-guessing his master. I mean, you watch how animals in the wild know just what to do, how to do it, who to do it to, without formal instruction, and how all of their relationships are symbiotic, not only with each other, but with their environments, and it has to make you believe in an overall scheme. If that's true, then there's a Schemer somewhere, right? Take a look in the sky at night sometimes, and just think for a few seconds, ponder the scope of it, dig the fact you're seeing these little beads of light that are actually posthumous signals from exploded stars billions of light years away. Sort of like here on Earth, with Elvis and Marilyn and James Dean and all—the Hollywood constellation of dead stars that still radiate. And what makes the god damn Moon come out at night and shed some light on the subject, and who tells it to punch out just as the Sun is getting his fat fiery ass up for the day shift? I'm telling you, there's something going on we don't understand. My infatuation with the female form distracts me from this obvious truth sometimes. Maybe that's why I spend so much time contemplating cheesecake. It's tangible, it's accessible—well, at least lately—and the mystery is right there for you to explore first hand, so to speak. To me, all the beauty and intrigue of the Universe is contained within one curvaceous female form. Heavenly body, indeed. But my fear, standing there watching Monica's ass as she took the holy walk alone along the Labyrinth, was that since female bodies are exceedingly temporal, the real truth, the everlasting, one and only one, was eluding me, and if the world ended before I figured it out, I might be in big trouble. We all might.

I decided I'd take on one last case before I retired: The Secret of Life As We Know It. If I cracked that one, I could live out my days in comfort and security. Sure, maybe I was being grandiose and preposterously ambitious, but really, I had nothing better to do with my life. Now that getting laid was no longer such an ordeal, I could redirect my energies toward a quest for loftier ideals and more substantial goals. And in a weird way, I had that psycho slasher sister to thank for my epiphany. Maybe she had a mission after all, besides her gig as a serial killer. God works in mysterious ways, she said. But mysteries are my specialty, babe. This was the way to go out, the big finish, the final case to end all cases. Of course, I'd still have to worry about paying the rent and eating and all, because jobs like this come cheap. Look at all who've tried and failed, wasted efforts for little or no reward. But I'm Vic Valentine, baby. And my destiny had finally presented itself to me.

"C'mon, babe, let's go to the Top of the Mark and celebrate," I told Monica as she finished the walk.

"Aren't you going to walk the walk?" she asked.

"Talk the talk, walk the walk—you name it, sweetheart. I've had a vision, an awakening, and you're gonna be the first to know about it."

She just stared at me, wide eyed. "Really? Have you like, flipped out finally?"

"Could be. Sleep deprivation and all, too much sex, my brain has been overly sapped or something, but let's have a drink and I'll run it by you."

"Sure." She reached over and kissed me, then quickly caught herself. This was a church, after all. I was so excited I could have had her right there in the middle of the Labyrinth, but that might not be appreciated by any but the most liberal of pastors. Even in San Francisco, I didn't want to take that chance.

The Top of the Mark has a 360-degree view of the City and the Bay Area in general. On a spectacular day like this, it was like living Cinerama. The bar was very chic but comfortable and they always played classic '40s swing and ballads over the sound system. It also always made me want to shout "*Made it Ma, Top of the World*!" a la Jimmy Cagney in *White Heat*. So far I hadn't gotten up the nerve. Maybe today would finally be the day.

Chapter Eight
LOOSE LIPS

"Vic, I changed my mind," Monica said to me, fright-eyed. "You're really cracked after all. I mean, you can't really be serious about all this."

"Why the hell not? I'm designated dick on the Case of the Cosmos."

"You're spaced out, that's for sure."

"Monica, c'mon. I mean, does the past week of events seem *normal* to you?"

"Your life has *never* been normal, Vic. Why lose it now? You're taking things *way* out of context. So you get laid a few times in a row. Big deal. Be grateful. You dwell on it so much, it was bound to catch up with you sooner or later, right? You're like a dog in heat that attracted the bitches all at once. So it's mating season. No reason to start looking for signs from beyond. Sex isn't an act of God, it's a force of Nature, Vic. Relax! Besides, I was the showstopper, right? Forget the others. Cheap warm-up acts. You can't even solve the mystery of your own life, Vic. You're like seriously deluded if you believe you can really figure out the meaning of life and clue everyone else in as your parting shot."

I sat back and sighed, surveying the vista of The City and the Bay. We were on the west side, facing the ocean and the Golden Gate. It was beautiful and inspiring. If only Monica would listen to me, the grandeur of the setting would be matched by the magic of the moment. "You just don't' get it," I said with a sigh. I finished my martini, Monica's suggestion for the occasion. "Someone up there is trying to tell me something, I just *know* it," I murmured, almost to myself.

"Are you telling me you're hearing voices now?" Monica asked me with a skeptical scowl.

"*No*," I said emphatically. "Why can't you give me any support in this? What is it you like about me, besides the cut of my jib? My personality, right? Well, this is it, babe. I thought you were so in love with me and all, but I guess not."

"*Fuck you, Vic!*" she said rather loudly, turning several appalled heads in the fancy joint. "What is this, emotional blackmail?"

"What? Where do you get that?"

"Just because you start giving me this weird crap about you being on a, um, uh, divine *mission* to save the world or something, doesn't mean I have to back you up. The fact that I'm pointing out how insane you're talking proves how much I really do care! What do you want, some dumb little airhead who just agrees with whatever you say? Screw that, Vic! Breakfast in bed is one thing, but if you want some little brainless bimbo to give you strokes, go back to Dolly or one of your other crazy women. You got me figured wrong." She crossed her arms, tense and hyperventilating.

Whoa. Time for damsel damage control. "Monica, cool it, no need to get touchy, jeez. I mean, all I said was, I want to do something meaningful with my life, not just waste it chasing skirts. When I say I want to discover the Secret of the Universe, what I really mean is—"

"Well? *What*?" Monica insisted. She was on the verge of bolting, I could tell. Maybe that was just as well, all things considered. Then she said bitchily, "And I'm not about to put up with you chasing skirts anyway. You're settling down now. With *me*. So get a grip, dude, and not the way you usually do, either."

"Aw, forget it. You don't understand, you never will. Just drop it."

"Oh, so now you're patronizing me? I'm just a stupid little girl, is that it? Well, I'm the one sitting at this table who went to college, remember."

I just shook my already spinning head. Women. *Woe-man*, as someone once said to me, I think my father. "Monica, look. This is about me, not about you, or me and you. I like you and all, you're very sexy and very sweet, and we're good pals, the best, but this is between me and myself, and if you can't hang with it, fine."

No dice. She was all ice. "That's nice," she snapped sarcastically. "Turn it around so it looks like I'm not standing by my man."

"Aw, boy. Forget it, Monica, just forget it. You're just as crazy and unreasonable as the *rest* of 'em."

At that point she stood up, threw her martini in my face, snarled, "*You're* the crazy one for pissing on the best thing that ever happened to you," gave me the finger, and walked out in a huff. Everyone in the room thought my table was suddenly of vastly greater visual interest than the panorama of San Francisco. I wiped the martini from my blushing kisser, smiled and shrugged in a casual "*What can you do?*" kind of way, and ran out after her. But the elevator door closed on me just as I reached it. She actually stuck her tongue out at me just before she disappeared from sight.

I actually felt guilty. Monica had been exceptionally kind to me lately, as always. She was right. She'd stuck around while all the others came and went, as it were. And I dismissed her as just another assembly line airhead. I just can't win. My spiritual quest was put on hold. I waited for the next elevator and descended to the lonesome depths of the Mark, then walked out into the lonely streets of San Francisco. The fog was drifting in and it was cold and windy, no longer sunny and scintillating. Everything had been going so well. What the hell happened? I was honest, that's what. Kills the mood every time.

Instead of returning to my Corvair I decided to walk up and down the hills and work off some weight. The weight on my mind was the flabbiest part of my anatomy, especially since Little Elvis was sound asleep, exhausted from his recent breakneck series of concerts. The Corvair was in a downtown garage, so I stuck to Union Square. I went into Lefty O'Douls and had a couple of bourbon shots chased by a beer, then walked up Powell to Lori's Diner for a solitary supper. I just couldn't figure out what had gone so wrong. Maybe the message in this was to finally forget women altogether, just concentrate on my mission. Yeah, that was it. God was telling me to stop being so easily distracted. Yeah, right. Whatever.

I was sitting at the counter minding my own business, steeped in my newfound resolve, when who should tap me on the shoulder but Judy fain, leader of The She Beams, and one delectable blond bosomy babe. I didn't know whether I was happy to see her or not. Then she kissed me flush on the mouth as she took the seat next to me, and I decided yeah, I was plenty happy to see her.

She had with her a bag of CDs she had just bought and was really excited about. "Check these out, Vic! New surf bands I never really heard of, well, heard of, but never heard. Have you? There's Shadowy Men On A Shadowy Planet, Deadbolt, and the Scandinavian band, Laika and the Cosmonauts."

"Wow." I looked them over. "These as good as Man...or Astroman?"

"I don't know yet. Hope so. Want to come over and hear them with me? I have the night off from rehearsal. I haven't seen you for a while, have I? Monica said you were in New Orleans for a

529

few days, that right?"

"Yeah."

"How come?"

"Vacation."

"Really? How was it? Me and the girls may tour there on our swing through the South. Our manager's trying to set it up. We're gonna hook up with Impala in Memphis if all goes well."

"Yeah? That's great."

"Vic, what's wrong? You seem, I don't know. Preoccupied."

"You could say that, yeah. How's the new album coming?"

"Great! We just laid down around four tracks, and they're unmixed, but you can hear a tape of 'em at my place, if you want."

"Sure. I've never really been over to your place much, have I?"

"No, you always just drop me off and split. Like last time. I still think of that night, Vic. All the time, in fact. What's with us?"

Oh no. "Wh-whaddya mean?"

"I mean *us*, dummy. Hey speaking of 'Dummy,' have you heard that album? By Portishead?"

"Just that song, what is it?"

"'Sour Times'?"

"Yea. I like it a lot."

"Good, we may cover it on the road. It has that spy sound to it, y'know?"

"Yea, it certainly does."

"It reminds me of you, actually. It seems everything reminds me of you lately, though. Vic?"

Concentrate, Vic. This is a test. Don't blow it. "Yea, babe?" I said nonchalantly, sipping my coffee and taking a bite of my sandwich.

"I'd like to see you again. I mean, *y'know*. Romantically. You're nothing like any other guy I know. I told Monica and she got really, I don't know, up on her hind legs about it, like she was jealous or something. I know you two have fooled around a little but there's nothing between you now, right, Vic?"

"Nope." That was true, too, at least at the moment.

"Good. I mean, do you know what I mean, Vic?"

"I, I think so." I was being obviously evasive, but I think she took it as shyness, a hallmark of the old, insecure Vic, not the half-Latin lover of modern times.

"You're blushing. That's so cute when you blush. Vic, I want you to answer me something. Truthfully."

"Shoot."

"Do I intimidate you?"

The waitress showed up right then to offer me more coffee. Judy passed on anything. I noticed she was wearing a tight mint green skirt with a matching sweater that was equally snug. She looked far more appetizing than anything on the menu. I'd lost my appetite, anyway. For my sandwich, that is. Little Elvis was wide-awake now, growling like an empty stomach.

"Vic, did you hear my question?"

"Yeah, babe. But I don't understand it. I mean, intimidated by what?"

"You're sounding very cool all of a sudden. You're not getting cocky, are you?"

"*Cocky*? Interesting choice of word, there. But no, no, Judy. I'm the same old Vic. Basically. I just don't see why you'd think you intimidate me, that's all. We've known each other a while and certain barriers have been broken."

"So why are you so stand-offish, then? I know you like me, a girl can tell, but you seem so distant. Do you think I find distance appealing?"

"Many girls do."

"When they're young and stupid. I'm twenty-five now, Vic. I don't have time to waste. And I want to tell you something *else*. Just because The She Beams are getting a lot of attention and we're cutting an album and all that, I'm still the same old Judy, too. And I'm really a one-guy girl. I broke it off with my fiancé because I wasn't sure I could be true, because I kept thinking of *you*, Vic. Then we spent that night together, and since then I've been really busy with the band, but I'm lonely, Vic. I really am. Let's go to my place for a nightcap and talk about it, okay? No strings, just *talk*."

"Pillow talk? I'm Rock and you're Doris, or vice versa."

"Not necessarily. It's up to you. No pressure. We're old friends, after all."

What the hell. The world wouldn't be any worse off in the morning. I'd save it tomorrow. Judy lived in a small but cozy flat on Telegraph Hill. She had taken the bus downtown so I drove her home in the Corvair. On the way she held my arm and kissed me, and I guess I kissed her back. Get it while the gettin's good, I figured. Though I had no intention at that point of sleeping with her. No way. That would be unethical. I couldn't be that big of a gigolo, I just couldn't, I kept telling myself. It wouldn't be right.

We'd just talk, listen to some music, drink some wine, I'd explain to her all about my new spiritual quest, she'd blow up and kick me out, and that would be that. A full evening of entertainment, Vic Valentine style.

First thing she wanted to do was play something for me she'd been working on. It was a surf instrumental version of "Stranger in Paradise," and it was a gorgeous, ethereal rendition. I just sat on her sofa looking around at her collection of seashells and tiki gods and other exotic artifacts as I listened and she played guitar wearing only her mint skirt and burgundy bra. She looked like a Christmas mermaid. The tropical ambience of her crib was enhanced by all the souvenirs she'd brought back from numerous trips to Hawaii and Tahiti and those places, all paid for by her mother Zelda, queen of the Elvis sex cult run by Deacon Rivers, her perverted paramour. Judy and Zelda had been estranged ever since I exposed the Elvis racket and the media caught wind of it, and Zelda went underground with Deacon Rivers in Miami. Judy didn't resent me for this. In fact, she seemed relieved, and grateful. *Really* grateful.

After she finished the number and I applauded enthusiastically, she crept over to me, kneeled in front of me, and unzipped my pants. Little Elvis stood at attention.

"Whoa," I said. "I thought we were going to *talk*?" As I said that, I looked at her smooth soft cleavage bursting out of the burgundy bra, and I just know my voice sounded weak.

She massaged my thighs and then started unbuttoning my shirt. "We can talk in the morning," she said as she climbed up onto my lap and put her arms around my neck so that her breasts were smothering my meager protests in the name of morality. But mortality was the real issue. The world could end any second, the way things were going. Maybe I was like the James Bond of the soul, converting women to my spiritual cause after winning them over sexually. Worth a shot, anyway.

Judy stuck her tongue in my mouth and I reciprocated. Our lips were all over each other in no time. We made love on the couch and then on the floor. Just before we were ready to get real gone she got up and quickly put on some Martin Denny music, or maybe it was Arthur Lyman, for that tropical island mood.

Later that night, as we lay naked in the middle of the floor, drinking Mai Tais and listening to the exotic music, Judy asked me, "Vic, do you love me?"

"Sure," I said too quickly, hence insincerely.

"No, I mean in a *romantic* way."

"Oh! Well, I guess, sure. Why not?"

"Do you *mean* that?"

"I….I…"

"Vic, what *is* it? When I met you, you were such a lonely guy, even kind of pathetic, and I felt a little sorry for you, you were so alone, just you and your cat, and now you don't even have the cat, but you've got someone who really cares about you, and you seem so, so, I can't tell *what*. Like you don't care, really, like it means nothing not to be alone anymore."

"Judy, it's like this. I went through a lot in New Orleans, it's a long story, but a lot's happened in general, lately, and I just feel it all means something. Everything's happening at once, like there's this big urgency. Remember I told you about those weird phone messages, musical selections, from like an old scratchy 45 or LP, all standards, like 'Cry Me A River' and all?"

"Yeah. You called the person The Phone Phantom, because you never found out who they were from."

"Not *you*, right?"

She laughed softly. "No, Vic. Sorry. I didn't really know you then. But what? Did you meet The Phone Phantom in New Orleans?"

"No. Just an old lover, and someone else, this crazy dame who told me I was on a mission for God."

"Like The Blues Brothers?"

"Yeah, right. No, really. I mean, the dame turned out to be crazy."

"*All* your women do, Vic. It's because your mother is crazy and you keep attracting the same type, so you can save women like your mother before it's too late and blah blah blah."

"Where'd you get all that?"

"I've talked to Monica about it."

I gulped. This could get touchy later, in a bad sort of way, and it would serve me right. I'd deal with it then. "So anyway, The Phone Phantom thing was really mysterious, like someone was sending me messages from beyond."

"Elvis?"

"Maybe. Or God."

"Same difference to my mother, only she thinks God rakes up leaves in Elvis's yard."

"Whatever. But my point is, and I know this will sound crazy, but I really think I'm marked to do something special. I was thinking maybe it was writing, or through my writing, but I don't know."

"You're not going to tell me you think you're the Messiah, are you?"

"Not quite, no."

"Not *quite*?"

"C'mon, I'm just kidding. Don't be like Monica and freak out on me right after we get intimate." *Oops.*

"*Monica*? What are you *talking* about? You told her all this? When?"

"Um, uh, earlier. Today, I think. Yeah. We had lunch."

Judy stood up and towered over, arms akimbo, her bare breasts shivering with anger. "What do you mean, 'after you get *intimat*e,'? Vic, did you *fuck* her? *Answer* me, god damn it! I want the truth! She told me she was going to seduce you as soon as she dumped her boyfriend, that little slut! Well, did you? Just tell me, I need to *know*."

I stood up and felt silly arguing this way in the raw. "Judy, please, settle down."

"Don't *touch* me, you creep. Just answer me. The *truth*. And don't lie, because I'll ask her and she'll brag if you guys did it. She's got this rivalry thing with me and you're like a prize to her."

"That's not what she told me, she—uh. Oh. Judy. C'mon, don't be like this. This was way before you and me, tonight."

"How long could it have been? You just got back from New Orleans, and it was while you were down there Monica broke it off with Steve and said she was going to go after you and I said not if I beat her to it. So she did beat me to it, but you want to parlay it into the whole band, I guess. You're the first She Beam groupie, Vic, congratulations. Now get out of here."

Now she was crying and I felt low and unworthy of her company. "Judy, you asked me to come over, you wanted to fool around, so why the drama?"

"Fool around, Vic? I *loved* you, you bastard. But you've changed, Vic. You've really changed, haven't you? You fuck your old lover in New Orleans? Answer me!"

"I, uh, I..."

"You *did*, didn't you? So what's that, three different girls in a *week*?"

For some reason I did a quick mental tally—the slasher sister, Rose, Dolly, Monica, Judy—and blurted out, "Five." I wasn't boasting or anything, really. That would be shallow, and stupid under the circumstances, but I was still on this honesty kick. Though my timing was a tad off, I must admit.

Judy picked up one of her pumps and threw it at me, followed quickly by the other. Both connected and hurt, but I deserved that and more. "God *damn* you, Vic! Get out of here! How *could* you?"

"Judy, we didn't have time to talk first, remember?"

"Oh, you are *so* pathetic, Vic. More than ever. I never want to see you *again*."

"Judy, please! How could I resist you? You're beautiful! You're talented, you're a great person, you've got an incredible rack, I just couldn't help myself, please!"

"Then what about all the others, Vic? Were they irresistible too?"

"Yes! I mean—shit."

"*Get out!*" Now she was threatening me with her glittering surf guitar. If she was willing to bash that over my head, she was really serious. I picked up my clothes on my way out the door, Judy behind me with the guitar held over her head like a surfer serial killer, and the next thing I knew, I was nude and shivering on her doorstep. Inside I could her sobbing. I knocked softly on the door and called her name and pleaded with her to open up, but it was no use. Time to call it a day.

I was ready to get dressed on the stoop before getting back in the Corvair when I heard a siren and lights flared and then two cops were sticking flashlights and guns in my faces and telling me to put my hands in the air. I was blushing and shaking and still naked except for my socks, and when I put my hands in the air I dropped my trousers around my ankles.

I tried explaining to the cops the extenuating circumstances of this suspicious looking situation but they didn't buy it. They knocked on Judy's door for verification of my shaky story but by this time Judy had turned out her lights and gone to bed, probably locking herself in the bedroom. The persistent knocking she no doubt attributed to me, so she ignored it. The cops made me finish dressing in the patrol car and then took me down to the North Beach precinct where I finished explaining with increasing exasperation. They called Judy and got her machine and she was obviously screening her calls. They left a message for her to call the station when she got home, because some babbling lunatic who claimed he knew her had been discovered naked on her doorstep. Their theory was that I was an overzealous rapist, hiding in the shadows but ready to go to work as soon as Judy got home. Fortunately Judy broke down and called the police station around four in the morning and exonerated me, but by that time, I was fed up with women and the human race in general.

Save the world? Hell, you could *have* it.

Chapter Nine
BABES IN BOYLAND

I was hanging out with Doc the next day at my favorite cafe, Rendezvous, which Judy once managed, since her mother Zelda had owned it, before she sold off all of her businesses in San Francisco to wander the globe with Deacon Rivers in search of Elvis. I'd told him all about what had happened with Monica and Judy. He shook his head through the whole thing, laughing, as usual.

"Vic, I gotta hand it to you—you keep coming up with new angles of self-humiliation," he said after I finished with me in the cop station, waiting for Judy to call. "But I gotta say—you had it comin'."

"Yeah, I guess. God punishing me, bad karma, whatever. But how do playboys and gigolos get away with it, Doc? This was new for me, and I've already blown it."

"Exactly, my man. You're a novice philanderer. Give it some time."

"Time is runnin' out, Doc. In a few years I'll be forty, and what have I got to show for it?"

"Shit, I left forty in the dust already, and I'm havin' a better time than ever. Anyhow, you got a ways to go before you reach that milestone, my man. Relax, or you'll look fifty long before your time. Hell, *sixty*, the way you're goin'."

"Doc, I been thinkin'."

"When'd you have time for that?"

"C'mon. You know that nun, that one who tried to kill me, right?"

"Most nuns will, given half a chance. What about her?"

"Well, she said some stuff that kinda got to me, about me being chosen and all."

"Chosen? For what? Lunatic's lottery? Champion chump?"

"Knock yourself out, Doc, you're a real riot. No, I mean—aw, forget it."

"Good idea. Anything that broad had to say ain't worth rememberin'. I'm surprised you ain't got nightmares and shit after all that." Doc shivered as he imagined the Hitchcockian encounter. Actually, the horror of that event had been somewhat offset by the subsequent erotic onslaught. Didn't matter, anyway.

"I have nightmares all the time, Doc. Even when I'm awake."

"Serious? Sounds like you have mostly wet dreams when you're awake, at least lately."

"In between."

"Hardly enough time there to enjoy a really good nightmare, Vic. Of course, now that no one's gonna be talkin' to you for a while, you may have a clean datebook."

"Meaning it's been dirty? *Filthy*?"

"Vic, calm down, willya? Why are you so damn defensive? So what—you played around and got nabbed. Happens all the time. Just be grateful you didn't get caught in bed with somebody's wife. Then you'd have a real problem, get an ass full of buckshot or someshit."

He looked away, finishing his coffee. Johnny Mathis was crooning "Chances Are" on the sound system. I had him.

"Doc, this new lady of yours, she a sister?"

"Naturally." He still wouldn't look at me, though, pretending to be absorbed in the melody. "Dude sang pretty good for a sissy, you know that?"

"Can the macho crap, Doc, and be straight with me. This sister, you mean as in black, not nun, I take it?"

He finally shot me a look.

"Have to be clear these days, Doc. Words have all these double and triple meanings, people get confused."

"Yeah—I bet you're still a '*dick*' in Monica's and Judy's book, but not the same kind you were yesterday."

"So this sister ain't somebody's sister?"

"Vic, chill with the word games, my man, you're givin' me a headache."

"All right, new tack. She somebody's wife?"

He flinched. I'd caught him off-guard for once. He nearly spilled his coffee. "Damn it, Vic, I thought you was retirin' from the detective racket?"

"Not yet, Doc. Need some background checks before I do?"

He narrowed his eyes with suspicion. "What you gettin' at?"

"Cheating spouses are my bread and butter, Doc, or used to be. Need to know if the lady's bein' straight up with you?"

"Vic, you're jumpin' to too many conclusions already. Nobody said the lady's wearin' a ring."

"Nobody had to."

Doc shook his head and looked away. Johnny Mathis began singing "Misty." He had something on his mind, all right. I'd hit one of his buttons for a change. It took my mind off my own madness. Just what I needed.

"I suppose you want to take this out in trade for your back rent, that it?" Doc said finally.

"Never thought of that."

"Bullshit."

"Fine idea just the same. How 'bout it? What's the situation? You met a lady who's steppin' out on her hubby, but she won't say who, but she drops little hints he may be a big shot, and you're worried about gettin' nailed and taken out by the unwritten law?"

"Vic, close up shop and reopen as a mind reader."

"Am I giving you a solid rundown or what?"

"Nobody's stoppin' you. Keep goin', Nostro-fuckin-damus."

"Thank you. My crystal ball also tells me you got the serious hots for this lady, more than you've had for any other dame in a long time, maybe ever, and she keeps sayin' maybe she'll dump the bastard and maybe she won't, but obviously she's unhappy since she's hangin' out with you, she digs your company, so what's stoppin' her from dumping the asshole? He loaded? She have kids? What's the deal? Now—those the questions you need answered, Doc?"

He sighed and looked at me with a mixture of amazement and disgust, a strange but common combination in my experience. "Basically, yeah, now that you mention it. You been keepin' tabs on me, motherfucker?"

"Like I haven't been preoccupied elsewhere."

"Well, how do you explain knowin' all this shit?"

"It's my business to read people, Doc. Besides, I know you pretty well by now. You got faith in me or what? I mean, the only reason I *do* know is because I found your mother for, remember? Consider this a follow-up job. You started out as my client, before you became my friend."

He nodded, reminiscing. "Yes, sir, poor old mother, wandering the streets of West Oakland, lost in a daze. She wasn't as gone as *yours* is, just old, but I was worried sick. You saved the day, man. We been bro's ever since, haven't we?"

"That's the truth. So, need some work done?"

He paused in thought. "Maybe. In exchange for back rent?"

I reached out my hand and he shook it, real business-like. "Deal."

Whew. My bank account had been on a hunger strike, my credit cards were over-maxed and the minimum payments were sucking up my savings, so this would turn out well, a boon for all.

Or so it seemed at the time. Me and my desperate optimism. When will I ever learn that pessimism is always my best bet?

Doc gave me a few leads and then went back into The Drive-Inn, and since Monica was working I didn't dare follow him. Instead I just went up to my lonely room and brooded, a sad return to my erstwhile pastime. No Puss. No pussy. The latter was just as well. The recent boon in poon tang had only resulted in alienating what few female friends I had left on the roster. Rose and Dolly only came back around because I'm the most dependable i.e. gullible sucker they knew, so whenever they're feeling particularly bored or lonely or horny, they drop me a line. And I bite on it, every time. In Rose's case, she went to somewhat elaborate extremes, not sure whether I'd fall for the same ploy twice.

And did I? In spades. And Dolly came to *me*, instead of baiting a trap in some distant place. Same result, though. They got what they wanted. And so did I, in the short run. But a piece of ass couldn't give you peace of mind, I was learning. Or at least, I *hoped* I was learning.

I put on some Frank and checked my phone messages. Nothing from Dolly or The Phone Phantom. A few potential client inquiries, missing pets and spouses and so on, and I jotted down some numbers to call back. I needed the work. First I'd take care of Doc, though.

All he really gave me to go on was the lady's address in the Western Addition, a description, and her name—Velda Hayes. Shit, sounded like a cross between Zelda, Judy's mom, and Velma, the B movie goddess back in L.A. I knew I'd get more details out of him sooner or later, but I didn't think I'd have to go to such drastic extremes. The truth was, I was only making that shit up about Doc seeing a shady lady married to a mystery man, but my instincts must have been inadvertently honed over the years. All I was going to do was stake out her place, which would be easy, since she hadn't met me and I could spy around incognito, snap a few pix of her hubby, maybe follow him around a bit, take a few more pix, and then Doc would be brought up to speed and my rent would be brought up to date. Simple.

Deciding I had no time to waste, I went directly down to the Corvair with my trusty snap-shooter and drove over to the address in the Western Addition. Velda Hayes lived in a beautifully restored Victorian amid a crumbling, gang-and-drug infested neighborhood. The Western Addition had the biggest population of blacks in the City besides Hunter's Point, but most of the Bay Area brothers and sisters preferred Oakland or Richmond, because there wasn't any of that pseudo-sophisticated white old money crap to deal with. Oaktown was down and dirty. So was the Western Addition, across Van Ness from downtown and the Tenderloin, blocks away from both affluence and the ghetto, but then you could say that about almost anywhere in this town. It was all crammed together in one overheated cultural boiling pot, cooled off by the fog.

Doc had met Velda about five months previously in The Drive-Inn, when she came in just to knock back a few shots and shoot the breeze with whoever was around. It was while I was in New York, and he never told me about it until recently. Monica wasn't there, on tour with The She Beams, so he had a clear field. She was about thirty-five, pretty well stacked, very classy, loved jazz and cocktails. Plus she was married. That first night she just complained to Doc about how miserable she was, and then he told her she should cultivate a life outside of her marriage, make new friends, *hint hint hint*. Normally Doc stayed away from such volatile situations, and he had a certain code of ethics he maintained, but Velda was such a hot number he couldn't resist. She came in for a few more visits with the Doc, and he suggested some radical treatment, a cure for the blues and the blahs, and the next thing you knew, they were back at his place, dancing to Count Basie and Woody Herman and Gene Krupa and Harry James, and then they got tipsy and wound up in the sack. Ever since then Velda would rendezvous with Doc at cafes and then they'd go to Pearl's or Bimbo's or Yoshi's or Kimball's for a nightcap and some jazz before retiring to his place. She wouldn't tell Doc where she lived or who she lived with, but one time he followed her cab from his house and found out her address, but then he was too timid and ashamed to stalk her and discover her secrets. That's where I came in. Doc was in love for the first time since I'd known him, about six years, and even if I didn't owe him back rent, I'd do this for him. I just had to know for myself whether Doc was wasting his time, fornicating and breaking spiritual rules for nothing. If he were in love, maybe the divine courts would show some leniency. Of course, I've thrown myself on the mercy of the same courts many times, but I always had the book thrown at me anyway. Hopefully Doc would have a bit more grace and understanding bestowed upon him, and maybe I would score some points as a matchmaker in heaven. Either that, or I'd fry as an accessory to adultery. Whatever.

It was an overcast day. I parked at a discreet distance from the Victorian and sat in my car listening to the radio, specifically KABL AM, which played a lot of sappy standards as well as a lot of swing and Sinatra. It was mainly geared for the geriatric set, but I'm an old-fashioned guy, out of sync with the modern world. I listened to it now instead of Live 105, the Modern Rock Station. Old before my time, like Doc admonished I would be. Didn't care. I kept that station on a pre-set, along with KCSM, the jazz station. I loved 'em. They gave me my soundtrack.

I had with me a latte in a to-go cup and there was a park nearby with lots of bushes to piss it out in. I just sat and waited. Doc had no date with her today, and far as he knew, Velda didn't work. There was no sign of life in the wide-open bay window of her house, so I assumed she was out. I kept waiting.

Around 6PM or so I saw her. Doc said she was voluptuous, but that was an understatement. He also said she was only half black, but not light enough to pass as white. He said she sort of looked like the young actress who played a half black half white chick in *Imitation of Life*, only an older version. He had it, all right. She was a bombshell, ready to blow. No wonder Doc wanted to light her fuse, even if she did belong in someone else's arsenal.

She was getting out of a car when I saw her, not a cab. The car was a sleek silver Mercedes Benz. I noticed a skull was painted on the passenger door. Hm. And whoever was driving the car gave her a big wet kiss through his window before she waved bye-bye and shimmied up the stairs to her door, where she blew the driver yet another kiss before disappearing inside. Then the Mercedes sped around the corner. I got the impression the driver wasn't her errant hubbie. After she was inside her house I got out of the Corvair, walked up the street, and knocked on the door, desperately thinking of what I would say when she opened it.

"May I help you?" he said with a sweet smile, opening the door wide, not a care in the world it seemed. She was wearing a tight red dress with sequins, and she had just kicked off her high heels and was in the process of removing her stockings, which my intrusion failed to interrupt. She slipped them off her fleshy calves and revealed red-painted toenails. As she bent over I saw down her ample cleavage. Her black bra could barely contain her massive hooters, and the simple effort of bending over seemed to wind her somewhat. In a few years she'd probably be a cow, and right now she wouldn't be deemed fit for a swimsuit competition, but what the hell, I'd rather have 'em a little over the limit than under.

Wait a minute. What was I thinking? This was *Doc's* woman. No, it wasn't. It was somebody else's. In any case, not mine. Take it easy, Vic. This is a job, a job for a pal yet. Calm down. No need to break my record, or Doc's heart, before he broke my head. Just stick to the case.

"Yes?" she repeated.

I looked up at her face now, and forced an overly friendly smile. "Hi. My name is V-Vinnie. I'm, uh, um, s-selling, y'know, stuff."

"Oh, sorry," she said, starting to close the door. "Not interested."

"Wait," I said, practically sticking my foot in the door. "I was just kidding."

Now her smile had turned to a frown. She stood there heaving, holding her stockings, staring at me with a wrinkled brow. "You sure you have the right house, mister?"

"Yea, the truth is, I'm actually a private detective, see." I pulled out my wallet and flashed my badge. "I need to ask you a few questions about your husband, if I may."

Now her expression went from curiosity to concern. "You mean Daryl?"

"Yea. Daryl Hayes. And you're Velma right?"

"Velda."

"Yea." I flubbed the name, thinking of my Hollywood friend, on purpose so she wouldn't think I was really after her. What a seasoned pro, a result of tossing salt over my shoulder all the time.

"I don't understand what this could be about," she said. She was visibly shaking. I almost felt guilty, but a sense of duty and honor superseded it, along with a little scoop of lust. She was one foxy mama. She actually looked like Pam Grier in her prime. This was not good.

"Well, it's nothing, really, ma'am. I was hired by a party I'm not at liberty to disclose on a case I can't divulge, which has nothing directly to do with your husband, but he may have inadvertently come into contact with some parties pertinent to the case in question, and I'd rather not alarm him by talking to him directly, because then he might accidentally, uh, alert the parties to the fact that I'm inquiring about them, and so I was wondering if you wouldn't mind answering a few simple questions for me, about your husband's business contacts, if they've ever been to this residence, or if you've overheard their names, or anything of that nature. Really, your husband won't be implicated. It's these other parties he knows who are the real culprits in the alleged, urn, y'know, thing." I was really slinging it, but she just smiled with bemusement through my whole spiel, and when I was apparently finished, she said:

"I don't believe it. You're Vic Valentine, aren't you?"

Ssshhhhit! "Um, yeah, how'd you know?"

"The name was on your license. *Detective*."

"Oh." I felt myself blush, always a handicap while on the job, especially in the midst of a bullshit undercover interrogation. It's also a drawback in poker, one reason I gave it up.

"I've heard Doc talk about you. You live above his office, right?"

"Um—"

"No use lying now, Vic. Doc wants you to find out about Daryl, right?"

"Well, uh..."

"Would you like to come inside and talk, or would you rather just stand out there and stammer?"

"Um, uh..."

She made an exasperated noise and was ready to shut the door in my face when I stuck a leg inside quickly followed by its counterpart on the other side of my erect pecker. I can't help it— whenever an attractive babe asks me into her home, I get a woody. Another handicap on the job, but with poker it's not a problem - unless it's strip poker, of course.

The Victorian was lavishly furnished and expensively decorated and after five seconds I was bored as stiff as Little Elvis. I hate that grandiose ostentatious kind of crap. Give me a neon-lit hotel room with a blonde in the bed and a saxophone outside the window anytime. I guess I'm just not the domesticated type. My dreams are pretty cheap compared to most American ideals. And I *still* can't afford them.

It was dark now so she flipped on a few lights as she led me down the long hallway past the living room and into the dining room. "Have a seat," she offered. The table was like something out of a European art film. There were bowls of real fruit, grapes and bananas and all, and the tablecloth looked like an emperor's cape. Paintings by famous dead geniuses lined the wall. They'd probably died penniless, poor bastards, and here Mr. and Mrs. Daryl Hayes used their stuff for opulent wallpaper while they ate like royalty on a holiday. What a world. Spilling over with justice.

What was really strange was that the decor didn't suit the neighborhood. Her mansion was flanked by crack houses. And she didn't seem worried in the least. About *anything*. Hm.

"So Doc told you about me," I said, a real blast of a conversation starter. "What'd he say?"

She was busy in the liquor cabinet. She made herself a gin and tonic and then proffered me a drink, but I passed. I had to stay as clear and focused as possible. I felt like I was leading a candlelight procession through a warehouse full of dynamite. The strain of the responsibility was getting to me, but one wrong move, one slip and BLAM!

"Doc thinks very highly of you," she said. "He trusts you more than he does anybody, he told me."

Oh boy.

"That's nice. I feel the same way about him."

"Take your coat off." I was still wearing my trench coat, my .45 in the pocket.

"Sure," I said, slipping it off and hanging it on the back of the chair I was sitting on. The .45 made a bumping noise as it hit the chair, but I didn't even blink. "Doc hasn't really said much about you at all."

"I know," she said, sitting in the chair next to me, sipping her drink. "We're supposed to be a secret item. I'm surprised he sent you to check me out."

"Are you pissed?"

"No. He's threatened to do as much. Jokingly, I thought. Would you like some music?"

"Um, what kind?"

"I like jazz. You?"

"Jazz is swell. My favorite, in fact."

She hopped up and went to a nearby stereo system, the dining room serenading set, which probably cost around a grand, and put on an LP. "This is a compilation of romantic stuff," she said. "I bring it to Doc's sometimes."

Sarah Vaughan began singing a tune I couldn't place, partly because I was trying to block the music out. I should've just said no when she asked if I wanted music. This was only going to make it harder, if you know what I mean and I think you do.

"Nice," I said as she sat down next to me again.

She bent over as she sipped her drink, and I looked at everything in the room except her cleavage. She was really beautiful. If I'd known just how beautiful, I would never have come here. Ever. Not until I had my rampaging libido in check. This was another test, I figured. Just what I needed.

"So, what are we going to do?" she asked.

"A-about what?"

"Doc. This situation. I already let my husband's name slip before I realized who you were. Daryl. Daryl Hayes. You going to tell Doc?"

"If he asks."

"What if I asked you not to?"

"I already told Doc I'd let him know what was up with you."

"Oh. As a *friend*, you mean?"

"Yeah, of course."

"You and Doc are close, huh?"

"Yeah. Like this." I held up my right index and middle fingers, locked together. "I'm close with Doc too, Vic. In fact, he lets me call him Curtis."

"That's good, because I get the idea he's in love with you."

She laughed, her mass of wavy jet-black hair falling in her face. "You're joking, right?"

"You think I'd go to this much trouble if I was?"

"I don't know. Pretty sloppy, just knocking on my door like that. Why couldn't have used more covert methods of finding out, like a real detective?"

"Because I'm a lousy detective."

"So I hear."

"Huh?"

She laughed some more, and as sweet as it sounded, it began to grate on me. "Doc apparently doesn't think highly of your skills. As a detective, I mean."

I shrugged. "I'm giving it up, anyway."

"That's probably a good idea. What are you going to do?"

"I'm not sure. But I didn't come here so you could ask me questions."

"Then why did you come?"

"To ask you. About your husband."

"Well, I'm not going to tell you."

"You aren't?"

"No way. Why should I jeopardize my situation by allowing some jealous fool to butt into my business and wreck my home life?"

"That doesn't seem very respectful of Doc's feelings."

"Who gives a damn? Want to see my doll collection? It's upstairs, in my bedroom."

My head was spinning like I'd been slapped. "Wait, back up a bit. You saying you don't care about what Doc thinks, or feels?"

"Not really. He's a good lay, but hell, honey, I got plenty of those. Daryl brings home the bacon, I cook it. But if he found out I went out for breakfast sometimes, he'd kill the bastard."

"Not you?"

"*Hell* no. He *loves* me."

"So does Doc."

"That's *his* problem."

I sat and sulked for a few seconds, then began to get up, but she hopped out of her seat and pounced on me. She was a big gal, and the sheer force of her weight pinned me down to my chair and she sat in my lap and began unbuttoning my shirt and kissing my throat.

Forcefully I gripped her arms and shoved her back into the table, but the next thing I knew I was staring into the business end of my own .45. She'd used one hand to unbutton my shirt and the other to stealthily pull my gun out of the trench coat draped across the back of the chair. Smooth.

She got up with the gun still sticking in my face and then ordered me to get up, too.

"Upstairs," she said. "I want to show you my doll collection. I get very offended when people say they don't want to see my doll collection. I've been collecting them since I was a little girl in foster homes all over the country, and then later my sugar daddies bought 'em for me, all over the world. Now only Daryl buys me dolls, but I still have a fantastic collection. Now I'm going to show them to you. If you don't want to see them, say the word, and I'll blow your honky head off. *Both* of 'em."

"Uh, Velda, look, I never said I didn't want to see your god damn dolls in the first place, but I got the impression you just wanted me to go to your bedroom, and I don't think that's a good idea."

She cocked the .45 and pressed it between my eyes. "Think it's a good idea *now*, sucker?"

"Lead the way," I said, breaking into a sweat.

She spun me around and pressed the gun nozzle to the back of my head and pushed me forward, into the hallway, up the dark stairway, and down the upstairs corridor. It was very dark but apparently she knew the way with her eyes closed. She stopped me in front of the appropriate door, kicked it open, shoved me inside, and flipped on the light.

She slammed the door behind her, still holding the .45 on me with a steady grip as she slipped out of her dress using her free hand. She kicked the dress away from her ankles and now she was standing there in her black satin slip, the shoulder straps of which she let fall down so that her huge breasts were almost totally exposed.

"You like that, white boy?" she said. "Want to see more?"

I didn't say anything, just looked away. She squeezed the trigger and blew a lamp to pieces.

It was only then I noticed the dolls. Literally hundreds of them, all shapes and sizes, from different decades, in different dresses from distinct periods. You couldn't see anything else, except I backed up into what must have been the bed. It was very creepy, let me tell you.

Velda was looking at me now with a glazed expression as the .45 smoked in her hand. "Don't you look away from me, white boy. Did Doc tell you my daddy was a white boy? *Answer me!*"

"N-no, he didn't mention it, actually. He did say you were half black, though."

"*See how you are?*"

"Pardon?"

"Why couldn't you have said half white? Because to you I'm a *nigger*, right?"

"I don't think that way, Velda. Actually, I find you *extremely* attractive, I can certainly understand what Doc sees in you. But let's not jump to conclusions."

"You calling me a *whore* now, white boy?" She stepped closer, and I stepped back, and fell onto the bed.

She laughed as she walked up and stood over me, pointing the gun straight at me, her finger trembling on the trigger. "My daddy thought my mama was sexy too, white boy. That's why he raped her. That's *all* you white boys want now, isn't it? So I don't wait for you to take it, like Mama did. She died giving me birth, Doc tell you that? No, I didn't even tell Doc that. I respect him, no matter what you may think, white boy. He treats me like a lady. I can't blame him for sending you to check up on me—it's my fault, really, I should've been able to tell he was falling for me and ended it, but he's so sweet. *Strip*."

"Excuse me?"

"You heard me. Now, before I blow that pink little penis right *off* you."

"B-but what about *Doc*? And your *husband*?"

She laughed. "Daryl should be home in about fifteen minutes, which gives us plenty of time. You're actually perfect, Vic. I'll let Daryl catch us, tell him you broke in and tried to rape me, he'll kill you in self-defense, then Doc will read it in the papers, and dump me. Save me the trouble of breaking his heart in person, because he'd never believe me anyway."

"What? *Why*?"

"Because his best friend defiled me, and because my husband is the number one drug lord in the Bay Area. Now strip, we're running out of time."

"But—"

She reached down and stuck the gun between my legs and hissed, "*Now*, white boy."

I guess somehow I failed the most crucial test of all, and this time it would mean permanent expulsion from the human race.

Chapter Ten
BEDROOM LIES

Naturally, under the circumstances, I had a little trouble getting it up as Velda pulled her slip over her head, keeping the gun trained on me even as she momentarily lost sight of me. I was too petrified to move anyway. Definitely, I was the Chosen One. Chosen for chaos and doom.

Then as Velda stood before me in all her naked glory, all I could think was, *What a way to go*!

She fell on top of me and I felt consumed by her flesh. Keeping the .45 in her right hand, she gripped the hair in the back of my head with her left as she stuck her huge tongue down my throat. Then as she ground her hips on top of me, she noticed I wasn't responding the way she wanted me to.

She sat back up, crushing me under her weight, her enormous brown breasts sagging over my pale chest, and replaced the her tongue with the gun. The muzzle bumped against my tonsils.

"Either I suck you hard or you suck *this* hard, white boy. Which it gonna be?"

Wide-eyed, I just nodded in complete agreement to her whims. She took the gun out of my mouth and kissed me, long and luscious, then her mouth worked its way down my body until she reached my flaccid penis. She took the shriveled little organ in her hand and her mouth, arousing it, over and over, then massaged it with her breasts, looking up and smiling, completely in control. At last I gave in and got a woody, much to her delight.

"About time, Daryl's almost home," she said climbing on top of me. The thought of that nearly sent Little Elvis back to the bleachers, but she put it in her and rotated her hips until we reached a rocking rhythm motion.

She closed her eyes and began to moan. I moaned as well, but more out of terror than pleasure. Then I looked over and saw that she had let the .45 slip from her grip.

My choice was simple, but by no means easy: Either I picked up the gun and backed her off of me, or I went through with what was potentially a phenomenal sexual experience. I thought of all that had recently happened to me, of the fact I'd already lost the trust of Monica and Judy. Doc would die inside if he saw this, or found out about it.

I picked up the gun and stuck it between her sweaty, jiggling boobs. She felt the cold steel against her hot flesh and slowly opened one eye.

"I've heard of *coitus interruptus*, but this is *ridiculous*," she said. "Put that down and finish this, white boy. I can't believe you don't want to finish this. Here I am, letting this be your last experience on this Earth, probably your greatest, and you don't want to. You must be joking."

"No, joke, Velda. Get the hell off of me. *Now*."

She massaged my chest and loins and reached down behind her and tickled my balls. "You sure about that?"

I pulled back the hammer and said, "I ain't the only thing pointing at you that's cocked and ready to shoot, big mama. C'mon. *Off*."

With a petulant pout she pulled me out of her and climbed off of me.

"Now. Put your clothes back on," I said, pointing the gun at her. "*Move it*."

"*Baby, I'm home!*" Just then the bedroom door burst wide open, and standing there gaping was a huge well-dressed black man, with an ear-ring and a nose ring and lots of rings on his fingers, all diamonds and gold. He was bald like Isaac Hayes, and had a deep, booming voice like Barry White. Not that I'm stereotyping or anything—these are legitimate reference points. Ostensibly this guy was Daryl Hayes, the man of the house, ogling a little white guy holding a gun on his naked, sweaty, shivering wife.

"Look, I can explain," I said feebly. "This isn't what it seems, please, *really*."

He lunged toward me with a primeval bellow, but then I shifted the aim of the gun his way. "Hold it, big guy. Now just listen, *please*."

"Oh my god, Daryl, you're finally *home*, my baby, he would've *raped* and *killed* me, oh my baby!" Velda screamed suddenly, jumping into Daryl's big, muscular arms as he just evilly glared my way, like a gangsta version of Lee Van Cleef. Problem was, I was certainly no Clint Eastwood in a Sergio Leone standoff. I wasn't The Man With No Name, I was the The Man *With* A Name: "Mud."

"I can't possibly imagine how you could talk your way out of this," Daryl said in a low, guttural voice, "so you might as well shoot us both while you got the chance, 'cause if you don't, you're so dead it ain't even funny." He was breathing so hard I thought steam was going to shoot out his of ears.

"How about this," I said shakily, trying not to let perspiration slacken my grip on the gun. "I put the gun down, get dressed, and we talk about it."

"About *what*, motherfucker? How good my wife is in the sack?"

"Look, man, I didn't come over here with any intention of doing your wife. She pulled this gun on me and forced me to, y'know." Then I realized that the truth was just too ridiculous to believe and clammed up. It was my gun, in my hand, and I couldn't prove she'd ever tricked me out of it. It just didn't make sense. He'd not only have to believe she stole my own gun from me, but used it to rape *me*. He'd also have to swallow me telling him his wife was a two or maybe ten or twelve-timing slut. Poor Doc. He deserved better. I wasn't sure whether I did. "You're right," I said with a fatalistic sigh. "I can't explain. You wouldn't buy the truth if I had it on videotape. I can't afford F. Lee Bailey, and I suppose we don't have time for that anyway, so you're right. Either I kill you, both of you, or I put the gun down and you kill me. And since I ain't never shot no one, I guess *I'm* the dead guy here." I uncocked the piece and tossed it on the bed, then slowly began getting putting my clothes back on. "If you don't mind, I feel a little embarrassed," I said in a trembling voice. "So before you kill me, you mind if I get dressed?"

Daryl just stood there staring at me intensely as I put on my pants and socks and shirt and shoes. When I was finished, I stood up and said with stoic defeat in my tone, "Okay, that's it. Go ahead, make my day."

Daryl gently released the sobbing Velda, still shivering in the buff, and walked over to me slowly. Inside I was saying prayers from as many different religions as I could think of, so I wouldn't miss out on the right one. I just closed my eyes tight, and tears dripped out and I was shaking as I felt Daryl's foul breath on me. I heard him picking up the gun from the bed. I heard him cock it. I heard the gun fired three times.

When I opened my eyes, I expected to be seeing either the Pearly Gates or Satan laughing his pointy ass off. Or being reincarnated into the body of a bunny rabbit, so I could hump till my heart's content and then get blown away all over again by a hunter's rifle. But instead I saw Velda lying dead on the floor.

I looked over at Daryl, who was sitting on the bed, his head in his hands, the smoking .45 by his side. I guess he felt my eyes on him, so he looked up, his face streaked with tears, and said in a hoarse voice, "G'wan an' and get outta here, boy. Best let me keep your heater, though. I'll dispose of it right quick, don't you worry. I won't let them pin this on you, and me, I can make it so Velda was never here, never existed. You don't know nobody who knows her, do ya?"

"No," I lied in a squeaky voice. Poor Doc. But hell, as it turned out, I'd saved his life. That could and would have been him lying on the floor instead of Velda, whose blood was billowing all over the nice shag rug, getting it gooey.

Daryl talked as if in a trance. "Good, 'cause if so, I'd have to smoke their ass. Reason I ain't rubbing *you* out, I *know* Velda's been steppin' out on me, and I ain't never seen a motherfucker choose to die befo' he'd smoke somebody else. You *hadda* been tellin' the truth then, scared as yo' ass was. I could just beat the livin' fuck outta you, and under other circumstances I would, just to warm up befo' cuttin' yo' wiener off and feedin' it the fish in the bay, as a kinda work-out, insteada goin' to the gym, but seein' Velda there like that, it likes to cut the heart right outta me. I *loved* that fuckin' ho, man, but if she stooped so low as to take home a pudgy little honky runt like you, then I knows things has gone too *far*."

I looked down at my gut. I wasn't pudgy. Of course, I wasn't going to argue the point at this moment. "Thanks for bein' so understanding," I whispered. "And believe me—this goes no further than this room."

He gave me a Mike Tyson time-for-the-knockout look. "That should go without sayin'. Now get yo' lil' white ass outta here befo' I change my mind."

I walked toward the door, casting sidelong glances at poor dead Velda, and as I opened it I turned and said, "Should I leave town for a while? 'Cause I'd get a sore neck watchin' my back all the time."

Daryl waved his big hand and shook his head. "That ain't my style, man. If I let you walk, that's it. I don't go breakin' my word 'cause of emotions. That ain't cool. I seen too many brothers die 'cause of that shit. You gots to control yo' emotions, you dig where I'm comin' from?"

I looked at him and nodded, passing up a prime opportunity to comment on the irony of his philosophy, given the current situation. "I hear ya. All right, then. Just let me say I'm sorry it worked out this way. I really was tellin' the truth, y'know."

He didn't say anything, just kept staring at his dead naked wife on the floor. I picked up my trench coat in the dining room on my way out. Billie Holiday was singing "Stormy Blues" on the stereo.

God, was I sick of grisly scenes of terror—so much so that when I got home, shaken and spent, I immediately popped in the most innocuous video in my collection, *Abbott and Costello Meet Frankenstein*. The boys would instruct me in the fine art of laughing at horror. I didn't laugh, though. I couldn't stop shaking long enough to even work up a smirk. The image of Velda lying dead on the floor with three bullet holes in her haunted me so much I prayed I'd fall asleep and have nightmares, because anything would beat the waking torture of mentally reliving that surreal slice of real life. But I couldn't sleep, either. After the flick ended I put on some more Billie Holiday as a sort of tribute to poor Velda, whose body would no doubt be dumped in an incinerator or something. Death, man. I hate it. I just *hate* it.

But beyond the everyday struggle I endured concerning the concept of mortality, I had one additional problem to confront on a (hopefully) more immediate basis: How the hell was I going to explain all this to Doc?

At least Daryl had said he'd make it so Velda just vanished from the face of the Earth—a depressing notion, but gruesomely convenient when it came time for me to concoct a scenario for Doc's benefit. I'd set out to help him, and later that same day, the love of his life was stone cold dead, murdered by her husband after catching us both naked in her bedroom, with me holding a gun on her. This would be good training for a possible future as a fiction writer, I deduced.

The problem was, the reporters of reality beat me to it.

The next morning I went down to Rendezvous, quickly bypassing The Drive-Inn, where Doc was opening shop, awaiting my report, and sipped a cafe latte. A *Chronicle* was lying on a nearby table. I idly picked it up, and down at the bottom of the front page, beneath all the routine headlines concerning global strife and the O.J. Simpson trial, I saw an item that froze my brain: REPUTED DRUGLORD DEAD IN DOMESTIC BLOODBATH.

Terrific.

All the proper names were there, and the story called it just as it must have appeared to whoever came upon the scene after I left: Daryl Hayes had come home, shot his wife, then put the gun to his temple and pulled the trigger. Murder-suicide after a particularly nasty squabble. The report mentioned the fact Velda was found nude, but had no further evidence with which to speculate. Good. Open and shut case. At least for the cops. Me, my troubles were just beginning. You see, Doc subscribed to the *Chronicle*.

By now he'd already read it, I was certain. I had two choices: leave town for good, or face the music, which would probably turn out to be a dirge.

I polished off my latte, stood up, put the paper under my arm, and marched down to The Drive-Inn.

Not only was Doc there, but so was Monica. And Judy, sitting at the bar. All my former friends were gathered in one place to chastise and possibly even draw-and-quarter me. Might as well get it over with, since I had no plans to leave town. No other city but San Francisco, international haven for outcasts and misfits and all around fuck-ups, would have me. I was already in exile. I had no other place to go.

I took a seat next to Judy, and they stopped talking about whatever they'd been talking about before I showed up. I just tossed the paper on the bar, front page lying open for all to see, then Doc, with a cool, detached, spooky expression, tossed his copy right next to it. Judy and Monica just looked down and didn't say anything.

"Maybe we'd better take this out back," Doc said with eerie smoothness in his tone. I took a deep breath and nodded.

"Sure," I squeaked.

I went behind the bar and followed Doc into the back alley as Judy and Monica silently watched. "Be right back," Doc said to them with that same aloofness. His calm demeanor was much more unsettling than an obvious outburst of rage would've been. I think he knew that, too. In his spare time, Doc studied to be a hit man, I think. He had the attitude down pat.

"All right, start talkin'," he said simply.

"You don't have anything to say?" I said.

"You first."

"Well, the article pretty much covered it."

"So you already knew about it."

"Um..."

"C'mon, Vic. Just be straight up. I know you went to check it out late yesterday afternoon, right? Like you said you was gonna do?"

"Well, yeah."

"And, so? You *meet* her?"

"Yeah, yeah, I met her, all right."

"Before she was ventilated by this asshole or after?"

"*Before*, of course."

Doc's eyes were glazed over now. Man, he could get scary. "Paper said they found her naked."

"Yeah, that's what it said."

"Could be this badass caught her with another man."

"Could be, yeah, that's one theory, sure." I was shaking now. Doc could tell something was up, he just couldn't say for sure what.

"You have any idea who that somebody may have been?" Doc asked me.

"Well, when I first saw her, she was..."

"She was *what*?"

"Well, gettin' out of a car, a Mercedes, and kissin' the dude in the driver's seat goodbye. Obviously they were tight."

"You mean drunk?"

"No, I mean *cozy*. Y'know."

"You tryin' to say Velda was a ho?"

"Well, if it quacks like a duck, it probably ain't a chicken."

Doc took a swing at me, but I ducked it, then he followed it up with an uppercut to my gut, which connected. I fell back against the brick wall, but didn't retaliate. I just let him get it out of his system.

"Sorry, Vic," Doc said, throwing up his hands, making me flinch. "I haven't heard the whole thing yet. It ain't like you to lie. I'm sorry. You were sayin'?"

"Well—you *sure* you wanna hear this?"

"Of course I do. You want that back rent taken care of or not? I need to know you earned your fee."

Did I ever. "Well, after the dude left, I went up and knocked on her door, and told her I was a P.I. and I needed to speak to her husband about a personal matter, and I showed her my badge and she made me, 'cause you told her about me, right?"

"Well, I never figured you'd be that *lame*, Vic. I thought this was gonna be a *covert* operation, not fuckin' trick-or-treat, knockin' on her door an' shit. What were you thinkin'?"

"*I* don't know, Doc. Anyway, she knew why I was there,

figured it out, and she invited me in, and we chatted a bit. And, y'know."

"And *what*? You come on to her?"

"Doc, c'mon."

"She come on to *you*?"

I paused too long. Doc began pacing back and forth in a minor frenzy, cussing and muttering and kicking cans and debris around.

"So you fuck her?" Doc asked me finally.

"Hell, no."

"She fuck *you*?"

"Well, she *wanted* to, but..."

"But you said no."

"Yeah, I mean no, I mean yeah, I said no. Of *course*, whaddya think? But she pulled a *gun* out on me."

"Velda carried a *piece*?"

"Well, it was actually *my* gun. She distracted me, and, well, one thing lead to another, and the dude busted in on us, and misinterpreted the situation, and next thing I knew, *bang bang bang*, she was dead on the floor."

"And he let you go."

"Well, sure. *I* didn't do anything."

"Shit. Just like that. *See ya, whitey, thanks for stoppin' by, but I gotta blow my brains out now*. It was like *that*?"

"No, not exactly. But he believed me when I said it was her, not me."

"Vic, you really expect me to *buy* this crap?"

"Well, it's *true*. Whaddya want me to do, make somethin' up?"

"You expect me to believe this nigga kingpin comes home and finds his woman with a sawed-off white boy, takes your word you're not messin' around, blows away the broad instead, and lets you *walk*? Uh-uh, no way, Vic. Come up with a better one."

I couldn't believe this. I was being almost totally straight with Doc—carefully editing out the sex scene—and he *still* thought I was a lying sack of dirt. How could I win? "Doc, if I was gonna lie, believe me, I would've come up with something a little less self-incriminating. Now, we friends or what? Why would I lie, Doc? The main fact is, this dame was nothin' but trouble, for *any* man. If I hadn't have been there, that could easily have been you dead, insteada them. She didn't love you, Doc. She knew how you felt, and she wanted to break it off, but she liked you, and she, well, she liked the *sex*."

"You stay the hell away from me, and from my store," Doc

said evenly, emotion bubbling under the calm surface. "And I want you packed up and moved out of that room upstairs, you dig? Judy and Monica are right—you're a sex maniac, man. You don't care who you screw, or screw over, for that matter."

I was almost in tears. "Doc, c'mon. After all we've been through, you're not even gonna give me the benefit of the doubt?"

"*What* doubt about *what*? The cops found her naked, shot by her husband, and you admit you were there."

"But if I'd really done anything with her, you'd think he'd have let me walk?"

"No. Know what I think? *You* shot him, made it *look* like a murder suicide. Oh, in self-defense, sure. But nonetheless, that's the only you coulda walked outta there alive. I know these brothers. They don't make deals. Dude caught you in the act, you blew him away, and then you shoot Velda too, Vic, just to make it look right?"

Now I was *really* crying. "Doc—you can't believe—I'd kill someone in cold blood like that, can you?"

"They said the weapon was a .45, found at the scene. If it wasn't yours—let's see it. You carryin', my man?"

I let my shoulders droop and face sag to my chest. "No," I said with a nod.

"I rest my case. You got a week to clear out. Old friend." Then Doc went back inside The Drive-Inn, leaving me there feeling more alone and lost than I'd ever felt in my entire lousy life.

I went out into the street and up to my office. And standing outside my door waiting for me was someone I was certain I'd never see again, even more certain than I was about Velda. It was Sister Sue from New Orleans.

"I thought you were in stir down in the Big Easy," I said gently, not wishing to alarm her with any sudden moves, keeping a wary eye on her hands. "How'd you get out this time? Back to finish me off? Well, hell, go to it. I got nothin' to live for anymore. I'm almost glad to see you."

"That's my sister Betty that's locked up, right where she belongs," Sister Sue said.

"Aw man, not *this* again. Please, just stab me and get it over with. I'm sick of this shit already."

"You don't understand, Vic. *She* was the crazy one, the killer. She posed as me just to confuse her victims, and contrived this entire story about me, when really, it was about *her*. *She* was the one molested by a priest, not I. I pity her, in a way, but I feel even sorrier for those she destroyed. You were the one that stopped her, Vic. See? You really *are* the Chosen One."

Oh man oh man oh man, when would it *end*? "Please just spare me the crap and kill me, all right? I just lost all my best friends in a couple of days, and I have no future, no reason to go on with this charade called Life. Just do your duty and put me out of my misery."

"That's what I intend to do, Vic. That's why I traveled all this way, to give you personal advisement and treatment, to set you back on your true path."

"All right, whatever, Just take off the nun outfit, it bugs me, Betty Lou."

"I told you, I'm *Sue*."

"Yeah, whatever."

"How can I convince you?"

"Well, let me see your wrist, where I shot you. Unless twins get moles and gunshot wounds in the same place, which I doubt, there should be a *bandage*."

She held up both wrists, and they were unmarked. Kiss my ass, Betty Lou had a twin sister after all, and she'd been sent to save me in the nick of time.

Chapter Eleven
PROSE AND CONS

What was I supposed to do, confess my sin-stained stories of decadent danger in a neon-lit netherworld of vamps and vice?

"I'm not here to judge your past," Sister Sue said as she sat across my office desk from me, and I leaned back in my seat, wondering whether I should just kick myself back out the damn window.

"Then why the hell, I mean heck are you here?" I asked rather rudely under the circumstances. After all, she was clearly on a mission of mercy. I just didn't believe I was worth it, and until she convinced me otherwise, I'd remain my typical surly self.

"I've tried to tell you—I'm here to show you your future."

"I thought we went already through this down in The Big Sleazy."

"You didn't allow me ample opportunity to prove the validity of my message." Man, she was so damn polite! If I were her I'd smack me hard in the kisser and walk out.

"Look, Sis, Rose—Betty's room mate?—she already told me it was *her* who sent me the plane ticket and all, so you can cut the malarkey about you sending it so I could get in touch with my inner savior and all that. I mean, what do you want from me?"

"Yes, it was Rose who sent the missive—but it was *me* who tucked in the typewritten note signed *your true love*. You see, I mailed it for her, and after all I'd heard about you, I realized you were Chosen for something special, and it was my personal mission to enlighten you."

I just shook my head and laughed. "I guess insanity runs in the family, Suzy, 'cause if you think I'm chosen for anything except oblivion, you're crazy. It's that simple."

"Rose told me you were stubborn, but she underestimated. You are truly a hard case. I have my work cut out for me, don't I?"

"Sister, c'mon, look. Let me save you a lot of trouble. Choose somebody else. If you only knew how screwed up I really am, you'd have a good long laugh. From here it looks like you could use one."

"I realize after your experience with my twisted twin, you may be skeptical in general when it comes to accepting anyone's version of the truth. I'll pray for patience."

"Sister, you're really beginning to get on my *nerves* here."

"Then I'll pray for patience for both of us, all right?"

"Aren't you due back at the convent sometime soon?"

"I'm on a sort of sabbatical, all expenses paid, only I told a little white lie and said I was visiting an AIDS hospice. It's all part of the overall plan, don't worry about me."

I stood up, couldn't decide where to go, and sat right back down. "All right, whatever. Can you just clue me in as to what exactly I'm, uh, Chosen to do, besides make a mess out of anyone or anything that comes near me?"

"*I'm* not a mess, Vic."

I laughed, then caught myself. "I rest my case."

"Are you insinuating I have a hidden agenda, that I'm psychotic like my sister?"

"Your idea, not mine."

"I find your suggestion troubling, but understandable. What can I do to prove my sincerity to you, Vic?"

Oh no. "You're not going to take off your, y'know, and, y'know."

"And what?"

"Never mind. Sister, look, it's *me*. All right? I'm a cynical bastard, warped by my own experiences, and it's nobody's fault but my own. I take full responsibility for my current sorry state. I've lost my best friends—all three of 'em—and all because I have poor judgment, to put it mildly. It seems I alienate the people I really need and attract the ones who will bring me down. I don't think I'm selfish, or even stupid, really, just misguided. I want..."

"Love?"

"Yeah," I answered too quickly. Damn, I had a hole in my hard-boiled armor-clad façade now, and she'd use it to penetrate even further into the vulnerable mush beneath it. "Yeah, I guess. But I want something tangible, not some hand-me-down philosophy or invisible deity. Whatever it is you think I'm chosen for, I just don't think I'm interested, much less qualified."

"Why don't you let me decide that?"

"Because, all best intentions aside, I want control over my own destiny, *that's* why."

"Have you ever heard of a Guardian Angel, Vic?"

Aw, man. "You're not gonna start laying this New Age jive on me, are ya?"

"Just listen, please. I traveled all this way—at my own expense, without an appointment, granted—but please, don't I deserve the chance to at least plead my case to you, or rather, your case?"

Big sigh. "Go on. I got nothin' better to do at the moment than listen to New Age psychobabble from a golden-hearted nun from New Orleans. Hey, are the cops down there really as crooked as they say?"

"Yes, but that's not my field of interest or expertise."

"I could tell you stories about dirty cops."

"Your father, yes, I know all about it."

"Rose?"

She nodded. "Can I continue with what I was saying now, please?"

I gave her the high-sign.

"You see, it was my sister Betty, not I, who was locked away with your mother in New York. From my sister I learned a lot about you, and also from Rose. We marveled at how coincidental it was, that my sister knew both your mother and the love of your life."

"Ex-love," I corrected her.

"Ex-life," she added wryly.

"Whatever."

"It's too bad you had a lapse in faith, Vic, because you could have averted so much pain in your life."

"With all due respect, Sis, religion didn't help my mother out much. Hey—your crazy sister isn't *really* religious, right? I mean, that whole story she told me, about you being a slasher nun, but now it turns out she was talking about herself, how much of that is true?"

"She was not a believer, obviously. She stole the clothes for her masquerade from me."

"Funny, Rose told me she had no idea you were really the same person."

"Because we're not, obviously. My sister is in a padded cell in New Orleans where she belongs, at long last, thanks to you. Would you like to call and verify?"

"Naw, there'd be a wound on your wrist if you were her. Unless it was divinely healed, and you escaped the cops and came here to finish what you started."

"You can frisk me for a weapon, if you'd like," she said almost seductively.

"Not now. Later, maybe." Control, Vic. Control. "I just find it really strange that Rose never saw the two of you together, you and your sister, I mean."

"Life is full of odd things. But the fact of that matter is, my sister and I didn't get along, never have. If I wanted to come by her place, I had to call first, make sure she wasn't home."

"Why would you visit her if she wasn't home, Sis?"

"To see Rose."

Always quick with the answer or rebuff. Her routine was well rehearsed, though I wondered whom else she'd practiced on. "How'd you meet Rose?"

"I stopped by unannounced, soon after my sister escaped from New York, and met her new room mate. Rose and I talked and got along wonderfully. Then my sister came home, saw me, and we had a scene and she said she never wanted to see me again."

"Betty Lou said your parents were rich, Houston oil."

"That's correct."

"So why'd she move to New Orleans if you were there and she never wanted to see you?"

"She loves the decadence of the Quarter. We used to visit there often as children, and it was so much more exciting than Houston, so she developed an affinity for it, and I suppose I did, too, though now I'm there because it's such a breeding ground for sinners. And anyway, despite her fears, she felt security in my company, even if it wasn't immediate. When Rose began attending services at our church, Betty Lou was actually jealous Rose was spending time with me."

"So why the hatred? Sibling rivalry?"

"She had trouble reconciling her lifestyle with mine, I suppose. Also, after her experience with that priest in Texas, she resented all religious symbols and lifestyles and those who practiced them, especially me."

"So that was true. Your sister was molested by a priest."

"Yes. Everything she told you about me was true, except it was really about her."

"How do you know what she told me?"

"I saw her, just before I left. I was worried about you, that her evil had destroyed you. But instead, you stopped you. You are Chosen, as I've said."

"Wait—you *knew* she was slicing guys up and shit?"

"Oh, yes."

"And you didn't stop it?"

"What could I do?"

"Turn her in!"

"I suppose I was in denial. She would call me late at night at the convent, and tell me of her crimes, treating it like a confession. Even though I'm not a priest, I had to respect the confidentiality of it, you understand?"

"Plus she was your own flesh and blood."

"Yes, perhaps that was a factor, I don't know."

"Plus the dudes she killed probably deserved it, in your book."

"My book is the Bible. I reserve judgment for the Lord. Besides, I had no idea who she killed. I still don't. I don't read the newspaper, and she didn't go into details. I don't think many of her victims have even been found yet, if any. She was exceptionally crafty and wily, a demented genius, in her own way, driven by mania and a lust for revenge against man and God and everything she blamed for her pain."

I nodded and let out some air. "So my mother was never converted into Catholicism, was she? Or *reverted*, rather."

"Not to my knowledge, no. Certainly not by my sister. She would only use that a pretense with men. I don't believe she ever had a conversation with your mother, who is autistic, I believe, no?"

"Yeah. Used to be just *artistic*. Fine line, I guess. You talk to Rose before you left?"

"Yes."

"She a nun now?"

"She's working toward a goal, yes. She said to tell you she thinks of you often, and to thank you."

"For what?"

"She didn't specify, said you'd understand."

"Yeah, I guess. Anything else?"

"Only that she loves you."

"Yeah, yea. You know the story about her son, right?"

"Sammy?"

"Yeah."

"Yes, she talks about it often."

"Personally I think she's on this nun kick as a guilt trip."

"I must say I agree."

"So you don't think she'll stick it out as a nun?"

"I'd rather not say."

"Between you and me."

She smiled. "But there is always someone listening."

"God?"

"At least."

"So what now? Part of my chosen task was to stop your sister, right?"

"That was a sign, yes. If you were just another lost soul, you'd be inside an alligator right now, or pieces of you would."

I swallowed hard. "Yes. So now what? I mean, I've screwed up big time just since I got back."

"Would you like to tell me about it?"

Why not. I told Sister Sue all about the fiasco with Velda and Daryl and Doc. I felt oddly comfortable talking to her now. I guess it was because she was a link to my mother, and to Rose, the two most significant female figures in my life. So far. She was also a very good listener. Hell, it was like relating traumatic events to a therapist, rather than a confession to a priest. I told her everything—the sex, the violence—and she didn't flinch. I suppose with a sister like hers she was hard to impress or offend.

When I had wrapped it up, she just nodded thoughtfully and said, "You don't really think your friend Doc believes you shot the woman or the man, do you?"

"That's how he acted. He was pretty insanely upset, more so than I've ever seen him."

"But he's in pain, confused. Give him time."

"Think so?"

"Trust me."

I shrugged. "Okay." I didn't go into my other dilemma, about sleeping with Monica and Judy within the same day and pissing them both off, because I didn't want to push it by coming off as a total heathen on a rampage. In a weird way, I was beginning to like having the Sis around. Maybe it was because she was so compassionate. I needed that gift just then, no matter what package it came in. I was in no position to turn away anyone who truly seemed to give a damn about what happened to me, because I sure as hell didn't. I asked her, "You mentioned Guardian Angels. That you? You my Guardian Angel?"

She smiled. "No. I'm only a messenger, Vic."

"Yeah? Okay. So? What's the message?"

"First you must accept Jesus Christ as your savior, and then we'll take it from there." Jesus. "Aw, can't do that, Sis. Sorry."

"You are still in denial?"

"Call it what you'd like, but I gave that up a long time ago. I mean, I believe in God and all, and maybe there was a Jesus and maybe there wasn't, but I can't buy into this organized religion thing. I just can't. It'd be too dishonest. Religion is politics to me, and I hate politics. Now, I'm sorry if I'm making you feel like you've wasted your time and all, and I like talking to you, but that's how the pancakes stack, Sister."

She looked down solemnly and said in a near whisper, "I see. Well, I'm not sure what to do now. I feel this strong need to give you some message, to guide you toward the right path, but not down it. Perhaps I've got my signals mixed."

"What made you want to become a nun anyway, Sister? You come from money, right?"

"Yes?"

"So, your folks religious?"

She smiled again, still looking down. It was getting to me. "No, my father was a drunkard and a womanizer and my mother the town character, as they say." Sounded something like the plot to *Written on the Wind* to me, but I was hardly paying attention anyway. I was dying to see her without the habit. She looked just like her sister, sans the manic glint in the eyes. Hopefully she hadn't cut off all her hair, either. Wait, wait, wait—cool it, Vic. This is a true blue nun you're sizing up. Back off.

During a pause I asked, "So why the religious route? The c-c-celibacy." Smooth, man. "And everything else. Don't you get lonely?"

She looked up from her lap, and her beautiful eyes met mine. *Ouch.* "I am never lonely, but sometimes, I do miss certain sensations. You see, Vic, I was much like Rose when I was younger. I, too, swung the pendulum all the way in the other direction, in order to cleanse myself."

"Of what?"

"I'd rather not go into it. But this is why Rose and I got along so well, I think. She reminds me of how I was before I changed."

"But you don't think Rose will go the distance, right?"

"I said I'd rather not say, and I still don't want to say. In truth, I just don't know. She seems sincere, but..." Her words drifted off with her gaze. She had withdrawn into some inner place I wasn't privy to. The expression on her face told me it was a sad place, but that was all.

"You all right?" I asked her.

"Yes, I—Vic, I feel I must tell you something. Personal, about *me*."

"Ah, that's okay, really, if it makes you uncomfortable, you don't have to."

"I was in prison. For prostitution, extortion, armed robbery, a while dirty list." She started weeping softly. I knew I didn't want to know anything about her. I just knew it. Too late now.

"Sister, really, take it *easy*."

"Call me Sue. My name is Susan Geyser."

"Geyser? That's funny, I mean your family being in oil and all."

"Yes, isn't it?"

"Hey, you need some like towels or something? Actually, I don't have any hankies, or towels, come to think of it, but I could run into the other room and get some toilet paper."

"No, no, Vic. It's all right. I feel like such a fool. I'm so embarrassed, baring my soul to a complete stranger this way."

"Hey, we're hardly strangers now, Sis, are we? C'mon, now, c'mon." I got up out of my chair and went over to comfort her. I put my hands on her shoulders gently and patted her back and her habit, feeling rather silly. As I did so, she reached back and held onto my arms and squeezed them, and then I'm not sure what the hell happened.

All I know is we were kissing when Doc knocked on the door and walked in. "Vic, I've been thinking stuff over, and..."

Sue stood up, and I stood back, and we both stared at Doc, who was staring back. It was then I noticed than Monica and Judy were behind him.

"You are a sick man, Vic," Doc said flatly, sadly shaking his head and walking back out.

"*Sick*!" Monica echoed with disgust, only louder. "*Vic*! *Ick*! *You sick prick*!"

Judy spit on the floor just before she slammed the door behind them.

"*Ooops*," Sue said. Now she was regaining her composure, smoothing out her wrinkled gown, adjusting her habit.

I just sat on the edge of my desk and buried my face in my hands. I felt like crying, or maybe laughing, but couldn't decide which so I did neither.

Sue touched my shoulder and I flinched, so she recoiled. Man, this was so awkward, I can't tell you. "Vic, I should go back. To New Orleans, I mean. It's been so long since a man put his hands on me—and I'm not saying this was your deliberate intention— but I just lost control."

"No, no, you didn't initiate it. And neither did I. I'm just *cursed*, I think. My whole fuckin' family. Oh, sorry."

"That's okay, Vic, I've heard worse. I'm an ex-con, remember?"

"Oh, yeah, yeah. What was your rap?"

"Ten to twelve."

"Do the whole stretch?"

She looked very sheepish. "No, I escaped."

"Really? How? Seduce a guard?"

She looked shocked. "How'd you know?"

I shrugged. "Doc stocks a lot of Women in Prison flicks." I shook my head in self-revulsion. "Doc. Shit. And the girls. Came back up to make everything right, just when we were both having a weak moment. I tell you, there's a curse on my stupid head. I just *know* it."

"Don't be silly, Vic. You're just an attractive, sensitive man, and women can't resist you."

I rolled my eyes. "Not until recently. What's up, Sister? Why is all this weird shit happening to me?"

"Call me Elizabeth, please."

"I thought your name was Susan?"

"My real name is Elizabeth."

"Geyser?"

"No."

I sighed. "What then?"

"I'd rather not tell you that yet. But at the convent, I told them my name was Susan Geyser as a cover."

"*Ooohhh,* so you originally went to the convent because you were in hiding, on the lam from the law in Texas."

"I joined the convent because I thought if I could save just one soul, I could redeem myself. You may be that soul, Vic. I had a wild time in Texas. I was a wanton, wanted woman. There and in Oklahoma. And Arizona. But that's all. No, wait, there was one warrant for my arrest in New Mexico."

"So where were you doing the time?"

"Illinois."

Oh boy. "Okay Elizabeth, or whatever, could you take off that habit now that we're being so informal?"

"Why?"

"I'd like to see your hair."

Keeping her eyes on me, Elizabeth slowly removed the habit and shook her out her full head of wavy red hair, darker than her twin sister's, but just as lovely. Stunning, in fact. "That feels good," she said.

I couldn't help myself. I leaned over and kissed her. She ripped the buttons off my shirt and then I practically tore off her gown and we did it right there in the middle of my office floor. Then we did it again in my bed. It was the miracle of "the burning bush" all over again. As she clawed the skin off my back Elizabeth confided that between prison and the convent she hadn't been with a man in three years.

Yeah, I was the Chosen One, all right.

Later, with her near-shredded gown and crumpled habit still on the living room floor next to my discarded garments, I made us a meager meal out of what I had around and brought it in to her, thinking: I've just desecrated a nun, I'm going to Hell, no matter what. I was a sexual deviant, a romantic outlaw. I was out of control. As a joke I put on "Personal Jesus" by Depeche Mode, timing it to play just as I walked into the bedroom with the breakfast tray. Man, was I a riot.

"*AAAAAAAHHHH*!" she shrieked as I entered, running right for me with a straight razor in her hand. I dropped the tray and wet myself simultaneously.

As I fought to catch my breath I realized she was doubled over with laughter. A couple of real comedians.

"What the hell's so funny?" I asked, failing to see the humor in her little gag.

"I'm sorry, Vic, I couldn't resist!" she said, jumping into my arms. "I feel so *free*!"

"Good for you, now help me clean this up."

She pointed to the wet splotch in my underpants. "You mean that?"

"No, I mean our dinner." She was still laughing. I still wasn't.

She then revealed the identity of the straight razor: It was her nail filer. "You're so jumpy, Vic." Then she began kissing me. "You are such a wonderful lover."

"Thanks, but I'd say your standards aren't too high after being in prison and the convent, three years without sex."

"I said three years without a *man*."

"You mean—oh."

"In prison, not in the convent."

That kind of turned me on. "You still like women?"

"Not really, not anymore, not now."

"But, what about Jesus?"

She looked lost and sad. "I don't know, Vic." Her eyes welled with tears. "I've been unfaithful to Him, haven't I? I lost sight of my purpose. I came here to help you and *I'm* the one with the problem, as it turns out."

I finished cleaning up the mess, still rather shaken and in a foul mood, but somewhat relieved that the tables had turned and she was no longer trying to force her brand of salvation on me. I didn't feel so guilty anymore, either. I didn't *rape* her, after all. And the lovemaking was incredibly intense and rewarding, because she was so pent-up and repressed. Me, I was used to it. Not so long before I'd been such a pathetic loser when it came to love. Now I was finally living up to my name. I was a walking romantic holiday.

I hugged her and we kissed a little and then I told her, "Look, just do me one favor, okay? Help me square things with my pals."

"You mean those girls?"

"Yeah. And Doc. Explain to them our situation, so they won't think I, y'know, made improper advances toward a nun. Tell 'em you had a sudden crisis of faith and were really horny and couldn't help it, and I was there for you."

"But, Vic, you aren't going back to them, right?"

"Who? Judy and Monica? They're just friends. Like us."

"But after what we just did, we're something *more*, right? I mean, I wouldn't give myself to just anyone. I broke my vows for you, Vic, remember that. That's no small thing."

Uh-oh. "Sue, uh, Elizabeth, listen: what we just did was *passion*, nothing more, nothing less."

She was glaring at me now with something resembling hatred. "No wonder your
friends don't like you. You really are a cold, selfish person, aren't you?"

"Huh? Wait a minute—I thought you were so *compassionat*e."

"Oh, is *that* was this was—*compassion*? Go to Hell, Vic. Literally." She got up and started putting on her under-things and then her rumpled habit and slightly tattered gown.

"What are you doing?" I asked her.

"I'm going back to New Orleans, back to the convent. You've taught me a valuable lesson, Vic. The outside world is full of people like you. And I thought you were so different. I should never have turned my back on my faith. I had a weak moment and you took full advantage of it, you *monster*. You're living proof of how troubled this world is in the End Times. All that I told you was not a lie, Vic. The world is coming to an end and you almost dragged me down with you. But don't listen to me, Vic. Listen to your friends—you are a *sick man*."

"What about me being Chosen and you not judging me and all that crap?"

"Oh, *now* you're interested! Well, too late, Vic. I'm going back to the convent and tell Rose how you took advantage of me."

"Please don't do that." I sounded so pathetic, just like my old self. "Please stay. I, I'm so alone. My cat's dead, my friends hate me, now I've made God's shit list, though I think I was born on it."

"Stop whining," she said, putting on her black shiny shoes. "I suppose you think it's funny I'm going back with a torn dress, don't you? Well, it so happens I have another one at my hotel. Goodbye, Vic. May God have mercy on you."

Then she walked out, and I didn't even try to stop her. Instead I sat down at my desk and started writing all this shit down, quickly, while there was still time.

Chapter Twelve
MOURNING SICKNESS

I kept writing and writing, often referring back to my journal, which I'd written in sporadically starting with the Rose/Tommy Dodge case. Since then I'd recorded some of my more amazing misadventures—the Elvis cult, my trip back East, the secret Hollywood movie—and now I had the real showstopper. I figured if I could just get all this into some kind of marketable form I would be able to call my own shots from now on. I'd be rich and famous and have lots of friends and women. Sure, I wouldn't be able to trust any of them, but so what? I didn't really trust any of them now.

No, that wasn't true. I trusted Doc. And Monica and Judy. I just no longer trusted myself.

My meandering mind didn't just stick to the facts, though. I kept going off into tangents not germane to the subject at hand. If I were writing for some college course they'd call me on that and grade me accordingly. But fuck 'em. I was writing this down for me right now, and later, if it gained an audience, so be it. If not, I'd simply try again.

Her erratic erotic behavior notwithstanding, some of the things Sister Sue or Elizabeth or whoever had said to me really stuck in my craw—particularly that Guardian Angel crack. I wondered if I really did have a Guardian Angel, and if so—was it Marilyn Monroe? Jayne Mansfield? If some departed soul from the '50s were watching over me, that would explain why I was so obsessed with that era. Rose used to tell me, when she was Valerie, back in New York, that I lived back then, in another body. I mean, I was born at the end of the '50s, but in my head, I carried on that stylistic and aesthetic tradition. Either Rose was right about her reincarnation theory, or else someone Upstairs had simply screwed up on my soul's paperwork, and I was born when I should have died. I just felt out of sync with the 1990s. Hell, I even felt out of place as a kid growing up in the late '60s and '70s. The early '80s, during the heyday of New Wave, were my most comfortable times, since the skinny tie set emulated the fashions and sensibilities of the '50s and early '60s in a warped, postmodern sort of way. All the punkettes idolized Bettie Page and her peers, decked out in dominatrix leather. Dead Marilyn and Dead Elvis were punk zombie icons, along with Sinatra, who was still alive but reinvented by the art crowd in the punk mold. The new wave scene was like the '50s reflected on a funhouse mirror in a carnival House of Horrors, and my outmoded sensibilities flourished.

But today, in this barren, postmodern wasteland, amid the end-of-the-century garage sale that passed as our collective culture, I felt alienated and lost. Was it just me? I mean, who else would be able to relate to this?

Doc could, to an extent, though being black, the past for his people certainly wasn't any rosier than the present. Or the future. But he liked cheesy monster flicks as much as I did. Monica was a punkette, so she had that same voodoo rockabilly take on things as her predecessors did during the old punk days, but she was too young to appreciate all my references, unlike Doc. Anyway, she probably thought Green Day was better than The Clash. *Kids.*

Judy was a surfer babe, weaned on The Ventures and Dick Dale and now joining the all-out neo-surf "movement" sweeping the underground like a fresh wave from heaven's reservoir, cleaning out all the grunge that had been collecting around the culture for the past few years. Judy even dressed the part, like a nouveau go-go dancer. But again, she thought what she doing was totally new. I think she considered Tom Cruise not only cute, but talented. I just can't hang with that, sorry. Give me a real man like Leo Gorcey over that plastic Ken doll with the rotating wardrobe any old day.

While I sat there scribbling into the sunset, I grew more and more melancholy and lonesome. As darkness fell it dawned on me why I had given up writing in the first place—the solitude. At least being a private eye allowed me the time and excuse to move around and mix it up. Also, unless my stuff was getting published, babes just wouldn't be swayed by my artistic integrity. It's just reality. That's why dentists are often boring but never lonely. Security.

I quit finally and ordered out for a pizza and flipped on the tube to the AMC channel. Just then there was an earth tremor, which lasted no more than ten seconds, but strongly rattled my apartment and my nerves just the same. To top it off, the opening credits of a Jimmy Cagney movie appeared on the TV screen just as the shaking ceased: *Kiss Tomorrow Goodbye.*

Whoa.

A message from God? Had I really gone one step beyond by desecrating that nympho nun on the run? Was the End of the World really just around the god damn corner? I was just starting to live, I thought. I'd reached a personal impasse, then what I considered to be an epiphany regarding the direction my life should take, and then the world ends? Naw, I still had five years at least—all the really hip Apocalypse pundits put the Last Hurrah at around the Year 2000. I never understood why God or Nature should adjust their destructive timetables according to the manmade Western Calendar, but apparently I was alone in this wonderment. So I still had a few more years to get published. But then so what? My efforts would be incinerated, along with Shakespeare's and Kinky Friedman's and everyone else's, from grocery lists to epic poetry. Man, did ordinary mortal life seem petty and pointless after an earthquake, even more so than usual. I didn't write for the rest of that evening. I didn't sleep until well after midnight, either, wary of aftershocks and that ominous movie title. I kissed Tomorrow good morning when it became Today, and went to merciful sleep.

The next morning I was awakened by a persistent knocking on my door. I wasn't expecting a UPS package and anyone who knows me at all knows better than to knock before noon, but I finally got up to answer it, grumbling and resentful, rubbing my bleary eyes.

As I shuffled through my office toward the door I wondered who it might be: an irate former client? A new one who didn't know my office hours? Dolly? Feds? Elizabeth? Only one way to find out.

"Yeah?" I said with obvious irritation in my voice as I swung the door open.

It was a mail guy, with a certified letter. Christ, what other suddenly love-struck ladies from my past were left? No matter whether this was a ticket to Cleveland or the French Riviera, no way was I rendezvousing with any more of my loony liaisons. I signed for the goddamn letter and practically slammed the door in the poor mail guy's face.

I looked at the envelope. Whoa. It was from the Chipper Monks Mental Home. I didn't like the feel of this already.

With trembling hands I tore open the envelope and shakily held the enclosed missive, which stated simply:

"*With deep sorrow we regret to inform you, Vic Valentine, of the recent death of your mother, Dorothy Violet Malone Valentine. She passed away quietly in her sleep from natural causes. Your aunt Florence is handling her estate. Funeral arrangements are scheduled for blah blah blah..."*

The services were being held that day. That bitch aunt of mine, whom I never got along with, had skillfully timed this notification to arrive just in time for me to miss the burial. I was effectively ostracized from the family. There was more regarding my mother's will, and apparently I was left a little money she had tucked away before being committed, ostensibly for my dead brother Johnny and Ito use for college or whatever. Aunt Florence was supposedly going to contact me in the near future with further details. There were a few significant ones missing from this succinct little chickenshit note in my shivering grasp. What did they mean by "natural causes?" My mother wasn't that old, only around sixty-five or so. Was it a heart attack? Brain hemorrhage? Stroke? Did Florence poison her own sister to alleviate herself of the financial responsibility and emotional strain? Had one of the orderlies suffocated her with a pillow? My imagination was going into grief-stricken hyper-drive.

I sank to the floor and squatted there for a long time, not even crying. I guess I was too numb, deep in shock. Funny, but along with the sadness was an odd sense of relief. I realize how cold that must sound, but you have to understand that my mother had been dead from a broken heart for a long time. Her soul was still trapped in this lifeless body, however, so to pass the time, she had become a mental recluse in an inner world of her own design, equal parts fantasy and memory. I didn't know if she was happier now, whether her spirit had evolved into some higher form, in a less stressful dimension, or she had reincarnated into a brand new body, or had simply ceased to exist. In any case, her suffering as Dorothy Violet Malone was over. But then so was the chance I'd ever see her again, as my mother. Would her soul be waiting for me on the other side, beckoning me from the end of that fabled tunnel of light people with near-death experiences have commonly reported seeing? Or would she only live on in my memory, until my own brain shut down forever? Depressing, any way you looked at it.

Maybe it really *was* the End of the World, and Ma had simply checked out early, along with Puss and Velda and Daryl Hayes. That didn't make me feel any less sad or lonely, however. Finally, the realization that my mother was gone and I'd never see her again began to sink in, gradually, then suddenly, and I sat there weeping in the middle of my office floor, just like a motherless child would.

An indeterminate number of hours later, or maybe just minutes, it was hard to tell since time had temporarily lost all meaning, there was another knock on the door.

"Get lost," I yelled to the unknown interloper, my voice cracking, giving away my mood.

It's Monica, Vic, open up. We really need to talk."

"I'm humping a nun, go away."

"C'mon, Vic. Doc's in trouble, we need you."

"In trouble? Like how? He's knocked up, you mean *that* kind of trouble?"

"More like he's missing. We haven't seen him since he went home for lunch yesterday, after we came to see you. And he didn't show up this morning, and he won't answer his phone. Judy and I went by his place, but nobody answered. We need you, Vic. We're worried."

"I thought you guys hated my guts?"

"No. We just think you're mixed up."

"Who isn't?"

"Beats me. I'm sorry for everything, and so is Judy, I think, but we can work this shit out later. Right now we have to find Doc. I don't want to call in the cops unless we have to. C'mon, you're a detective, right? And you're our friend."

"I *am*?"

"Damn it, Vic, open the fucking door! Of *course* you're our friend, *c'mon*!"

Wearily I rose and opened up and Monica fell into my arms and we held each other tightly. I was still clutching the certified letter, and Monica happened to read it as it dangled from my limp hand.

"Oh my god, Vic, your mother's *dead*?"

"Huh? Oh yeah. So it says, so it says," I said with a sniffle.

"When'd you get that?"

"I dunno. This morning."

"Oh, Vic, I'm so sorry."

"I guess I deserve it, the way I've been acting."

"Who was that nun we saw yesterday? You getting religious in a perverted way?"

"Did I look like I was getting religious to you?"

"Not exactly, but you can explain later. Right now, let's find

Doc."

"Okay."

"You sure you're up to it, with this bad news and all?"

"Doc may be in trouble, we can't afford to fuck around. Anyway, the funeral is today, back East, so it's a done deal, already. You and Doc are my family now. Let's go get him."

I led Monica down to my Corvair. We stopped for some fast food and coffee so I would feel energized, and then I drove directly to Doc's house in the Sunset District. He rented the top story of an old restored and converted Victorian as a private flat. Monica and I poked around outside on the stairs and porch and couldn't find any evidence of Doc's whereabouts. His car, an early '60s model bronze-colored Impala, was still parked on the street. After repeatedly banging on the door I walked around to the front window, took out my gun, told Monica to scout around for any nosey onlookers, and then smashed in the glass. I opened the window and we both climbed in. No cadaverous odors greeted us, thankfully, but after some snooping around the apparently undisturbed interior I came upon a distressing clue:

At Doc's supper table, in the dining room, surrounded by the movie memorabilia that cluttered his place like Forest J. Ackerman's museum mansion, was a picture of Velda out on Fisherman's Wharf. She was standing against a backdrop that included Alcatraz and a bunch of docked boats. She was smiling and looked very beautiful and happy and, well, alive. At least, this was my impression when I put the two halves back together. Next to the torn snapshot was an empty bottle of whisky and an equally empty whisky glass. But those weren't the clues to his current whereabouts. The clue came in the form of a vase of dead flowers with a note that said in a scary scrawl, "*Love always, your dead whore, Velda. P.S. I'll see you soon, motherfucker—Love, Daryl.*"

"They got him," I said solemnly.

"Who?" Monica said, reading the note with huge terrified eyes.

"Daryl's people. They must've known she was seeing Doc on the sly, and blame him for their boss's untimely demise, even though it was self inflicted."

"You think, my god, Vic, you think they *killed* him?"

I shuddered, hoping she wouldn't notice, because it wouldn't help Doc if we all gave in to panic. I had to stay strong until I got some hard facts, but inside, it caused me a great deal of pain to think Doc would've left this world in a violent fashion and with us on such rotten terms. Between this and my mother's death, I barely had the power to walk, much less pick a direction. But I had to keep moving, like a shark, or drop dead where I stood.

"I'll take it from here," I told her. "You get back to The Drive-Inn, run things till you hear from me."

"I closed it up to look for Doc."

"Re-open it. That's what he'd want, right? That shop is his legacy to the world. He was, I mean, is very proud of it. Carry on in his spirit. You'll do him proud, wherever he is."

She started to cry. Dames. "You talk like he's already dead, damn it!"

"No, I don't think he's gone. I just have a gut feeling."

"You mean you just *hope*. That's not the same thing."

"Sometimes it is. C'mon, where I'm going, it's too dangerous."

"Don't patronize me with this macho shit, either."

"Monica, c'mon. I'll drop you off at The Drive-Inn. Maybe Judy could help you out or something, keep you company till I get back."

"From where?"

"First I'm gonna, well, I won't tell you, cause you'd just follow, right?"

"Probably. You may need help too, Vic."

I kissed her on the forehead. "You'll help by doing as I ask, sweetheart. Really. I don't want to have worry about losing you, too."

She looked into my eyes soulfully. "I really mean a lot to you, Vic?"

"You know it, babe."

"Really? Do you love me?"

"Sure, in a way. You know that."

"But, you know what I mean. As a woman."

"What else, as a pomegranate?"

She let out a little laugh that sounded more like a bleat. She was still sobbing. "Vic, if I lose Doc, you'll be my only real friend in the world."

"What about Judy?"

"She's not *you*. We're not as close."

I gave her another little hug and kissed the top of her head. "All right, now, don't worry about it. I'll get Doc and everything will be back to normal."

"He doesn't really think you killed Velda, you know."

"I know. He was just flipped out."

"He felt really bad. About losing her and you in the same day. He blamed himself for both."

"What? Velda too?"

"Yeah. He figured if she wasn't fooling around, she would still be alive."

"Takes two to tango, kid."

"Doc still feels responsible. And he said even if you are sick, he still loves you and shouldn't have said what he said to you."

"Sick? You think I'm *sick*?"

She just shrugged. "Just lovesick, maybe."

"Yeah," I said. "Sick of love. C'mon, let's get outta here. Any time we waste now in on Doc's clock."

I took her back to The Drive-Inn and dropped her off, then headed straight for the Hayes house in the Western Addition. Yellow police tape was all around the crime scene, blocking interference from strangers, and all the lights were out. I wondered where Daryl's boys hung their hats. I assumed this was their hood, so I looked around for the nearest bar, so I could make inquiries. I checked the chamber of the .45. Almost full.

The bar I went into was called The Jungle Hut. It was part tiki bar and part hellhole. I was the only white boy in the vicinity, much less the bar itself. It was practically deserted except for some homies playing pool in the rear and a couple more sitting at the bar. Loud, abrasive hip-hop blared from the juke. I hated it, but kept my opinion to myself.

I could feel unfriendly eyes on me as I sauntered up to the bar and sat down and asked for a whiskey sour from the bartender, who was relatively gregarious, in his 50s and obviously wishing someone would play jazz instead of rap for a change, though the customers made the call since they paid the bills. I wouldn't say we had an instant rapport, though. He gave me my whiskey sour, took my money, and went back to the sports page.

The homies at the bar were talking about the O.J. Simpson thing, how they thought he was totally innocent and had been set up. I didn't offer any conflicting theories. I just drank my beer and waited for an opportunity to query the bartender in a discreet but no-bullshit fashion. I didn't have time for subterfuge, or the energy. I merely wanted to cut to the chase.

Someone cut to it for me, and I wasn't the pursuer, either. "Hey, white boy," I heard someone say, someone who had their big hand on my humble shoulder.

I turned to see that a big brother in a leather coat and wearing shades was breathing down my back. Another brother was behind him, also wearing shades, but standing pat impassively. "You mean me?" I said.

"No, the *other* white boy. We noticed you're packin'."

"How'd you notice that? I'm not flaunting anything. None of your business whether I carry or not."

"In here it is."

"Yeah? How's that?"

"Give me the piece or leave. That simple."

"What if I do neither?" I was shaking, though, and he could tell.

A feint smile flickered across his face. "You wanna *fuck* with me, white boy? *Here*, on *this* turf, where you ain't got a friend in the world?"

"Oh, I got a friend around, I think. I hope."

"Anybody I know?"

"Maybe. Name's Curtis Jackson, but he goes by the moniker of Doc Schlock."

No smile, no reaction, just silence for a few tense moments. Then: "You bring that piece in here because you lookin' for your friend?"

"I carry a piece wherever I go. I'm a private detective. I have a license which I'd be all too happy to show you."

"You a dick, white boy?"

"You mean as in short for detective?"

"I mean as in a short detective, with a little white dick." I heard the homies nearby laugh. The bartender just kept his nose in the sports section. I guess he learned a long time ago to mind his own business.

"Yeah, I'm a dick all right," I said, still shaking, but speaking calmly. "A dick looking for a hole."

"Want me to dig one for you?"

"Naw, I mean a hole like a black hole."

I could feel the entire room bristle with tension. Even the jukebox was quiet now, and that was good.

"You lookin' at one big black motherfucker who's gonna swallow you whole, less you can come up with a better explanation why you sittin' here in this bar talkin' shit with a heater bulging in your coat."

"I told you. I'm lookin' for my friend."

"What makes you think he here?"

"Not here, but see, he was a friend of Velda Hayes."

"Velda Hayes? Daryl Hayes's wife?"

"Yup, that's the one."

"She dead."

"Yeah, I know."

"He dead, too."

I gulped. "Doc?"

"Daryl."

"Yeah, I read it in the papers. Too bad. Sad story."

"So, what makes you think yo' friend is here, if Velda ain't no more?"

"Maybe he was invited to the wake."

"Ain't no motherfuckin' wake. She wadn't no fuckin' Irish bitch. I think you best come out wit' me."

"Yeah? Where to?"

"Anywhere I say, white boy. Get up."

I finished my whiskey sour in a gulp and tossed a few bucks on the bar, stood up, and then with one sudden motion, pulled out the .45 and stuck it the big brother's forehead. Nobody moved. The bartender turned to the next page. The homies at the bar and in the back watched with something approaching awe, either at my courage or stupidity or both. The brother behind the big brother stood perfectly still, a neutral observer until further notice.

"You got balls, white boy," the big brother said, not even breaking a sweat. "But not after we're through with you. We cut 'em off and feed 'em to my motherfuckin' *dog*."

I cocked the .45 and I noticed him swallow. "Look, man, for all I know the world could end any minute, for all of us, and that's how I'm living my life these days, like there's no tomorrow, so save the tough talk and tell me where my friend is."

"You think I know, huh."

"I hope you do."

"For my sake?"

I shrugged, realizing the spot I'd put myself in. "Mine, too. *And* Doc's."

Big Brother smiled faintly again and said, "Put that gun away and we'll talk some business. Fair enough?"

"I do that, you might just kill me."

"Maybe. But if you shoot me, you may never find your fuckin' friend, not in this world, no matter when the fuck it ends. Think it over, but quick. I ain't got no more time for this shit."

I thought it over. I uncocked the piece and put it slowly back in my pocket, silently praying to my Guardian Angel.

Chapter Thirteen
SEX SUCKS AT LAST

Big Brother was watching me.

"You either real stupid or you just sick of livin'," he said slowly as he moved towards me. "Maybe both," I said. "My cat died, then my mother. Maybe Doc, too. Might as well make it an all-around parlay."

He stepped back a bit with a curious frown on his face. "Yo mama died?"

"Yeah. Just found out today. And now it looks like I lost my best pal, too."

Big Brother looked at his backup bro'. "This boy out of his mind wif craziness and grief," he said. "If what he sayin' is true." He looked back at me with a mixture of pity and skepticism. "'Course, I cain't think of no other reason he be this motherfuckin' stupid as to stick a smoker in my face, then put it away like nuffin' happened. You *gots* to be crazy."

I nodded in complete accord. Oddly enough, I wasn't shaking anymore. You see, there had been some truth in what I said. I wasn't just bluffing when I agreed that I was tired of living. But I was also afraid to die. It's a very stressful conflict. "That's me, man, stupid and crazy and tired. Got nothin' much left to lose. Look, if you know whether Doc is alive or dead, I'd just like to know, that's all. See, I'm about to retire from this detective biz anyway. I ain't no hot dog on a vendetta. If I was, I'da just burst in here with an Uzi and blown everyone away, or as many as I could before you got me, which would be inevitable under the circumstances." Then I put my hands in my trench coat pocket, and realized I was carrying an even more potent weapon—the notification of my mother's death. Proof. I pulled it out and handed it to Big Brother, who took it warily, handling it like it was used toilet paper.

"What the fuck is this?" he inquired.

"Evidence I ain't lyin'. About being insane with grief, I mean. Look at the date, too. I just got that this mornin'."

Big Brother looked it over carefully, then read it aloud for all to hear, carefully enunciating each syllable, either because he was extra polite or practically illiterate. I didn't venture a guess, just listened along with everyone else. After he was finished, he just nodded with curt sympathy, handed me back the letter, and said:

"So, I don't unnerstand, shorty. What the fuck you want from us, 'xactly?"

"I *told* you. The *truth*. You know whether my pal Doc is alive or what? I ain't accusing you or anyone you know personally of rubbin' him out, but this looks to be a tight-knit little 'hood, and you musta heard something. Besides, I read it on your face when I mentioned his name. You wouldn't be waitin' this much time on me if you weren't the least bit interested, like if I'm workin' for the cops or somethin', which I'm not. I'm not working at all. I'm not here as a law officer or investigator, just a friend with nothing left to lose. I pack the rod wherever I go, even sleep with it under my pillow. (A lie, but what the hell.) No offense, man. If you know somethin', no details, just the hard facts, that's all I need to know, so I won't waste time and worry waitin' for him to show up when he's six feet or sixty fathoms under by now. I thought someone in here might know, or know someone who does. Just a long shot. Take it or leave it."

Big Brother was mulling this over, I could tell, as he continued to size me up. He admired my *chutzpah,* which was really apathy, honed by my recent experiences with death, the ultimate party pooper. At that point, I really felt like I had nothing more to lose.

That was when Big Brother looked at me pensively and said, "Let's go, short shit. I show you right where yo' friend is."

"So he's still alive?"

He grinned, revealing a golden molar. "I don't wanna spoil the surprise, now. Let's go."

"You might just take me out and shoot me for dissin' you, and in public yet, whether you feel bad about my Ma or not."

He nodded. "That's just the chance you gonna hafta take now, ain't it?"

Stoically I nodded and said, "Let's do it." Then to myself I silently added, *See ya soon, Big Brother*, and his second led me outside. Behind me I heard some low mumbling and the bartender shuffling his newspaper obliviously. Probably figured he'd served me my last beer, if he considered me at all.

They led me into their shiny sleek big bad black Cadillac, a real gangsta-mobile if I ever saw one. The upholstery was a deep royal red. These guys used their money wisely, even if they obtained it stupidly. I didn't express any curiosity as far as their income went. I just quietly admired the spoils of their profession, which had something to do with narcotics, if they trafficked with the late Daryl Hayes, a fairly safe assumption so far. I just climbed into the back seat and kept my cool, which was about all I had in my favor, next to the .45 and my mother's death notice. Who'd have ever figured I'd engender sympathy with such a thing from such a dude at such a moment? Maybe I really did have a Guardian Angel after all. If so—good work, Marilyn. (I'd just assume she was Marilyn Monroe until I was given a contrary sign, which may very well never come anyway, since Angels apparently thrived on conjecture.)

They hadn't asked for my gun yet, which was nice, but when the Caddy sped around the corner and down a few darkly unfamiliar blocks and then slid into a waiting garage and the door slammed shut behind us, I grew somewhat apprehensive, and felt compelled to voice my concern as diplomatically as possible:

"Where in the hell are we?" I piped up in the blackness. I could barely see them now. "Unless you're really The Green Hornet and Kato, and this is Black Beauty, but somehow I doubt it."

I heard them get out of the car and then open my door for me. "When I was a kid," I heard Big Brother say as I stepped out, "I couldn't play no Green Hornet or Batman or Spiderman or Tarzan or Lone Ranger or *none* of that shit. I couldn't even play a fuckin' Indian if we played Cowboys. I always had to be a motherfuckin' native in the jungle or the motherfuckin' Black Panther. Shit really pissed me off, and still does, when I think of it."

I contemplated what he'd just told me. I never had that problem as a kid, and never realized how lucky I was being able to portray almost any hero in the popular media, even the Japanese ones, like Ultraman, if I so chose. I had to ask him, though, "You mean the Oakland radical kind of Black Panther or the Marvel comic book hero?"

I heard him chuckle. He was still a shadow in the dark. "First one, then the other. Right this way, shorty."

That was food for thought, which I stashed away until later. "The name's Vic Valentine," I said, following his footsteps.

"Yeah, and I'm Aquaman," he said. "Just shut the fuck up now."

"I'm half Italian, y'know," I said perhaps a tad too nervously.

I could hear him stop and turn in the dark. "What the fuck I just *tell* you? What the fuck I care you half wop? Fuckin' greaseball used to fuck my sister then beat her. I *buried* his greasy ass. Got any *more* to say?"

I nodded loud enough for him to hear, and we commenced walking. Big Brother's second was right on my heels. I didn't like this, and softly fingered my .45.

Big Brother stopped suddenly and I bumped into him. I mumbled an apology that he ignored, though I could tell he was a little peeved by my Caucasian clumsiness. Then he rapped on a door, I mean he knocked, that is, apparently in some secret code. The door opened and I was pulled and shoved inside at the same time and as I stepped into the next room I saw several things that inspired mixed emotions:

First, I noticed about ten other homies with their guns out, all cocked and pointed my way. I'd be a rusty sieve before I could even touch the trigger of my .45. so that was out. Figured. They were all more casually dressed than Big Brother and his second, wearing loose sweat jackets with hoods and baggy pants and all. Little plastic sacks of white stuff lay in piles next to mounds of money. The array of weaponry in the room, both in their hands and lying around on the floor like so much clutter, was astonishing. It was a veritable arsenal. Most of the heaters pointed at me looked like the thing Robocop used to tote around. And then in the center of the small, dimly lit, dirty room was Doc, tied up, lying on his side, his eyes swollen, his nose and mouth bloody. When he saw me, he brightened up a bit, but then when he saw that I was the bulls-eye in everyone's target, he resumed his expression of hopelessness and despair.

There were a number of demands for my identity, and when everyone had quieted down, Big Brother calmly explained, "This here is a friend of Lover Man down there. He's a private little dick, pokin' his pink little motherfuckin' nose around, lookin' for his friend here. Well, he found him."

Then there was a unanimous outcry for my instant violent death. Doc just shook his head sadly, looking at me through his black and blue peepers with resignation and empathy and gratitude, because he knew I was in this fix in a half-assed attempt to save his ass. Now it looked like I'd just be joining him. Oh well.

Big Brother told everyone to pipe down and put their gats away. "White boy just lost his Mama, have some respect."

"My cat, too," I unwisely chimed in.

"Fuck yo cat, I use 'em for target practice," Big Brother said. "Then feed 'em to my dog. You wanna meet my dog?"

"Uh, maybe later," I said. "Right now, me and Doc should get goin'."

That really cracked everyone up, except Doc and me, that is.

"Where you figure on goin', Flash?" Big Brother asked me.

"Uh, home, I guess, maybe stop off for a quick bite, I don't know. What's the difference? Doc looks like he's paid for his indiscretion, and me, I'm just out of my mind with grief, but I never stepped on your toes."

"You fo-gettin' somethin, aintcha?" Big Brother said ominously.

"You mean back at the bar? I thought that was bygones be bygones by now. My mother and all, you know."

"That don't 'splain why you fuck Daryl's wife, do it?"

Well, I nearly shit my pants right there and then, but even my crap was too scared to come out. Doc just buried his head into the floor and refused to look at me.

"I think you must have me confused with somebody else," I said meekly. "I mean, why would Velda go for a little vanilla truffle like me when she could have Doc?" That was dumb, real dumb. My nervousness was going to blow an already volatile situation sky high if I didn't put a sock in it.

"How you know her name is Velda den?" Big Brother asked me.

"I, uh, D-Doc told me about her. But y'know, she never told Doc she was married, y'know."

"How you know *that*?"

"She, she *told* me, that's how. When I went to see her." I figured they'd clocked my entrance and exit. Hell, for all I knew at the time, Doc was just bait, and they blamed me for their leader's bad call. Hopefully they hadn't been hiding in the god damn closet when Velda seduced me. Though they have seen her sit on my lap through the front bay windows...

"So you admit you visited Velda," Big Brother said, part Perry Mason, part Ice-T. The room was deadly quiet now.

"Yeah, you know I did, that's why you made me in the bar, right?"

Big Brother nodded. "Yeah, we been watchin' you."

"So Doc was just bait, right? Then let him go and deal with me."

"Uh-uh. He stepped outta line, too. He know you were doin' his woman, who wasn't even his woman?"

I couldn't even look at Doc now. Without even thinking, I tossed out a wild card, since I had only one hand left to play, if that. "According to Velda, Doc and me weren't the only ones, man. She told me she was doin' all of Daryl's men on the sly— even *you*."

There was the unsettling clicking of many guns being simultaneously cocked, but not all were pointed at me now. They seemed to be pointed at each other. I'd hit a nerve by accident. "You best shut the fuck up now, lest you wanna take a bloodbath," Big Brother said slowly.

"Hey, man, I'm bein' as straight with you as you are with me. See, the day I went to see Velda— and it was only once—I saw her gettin' out of a Mercedes Benz, a silver one, with a skull painted on the side door, and she kissed the driver on the way out. You know me and the Doc here don't breeze around town in that kinda glamour, not that it's out of our class, it just isn't our style. I notice you drive a real nice Caddy, man, so I ain't sayin' it was *you*. But who else you know who drives a silver Mercedes Benz with a skull and would be smoochin' with your boss's lady in plain sight? Anyone?"

The following moment was tense, to say the least, the air fraught with paranoia and unspoken accusations. Then Big Brother suddenly turned around to his second, who handed him a badass looking machine pistol, and Big Brother faced the assemblage and abruptly mowed down a dude in the back of the room. All the homies cussed and then the next thing I knew there was a lot of name calling featuring the F word. Everyone accused everyone else of boning Velda, and apparently the room was almost as full of guilty consciences as it was of guns, drugs, and dough. As the hostilities increased I grew more and more insecure about my imminent health, and Doc just cowered on the floor. I thought I could him whimpering, but maybe he had just found religion and was praying. Me, I was paging my Guardian Angel and anyone else who happened to be on the same frequency. The volatile situation heated up steadily as everyone began making loud macho threats with their heaters, then Big Brother made it all the more precarious by blowing away another brother who accused him of stealing the other dead dude's Mercedes to go visit Velda and set him up. I managed eye contact with Doc and signaled for him to try crawling over in my direction, because the fuse was lit and it was just a matter of time before the whole room went boom.

Just as Doc started slowly rolling my way there was a sudden outburst of gunfire, an exploding firestorm of mayhem that left ringing in my ears and spots in my eyes after the last shot had finally been fired. I also had a hell of a headache and an empty bladder. I waited for the smoke to clear and then I leaned down and looked for Doc. He was still moving, but no one else was. Even Big Brother was sitting up stiffly against the wall with his chest full of big bloody holes and his eyes wide open, staring into eternity. It was a sickening sight, but I had no time to mentally editorialize or spiritually reflect on the matter right then and there. I scooted over to Doc and tried to untie him, but the knots were too tight and I'd need a knife, so instead I led him back out the door I'd entered. We stumbled around the dark garage as sirens wailed in the distance. I couldn't find the goddamn way out of the garage, so we ran back into the room full of fried homies. Then, since Doc was out of it and couldn't make any sensible decisions, I elected to pocket a few wads of cash, carefully skipping the bills splattered with blood. Why the hell not? The drugs I left behind for the cops, though. Okay, maybe taking ill gotten gains from dead dopers was technically immoral, but the way I figured it, it was a combination of my fee for the rescue case and reward money for indirectly helping to dispose of a societal menace. It was a reasonable justification, enough to ease my conscience long enough to scavenge and scram.

We went out through the other door, which led into a hallway. We chose what I deemed to be the rear entrance and then we found ourselves in a normal backyard with laundry lines and barbecue pits. I heard children laughing and playing nearby. Despite the overall rundown nature of the environs, it hardly seemed a likely site for a massacre, though all the elements had been in place long before I showed up. I just happened to be an accidental catalyst. Obviously tensions had been running high for a while, all because of Velda's indiscriminating libido.

Doc was in bad shape and breathing heavily but I practically dragged him through the yard and down the street and up another until I saw a taxi and flagged it down. We got in and I told the cabbie to head for the nearest Emergency Room pronto, my friend had just been beat up and mugged by a gang of roving thugs. The cops were on the way, I told him, hence the sirens, but we had no time to fill out a report and answer questions, my friend needed immediate attention. The cabbie was hesitant until I dug into my wallet and flashed a fifty, then he peeled out. Human nature can be so touching.

Doc pretty much passed out on the way, and I had a little time to ponder what had just happened, and it hit me that a whole gang of drug dealers had wiped themselves out because of one dizzy deceitful dame. I couldn't decide whether that was good or bad, then figured it was just status quo in the topsy-turvy world of men and women, at least these days, but maybe always, one way or another.

What was even more amazing to me was that Doc and I had walked out of that mini-holocaust alive and in relatively good shape. Hell, if I hadn't have interrupted the proceedings right when I did, Doc might've been doing an off-key duet with Marvin Gaye by now. I chalked this up to the unseen meddling of my Guardian Angel, whether she was Marilyn Monroe or Clarence from *It's A Wonderful Life*. I heard the ding-ding of a cable car on the way to the hospital, and wondered if my Angel had won his or her wings.

The doctors in Emergency wanted to know why Doc was tied up, and I concocted a quick fable about a Houdini-type magic routine gone bad, just before the mugging by unknown assailants, and they reluctantly bought it. I didn't want to get bogged down with logistics right then, largely because of the illicit bulge in my pocket and largely because I was plum tuckered out. A report was made out anyway, but I ducked out before giving my name or any other details. Doc would recuperate and come home soon. I'd send Monica and Judy to check up on him. I just didn't want any further entanglements with the law or the lawless. I just wanted to lay low for a long, long time.

When I got home I called Monica down at The Drive-Inn and she came up and I told her all about the sordid series of events, including the carnage, something I'd never witnessed except on celluloid and which kept me away from anything more violent than Bugs Bunny cartoons for a long time after, but I didn't tell her about the dough. I'd made off with a good solid amount, I won't disclose exactly how much, but enough to buy me plenty of time to ponder my potential as a poet, a person, and a private eye.

We were in my office later that night, and Monica, who closed The Drive-Inn up early, was sitting across from my desk. Judy was rehearsing with The She Beams, and has yet had no idea what had transpired.

"I don't know what to say," Monica said softly. "You're a true hero, Vic. But I still don't understand why you just left Doc in the hospital, all alone."

"I told you, I don't want to get any more mixed up with the

media or the cops or anybody. Doc'll be out in a coupla days, and I'll make it up to him then."

"I guess this makes your friendship solid again."

"Yeah, I hope, but I told you why they all started shooting right?"

"'Cause of Velda, cause you said she was sleeping with some of 'em."

"*All* of 'em, the way it looked. That beat Doc up as much or more than they did, on the inside. It's ironic, y'know? Usually I'm the one all fucked up after a tryst with a promiscuous flake, and now Doc is laid up with broken bones and a broken heart. Anyway, before I lit the fuse, it kinda came out that I visited her, too."

"So you *did* sleep with her!" Monica gasped.

"Not exactly. She practically raped me at gunpoint. C'mon, Monica, give me *some* credit."

"I didn't think you'd even touched her, but then we walked in on you and that *nun*."

"That nun was the psycho from New Orleans, Monica."

"What? I thought she was locked up?"

"That's her *sister*."

"But I thought it was the sister who, I mean, the Sister didn't really *have* a sister."

"Never mind, I'm getting a migraine, I think. I'll explain later. But my point is, I hope Doc understands the circumstances and forgives me."

"Well, you did prove how much you care about him by going into that drug den to get him out. That was really brave, Vic."

"Yeah, well, after that notice about Ma, and all the other stuff, I just didn't care what happened to me anymore, in a way. I wasn't really brave. I was just sorta crazy. But I'm over it now. All that gunfire at close range woke me up. I might as well live."

"You still on that find the Secret of Life kick?"

"Naw, fuck it. I don't know what the hell's going on, and why should I?"

She giggled. "I'm glad you came to your senses. You really freaked me out with that. You were like that guy in that movie, Elmo Gallant or something."

I rolled my eyes. Kids. "Burt Lancaster as Elmer Gantry."

"Yeah, whatever."

"So you forgive me now, I take it? I've redeemed myself?"

She grew somber. "Yeah, I guess so. You still have to talk to

Judy, though."

"I will, but you have to promise me you'll put a cap on this rivalry thing with her. You guys are band mates now, after all. You gotta harmonize, if you catch my drift."

"I'll try, but I still have feelings for you, Vic. So does she."

I fought that impulse to be an asshole that all guys get when their luck changes after a devastating drought. "Monica, we're *friends*. We can't be messin' around like that anymore, y'know? Much as we'd like to. It's just be too sloppy."

"What about you and Judy?"

"Not her, either. I'll talk to her, don't worry. It's my fault, I know, for not drawing the lines sooner, but what can I say, both of you babes turn me on. But I'm gettin' too old to complicate my life my foolin' around with friends. We're not in love, Monica, c'mon. And neither are Judy and me. We're all just lonely, that's all, but we need to keep things clear, or else, look what happens. I mean, it's tough, controlling natural impulses, but I guess that's why we have brains as well as genitals. We gotta think with the right organ or *else*. I mean, look at that mess I just left. A room full of smoking corpses, all cause people were screwin' without thinkin'. Jealousy rears its ugly head, and then someone blows it off."

She looked sad now. "I thought we were making love, though, you and me, I really did. I guess not, or you wouldn't have run to Judy straight from me."

"Monica, look, despite what it might look like, I don't sleep with just *anybody*. Only women I feel a real affinity for. It just so happened that *all* the women I care about in the world lined up at once and I was so lonely I couldn't resist. All right, except the nun, or the *nuns*, but all the others, including *you*. But now I feel like I'll never have sex again. All those dead bodies sort of cured me of my terminal horniness, I think. Lust has lost its luster, you might say."

"I can't believe you're saying that."

"Believe it. Now go on, go see Doc. How's school, by the way? You study Art, right?"

"God, Vic, that's the first time you've asked me about that since I first told you about it like a year ago."

"I told you, babe, I care." In fact, it had just that moment reoccurred to me.

"Well, I sort of dropped out, cause I was so busy, with the band and work and all, but I'm slowly picking it back up, one course at a time."

"Good." I got up, walked around my desk, and kissed her on the forehead. "Keep it up."

"I would if you'd let me."

"Now, now," I said with avuncular authority. I went into my pocket and handed her a few hundreds. "Take this and pay for Doc's hospital bills. Shush, now, don't ask me where I got it, it's from my savings. Now *blow*." She took the money with a shrug. I patted her on the butt on her way out. It's just who I am.

After she was gone the loneliness set in, and I wondered how I would make it without intimacy. Part of me—and you know which part—still wanted to continue being physical with both Monica and Judy, but experience had taught me that wouldn't be prudent if I still valued their friendship. I felt lucky, in a way, and my confidence soared because of their affectionate attention. I was back in the saddle, romance-wise, but I felt like my horse had been shot out from under me. I just sat there in the dark, listening to Sinatra, tossing darts at my heart-shaped dart board, behind which was the safe containing my secret stash, and tried to decide what to do next with my lousy lonesome life. I spun around in my chair and stared out at the street below and thought: Made it, Ma. Top of the World.

Chapter Fourteen
CALL ME CLUELESS

The next morning as I was making breakfast I heard this scratching at my door. At first I ignored it, attributing it to a giant rat or mutant insect escaped from a nearby laboratory that I'd shouldn't touch or confront, but it was so persistent, I finally had to open up and check it out.

Sitting there on her ample laurels was a tubby Tabby, with creamy orange fur, looking up at me with soulful eyes and then letting out an adorable chortling sound like Gizmo in *Gremlins*. She (I found out her gender soon after, but guessed correctly right away) proceeded to waltz inside and make herself at home. It was then I noticed there was a note tied around her neck. Great. More mysterious missives from mad missies. The cat would probably explode, too. What the hell. I reached down and petted the purring pussy, which was very friendly, I must say, and removed the little note from her cuddly neck. It said simply, in very feminine handwriting I didn't recognize, "Puss sent me."

I went outside and looked around and saw no one. Apparently this cat was an independent operator, and my Guardian Angel was acting as unseen liaison between Puss and the Tabby, whom I immediately dubbed Cheesecake. It just came to me immediately, since she was so soft and creamy and roly-poly, plus I was really into '50s pin-ups and that just seemed like a natural moniker for a female feline in my possession.

I reached down and picked her up and she licked my hands and face and climbed all over my shoulders like an animated fur-piece. "Did Puss really send you, Cheesecake?" I asked her, not yet realizing she was a she, but suspecting, since her meow and manner were so decidedly feminine. I played with her a bit and then put her down and went down to the corner for some cat food and litter and all the stuff I'd tossed out when Puss died, thinking as I did: Was Puss my Guardian Angel now, or was he just sitting on Marilyn's lap?

I called Monica and told her.

"I swear, Vic, it wasn't me," she said sleepily. "But that's really cool. What are you gonna call her?"

"Cheesecake."

"What? What's with you? The last one was Puss. What will the next one be called—Muff? Snatch? *Nookie*?"

"Yeah, yeah. So it wasn't you."

"Believe me, Vic, if I wanted to give you a present like that, I'd be up front with it so I'd get all the credit. I don't think it was Judy, either. I spoke to her late last night and I think she's a little mad still."

"Yeah, whatever. How's Doc?"

"Oh, fine. Well, better. He'll be out later today or tomorrow. He asked where you were. He wants you to come see him."

"Well, it's complicated. I'll just see him when he gets out. He still pissed at me too?"

"Couldn't tell. It'll be okay. I can't wait to meet your cat, but right now I have to open The Drive-Inn. I promised Doc I'd take care of things till he got back."

"Good. Tell Judy if you talk to her I'll see her later, huh?"

"Okay. I'm glad we talked, Vic. That cat's a good sign, I think."

"Yeah, from *somebody*. See ya."

I hung up. Cheesecake was making herself at home, purring and mewing. Man, she was chubby, though. Well, voluptuous, or perhaps, more accurately, *zaftig*. But then so were many cheesecake calendar subjects. She obviously wasn't some scrawny street urchin picking some sucker at random to nurse her back to health. Whoever sent her had taken good care of her, and since she was already a girl, I wouldn't have to worry about her getting urinary tract blockage and having to pay to get her dick whacked off. She was already there. It felt right to take her in, and my loneliness was instantly abated, but that note was a tip-off that something weird was up Of course, weird in my life doesn't necessarily mean unusual.

I finished breakfast and introduced Cheesecake to the Chairman of the Board and then sat down to write, but for some reason, it just wasn't flowing. Maybe I needed time to assimilate everything. I felt like there was something missing, an overlooked task, one last obstacle to my ultimate piece of mind. I sat there thinking about Ma and her unfinished life and unrealized dreams and then it hit me:

Her letters. I still had to open and read the sack of letters sent from the Chipper Monks in my closet. At that point they were my only heirlooms, and probably always would be, since Aunt

Florence would no doubt see to it I was totally cut out of my mother's meager will. I had no more time or excuses to procrastinate. I had to read those letters for an explanation of my past and maybe even a clue to my future.

Hesitantly but resolutely I went to my closet and took out the sack and dumped the pile of letters onto my desk. I recalled reading a few before I stopped opening them, and they were so disturbing, full of meaningless manic ranting about UFOs and conspiracies and even darker demons that I just gave up. It was too intense, too stressful to share her sickness with her, mostly because of the emotional proximity. But now I was older, and she was gone, and these were my only link. I picked an envelope at random and gently tore it open as Cheesecake hopped up on the desk and sat on the stack, purring. I was really glad she was there to share this experience with me. I don't think I could've handled it alone.

The letter I chose was postmarked much earlier, after I'd first arrived in San Francisco and tried to make my mark as a freelance journalist. It seemed to follow the old general depressing haphazard line of paranoid rambling, so I skipped through it and opened another, and another, and another, until there were two piles of letters, one opened and half read and one unopened and unread. I felt overwhelmed an odd sense of desperation and hopelessness, got up, paced the room, listening to Frank, Cheesecake at my heels, and when I felt mentally and emotionally rested, I tackled the remainder, praying I'd find just one lucid letter to perpetuate a positive memory of Ma.

It took a while, but I found it. Amid all the sadness and madness was a letter postmarked around two years earlier. Unlike the others it was neatly written and folded. Here's part of it:

"Dear Son—I am sorry it has been a long time since I have written you but I have been away. I can't tell you where because I don't know where. Maybe it was in a bad dream, but I'm back now and I want you to know I miss you terribly and wish you would come visit me soon. I know you are far away and that is good but please if you can try to see me now before I dream again. I can't control the bad dreams, you see, they just overtake me like the tide. Remember those trips we used to take with your father and brother? I think about them all the time, the woods and the rivers and the picnics and smell of campfires and music on the radio. I miss music. I want to play the music I hear in my head sometimes. I wish when I die I go to a place like the forest where music plays

constantly. Maybe there I will see Johnny and your father again, but before I go there, please come see me. Hurry, before it's too late and I won't be able to talk to you anymore in this world..."

Well, it went on, but that was the gist of it. No mention of the usual fears and threats, just straightforward human frailty and passion. At least I finally did go see her the previous year, without even reading this moving summons, but I was too late—the tide had overtaken her again by the time I got there, except for one brief instant when she reared her head out of the waves and kissed me goodbye, as if she knew that was the last time I'd ever see her. In this world, at least.

I put all the letters away neatly into the sack, except for that last one, which I tucked into my desk to be re-read over and over again in the future. I felt a connection with Ma, with her real inner spirit and not the damaged shell that wasted away in the mental home, but nothing was really illuminated as far as my life went. The letters held no clues as to why I kept attracting lost women like my mother, over and over, without any encouragement or solicitation on my part. Or, wait. Was I subconsciously beckoning these women to me? Or did I have some weird karma to work out, or was I simply cursed, or were all women crazy and mine were just being honest with me? No, most of the women I knew, including my mother, were victims of brutal, abusive, insensitive men. But I was so nice. Maybe that was it. Maybe I should start being brutal and insensitive. No, I couldn't do it. I was stuck with my lonely code of ethics. If I just swore off the opposite sex forever, that would effectively eliminate the dilemma, and I could preoccupy myself with more noble pursuits.

Yeah, like what?

Whatever.

I petted Cheesecake and then went out for a bite. Tentatively on the agenda was a visit to Judy to patch things up once and for all so I could move on to wherever I was going next, but the path seemed just as dimly lit and randomly winding as ever.

I went down to Rendezvous and killed some time, afraid to read the paper for fear of what I'd find there—more odious bulletins decisively impacting my little life. So instead I wrote in my little notebook, more entries for my dinky diary. I sat there for hours listening to big band swing on the sound system, and then some mellow jazz tunes as the day descended into night, and I continued to scribble and nibble and dribble, just like those cafe-dwelling pseudo-literary snobs and drips I once ridiculed. I recalled what a friend of mine back East once told me: *Writers don't get laid*. Yes, they do, I countered. Look at me. *Not good ones*, he said. Maybe now I'd become a good writer and not have to worry about nookie anymore, or at least until the quality of my work began to suffer from lack of amorous nourishment. My stock had gone up, and I was well stocked, enough to last me through several notebooks. For once, a lack of sexual prospects didn't bother me. I could concentrate on my work now, my mission in life. Getting laid would only distract me. Time was running out. It was time to work. At least until my hand got cramps.

I finally quit and went out to North Beach for some spaghetti with marinara at the U.S. Restaurant on Columbus Avenue, a fine dining establishment. Then I popped over to Judy's flat on Telegraph Hill.

"Got a minute for an old friend?" I asked her when she opened the door.

"Vic," she said, not smiling. "You should have called."

"Why? You have a guest?"

"No, but..."

"But what? You're not gonna let the cops bust me for trespassing again, are you?"

She snorted, suppressing a laugh. Hardy har har. "No, not yet, you're still dressed. Come in, damn it."

"How can I resist such an invitation?"

I stepped inside and we sat on her sofa and I looked at her seashells and she got us some drinks and then I told her all about my most recent flirtation with death. Chicks like it when you tell them about your other dalliances. It presents a challenge.

"I can't believe that," she said with awe.

I shrugged with weary worldliness. "What can I say? I've got an angel on my shoulder, I guess. An angel with a tommy gun, that is."

"I mean that you didn't go visit Doc in the hospital."

"Oh. Well, I just didn't want to deal with cops and all. I've had enough of that. I don't want to be linked to that massacre and go through all that legal razzmatazz. I just want to take it easy for a while, not think or worry or anything, y'know? Just figure stuff out."

"You mean like seducing nuns, whether or not that's a good idea?"

I told Judy all about Sister Sue or Elizabeth or whoever she was. Judy just nodded with a very bored expression, like this was par the course for me, which it was.

"I pity any girl who really falls for you," she said when I'd finished.

"Thanks. So you're sayin' you're off the hook?"

"You mean with you? C'mon, Vic, I was just lonely. I like you, in spite of everything, but I've got my music, and you've got— what *have* you got?"

I shrugged. "That's what I have to figure out, baby cakes."

"You still a detective?"

"I still have my license, yeah, but, I don't know *what* I want to do next, Jude. I really don't. I may just move someplace new and start all over, like Seattle. I've always dreamed of living there, for some reason, even before I moved here from New York. I think it would suit me."

"*Seattle*? Really? You never told me that!"

"You never asked. I miss seasons, like what I grew up with, too, but I don't want to actually live back East again. Too many ghosts from my past would haunt me, just like they do here now, actually. At least there's the fog. But there's no *autumn* in California, just this Indian summer shit. Plus it's so *green* up there, or so I hear. Aw, hell. It's just a fantasy, really. Something to look forward to, even if I never actually get around to it. Otherwise I just feel so *stuck*, like life is just passin' me by, y'know?"

"Yeah, I understand. I like it up there too, so pretty, but it *rains* so damn much."

"Exactly!"

"You just *like* being depressed, I take it."

"Actually, the *sun* bums me out. But I'm bummed most of the time anyway, so I guess the weather doesn't really matter much these days."

"Oh. Monica told me about your mother, I forgot all about that. I'm sorry, Vic, I really am." The hardness in her tone was relenting now.

"Thanks."

"I guess that takes the wind out of your sails. At least my crazy old mother is still alive somewhere."

"You talk to her lately?"

"She left a message. She's still in Miami, and the band's going to stop through on a tour this summer, so I might see her, or she might come out and see me."

"Do it. Life's too short for petty grudges."

"Vic?"

"Yeah, babe?"

"Can I give you a hug?"

"Thought you'd never ask."

So we embraced and kissed a little but that was it. The mutual attraction was still there, diluted by recent events, but frustratingly evident. We both realized it wouldn't be wise to take it any further, not now, anyway, not until we both figured out our own solitary situations. Then perhaps we could share what we built up. Yeah, and maybe there would one day be world peace and a cure for cancer and AIDS and Elvis would play Vegas on New Year's Eve 2000. Yeah maybe.

I told her about Cheesecake. "I guess you know nothing about it," I said.

She shook her head. "Sorry, I was still mad at you. Maybe it was The Phone Phantom."

"Yeah, maybe."

"Or Monica? She's the cat lady."

"I asked her already, no dice."

Right then the phone rang. Judy went to answer it and came back a minute later.

"Speak of the devil-ette, that was Monica. Doc's coming home right now. I have The She Beams on call so that we can do a welcome home gig at The Drive-Inn."

"That's great. I'll be there."

I stood up and she walked over and hugged me. "Want to come with me?"

"Naw. I'll just see you there." I kissed her on the tip of the nose and then walked back down the hill to my Corvair and drive home.

Well, I had all my friends again, at least. As long as Doc forgave me, and I'd think he would, under the circumstances. I was sitting at the bar of The Drive-Inn when Monica came in with him. The She Beams hadn't showed up yet, and the place was closed to the public until they did. We just wanted some quality time alone with Doc first. Monica took him back to his apartment first to get dressed and cleaned up, so by the time I saw him, he looked like a million.

When he first saw me, he froze, and so did I. He walked, or rather, limped over with a stern expression on his battered face. I looked back at him somewhat nervously, and then he broke into his trademark gap-tooth grin—in fact, the gap was even wider now, since getting roughed-up—and I knew Doc was back.

We hugged and all that crap, and mutually apologized and

when we were done getting sentimental and sloppy he went behind the bar and heaved a big sigh. "Good to be back, I gotta say," he said. "Why didn't you come visit me, Vic?"

"I just, I dunno, Doc. After I dropped you off, I just kinda freaked out."

"You took some of that dough, didn't you?"

I squirmed in my seat. Monica chided me with her eyes.

"Well?" Doc said.

"Yeah, some. So what?"

"I figured that was it, so I didn't say nothin' to the cop who made out my report. He asked who dropped me off and I said I didn't know you, and he forgot about it, figured you were just a good simian."

"Samaritan."

"You heard me."

"It's good to have you back, Doc."

"*How* good? You gonna give me some of that loot?"

"You *better*," Monica said.

"Well, sure, Doc. In fact, I'm gonna pay my back rent out of it."

"That's good for a start."

"Doc, c'mon. I need the time to relax and not worry about makin' a living for a while."

Doc nodded. "Monica told me about your Mama just a little while ago. Sorry to hear it, Vic. Truly, that's a damn shame."

"Yeah. Thanks."

"So what are you gonna do after you're through mournin'?"

"That's the big question, Doc. I'm writing and all, but, we'll see."

"Well, you did spring for my hospital bills, so just give me my fuckin' rent money, and we'll call it even. Keep the dough, Vic. Coast for a while. You deserve it."

Then Monica gave me a kiss on the cheek and I felt all warm and fuzzy inside. Judy and The She Beams—Suzy from Japan, Esmeralda from Spain, and Nikki from Jamaica—showed up just then and everyone hugged and all and then they set up their instruments and opened the door for the public. Judy had invited some of her pals and so had Monica, so the joint would be jumpin'. Me, all my pals were already there.

An hour later The She Beams were rocking the joint and Doc was getting a buzz on and having a grand old time. His brush with death was practically forgotten now. I took him aside at one point to ask him about his true inner state.

"You miss Velda?"

"Who?" he said.

"'Nuff said."

"You miss Rose?"

"Who?"

He shook my hand. "Hey, speakin' of pussy, I hear you got a new cat. Monica just told me."

"Yeah, but I don't know who it's from."

"Maybe nobody. Maybe she just showed up."

"She did, but there was a note around her neck—said *Puss* sent her."

"Well, there ya go. What's the mystery?"

"Doc, Puss is a dead cat."

"Maybe he's an angel now, lookin' out for ya. Just goes to show you, Vic—you never know what's around that next corner."

"Good or bad."

"That's life."

"No shit, Doc."

"Well, stop beatin' yourself up tryin' to figure it out. Just roll with it, my man. Just roll with it. Roll till you stop rollin', or somethin' stops you, whether it's a stone in your kidneys or a bullet in the brain. Who knows, maybe your Mama's up there with Puss, and they *both* sent this new cat to you. What's her name?"

"The cat? Cheesecake."

Doc cracked up. "C'mon, let's go check her out."

So Doc and Monica and The She Beams took five and came upstairs to meet Cheesecake, whom we interrupted tearing my room apart. All the girls thought she was just adorable and took turns petting her, while Doc just sat on my desk with a bottle in his hand and took it easy. Monica picked Cheesecake up and looked her over, confirmed her sex, and said she'd take Cheesecake down to the vet the next day for a complete checkup, and I said that would be swell.

"Yeah, she's Cheesecake, all right," Doc said, looking at my framed portrait of Bettie Page and my autographed still of Mara Corday. "Just don't get *confused* and too lonely one night."

"Yeah, yeah. Don't worry, Doc."

"Well, we're goin' back downstairs now, wanna come with? The party's just beginnin'."

"Naw, I'm kinda beat. It's after midnight, Doc."

"Time's a matter of perspective, Vic, just remember that."

"That's real profound, Doc. Thanks."

He slapped me on the shoulder and leered at me with glassy-eyed sincerity. He was pretty loaded. "I understand. Your Mama, right?"

"Partly, I guess, yeah. Hey, Doc, think the world's gonna end soon?"

He just shook his head and belched and said, "Vic, we're still here, after all that's happened, and that must mean *somethin'*. Why worry about when the party's gonna end? It started already, didn't it? Had to be a reason for that, I mean, parties don't get started just so they can end. Too late to worry about that, Vic, we're already in it. And it'll go on till it's time to go. What time is the party over? Who gives a damn, Vic! Just enjoy yourself till the booze runs out and the broads fall asleep."

I sighed. "Whatever," I said. Then Doc gave me another tipsy hug and Monica and Judy and all The She Beams each gave me a kiss as they filed out my door, and then it was must me and Cheesecake and the Chairman and a room echoing with unfulfilled promise.

I noticed the red light on my answering machine was flashing. Reluctantly I checked the messages, since I wouldn't be able to sleep wondering who they were. Might as well get it over with.

The first one was from Dolly: "Hey, Vic, it's me. Doll. I'm in, I don't know *where* I am, it doesn't matter. But I'll leave my number, so you can call me, if you want. I miss you, Vic. I think there's a chance for us, I really do. I've never loved anyone like you, Vic. Just remember that, Vic. I mean, I've never loved anyone like I love you, but, yeah, also—I've never loved anyone like I love you. I don't think I've ever loved anyone, period, except, well, I'm getting all misty and I'm a little stoned but I'll give it up if you call me, Vic. *Please*. Tonight. I love you, here's the number..."

Beep.

Next: "Vic, this is Rose. I'm leaving tomorrow to do Missionary work in Salvador and some other places, and I've been thinking, Vic, and I think—I want you to help me rescue Sammy, and then we can, I know this sounds *crazy*, but we can run away together, to some romantic place, and start over, all over, and I know, this sounds crazy, but if I don't hear from you, I'm afraid I really will devote my life to this work, and while that will make me feel clean. I'm so *alone*. I miss Sammy, and I miss you. Call me, Vic. The number is..."

Beep. Next:

"Vic, this is Elizabeth. I'm still in California. I don't think I can return to New Orleans now, after what happened, and I can't stop thinking about you, Vic, and what happened between us, it was so, so *spiritual*, in a way, and I think that's why I felt compelled to connect with you all along. Anyway, I'm in Monterey, and here's where I'm staying. Please call me, Vic..."

Beep.

There was one more call, from a potential client, a desperate sounding lawyer who needed some surveillance shots of a clandestine affair between his wife and his boss. He was probably loaded and I could milk him for a bundle. *His* number I took down. The rest I erased.

I guess I'm a real dick after all.

The End of

DIARY OF A DICK

But

Vic Valentine will return in

HARD-BOILED HEART

Bonus:

BRAIN MISTRUST

A Vic Valentine Vignette

Originally published in *The Shamus Sampler 2*, 2014

Chicago, 2005

I was getting blown by the Windy City, and for once, I was hoping I wouldn't be swallowed whole.

The big question was how did I wind up in Chicago, anyway? The PI license in my wallet insisted my name was Vic Valentine, and my residence was in San Francisco. That part I vaguely remembered. The rest was a big, gaping void that I needed to fill with some hard facts, but quick.

I knew I was in Chicago because there was a folded *Tribune* on my bedside table, next to the radio clock and phone. I looked at the date. It seemed like I'd lost a few days, since last thing I remembered it was Saturday. Apparently today was Wednesday. At least it was still the same year: 2005. I got up and went to the window. I'd been to Chicago a few times on cases, but I didn't recognize the precise neighborhood. But it looked, felt and smelled like Chicago, all right. Every big city has its own unique aroma. You don't always get a whiff of it at first, but after a while, that special scent makes any town as instantly distinctive as perfume on a pig.

The last thing I remembered with any clarity: I woke up in a generically appointed hotel room next to a reasonably attractive red-haired woman in her middle thirties or so. She was snoring, which detracted somewhat from her overall allure. She was lying on her belly but I had a nice view of her left tit from the side, and from that angle at least it looked quite round and succulent. Her ass was plump and juicy with just the right amount of cellulite, which I love even more than celluloid, and almost free of blemishes and zits. There was just one big red pimple with a whitehead, ready to pop, but I resisted the urge to squeeze pus out of a shapely stranger's butt cheek. When she let out an involuntary fart, which puffed almost visibly into the air, her physical appeal was again somewhat diminished. My groggy state of mind extended to my penis, so my sex drive was stuck in neutral anyway. For all I knew, we'd already been intimately acquainted, anyway. There was a sexual stench wafting up my nostrils, and then I noticed I was wearing nothing but my socks. Clue number one. My Fedora, shiny suit, skinny tie, white shirt, and sharp black shoes were strewn across the floor beside the bed. Next to them was what appeared to be a wrinkled pink waitress outfit and dirty white tennis shoes, made for walking. Clue number two.

Rather than attempting to mentally reconstruct our passionate tryst, I gazed passively at her naked body and tried to envision her in various unattractive poses, like sitting on the toilet, taking a crap, straining and squinting, the twisted folds of her flesh distorting her feminine figure. I often do this to put human beauty into proper perspective, so I can deal with people in their organically honest forms. One's appearance almost always relies on cosmetic circumstances like lighting, makeup and situation. And of course, subjective tastes. Our bodies are collectively in various stages of deterioration, depending on factors beyond our control, like age, and others we can but don't always keep in check, like abuse via various substances, including food. We're basically just temporal blobs of corporeal mush, tragically vulnerable to the elements as well as the random ravages of time. We often emit foul odors and exhibit natural behavior in common with most species considered inferior. Like we're the true inheritors of the Earth and dominant custodians of the planet. Nice job, by the way. Look around. Who are we kidding? Not me.

Then she moved her head, opened her eyes, and looked at me while I was still standing at the window, looking at her.

She sat straight up, pulling the sheets around her jiggling

breasts, which were indeed spectacular, and shrieked. I have been greeted with that reaction first thing on many a misguided morning, so at least there was *some* reliable continuity in my life. Her face was soft and pretty in a plain way, and while she was no high fashion model, thankfully, her old fashioned curves were a sight for sore eyes. As the saying goes, beauty is in the eye of the beholder, and her big, pointy nipples were getting along just fine with my popping pupils. Little Elvis began to stir.

"Who the hell are you?" she asked me with urgency in her crackly voice.

"I was about to ask you the same question," I said.

"What, you don't know who you are, either?"

"No, my name is Vic Valentine. I'm a private dick—pardon the pun—from San Francisco. I just don't know how I got here. *Or* you."

"Well, don't ask me!"

"You mean *you* don't know who you are, either?"

"No, I don't know who *you* are!"

"But I do. And I introduced myself. Your turn."

"M-my name is Dottie. Dottie Evans."

"But of course it is. You're a waitress. Makes sense in this epic B movie I call 'my life.' Better than 'Marge,' I guess."

"Oh, yeah? So you're name is what again, Rick Romance or something? *That* for real?"

"Vic Valentine, I said, and yeah, it's for real. But are you? Maybe I'm just dreaming..." I thought of Sean Connery as James Bond, encountering Honor Blackman as Pussy Galore for the first time in *Goldfinger.*

"I know, right?" Self-consciously, she pulled the sheet tighter around her. "Did we...did we...*make* it?"

"You mean 'fuck'? In my professional opinion...yeah, looks that way. Sorry."

Then she blushed and her thickly lashed brown eyes fluttered for an instant in embarrassment as she sized up her mystery date. I was starting to like her, whoever she was. "Well, I guess I could've woken up next to worse," she said, flattering me. But then she just had to add: "God knows I have. *Plenty* of times."

Uh oh: better add a checkup at the local clinic to my itinerary, I thought. I didn't notice any used condoms around, but I did recognize some familiar white stains on her thigh, because I'd seen similar sticky spots on my own thigh before, from the same source, when I was alone.

Then I suddenly remembered something else: I owned a cat who was getting on in years. Who was taking care of him while I was away on mysterious business? My friend Doc Schlock? No, I recalled clearly that Doc was currently in the hospital being treated for some pancreatic problems. Monica—my sexy young gal-pal—was left in charge of his establishment, a combo video store/bar called The Drive-Inn, above which was my studio apartment/office. My next move would be to call her not only to check up on my cat, but to find out if she knew why I woke up in Chicago and not back in Frisco. Yes, I said *Frisco*. I'm originally from New York. I'm not a Bay Area native so I didn't go for that local civic pride jazz. Even though I'd been stuck in California for years, I never identified with any particular place as my home. I'm merely a citizen of Earth. There's enough shame in that, anyway.

First things first. "So where do you work, Dottie?" I asked.

"Why?"

"Because maybe we can figure out where we met, and take it from there. I assume a diner?"

"Well, yeah. But that's not the last place I remember."

"What is?"

"A bar called the Green Mill. I *think*." Dottie got up from the bed, the sheet still tight around her voluptuous body, and ran to the window next to me. I stepped aside, giving her wide berth. Despite my natural attraction, I was a little afraid of her, too. "That's it!" she said, pointing down the street. "We're still in the same neighborhood!" I hadn't noticed it before because my vision was somewhat blurred but that settled it. We were in the Uptown District.

"So you don't live here?"

"In *this* dump? Honey, I'm a waitress, not a hooker."

Well, that was a relief, I thought. At least I wouldn't owe her money.

"Get dressed," I said. "Let's go to the Green Mill and ask some questions."

"You think we were drugged?"

"Hey, the last thing I remember was being at a bar in San Francisco, called The Drive-Inn. So if somebody spiked both our drinks, they obviously did some traveling in between."

I couldn't help looking at her with obvious lust, both heads throbbing. She noticed, and returned the leer. Next thing I knew, we were back in bed, frolicking like frisky honeymooners. Since I didn't have any condoms, obviously, and we were now fully aware of our actions, at first we just engaged in vigorous oral sex. But after a while we just said "fuck it," literally, and took the perilous plunge back into the amorous abyss.

Four hours later it was getting dark and the iconic, green neon sign of the Green Mill was beckoning to us through the somewhat misty veil of the evening. It was the nexus of winter and spring, when the weather couldn't make up its mind which climate to cater. At least Chicago had seasons. Having grown up back East, I still missed them.

Dottie and I got dressed and walked down to the Green Mill like we were a cozy couple with a cherished history, as opposed to two total strangers who had nothing in common but shared bodily fluids and a 72-hour blackout. Whatever or whoever brought us together might be in for a grateful handshake.

Sometimes I stop and savor random moments, any random moment, with the bittersweet awareness that whatever it is will never be precisely repeated or possibly even accurately remembered, even if it is recorded, since photos and films, like memories, are intangible evidence of a particular instant that is forever lost immediately after it is experienced. That makes me very sad. I'm not sure why. I guess because it's a constant reminder of our mortality. Life is so damned elusive, persistently slipping through our grasp at a gradually accelerated clip no matter how hard we hang on to it, like realizing you're dreaming halfway through the dream, afraid you'll wake up any second, and it will all suddenly be gone, just like that.

This was one of them.

The Green Mill Cocktail Lounge had once been owned by Al Capone, and indeed there was a shrine devoted to him behind the bar. The legendary club had also been featured in the old Michael Mann flick *Thief,* one of my favorites. Other than that, it looked pretty much like any other dimly lit neighborhood dive, with comfy booths and a little stage famous for blues bands and poetry slams. Framed photos of the city's checkered history lined the wood-paneled walls. The Journeymen were singing "500 Miles" on the jukebox as we walked in, and I suddenly suffered an acutely melancholy pang of loneliness, like I was missing home, or at least the place I knew best.

I ordered Dottie a Cosmopolitan and me a Manhattan and excused myself to go the head, though I really went to the payphone to call Monica collect back in Frisco. Okay, *San Francisco.* Unbunch your panties already.

"Hey Monica, it's me, Vic."

"Vic! Where the hell *are* you?" She sounded very concerned.

"Chicago."

"Chicago? But you said you were just going upstairs to take a nap! What the hell?"

"Yeah, I know. I mean, I don't know. How's my cat?"

"Well, when I didn't see you yesterday I went up to check on you, and since you weren't around I took the liberty of feeding him." Monica had a key to my pad. I trusted her. Plus it came in handy for emergency booty calls.

"That's cool, thanks. Big load off my mind."

"So what the hell are you doing all the way in Chicago all of a sudden? You were just complaining to me how broke you are! Did you get a client and skip town without even saying goodbye, just like that?"

"I don't know! Maybe!"

"*Maybe*? What the *fuck*, Vic?"

"Monica, to be honest, I just woke up here. This morning, I mean. And I have no idea how the hell I got here."

"Where exactly are you right now?"

"A bar called the Green Mill, down the block from the joint where I woke up."

"Are you alone?"

"Ah, no. No, I'm not."

"A chick?"

"Yeah."

"You bang her already?"

"Yup."

"Figures. At least you didn't wake up with a guy."

"Or worse."

"Though *that's* a story I'd *love* to hear."

"Don't hold your breath, baby. Anyway, the chick has no idea how she wound up in bed with me, either."

"Is she cute, at least?"

"Yeah, she's sweet, too. No sign of foul play. Except for the mutual amnesia. And the fact that she's an actual resident, and I'm an unwilling visitor."

"How can you be sure you're unwilling, if you don't remember how you got there?"

"Good point. Do you remember seeing me in the Drive-Inn with anyone else, perchance?"

"You mean Saturday night? No, you were alone as usual. In

fact, we were supposed to get together later that night, but I told you I was too tired. Then I didn't hear from you Sunday, so I thought you were mad at me. That's when I went upstairs to look for you and fed your hungry cat. I figured you were gone on a job, since I knew you were in the middle of some kidnapping case, but it was weird you didn't check out with me first, like usual. Just in case something happens to you."

"And so it did this time. What's the last thing you remember about me?"

"Toasting Doc's health right here at the bar, then calling it a night."

"That's *it*?"

"That's it."

"Damn."

"Vic, I'm worried about you. Just come home and we'll figure it out from here, okay?"

"I don't know. I guess you're right. But the answer must be right here in Chicago. I think I'll poke around for some clues before I split town."

"And that ain't all you'll be poking, right?"

"I gotta go, I left her alone at the bar."

"Just be careful, Vic."

"I will. See ya soon."

"I *hope* so."

"Me too."

I hung up and returned to the bar. Both our drinks were sitting there, untouched, but Dottie was gone. When I asked the blasé bartender about her, he just shrugged.

I downed both cocktails before I decided I was hungry. Famished, in fact. I paid the bartender with my credit card (at least I hadn't been rolled during transition) and headed back to the hotel, praying I'd find Dottie there.

That's when I began wondering about a fundamental fact: I had the key to our room, but I didn't remember checking in.

I went up to the desk clerk on duty, a nervous little guy, and asked him if he remembered me.

"No," he said, his face twitching with telltale tics as he finger-combed his pencil mustache.

"So who checked me in?" I asked.

"I don't know. Whoever was on duty. I was off last night."

"So you know I checked in last night?"

"It says so on the record, sir."

"I see." But actually, I was flying blind.

I went up to the room half-hoping to see Dottie, but fully expecting it to be empty. It was. I checked the closet. No clothes, no luggage, no sign of any life at all.

It dawned on me I should probably get checked out by a doctor, especially since my crotch was starting to itch, on top of the mental blackout. But my growling stomach demanded immediate attention. My brain could wait. Anyway I'd already given my cock's indiscriminate desires top priority, and look where it had lead both of us: Nowheresville. Our natural habitat.

Fortunately there was some cash in my wallet, enough for a cab across town. I craved some Chicago pizza. I grabbed the newspaper off the bedside table for some reading matter, told the rat at the desk to call me a taxi, then headed over to Gino's East, the one inside the Loop, since from there I could hop a train over to my favorite local bar, Miller's Pub, across from the Art Institute. Funny I could remember that joint, but not how I got here this time. I also remembered the best Chicago-style pizza I'd ever had was at Zachary's. Back in Oakland. But that was a little beyond my cab fare budget at the moment.

I voraciously devoured an entire medium-sized deep-dish cheese-and-spinach pizza, which would no doubt plug up my bowels for days, but I always had trouble taking a shit when I was out of town anyway. Also sleeping. But I didn't have time for that, anyway. Yet I did have time for two ass-kicking Gibsons at Miller's, which is where I was, idly looking over the *Tribune* I'd brought with me, when I finally noticed a small item on the bottom of page five: *Local Waitress Missing; Police Hunt for Private Eye Suspect.*

Gin dribbling down my chin, I quickly read the rest of the short article, which I hadn't even noticed before. This was printed and distributed while I was actually *with* Dottie that very morning, so obviously it was a set-up. Not many details, but enough to ruin my day: my name, Dottie's name, and her picture. I was listed as "a person of interest" since I was last seen with her at the Green Mill Cocktail Lounge.

By this time I was four or five sheets to the wind, and the wind was blowing pretty hard as I staggered outside, hailed another taxi, and headed right back to the hotel—where the cops were waiting to pick me up. That ratty desk clerk had dropped the dime on me.

Oh, and they'd found Dottie. Floating nude and dead in Lake

Michigan.

Sitting handcuffed in the backseat of the black-and-white on the way to the nearby precinct for questioning, it hit me that I was in my forties and still alone. Sure, I got my share of pussy, but I never really connected with another human being the way I did with my cat.

Though they couldn't charge me with anything yet, the fact that I couldn't provide any details that countered the overwhelmingly incriminating evidence meant they had sufficient cause to hold me. Plus I was too plastered to make my own case with any sort of rational coherence. I drunkenly insisted I'd been framed—doped then duped, a randomly selected patsy transported from the Coast, the perfect fall guy since I was a transient out-of-towner. True, I had no homicides on my record, but enough shady activity committed in "the line of duty," dating back the past fifteen or so years, that a jury wouldn't have a lot of trouble believing I was capable of suddenly snapping. Anyway, this is what the two assholes interrogating me believed, and I was in no condition to argue.

The coroner was conducting initial tests on Dottie's corpse as we chatted. They took some blood samples from me. Her dead body had been pumped full of semen, most likely mine, but the question remained whether she'd been raped, her corpse had been violated, or I just happened to be the innocent sap who gave her a farewell fuck for the Long Road. The DNA results would take a while to come back in. Meantime, I had free room and board, courtesy of the City. Broke as usual, I made the most of it and looked on the bright side of a dark situation. It was all I could afford.

Dottie's death was ruled a suicide by both the coroner, who found no evidence of physical abuse, and the homicide detective, a fairly nice guy named Phil, who'd been assigned to the case. A reliable witness jogging by had actually seen her strip then wade into the water on the North Side, as if in a trance. This testimony was corroborated by a few other bystanders who had read about her in the paper. Back in her little studio apartment the cops found a note which provided the final missing piece. In her own affirmed handwriting, Dottie had written: *One last fling, then the pain is over*. Whether she meant fling as in an affair or a fling in the lake—or *both*—no longer mattered. She was gone.

One last detail: my fingerprints were all over the joint. That also didn't matter now. They just figured I had been her choice for a last hurrah. The cops laughed at the notion, right in my face, but I didn't let it get to me. In any case, I was released as soon as soon as the eyewitness accounts were confirmed. I was back on the mean streets. But I had some questions of my own that still needed answers.

I headed back to the Green Mill. Ironically, the Journeymen were still singing "500 Miles" on the juke, as if in a continuous loop. The hazy, surreal memory of Dottie was already haunting me.

"Manhattan," I said to the bartender. Different dude than when I was with Dottie just before she disappeared, ostensibly to go drown herself. He was a young guy, in his twenties, probably a musician, but definitely not a generic hipster. He immediately came across as authentic, confident, and friendly. His name was Tim.

"You sure?" he said to me with a curious smile.

"Uh, yeah? Why not?"

"I'd think after the other night you'd want to dry out for a while."

"Other night? What other night? I didn't see you last time I was here."

"That must mean you've been back since, then."

"Since when?"

"You really don't remember?" He grinned without condescension, just genuine surprise. "Wow, you guys really *were* wasted, huh?"

"'Guys'?" I said. "What other guy? Who was with me?"

"Figure of speech," he said. "Actually, it was a girl. A woman, really. Friend of mine."

"Dottie?"

"Yeah. At least you remember her name, dude!"

"Yeah, you haven't heard, I take it."

"Heard what?"

I figured news of Dottie's death hadn't even made the news yet. Maybe it never would. In the scheme of things, she was nobody, just another poor, nearly anonymous stiff in the morgue. Her few friends would find out soon enough. I decided not to be the bearer of bad news. "Never mind. So tell me—what's your name again?"

"Tim."

"Tim. Tell me, what did you know about our friend Dottie?"

"Well, what exactly do you need to know?"

"Little things. What she liked, what she didn't like, stuff like that."

"Can't you just ask her yourself?"

"Well, I'm leaving town soon, doubt I'll ever see her again. Didn't get her number. You know how it is." I winked.

"No I don't," he said, making me feel slimy.

"Well, anyway, I *liked* her, but didn't want to get too attached since I'm just passing through town, dig?"

"Yeah, that figures."

"What figures?"

"Dottie was always attracted to that type."

"What type you mean, exactly?" I tried maintaining a pleasantly clueless expression.

"You know, the 'just passing through' type. She even had a kid with one. Dude from California. She was just out there visiting him, too."

"Who?"

"Her kid. Lives somewhere near San Francisco? Burlingame, I think. With his dad. Dude makes a lot of bread, works with computers or something. A consultant, I think she told me."

"Yeah? She didn't mention either to me. How'd they meet?"

"At the coffee shop where she worked until recently. Not too far from here."

"Recently?"

"Yeah, she got canned after like ten years, kept showing up late for work, which really wasn't like her. She was always a bit of a lush, but she started drinking a lot more recently. She didn't even tell 'em first that she was going out to California, so they fired her. She came here straight from work and told me all about it. It was really a shame. She'd been going downhill for a while, but I thought she'd cleaned up her act since she started going to, y'know, AA meetings and all. Then she showed up here with you that night, smashed out of her mind, I assumed because she was so upset she'd lost her job, and I guessed things didn't go so well on her trip. Man, she was totally out of it. And so were you, frankly. I finally had to cut you both off. You *really* don't remember?" I shook my head, and he continued: "Y'know, actually, I heard cops were asking around here the next day, but not during my shift. Her landlord was worried about her, or something, since she didn't come home that night to feed her cat, which also wasn't like her. I guess she was with you the whole time." He eyed me with some polite suspicion. "I hope everything is okay now?"

I nodded. "As far as I know," I lied.

Oddly, it was all starting to come back to me. I *hadn't* been drugged as part of some nefarious conspiracy after all. I wasn't set up by the estranged California father of Dottie's love child to murder her back in Chicago. Somehow I'd hooked up with her, we went on an epic bender, and I actually came home with her. *All* the way home. I vaguely recalled a snippet of conversation. *"Your place or mine?"* she had asked. I guess I chose hers.

Then the cerebral damn broke, and almost everything flooded back in one wild *whoosh.*

Her ex was actually a client of mine. Richard Something. Wealthy Silicon Valley type. He had hired me to find his missing kid. Following a late night tip from an underground informant, I did find the kid —at the airport. With Dottie. I immediately called Richard from San Francisco International and he came right over and picked up the kid. Dottie was left a hysterical mess. I felt guilty for my part in her misery, and wanted to console her. We went to the airport bar and started drinking...

It had all been an alcoholic blackout. For *both* of us.

I'd encountered these sorts of incidents before, during the course of several investigations, but never actually *experienced* one until now. One type of blackout is called "en bloc," wherein the inebriated party can't recall *any* events within the perimeters of a certain adversely affected time period, even when prompted via hypnosis. The other type was called "fragmentary," which is probably what I was suffering from, since bits and pieces of the recent past were beginning to resurface in my murky mind. The cops probably fingered me because we were fellow passengers on the same flight, and I was the last person seen with her in public.

Was I really *that* much of a drinker, though? I knew I'd been depressed lately, more so than usual, since I was worried about Doc's medical condition, and he was my best friend. I was also losing sleep over my rapidly advancing age. As well as mounting debts, no alternate career prospects, and the aching lack of a life companion with whom to share my woes. My loneliness was literally killing me.

Though I couldn't lucidly recall every single moment leading up to the Green Mill, my fingerprints at her pad must've meant we went to her place first, directly from the airport, then she must've gone to work, and I guess I had gone with her, probably expecting a free meal, since bottom feeding was my style. Obviously she was in no condition to wait tables, so they gave her walking papers, which led us both back here. Not sure why we went to a nearby hotel instead of back to her place, except for the convenience of proximity. Plus, like Tim pointed out, we were both stoned beyond reason. We probably just stumbled down the block, tumbled into bed, and then woke up a day or so later virtual strangers, the booze having worn off by then.

Funny thing was, even sober, we actually liked each other. I guess she didn't like me quite enough to cancel her final plans, though.

While I had been sitting there contemplating all this, Tim had been mixing my Manhattan, which he set down in front of me with a customary if cautionary smile.

"Here's to Dottie," I said.

"Cheers," he said, still blissfully oblivious to her permanent absence from the planet.

I stared at my Manhattan for a long time without taking a sip. Then I decided to order a different drink.

Sinatra went from singing "Chicago" to "My Kind of Town" on the juke while I slurped my heavily creamed coffee. Fate is my pimp, but God was my DJ. Perfect exit music. I had to get out of there fast before "500 Miles" returned via inevitable rotation. I gulped it down. The caffeine rush gave my battered system just the jolt it needed. I got up, nodded at Tim, and left some bills on the counter.

As I left the Green Mill to hail a cab for the airport, I kept scratching my itchy crotch as discreetly as possible. At least Dottie had left me something to remember her by besides that damn song, which played in my head all the way home.